STORY OF A SOCIOPATH

Julia Navarro
Story of a Sociopath

Julia Navarro is a journalist, a political analyst, and the internationally bestselling author of six novels, including *The Brotherhood of the Holy Shroud* and *The Bible of Clay*. Her fiction has been translated in more than thirty countries. She lives in Madrid.

www.julianavarro.es/en

STORY OF A SOCIOPATH

A Novel

Julia Navarro

Vintage Books
A Division of Penguin Random House LLC
New York

A VINTAGE BOOKS ORIGINAL, NOVEMBER 2016

Translation copyright © 2016 by Joanna Freeman

All rights reserved. Published in the United States by Vintage Books,
a division of Penguin Random House LLC. Originally published in Spain
as *Historia de un canalla* by Penguin Random House Grupo Editorial,
S. A., Barcelona, in 2016, and subsequently published in the United States
by Vintage Español, a division of Penguin Random House LLC, New
York, in 2016. Copyright © 2016 by Julia Navarro.

Vintage and colophon are registered trademarks of
Penguin Random House LLC.

The Cataloging-in-Publication Data is on file at the Library of Congress.

Vintage Books Trade Paperback ISBN: 978-1-101-97325-7
eBook ISBN: 978-1-101-97326-4

Book design by Steven Walker

www.vintagebooks.com

Printed in the United States of America
10 9 8 7 6 5 4 3 2 1

To my friends Margarita Robles, Victoria Lafora, Asun Cascante, Lola Travesedo, Asun and Chus García, Carmen Martínez Terrón, Irma Mejías, Lola Pedrosa, Pilar Ferrer, Consuelo Sánchez Vicente, and Rosa Conde, who are always close to me, however far away they may be.

And to Maia, who is eight years old and already striding through life.

To Fermín and Álex, always.

Acknowledgments

To Doctor Isidre Vilacosta, for answering my many questions on heart disease, and Doctor Pedro Górgolas, for resolving other questions on medical matters. If any errors remain, then I am responsible for them. Thanks to you both for your patience.

And thanks to the team at Penguin Random House who have, as always, smoothed this book's path to its readers.

STORY OF A SOCIOPATH

I'm dying. It's not that I'm terminally ill or that my doctors have declared me a lost cause. The last time they saw me was to tell me that I was in pretty good shape, especially for someone who's suffered a heart attack and had valve replacement surgery. My blood sugar levels are a bit high, and so is my cholesterol, and my blood pressure's on the edge, but it's nothing, they say, that can't be fixed by taking a few pills every day, going on a diet, and giving up cigarettes and alcohol.

"Go for a walk. The best thing is to go for a walk. It's the best medicine. Lots of people with your medical history would be pleased to look like you," the doctor said, trying to cheer me up.

I'm not that much older than him, eight or ten years at the most. I didn't say anything. Why should I? I know that I'm dying and I don't need blood tests or cardiograms to prove it. How do I know? I know because I look at myself in the mirror every morning and see the brown patches that have sprouted on my skin. And not an inch of my skin that hasn't lost its elasticity.

I look at my hands and what do I see? Blue threads showing through the skin. The same blue threads that crisscross my legs. They are veins, as hard as stone now.

"You are more interesting than you were when you were twenty," the hypocrites say. Liars. Especially the women. The only thing interesting about me is my bank account and my entry in *Who's Who*.

It's been a while since I realized that other people don't see you for who you are, but rather for what you have, for what you represent. The same gray hair, the same grayish skin: these would be looked at with indifference or even disgust if I were one of those wretched creatures who can be found in any corner of the city.

How much longer do I have? A day perhaps, a week, five, six, ten years . . . or maybe tomorrow I'll wake up with a sharp pain in my chest, or find a lump while I'm in the shower, or faint in the street, and the same pleasant doctor will tell me that I've got cancer somewhere, in my lungs, my pancreas, wherever. Or he'll tell me that my tired heart has given out again, and I'll need a new valve. From one day to the next death will show her face.

But I don't need a lump, or a fainting fit, or my heart to beat out of time. I know that I am dying because I've reached that age when there's no more fooling yourself and you sense that you are living on borrowed time.

Tonight death has filled my thoughts and I've started to wonder what the last minute of my life will be like. I'm afraid that it will be in a hospital bed, without any power to make decisions about my own existence. I imagine myself incapable of moving, incapable of speech, communicating by signs or with glances, with nobody able to understand or share my suffering.

We don't choose where or when we are born, but we should at least be able to decide how to confront the final moment of our lives. But that's denied to us as well.

When I know that the hour has come when death will visit, I'll try to work out how to greet her, how to avoid her for a while, but above all how to start the trek into nonexistence.

And so, as I await that treacherous knock on the door, tonight I am overwhelmed by memories of my life, and they all leave the taste of bile in my mouth.

I'm scum. Yes, I always have been and I can't make myself

regret being scum, for having been scum. Although if what the physicists say is true, and time is just a construct of the human mind, we should have the chance to walk backward, to live the life we could have lived but did not.

Am I wrong if I think and say that we would all change parts of our past? That we would do things differently from how we have done them? If we could retrace our footsteps . . . Maybe even I would behave differently.

There are people who say, out loud, that they regret nothing. I don't believe them. Most people have consciences in spite of themselves. I was born without a conscience, or at least I never knew where to find one, but perhaps one will knock on my door tonight. But I will try not to let her in, because nothing can change the things that torment us.

Tonight, as I look death in the face, I'll go over what I have lived through. I know what I did, and what I should have done.

CHILDHOOD

1

I must have been seven or eight years old, and I was walking along with the woman who looked after me and my brother. It must have been halfway through the afternoon, the time when we got out of school. I was in a bad mood because the teacher had scolded me for not paying attention while she explained something or other.

My brother was holding María's hand, but I preferred to go at my own pace. Also, María had sweaty palms and I did not like the touch of her wet skin on mine.

I was running from one side to the other, ignoring María's complaints.

"I'm going to tell your mother. You do this every day: you let go of my hand and you don't even hold it when we're crossing the street, and you never look to see if a car is coming. One day something terrible will happen."

María was complaining but I wasn't paying her any attention. I knew her string of reproaches by heart. Suddenly I saw a little bundle lying in the gutter. I went over to see what it was. I gave it a nudge with my foot and to my surprise saw that it was a bird, one of the many sparrows that filled the trees of the city. I thought it was dead and gave it a little kick that put it farther from the curb. I went over to it, curious to see where it was, and I saw that it was moving, slowly, as if breathing its last. I stepped down from the curb and gave it another kick. The sparrow's neck twisted back on itself.

"But what are you doing, there in the middle of the street? I'll tell your mother today for sure. I can't take it anymore."

María took me by the hand and made me walk alongside her. I was extremely cross that she was pulling me along, and as soon as her attention wavered I kicked her in the calf.

I don't regret the kick I gave María that day, but I can't forget the motionless body of the sparrow. It was me who had caused it to breathe its last.

"Jerk!" Jaime said, looking at me disapprovingly. I don't know if that was for kicking María or for having kicked the sparrow.

"Shut up or you'll get one too," I said crossly.

Jaime said nothing. He knew that as soon as he dropped his guard he would have to take another kick from me, or even a punch in the ribs. I was two years older than my brother, so he was always at a disadvantage.

"I'm going to tell your mother. I can't deal with you. If you carry on like that I'm not going to pick you up from school anymore. You're a very bad little boy."

Bad. Yes, that was the teacher's favorite assessment too, as well as María's and even my mother's.

My father told me off, but he never said I was "bad." He knew me too well to send me away with that silly phrase, "You're a bad little boy."

If I could go back in time the scene would be similar:

I would be walking with María and Jaime, without minding that I was holding my nanny's sweaty hand. I would have told her that I was in a bad mood because my teacher, Miss Adeline, had scolded me, and María would have given me some words of comfort. Something like, "Don't worry, it's nothing serious to let your mind wander every now and then, tomorrow you'll listen and Miss Adeline won't be upset anymore."

I would have seen the little bundle moving on the sidewalk and would have asked María if we could have a look. "There's something over there, look. Can we go and see?"

María would have grumbled: "Who cares what it is, let's go, we're in a hurry," but she would have given in. When I realized it was a sparrow, I would have picked it up carefully. Jaime would have looked at it with curiosity and would have said, "Poor little thing!" And the two of us, our hearts touched, would have begged María to let us take the sparrow home with us. My mother was a nurse, so she would have been able to do something to save the little bird's life. We would have kept it for two or three days, and once it was better, we would have given it its freedom.

But that didn't happen and I'm not sorry.

That afternoon, when we got home, my mother was getting ready to go to the hospital. She was on the night shift that week and seemed tired, and that was probably the reason why she paid little attention to María's complaints. She barely even scolded me: "When are you going to learn to behave? What will I do if María loses patience with you and leaves? I have to work and I won't be able to do that without her."

"You could find someone else to look after us," I said defiantly.

"As if it were that easy! María is a good person. And you're a very bad little boy! I don't know what we're going to do with you. Go to your room and do your homework. I'll talk to your father and he'll tell you what your punishment will be. And now I have to go."

"Like you always do. You're never here."

I knew what I was doing. I wanted to hurt my mother, who felt guilty for not spending more time with us. I had overheard her more than once talking with my father and blaming herself for spending more time at the hospital than at home, and although my father would console her by telling her that the important thing was the love she gave us and not the time she spent with us, my mother couldn't help feeling that she was doing something wrong. So I hit her where it hurt her most.

She looked at me, and I saw a spark of sadness in her gaze, and then a burst of anger.

"Go to your room!"

On my way there I took the opportunity to give Jaime the kick I had promised him, and he gave a howl that drew my mother's attention.

"What's going on here?"

"Thomas kicked me!" my brother said, in tears.

"María, please, take charge of the children . . . I have to go. And you, Thomas, go to your room, and we're not going to take you anywhere this weekend."

"What do I care? It doesn't matter to me! And I don't want to be with you anyway. You're not a good mother. You're not like my friends' mothers. You're never here."

My mother didn't even look at me. She left the house and slammed the door. I suppose it was her way of controlling her anger and not giving me a smack on the head.

Yes, that afternoon should have been different:

"Mama, Mama! Look, we've found a sparrow and it's hurt, will you help us make it get better?" That was what I would have said while my brother, Jaime, tugged at my mother's dress.

"I'm in a rush, but I'll have a look. Let's see . . . Its leg is broken, but it's nothing serious. Go and find a thin piece of wood, one of your pencils would be good. Look, we'll put a splint on it and in a few days it will be better and ready to fly away. Thomas, go and ask María for a shoe box and some cotton balls. We'll put it there so that it's nice and warm."

"Can we keep the sparrow forever?" Jaime would have asked.

"No, its mother will be looking for it and she will be worried. Also, birds should be free. When it's better I'll go with you back to where you found it, and we'll let it go so that it can go back to its nest."

"Thank you, Mama," I would have said, and would have leaned over to give her a kiss.

My mother would have stroked my head and said to us: "How good you are. That's what I like, that you feel sympathy for suffering creatures, even ones as small as this little bird."

Yes, it should have been like that. But what happened was that I spent the rest of the afternoon in my room without bothering to do my homework, taking all the toys out of their boxes and strewing them around the room in the knowledge that María would have to pick them up, which would make her doubly annoyed, not just because of the extra work but because she had a bad back as well.

When my father came home a little before dinnertime, María was complaining.

"What's happened, María? Have the children been naughty again?" my father asked.

"Jaime is a little angel, sir, he never makes any noise, but Thomas . . . He's a very bad little boy, sir, he just thinks up ways of annoying other people."

"Come, come, María. There are children who are more lively than others, but that doesn't mean they are bad. Tell me, what has Thomas done?"

María told him what had happened that afternoon and he called me into his study. As I knew that María would complain about me, I had already taken my revenge. While she was speaking to my father I had gone to the kitchen and poured the contents of the salt shaker into the soup she was making. She'd have to start again from scratch.

My father was a lawyer. He worked a great deal. He left the house early in the morning and didn't come back until it was night. It was unusual for him to have dinner at home. I never complained that he didn't spend more time with us. I thought his work was important and I felt very proud of him. He was always elegantly dressed, even on weekends when he took his tie off. But my mother, whenever she took off her makeup and got into her housecoat, seemed to me to hunch over, to become insignificant.

"Didn't you feel sorry for the sparrow?" my father asked me.

I thought before replying. I knew that I had to find the right words to get him on my side.

"I thought it was dead and . . . well, I didn't realize. I didn't think."

Thinking. That was my excuse. My father always excused me by saying that I was a scatterbrained child who never stopped to think, and that was why I got into trouble.

"But you have to think, Thomas. I've told you that before. If you'd stopped to look you could have saved the sparrow's life. Your mother would have helped you. As for kicking María, I can't allow you to do things like that. María is an adult, and adults need to be treated with respect. And you kicked Jaime as well: Aren't you ashamed to have hit someone smaller than you?"

I lowered my head. Knowing my father, I was sure that he was trying to work out which punishment to give me that wouldn't be too severe. Finally he found it.

"Look, you're going to have to read a story that I'll give you, about a boy who is always causing mischief, but one day something happens that makes him change his behavior. And then, when you've read it, you can come and talk to me about it. You'll learn something this way."

"Mama said that you wouldn't take us anywhere this weekend," I whispered in my most innocent voice.

"Well, Mama was cross. She works a lot, poor thing, not just at the hospital but also here, looking after all of us. I'll talk to her."

At this moment, we heard María start to scream.

"He's a devil, a real devil! Lord, who would do such a thing?" she said, coming into my father's office.

"What has he done now?" he asked in alarm.

"He's poured all the salt into the soup. I can't take it anymore! I've been on my feet since seven o'clock this morning, and now I've got to start all over again. I'll have to make another pot of soup."

When María had left my father's office he looked at me severely.

"I don't like what you've done. María doesn't deserve for you to treat her like that. You need to go and apologize. Then go to your room and read what I've told you to read. You have to have read everything by dinnertime."

When my father looked at me severely it gave me an unpleasant scratchy feeling in my stomach, but even so I wasn't prepared to apologize to María.

I could have done so. But I would have liked María to have told my father that I had behaved myself, that I had done my homework without complaining and had even helped Jaime do his.

My father would have been happy and would have sat me on his knee. He would have suggested that we spend some time reading one of the books from his library, which he guarded as if they were treasures. I would have enjoyed this moment of intimacy with my father because, after having read for a bit, he would have asked me about my friends, my teacher, the lessons I had learned. It's likely that, as a reward for my good behavior, he would have let me fill his pipe and we would have made plans for the weekend. Who knows if he would have found the time to

come with me and Jaime on a bike ride, or even to go and have
a meal at a restaurant somewhere.

None of that happened. I went to my room and kicked the
radio-controlled car, then sat on the floor in the middle of the
chaos I had created. I had no intention of reading the story. I had
a knack of getting away from my father's questioning. I read a
couple of paragraphs per page and then, when he questioned
me, I would give him answers based on what I had barely read,
pretending to be nervous. I didn't care about lying to him, even
if he was the only person for whom I felt any affection. That's
how I was. That's how I am.

Miss Adeline was a good, if demanding, teacher. She never raised
her voice and never slapped anyone. My classmates seemed to
like her, but I hated her as much as I hated María. Everything
about her annoyed me. Her yellowish face, the eyes that seemed
to shrink when she looked at you, giving the impression that she
was peering into your mind. Her monastic clothes: she always
wore skirts and sweaters in dark colors, thick tights, flat shoes.
She was around forty years old when I entered her class and
they said she'd already been at the school for twenty years, and
was bound to retire there.

She was friendly and patient with her students without being
affectionate, and was always ready to repeat the day's lesson
over and over until she was sure that we had all understood her
explanations.

I regularly complained to my father about Miss Adeline. I
said that she was out to get me, that she scolded me for no reason
at all, that she didn't explain the lessons well. My father believed
me and from time to time asked my mother to talk to the teacher.
Her reply was always the same: "I would, but as it's Thomas, if

he's being scolded it's because he deserves it. You'd have to be a saint to put up with our son."

I prepared my revenge meticulously.

One morning, during recess, I deliberately beat my head against the wall. I hurt myself and immediately began to get a swelling that turned my forehead red. Before recess ended I went up to the classroom, knowing that Miss Adeline would be there correcting our homework. When she saw me come in with my red face she got worried.

"What happened? Did you fall over? Come here and show me."

I went over to her slowly, while my fellow students were coming up the stairs and going to their classes. I timed things so that when the door to our class opened the teacher was holding my head and looking at the bruise. At that moment I started to shout at the top of my voice.

"Don't hit me! Don't hit me!"

My classmates, coming into the class, didn't know what was happening. Miss Adeline seemed to be holding me while I was shouting, and I shouted so loud and so long that Miss Ann, the teacher in the class next door, came into the room to see what was going on.

"She's hitting me! I didn't do anything!" I shouted, in the face of the other teacher's incredulous stare.

"Good Lord, Adeline, what's going on here?"

"Nothing, I swear. Thomas came in with a bruise on his forehead. I was just looking at it."

"Please, stop her from hitting me again," I whimpered, as though I were afraid.

Miss Adeline looked at me in confusion and let go of my arm. Which let me perform one final trick: I fell to the floor as though I had been pushed.

"But, Adeline!" Miss Ann exclaimed without much understanding what was going on. "Come on, Thomas, get up. We'll take you to the school nurse. She'll make you better. And you, Adeline . . . I think we'd better go to the principal to sort this out."

For all that my teacher swore to Mr. Anderson, the principal, that she had not hit me, and although my classmates could not say for certain who was telling the truth, the bruise served as evidence for my case.

Mr. Anderson called my mother at the hospital and asked her to come to school right away. Meanwhile, I whined and complained about how much the bruise hurt. My tears were as heartfelt as those of Miss Adeline, who had collapsed when she saw that the principal seemed prepared to believe me more than her.

"What happened?" my mother asked in alarm as she came into Mr. Anderson's office.

"Calm down, your son is all right," the principal replied, agitated. "Although we don't really know what happened."

"But how can you doubt my word?" my teacher said.

The principal didn't reply, and at that moment I knew that I had won the battle.

My mother listened in silence to Miss Adeline's explanation. My teacher swore what was in fact the truth: that I had already had the bruise when I came into the class, and when she had tried to see what had happened, I began to shout and accused her of hitting me.

"Well, I don't know what to say. I am sorry about this incident, and I assure you that nothing of this kind has ever happened in my school. Miss Adeline is a teacher whom the children love and we've never had any complaints about her behavior, but . . . I don't know, maybe Thomas made her more nervous than usual; you know that he is a slightly unruly child." As he spoke, the principal wrung his hands.

"What happened, Thomas?" my mother asked me in a tired voice.

I could tell that she did not fully believe that Miss Adeline had hit me. She guessed something had happened but was unsure exactly what it was.

I didn't answer, but I cried all the harder and hugged her around the waist. My mother pulled me to her and tried to console me. I looked at Miss Adeline out of the corner of my eye and knew that she had been beaten.

I thought it better not to utter another word and just to keep crying, in case I contradicted myself. By this time, my face was almost entirely red and my eyes were swollen from crying. It was an extraordinary piece of theater, a professional actor couldn't have done any better, and in spite of her initial doubts my mother ended up believing me. She knew me well, but not well enough to believe me capable of such villainy.

"I hope that you will take this seriously. What has happened to my son is unforgivable."

"Yes, yes . . . of course we will have to do something. I will call a meeting of the entire staff."

"You'll have to do more than that, Mr. Anderson. I don't think that the parents of the students will be able to remain calm once they know what happened to my son. Today it was Thomas who was the victim, tomorrow it could be any one of their children."

For the first time I saw that my mother was moved by my tears, perhaps because it was hard for her to see me crying. That was what convinced her.

The next day I did not go to school. My mother didn't even wake me up in the morning. When I opened my eyes it was already midmorning and I saw her sitting on the edge of my bed, looking at me closely. I was shocked, but I calmed down when I saw her smile and she took me by the hand. I think she felt guilty that she hadn't trusted me from the start.

"You won't have to go to school until Mr. Anderson sorts out what he's going to do with Miss Adeline. And better for him if he decides sooner rather than later."

"Didn't you go to work?"

"No, I'm staying with you today. We'll go out for a walk and then go and find Dad in his office, is that a good idea?"

"And what about Jaime?" I wanted to know if I would have to share my parents with my brother.

"María will look after him. Today it'll be just the two of us."

When I went back to school Miss Adeline was no longer there. She had been fired. Not just that, but the school had passed her case along to the state education authorities, which meant that she would be punished and her career as a teacher was over.

I congratulated myself on my success. She was a very stupid woman to try to stand up to me.

I heard a couple of teachers complaining about Miss Adeline's bad luck. I found out that the woman who had been my teacher was a widow with a disabled daughter. If she didn't go back to work then both of them would be forced to rely on charity. None of this gossip affected me.

Do I regret what happened? It was so long ago! I have never been blind to the cruelty of my behavior. If only I could live through that moment once again . . . I know that I could have protected Miss Adeline from her punishment.

When my mother asked me, "What happened, Thomas?" I should have told the truth:

"Mama, I'm angry with Miss Adeline. She gives me a lot of homework and she's very demanding. I wanted to hurt her. I gave myself the bruise. I'm sorry, Mama, sorry for lying."

I can imagine the stunned look on Mr. Anderson's face, the relief on that of Miss Adeline, the anger in my mother's eyes.

"So you tried to fool us all . . . What you've done is difficult to forgive, you almost got Miss Adeline into a lot of trouble. I don't know what I'm going to do with you, you little devil!" she would

have said, trying to stop herself from giving me a slap right there, in front of the principal and my teacher.

For his part, Mr. Anderson would have scratched his head, which is what he usually did whenever he had to make a decision, and looked at me severely.

"Young man, what you have done is very bad and will naturally have consequences. You must understand that we will have to take severe measures. And as for you, Adeline . . . Well, I hope you will forgive us for this difficult incident, but you must understand . . . Thomas's accusation was so serious, and with the bruise as well . . . Who would have thought that a child could go so far as to hurt himself!"

"I am sorry, I am very sorry, Mr. Anderson. I hope that Miss Adeline can forgive us. Knowing my son, we shouldn't have doubted her version of the events. I don't know how I can apologize, or how I can make amends . . ."

Miss Adeline would have wiped away her tears with one of those spotless handkerchiefs she always carried in her bag and, with great relief, would have accepted my mother's apologies, although I suppose she would have looked at the principal fairly reproachfully. As for me, I am sure she would have looked at me in terror, as if I were the devil himself.

"I think we adults should talk about this disgraceful incident. Thomas, go to your classroom, and we'll call you in a while."

I know that I would have cried even more fiercely then, as fiercely as I cried to support my lie, begging forgiveness from my mother, my teacher, the principal.

Yes, that's what I should have done. What would have happened? My mother would doubtless have scolded me, and they would have punished me at school and at home, but I've never cared about being punished. No, if I didn't tell the truth it was not because of cowardice but out of sheer wickedness. I know that's how it was.

———

My mother always compared me with Jaime. Perhaps that is why I hated my brother so much.

"Look at your brother. He's only six but he's much more responsible than you are." "Look at Jaime, he cleaned his room without needing to be told." "What good grades Jaime gets! Straight A's, and you . . . you're a problem, Thomas. You don't study, you behave badly, you're completely disorganized; I don't know what we're going to do with you."

Those were some of the phrases my mother used most often. And every time she held Jaime up to me as an example, my hostility toward him only increased.

I must have been about twelve when I decided to get rid of him, and it was all my father's fault. I had grown accustomed to my mother's scolding, now that she was incapable of hiding how much I irritated her and how content she was with Jaime's behavior. She kissed him and enjoyed hugging him, and smiled, whereas I would not allow her these gestures of affection and she would scarcely brush my cheeks with her lips and then move away as if I disgusted her.

But not only my mother gave my brother her brightest smiles. My uncles and aunts, my cousins, my parents' friends: all of them always had words of praise for Jaime. It is true, I gave them no cause to praise me. I was unfriendly, I didn't let anyone kiss me and I tried to ruin everyone's visit. One afternoon when my aunt Emma, my father's sister, came to visit, I opened her bag and emptied it by throwing its contents out the window. The porter came up to tell us that various flying objects had come from one of our windows: a packet of tissues, a purse, a wallet, some keys . . . Of course, this was not the worst thing I did: on another occasion I kept myself busy cutting the sleeves off her coat. She often told my father that I was a very problematic child and that I should see a psychologist. But all her advice went unheeded. I think my father thought that his sister Emma didn't know much about children. She had married young and had soon been widowed, before having children. Her husband had been afflicted with a raging leukemia, and after his death she had never married again.

My father scolded me but without much conviction, and my mother would often slap me.

"This child will be the death of me!" she used to shout.

I have already told you that I thought I could rely on my father's unconditional support. In fact I was convinced that he was the only person who loved me more than Jaime. One Sunday morning I found out that I was mistaken.

Sunday was María's day off, and so my mother got up to make breakfast while my father finished getting dressed. While they had breakfast in the kitchen, Jaime and I were allowed to sleep in a little.

That Sunday I woke a little early and, after checking that my brother was still asleep, I went to the kitchen, knowing that I would find my parents there. At last I could be alone with them, without Jaime around! But I didn't go into the kitchen, as I heard my father talking about me.

"The poor boy is a disaster. He's not handsome, he has no special talents, he hasn't got the mind for studying. What are we going to do, Carmela? He is how he is, but he is our son and we should accept him. At least we have Jaime to make up for him. Thank God that boy's got everything."

If he had slapped me it would have hurt less than the words I had just heard. Up to that moment, nothing had really hurt me. Not the punishments at school, not the blows I got when I fought with some boy from my class, not my mother's scolding . . . Nothing had provoked the sense of pain that started in my stomach and expanded until I could barely breathe.

It wasn't that my father was complaining about me: I could have withstood that. He was pitying me, and that was a humiliation I did not know how to deal with.

It took me a few seconds to be able to move again. I decided to continue listening, but I saw my mother looking toward the door as if she guessed there might be someone there, so I walked backward silently and went to my room.

Jaime was still asleep and I stood next to his bed in order to look at him. My father was right. We were not alike. Jaime's face reflected the goodness of his character and, yes, unlike me, he was handsome.

I felt the need to punish my parents for their obvious lack of love for me. I could no longer fool myself into believing, as I had up to this point, that I was my father's favorite. I had been convinced that this was the case; everyone else preferred Jaime and made no attempt to hide it, but my father was always pleasant to me and showed me affection. Now I knew that he did so because he felt he had no choice.

The idea came quickly into my head. My parents would be unable to bear the pain of losing Jaime. I had to get rid of him but I didn't have much time. The routine was always the same on a Sunday: at any moment my mother would come and wake us up and tell us to go to the kitchen while she got dressed.

I took the pillow from my bed, my mind made up that I would press it over Jaime's face until he stopped breathing; but that would have consequences for me, and I thought that it would not be fair that I would also be punished for the death of my brother. I had to find another way to get rid of him.

I don't know why I looked toward the window, but I immediately smiled. I had found the way.

I opened the window and looked down to the street. Our apartment was on the ninth floor. If I could get Jaime to lean out, then it wouldn't be hard for me to give him a push. He'd fall, and at this height there was no way he could survive.

I woke him up by pulling his duvet off and pinching him.

"Get up! There's a cat out on the window ledge. It's very small and it's about to fall."

I knew that my brother would not be able to resist taking a look. He liked animals, especially cats.

Jaime jumped out of bed and walked barefoot to the window. He stood on tiptoe to take a look.

"I can't see it. It must have fallen down. Poor little thing."

I just needed him to lean out a little more so that the push I was going to give him would be barely noticeable.

"You won't be able to see it like that. You need to lean out a little farther."

Jaime must have had a guardian angel. Having a brother like me, it was more than likely. While I was helping him to lean out farther, getting ready to give him a little push, we heard my mother shout.

"What are you doing? Jaime, come here at once and you . . . you . . . How could you let your brother climb up to the window like that? He could have fallen. You're so irresponsible."

Jaime ran to hide in my mother's arms, and she held him fearfully and close. She looked at me and I could see the mistrust in her eyes.

"Thomas heard a cat meowing," Jaime said in explanation.

My mother walked over to the window and looked to see if there was a cat; then she shut the window and grabbed me fiercely by the arm, shaking me as though I were a sack of potatoes.

"There's no cat! What were you up to?" And she gave me a pinch.

"He didn't do anything," Jaime protested, not understanding my mother's reaction.

I didn't even bother to defend myself and looked her up and down, trying to fix all the hate I felt on her with my gaze. It must have had some effect, because she left the room with Jaime, telling him to take a shower at once: she would bring his clothes to the bathroom. When she came back to the bedroom she stood in front of me. She seemed to be searching for the right words.

"I don't know what went through your head, but I swear, if you put your brother in danger ever again then . . . then you'll go to a boarding school, Thomas, a boarding school where they'll keep you on the straight and narrow, where they'll get those demons out of you."

I remained silent. I knew that my mother was driven half desperate by my lack of a response.

She looked at me again and left the room, slamming the door. I wondered what would have happened if I had thrown myself into the void. Would they mourn me? For a moment I wanted to think that my father would regret it, but I could no longer fool myself. I had heard from his own lips just what he thought of me. And as for my mother, I was sure that after everything had settled down, my absence would be a relief to her.

No, I wouldn't throw myself out the window. There was no better punishment than for them to have to keep putting up with me.

I left the room and went toward the kitchen to have breakfast. My mother, her nerves frayed, was telling my father what had happened.

"I'm telling you, we need to be careful with him. Thomas is jealous of Jaime."

"Carmela, I don't know what you're thinking, but in this instance you must be mistaken. I don't think that Thomas would . . . Well, don't blame *him* that Jaime was climbing out the window."

"But he was behind him . . . He was helping him lean out . . . John, I know our son, I know what he's like . . ."

"But aren't you exaggerating just a little?"

"We have to get him away from Jaime. We could change his room, put him in the guest room, which is a long ways away from his brother."

"Come on, don't exaggerate! And the guest room is very small. It wouldn't be fair for Thomas. You always said that when the children were bigger you'd turn the playroom into Thomas's room."

"But he'd be too close to Jaime. He'll be fine in the guest

room. Thomas doesn't need much space. Why does he need a big desk if he never studies? Have you ever seen him with a book in his hands?"

My father ended up giving in to my mother. I felt defeated.

How should this have taken place? Like this, perhaps:

When I heard my father referring to me so pityingly I should have gone into the kitchen. When they saw me, he would have been uncomfortable:

"Thomas, what are you doing here? It's very early. How come you're awake?" he would have asked, fearing that I had heard the last fragment of conversation.

My mother would have looked at me with her usual mistrust, sure that I had been listening behind the door, and I would have said:

"I woke up a while ago and I was hungry. And . . . well, I thought that if I got up earlier then I could be with you for a while."

My father would have felt ashamed, guilty about having expressed such a negative opinion of me. As he was a good man, he would have come over to me and ruffled my hair, and asked me to sit down.

"Well, we like spending time with you as well. Isn't that right, Carmela?"

"Dad, I heard you . . . You said that I'm not handsome like Jaime and that I don't know how to do anything. You're right, I need to make more of an effort. But I love you, I love you both very much, you and Mama, and Jaime too. I'll try to do things better, I promise."

I'm sure that my father would have embraced me and that even my mother would have been unable to do anything other than succumb to this humble confession.

I would have enjoyed that embrace, feeling comforted in hav-

ing managed to make my parents see that there was more to me than this little monster who ruined their days.

After breakfast I would have said to my mother that there was no reason for her to worry about Jaime.

"I'll wake him up and have breakfast with him while you get dressed in peace."

I know she would have agreed, silently blaming herself for not being able to love me more.

Jaime would still be asleep when I went back to the bedroom. I would have sat on the edge of his bed and woken him up by blowing on him, because he'd think that was funny. I would have gone with him to the kitchen and filled his mug with milk and found him some cookies. Then I would have stayed by his side until he finished his breakfast.

Yes. That's what should have happened. It would doubtless have awoken in my mother some feeling of benevolence toward me, and my father, although aware of my flaws, would have felt moved by my attitude.

But it happened in the way I have told you, so I found myself thrown out of my room, although I admit I didn't much care about that. In spite of the size of my new room, it was, just as my mother had said, a long way from Jaime. And it was mine. I could enjoy my solitude without having to put up with my brother's permanent presence.

I asked myself how it was possible that my mother could know me so well. In spite of myself I admired her for that. I wasn't surprised that the next day, Monday, she asked María not to let Jaime out of her sight.

"Don't you worry, I know just how Thomas can be, and how you've got to have a hundred eyes on him all the time. I don't know what's wrong with that boy."

My mother nodded. She mistrusted me so much that she feared for my brother.

Jaime said that he missed having me in the room with him, a statement that earned him a kick in the shin.

"Well, I don't miss you at all. At least I don't have to put up with your silly face all the time, looking as though butter wouldn't melt in your mouth."

He didn't even complain. He put up with the kick just as he had put up with the many slaps that I had given him over the course of our short lives.

Everything about Jaime bothered me. The innocence in his face, his discipline in his studies, the fact that everyone liked him, not just because he was a pretty boy, but also for his open and cheerful character.

María used to say that Jaime was filled with good ideas and that I was filled with bad ones. She was right. That's how things were; that's how things have continued to be.

I didn't try to get rid of my brother again. Instead I opted for indifference. An indifference that would help to harm him because despite all my rejections, he, the trusting fool, loved me.

I decided not to talk to him. I didn't reply when he spoke to me, which made him very sad. My mother scolded me for my attitude, but I had decided to ignore her as well. No matter what she said, whenever she spoke to me I looked away. I even started humming to show that nothing she could say to me would ever matter.

My father tried to get me to explain why I behaved like this, but I just shrugged.

"Thomas, you're not a baby anymore, you can't behave like this. Mama is suffering and Jaime loves you very much and can't understand why you ignore him. Can you tell me why you are acting this way?"

No, I couldn't tell him. He must have realized that I hated my mother and my brother. And the cause was nothing more than that Jaime looked physically like my father: thin, blond, his eyes halfway between gray and blue, his skin as white as milk. And I . . . I was just like my mother, but those parts of her that might appear attractive were a disaster in me: short for my age, dark-haired, swarthy. I still remember the day when one of the girls in my class said I looked like I'd been put in a toaster. I gave her a push and a slap. Joseph separated us: he scolded her for having compared me to a piece of toast and berated me for having hit her.

Joseph was the class leader. He didn't do anything to make himself so. He simply was.

He wasn't one of your typical horrible nerds. Quite the opposite, in fact. If someone came to class with their homework unfinished, Joseph would lend them his exercise book so they could copy his answers, and in tests he did everything he could so that the person sitting next to him could sneak a look at his paper.

Strong and tall, always smiling, he was friends with everyone and the teachers' favorite. He didn't even try: he was just himself, and everyone liked him.

The rest of my classmates barely spoke to me. It was Joseph who invited me to play soccer with the rest of the class and who brought me into the conversations on the playground.

I realized that, if not for him, everyone else would have ignored me altogether. They didn't like me, and they had reason not to. I had hit them; I had torn up their exercise books or shredded their textbooks. They would have avoided me like the plague had Joseph not used his leadership skills to make sure I wasn't abandoned.

I must admit that I had conflicted feelings about him. I admired him, yes. I could not deny that he was the best one of us all, and I would have liked to have been his friend; I fantasized about being his only friend. But I knew that this was not possible. Joseph treated me like a classmate, but he was not my friend. We never exchanged secrets and never saw each other outside of school. I knew that Joseph went out with some of our classmates on weekends. I heard them talking about the basketball game they had gone to with their parents, or the movie they had seen, or the Saturday afternoons they had spent playing basketball. It hurt me not to be a part of Joseph's life. For him I was just one among many, although I must admit that he never abandoned me when another student muttered about me, accusing me of destroying his exercise book, or stamping on his ballpoint pen, or throwing a textbook into the street on a rainy afternoon.

I wished Joseph had counted me among his friends, his true friends, the ones he spent time with hanging out around the school gates. But he never did. I did not exist for him outside the school; even so, he was the only person who stood up for me against my teachers and classmates.

I think we must have been sixteen or seventeen, I don't remember very well, when Claire came to the school. She was French, and, as they explained to us, her father's company had sent him to work in New York, so she had to come and finish high school with us.

If Joseph had been the class's sole leader up to that point, from this moment on Claire shared this leadership with him. The girls admired and envied her equally. And as for us, well, we all fell in love with her. It wasn't that she was a beauty, but her way of talking, of moving, the way she dressed, all made her different. The girls all tried to imitate her, unsuccessfully. She was different—she was French.

I was charmed by Claire until I found out that she and Joseph had fallen in love. They didn't do anything special to show it, but it was impossible not to see the glances they exchanged, or how they tried to touch each other whenever they were close enough, or how Joseph suddenly started to ask for her approval of everything he did, or how, if she had on a new pair of pants or a tight top, she would look at him out of the corner of her eye to find out whether he liked it.

The others accepted that something special was beginning to form between Claire and Joseph, but I could not bear it. I felt doubly betrayed. Why had this girl not chosen me? Why had everyone else stopped existing for Joseph?

It became normal for them to leave school together and for him to drive her home on his motorbike. On Saturday afternoons, when he used to meet up with his friends and play basketball, he would now catch a movie or go out for burgers with Claire. No one else mattered anymore. I asked myself if they even saw us, or if we were just part of the scenery.

I couldn't help feeling resentment toward Claire. She had broken the status quo at the school, which made me more alone than before, and I could not put up with that.

I had to find a way to make Joseph break up with her. It would not be easy, because it was clear to everyone that they were in love, and first love leaves space for nothing and no one else within its boundaries.

My mother realized that something was happening. She mentioned it one night at dinner.

"I don't know if you're planning something or if it's just that you're growing up, but you've gone a few days without causing any problems around the house."

"Don't be like that, Carmela, can't you just accept Thomas's good behavior for what it is?" my father scolded her.

At any other time I would have been annoyed by my mother's comment, but I paid no attention to it. Nor did I thank my father for his support, even silently. I was obsessed with finding a way to have Claire disappoint Joseph and to have him stop devoting all his attention to her. Then everything would go back to how it had been.

Jaime looked at me curiously. It was a relief for him that I had other things on my mind, because I hadn't tormented him for several days. The last time I had paid my brother any attention was when I poured ink over the drawings that he was supposed to hand in at school the next morning.

It was not easy to find a way to get between Claire and Joseph. My idea was that the only sure way to provoke Joseph's rage was for him to see Claire kissing someone else, but it would be difficult to ensure that this would happen. I had only one option: I myself should kiss her. The problem was that she barely noticed my existence.

I prepared my plan down to the last detail. Nothing could go wrong, or else not only would I show my hand, but neither Joseph nor the rest of the class would ever forgive me and I would be a pariah forever.

It had to be on a Wednesday. That was the only day that Joseph did not walk Claire to class. On Wednesday he had violin lessons first thing in the morning, and arrived only just in time to go to school. I would have to take advantage of the timing to accost Claire, who, I had noticed, was usually the first student to get to class.

I was very nervous on the Wednesday I had chosen. I was not one hundred percent certain that all the elements of my plan would come together.

I left home early and when I got to school neither Claire nor any of my classmates had yet arrived. The drama had to play itself out in the span of a very few minutes; that was all the time I had.

As always, Claire arrived ten minutes before the class began and was surprised to see me in the classroom with my head in a physics textbook.

"You're here early!"

"Yes, I'm just going over a few things. I don't understand physics very well . . . I'm not that good at it and we've got an exam in a few days."

"If you want, I could give you a hand. What don't you understand?" she said, coming closer.

"This," I said, pointing to the open page while I looked at her out of the corner of my eye. I couldn't rush this part.

She sat down next to me and started to explain one of the physics problems. I looked at her with attention, as if I were really interested in what she was telling me. When I heard footsteps in the hallway I acted quickly. I grabbed her by the neck and forced her down onto the table, then I started to kiss her. She tried to struggle free but I wouldn't let her go; we struggled and I undid a few buttons of her blouse.

The door opened. Some of our classmates started to come in, but stopped in the doorway as they saw me on top of Claire.

I stood back and she climbed to her feet. There were at least half a dozen students looking at us.

"It was him . . . the son of a bitch . . . He forced me," Claire babbled.

"What are you saying? You kissed me!" I replied.

She started to button her blouse and straighten her skirt. She seemed confused as well as ashamed at our classmates' recriminatory gazes.

"It wasn't me . . . He threw himself on me . . . I was helping him with his physics . . ." Claire tried to explain.

The murmurs had grown louder and the students now entering the class heard from the lips of those who had first come in what they had seen.

"They were kissing," one girl said to another.

"Making out? If we'd been a minute or two later, who knows what we'd have seen!" said another girl.

"What about Joseph?" said Ian, who shared Joseph's desk.

"We'll have to tell him," said Simon, the class geek.

"Don't be a dick! I'm not going to say anything. If Claire's tired of Joseph, then she should tell him herself. That's the least she should do," another girl said.

"But I didn't do anything!" Claire shouted.

"But we saw you!" Simon exclaimed.

"You didn't see anything! This *cochon* attacked me!" Claire said.

"Right . . . He attacked you . . . Is that the best you can come up with?" said the ugliest girl in the class.

I hadn't said a word. It was better that the others speak. Up to this moment no one had blamed me for anything. Even among us, who were still young, the old prejudices still flourished. The girls in the class had never really liked Claire because she was, if not the prettiest, then the most attractive, and all the boys preferred her to any of the other girls. As for the boys, the old cliché about self-confident girls came into play: they were easy prey and anyone could take them.

Suddenly their envy had bubbled up: the girls were envious of Claire, who was different from them, and the boys were jealous that they had not been chosen over Joseph.

Our first class was physics and Joseph arrived at the same time as the teacher.

"Phew, I nearly didn't make it, I missed the bus!" Joseph said, not speaking to anyone in particular.

Everyone carried on murmuring and the teacher ended up getting upset.

"What's got into you today? If you keep talking then I'll stop teaching."

No one would admit to not having seen us kiss, and as the story reached Joseph and grew more detailed, it became Claire who had thrown herself on me.

I looked at Joseph out of the corner of my eye, and saw him listening to what Ian was telling him. Ian sat at the desk next to him and was also his best friend. Joseph's face seemed to be collapsing as he listened and there was a moment when our eyes met. I could see pain, disappointment, and anger there. I could not hold his gaze, so I lowered my head to keep looking at Claire out of the corner of my eye. I could see her indignation and disgust, but no surrender, and I admired her for that.

The teacher ended the class ten minutes early because no one was paying attention and the murmurs kept getting louder.

Joseph came straight over to my desk and stood in front of me.

"They were right when they said that you were a pig," he said, managing with difficulty to restrain himself from hitting me.

I shrugged, but this time I did hold his gaze.

"Don't get mad at him, get mad at the one who started it all," one of the girls said.

"Jennifer's right. You tell me who could resist a girl throwing herself at him," another student said.

"Motherfuckers!"

Joseph's exclamation surprised us all. Until now we had never heard him swear.

"Ask Claire what happened," Jennifer suggested, maliciously.

But Joseph just took his books and left the classroom. Claire went after him. Joseph's voice came to us from the hallway.

"Leave me alone! Go and find someone else to make out with."

"I didn't do anything, I swear it was Thomas who threw himself on me . . ." Claire whimpered.

Their voices faded down the hallway but I was satisfied. I knew that there was no way that Joseph could forgive Claire, not because he didn't want to, but because he felt humiliated. If he had forgiven her, then everyone in the class would have said that he was a wuss.

From that day on I found myself in a new situation. A lot of the girls who had previously ignored me now seemed to find me interesting. Some of the boys also treated me differently, with more respect, as if I had accomplished some great deed.

I don't know how Claire and Joseph managed to avoid each other after that, as they had classes together every day. He spoke only to his group of close friends; as for Claire, everyone ignored her. No one spoke to her, they treated her like an outcast. When the year was over she left the school and we never heard anything more from her.

What did I gain from my despicable action? Actually, nothing. I got rid of Claire but lost Joseph forever. Because Joseph did not forgive me. He never spoke to me again and steered clear of me whenever he saw me.

I have to admit that I enjoyed the situation for a while. I was comforted by the knowledge that I had been able to execute a plan that, for all its wickedness, was nonetheless difficult to pull off.

I know now that this victory did not taste like success. I could have called it off but did not:

When Claire came over to me, innocently, to help me with the physics problem, I should have backed out of the plan. I could have listened to her explain how to solve the exercise and then thanked her.

"Good thing you told me how to do it. I was trying to work it out last night and couldn't manage. And I'm sure that the teacher will call on me to explain it today. You know how he likes to catch us off guard."

"I don't mind helping you. I'm good at physics and math," she would have said.

Then I would have said something to Joseph like: "Claire helped me with the physics problems. She's pretty smart." And he would have been proud of her.

Yes, I could have stopped then, or even fixed things later.

When Claire insisted that it was I who had thrown myself on her, I could have admitted it.

"You're right, I'm sorry. I don't know what came over me. I . . . Well, I'm sorry."

The girls would have called me "pig" and the boys would have thought I was a loser. Joseph would have gotten angry.

"If you go anywhere near Claire ever again, I'll break your face."

"Joseph, I'm sorry. I . . . I don't know why I did it. Please forgive me."

"I've warned you, don't even think of getting close to her again."

I know that the rest of the class would have laughed at me and blamed me. They would have shunned me, but in the end perhaps Joseph would have forgiven me. I don't know. And as for Claire . . . Well, I don't think she would have forgiven me. She would have decided I was "horny" and, once she had gotten over her fright, she would have laughed at me, along with the other girls.

But I didn't do any of that, and so I ruined the first flowering of true love between Joseph and Claire, and probably, despite the years that have passed since then, neither has forgotten what happened, and neither has forgotten me. Their hatred has probably followed me throughout my life, even though I, as the years have gone by, stopped thinking about them until today.

What happened that day taught me that I was very good at causing trouble, and reminded me that I had unfinished business with my mother.

I never understood why my father had married her. They were so different. He was a perfect WASP. His family was rich. My grandfather James was a lawyer and my grandmother Dorothy was from an elite family, so my father and his sister, my aunt Emma, were both able to go to Harvard. She majored in classical literature; he studied law. And the education they received there marked their ways of being in the world from then on.

My mother was born in Miami, the daughter of a Hispanic father, an immigrant who married an American woman as poor and as graceless as he was. When my maternal grandfather arrived in the States, he had with him the address of a Catholic charity that helped immigrants. My grandmother worked there. I've always thought that my grandfather must have married her just to get citizenship, because she never could have been attractive. But they had worked hard to fulfill their American Dream and my grandfather, who was an accountant, managed to attain a certain degree of wealth and status and so, not without sacrifices, they were able to send my mother and my uncle, Oswaldo, to a private school. In the case of Uncle Oswaldo it was a wasted investment, because he never liked studying, but my mother dreamed of becoming a nurse and eventually managed to do so.

My mother spent her childhood in Miami; later, when she was a teenager, the family moved to New York City. My grandfather had gotten a better job. Even so, they couldn't afford much in the way of extras, and my mother used to tell Jaime and me how she had done everything, babysitting, flipping burgers, selling T-shirts, anything that would help pay for nursing school. She didn't go out much, and spent only what she had to: her sole goal was to end up a qualified nurse.

My parents met on one of those days when rain spoils the end of a New York summer; she was working in a hamburger joint near Rockefeller Center. She was walking through the rain without an umbrella and met a young man who had one. She didn't know him, but asked if she could share his umbrella, and where he was going. Although he was disconcerted, the stranger not only agreed to share his umbrella, but also walked the young woman to the subway.

When we were younger my father would tell Jaime and me that he had fallen in love with my mother as soon as he saw her.

I didn't understand this. I could not understand what anyone could find attractive about my mother. Her skin was dark and so was her hair, and her black eyes declared her Hispanic origin. She was always on a diet because she had a tendency to get fat. Her backside was too big and this stopped her from being elegant, for all that my father tried to teach her about dressing and behaving in accordance with his own family's standing.

Years later, when the animated movie *Pocahontas* came out, I was appalled to see how much the Indian princess looked like my mother.

It didn't help that I looked like her. My hair and dark eyes were my genetic inheritance from her, as was my tendency to put on weight. Jaime looked like my father. He had the same blond hair and the same blue-gray eyes, although Jaime's were a little darker. Like my father, Jaime was tall and slim; they both had a natural elegance lacking in my mother and me. It didn't matter that my mother wore designer clothes, nor that her elegant bags were the envy of all her coworkers at the hospital. There was always something vulgar about her. I compared her with my paternal grandmother, Grandma Dorothy, who was elegant even when dressed in clothes for the country. I suppose her height and thinness contributed to that.

I was ashamed of my maternal grandparents. Grandpa Ramón and Grandma Stella were vulgar if you compared them with the Spencer side of the family, but I forgave Stella because, although she was fat and ugly, she was at least of pure American stock. But my mother had not taken after her at all, did not have her blue eyes or chestnut-brown hair. Ramón's genes had dominion over Stella's.

My grandparents' greatest achievement was their oldest child becoming a nurse. To my relief they lived in Queens, a long way from Manhattan, and when I went to school I was the only person who knew anything about this borough. None of my classmates had ever set foot outside Manhattan.

When my maternal grandparents came to visit us they looked out of place. It didn't matter how pleasant my father was toward them, or that my paternal grandparents treated them politely. We had nothing in common with them, nothing to say to them, nothing that tied us to them except for my mother, and that was not enough for me.

But if my grandparents made me feel ashamed then Oswaldo, my mother's younger brother, made me feel even worse. He looked like what he was: a son of an immigrant who, because he had failed at school, earned his living with a little studio that he had set up himself. He laughed loudly and ate as if he were always hungry, and more than anything else I was disgusted by his fingernails, which always showed traces of paint.

My mother was aware that her family did not fit well with ours, but even so she had no pity for my father or my paternal grandparents, and from time to time she inflicted her relatives on us. The worst of it was always the Christmas meal. My Spencer grandparents went down to Florida after Thanksgiving and didn't return until the beginning of the new year, so we always spent Christmas in Queens. Jaime did not seem to notice the change from one side of the city to the other. For me it was like crossing a border into a different reality. From Manhattan into an immigrant borough in which the human texture was different, just as the shops on Fifth and Madison Avenues were different from the little businesses in Queens.

My mother was proud of her Hispanic ancestry and had given us both Spanish names. She had also insisted that Jaime and I be baptized Catholic, even though my father was Episcopalian. But I resisted and refused to be called Tomás instead of Thomas, and eventually she gave in.

I must say that Jaime seemed to find my maternal grandparents pleasant company and was always affectionate with them.

I was embarrassed to be seen with them, so I preferred to visit them in Queens rather than have them come visit us in Manhattan, where I shuddered to think that I might bump into a classmate and have to explain that this man with odd features and olive-green skin was my grandfather.

And I was not wrong: in spite of all the discourses about equality, I knew that Hispanics in the United States were barely above black people on the social scale.

Yes, I know that Clinton came to power on the back of the black vote and Obama came to power on the back of the Hispanic vote, both of them important minorities in the service sector. But I did not want to have anything to do with them.

My mother never stopped telling me that I had been a difficult child from the day I was born. It took me fourteen hours to come into the world, and I caused her so much pain that she said she would never forget it. For the first few months of my life I never stopped crying and never slept the whole night through. So my mother and I got off on the wrong foot, unlike with Jaime, who apparently came into the world almost without her noticing and never gave her a bad night.

I was an angry little boy, and from time to time my mother slapped me. I defended myself, of course, and as soon as she slapped me I would give her a kick, which made her cuff me. Even so, I should say that it was I who pushed her away whenever she tried to kiss me, or hug me, or pick me up. I couldn't bear physical contact. I remember one day, when I was seven or eight years old, she tried to give me a kiss on the sly and I kicked her away, saying, "Leave me alone, you smell bad." I didn't like the way my mother's skin smelled. It was a thick, deep smell, too much like the way I smelled myself.

When Jaime was born, I must have seen how my mother gave herself over to coddling him. Jaime didn't reject her; in fact he was anxious for any display of affection. And my mother seemed to enjoy the fact that here at last was someone who would allow her to shower him with all the kindness that I had rejected. She smiled happily when she saw him, she picked him up in her arms and gave him hugs, she spent hours looking at him and rejoicing in how beautiful he was.

My father would try to calm her down, point out that I was in the room as well, that she shouldn't distinguish between us. Then she would stretch out her hand and ruffle my hair, but I would walk away and she would look sadly after me.

My lack of affection turned into hatred. Our relationship became a permanent battle and later, proud at having broken up Joseph and Claire, I decided that the time had come to win the war with my mother.

I had to separate my parents. I wanted to force my mother to move out of our apartment. I thought that I would stay with my father, and that Jaime would go with her.

The challenge was figuring out how to accomplish this. The more I thought about it, the more difficult it was to incriminate my mother. She was dedicated to her family and to her work, and everyone who knew her liked her. Even my paternal grandfather, always a demanding man, was pleasant toward her.

I started to sleep badly, obsessed with finding a way to make my parents break up, and on one of these sleepless nights I realized that the only way to find something to use against my mother would be to follow her.

But it was not easy to leave the apartment without a good excuse. My father was very strict about how we structured our time, and my mother always wanted to know where we were, and with whom, so I told them that I needed to start running, that going out for a jog was something I needed to do to relax.

They grew accustomed to seeing me head out at any hour of the day dressed in a tracksuit: in the mornings before I went to class, at night before dinner, some afternoons.

"Well, you've certainly gotten into running," my mother said, who could not understand why I was suddenly so keen on sports when up to then I had been no fan at all of physical exercise.

"He's getting bigger, he's growing up. Don't complain, Carmela, it's better that Thomas goes out jogging rather than sitting around here wasting his time," my father said.

My mother worked as an ER nurse at Mount Sinai Hospital, not that far from where we lived. All you had to do was cross Central Park to get to the hospital, which was between Fifth and Madison. When the weather was nice, she would walk there: it took her about thirty minutes. My father didn't seem to understand why she insisted on working so much, given that we had more than enough money to live comfortably. Sometimes I heard them talking about that. But it had been hard work for my mother to become a nurse.

Running was an excuse for me to follow her. We lived close to Central Park, on West Seventy-Second Street: a street that became famous because John Lennon lived there, in the Dakota at Central Park West, until a madman killed him.

I knew my mother's schedule by heart: when she went in and out of the hospital, what shifts she worked.

I used to go to the sidewalk across from the hospital and hide. I could see people coming in and out of the building, but it was hard for them to see me.

Sometimes my mother would come out of the hospital alone, sometimes with her coworkers. I usually saw her leaving with another nurse, Alta Gracia, who, as well as being her best friend, was also Hispanic.

I still think that Alta Gracia is a surprising name. Apparently it refers to a Virgin celebrated in the Dominican Republic, which is where my mother's friend was from.

They usually stood at the entrance for a few seconds talking before saying goodbye. Other times they would walk a little way together. I was surprised by how absorbed they became in their conversations. And the way they laughed. Yes, that open and free way of laughing, guffawing almost, without caring that people stared at them.

I was frustrated to find that my mother had a routine from which she never deviated, not even by an inch. It didn't matter if it was two o'clock in the afternoon or ten o'clock at night: when she left the hospital, she went straight home.

I thought about going into the hospital, but it would have been difficult for me to spy on her there. And security might have caught me.

I spent a month spying on my mother and was about to conclude that there was nothing going on that I could use against her, when one afternoon something odd happened.

I saw her leaving with Alta Gracia. They were walking fast

and looked very serious. They walked arm in arm. Where were they going?

They walked up Madison Avenue, into Harlem, for half an hour. I followed them to a group of low buildings on 130th Street. They went up some stairs without looking back and Alta Gracia took out a key and let them into the building.

Who lived there? What were they doing there? I didn't know where Alta Gracia lived, but perhaps it was here: I had heard my mother say that she lived on her own.

"She doesn't want to get involved with anyone, and she really doesn't want children. She says she prefers to enjoy life," she had once said to my father.

"She's young now, but when she's older she'll miss having someone to share her life with," my father said.

"Well, you can share your life with someone without living under the same roof or bringing children into the world," my mother replied.

I don't know why I remembered that conversation at this particular moment. Perhaps because I was trying to find a reason why my mother might go into that particular building. Perhaps they had decided to have tea together, or were visiting someone. I couldn't think of any other reason.

I saw someone closing the curtains, but I didn't have time to see who it was. I was annoyed, but it wouldn't really have been possible to see what was going on inside given that I was on the opposite sidewalk, hiding behind a car.

My mother came out an hour later. I was surprised, because she looked hot and it was a cold day. Alta Gracia said goodbye and kissed her on both cheeks.

I started running home. It was evening and I had been out for more than two hours.

I got back after my mother did. She had taken the subway and the crosstown bus, so she was there before me. My father got back only ten minutes after I did.

"How was your day?" he asked my mother.

"Crazy. We were working flat out and Dr. Brown chose today of all days to get sick. His wife called to say he wouldn't be coming, he has the flu. And as if that weren't enough, two nurses on my shift took the day off. One of them because her son had broken his ankle playing basketball and she'd been called to go pick him up from school. And the other one's father died suddenly. So I didn't stop at all today. I'm tired. I'm going to take a shower and go to bed."

"Aren't you going to have dinner with me and the children?" my father asked, slightly surprised.

"If you don't mind, I think I'll go straight to bed. I'm exhausted."

My father did mind, but he didn't say anything. María served dinner like she did every night. I was confused: I wondered why my mother hadn't said anything about going to Alta Gracia's, if indeed she lived in that mysterious building.

Jaime didn't shut up, telling my father about the baseball game he had played that afternoon. My father seemed to be listening, but I thought I could detect a shadow of worry in his eyes.

After supper he went to his study to read, as he did every evening, and to smoke a cigar. Jaime and I went to watch television for a while in the living room while María cleaned up in the dining room, and then we went to bed.

I didn't sleep that night either, as I wondered whether my mother would tell my father where she had been.

The rest of the week my mother kept up her normal routine. Even when she left with Alta Gracia she didn't hang around and came straight home.

I thought about going back to the building in Harlem to see if Alta Gracia really lived there. I did that one Saturday afternoon. I lied to my father, saying that I had agreed to meet up with a friend to go running.

"That's a good idea, it's always better to run with someone else than to do it alone. But you should think about doing things other than running. You're old enough to start going to the theater, to concerts, to take an interest in cultural things. Maybe you could go somewhere next week, perhaps with this friend of yours, or even with Jaime."

I didn't reply. I shrugged. I didn't want to go against my father. In fact I had no friends, nobody I could go with. But my father didn't know that. And if I had a choice, I would never go anywhere with Jaime. I still hated my brother.

I spent four hours watching the building where I thought Alta Gracia lived. But I didn't see anyone going in or coming out. I was tempted to go over and ring the bell, but if Alta Gracia had opened the door then I would not have been able to justify my presence. I went home, frustrated at my failure.

My parents had gone out to dinner and Jaime was in the country for the weekend, at the house of one of his friends from school.

María was in her room, and when she heard me come in she came out to say that she had left me dinner in the kitchen. I didn't reply. I went to the kitchen for the tray and then sat in the living room in front of the television, enjoying the solitude that I liked so much.

There weren't many occasions when I had the whole apartment to myself.

But I could not concentrate on the movie I was watching. The mysterious building in Harlem was turning into an obsession. I had to find another excuse to go back and stake it out. It wouldn't be easy, because my father liked to spend the weekends with us. On Saturday or Sunday mornings we would go to gallery exhibitions; my father was an expert on modern art. He had a good eye for discovering up-and-coming artists and he was extremely proud of his collection. There were thirty or so paintings distributed throughout the house, to my mother's despair, as she could not derive the same pleasure as my father did from these canvases in which the artists had created worlds that she could not understand.

After visiting these galleries, my father would take us out to lunch at an Italian restaurant and then we would go home. Jaime would go to his room to study, my mother would sit down to watch television, and my father would cloister himself in the study to smoke and work on his cases. I would also hide in my room and open a book just in case my father came in to ask me what I was doing, but all I did was think about how to split up my parents. There was room in my head only for planning vengeance against my mother.

I had no excuse that Sunday to get away. My mother was in a bad mood and so was my father, although he, unlike my mother, never overtly showed his moods.

It was not until Monday that I was able to go to Harlem again. I spent more than an hour there outside the building, expectant, but again I saw no one come in or go out.

I must admit that Harlem made me feel a little anxious, although I heard my parents saying that the neighborhood was now much less dangerous than it had been. It would still be several years until Bill Clinton, after his presidency was over, would set up his office in the heart of the neighborhood.

Over the next few days my mother continued with her habitual routine. She left the hospital and went straight home, and not one single day did I see her leave with Alta Gracia.

I had to wait a whole week until I again saw them heading off to the mysterious building.

They walked quickly, arm in arm, murmuring to each other. They looked worried, and I thought that my mother might suspect that she was being followed, as she stopped dead in her tracks and looked back. She didn't see me because I had crouched down in time, but once again my mother revealed herself to have a well-developed intuition where I was concerned.

They went quickly into the building and this time I saw that it was Alta Gracia who closed the curtains. I cursed her for it.

My mother left two hours later. I was nervous, because María must have been worried that I was not yet home, and she was perfectly capable of calling my father or my mother.

My mother came out of the building looking upset. I didn't wait. I quickly hurried off to the entrance to the nearest subway station to try to get home before she did.

I managed it, but barely. My mother must have caught the next train because she got home only ten minutes after I did.

María confronted me.

"Would you mind telling me where you have been? You're not fooling me, or your mother, with these tales of going out running. Lord knows what you're getting caught up in . . ."

"You're always so nice to me. You think I'm the absolute worst," I said, angrily.

She didn't reply, but I was sure that inside she was in fact thinking that she didn't know anyone worse than me.

When my father arrived, my mother was already in the living room, watching television.

I was surprised to see that when my father went to see her and give her a kiss, she reacted indifferently to him.

"How was your day?" he asked.

"I didn't stop for a moment. I'm going to go to bed soon."

It was the second time that my mother, after one of her mysterious visits after work, had decided not to eat with us and had instead gone to bed early. My father said nothing, and left the room to go to the study and put down his briefcase.

The next morning, over breakfast, my mother seemed once again in a bad mood, and was distracted as well. My father paid very little attention either to Jaime or me and left the table before we had finished eating, claiming he had to go speak to a client.

That evening everything was normal once again. My father came home early and my mother seemed to have regained her good temper.

I didn't know what to think. I was sure that there was some secret at the place where my mother went with Alta Gracia, but I could not imagine what it might be. What was clear was that these visits affected my mother greatly.

If not for the fact that I wanted to cause her pain and was

now curious about what she was doing, I would have stopped following her. I was tired of running so much. One morning after breakfast, María even told my mother that I was looking a lot thinner.

"Well, it's not a bad thing for him to have lost a few pounds. Thomas is built like me, and it's not good for a boy to have so much weight in his butt," my mother said, looking at me, unaware of how much her comments hurt.

"If you think that it's okay for you to have a big butt, then you're wrong. You look like a mushroom," I said insolently.

"How dare you!" My mother was shocked to hear me talk back to her.

"You give me your opinion of my butt, and I'll give you my opinion of yours. I've inherited the worst part of you even though you don't have anything at all I would like to inherit."

"Don't talk back to your mother!" María said.

I didn't give them a chance to say anything else, because I left the kitchen, slamming the door.

"You go too far all the time," Jaime said as he followed me out.

I cuffed him so hard that tears came to his eyes. I couldn't bear him, but I consoled myself by thinking that soon I would be rid of both him and my mother.

I had to wait another week before my mother broke her routine again and returned to the building on 130th Street with Alta Gracia. It was the third time, and always on Thursday. Did this have anything to do with the fact that my father always came home later that night? On Thursdays my father and his partners met to talk over the week's work, so he never got home before eight.

This time, once again, I was unable to see what was behind the curtains.

I decided to stop spying on my mother, and instead to concentrate on the building. But I introduced a new factor: instead of running from one side of the city to the other, I got myself a bicycle. My father thought that it was a good idea for me to add cycling to my new list of sports, but my mother and María looked at me suspiciously.

Finally I managed to get somewhere: I saw Alta Gracia coming in and out of the building on three or four occasions. So either she lived there, which was the obvious conclusion, or else she was going there to see someone.

I kept asking myself why my mother always went happily into the building but came out in a bad mood, her face drawn.

On one of these Thursdays, my father came home in a good mood. He told us he had won a delicate case that he had spent months working on. "It's a great victory for the firm to win this case," he said, and did not give my mother the option of going to bed early, as she now did almost every Thursday. She barely spoke during the meal and seemed listless and upset as she poked at her plate of fish.

Jaime asked my father to tell us all the details of the case and why it was important, and he complied, ignoring my mother's pale face and her evident lack of desire to hear about it.

That night I made a decision. I would take my camera with me in my backpack and photograph my mother's entrances and exits. I was sure that she had told my father nothing of her visits to that mysterious building. It would be good for me to have some evidence of her secret.

My mother began going to the building without Alta Gracia, and after I waited for her to come out one Thursday, luck was on my side. When the door opened and my mother came out, she was with a man. I started to take photograph after photograph, asking myself who this unknown person could be. My mother was gesticulating. She seemed angry, and suddenly he took her in his arms and held her for a few seconds as I took several more photographs. She cried and he wiped her tears away, which was a clear sign of their intimacy. Then they said goodbye with a kiss on the cheek.

I pedaled home as fast as I could, anxious to get back before she did. I managed it. I was in the hall when she came in. There were no marks of tears on her face when she opened the door. She said hello to me, and seemed irritated.

"Shouldn't you be studying?"

"I was just going to the kitchen to get some tea," I said.

"It's no time to have tea, it's nearly eight. Your father will be back soon."

I waited for my father to come home. My mother had gone to her room and he went there after saying hello to Jaime and to me. The three of us had dinner alone that evening. My mother didn't bother to join us.

"She's tired," my father said, making excuses.

"She's always tired on Thursdays," I replied.

My father looked straight at me, surprised by what he had just heard. He paused for a second, as though he were processing my comment.

"Your mother's job isn't easy. There are days that are harder than others."

"Well, it seems that Thursdays are the worst day of the week. She hardly ever has dinner with us on Thursdays anymore," I insisted, mercilessly, in the face of my father's unresponsive surprise.

We ate almost in silence, for all that Jaime tried to keep the conversation going. When we finished eating my father went to hide in his study and smoke his cigar, and, I hoped, to allow the seed of the confusion I had planted with my comments to start to sprout.

My mother didn't have breakfast with us either. My father excused her again.

"She's on the night shift, so it would be good for her to sleep a little more."

"Right," I said, and gave him a significant look.

"Poor Mama, I don't know how she manages to work all through the night," Jaime said, unable to read the meaning underneath my words.

For the next few days my mother seemed upset, as if nothing and nobody surrounding her were at all important. I realized that during breakfast and lunch she made a huge effort to participate, but she didn't care about anything Jaime or I, or even my father, said. When María asked her how to organize something around the house, she left it up to her to make the decision.

I was impatient for Thursday to come around. I wondered whether I would see the man again. I wanted to take a photo of them together, to have a good collection before sending the pictures to my father.

That is what my plan was, to send my father the photos of my mother going into the building, alone and with Alta Gracia, and, most importantly, showing her in the arms of the unknown man. I would send them with a brief note: "Your wife is cheating on you." Yes, that would be enough for my father to talk to her, and she would have no other option than to admit she had a lover. Because at the time I was firmly convinced that my mother went to the building in Harlem to meet this man, and that Alta Gracia facilitated their secret meetings.

I wanted to take a good photograph of the unknown man. The photos I had taken at a distance with my camera from my hiding place were not able to show his features in detail.

The next Thursday my mother went to the building with Alta Gracia and came out alone a couple of hours later, and no one saw her to the door. Now it was I who could not control my bad temper, and I joined my mother in refusing to eat dinner with my father and brother that evening.

María, without wanting to, helped me instill greater suspicion in my father's mind, because when I said that I wasn't hungry, that something I had for lunch had disagreed with me and that I was going to bed, María muttered grumpily, "Just like your mother, every Thursday."

My father looked at her reproachfully, but María didn't even realize that we had heard what she had said.

Two more weeks went by before luck came my way again.

My mother went to the building without Alta Gracia. She was walking fast and seemed impatient. I was waiting in my hiding spot among the trees and what happened next was what I least expected. Before my mother reached the building, a man caught up with her and called her by name. She turned around and they kissed. It was an innocent kiss, like two friends give each other when they meet. Then he took her by the arm as if they were the best of friends and went up the steps to the door. The man took some keys out of his jacket pocket and opened it.

I had been taking photos the whole time. I rejoiced to think of the expression of surprise on my father's face when he saw the photos. He would be bound to ask my mother for an explanation and she would find it hard to think up an excuse, because these photographs would give my father proof of her infidelity.

I waited patiently for them to leave, but to my annoyance the man did not come out to say goodbye. Although I could have accepted my lot then, I decided to come back one last Thursday. The more photos I could send my father, the more convincing would be the evidence he could use against my mother.

Luck was not always with me, and I had to wait almost another month before I got to see her with the man again. This time they came out of the building together and walked for a good distance, talking to each other: she was holding his arm and they seemed very involved in the conversation. I followed them for a while. My mother, who was short, stood on tiptoe to kiss him goodbye and once again he held her for a few seconds in his arms.

What was the man like? Normal. Nothing about him stood out. He wasn't tall or short, or fat or thin. His hair was dark brown, almost black, but he didn't appear Hispanic. He was wearing cheap clothes, the kind that you find in any mall. Even so, he gave off a certain air of solidity, security. He didn't look like he was just anyone.

I decided that the photos I had already taken would be enough. The next step was to find a place to get them developed. It couldn't be near my house. It had to be in another neighborhood. Luckily, a city like New York allows you to be anonymous.

I got them developed the next day in Chinatown. My plan involved tying up my right arm in a sling. I went into a camera shop and spoke to a very friendly Chinese woman: I insisted that I needed to have the photographs at once. "Tomorrow," she said, but in the end she gave in and said I could have them in three hours. I had an envelope with me and asked her to write down the address because my right hand was bandaged. She did not complain and even told me where the nearest post office was.

I had abandoned the idea of adding a note saying, "Your wife is cheating on you." The photos themselves told a sufficiently obvious story. They were clear proof of my mother's betrayal.

All I had to do now was wait a few days for the envelope to arrive at my father's office, which was the address I had had the woman write. I must confess that I felt a little nervous as I waited for the big day to arrive. Every afternoon when my father came home from work I looked at him, to see if he was angry or upset. And finally the great day came.

That Monday my father came home earlier than expected. My mother had been on duty the night before and was at home. Jaime was in his room studying and I was drawing a picture.

"Tell my wife to come into the study," my father said to María as soon as he had come through the door.

"She's in the kitchen," María said, a little surprised by my father's sullen tone and bearing.

But he said nothing and went straight to the study. My mother went there a few seconds later, confused by his request. She didn't shut the door and I hid in the hallway, excited to imagine what would happen next.

My father handed her the envelope without saying anything. She looked at it uncomprehendingly.

"What is this?"

"You tell me."

She opened the envelope and took out the photographs. She went through them one by one; there were more than twenty of them. Then she put them back in the envelope and handed it back to my father.

"It's you who needs to give me an explanation. Are you spying on me?"

"*I* need to give you an explanation? Well, you've got nerve at least."

"Juan, don't raise your voice . . ." When she was nervous, my mother would use the Spanish version of my father's name.

"Don't call me Juan and I'm not raising my voice. I'm asking you for an explanation and you have the nerve to tell me that I should be giving you one."

"Yes. I want to know who took these photos, who has been following me, and why. And you have the photos, so you should be able to give me an explanation."

My father barely managed to contain his indignation. I saw his clenched fists held down at his sides and my mother in front of him, looking him in the eye, defiant.

"They came to me in the mail this morning."

"Who sent them to you?" my mother insisted.

"The charitable soul who found you out neglected to include a business card," my father replied.

"Right . . . And this 'charitable soul,' as you call him, what exactly has he discovered?"

"Who is this man, Carmela? Why do you go to this house?"

"You're asking me for explanations?"

"Are you surprised?"

"We've always had a relationship of mutual trust," my mother replied. "I've never asked you about your dinners with clients or why you stayed late working in the office. And I wouldn't be suspicious of you if tomorrow I came across you walking down the street with a woman I didn't know."

"You're good at this, Carmela! You'd have made a great law-yer. Turning the victim into the aggressor. Amazing!"

"No one has attacked you, but you are attacking me. I insist that you give me an explanation."

I had never seen my father so angry. He was an even-tempered man who never raised his voice. This was the first time I had heard him shout.

"Where do you go on Thursdays, Carmela?"

"Thursdays! Goodness, you're so on the ball that you can even put days of the week on these photos."

"You owe me an explanation," my father insisted. "Or else . . ."

"Are you threatening me, Juan?"

"I'm asking for an explanation. Nothing more."

Up to that moment they had been standing up, facing each other. Now my mother sat down in an armchair, first lighting a cigarette, even though she knew it annoyed my father greatly when she smoked.

She greedily sucked in the smoke while my father remained standing.

"I suppose you know that in this country you can die with-out good medical insurance, without anyone feeling the need to look after you in a hospital like you deserve. That there are treatments you don't get if you can't pay for them, no matter how sick you are. The man in the photo is . . . He's a friend of mine and Alta Gracia's. He worked in hospital reception for a while, then they fired him, you know how these businesses are. They thought that a younger, more attractive woman was better than a middle-aged man. And he, well, he worked at the jobs he could get, and now he keeps the books for most of the businesses around where he lives. He's a good man. When they threw him out of the hospital his wife abandoned him. She took their two little children and he hasn't heard anything about her since. Now he lives with his daughter Natalie, from his first marriage. She's twenty years old and has cancer, and she's not going to get better. She needs palliative care, but he doesn't have the money to pay for it. So Alta Gracia and I help as much as we can. I go and help wash her and . . . well, I give her morphine injections for the pain. I help them. I usually go on Thursdays, which is when Alta Gracia has her guitar lessons. I spend two or three hours there; I wash her, I change her sheets, I give her the morphine . . . Natalie is aware that she is going to die, that she's living on borrowed time. The doctors told her that she wouldn't live more than six months, and the end is near. And if you want to know more, I'll tell you. I think George is a good man. I don't do what I do just for his daughter, but also for him. He's a good man, an upright man, who has been denied all the good that he deserves. You wouldn't like him, and do you know why? Because George is a loser and you don't want to hear anything about losers. Life has been good to you. You haven't had to struggle to get what you've got; it was always there, and all you had to do was stretch out your hand and take it. The rest of us have had to fight to make our way. I've been lucky; George hasn't, and he's been left behind."

They didn't say anything. What more was there to say? I scarcely dared breathe for fear that they would realize I was there.

"Why didn't you ever tell me about this man and this girl?" my father asked in a hoarse voice.

"I don't know. I suppose because it has nothing to do with you. Why should you care what happens to someone you don't know?"

"George is a part of your life you don't share with me, is that it?"

"I don't know. Maybe."

"When someone's hiding something . . ."

"Yes, they end up looking suspicious."

"What is there between George and you?"

My mother said nothing. She seemed to be trying to formulate her answer as if she were afraid of what she was going to say.

"Nothing to be ashamed of. But I do feel close to him, close to his pain. I admire him, okay? Yes, I admire him because in spite of everything he hasn't given in. He's lost his wife, his two young children, he's about to lose his daughter forever, and he still keeps on fighting. I don't know where he gets the strength to carry on."

"What do you want to do?" my father asked, aware now of the depth of feeling that existed between my mother and George.

"What do you want to do, John? You sent people to spy on me."

"I didn't send anyone. I don't know who sent me these photos."

"You might not know who, but the reason is clear: there's someone who wants to hurt me, who wants to hurt the both of us," my mother said.

"Well, they've done it," my father replied.

"George is not my lover," my mother said in a low voice.

"Yes, but you yourself have said how important this man is to you. You spoke about him in a way that I don't imagine you'd speak about me. Sometimes the betrayal is greater when it has nothing to do with sex. Carmela, it's you who has to explain yourself, to tell me why you didn't share this with me, why you pushed me to the side. I think that both of us know the answer."

My mother seemed to be afraid. The security that she had so rejoiced in was starting to melt away. My father was standing, facing her, looking at her as though she were a stranger. She had wounded him deeply. All the certainties of his life were falling apart in front of his eyes.

I wanted to shout, that's how happy I felt to see my mother about to be ruined. Yes, ruined! And by me! I was sure that my father would not be able to forgive her and that they would end up separating. They had no other option.

"I've got work to do. I'll sleep here," my father said, making a sign that my mother should leave the study.

"Juan, we can't leave things like this. I . . . Perhaps I wasn't entirely aware of how important it was, what I was doing."

"I'm not blaming you for wanting to help someone who worked with you. You know that that's not the problem. I'm not a monster. The question you need to answer, and answer to me, is why you hid what you were doing, why you couldn't share it with me, why this man is so important to you."

"There was nothing between us, I swear!"

"Please, Carmela, that's not what we are talking about and you know it."

My father had decided that the conversation was over, and my mother did not seem to have the strength to continue. I hurried away, scared that she would find me. I couldn't sleep that night, as I was enjoying my triumph.

Our lives changed. The change was not rapid, but it was clear. I waited desperately for my parents to tell Jaime and me that they had decided to separate, and I grew impatient that days went by without either of them saying anything.

They didn't say anything, they didn't speak, apart from saying, "Please pass the sugar," or, "Would you mind giving me that cup?"

María noticed the tension between my parents and seemed to have been struck dumb, and she even stopped annoying me with her constant reproaches.

Jaime was worried. He knew something was happening but did not know what it was.

"I don't know what's up with Dad and Mama. They're not talking at all. It's like they're . . . not angry, but distant. Don't you think it's strange?" my brother asked me one day.

I shrugged, as though I didn't care. I don't think Jaime

expected this reaction, and he kept on talking to me even though he was in fact talking to himself.

"Dad sleeps in the study a lot. I heard them talking a few days ago. Mama asked him to come back to the room they always used to share, and he said that he was busy with a case and that he'd sleep in the study that night as well. I hope it's nothing serious; I'd hate it if our parents split up. I love them both so much."

"You stick to your own business and leave them to deal with theirs. Why do you care what happens to them?"

"Of course I care, and you should care too, they're our parents . . ."

"And they're old enough to know what's best for them. And don't be dumb, you're not a kid anymore."

One afternoon when I came home I saw that the study door was shut. I wanted to go in, but María stopped me.

"Your parents are talking and they told me that no one was to disturb them. You'll have to wait."

"Have they been talking for a long time?" I asked.

"More than two hours. Don't be nosy. Go to your room. You must have some homework to do."

At last! I thought. At last they're talking, deciding how to manage their separation. That's what they must be doing, I thought. But I was wrong. My parents came out of the study having made an agreement: they would carry on living together. That weekend we resumed our custom of eating out after going to the exhibitions our father wanted to see.

We returned to our routine, but did so without much enthusiasm. I was furious that I hadn't achieved my goal of breaking up my parents, and my parents seemed to be resigned more than anything else. The only person who seemed happy was Jaime.

No, I hadn't managed to break them up, but I consoled myself with the thought that I had destroyed my father's trust in my mother, and that she would never be able to recover it. It seemed that they had stopped being happy, although they went back to sharing a room.

My father treated my mother with a coldness that was not at all a matter of calculation, but rather the result of something having broken inside him that could not be repaired. My mother stopped laughing. She seemed to stop caring about her looks; she got fat. Worry made her eat more than she should have.

I asked myself why they had decided to stay together if it was clear that they now felt very separate from each other. But I could not figure out a reason.

Now it was my father who sometimes came home late, while my mother stopped going out on Thursday afternoons.

I broke their life together, and although I enjoyed this at the time, now I realize how useless my triumph was. I shouldn't have sent those photos to my father. No, I definitely shouldn't have done that.

If I could turn back time I would go back to the afternoon when I had the photos developed. Yes, I should have stopped at that moment. I imagine how things would have been:

The Chinese sales assistant would have asked me when I needed the photos. As soon as possible, I would have insisted. Then I would have asked her to write my father's address on the envelope and I would have set off toward the post office. Imagine the scene. Once all the stamps were in place, the post office clerk would have stretched out his hand for the envelope, and I would have taken a step backward.

"Do you want me to mail it or not?" he would have asked, surprised at my reaction.

"It's just that . . . Well, I think there's something I forgot to put in it . . . I just remembered . . . I'd better check and bring it back."

I would have pressed the envelope to my chest and once I was safely out in the street I would have gasped for breath, asking myself why I hadn't done what I promised myself I would do.

"It's a crime what you were planning to do to your parents," I would have said to myself. "The truth is that your mother hasn't done anything serious enough to you for you to try to destroy her. You're going to hurt Dad a lot, and he won't recover from this."

I would have struggled with myself for a long time. I would have gone over the list of grievances I had against my mother and then would have thought about the harm I was about to cause my father. He had shown me infinite kindness, even though I had always been the person I was. No, he didn't deserve to be punished this way. Perhaps my mother did, but not my father.

I could have carried on with my little petty revenges against her, there was always something to do, but there was no need to destroy my father.

Walking up and down while I marshaled my thoughts, I would have eventually come to a decision. I would have gone over to a storm drain, opened the envelope, and torn the photographs into unrecognizable pieces and dropped them through the grating.

As I tore them up I would have felt a slight discomfort with myself for having been so soft, for having felt compassion for my father and allowing that to stop me from taking revenge on my mother.

When I got home, I would have found my father in the study, absorbed in some papers.

"Come in, Thomas, come in. How was school today?"

We would have spoken for a while about nothing much: my classes, my classmates, María's last complaint about how untidy my room was, and we would have heard my mother's key turn in the lock, heard how tired she was as she came in. She would have come over to my father to give him a kiss on the cheek, then squeezed my arm and said hello, and then gone to say hello to Jaime in his room.

Yes, everything would have been the same as it had been up to then. My mother would never have abandoned us for the man in the mysterious building. It was just an illusion, a means of feeling alive, of overcoming her deadening routine.

Marriage to my father had played a key role in her personal and social ascent in the world. She, the daughter of an immigrant, had been transformed into an East Coast upper-class wife. Yes, she had come a long way, not just because of her education and her work, but also because her place in the world had been transformed when she married John Spencer.

She liked calling my father Juan, but that was a joke between the two of them. John Spencer was a respected lawyer, as his father and grandfather and great-grandfather before him had been. He had a spacious apartment in Manhattan, insurance in case of sickness or unanticipated expenses, and a dozen good friends with whom he could spend weekends sailing off Newport, as well as traveling every now and then to Europe.

They had a good life in which nothing was lacking, and my mother enjoyed all the advantages she had not had as a child living in Miami and, later, in Queens.

No, she would not have taken any step that would have cost her all this. I was sure of that.

That night, I would have felt a bittersweet sensation in my stomach. Bitter because I had not delivered the coup de grâce to my mother, sweet because I had saved my father.

I would have observed her, at dinner, and said to her wordlessly: "You owe me your life, this life that you are enjoying, and if I wanted to I could tear it away from you." I would look at my father and at Jaime and think that, even though they didn't know it, they would always be in my debt for having allowed them to remain ignorant of my mother's lies, to keep them living this life that flowed peaceably, without great upheavals.

More than once, I am sure I would have regretted my decision not to keep the photographs in the envelope. Yes, every time my mother stood in my way, every time we confronted each other, I would have made the decision to go back to that building, Thursday after Thursday, until I could take more photographs of her together with that man. She didn't know it, but I would always have her fate in my hands, and that would make me feel good. Even so, the important thing is that I would not have brought sadness into my house.

But instead I chose revenge and took pleasure in it. There was a victim, my father, who would never again be happy.

Was I pleased with myself? Yes, at that moment I was pleased with what I had done, and didn't regret it. And now it is too late for regrets. It would be hypocritical of me to regret it, and I will not, but I know that the day I sent that envelope I changed the direction of both my parents' lives.

YOUTH

2

I didn't have the grades to get into Harvard, so I broke the family tradition that the firstborn son should study at that institution, which shelters the best and the brightest, and eventually take up law there. That honor fell to Jaime, my perfect brother.

My mother was not upset that I would not be able to study at Harvard.

"Jaime will do it," she said, as my father was bemoaning the fact that I would not be following the family tradition.

"Yes, I know, but I would have liked it if Thomas . . ." my father insisted.

"He's never liked studying; it will be difficult to get him into any college. Let him decide what he wants to do."

"He's said that he wants to go out to work, but I won't allow it. There's no need for him to do so, but he does need to educate himself," my father replied.

My mother said nothing. She never stood up for me; she thought I had no talent for anything. Or at least that's what I thought.

Despite my insistence that I didn't want to keep studying, much less go to college, my father insisted that I do something. "Whatever you want, but make it something you like," he said.

"I'd like to make ads," I said, just to say something, although the truth was that ever since I was a child I had tuned out whenever the commercials came on the television.

"Well, that's not a bad idea . . . I didn't think that the life of an adman was something you might like. Well, we'll find a good place for you to study," my father said.

"I don't want to go to college. I'm sick of studying. Can't you get me a job at some firm one of your friends runs?"

"We'll try to find a proper place for you to study. If you want to be an adman then you need to work at it."

There was no way to change his mind. He was inflexible. I could have refused; I was old enough now to go out into the world by myself. I don't think that anyone, with the possible exception of my father, would have minded if I had gone to the other side of the country.

My paternal grandfather had retired and left the law partnership in my father's hands, and now he was enjoying traveling with Grandma Dorothy. As for my maternal grandparents, I didn't care about them, I never treated them with affection and they were always withdrawn with me. They were a mirror in which I did not like to see myself reflected, especially when it came to my uncle, Oswaldo.

I also don't think that Jaime would have noticed my absence all that much. His only aim was to be like my father, so he spent all his time studying to get into Harvard. I suppose he dreamed of one day taking over my father's place in the law firm. And my mother . . . Well, I really don't know about her, but given that she was always complaining about me, perhaps she would have felt relieved if I had gone to live in Los Angeles, which was something I was always threatening them with.

But in the end I made a practical decision. Had I left, it would have meant trying to find my own way in the world, taking whatever job was necessary to survive, and losing all the privileges that had up to that moment accompanied me through life.

"All right, Dad, I'll study, but I won't go to college. I've spoken to a training center, a kind of academy; they'll let me in and I can study advertising there."

"An academy? What could you possibly learn there?"

"Don't think it's the easy option. It's called the Hard School of Advertising, it doesn't sound all that bad. It's in SoHo."

"That's a strange location for a school," my mother murmured.

"Why? It's a neighborhood where things happen," I replied defensively.

My father, aware that it was the most he could ask of me, accepted this in the end. My mother seemed indifferent: for all she tried to hide it, I knew that she had no faith in me whatsoever.

The owner of the academy, Paul Hard, seemed a very strange man. A loser who did not give in even though he was aware that his moment had passed. From the start I knew that he was a scrounger, a survivor who would do anything just to keep on living a couple of minutes more. He also saw that, out of all the academy's students, I was different; all he needed to do was find out how, and why.

Paul had been a successful creative director and, his résumé claimed, he had worked in two of the most important ad agencies in the city. He never told us students why he had been fired, but we found out that after leaving the last agency he had spent several years out of work, finding odd jobs as a traveling salesman, or designing business cards for local shops. This barren period had coincided with his third divorce. That wife did not want to share her life with a failure, so she left him for another creative director, an old friend of Paul's with his own business in San Francisco.

The Hard School of Advertising brought me into contact with a reality that was very different from the one I had been accustomed to.

We students were a mixed bunch. We weren't all the outcasts of society. Some of us were poor little lambs who had lost their way, the sons of rich families, who had ended up there because no college worth going to had accepted them; others, like me, were those who had no plans to do even the smallest amount of work, but didn't want their parents to see that they were doing nothing.

Paul had rented part of an old warehouse and remodeled it himself. He had taste and imagination, so the inside looked decent despite its shabby exterior. There were other teachers and former stars, just as Paul himself had been.

"You are going to spend the next two years with us, so it's better for you to make sure things are clear from the start. This isn't college, but the three of us know more than all the snooty professors at Harvard. We know all the tricks of the trade and that's something they don't teach you at any university. You're going to learn more than you might imagine, but I'd better warn you from the start that the people who survive here are those who manage to forget their goody-goody attitudes. When it comes to getting an account, there are no rules."

I liked Paul's welcome. No pretentious words about what our futures held for us. He didn't feel that he owed us anything. We were just a way for him to pay his bills and survive, but he was going to teach us what he knew.

Paul always wore a jacket. In winter he alternated two worn-out cashmere jackets, souvenirs of the time when he had been a successful executive. In summer, it was crumpled linen jackets, which had seen better days.

The classes started at eight and finished at noon and I must say that I was never bored. The teachers explained what they knew and how they had done their jobs; they explained the campaigns they had taken part in and got us to invent our own campaigns for all kinds of products. There weren't many of us, no more than fifty, so we were divided into working groups. Each group pretended to be an advertising agency, and we competed against one another to win the accounts, whether they were for sausages or makeup or bathroom cleaner.

There were a few very smart girls in my group, and the hard parts of the tasks always fell on their shoulders, especially on Esther's, while the three or four boys, like me, tried to avoid doing any work at all.

I liked Esther. She was Italian-American. Her family had a restaurant, where her father worked, along with her grandmother, two uncles, and her older brother. But she was not prepared to spend her life sweating over a stove or waiting tables. She knew what she didn't want to do and she enrolled in the academy because it was the only school her parents could afford.

But I got along better with Lisa. She lived with her parents in a luxurious duplex on Fifth Avenue, facing the park. She had been expelled from several all-girls high schools. She had ended up at the Hard School of Advertising to annoy her parents, who had imagined another future for her. She went there because she had to go somewhere. New York winters were too cold for her to be out on the street, and she couldn't go to her usual hangouts because she might see someone she knew, so she went to the academy, put on her headphones, and tuned out. Until one day when Esther stood up to her.

"I'm not going to do all the work myself; the guys do little enough as it is, but you don't do anything. So roll up your sleeves or switch groups."

Lisa went to complain to Paul about Esther's attitude, but he didn't care.

"I don't mind if you come in and don't do anything, as long as you pay your tuition, but I'm not here to deal with your whining. Sort it out yourselves."

She wasn't used to being treated like that, but she realized that Paul wasn't going to care about her poor-little-rich-girl complaints. He had accepted her for one reason only, her tuition payments, and as far as everything else was concerned he didn't care if she came to his classes or sat in the hall. He didn't care about teaching us anything. He said that he wasn't our father and that we were old enough to make our own choices. I think that his indifference in fact led lots of us to be interested in what he had to teach us. He didn't care; he wasn't going to fight any wars to make us love advertising. We were a group of more or less useless young people and that wasn't his problem. It was up to us.

If there had been a spark of anything good in me, I would have tried to become Esther's friend. She was intelligent, dogged, and ambitious, and it was clear she would take any chance as long as it kept her from seeing the family restaurant looming on the horizon.

But birds of a feather flock together, so I spent most of my time with Lisa, in whom I recognized my own darker instincts.

I knew that I would never be able to trust Lisa, that she was capable of any kind of wickedness just for kicks, and that she took revenge on anyone who crossed her. I didn't doubt for a second that one of these days she would destroy Esther. She pretended not to pay her any attention, but this was her way of blindsiding her. Yes, she was capable of fooling everyone but Paul and me. Paul was not taken in by Lisa and knew how to put her in her place. As for me, it was interesting to have her near me so that I could watch her; also, she was attractive and dressed well, and we had fun together.

My father and Jaime, even María, seemed to approve of my friendship with Lisa. She had come to visit us a couple of times at home, and had been charming and well-mannered. Also, my father knew about Lisa's father, Mr. Ferguson, a meat magnate. Apparently he owned thousands of head of cattle, reared for the slaughterhouses. I made fun of her and called her a "steak princess."

Lisa was not able to deceive my mother. They immediately felt antipathy toward each other.

"She's not a nice girl," my mother felt brave enough to say on the day they met.

"How do you know? You've barely spoken to her and you

say she's not a nice girl. You know what, Mama? You think you're better than everyone else, that no one's superior to you."

"Thomas, don't talk like that to your mother. She was just giving her opinion," my father said.

"Right, but you thought she was great," I replied.

"Yes," my father admitted, a little flustered because he didn't want to have a scene on account of Lisa.

"Well, when Mama knows her a little better she might change her mind," Jaime said, trying to find a happy medium.

"Mama doesn't like anything that I like and she's perfectly capable of condemning someone after knowing them for five minutes," I insisted.

"You're right, it was a hasty opinion. I'm sure she's a good kid, but those eyes, her way of looking at people . . . I don't like it. I don't know why. I'm sorry I annoyed you, Thomas," my mother said, which satisfied me.

"Well, the important thing is that Thomas likes her, and we'll get to know her as time goes by. She could come sailing with us in Newport one weekend. Would that be a good idea, son?" my father suggested.

"Yes, that would be great. The Fergusons have a house in Newport as well. Oh yes, they've invited me to a benefit dinner at the Plaza this weekend. Lisa's mother runs a charity that raises money for African children."

"At the Plaza? Excellent," my father said, who seemed satisfied that I had been invited to an important social engagement outside our normal group of friends.

"I'll tell María to take your tuxedo to the cleaners," my mother said, in an attempt to appear conciliatory.

I enjoyed the benefit dinner. Lisa made up a game where we had to decide what animals all the friends of her family were like. Every new comparison made us burst out laughing, and I must admit that we were both very witty.

If my mother didn't like Lisa, then I didn't like hers either. Her mother saw what was obvious, that we were too alike for any good to come from our connection. But just like my mother, Lisa's mother didn't dare put obstacles in the way of our friendship: she knew her daughter well and was aware that if she criticized me too much she would only push us closer together. So she tried not to make it too obvious how much she disliked me.

Although we had already slept together several times, that night Lisa wanted to have sex in one of the women's restrooms at the hotel.

"It'll be exciting," she said as she dragged me by the hand.

I didn't think there was anything exciting about locking ourselves in a stall—quite the opposite, in fact—but what Lisa really wanted was for someone to find us and for all her mother's friends to hear about it.

I followed along. We entered the restroom at just the right moment, while a friend of Lisa's mother was touching up her makeup and chatting with a friend of hers.

Lisa pretended she hadn't seen them and pushed me into a stall. She started to whisper obscenities while she unzipped her dress and pushed me up against the wall. I wasn't capable of fully inhabiting my role. Not just because of the scandalized whispers of the ladies who were still outside, but because I didn't feel completely comfortable in the situation. I did what I could, which was not much.

"You're a fag," Lisa whispered in my ear.

Then she started to moan as though we were really having unforgettable sex. Well, it was definitely going to be unforgettable, because all her parents' friends and mine would find out about our exploits.

Lisa opened the door while she was still half out of her dress and I was crouched down looking for my bow tie, which she had thrown onto the floor. The women scolded me for coming into the ladies' room, and were scandalized by Lisa's attitude. She didn't bother replying; she zipped up her dress, touched up her lipstick, smiled, and took me by the hand to lead me out of there.

"We've gone a bit far," I ventured.

"Don't be stupid. We've done something they'd love to do but aren't brave enough to go through with."

I wasn't sure she was right, but I said nothing. Although I didn't want to admit it, she controlled our relationship.

When we got back to the table, her mother looked at us so angrily I thought she was going to hit us or throw us out. Mr. Ferguson grabbed his wife's arm in an attempt to hold her back, and couldn't meet Lisa's eyes as she stared at him defiantly. The rest of the guests at our table were so uncomfortable they didn't dare look at us.

But Lisa still had not finished embarrassing her parents. As soon as we sat down in the midst of an ominous silence, she got up again and looked at everyone scornfully.

"Let's go, Thomas, these old farts bore me. Don't complain, Mother dear, I've done my bit and come to your dull party. I hope next time you won't insist on my accompanying you to fulfill your social obligations."

Lisa's mother stood up and was still for a moment as she looked at her daughter. Then she gave Lisa a slap that sounded as though someone had broken a glass. All the guests looked on in shock. I didn't know what to do, but Lisa decided for me: she took hold of my hand and made me follow her. I didn't dare say goodbye to the Fergusons.

I know that I blushed. I had not until this moment been capable of making a show of myself in public. Yes, I had done a few things I was embarrassed of, but these had always stayed private or, at the very least, had occurred in such a way that none of the witnesses could accuse me directly, or have anything to pin on me apart from their suspicions. But the scene that had just played out left us both exposed.

We left the Plaza, followed by the recriminatory gazes of

everyone we passed. She smiled defiantly, but I felt too confused to do anything other than look straight ahead and walk faster as I tried to escape.

It was cold in the street and snowing. All the cabs that passed us were taken. Lisa held me tighter by the arm, scared of slipping. Her feet sank into the snow. It was not easy to walk in those fragile high heels.

"This is hopeless."

"Well, what now, then? I can't walk in these. My feet are soaked," she said angrily.

At this moment I would have gladly abandoned her in the street, but I didn't dare. We walked until we spotted a café and I suggested we go in.

She said nothing, but tried to walk faster to get there sooner.

When we got inside Lisa was soaked. Her updo had collapsed and water had sluiced down her face, taking with it layers of makeup and eye shadow. The mink stole her mother had lent her was equally wet and had not protected her silk dress, which now stuck to her body. And as for her shoes, they were completely useless.

"Sit down," I said, and took her to a corner table. "I'll order us coffee."

"I don't want coffee. Get something stronger."

"Like what?" I asked in irritation.

"Is gin all right for you?"

"No, it's not all right. You've had enough for one night and you're frozen: you need something hot."

"Get me some gin and stop preaching."

The waitress looked at us from a few feet away. She didn't seem at all surprised to see two sodden figures in a dress and a tuxedo. Her gaze was both indifferent and condescending, more or less half one and half the other.

"Gin for both of you?" she asked before I could say anything.

"Gin for her, and a strong coffee for me."

"Anything to eat?"

"No, we've just come from a dinner."

"Right."

I called several car services without success. Lisa looked at me angrily, as if it were my duty to find a cab.

"The only other thing I can do is call my brother and ask him to come pick us up."

"Your goody-two-shoes brother has a car?"

"Well, he could take my mother's car keys."

"How old is he?"

"Seventeen."

She was making me nervous with her questions. Why should she care how old my brother was? Also, I wasn't sure that Jaime would pick us up without telling my mother.

"Call Esther."

"Esther? You're crazy. Do you really want to wake her up at this time of night?"

"She's a good girl, and she won't mind doing us a favor. Good girls don't leave people they know abandoned in the street when it's snowing. You wouldn't go rescue her, and I wouldn't either, but she'll come rescue us."

She was right. To my surprise, Esther agreed to come. Lisa gave her the address of the café and said thank you.

"Well, she is a good girl," I said in surprise.

"And she likes you. Don't tell me you haven't noticed? Thomas, the whole academy knows. Why else do you think she lets us copy her work? She's a stupid little good girl."

Half an hour later Esther turned up at the café. She didn't blame us for anything or ask us any questions; she just took us home. We dropped Lisa off first, and then she took me home.

"Thank you, Esther, you saved our lives. We got unlucky with the cabs tonight." I felt foolish, trying to apologize.

"Don't worry. You'd have done the same for me."

No. I felt the urge to say that I wouldn't have done the same, not for her, not for anybody. That I wouldn't have left my house at eleven o'clock at night in a snowstorm to find a couple of classmates who didn't even behave like classmates should. But I shut up and nodded. I think she knew deep down that I wouldn't have gone out of my way to help her, not in circumstances like these or in any others.

My house was silent when I arrived, but I was shocked to see a light on in my father's office. I tiptoed past the door, but I hadn't taken more than a step when I heard my father's voice.

"Thomas."

"Yes, Dad."

"Your mother and I are waiting for you. Come in."

The presence of my mother meant a storm was coming. They must have already been made aware of the scandal that Lisa and I had unleashed. My father knew a great many of the Fergusons' guests, and one of them must have hurried to tell them about our behavior.

My mother, wrapped up in a robe, sat in an armchair. She looked at me bitterly, once more regretting the lack of communication between us.

"What happened? How could you behave so . . . so terribly? I'm ashamed of all the things I had to hear about you and this girl . . ." My father's upper lip trembled, an unmistakable sign that he was upset.

I said nothing. I didn't know what to say and I was not feeling strong enough to be insolent, which was what my mother wanted from me.

"I want an explanation, Thomas," my father insisted.

"I can't give you one," I replied in a tired voice.

"You can't? You can and you must." My father's voice was filled with indignation, but also pain.

"I don't have to explain anything," I said, and turned toward the door.

"You slimy little bastard!" my mother shouted.

I turned toward her, furious. She was still seated, but you

could see the tension in her body and her face. If she had dared to do it she would have hit me.

"Carmela, please!" My father looked at her in anger.

"He has to give us an explanation. He's made you look ridiculous. Yes, you: it's you who knows all these important people. You yourself said that there were clients of yours who would be at the dinner, and some of your classmates from Harvard, and, best of all, the wife of one of your most important clients, that unbearable Donovan woman, who has taken it upon herself to make sure everyone knows what kind of a son we have."

I felt nervous when I found out that Martha Donovan had been at the dinner. I hadn't seen her, but that was not surprising; there had been more than three hundred people there. My mother felt no affection for this woman, who represented everything that she was not. Martha Donovan was the daughter of one of the steel kings. Her family was East Coast aristocracy, she had gone to Radcliffe, and she was married to Robert Donovan, one of Wall Street's most influential bankers. You did not want to be on Martha Donovan's bad side if you wanted to be received in New York society. And my behavior had made my father look bad.

"I'm not going to give you any kind of explanation, and I don't have to. Good night."

"Thomas . . ."

But I did not respond to my father's call. I went to my room and bolted the door, knowing that one of them would try to come ask me the reasons for my behavior.

What happened did not have to happen. I have never felt proud of that episode with Lisa, but neither have I regretted it.

Things should have gone differently, yes, but I was not brave enough to tell Lisa what to do:

When she ordered me into the restroom I should have said no, although she would have blown her top and insulted me. Lisa

*could have thrown me out of the dinner, but I should have taken
that risk. If she had done so then she would have been the one
making a fuss, and I would have been the offended party. What
should I have done when Lisa insisted that I follow her to the
restroom?*

"No, and I mean no. Are you crazy? If you want to cause a
scandal tonight I'm not going to be any part of it," I should have
said.

*Lisa would have been surprised at my refusal to participate in
one of her games.*

"Come on, don't be a coward. I'm desperate to have a quick
fuck. Do you want me to find someone else?"

"Do what you want, but I'm not going into the women's restroom with you. At least have a bit of taste when you're trying to
find somewhere to have sex."

"Now who's fussy! Any of the men here would die to do it
with me, wherever we went."

"Well, I suppose you've got a lot of people to choose from,
then. Go and ask around, see how many go with you. Tell me
how it went."

"You're an idiot! Was this why I insisted that my mother
invite you? Why don't you get out of here, you snob? Go back to
your mommy."

"Are you sure you want me to go?" I would have said, looking
firm and serious.

"Yes, get out! I'm sick of you. You're so boring."

*Lisa would have turned to the guest on her left and ignored
me for a while as I asked myself what to do.*

*Suddenly, Lisa would have spoken in a loud voice to her
mother.*

"Mother dear, you're right: Thomas isn't the one for me.
Can you ask him to leave? He's making me feel uncomfortable
and . . . well, either he goes or I do."

*The guests at our table would have waited, silent and expect-
ant and probably a little uncomfortable. Mr. Ferguson would*

have cleared his throat, looking at his wife in search of an answer. His wife would have smiled and looked at me, waiting for me to show a spark of dignity and leave, which is exactly what I would have done.

"If you don't mind . . . Thank you so much for your kind invitation. The dinner was a great success. How could it fail to be, given the worthiness of the cause? Good night."

And, looking straight ahead, I would have left the dining room with a steady stride in the face of the astonished guests, in an overt display of dignity. Yes, I could have felt proud of myself. Also, Lisa would have been furious at my rebellion and that would have raised me in her esteem. She was only ever interested in things she could not control.

My father would have been surprised to see me come home early. I would have told him part of the truth—that I had argued with Lisa over a matter of no importance. Although he would have liked to insist, my father would not have pressured me to tell him the cause of the argument. My mother would have given no sign of interest, and so I would have saved myself from having to give her an explanation too.

Or else I might not have been capable of standing up to Lisa and would have followed her to the restroom. But once we were there I should have refused to take off my pants.

"This is ridiculous. Do you think we can do anything here? I don't feel like it."

"You're a fag."

"I don't care what you say. Let's get out of here."

I should have opened the door to the stall and faced up to the recriminatory gazes of the scandalized women.

"I'm sorry, this was stupid. A stupid bet. I hope we haven't disturbed you too much."

Of course, they would have told the rest of the guests, but it wouldn't have been as bad.

Or else Lisa, to hurt her mother, would have decided to say that she was bored with being surrounded by old farts and would have left, asking me to accompany her. And I would have had to be firm with her.

"Lisa, it's a great party and I don't see why we need to go. Thank you very much for inviting me to spend such a special night with you all. I could not have had more pleasant dining companions."

I can imagine Lisa's anger. She would have kicked my shin and elbowed me in the kidneys, insisting that we leave and insulting her mother's guests. I would have had only one option.

"I think it would be best if I escorted Lisa out. It would not be fair to allow her to ruin a night as wonderful as this one. I'm very sorry to have to leave, but it's better if I go with her. Don't worry, I'll get a cab and take her home."

At this point, Lisa would have stood up and headed toward the exit. I would have followed her angrily.

"Is this how you leave me in front of your parents? What will they think of me? There are people here who know my parents! I don't need to make a fool of myself just for you. So this is it. I'm sick of your whims and childish behavior. Grow up. You're a woman, not a baby."

I should have realized that what we were doing was not good. Above all, I should not have been afraid to stand up to Lisa.

My last chance would have been when I got home. Yes, at this point I could, perhaps, at least in front of my parents, have lessened the impact of what I had done.

When I saw the light in my father's office it should have been me who went in and showed my face.

"Thomas, come in. Come here. What happened? They called us. How could you have behaved so badly?"

"Dad, I'm sorry, you don't know how sorry I am. There's no excuse for what I did. Lisa . . . well, Lisa is a little difficult. It's hard to disagree with her and sometimes . . . She gets along very badly with her mother and wanted to upset her, to make her ashamed in front of her friends, and I was a part of it. I don't

know how to apologize. Don't think that I'm proud of what I've done. If I could go back in time, if I could make things better . . ."

My mother would have looked at me in disbelief. She would not have been prepared for any contrition on my part, and far less for me to say something like this to her face.

"You've made us all look ridiculous, especially your father. That Donovan woman called . . . You can imagine what this is going to cost him. You're an ungrateful little bastard!"

"Carmela, please, I don't want to hear you say that! Thomas, are you aware of the damage you've done, not just to us but to yourself? We have a reputation, a good name. There are lots of doors that will open to you in this life, simply because of who you are, but they can also close, forever, if you behave inappropriately. I can't believe what we've been told."

"Shamefully, no one has exaggerated anything. I'm sorry for how I've behaved tonight. It's not an excuse, but I let myself get carried away by Lisa. I . . . Believe me that I'm embarrassed and willing to do anything to try to fix this, even if it turns out to be impossible . . ."

"Of course it's impossible!" My mother would not be able to control the bitterness that my behavior had provoked in her.

"I could apologize. I don't know, maybe I could write a letter to the Fergusons' guests, or at least the people you know. To the Donovans, of course. I'll send them some flowers . . ."

"Flowers? Do you think that old bat is going to be satisfied with a bunch of flowers? She'll be telling all of Manhattan that you are a savage with no upbringing. She'll be closing doors against you as we speak, and you will never be able to open them again. I hope that what you've done doesn't affect your father's firm or your brother's future."

"You care about everyone except me," I would have replied, hoping to move her.

My mother would doubtless have calmed down. After all, she did love me.

"That might be a solution. Perhaps it won't fix anything, but it would at least be a suitable gesture that they would have to acknowledge. Yes, send them some flowers and a note of apology. And you should apologize to everyone who was there, all the people you remember seeing. Write to them and tell them that it was immature on your part, that you're sorry, that you're trying to work out how to remedy what you did. Tomorrow you can start writing those apologies and we'll send them out at once," my father would have said.

"Do you think it will help?" my mother would have asked, hopefully.

"It will be better than nothing. If he apologizes then there will be people who accept that it was nothing but childish behavior. It's the only option."

"Dad, believe me when I say that I'm sorry. I . . . I feel ashamed and I'm sorry if my behavior this evening hurt you. It was not my intention . . ."

"You haven't behaved well, but I'm pleased that you realize your mistake and are ready to apologize. The important thing is to recognize your errors so as not to make them again."

What a scene! My father would have forgiven me. I know. And my mother would have been vanquished by my attitude and would have tried to hug me.

I would have spent the rest of the night writing these apologies and would have surprised my father at the breakfast table by handing them over for his secretary to mail.

And as for Lisa, it would have been best to break up with her once and for all. Nothing good could come from our relationship.

Yeah, that's what didn't happen. I slept well that night, probably as a result of the tension and what had happened, and the next day I was pleased to see Lisa at school. She was radiant, in tight-fitting jeans, boots that came up to her thighs as though she were a musketeer, and a pale pink sweater that showed off her curves.

"What a night last night, right?" was how she greeted me.

"My parents were furious. They're not going to let this one slide," I said grumpily.

"Do what I do. Tell them to go screw themselves. My mother tried to give me one of her stupid talks this morning, but I shut the door on her. Then my father tried to do the same. They threatened to take my allowance. 'You won't have two cents to rub together,' my mother said. My father tried to get me to apologize to the guests. He wants me to write to everyone who came. They're nuts! The funniest part was when my mother shouted through my door that she wanted to send me to a clinic because she thinks I'm fucked up in the head. Bitch! What did your parents say?"

"My father wants me to apologize, and I think that'd be enough for him. As for my mother, well, I've told you about her. Nothing's good enough for her. She's not speaking to me for the time being. My father left before breakfast, and my mother looked right through me when I came into the kitchen."

"At least they don't try to mess with your head with all the crap they talk. You know we're in the papers? A couple of gossip columnists who were at the party pointed us out as two extravagant, bad-mannered kids, and said our behavior was the result of having grown up spoiled. Look, I brought the article."

Lisa seemed proud that the gossip columnists wrote about what had happened and said that we'd done whatever we could to draw attention to ourselves. One of the journalists wondered what right we had to behave like "rebellious youth" if we had had such privileged upbringings.

These articles made Lisa happy, but they upset me. I didn't like people talking about me at all, let alone in the terms these journalists used. At this point Esther came by. Lisa ignored her and walked off.

"She could at least say hello!" Esther complained.

I didn't say anything, and shrugged. I felt uncomfortable that Esther had been a witness to our unfortunate adventure.

"We were in the papers," I said, apologetically.

"I know, you're the only thing anyone's talking about. I heard Paul saying that you're not going to fool him and that he's going to keep an eye on you because he doesn't trust you."

It bothered me a great deal that Paul could have said such a thing about me and Lisa. Who was he to judge?

"He's more of an asshole than we are, so we've got nothing to blame ourselves for. And what does he care what Lisa and I do in our spare time?"

"It was just a comment. I don't really think he gives a damn about you."

I should have thanked her for what she had done, but I couldn't find the words. I hated Esther's air of superiority. She had behaved like a proper friend, but I refused to accept that I was in her debt.

We went to class without talking. Lisa was already sitting there, looking at her nails as though she didn't care about anything. I sat down next to her, as always.

"Everyone's looking at us. Everyone's jealous," Lisa whispered.

"I don't think so," I replied.

"They don't dare do the things we do, and that's why they're jealous," Lisa insisted.

Paul came into the classroom and didn't even look at us. He started to explain how to woo the people whose job it was to decide whether you got an account.

More than anything else, Paul's classes were about how to get accounts and how to stop other people from getting them. He usually said that advertising required talent and that was not something he could teach us. "You've either got it or you don't, and I don't care whether or not you do."

It was clear that Esther was a favorite of Paul's. He admired her intelligence. She was capable of finding the right phrase for selling anything, whether it was soap or frozen vegetables. After Esther, I was the fastest and the cleverest when it came to thinking up a slogan. To my surprise, and to Paul's as well, I guess, I seemed to have a knack for advertising. As for Lisa, she never managed to come up with anything. She was there because she had to be somewhere, but she didn't care about anything that Paul was teaching us.

"Miss Ferguson," he said to her one day, "why don't you just give up coming to class? You know I'm going to pass you whether or not you come, and I don't care what you do. As long as the tuition checks keep on coming. What I can't stand is your yawning. You don't like getting up in the mornings, and I don't either, but I have to be here to get your money."

"Mr. Hard, there's nothing I would like more than not to have to come here, but for the time being I'll keep on keeping on. I'll try to keep my yawning down to a minimum."

My relationship with my parents took a long time to get back on track. My father had been truly ashamed when he read in the newspapers what Lisa and I had done at the party. He, who was always so well-mannered and restrained, now found himself having to stand up for me whenever one of his friends made an expression of sympathy for the public shaming he was now having to go through. As for Lisa, she was no longer welcome in our house, and I wasn't welcome in hers. We both knew that we had crossed a line, and that it would not be wise to impose ourselves on the other's family.

My mother spent several days refusing to talk to me, and my father addressed me only in monosyllables. I didn't care all that much, but it was a little awkward. After the incident our weekend lunches out in the city were canceled. I didn't want to go, and they didn't want me to go, so Dad and Jaime would go to exhibitions by themselves and come back home for lunch. My

mother would sometimes go with them, or to the salon. I also
stopped going to Newport on weekends with my family. What
annoyed me most about this incident was that it seemed to have
brought my parents together again.

Lisa and I would spend weekends together. We would go to
a hotel and enjoy doing nothing. We would get there on Friday
evening and stay until late Sunday afternoon. We walked around
the city, slept until midday, and tried to find places to go where
we wouldn't have to see anyone who had anything to do with
us or our families. It was at one of these places that Lisa picked
up her coke habit.

The dealer was an attractive guy with broad shoulders who
looked like he could do anything. His name was Mike. Some
called him "Muscle Mike." He worked in PR, if anyone could
believe that a place like the club where we met him might need
PR. Lisa liked him—that much was clear. She always insisted
that we go to his place and looked for him as soon as we got
in. When we went out on the dance floor he would come dance
with us, and it was obvious that I was not needed there. They
laughed, and looked at each other, and every now and then he
would make a sign and they would disappear into the bathroom
to do a line or two. I steered clear of all that. I didn't want to do
drugs, at least not with that guy, for all that Lisa insisted.

One night they took longer than usual to come back. I went
to find her and ran into Mike. He was pushing Lisa up against
the wall and her panties were down.

I didn't even get angry. I realized I didn't care. When Lisa
came back she looked at me defiantly.

"Don't follow me."

"I didn't follow you."

"I do whatever the hell I want."

"Of course, like I do."

"Mike's an interesting guy."

"He's a dealer, but if you like him, go ahead."

"You don't care?"

"No."

I have never been more sincere than I was at that moment. I hadn't felt anything when I saw her, panties around her ankles, pressed up against Mike's body. My indifference surprised even me.

"It's better like this. I won't come back to the hotel with you tonight. I'll go to Mike's: he's having a party. I don't know if I'll come back tomorrow either."

"Don't worry."

I think she was as surprised by my attitude as I was, and maybe even a little upset.

"Hey, don't pretend like you don't care."

"But I don't, Lisa. I swear I don't care at all what you do. Go on, go and have a good time with Mike. He's waiting for you at the bar."

She went. She left with him and from the way she looked at me I could see that she was angry. She would have liked for me to suffer, and maybe even to try to stop her from leaving, and for Mike to give me a real beating. But if I didn't complain it wasn't because I was scared of what Mike might do to me, but rather because I realized how little Lisa really meant to me. We had been together for a year, but the only thing holding us together was the wickedness that we both held inside ourselves. And that was a very fragile connection.

I enjoyed being alone in the hotel all weekend. I didn't expect her to come back, and I wouldn't have wanted her to; I liked to feel myself master of my time without having to share it with anyone. I felt free for the first time, and I liked the feeling.

We met up again on Monday at school. Lisa looked terrible. I sat down next to her as I always did.

"I'm exhausted. Mike is an animal."

I nodded. I was sure of it. Mike was an animal in every possible sense.

"But we can keep sleeping together whenever we want. He won't care."

I didn't care either. It would be good for me to have a guaranteed ration of sex, at least until I sorted myself out. My relationship with Lisa had taken up all my time and for the moment there was no one else. There was no reason why I should give up on Lisa while I was waiting. I thought about my mother. If she knew what had happened she would have been happy, if only because it would give her a chance to say, "I told you that girl was a slut, but you were the last person to find out."

Lisa started to miss class. If I had had any feelings for her, I would have been worried to see how she was getting hooked on cocaine and other substances. Mike had found the ideal client. The Fergusons were rich and Lisa always had money. She could pay for her drugs on delivery.

"I feel sorry for Lisa," Esther said one day when Lisa came to class sweating, her hair out of place and her eyes bugging out of her head.

"She's a big girl."

"Yes, but that doesn't mean that she knows what she's gotten herself into."

"What has she gotten herself into?" I asked angrily.

"Come on, Thomas, even an idiot can see that she's on something. Look at her. What's left of her?"

"She's the same as she always has been, Esther."

"If she were as much my friend as she is yours I'd try to help her. But we've never gotten along, so I can't do anything. But you should do something."

Esther's comment irked me. Why should I get mixed up in Lisa's life?

Paul didn't like the state she was in that morning, so he sent her home.

"Miss Ferguson, I've said in the past that I don't care what you do. But I don't want drugs in my academy. I don't have much reputation left without you getting rid of the last scraps of it. Come back in six months. The class will be over, you will have passed, and your parents will be happy with the shitty diploma I give you."

Lisa didn't pay him any attention and instead sat down next to me.

"I don't like the superior look your friend Esther's giving me."

"Since when do you care how other people look at you?" I asked indifferently.

"So you've found someone new. You like that little two-faced skank."

"Lisa, leave me alone. I don't poke my nose into your life, so don't poke yours into mine."

"So you are sleeping with her."

Instead of replying I decided to listen to what Paul was telling us about how to con clients. I knew that Lisa hated to think that I might have something going on with Esther. She wouldn't have cared if I had gotten involved with anyone else, but she hated Esther because Esther was everything she would never be. Esther took life seriously because she knew she had to, if only to escape her fate at the family restaurant. Esther was the one who pushed herself the most to understand the lessons that Paul and the other teachers were passing on to us.

Lisa nudged me and kicked my shin to get my attention. But I didn't want to speak to her, much less have an argument, given the state she was in. She had gone too far with the cocaine or whatever it was.

Suddenly she ostentatiously pulled up her sleeve and showed me a number of injection scars on her arm.

"You're crazy," I said in a whisper.

"And you don't know what you're missing. You're a little mouse, Thomas, scared of life. You'll never stop being a middle-class kid who wants to pretend to be a bad boy, but the worst thing you've ever done in your life is talk back to your mommy and daddy."

Lisa started to run her hand over the bruises that surrounded the puncture marks.

"What are you on?" I asked.

"Why do you care? Want to try it?"

"No, I don't, and if you looked in the mirror you'd be terrified of what you've become. Know what? You're not crazy, you're just dumb."

Lisa looked at me in confusion. She didn't think I was capable of standing up to her. She was about to reply when Paul spoke to us angrily.

"Miss Ferguson, Mr. Spencer, would you be kind enough to let me teach this class? Perhaps you'd like to go for a walk?"

"I'm sorry," I muttered, as I looked away from Lisa's arm.

"Let's go," she said, and stood up.

I remained seated, looking straight ahead, pretending to ignore the fact that Lisa had gotten to her feet. She stared at me, not understanding why I was behaving like this, but didn't say anything and just left the class, slamming the door behind her.

I stayed at my desk, but I stopped paying attention to Paul and asked myself why I hadn't gone with Lisa. It didn't take long to come up with the answer: I didn't care if other people ruined their lives, but I wasn't prepared to ruin my own, and so I knew that I wasn't going to line up alongside Lisa. I had been shocked by the marks on her arm. It was clear that she was now lost forever, but I didn't want to get lost with her.

After class, Esther came up to me to scold me for not having gone after Lisa.

"You're not a very good friend. Aren't you worried what might happen to her?"

"No, not in the least, and I don't know why you're worried either."

Lisa came back on the day that we had to hand in our final paper for the year. I must confess that mine was mediocre, that I hadn't bothered to make any effort, knowing that Paul would pass me no matter what I handed in. As for Lisa, she sauntered in without even a pen, but though she was obviously still on drugs, she seemed more clearheaded than the last time she had come to class.

"Hey, you've changed. You've even done your paper for Paul."

"Well, I didn't bust my ass, but I've got something to hand in, yes," I replied indifferently.

"And the two-faced skank?"

"Who do you mean?" I asked, knowing she was talking about Esther.

"Your little Italian friend."

"I suppose her work will be the best, as always."

I could see in her eyes that she was trying to think up some way of ruining things for Esther, but I didn't pay any more attention, as Lisa sat down next to me and started to get me up to speed with the latest on her crazy life. She almost paid attention in our economics class. When the professor left the room for a bit, most of the students followed him to go and smoke outside. Esther went too, even though she didn't smoke; she probably just wanted to keep talking to one of the girls.

Lisa got up and went to Esther's seat. I saw her open the file on the desk and examine it until she found what she wanted. It was Esther's final paper. Lisa's smile was a warning. She started to tear up the pages in a rage until they were little pieces of confetti that fell to the floor, where she stamped on them furiously.

I watched her, knowing how upset Esther would be. But it would be a lie if I said that I cared how Esther felt, and so I let Lisa do what she was doing.

When the others returned, followed by Paul, Esther's work was sprinkled all over the floor. I saw how shocked Esther was by Lisa's defiant gaze and then how stunned she was when she saw her folder open and empty.

"But . . ." Esther started to cry when she realized what had happened.

"What is it?" Paul asked, coming over to Esther's desk.

There was no need for her to say anything. He immediately guessed that Lisa had been the cause of all this destruction.

"Do you feel better, Miss Ferguson?" he asked Lisa, looking at her angrily.

"Yes, I feel great, Mr. Hard."

"Excellent. Now, please do me a favor: leave and don't come back until I hand out the diplomas. You can come with your parents and pick up yours. They might even be happy, because I think that that shitty little diploma is the only qualification you'll ever get in your life."

Then he turned and walked up to the board, while Lisa waited, not knowing whether to go or to stay, and Esther sobbed disconsolately.

"Esther Sabatti graduates with honors, with a special mention for her coursework. Now, the rest of you, give me your papers. You know that you've all passed anyway."

Esther looked at me, trying to find an explanation. She assumed, as did the rest of the class, that I had been a witness to Lisa's act. I looked back at her and shrugged.

Lisa left the room with the same air of superiority she always had, even though she had disgraced herself. She still saw herself as the rich girl whom no one could stand up to.

The murmuring in the class was too loud even for Paul. All the students were blaming Lisa and they looked at me out of the corners of their eyes, as if I were also somehow to blame for the disaster. I decided to distract myself, and looked at Paul as though he were saying something that really piqued my interest. Esther looked away from me eventually, disappointed in my attitude.

Esther has never understood why I allowed Lisa to destroy her work. She can't accept that I'm indifferent to wicked behavior and that I myself have too often slipped into that entrance to hell where one only wants to cause harm to others.

Esther would like me to have behaved otherwise:

Of course I shouldn't have allowed Lisa to fall into Mike's hands. The night she told me she was going to a party at her dealer's house I should have gotten her away from that wretched place, no matter how much she protested. I suppose we would have had a huge fight, but even so, I know that Lisa would have listened to me. I was her best friend—really her only friend, the only person with whom she didn't have to pretend to be anything but who she was. The person she could trust because she had recognized in me the same darkness that closed her off from the world.

"Don't go. He's in some deep shit and the only thing he wants from you is the money you pay him for drugs. You're a gold mine to him, rich and impulsive—his best client. You can't think you mean anything to him? He sleeps with you because it's part of his job, and it's obvious that you're not his type. You're still not cheap enough to be his type." That's what I should have said to Lisa.

"You're just jealous! Look what we have here. Young Mr. Spencer is jealous," she would have answered.

"Don't be ridiculous. I don't care who you screw around with, but this guy is worse than a con man. He'll bleed you dry and when there's nothing left to take he'll kick you out onto the street. Did you know that he's a pimp too? That he has a bunch of girls hooked on crack who he uses to foot the bill for his drugs?"

"And you think I'm going to end up like that? You're crazy, Thomas Spencer!"

"You know I'm right, Lisa, so let's get out of this dump and never come back. We're not missing out on anything here. If

you're really feeling adventurous, how about we go scale the Statue of Liberty, totally naked? Maybe we'll end up on the front page of the New York Times.*"*

I would take her by the arm and, overcoming her resistance, drag her outside the club. Mike would follow us to see where we were going and I would confront him.

"Lisa doesn't want to go with you. Let her go," Mike would say, getting cocky.

"Get out of the way. We're leaving. Go find some other idiot to leech money off of—you've had enough from this one. If you don't, you'll find yourself facing the entire police force of New York. Her father is a major donor to the police orphans' fund, you know. I'm sure there are plenty of volunteers who'll do him the favor of locking up the dealer who's harassing his little girl."

Mike would hesitate, but then he'd leave. Guys like him don't want any more problems than they've bargained for. Lisa and I would be able to leave the place without anyone getting in our way.

"Who the hell do you think you are to tell me what I can do? Get off me! I'll go wherever I want, and don't you dare talk to my parents about Mike or anything else."

"I will talk to them, Lisa, I will, and I'll convince them to talk to their friends in the police so they'll pay Mike a visit. You'll see how happy that makes your dealer, and how he'll welcome you if you try to go back to him."

Yes, it could have happened like that, although I wonder whether it would have made Lisa renounce Muscle Mike or whether she would have ignored my threats. I had my chance to save her, to stop her from ending up a burnout. I could have talked to her parents and risked having Mike's friends pay me a visit and beat me to a pulp. But none of that happened, just as I did nothing to stop Lisa from destroying Esther's end-of-year project.

I've never understood why Esther bothered to be my friend, why she forgave me for all the sins I committed against her. That was the day she started down her long path of forgiveness.

Esther would have wanted me to stop Lisa from destroying her work:

Lisa opened Esther's file and began reading the first pages of her end-of-year project. A veil of anger and malice fell across her face. I knew her well, and so I knew that the worst possible idea was flashing through her mind. I should have thrown myself in front of her and taken those pages from her hands. She would have struggled to get her revenge against Esther, but it wouldn't have been hard for me to stop her. Lisa barely had the strength to stand; the drugs had worn her out, so just one light touch could have pushed her away. Then I would only have had to put the pages back in the file, close it, and get Lisa away from it, no matter how much she protested.

"You're an asshole! What's going on? Are you screwing her? I always knew you'd end up being whipped. She's a bitch! Don't you see that? She's wanted to jump you since day one and now . . . I'm . . . I'm away for a little and when I come back you're screwing her, you bastard!"

Lisa would have insulted me with increasing volume until everyone could hear her. But nobody would have paid her much attention. They hardly felt sorry for her. The people who went to Paul's academy did so in a desperate bid to escape what destiny offered them. They were hardhearted because life hadn't treated them kindly, so they cared little about spoiled rich girls like Lisa who showed up at the academy because they had nowhere else to go.

"Don't be stupid. What does Esther matter to you? Leave her alone. Destroying her work won't help you in the slightest. She's worked hard on it, but we all know that Paul will give us all our diplomas anyway, even you. The only thing you'll do is make a

fool of yourself, and make everyone think that you did it out of jealousy, because you can't bear that Esther is everything that you aren't. And yes, also because you think I'm sleeping with her," I would have snapped.

Lisa would have raised her hand and slapped me with her feeble strength. She wouldn't have been able to handle being forced to look in the mirror and confront reality.

I would have put up with her slap while taking away Esther's file and forcing Lisa to sit down.

On returning to class, the rest of our classmates would have regarded the embers of our argument with indifference. Paul would have paid us no attention, and while Esther might have looked at us with curiosity, she wouldn't have come close to guessing the reason behind this animosity between us.

I know that Lisa would have looked at Esther with hatred, and perhaps even have spat out some insult, something that would have stung her, but she couldn't have done any more than that because my hand would have been on her arm, holding her back.

Yes, it should have happened like that but it didn't, and as the years passed Esther would continue lamenting the incident, and reproach me from time to time for what I allowed Lisa to do.

What did happen that day was that, after Paul's class ended, Esther came up to me with eyes reddened. I tried to avoid her. I had no wish to talk to her.

"What has the world done to Lisa for her to end up so evil?" she asked me.

"Evil? She isn't evil. It's just that she has a strong personality and doesn't know how to control herself."

"Right . . . So destroying my work is a product of her personality. How generous you are when it comes to defending her!"

"It's just that I don't judge her—and why should I? People are the way they are, and Lisa is prone to temper tantrums."

"And what if she had destroyed *your* work?"

I shrugged my shoulders. I really wouldn't have cared. The reason I'd spent two years at Paul's academy was the guarantee that I'd receive his "crappy little diploma," as he called it, even if I hadn't bothered to attend at all. The rules were clear from the very start. If I had done any of the work that we were given, it was only because I decided to do it, not from fear that someone might rebuke me.

"You're already graduating with honors. What more do you want?"

"It was good work, Thomas. I tried so hard to do the best that I could. I spent weeks working on it and now . . . Yes, Paul is letting me graduate with honors because of what happened, but do I deserve it? I don't want it if he doesn't know for certain that I deserve it. I told him to just give me a passing grade."

"You're so dumb! Everyone knows you're the best student, the only one who has actually taken this place seriously enough to get your diploma, and the only one who has done the impossible and absorbed the knowledge of these strange professors, Paul included."

"I don't want gifts and I don't want pity—I only want what I deserve. That's why I'm going to reject the honors citation."

"You could redo the project."

"No, I can't. I have to help out at the restaurant over the next couple of days. We have a ton of reservations for wedding receptions."

"Your parents will be pleased," I said, for the sake of saying something.

"Yes, of course they are. Winter wasn't good. We've barely managed to hang on to our long-standing customers. It's not that we've lost them, it's just that now they spend less . . . Everyone wants to save money, and my parents have lowered their prices so much that now we're barely making a profit."

"At least you haven't had to close."

"Tell me, Thomas, why is Lisa like this? I can't figure it out. She has everything she needs to be happy, and yet . . ."

"Don't judge her. You can't understand her. Don't keep going over it. Just forget about her. I doubt you'll ever see each other again once the semester is over."

"Yes, it would be hard for us to run into each other. I live in Little Italy and she lives in the heart of Manhattan. I doubt that she can see the street where I live from her parents' penthouse apartment."

"Social envy," I remarked sarcastically.

"I'm just describing reality. Kids like you have no idea how hard it is to get by."

"We've been lucky."

"Yes, luck has been on your side. Who knows why?"

"You think we don't deserve it?"

"Who knows?"

To be honest, I didn't care what Esther thought. We stopped talking because Paul came up to us and I took the opportunity to leave. I didn't feel like continuing the conversation.

I didn't try to find out what happened to Lisa. I imagined that she'd keep buying coke and other shit from Mike and that he'd keep screwing her to keep her happy. She was a good client, and a guy like him had no problem pulling her panties down against the bathroom wall of the dive bar where he worked.

The day of my graduation, my parents insisted on coming with me. My brother Jaime made sure that nobody would miss it—he took it as given that the family had to be together for such an occasion.

"It's an important day for Thomas. He has to know how proud of him we are for getting this degree. The boy has tried so hard . . ." my father said to my mother.

"Do you think this diploma is worth anything? You know better than I do that it's a third-rate academy. I doubt any advertising agency is going to hire him when he shows them this sham diploma," argued my mother.

"Don't be so negative. You should be satisfied that Thomas has done something," insisted my father.

"I don't know why Jaime has to come," replied my mother.

"Jaime loves his brother. To be with him on such a special day—he wouldn't miss it for the world."

"Don't be stupid, Juan. This isn't a special day for Thomas. It's all the same to him."

My mother was right, but I didn't bother to tell her that. I didn't want to give her the satisfaction, so I accepted that they were coming with me.

My father's chauffeur was waiting for us at the door of the house.

I had to elbow Jaime because his sunny brightness was getting on my nerves. He wouldn't stop congratulating me, as if I had gotten my advertising diploma from Harvard instead of the Hard School of Advertising. But my brother had always been simple.

"Leave it, Jaime," my mother said, also irritated.

The chauffeur dropped us off at the door of the academy. My mother took a deep breath, as if she were making an effort to control herself and not run away. Jaime looked around curiously and I noticed him loosen his tie, as if he had suddenly realized that his navy-blue suit and striped tie were out of place here. My father seemed not to notice his surroundings, and smiled at me affectionately, gesturing for me to lead them into the academy. He didn't seem surprised by its run-down appearance.

Paul came over to greet us. He was wearing a nice suit, though it was old-fashioned—I imagine he'd bought it when things were going well, when he was working at one of the large advertising agencies.

My father shook his hand and told him how pleased the family was that I had successfully completed my studies in advertising. Paul frowned until he realized that my father was being sincere. As for my mother, Paul sized her up in a single glance. He noted her discomfort.

"Mrs. Spencer." Paul kissed my mother's hand exaggeratedly. "It's a pleasure to meet you."

At that moment Esther arrived, accompanied by her parents and her brother, and we had no choice but to greet one another. I introduced her to my parents and for a few moments the two families exchanged banalities. My father seemed charmed by Esther's parents, and I thought about what a hypocrite he was. What did a brilliant, well-off Manhattan lawyer have in common with a family who cooked Italian food for a living? My mother shook their hands and stood rigidly by my father's side. As for Jaime, he made such a show of friendliness that it annoyed me. He seemed interested in everything Esther's brother had to say, and smiled like an idiot at her mother, whom he praised for her tasteful hat.

It seemed that Esther was as uncomfortable as I was, and we left our parents behind as we headed to the classroom that had been repurposed for the ceremony.

"I couldn't stop them from coming," I said, excusing my parents.

"And why wouldn't they have come? It makes sense that they want to share this moment with you."

"God, you're so dumb! You know that the diploma Paul's going to give us is a piece of shit, that it's not worth anything. The only reason we've spent two years here is because we couldn't go anywhere else," I replied angrily.

She didn't shrink away, but faced up to my anger.

"*I* couldn't go anywhere else, but *you* could've. Of course you could have. Your family had the money for you to be able to go to a good college. If you're here it's only because you decided to be. You're an idiot, Thomas, a total idiot, because you don't know how to take advantage of all the things life has given you. So don't belittle this place, because it's the only school I could go to, and that was due to my parents' hard work, and my own. Do you think it's fun, waiting tables and helping to peel potatoes and carrots?"

I had no time to answer because at that moment it seemed that a new arrival was causing something of a disturbance. Then I saw Lisa enter, followed by her parents.

Mrs. Ferguson seemed as uncomfortable as my mother. I'm sure she was asking herself what she was doing in a place like this. If her friends could see her now . . . As for Mr. Ferguson, he hadn't managed to become the greatest meat producer in the country without being able to face any situation he came up against. I watched him greet Paul and the other professors as if they were old friends.

Lisa didn't even bother to look at me. She was a little thinner and had dark circles under her eyes. She didn't seem to be high, or at least not so high that she wouldn't be able to handle the ridiculous ceremony where they'd hand us our useless diplomas.

Mr. Ferguson greeted my father, and Mrs. Ferguson did the same with my mother. Paul motioned for us to sit together. It wasn't a good idea but I could do nothing to stop it, so much to my dismay I ended up sitting next to Lisa.

"You bastard," she whispered to me, but not quietly enough for the people around us not to hear.

"How kind you are. It's good to see you, and still standing too." I wanted to offend her just as badly. Paul glared at us and with his powerful voice called for silence from all present. The ceremony was about to begin, and standing on the dais, flanked by the other professors, he seemed to be taking this dog and pony show seriously.

The first lie he told was that having us as students had been a privilege for his academy, because we were all brilliant young people eager to learn. The second lie was that we had exceeded all expectations and from this day forth could compete with the very best in the world of advertising. "You will go out fully prepared and with a diploma that may be modest, yes, but one that is recognized by those in the business. And so, ladies and gentlemen, your future shall be whatever you wish it to be," he concluded, as the guests traded looks. Then he read out our names, and we went up one by one to receive our diplomas. We shook hands with Paul and the other professors, and returned to our seats amid applause from family and friends.

An hour later the farce was over. I, like my mother, had wanted to get out of there and not waste any more time, but Paul had pushed together a couple of desks and covered them with a tablecloth, on which were served drinks and some paltry canapés. My father said we should at least stay a few minutes so as not to offend him.

I wouldn't say I was surprised when I saw Lisa approach Esther. I even leaned back against the wall, ready to enjoy the show I was sure Lisa was about to put on for us.

"So you managed to get your diploma even though you couldn't present your end-of-year project? Who did you have to sleep with for them to give it to you? With that killjoy Paul? Did you screw him? Well, I guess you poor types will do anything to get ahead."

A hand closed around Lisa's arm, and she found herself facing the angry glare of Esther's brother.

"What did you say?" asked young Roberto.

"You heard me," she replied, unfazed, even though he was a head taller than her and strong as an ox.

"Apologize to my sister for what you just said," he demanded.

The Fergusons came over, alarmed. Mr. Ferguson attempted to intervene.

"Young man, let go of my daughter. I don't believe this is the way to make things right."

"She has to apologize to my sister, and loud enough for everyone to hear it."

"Lisa, my girl, apologize, it was a silly thing for you to say. I think it's just a young girls' rivalry," said Mr. Ferguson, turning to everyone there to try to defuse the situation.

"Your daughter is a bad person, Mr. Ferguson, but you already knew that. What I will not allow is for her to insult my sister, to defile her in this way simply because she's jealous. So either she says sorry . . ."

Roberto's fingers gripped Lisa's arm tightly, so tightly she couldn't help but grimace in pain.

Paul approached, alarmed by what was happening, and regarded Lisa with hostility.

"Miss Ferguson, I'm not asking you to apologize to me—I know you like to make a scene—but you should apologize to Miss Sabatti, who you . . . Well, you've done everything you could to torment her since the day you first met.

"Please apologize and then that's that. Your classmates deserve to look back on this day happily."

Esther's parents seemed distraught. They couldn't understand what was happening and looked in anguish at their elder son, fearing that the situation would escalate.

Knowing Lisa as I did, I knew that she wasn't about to rectify the situation, certainly not in public.

My father came up to me followed by my mother, who seemed worried.

"Lisa is behaving appallingly," my father said to me quietly.

I shrugged. I had no intention of defending Lisa, nor did I want to agree with him.

Esther remained silent, nervously wringing her hands, her face reddened with humiliation.

"Forget it, Roberto. She's not worth it. That's just how she is. Everyone knows she is how she is and I am how I am," Esther managed to say, trying to get her brother to let go of Lisa's arm.

But her words angered Lisa even further, who reacted like a viper that had just been stepped on.

"The little slut playing the innocent. Who do you think you're fooling? We all know that Paul drooled over you, and you let him in order to guarantee your frigging diploma. You've really fooled your family! Do they know that you wanted to screw Thomas too? You'd do anything to climb the social ladder. The little cook becoming Thomas Spencer's wife. I heard you say you were going to sleep with him to get pregnant and then either force him to marry you or pay child support. I dare you to deny it!"

Esther didn't bother to deny it, but instead slapped her so hard that the imprint of her fingers remained seared like scars across Lisa's face.

Mrs. Ferguson screamed in horror. Lisa didn't even cry out. She fixed her gaze on me and exclaimed, "Ask Thomas. He knows I'm telling the truth. He ran away because he knew the little bitch tried to reel him in and seduce him."

All eyes turned to me but I said nothing. I stayed silent, impassive. I wasn't even moved by Esther, who was looking at me and waiting for me to tell the truth.

Mr. Ferguson came forward to try to rescue his daughter, but Paul stepped in to stop him.

"You're a liar, a villain, an immoral drug addict. You'll end up in the gutter. Oh yes, one of these days they'll find you dead with a needle in your arm. Get out of here. You sully all of us with your presence."

Paul's words surprised us all. Lisa looked at him with hatred in her eyes.

"Let go. Let her leave," Paul asked Roberto.

"She has to say sorry," Roberto demanded, holding Lisa's arm ever tighter and shaking her.

"Enough!" yelled Mr. Ferguson.

My father approached Roberto and Lisa and I feared he'd say something.

"Miss Ferguson, you should save yourself and the rest of us from letting this unpleasant scene go on any further. You have offended Miss Sabatti and you must apologize. Do it," he said.

"Never," replied Lisa.

Esther slapped her again, this time with so much anger and

despair that my father tried to hold her back while Mr. Ferguson tried to get Roberto to let go of Lisa.

"Are you having fun?" my mother asked me, lighting up a cigarette and ignoring the fact that smoking wasn't permitted inside the academy.

"Sure. Those two should start punching each other and then the scene will be complete."

"Lisa has no shame, and it seems you don't either," muttered my mother.

"I've inherited quite a number of your bad qualities," I said.

Just then Lisa screamed. Esther's blows continued to rain down, and even though her father tried to hold her back he could do nothing to stop her.

"Esther, my girl, leave her, leave her!" her father pleaded.

But Esther wouldn't listen to anybody. She needed to hit Lisa to cleanse herself of her humiliation and shame.

"I'll sue you!" yelled Mr. Ferguson to Esther.

My father intervened again, and to my surprise turned to face Mr. Ferguson.

"I would be honored if Miss Sabatti would allow me to be her lawyer. She should be the one to sue your daughter for slander, and we will seek compensation. What has happened here is intolerable."

My mother also looked at my father in surprise. What did this girl matter to him?

Eventually the Fergusons managed to free their daughter. The families of the other students hurriedly said goodbye to Paul and the professors. Nobody wanted to stay a minute longer. It had been a first-class spectacle, but not a pleasant one. They'd have plenty to talk about and plenty of people to criticize.

"You should have defended Esther by telling the truth."

It was the first time Jaime had ever reprimanded me. His reproach infuriated me. But that was my brother's way, just like it was my father's way to side with the weak. Right at that moment my father was trying to console the Sabattis, assuring them that nobody had believed a single word Lisa Ferguson said. My father was so naïve.

Esther passed me without a glance. I wondered if I should say something, but I resisted the impulse. I was not in the mood for her admonishments.

"Your brother is right," said my mother.

"Right? How is he right?" I asked bad-temperedly.

"That bitch of a friend of yours has made a fool of Esther. Some of your friends will believe Lisa—people always prefer to believe the worst."

"And they're almost always right to believe the worst," I assured her.

I started to turn away but Jaime put his hand on my shoulder, forcing me to turn back. I was close to punching him but Paul came up to us.

"Your friend will end up dragging you down with her. Watch out for her," Paul said to me.

"Don't exaggerate. She was just on edge and you already know that she doesn't get along with Esther," I replied, without much conviction.

"You are not as smart as you think you are, Mr. Spencer; you must be the only one who hasn't yet realized that you've been no more than a puppet in Miss Ferguson's hands."

Paul's claim irritated me. So that motley crew with whom I'd studied thought me little more than Lisa's plaything.

"I don't know what you're talking about," I responded angrily, and before he could reply I headed for the exit.

I couldn't bear that place for another second. What's more—I have to confess—Paul had hurt my self-esteem.

Jaime followed me, as did my mother, while my father said goodbye to the Sabattis. I didn't feel comfortable until I was in the car. I suddenly needed to distance myself as quickly as possible from Paul's academy and the two years I'd spent there.

"Lisa Ferguson's behavior has been disgraceful," said my father to no one in particular.

"She's a bad person," said my brother.

"What do you know? You don't know her. You don't know anything about her."

"You don't have to be a mind reader to see what kind of a person she is," Jaime replied.

"That poor girl . . . Lisa has destroyed her reputation," my father continued.

"You're being melodramatic. I don't understand why you're all reading so much into a catfight," I insisted.

"No. That wasn't a catfight. I don't know what idea you have of women but Lisa is surely the worst you will ever meet. I think she's your perfect match," announced my mother.

I felt like slapping her. I imagine it showed on my face because my father scolded her.

"Carmela, don't make Thomas feel guilty about what happened. But, son, your mother is right. What she did to Esther is unforgivable."

"Why didn't you defend Esther?" asked my brother.

Jaime's insistence was getting on my last nerve. He would have behaved like a knight in shining armor, but I wasn't like him.

"How about you leave me in peace, okay?"

No one said another word. We arrived at home and I shut myself in my room, while Jaime talked with my parents in the study.

I knew that they were criticizing my attitude, thinking I was lacking in manners.

I sat on the bed going over what had happened and reached the conclusion that if I hadn't defended Esther it wasn't because I was afraid to confront Lisa, but rather, I told myself, because I didn't care about either of them.

What my parents and my brother thought I should do is not what I did:

When Lisa accused Esther of sleeping with Paul, I should have intervened. I should have said that it was all a sick joke, and I should have gotten Lisa out of there. I know I could have handled her. She would have protested but then followed me, and the whole regrettable scene would not have happened.

Lisa had nothing to lose—she loved scandals, so none of the events that she set in motion mattered to her. Yet I knew that the scene would destroy Esther. Lisa's claim that Esther had slept with Paul and that she had tried to do the same with me was slander that I knew would spread like an oil slick. My mother was right that people always prefer to think the worst of others in order to feel less miserable about themselves.

"Be quiet, Lisa! How dare you say such things? You know that Esther is the best student here, the best of us all, the only one who deserves to graduate with honors, the one who truly has talent. How dare you insinuate that there's anything between her and Paul? You know that's a lie. Esther would be incapable of doing anything like that."

Yes, that should have been my speech. My father and my brother would have looked at me with pride, and my mother would have been surprised by my courageous behavior. Naturally Lisa would have turned on me, launching into her second accusation: that Esther was a manipulator, capable of sleeping with anyone in order to climb the social ladder, and the idiot she had under her thumb was me.

My reply would have had to meet the standard of my previous words. I could have taken a couple of steps back and looked at Lisa, scandalized. And then I could have approached Esther, saying loudly:

"Esther is my most selfless friend. No one who knows Esther could believe such a story. It's just slander. You can't stand that she's a good and honest person, perhaps because that would be beyond you. I won't allow you to ruin her name or the friendship I have with her. I don't know what's going on with you, Lisa,

and I'm sorry to see you in this state, but your words reflect back on you. You're ridiculous. You're pitiful."

That last part would no doubt have further enraged Lisa. I'm sure she would have tried to slap me. But at that point I would have loudly apologized to all those watching the scene and, taking Esther by the arm, would have invited her to leave with me. My parents and the Sabattis would have followed us, and Paul's unsuccessful end-of-year party would have been over.

The Fergusons would have dragged Lisa away, ashamed of her behavior. And I would have seemed almost like a gentleman to everyone present.

But I did none of that. It never even crossed my mind to do anything like that.

The actions I did not take that day are part of another life—a life that now, as I decline and am on the verge of, yes, death, I wonder if I should have lived.

As time passes, I'm beginning to think that if I had acted correctly I might have been proud of myself, but I can't be sure of that. Back then I saw my future as just a fraction of eternity and felt no need to be noble or to do any good. I asked nothing of myself. I accepted myself as I was: no more, no less.

I can still remember how uncomfortable dinner was that night.

My mother was in a bad mood and when our eyes met I could see how disappointed she was in me. Jaime seemed saddened, as if those scenes he had experienced were out of some nightmare. He watched me out of the corner of his eye, searching my face for answers. It was my father who broke the silence when we reached the second course.

"Thomas, I'd like you to think about what happened. You'll agree with me that you should have intervened."

"And what do you think I should have done?" I asked, to provoke him.

"Told everyone that Lisa was lying and stood up for Esther. That girl doesn't deserve to be treated this way. As for Lisa . . . I won't tell you what to do, but that girl can only bring you trouble. I feel sorry for her parents. Mr. Ferguson has worked hard to become a great businessman. And Mrs. Ferguson has always been generous with the organizations that need her help."

"Oh yes, she does love her charity galas. They're a great opportunity for her to show off her jewels and for the papers to highlight their generous donations, to legitimize their fortune. And Mr. Ferguson is a humble cattle rancher who has cleverly managed to get his prepackaged meat sold in supermarkets across the country. He's a butcher who got lucky, hardly aristocratic enough for the hypocritical tastes of the great families of New York. But this is the land of opportunity—if you get rich, you have a guaranteed seat at the table of high society. If Mr. Ferguson weren't a wealthy butcher they would laugh at his accent, at his ridiculous hat, at that folksy attitude he likes to cultivate. Mrs. Ferguson hasn't stopped being what she was either: a teacher from the Midwest who's come up in the world. The designer labels, the jewelry, the French manicure—they haven't turned her into the great lady she claims to be. Isn't that right, Mother? That's what you always say. 'A monkey dressed in silk is still a monkey.' You said your grandmother taught you that."

My mother knew that everything I had just said about Mrs. Ferguson expressed the same opinion I had of her.

"Where did all this hatred come from?" asked my mother, barely restraining her desire to slap me.

"This *is* the land of opportunity," my father interrupted. "There are no aristocrats here, just people who will judge you based on how hard you try. Mr. Ferguson is an example of how far you can get if you work hard. Here nobody asks where you came from, only what you do and what you're prepared to do. That's how Mr. Ferguson has earned the respect of all who know him. Do you know how many families he gives work to? And your comments about Mrs. Ferguson are out of line. The jewels she wears are the result of her husband's efforts—she's allowed to feel proud of him. It's easy to remain indifferent when someone asks you to support a good cause, but everyone knows that they can count on her, and that is very laudable on her part."

"If you say so," I replied.

"You have no right to judge the Fergusons, but you should have enough sense to know that Lisa is heading in a bad direction. That girl has decided to throw her life away," insisted my father.

"If her father had worried more about her instead of spending night and day selling his goddamn cattle," I replied, "and if her mother had spent less time at the salon trying to be someone she's not, then Lisa—"

"You mean that Lisa is the way she is because of her parents?" There was an implicit reproach in Jaime's question.

"We are all who we are as a consequence of something," I said firmly.

"Bad people always look for excuses to justify the way they are," declared my mother.

"If you say so."

Without telling me, Jaime had decided to frame the ridiculous diploma that Paul had given me. For some reason, my brother wanted to showcase the piece of cardboard that announced I had graduated from the Hard School of Advertising.

In the fall my brother would enroll at Harvard and, from that moment on, there would be no way to deny the obvious differences that would exist between us. But he did love me.

I had to start thinking about what I was going to do with the rest of my life. I knew that it would be difficult to find a job if my only credential was a diploma from Paul Hard's academy. Either my father would have to ask a favor of one of his friends or I'd have real problems, as no advertising agency would bother to interview me. My father expected me to ask him—he was too polite and respectful to try to impose his help on me. My mother didn't seem to care that I was wandering around the house with nothing to do. The truth is, that summer crept up on us, and perhaps they thought it wouldn't hurt for me to have some vacation before I tried to enter the working world.

It was Aunt Emma, my father's sister, who triggered the decision I'd eventually make.

When the weather was nice we usually spent part of our vacations at her house in Newport. It was a large house, and from the tall windows you could make out the sea. She liked having us there. She'd inherited the house from her husband. I suppose they'd both thought they'd fill it with their own children. But bad luck had haunted my aunt, leaving her without a husband or children. She had to make do with Jaime and me.

I always managed to squirm out of family responsibilities, but on this occasion, out of boredom or a desire to leave the city, I agreed to go with them. Aunt Emma had insisted we spend at least a couple of weeks at "the cabin," as she dubbed her Newport house. The grandparents would come too. This family reunion seemed to excite both my father and Jaime, while my mother resigned herself to two straight weeks in Newport. Because I gave in to boredom and because my mother always gave in to my father's demands, we all ended up installing ourselves in Aunt Emma's house on Ocean Avenue—and it was well we did so, since at that time the humid heat was unbearable in New York City.

Aunt Emma liked to organize our stays as if they were military operations. In the morning she would gather everyone in the kitchen and spend some time discussing what we would do for lunch and dinner. Then she made sure that there were fresh flowers everywhere in the house and that my father had his favorite newspapers.

My grandfather and father would leave early to play golf. My grandmother Dorothy would also rise early to take a walk with her ridiculous Yorkshire terrier, and then she would spend the rest of the morning with some friend. As for my mother, she would get up late and usually stay on the porch reading, ensuring that not a single ray of sunlight would touch her and further darken her skin.

Jaime had friends whom he'd usually go out with, to play tennis, to surf, and to flirt with girls. I was the only one who had no agenda, because, in truth, I didn't want to do anything.

I would usually go for a swim as soon as I woke up. When I was younger my mother had tried to prevent me from going out in the sun so that my skin wouldn't get darker, as had happened to her. But I had already convinced myself that it was her fault that, due to my genetic inheritance, I would never have white skin, so I no longer bothered avoiding the sun.

The rest of the day I tried to slip away from whatever plans Aunt Emma concocted, which usually consisted of having cocktails, or tea, or going to some neighbor's house or inviting them over. She liked to see the house filled with people.

I don't remember if it was the third or the fourth day after we arrived in Newport when, at one of the few dinners where there were no guests, my grandfather James asked me what I was going to do with myself.

"He has all summer to think about it," my father replied on my behalf.

"Well, there's not much to think about—Thomas wants to work and if he needs a leg up you know you can count on me. I have a couple of friends with good connections at advertising agencies. I could talk to them. What do you think?"

It annoyed me that my grandfather was insisting on talking about my future, and especially that he wanted to organize it for me.

"Leave the boy alone, James. When he gets back to New York

he'll have plenty of time to think about what he's going to do. For now he has to enjoy this short vacation," my grandmother Dorothy intervened.

"James is right. Thomas needs to decide how he's going to face up to his future," said my mother, in support of my grandfather.

Suddenly all eyes turned to me. My grandfather was spoiling the dinner for me. Even naïve Jaime realized that I was getting angry and tried to change the subject.

"Grandpa, why don't we go out sailing tomorrow? I've been looking at Aunt Emma's little sailboat and it's in good condition. We could—"

"Of course it's in good condition—I don't sail often but from time to time I enjoy the solitude of the sea," said Aunt Emma, reminding us that she knew how to sail unaided.

But my grandfather didn't give in and ignored Jaime and Aunt Emma.

"You have to work, Thomas. There's a lot of competition out there. Kids willing and able to take on the world. You can't wait around," he insisted.

"The truth is, I have no desire to work," I said, to provoke them.

"What? So what do you want to do?" asked my grandfather angrily.

"Nothing. I honestly want to do nothing."

"But you have to do something." My mother's voice carried that note of hysteria that always came up when she was talking about me.

"And he has to decide tonight? Come on, James, leave the boy alone. He's on vacation. When he gets back to New York he'll have no choice but to decide what to do, but for now he has the right to relax like the rest of us." Grandma Dorothy had aligned herself with me to avoid an argument at the dinner table. She detested scenes.

Suddenly Aunt Emma intervened. She looked at me as if an idea was coming to her.

"And why does he have to work right away? In England it's common for young people leaving college to take a gap year. They travel, see the world, get their heads straight, and then when they get back they return to reality, which means finding a job and a nice girl to marry."

"I suppose this gap year is within the reach of all English kids," said my grandfather bad-temperedly.

"But in Thomas's case . . . If he decided to do it I don't think he'd have any problem, right, John?"

My father didn't know how to respond, but my grandfather did, saying that Emma's idea was utter nonsense. I saw that my mother was about to say something but I cut in.

"You know, Auntie, you've given me a great idea. I'll take a gap year. I'd like to spend some time traveling through Europe. I want to get to know London and Berlin."

"But . . ." My mother's surprise was evident.

"Well, we'll have to talk about it." My father seemed uncomfortable.

"Well, it seems like a good idea to me." That day Grandma Dorothy had become my greatest ally.

My grandfather looked at her with disgust. He didn't like my grandmother to take the opposing view, least of all in public. But she pretended as if she hadn't noticed my grandfather's consternation.

"In any case, it'll be Thomas who decides what he wants to do. We can advise him, but we can do no more than that," said my father, who seemed to want to change the conversation as much as Grandma Dorothy did.

"So if Thomas decides to do nothing you will abstain from interfering," my grandfather reproached my father.

"Come on, Dad, it's not like that. But I do think we must all seek out our own paths, and however hard it is we must allow our children to choose their own way. Thomas will decide what he believes is right for him, and of course he knows he has to do something: he can't just sit there twiddling his thumbs. Now what do you say, Dad, shall we play some chess after dinner? You beat me yesterday and you owe me a rematch." My father wasn't prepared to continue an argument with his own father.

That night, thinking about Aunt Emma's crazy idea, I could hardly sleep. Yes, why not go? I felt no particular attachment to my family, except to my father. And New York's advertising agencies weren't going to fall over themselves to hire me. The question was whether my father would be willing to help me financially so that I could go off on a journey with no practical purpose. Would he? Would my mother let him?

I decided to talk to him once we returned to the city and could be alone. I didn't want any intrusion from anyone else.

As I couldn't sleep I went down for breakfast shortly after dawn. Aunt Emma was the only other person awake.

"Where are you going so early?" she asked.

"If you lend me the boat I could go out sailing for a while."

"Your brother said last night that he'd like to go out on the boat today. Why not wait for him and go together?"

"Because I like to be alone and Jaime never stops talking."

"Poor thing, he's always trying to figure out how to please you but you're immune to his attempts. You're lucky to have him as a brother."

"Even an idiot would know by now that I'm lucky to have Jaime as a brother. You all won't stop telling me," I protested grumpily.

"So, are you really thinking about leaving?" My aunt changed the subject to avoid clashing with me.

"Yes, that was a good idea you gave me. After all, I've got nothing better to do."

"It'll do you good to grow up and appreciate what you have."

"Huh, so you think I'm immature!"

"Of course you are—same as any boy your age. You're still confused by life."

"That's textbook psychology."

"I don't need to read a textbook. This is how it is with many young people. You're nothing special."

"I'd like to go to London. What do you think?"

"You'd like London, but if you want to do something new, something surprising, go to France, or even farther south, to Italy, Greece, Spain . . . That's if you do want a change in your life. London is good too, and you'll find it easier because of the language."

"Do you know Europe well?"

"No, not that well. But when I married we went there. We spent a whole summer traveling from place to place and I fell in love with Italy. Perhaps I'll go back one day. Oh! By the way, the Fergusons arrived yesterday. Their daughter, that friend of yours, Lisa—she looks like a ghost."

So Lisa was in Newport. I wasn't too surprised because I had spent more than one weekend at the house the Fergusons owned, not very far from Aunt Emma's. Of course, the Fergusons' house was a three-story mansion, with a Carrara marble floor in the ballroom and a Versailles-style garden that extended down to the beach.

"It's a shame that a girl who has everything should waste her life on drugs. She could turn up dead any day," said my aunt.

"And how do you know she's on drugs? You don't have to listen to people's gossip," I snapped.

"It's not gossip, Thomas. Everybody knows it. Her poor mother is desperate. She doesn't know what to do with her."

"Well, if she wants to do drugs then let her. Why not?"

"You're too young to be so cynical. I can't believe that you'd be so indifferent to what's happening to Lisa. That girl liked you and you liked her. You were inseparable, though I'm not surprised that you don't see her anymore."

Aunt Emma never ceased to surprise me. It wasn't like her to parrot gossip. She annoyed me too. Yes, she annoyed me with her insinuation that Lisa had ditched me. I must be the talk of the town for the idle ladies of Newport.

"There was never anything serious between us. We were just friends, no commitment, so she didn't leave me and I didn't leave her. If she wants to destroy herself I won't be the one to stop her."

"If you say so . . . Anyway, I'm late. I'm going to go with the cook to buy everything we need for the get-together tonight."

"I didn't know you were throwing a party."

"Well, it's not a party exactly. A few friends are coming by to have drinks and something to eat, but it will be an informal gathering, just to have a good time. And I want no excuses: you must be ready by six."

"Are the Fergusons coming?"

"I haven't invited them. Your parents wouldn't feel comfortable after what happened at your graduation. And I imagine you wouldn't either. Anyway, they're not my friends, only acquaintances."

"It makes no difference to me. I'll go and see Lisa in a little while."

I actually had no desire to see Lisa, but it was a good way to unnerve all those stuck-up types among Newport's high society. If they saw us together they'd have something to talk about.

I waited until ten to go to the Fergusons' house. By then my father and grandfather had gone to play golf and Jaime had convinced Aunt Emma to lend him the boat to go sailing with a couple of friends. My mother had said she was going to the hairdresser's, not trusting that the night would be as informal as Aunt Emma claimed.

The maid who opened the door told me that Lisa was sleeping. I was about to leave when Mrs. Ferguson saw me.

"Thomas, what are you doing here? Come in, come in . . . Lisa is sleeping. She's not well."

She invited me to stay for coffee as she explained that she was trying to convince Lisa to be admitted into a detox center. She refused, but perhaps I could help them to convince her.

"The doctor says that Lisa is very ill. She has . . . well, she has . . . she has AIDS. You know, the needles . . . She wasn't careful enough and that horrible man, that Mike, he didn't even try to protect her. He could have stopped her from injecting herself with any old needle.

"Why, Thomas? Tell me why Lisa felt the need to resort to drugs. What did we do wrong? What is it that we haven't given her?"

I was tempted to tell her the truth: that her daughter was a bad person, just like me. That that was why we were friends, because we recognized the evil in each other, and she shouldn't look for anyone to blame. There wasn't anyone else to blame— other people weren't the problem. If it hadn't been Mike, Lisa would have found some other way to destroy herself. The truth was, the only thing that differentiated Lisa from me was that I didn't care about destroying other people as long as I saved myself, while she had no problem throwing her lot in with others as they destroyed themselves.

But I didn't tell her mother that. I just listened and nodded. I think what Mrs. Ferguson really needed was to vent her anguish by talking freely with someone who wouldn't judge Lisa. And I would not.

"She's taking methadone. The doctor says that'll stop her from suffering from withdrawal symptoms. Above all he recommended that we remove her from . . . well . . . the circles she was moving in in New York. You know . . . but . . . she's so on edge . . . she says horrible things. I hope that here she can get a little better. Miss Harris seems very efficient and she's taken care of patients in similar circumstances."

"Miss Harris?" I asked.

"The nurse. She was recommended by the doctor who treats Lisa. She controls the dosage of methadone Lisa gets each day, as well as the AIDS medication. My God, I don't know what we can do!"

"She'll be all right," I said, just to say something, and got up to leave.

"No, don't go . . . I'm sure Lisa will want to see you. I'll ask Miss Harris if Lisa has woken up yet. Wait here."

I didn't want to sit down and make conversation with an invalid, and that was what Lisa was, if I'd correctly understood what her mother had told me.

Mrs. Ferguson came back, accompanied by a tall, heavyset woman with short hair and a patronizing smile.

"So this is Mr. Spencer." She shook my hand. "Lisa has talked to me about you. It'll do her good to see you. If you'd be so kind as to wait a little, in twenty minutes she'll be ready to go down to the garden. It's the best place to sit and talk. And she'll get a bit of fresh air. But I have to warn you: she'll try to convince you to help get her some drugs. It doesn't matter what she says; you, Mr. Spencer, must be firm and help us make her understand that she's playing with her precious life. You could be of great help to us. She trusts you."

Mrs. Ferguson took me by the arm and led me to the garden, where Mr. Ferguson was currently engrossed in reading the papers.

"Benjamin . . . Thomas has come to see Lisa. Miss Harris will be down with her in a few minutes. It'll do her good to be with Thomas."

From his expression I could see that my presence made him uncomfortable. He got up to shake my hand. The last time we'd seen each other had been the day of the graduation. The scene Lisa made had shamed her father, and he knew that his daughter and I had stirred up other trouble together as friends.

We made small talk. Mrs. Ferguson tried to focus the conversation on Lisa's condition but her husband was too reserved to talk about it.

Miss Harris appeared with Lisa. She was holding her arm, seeming to support her.

Lisa's face showed signs of her sickness. Of AIDS, and the drugs too. She looked at me angrily, as if my presence displeased her.

"What are you doing here? Get out" were her first words.

I didn't even reply. I got up to leave. I nodded slightly at Lisa's parents.

"What manners!" exclaimed Miss Harris. "That's no way to greet a guest. Mr. Spencer will stay awhile. I'm sure you'll enjoy talking about things . . . It's been a while since you've seen each other, hasn't it?"

The Fergusons and Miss Harris left the garden, leaving me alone with Lisa, whom they had sat in an easy chair beneath a sunshade.

Lisa looked at me defiantly. She was waiting for me to obey her, to leave without protest, which is what I was intending to do. But a second later she changed her mind.

"Well . . . maybe you can be useful for something," she said as if she were talking to herself.

"Don't believe it—I haven't changed. I'm still good for nothing," I told her.

"Can you get me coke, speed, heroin? Anything . . . They want me to give up the drugs. But I don't want to. Now . . . well, I don't feel good, but I'll get better and I'll leave. I'm sick of the condescending way they treat me. And that Miss Harris is awful. She won't let me out of her sight. She brags that none of her patients have ever managed to slip past her to score. She gives me methadone like you'd give candy to kids, if they behave themselves. She's a bitch."

I stayed standing, looking at her. It was hard to recognize Lisa in that drawn, jaundiced face and that cartoonishly skinny body. She still had the same defiant look, but her eyes seemed to belong to a person who had already lived many lives and was closer to death than life.

"You look bad—seriously bad. Have they told you how long you've got?"

"You son of a bitch! You think I'm going to die? Well, so what? If it doesn't matter to me then there's no reason it should matter to anyone else."

"You don't care if you die?"

"I don't know . . . I don't think so . . . Why should I die? They're all idiots. If you control what you take, if you don't go too far, you don't have to die."

"It doesn't exactly seem like you've been able to control it."

"I'm worn out."

"Yes, you really are."

"Get me something. I managed to talk to Mike before they brought me here. He has a friend who works at a bar—it's not far from Newport . . . You could go and bring something back for me. Oh, and buy syringes."

"And Miss Harris? I don't think she'll fail to notice that you've started using again."

"I go to the bathroom alone."

"Right."

"Will you do it?"

"No. I don't want to get mixed up with Mike's friends. He and his buddies are scum."

"And you think you're so much better?"

"I'm not that level of scum. And I'm not going to take my chances on you, Lisa. I don't want anything to do with drugs. You already knew that."

"You're a coward."

"Maybe, but one thing I am sure of is that I don't want to depend on anything that I'm not able to control."

We fell silent. Lisa looked at me angrily while considering how to wear down my resistance. I raised my eyes to the house and saw Mrs. Ferguson and Miss Harris peering out the living-room windows.

"I'm leaving, Lisa. Be well."

"You could at least take me to that bar. I'd go in to pick up. You'd just take me there and bring me back. That doesn't commit you to anything."

"It depends."

"Depends? Depends on what?"

"If you shoot up too much and die. Then I'll be accused of having taken you to that bar. No, I don't want to get mixed up with drugs. You figure it out yourself."

"You're a son of a bitch."

"You already told me that. Goodbye, Lisa, and good luck."

She didn't try to stop me. She sunk back into the chair and looked away as if I weren't there.

Mrs. Ferguson and Miss Harris wanted to know what had happened, why I was leaving so quickly. I hadn't even sat down next to Lisa.

"She's not in a good mood and she doesn't want visitors," I explained.

"But you'll come back? You'll really come back to see her? She values you so much . . ." Mrs. Ferguson was like a castaway swimming toward a mirage.

I left, followed by the severe gaze of Miss Harris, without saying whether I would return.

I stopped thinking about Lisa. Well, I stopped thinking about her until four days later, when I unexpectedly found her hitch-hiking along the highway.

She looked awful. She was dressed in jeans and a T-shirt, but she was so skinny it looked like they were about to fall off her body. Even the sneakers she was wearing seemed too big. I stopped the car when I saw her.

"Where are you going?"

"Where do you think? I climbed out the window once Miss Harris dozed off—thanks to the Valium I dissolved in her milk. So, will you take me?"

"It depends."

"You only have to take me just over a mile from here. Leave me on the road and I'll find my own way back."

"It doesn't seem like you're having much luck hitchhiking."

"People in Newport are stupid. They don't trust anyone."

"It's probably because you look like a drug addict, which you are."

"Are you taking me or not?"

"You're going to Mike's friend's bar?"

"What does it matter to you where I'm going? I don't have to tell you. Look, we know each other, and you found me on the highway hitchhiking. I'm going to a friend's house nearby. Does that explanation work for you?"

"If you say so . . ."

"Yes, I say so. I'm going to a girlfriend's house. Doesn't that seem innocent enough to you?"

I hesitated a moment but told her to get in the car. Her choice. I'd leave her on the highway a mile up the road. Then I'd go. Let her make her own way back.

Aunt Emma gave me the news the next morning. Lisa Ferguson had been found dead in the bathroom with a syringe in her arm. They had taken her body away for the autopsy and the police were analyzing what was left in the syringe.

I decided that, to dispel any suspicion, it would be best to say we had met by chance the previous evening.

"I saw her yesterday and she seemed better to me," I told Aunt Emma.

"You saw her? Where? I thought you went to meet your father at the country club."

"And that's what I did, but I saw her on the highway hitch-hiking. She was going to a friend's house and I took her a mile or so."

"You have to tell the Fergusons!" exclaimed Aunt Emma.

"Okay, I will . . . But she seemed fine when I saw her. They wouldn't have let her go out if she wasn't."

"It seems she escaped out the window."

"But Miss Harris never let her out of her sight."

"You know what Lisa did? She drugged her glass of milk. The nurse fell asleep."

"I'll go straight to their house. They'll be devastated," I said, without the slightest hint of emotion.

"We'll all go. Your father and mother will want to go too. Fix yourself up a bit and . . . Well, the police might want to ask you a few questions. Where you saw Lisa . . . Things like that."

I went with my whole family to the Fergusons' house. My grandparents wanted to come with us too. It irritated me that my brother Jaime seemed upset.

"What does Lisa even matter to you?" I snapped as I saw him stifle a sob.

Mr. Ferguson told us that the funeral would be held in a couple of days.

"We have to wait for the results of the autopsy."

"I saw her and she seemed so well . . ." I said, as if my seeing Lisa had been the most normal thing in the world.

"You saw her? Where? What time? Why didn't you tell us?" Mr. Ferguson had suddenly become alert and looked at me with distrust.

"Well, I was driving to meet my father at the country club and I saw Lisa hitchhiking on the highway. She told me that she felt great, and that she was going to a friend's house a mile or two down the road. So I took her that mile or so and dropped her off on the highway. She didn't tell me but I imagine she was going to Mary Taylor's house—she lives around there . . ."

"You have to tell this to the police," said Mr. Ferguson. "You could be one of the last people who saw her yesterday."

"Sure, I don't mind, but . . . I was only with her a couple of minutes, and she seemed fine."

"Not . . . she wasn't . . . I mean, she wasn't on drugs?" Mr. Ferguson wanted to know.

"She seemed normal to me."

"What time was this?" he insisted.

"Around five . . . what time did I come for you at the country club?" I asked my father.

"Yes, it would have been after five. After playing golf I had a drink for a while with Donna and Tom Willis," my father recalled.

Mr. Ferguson called the detective who was conducting the investigation, and he arrived almost immediately.

The detective repeatedly questioned me about my brief meeting with Lisa. I imagine he was so insistent because he wanted me to add more details. But I stuck to what happened—with the exception of my conversation with Lisa.

"We still don't know where she went and who gave her the drugs. It seems you were the last person who saw her."

I cursed Lisa inwardly. I should never have let her into my car. I knew that I would end up being implicated, whatever happened.

Not only my family, but also all the staff at Aunt Emma's house had to give detailed accounts listing everything they knew I had done that day. They could confirm that I had gone out with Jaime and his friends to sail in the morning, and that I was lounging around at home from noon until my father called, asking me to come get him.

The detective wanted to know where and through whom Lisa acquired the drugs. After making inquiries, not just in Newport but also through the police in New York, he had to accept that no person nor any episode in my life could link me to drugs.

One week later, with Lisa now buried, the police detective insisted on speaking with me again.

"Do you know a 'Muscle Mike'?"

"I've already explained that I did. He was the PR guy for a club I went to with Lisa sometimes, and I never liked him."

"Apparently Lisa dumped you for this Mike."

"Lisa and I were just friends. We never had a serious commitment. Sure, when we met Mike I stopped seeing Lisa—I didn't like that guy."

"Did you know he was a dealer?"

"You didn't have to be a mind reader to figure that out. Plus, once Lisa started going out with Mike . . . Well, it was obvious that she wasn't well."

"This Mike, did he come to see her in Newport?"

"I don't know. I only saw Lisa two times here. At her house and on the day I found her on the highway, and we didn't talk about Mike."

"Did Lisa know anyone in Newport who could be connected with Muscle Mike?"

"I don't know. She didn't say anything to me about that."

"You don't seem very upset by your friend's death."

"You want me to break down in tears? Lisa's death has affected me just like everyone else, but I'm not the type of person to display my feelings. The way I feel is my business."

"You're much too composed. Way too much, given your age."

I shrugged. I didn't feel guilty about Lisa's death and so didn't give the cop the slightest glimpse of anything more than what I wanted to tell him. He was an old hand, and could tell that I knew more than I was letting on, but he also knew that I had nothing to do with Lisa's death.

"If you remember anything that could shed light on what happened that night, with Mike or with anyone connected to him . . ."

"I'm sorry, I can't help you. I've already told you everything that happened in the few minutes I saw her that evening."

"She shot pure shit into her veins. Whoever sold it to her knew what could happen to her."

I nodded. I agreed that Mike's friend and Mike himself were scum.

So many years later I wonder about that late afternoon when I met Lisa on the highway.

Could I have prevented her death? That day, yes, but Lisa was doomed. If it hadn't been that day it would have been the next. It was only a question of when she could escape from Miss Harris. It's what she did. So I didn't feel guilty about her end. Although things might still have played out differently:

When I saw Lisa walking along the edge of the highway, I should have asked her to get in, knowing where she was going.

"Come on, I'll take you home."

"Fuck off," she would have answered.

"Get in, Lisa, quit being so stubborn."

"I'll get in if you promise to take me a little farther on. I'm going . . . Well, you know where I'm going. You could come with me."

"No. I'm not going anywhere they sell drugs."

"If you were that fussy you'd never be able to leave the house. They sell them everywhere. Even those fancy clubs we used to go to."

"If you say so."

"Don't play Goody Two-Shoes with me. You know there are drugs everywhere. You only have to snap your fingers and they'll bring them to your door."

"And you want to keep snapping your fingers, don't you? You're going to kill yourself, and what's worse, you're wasting away so much that you're nothing but a wreck."

"*Charming as always. Save your sincerity. I don't need it. Don't pretend to be the sensitive one—it doesn't suit you.*"

Meanwhile I would be turning the car around to take her home. She would protest.

"*Hey, what are you doing? Turn around right now or I'll throw myself out of the car.*"

"*No, I won't. And don't bother trying to open the door because I've locked it.*"

Lisa would have thrown herself at me, not caring that we might crash.

"*You bastard! You have no right to kidnap me like this. Stop the car right now!*"

"*No, I'm not stopping. I'm taking you home. You're crazy if you think I'm going to help you kill yourself. Do it when I'm not around.*"

"*Stop, you bastard!*" *Lisa, hysterical, would try to hit me or wrench the wheel from my grasp.*

"*Keep still! You know that I'm not going to take you to Mike's friend. Go some other time, and try not to run into me on the way.*"

Mrs. Ferguson would be shocked to open the door to find Lisa and me struggling.

"*My God! But . . . Lisa . . .*"

"*It's okay, Mrs. Ferguson. Lisa is fine. She went out for a walk and I've brought her home.*"

"*A walk? Miss Harris didn't tell us that Lisa went out . . . Miss Harris, Miss Harris!*" *Lisa's mother would call in vain for her daughter's nurse.*

"*Let me go! Who do you think you are? I'm sick of this shit. And don't you go playing the hero. Don't fuck with my life! Get out!*"

"*Oh my God! Lisa, my girl, calm down. Thomas only wants to help you . . . Miss Harris!*" *The tone of Mrs. Ferguson's voice would be hysterical, especially given the absence of Miss Harris.*

"*What's going on?*" *Mr. Ferguson would appear in the hall, at first not understanding what was going on.*

"*Good evening, sir. I've brought Lisa home.*"

"*Lisa? But wasn't she resting in her room? I didn't know that she went out. Miss Harris . . .*" *Mr. Ferguson would look at Lisa and me in confusion.*

"*I'm afraid that Miss Harris is indisposed,*" *I'd reply.*

"*Indisposed? And why did no one say anything? . . . None of the maids have told us . . . Oh my God!*" *Mrs. Ferguson would resume wailing.*

"*Shut up! Leave me alone! And let me go or you'll see what happens!*" *Lisa would scream.*

But however hard she would try to pry my hand from her arm, she wouldn't be able to. She was too weak, too emaciated, too sick.

A maid would appear in the hall to inform the Fergusons that Miss Harris was unresponsive. Mrs. Ferguson would let out a wail, overwhelmed by the situation. She would run to Miss Harris's room, followed by the maid. Meanwhile, Mr. Ferguson would hesitate, wondering if he should take charge of Lisa. He'd look at the two of us as if we were both strangers, but I'd sense that he feared how Lisa might react. Finally he'd decide to ask me to help him take his daughter to her room.

Lisa would try to bite my arm. She'd do so with more anger than force. But I would have stayed firm and taken her to her room, followed by Mr. Ferguson. And at just that moment Mrs. Ferguson would reach Lisa's room, crying and calling for a doctor.

"*She's dead! She won't talk, won't move . . . My God, what are we going to do?*"

"*Mrs. Ferguson, I don't think Miss Harris is dead, I think . . . well, I think she's been given some tranquilizers, a couple of pills that the doctor prescribed for Lisa,*" *I'd say.*

"*But she's not moving! She's not breathing!*" *she would insist.*

"I'll call a doctor. Please, Thomas, don't go. You can see that we need you here. If you'd be so kind . . ."

"You can count on me, Mr. Ferguson, but let me call my father. I was on my way to pick him up at the country club and I'm almost an hour late."

Mr. Ferguson would approach Lisa apprehensively and grab her arm, forcing her to sit on the bed. Lisa would turn against him and I'd have to intervene so she wouldn't knock her father down.

The maid would take charge of the situation and say that she would call the doctor.

When Dr. Jones arrived Miss Harris would still not be showing any signs of life, and Lisa would be suffering convulsions due to her withdrawal symptoms.

The doctor would confirm that Miss Harris was still alive, and it was just taking a long time for her to wake up from the sleep induced by the high dosage of Valium that Lisa had administered. As for Lisa herself, he'd recommend the most prudent course of action—committing her to a specialized detox center.

"I'm afraid one nurse, even one as highly valued as Miss Harris, is not enough to control Lisa. There are some very good, very discreet clinics. I recommend that she be admitted as soon as possible. It would be the best for her and . . . also for yourselves."

The Fergusons would agree. It was the only option, and even that wouldn't fully guarantee that Lisa would get better. She wouldn't want to go, but they had to try.

I would become the hero of Newport. The Fergusons would tell their closest friends about my feat. How I had found Lisa hitchhiking on the highway and returned her home in spite of her protests. God knows what misfortune she had avoided. All alone there on the road . . . but fortunately I had appeared and had taken charge of the situation. It was lucky that I was such a good friend to their daughter, always attentive and patient.

Maybe someday . . . if Lisa recovered . . . who knows . . . We made such a good couple and were such close friends . . .

My father would go on and on about how proud he was of me, and my mother would have to acknowledge that my intervention may have saved Lisa's life. And my grandfather . . . well, my grandfather would have told anyone who would listen that his grandson was a true gentleman who had not hesitated to take care of that poor girl.

Yes, it could have been like that. But the truth was that not for one moment did any of that occur to me, nor did I have any intention of helping Lisa. I didn't want to get mixed up in her sordid life, so I abandoned her on that road with full knowledge of what might happen.

The detective, reluctantly, had to accept that I hadn't committed any crime. His old bloodhound's nose told him I knew more than I was letting on, even though what I knew had nothing to do with Lisa's death.

"You know something? I think you're afraid."

"Afraid? What would I be afraid of?" I asked.

"Of whoever sold the drugs to Lisa. Of Muscle Mike, the PR guy at the club who was dating your friend. Of the dealers who work with him. You shouldn't be afraid of them. We can protect you. The only thing I need is for you to tell me the truth about who Lisa was meeting that evening," he insisted.

"I don't know. She didn't say."

"Are you sure?"

"That's all I can tell you."

We locked eyes. He knew he couldn't force me to say another word. I suppose he gave up, because I never saw him again.

We returned to New York, and while my parents resumed

their routines I spent my time hanging around, until one day my father surprised me by inviting me to lunch at a restaurant near his office.

I imagined that he was going to deliver some long sermon reminding me that the time had come for me to do something "useful," as he kept saying to me.

"I've been wanting to have a quiet word with you for some time," he told me, smiling, while looking distractedly at the menu the maître d' had handed us.

I didn't reply. Why should I? I knew what to expect from him.

"If it suits you, I'll order a couple of nice tenderloin steaks and a Caesar salad. And some wine, we'll get a good bottle of wine."

I enjoyed watching how he put off the conversation he had been wanting to have with me. He didn't start until they brought us our steaks.

"So, Thomas, I'd like to know if you've made a decision about what you want to do. Both your grandfather and I are prepared to talk to our friends. We can open some doors for you; then it will be up to you. Your grandfather is a friend of Martin Snowdon's—he's retired now, but his eldest grandson runs the Snowdon advertising agency. Martin owes your grandfather a couple of favors. Our office has always handled his family matters. So he'll be happy to help. What do you think?"

I paused a few moments before replying. Not because the proposal had taken me by surprise. I knew that both my father and my grandfather were well connected, and they'd use their networks on my behalf.

In our world, these things happened every day.

"I don't want to stay in New York. My intention is to leave."

Now it was my father who remained silent. He hadn't really taken the idea seriously.

"Right. Well, it's not that it seems like a bad idea, but . . . don't you think it would be a waste of time? Here you could get a job, but in Europe . . . I don't know, you might find it difficult to find something that's worth the effort."

"Yes, you might be right, but the one thing I know for sure is that I want to leave behind what my life has been so far."

"You haven't had it that bad," my father reproached me. He seemed hurt.

I shrugged. I couldn't blame him for anything, he was right about that, but I think he never realized that I wasn't happy, given what I had on paper: a family with enough financial means that I never had to worry about anything.

"It would kill your mother if you left."

I couldn't help but laugh. He was a good man, too good, and therefore could not imagine that a mother and son could be irreconcilable enemies.

"You think you don't matter to her? You're wrong. You are very important to her, much more important than the rest of the family."

"Come on, Dad! You know that Mom and I don't get along. If I go she'll feel free. You'll see."

"You don't know your mother. It's just that the two of you both have strong personalities. You've always wanted to do your own thing, and your mother hasn't allowed you to. That's natural."

We talked for a long time, but he couldn't convince me to stay.

There was no going back. I would have liked to laze around a little longer but my father wouldn't have it, so a month later I found myself on a plane to London.

Jaime, always so sentimental, forced me to endure a tearful farewell. My paternal grandparents came to say goodbye. As for my mother's parents, I was the one who strongly discouraged them from coming. They were determined to at least come into Manhattan to say goodbye, but I stood my ground. I couldn't shake off Uncle Oswaldo, however. My mother's brother turned up at the apartment on behalf of the whole family with a package in which, I was told, there was a cake that my grandmother Stella had made for me to eat on the journey. I looked at him with such contempt that he didn't insist on accompanying me to the airport.

3

London was a great surprise to me. I found it as impressive as New York, though different in many ways.

A taxi took me to the Hotel Kensington, which my father had recommended. I couldn't stay there for long. It was too expensive. My father had given me enough money to live fairly comfortably for a couple of months, but I didn't want to have to call him to ask him to add to that fund. So, in addition to finding a more affordable place to live, I had to look for work.

I'd researched the then fledgling advertising and communications agencies in London, and decided to start by paying them each a visit. I'd hand over my ridiculous ten-line résumé, which stated that I had obtained a diploma in advertising from the Hard School of Advertising in New York. It was hardly a decent letter of introduction.

On the first day I visited seven agencies. None of them allowed me past reception, and even seemed reluctant to let me leave my résumé.

"Send it in the post," I heard several times.

But I had nothing to do, so I went around town and kept myself entertained, and started to get to know the city.

After a week I was beginning to worry. It seemed finding a job wouldn't be so simple.

I spent one morning visiting the British Museum and in the

afternoon decided to walk through Hyde Park, but the rain stopped me. I went into a movie theater, but I couldn't concentrate on the movie, so I returned to the hotel and sat at the bar.

The bartender was a Polish immigrant who always poured me far more whiskey than his superiors would allow. When I asked for another he looked at me and seemed to hesitate before asking me a question.

"You seem worried," he said as he served me my drink.

"Well, I'm still getting used to the city."

"Will you stay long?"

"In London? That depends on if I find work. In this hotel, another three or four days. I'm looking for an apartment."

"I see. So you're like all the rest of us, looking for work."

I was about to get angry at his impertinence, because he was looking at me as if I were his equal, but instead I thought I might be able to take advantage of the situation.

"Yes, essentially; I'm looking for work and a place to live."

"What do you do?"

"I'm in advertising."

"Well, start thinking otherwise, and focus on finding whatever work you can get. In London there's always a demand for waiters, janitors, cooks . . . A friend of mine—he's a mathematician—just got a job as a waiter at the Dorchester. I think they need another. If you want I can call him and find out if there's still a vacancy. The pay isn't bad, and then there're the tips."

A waiter. How could this man think that I'd allow myself to become a waiter?

"And have you always been a bartender?" I asked him.

"I have a degree in Slavic literature, but here, this is how I earn my living. It's what there is."

"But you couldn't find anything related to your studies?"

"Well, no, otherwise I wouldn't be serving cocktails. I might get to teach some classes at a college on the outskirts of London. It's in a district of immigrants, and there they don't care if the teachers aren't British. God willing I'll be lucky, but I'm also not holding out hope. I've spent five years in London and this is the best job I've had since I got here."

"Where did you study?"

"At the University of Warsaw. They don't need specialists in Slavic literature around here. If I were a doctor, a physicist, an electrician, or a pharmacist perhaps I might stand a chance. And I don't think you'll have any better luck in advertising . . . but who knows? Would you like me to put you in touch with my friend for that job at the Dorchester?"

"No, thank you, I don't think that will be necessary. I'll figure things out."

"I suggest you rent a room in someone's house. It'll be cheaper than a hotel, and certainly a flat, unless you share with someone. I'm renting a room in the house of an elderly couple— they subsidize their pensions by renting out the two rooms their children left vacant when they moved out. They're good people. He's worked all his life on the Tube and she worked for a cleaning company. The rent's cheap."

The bartender had taught me a lesson in reality in just under a quarter of an hour. Suddenly I realized that the rules of the game had changed, that living on my own meant leaving behind the way of life I'd had up until now. In all probability, no advertising agency would open its doors to me, and so I'd have to get used to the idea of doing any job, even being a waiter at the Dorchester.

"Thanks for the advice."

"No problem. Advice is free, although it shouldn't be," he replied, looking at the miserly tip I'd left on the bar.

I had no wish to keep talking to him, so I left the bar and went back out on the street. But I had nowhere to go. I was tired and it was raining, so I went back inside and up to my room, where I was beginning to feel like a caged animal.

I had a few advertising agencies left to visit, but I knew it was pointless for me to go knocking on doors, so I mass-mailed my résumé even though I knew it was a waste of time.

I started to flick through the job ads in the *Times*. The bartender was right: there was demand for cooks, waiters, janitors, salespeople . . . Then I noticed an ad for a PR assistant for a shopping mall. I didn't know what being a PR assistant would entail, but it didn't sound as bad as becoming a waiter, so in spite of the rain I decided to go introduce myself.

The mall was located in Canning Town, a modest neighborhood of blue-collar workers and immigrants. The mall itself stuck out like an eyesore, dominating one of the blocks. It seemed out of place in this district.

The security guard at the mall offices told me that it was late and there almost certainly wouldn't be anyone in the PR office, but I insisted that he call. I was lucky: the staff still hadn't left. I was received by a secretary, grumpy because she had been about to leave and had to delay her departure because of me.

The surprise was that the PR person was a woman, not a man, and also that she wasn't bad looking. Blonde, with slightly prominent blue eyes, dressed in a gray—no doubt designer—pantsuit and a white silk blouse. She was balanced on a pair of incredibly tall high heels.

"I'm Cathy Major," she introduced herself, shaking my hand and looking at her watch impatiently.

"Thomas Spencer. I came about the job . . ."

"So you're looking for work. Do you have experience?"

"No. None. I just finished my studies in advertising at the Hard School of Advertising in New York, so I haven't had the chance to work yet."

"Leave your CV and we'll call you."

"No, you won't," I replied, annoyed.

"Probably not. And now . . . it's late and I'm on my way out."

"I'm not surprised you need someone. This mall is dead. I've seen barely a dozen people. Don't you have any ideas about how to get people in? Maybe you should change the name. Green. Who decided to call a shopping mall Green?"

Cathy swallowed and looked me up and down. I could tell

that she was hesitating between sending me away and giving me an explanation. She chose the second option.

"This is my fourth day on the job. All that still has to be done. I need an assistant with experience, with new ideas. The owners of this shopping center are on the verge of bankruptcy. Barely any of the shops have been let."

"I can think of a number of things you could do to get people to come," I said boldly.

"Oh, really? So I'm standing in front of an advertising and communications genius and I didn't even realize." Her sarcasm irritated me.

"You've nothing to lose by hiring me. If you don't like my ideas then fire me. Give me a couple of months and you'll see."

"I don't even know if *I'll* get a couple of months, so I can hardly guarantee that for you."

"Tell me what's going on."

"A pair of builders managed to get the council to give them the permits to demolish a couple of run-down houses, then build a shopping center, with the level of success you've seen here. Which isn't surprising, given the neighborhood we're in."

"And what neighborhood are we in?" I asked with concern.

"Where have you come from?"

"New York."

"Right. Well, you should know that the area is dying. There're old people living here, retired people with little buying power, and they all prefer shopping in the traditional local shops. But above all there are immigrants. The rent here is cheap. Lots of these old retired people usually rent out their rooms. This is no place to open a shopping center."

"You don't seem too thrilled about your job."

"I've got nothing else. Otherwise, I wouldn't be here."

"What have you promised the owners of the mall?"

"That I'll do what I can, nothing more."

"How many people are there on your team?"

"Are you joking? The team is me and the secretary, Mary."

"Hire me. I'm from New York and I've got plenty of ideas that could help you. How many candidates have you interviewed?"

"Just one, apart from you."

"So it doesn't seem like you've got a lot to choose from."

"You're wrong. I have a stack of CVs I've been sent and tomorrow I'm seeing seven other candidates."

"Don't waste your time. Hire me. You won't regret it."

She did it. She hired me. I had no interest in that shopping mall, and planned to spend no more time working there than was absolutely necessary.

When I got back to the hotel I went straight to the bar. I wanted to boast about my good luck to the Polish bartender.

Two days later I was not only working, but had also moved. I was renting a room from an old widow whose house was about half a mile from the mall. Mrs. Payne was the sister-in-law of the mall's security guard—for her there was no higher recommendation than his word.

"I don't like to let just anyone into my house, but my brother-in-law Tom says you're to be trusted. Tom and Lucy, his wife, are good to me. You know, Tom owes his job to Ray, my late husband. It was Ray who hired Tom at the security firm. My Ray was the supervisor and everyone was fond of him. But as you can see, God chose to take him away and leave me alone."

The Paynes hadn't had children and the pension that Ray had left his wife was modest, even by the standards of this neighborhood.

Though the room was small it came with some furniture: a bed, a built-in wardrobe, a desk and chair, and a chest of drawers.

The furniture was cheap, although it must be said it all gleamed. Mrs. Payne seemed to amuse herself by waxing anything that crossed her path.

The only problem was that we had to share a bathroom, and she turned out to be very strict when it came to the water bill.

"No baths here—a quick shower will do you," she said on the day I moved into her house.

From Mrs. Payne I learned that Cathy Major had worked at one of the best PR firms in London.

"But she made the mistake of jumping into bed with her boss, and these things always end badly. It seems his wife found out and demanded that he sack her. And that's what he did. But the worst thing is that Miss Major caused a scandal, and that left a very bad impression on the agencies in the City."

Mrs. Payne had obtained this information from her brother-in-law, who seemed to be up to date on the life stories of all those who were working at Green.

I have to admit that I liked Cathy. Not because she was particularly friendly but because she held no surprises. She was direct and didn't mince words. And she didn't try to hide the frustration she felt from working at a mall in a distant neighborhood where there wasn't an ounce of glamour. Even so, she came to work dressed like the executives who are so prevalent in the City. She must have still had a well-stocked closet because she never lacked for designer suits, bags, and shoes that seemed so out of place in Canning Town.

"Right then, clever boy, the hour of truth is upon us. Tell me what ideas you've got so Green doesn't end up closing and you and I don't end up out of a job."

"The first thing is to get clients. There are only ten shops open and from what I've seen there's space for a hundred and fifty."

"You and I aren't here to find clients. We're here to publicize the place."

"We need publicity aimed at commercial clients, to get them interested in opening a business at Green. The first thing we have to do is convince the bosses to rent out the units at low prices, at least for a couple of years."

"What are you talking about? Perhaps you don't understand that our job consists of attracting customers to the shopping center. We're not here to worry about renting out the shops."

"Tell the bosses we want to talk to them. You can't publicize what doesn't exist, and that's what this mall is—it's dead."

"They won't like it, and they might sack us."

"We're their best chance. Right now all they've got is a building that will end up out of business if they go on like this. Call them, Cathy."

"Do you know what it took for me to get this job? I'm still on probation, and so are you."

"I know, but we have to play hardball. We have no other option."

"And if they sack me I certainly won't have any other option, and I think you won't either."

"Trust me."

"Never. You can't be trusted. I've known enough men in my time to figure out that you're a nasty piece of work."

"So why did you hire me?"

"Because you seemed clever. The problem is now you're trying to be too clever by half."

"Call, Cathy. They might fire us today, but if we don't do anything they'll fire us next week."

She made the call. The next morning, two sour-faced types received us in their office, a couple of blocks away from Green.

They were a pair of smartasses. Mr. Bennet and Mr. Hamilton had started from the bottom, first doing odd jobs, then working for a construction company; later they decided to go independent and set up a small business renovating houses. They were no more than two construction workers who had gotten lucky, playing at being businessmen. And they were about to go bankrupt—they had invested all their profits in launching a mall in their neighborhood, convinced that this would catapult them up the social ladder so they could rub shoulders with the real developers who had offices in the City.

Cathy knew how to impress guys like them, and appeared dressed in an Armani jacket and sky-high heels that made the three of us seem insignificant.

"I want you to meet Thomas Spencer. I've hired him as an assistant. He has the best credentials: he graduated from the Hard School of Advertising in New York."

Paul Hard would have laughed if he'd heard Cathy mentioning his academy as if it were some elite school. But a degree, to Mr. Bennet and Mr. Hamilton, was like some unobtainable treasure.

They each shook my hand and I felt like I was being observed with equal parts curiosity and distrust.

"We've been working on a couple of ideas that we think will be effective for Green. Go ahead, Thomas, I'll leave it to you to explain the plan we've come up with."

I wouldn't say I was surprised by the audacity with which Cathy assured them that we had been working on some ideas. She'd just introduced "my ideas" without even knowing what they were. But that was her way of making clear that she was my boss and wasn't about to let me put my name on anything.

I hadn't prepared any concrete plan of action, but I was good at improvising. Frankly, the ideas came to me as I talked.

"I'll give it to you straight. We can't launch any kind of ad campaign when there are only ten stores open. The first thing that has to be done is increase the number of rentals, and we can't do that alone—it depends on you."

"So you think we're doing nothing? That we opened Green just to look at it?" mocked Mr. Bennet.

"It's clear that you don't know how to sell what you've got, gentlemen. Maybe in a few years' time there'll be business owners fighting to rent units at Green. For the time being, you're the ones who have to convince them to do so."

"And how do you want us to do that?" asked Mr. Hamilton suspiciously.

"With a publicity campaign—we tell people they'd be idiots not to open a shop at Green, and that they can't miss the opportunity to rent an incredible space at a bargain price. You're currently renting out the fifty-meter units at one thousand five hundred pounds a month. Lower the price to three hundred pounds. And the hundred-meter units you rent out at six hundred pounds. And—"

"You're crazy!" Mr. Bennet interrupted.

"No, Mr. Bennet, I'm giving you a solution."

"That'll ruin us completely," he exclaimed, furious.

"On the contrary, this is to recoup your initial investment and will end up making you money in the long term. No, it won't happen overnight, but at least the center won't end up becoming a magnet for squatters, which is what will happen if you carry on without renting out the units," I insisted. Cathy cut me off. Then it was she who continued talking, jumping on board with all the ideas that I had just sketched out. I realized that Cathy was fully capable of robbing your wallet without even blinking.

"What Thomas and I are proposing is an option that's worth considering. Imagine Green with all the shops up and running. Clothes, music, electronics, food. People—it's about getting people to come, to get used to the idea that when you need something, you go to Green, but not just to buy. It's also a place to browse, to pass the time. Because of course Green should have a cinema, a kids' playground . . . Essentially, you have to turn this into the leisure hub for the neighborhood and the surrounding areas. You have to have an aggressive pricing policy. We will draw up the campaign."

"Right. Do you know how much it cost to set up Green? You haven't the faintest idea how much money we've invested here. We have to pay off a ton of loans to the banks. And you're suggesting we give our shop rentals away? Is this the only idea you've had?" Mr. Bennet's tone of voice left no doubt that he was angry.

"We can visit the retailers in the area, and explain to them individually the advantages of renting a unit at a low price. They have to invest, yes, but the investment is small if the price of the unit is," I said firmly.

"And who will pay off our debts?" insisted Mr. Bennet.

"How are you paying them now? You're not, are you? Or you're having such a hard time paying them you could go bankrupt at any moment. You'll lose Green and maybe end up in bankruptcy court. You'll see. We could waste your money for a couple of months on an ad campaign that wouldn't lead anywhere. If that's what you want, great. We'll do an ad campaign that'll increase the shortfall you already have with the banks," I argued.

Mr. Bennet opened his mouth to speak but Mr. Hamilton stopped him.

"This isn't what we were expecting of you, Ms. Major. Really, you didn't say anything about this to us when we hired you," he said, fixing his gaze on Cathy.

"Mr. Hamilton, ever since you hired me I've been meticulously studying the situation at Green. I assure you that I've reviewed every possible solution over and over. But in the end Thomas and I arrived at the same conclusion. We are professionals, honest professionals. After all, our reputations are on the line—we can't accept a job only to fail." Cathy spoke with such conviction I felt like laughing at her.

"Right, we'll think about it. Everything you've said to us . . . we have to think about it. We'll talk and give you an answer. Or perhaps we'll sack you, since you're so sure that if we don't carry out your plan, Green will be a failure. Shall we leave it there?" Mr. Hamilton looked at the two of us, knowing that he had surprised us with his response.

"Fine, very well. That's only fair. Think about it, and when you've decided we'll talk," replied Cathy in all seriousness.

When we left the office Cathy turned to me furiously.

"You idiot! They're going to sack us. How could you tell them that if they didn't do what you said there was nothing we could do and our jobs would be useless? I don't know about you, but I need the money those two cretins pay me. Things aren't going great for me right now . . . I don't think I could find another job so easily."

"Don't shout. Calm down. We're not going to lose our jobs. They'll agree to it. They have no other option," I assured her.

"Oh, really? So, along with that ridiculous diploma you have from the Hard School of Advertising, you've also got one from a correspondence course in finance? You've got some nerve."

"Some nerve for saving your job. How much longer do you think those idiots were going to pay you for twiddling your thumbs? They may be a pair of hicks, but they aren't so stupid as to waste money they haven't got."

"And now what do we do?"

"Well, we make a list of potential clients and design a catalog for Green that we'll give to all the local business owners, and send out to leisure companies, movie theaters, restaurants, playgrounds, and we'll draw up a nice ad for the *Times* offering units at Green at low prices. We'll have everything ready by the time those two call."

"To sack us," groaned Cathy.

"To put us in charge of everything. They don't know how to do any of this."

"I made a mistake in hiring you."

"I hope you treat me to a nice dinner when Bennet and Hamilton call to tell us they've accepted my idea."

"Our idea," she corrected.

"Yes, I saw how you jumped onto everything I proposed. Such gall!"

"Hey, you came to me to ask for a job and I'm responsible for everything that comes out of my department, including all your ideas. As long as you work for me your ideas don't belong to you. Let's get that straight."

"Unless they fire us."

She didn't reply, and I knew why. If the bosses decided to

reject my proposal she would do whatever it took to fool them awhile longer. Naturally she'd offer them my head. I couldn't trust her, just as she obviously couldn't trust me.

We got to work. Cathy was talented. Within a couple of hours she'd drawn up the outline for a catalog for Green. I had taken on the easy task: writing the text for an ad that would go out in the *Times* and other papers in the event our bosses gave us the go-ahead.

We had the secretary look up the names and addresses of the major companies in the leisure industry, as well as the most prominent retailers in the local area. Mary protested the increased workload, but Cathy put her in her place, reminding her that she'd fire her if she complained again.

"You see, Mary, I don't give a damn who my secretary is. I'm in no way tied to you. So if you're not prepared to do the work, get out of here. If things go well you'll have to do this and much more besides, and overtime as well. So you decide—stay or go? And if you stay you can forget about complaining, because I'll have you out the door without thinking twice," said Cathy without blinking.

Mary looked Cathy up and down. She had been hired a week ago and so far had done nothing but read the paper and answer phone calls from the occasional clueless person. The work had seemed a cinch and the boss easygoing, but suddenly it appeared that things were about to change. She thought before replying.

"I need the money."

"Right, then shut up and do as you're told. Hey, and no long faces! I like it when people smile. I want a pleasant work environment," warned Cathy.

"Are you going to pay me to smile?" asked Mary sarcastically.

"It's already part of the salary," replied Cathy icily.

Mary realized that if she wanted to keep her job she had to back down.

"So when do you want this list you asked me for?"

"Now."

We worked ten-hour days for the rest of the week, and by Friday Bennet and Hamilton still hadn't called.

Cathy looked nervous. I was worried too, although not enough to affect my mood. Plus, I had made myself out to be the guy who was perfectly sure of himself, capable of handling any setback.

We waited by the phone all day, but none of the calls we received were from Green's owners. At around three, Mary asked Cathy's permission to leave.

"I doubt anyone's going to call at this hour," she said.

"We'll all leave at five. And as far as I know you've still some work to do," replied Cathy, happy to annoy Mary.

I said nothing. It was all the same to me if I stayed in the office till five. I had nothing to do and I was starting to get bored of watching TV every night with my landlady.

Naturally nothing happened. In fact, the telephone hadn't rung since midday. Friday afternoons were difficult because everyone was out of their offices.

At five on the dot Mary picked up her coat and left with a blunt "See you Monday."

"I can't stand her," Cathy said to me.

"Then fire her."

"You wouldn't care?"

"Mary means nothing to me. Neither do you," I replied in all sincerity.

"You never hold back from saying what's on your mind."

"And why should I? I don't owe you anything."

"You owe me for this job."

"No, I don't owe you for that. You gave it to me because you knew how hard it would be to find anyone who thought it was worthwhile to work here. None of your friends from the City would even consider visiting you here."

"What are you doing tonight?" she asked me with curiosity.

"Nothing."

"Let's go out for dinner, my treat. Afterward the drinks are on you."

I accepted. I had no better plans and I was sure that we would dine well. Cathy wasn't the type to waste her time at burger joints.

She took me to Gastronhome, a French restaurant in which there wasn't a single table free, but on seeing Cathy the maître d' assured us that we would be seated in minutes. While we waited we were brought a couple of glasses of champagne.

The dinner was worth the wait. A vegetable tart and sole meunière accompanied by a Chablis, and to finish, an apple tart with a glass of Calvados.

By that point the alcohol had loosened us up, and we laughed over the smallest things. We started to criticize our bosses, the far from distinguished Messrs. Bennet and Hamilton, then moved on to Mary, not forgetting about Tom the security guard and of course his sister-in-law, my landlady Mrs. Payne. We got tangled up in a discussion about whether advertising was more effective when explicit or subliminal. By the end of it we were sizing each other up, deciding if it was worth our time to jump into the sack. Cathy decided that it was.

"Let's go to mine for a nightcap."

I eagerly accepted. It was my lucky night. I'd had a free meal and on top of that Cathy had invited me to her place. We had a good time, but she made it clear that what happened wouldn't change the relationship between us. She didn't invite me to spend the night, but asked me to leave almost as soon as the sex was over.

"Don't get any ideas. I only invited you out tonight because I had nothing better to do," she warned me.

"Same here," I replied.

"You're not bad but you're not my type. Besides, you have no future."

"You're wrong about that last one, and you know why?

Because I've got nothing riding on life. The truth is, nothing matters to me."

"What a cynic!"

I was still in time to catch the Tube back to Mrs. Payne's house where, to my surprise, she was awake and waiting for me.

"But why didn't you tell me you'd be back late? I've been worried about you."

"Mrs. Payne, thank you for your concern, but there was nothing in our contract about me having to tell you what time I'd be back to go to bed. Sometimes things come up."

"Yes . . . but . . . but still, it would be nice if you were kind enough to let me know. I don't like lodgers who keep strange hours."

"If you're not happy with me . . . well, I can always find someplace else."

Mrs. Payne was alarmed at the thought of the room going empty, so she tried to smooth over the situation.

"I hope you don't mind me worrying about you. You know, so many things happen in big cities . . . Of course you can come home at whatever time suits you."

"In that case I'll stay. Good night, Mrs. Payne. Sorry to have inconvenienced you."

At eight o'clock on Monday morning Mary answered the first phone call. Mr. Hamilton asked for me. He wanted to know if I could come by the office to have a meeting with him and his partner, Mr. Bennet. I didn't even ask him if I should bring Cathy, who still hadn't arrived at the office.

"Shall I tell Ms. Major to go to—" Mary started to ask me.

"No," I interrupted, "Ms. Major is not included in this appointment. I'll call her."

Mr. Bennet seemed nervous and left it to his partner, Mr. Hamilton, to begin the conversation.

"We've been going over your proposal and we don't like it

but it looks like you're right: it's our only option. We've managed to get an extension from the bank. They're willing to renegotiate the terms as long as we start paying back some of the money. This means a higher interest rate and, what's worse, we won't make a penny out of Green, but at least we'll pay back part of the money we owe and for the time being we'll avoid foreclosure."

"This bloody shopping center has ruined us," Bennet chimed in.

"It'd be worse if we ended up in court," Hamilton reminded him. "Now it's just about buying some time."

"You're too optimistic," Bennet interrupted.

"Right, let's focus on the subject at hand," said Mr. Hamilton. "We can't rent out the units for three hundred pounds—it has to be a little more than that. The fifty-meter units for five hundred pounds, the hundred-meters for nine hundred pounds, and the hundred-and-fifties for one thousand two hundred pounds. We're also prepared to lower the price if someone rents more space, for a supermarket or cinema or whatever. Renting in Green will be a bargain. And it will be you, Mr. Spencer, who'll be in charge of finding clients. We're builders and we've never had to look for customers before. We just build and sell. That was easy."

I gave him a list with the names, addresses, and numbers of several retailers, as well as the major business owners in the leisure sector.

"I've done my homework," I said, looking at the two of them.

"Well then, get to work," urged Mr. Bennet.

"I will, but I need you to be in agreement. Have a look at the list."

Mr. Hamilton quickly scanned it and passed it back to me.

"We don't know who any of these people are, and we don't care who you call. What we want is to rent out these shops," said Hamilton.

"Do what you have to do," added Mr. Bennet.

"I'll consult with you on all the steps I have to take, but I don't want any interference."

"What do you mean?"

"I want to do this my way. I want to be in charge. When I call the men on this list, I'll be speaking with the executives. I want to be the project manager."

"But Cathy . . . I mean, Ms. Major, she's . . ." Mr. Bennet spluttered, without daring to name Cathy as my boss.

"Come on, Bennet, so far the girl's just been twiddling her thumbs wasting our money. We both know that if we take this risk we have to let Mr. Spencer run the show."

"It doesn't seem very loyal . . . She . . . well, she's very well known in advertising," insisted Mr. Bennet.

"Put Spencer in charge, even if you do have the hots for that girl. She'll have to get used to the new situation," replied Hamilton.

I immediately understood that Cathy had gotten the job because of her looks. Of course Bennet would have the hots for a woman like that. He would never have dreamed he could come within ten feet of a woman like Cathy. She was out of his league, but destiny had placed her in the position of having to smile at him. Had she gone to bed with him? No, she was too smart for that, but no doubt she was leading him on. I made a decision. If I were going to be the boss of this stupid venture I'd have to rid myself of Cathy. She wouldn't agree to us swapping roles: me the boss and her my assistant. Hamilton was on my side while Bennet was still drooling over Cathy, so I decided to play dirty to get her out of the way.

"Mr. Bennet, Ms. Major is no doubt a talented woman, but one with a bad reputation. Her departure from the City was the subject of a lot of gossip. Her affair with her boss . . . Well, there were personal matters that ended up embarrassing everyone involved. It seems that Ms. Major sought revenge by going public with their relationship. In the City they say that she's capable of doing anything to get her way. If you want me to take charge you should let me choose my own assistant. I don't think that Ms. Major is going to resign of her own accord and I don't want to waste my time on domestic quarrels."

"Oh yes, she's the type who threatens to call your wife to tell her she's slept with you if you don't do what she says. I told you so, Bennet." There was a tone of reproach in Mr. Hamilton's words to his partner.

"I don't think that . . . Well . . . It doesn't seem right to fire Ms. Major," grumbled Bennet.

"I know she has you by the balls but you heard what Mr. Spencer said. This kind of woman can ruin a man's life. You wanted to aim high, Bennet, and we can't afford a scandal. Remember that our wives are in this as much as we are. The last thing we want is for your wife to get jealous because of Ms. Major."

"You two decide." I stood up to leave.

"Sit down! Sack her, do what you want, but I'll slice your balls off if you haven't rented out all the units in Green within one month." Hamilton's tone left no doubt that he was willing to make good on his threats.

"I can promise to do my job, but I can't promise miracles. If I haven't rented out at least half of the units within a month, then fire me."

"We will, in addition to slicing your balls off," confirmed Hamilton.

Just then Hamilton and Bennet's secretary opened the office door, followed by Cathy.

"Well now, I didn't know that we had a meeting this morning. I suppose you have an answer to my proposal for Green . . ."

"Yes. Mr. Bennet and Mr. Hamilton have made a decision, and I've made mine too," I said, looking at her coldly.

"Oh yes? I'm dying to hear the news," she said, looking at Bennet with a smile full of promises.

"The first piece of news is that these gentlemen have agreed to my plan. The second is that from now on I'm in charge of the project. And the third is that I'm free to choose who I want to work with and I've decided to let you go. I'm sorry, Cathy, but I don't think you're the right person for this project. It's too big for you. It's not just about advertising, but about saving the business, and to do that you have to roll up your sleeves and hit the streets. You wouldn't know how to do that."

"You're insane! You think you can sack me? Mr. Bennet, tell him . . . get him out of here. What are you thinking?" Cathy seemed on the verge of hitting me, looking at Bennet with the certain knowledge that he would defend her.

"Ms. Major, we have accepted Mr. Spencer's conditions. We'll write you a check for your pay to date," Mr. Hamilton told Cathy, not giving her a chance to respond.

"I'm sorry," Mr. Bennet managed to say.

"This can't be happening!" Cathy sounded hysterical.

"But it is, my dear, it is," I interjected.

She locked her eyes on me and then on Bennet, who couldn't meet her gaze. Cathy was smart enough to realize that she had lost. She paused a moment to compose herself. She didn't even look at me as she spoke to Mr. Bennet.

"I won't go until you pay me right down to the last penny."

"But right now . . ." he mumbled.

"Now, Mr. Bennet, right now." Cathy's voice was threatening.

Bennet looked at Hamilton, who stepped in, knowing that Cathy wouldn't leave without her money.

"We'll write you a check," Hamilton suggested.

"No, no checks. I don't trust you. You've already shown me what kind of men you are. You'll pay me in cash. I'm not leaving until you pay up."

The time had come for me to go. I had no role to play in this scene.

"Gentlemen, I'll keep you informed." I left the office without giving them a chance to say goodbye.

When I returned to the office at Green I asked Mary to clear out all of Cathy's belongings.

"Ms. Major doesn't work here anymore. Put all her things in a box. Oh yes—and I'm the boss now. So if you want to work here these are the conditions: there are no fixed working hours. You will be here until I leave. I want no complaints or objections. And I warn you that I'm short on patience. If you want to, then stay; if not then you know where the door is."

Mary looked at me in silence and went to clear out Cathy's office, which in reality was little more than a cubicle surrounded by a glass partition.

Cathy arrived an hour later and Mary handed her the box. I saw that she hesitated over whether to hurl some insult at me but thought better of it. Or perhaps she had too much class to make a scene for a nobody like me.

She left with a brief goodbye to Mary; as for me, she didn't even look my way. I imagined I would miss her. I didn't have her knowledge or her experience, both qualities that I would need to successfully bluff my way through the offer I had put on Bennet and Hamilton's table. Why had I fired Cathy? Because I felt the urge to try my luck. I wanted to be the one who, for the first time in my life, took the reins of something, even if it was a doomed project like Green. I wanted to give the orders, to do things or not do things according to my own will, without anyone questioning me. Cathy would only be in my way.

I savored the moment. Mary watched me out of the corner of her eye. By that point she had realized that I was a scorpion who could strike at a moment's notice. Even if she became the perfect secretary I could still fire her at any time for reasons that she wouldn't understand and I wouldn't bother to explain.

I don't regret what I did, but neither do I recall the incident with satisfaction. I owed Cathy for helping me when I didn't have the first clue what to do with my life. We could have worked together to pull off that plan to save those two social-climbing construction workers, which is what Hamilton and

Bennet really were. I didn't care about them or Green, so if I'd looked beyond the vanity of being the boss there was no reason I couldn't have continued working with Cathy.

I'm sure I should have behaved very differently than I did:

When Mary passed me the call from Mr. Hamilton I should have told him that Cathy hadn't arrived yet, and that as soon as she reached the office we'd come over to see them. Or maybe I could have gone ahead, but insisted that Mary tell Cathy to head immediately to Hamilton and Bennet's office.

"Mary, try to find Ms. Major and tell her to go straight to the bosses' office. I'm going now, but she should hurry."

When I arrived I should have told Mr. Hamilton that Cathy and I would take charge of the matter, that we were capable of moving it forward. I could even have suggested that Cathy's contacts in the City meant there were doors open to us that would otherwise have been out of our reach.

When Cathy rushed in late to this unexpected meeting, I should have filled her in and allowed her to be the one to take charge of the project.

"Cathy, Mr. Bennet and Mr. Hamilton have accepted our proposal with some modifications. See what you make of it. They suggest we increase the rental prices, but not by too much . . ."

She would have accepted, of course; it was all the same to her whether we rented the units at five hundred pounds or a thousand. All that mattered to her was keeping her job as long as possible, just like me.

"The increase isn't important, but under these conditions it'll be more work for us to rent out the units at Green. We'll get straight to work and do whatever we can to make it happen. Won't we, Spencer? Gentlemen, we'll let you know when there's news—hopefully good news," Cathy would have said.

Then we would have left that showy, tacky office and hailed a cab to take us to Green. Maybe later she would even have taken

*me out for dinner. She was generous. Then I would have worked
hard making calls, saving the important ones for her. It would be
absolutely clear that she was the one in charge.*

But none of that happened. Nothing in that scene took place. So
I became the boss and the head of a failing project, knowing no
one in London, only going by the list drawn up by Cathy Major.
Taking advantage of her work. My conscience still didn't waver.
To be honest, it has never wavered.

What I did was get straight to work. I hadn't a minute to lose.
Hamilton was fully capable of carrying out his threats.

"Mary, find the list of potential clients and get me Mr. Bradley."

"The multiplex guy?"

Two minutes later, Mr. Bradley's assistant was asking the reason for my call. I explained briefly. The company that owned
Green was offering the space required for a multiplex movie
theater at a bargain price. The assistant asked how much this
supposedly bargain price was. I told him and the line went quiet.

"Okay . . . This is all very interesting, but shouldn't you send
us some information about what Green actually is? How many
shops are open, number of residents in the area, links with other
parts of London . . . ? I mean, a brochure, as it's usually done?"

"Well, you see, the reason I'm calling is because I know
Mr. Bradley's reputation. I'm reaching out personally as a courtesy before our brochure is sent to other businesses in your
sector. In any case, you'll get the brochure in a couple of days.
Naturally, I'd like to set up a meeting with Mr. Bradley, unless
you tell me he's not interested, in which case I won't pursue."

The assistant didn't seem to know what to say, and opted to
ask for the number where he could reach me.

"We'll call you as soon as we receive the brochure," he told
me before hanging up.

I had learned my first lesson. No one would see me without
a prior calling card, and that card had to be a glossy catalog with

photos of Green and information about its business opportunities. Mary and I worked for the rest of the day. As soon as we finished the brochure we'd send it to the printers; then we'd find a courier company to deliver the catalogs to potential clients. I gave the operation four days to be carried out.

Mary knew of no printers capable of producing our catalogs in just a few days, so I turned to the security guard, who apparently knew how to find anything. He gave me the address of a printing business belonging to his brother-in-law's friend.

"They're short on work right now. You know how it is: lot of businesses closing," he explained as he wrote down the address for me.

I was thankful that was the case, because it meant I could put pressure on the printers to work fast. And that's what I did. Even so, things went slower than expected. To begin with, I had to redo the brochure design four or five times until I found a look that satisfied me. It had to be modern, contain enough information but not so much that it overwhelmed potential clients, and, above all, convey the idea that the offer was irresistible. The problem was that I knew nothing about design. But I did the best I could, and two days later I had created the catalog.

"What do you think?" I asked Mary.

"Fine," she replied tersely.

"So you don't like it."

She smiled and asked if I wanted tea, leaving me in no doubt that she didn't like it at all. Even so, it was the best I could do and I sent it to the printers.

The catalog didn't turn out so badly thanks to a couple of suggestions made by the printers.

Mr. Hamilton called to ask me how things were going and I promised that we would have results very soon.

"The banks won't wait," he warned me.

While I was waiting for the catalog to reach major potential clients, I spent my time visiting the most solvent-looking businesses in the neighborhood one by one. I convinced three of them to try their luck at Green: a sports store, a Chinese-run store that sold everything, and a bakery. It was a start, though I urgently needed more contracts. I asked the Chinese owners to put me in touch with any of their compatriots who might be interested in setting up shop at Green, but without success. So I had to turn to Mary to dig up information about the kingpins who ran the import businesses from China. If we could rent a couple of units to them, we'd be saved.

Eventually I came across Mr. Li, the owner of several supermarkets in London as well as a couple of cheap toy stores. I convinced him to visit Green and he seemed to like it, because he rented five units from me. I demanded in the contract that the shops be decorated according to Western tastes, with some restraint; no lanterns or any of those decorative elements that would remind people that these were Chinese shops and would put off customers.

In fifteen days I managed to rent out eight units. It wasn't much, but I considered it an achievement.

Mary had suggested that we put an ad in the *Times* advertising the units, and especially the prices.

"Good idea, Mary. Then everyone will know that Green exists and that it's a bargain to open a business here."

"It's not actually my idea. Ms. Major told me that this is what she would have done if Mr. Bennet and Mr. Hamilton accepted her plan."

"Enough about Cathy. The whole cheap-rent idea was actually mine."

I had been telling the truth, but Mary had looked at me skeptically. She had the lowest of opinions of me. If I was capable of getting rid of Cathy, I must also be capable of stealing Cathy's ideas.

I sent Mary to place various ads in the *Times,* the *Guardian,* the *Sunday Times,* and the tabloid papers that everyone reads on the way to work.

Two days later Mr. Li surprised me by turning up at my office with a proposal.

"How many units can you rent me?" he asked, with no preamble.

"How many do you need, and for what?"

"I have some friends interested in opening shops."

"Okay. Are these friends Chinese?"

"Yes, Chinese."

"What kind of businesses do they want to open?"

"Oh, everything! Restaurants, supermarkets, clothing ... All Chinese, only Chinese—a major Chinese shopping center," replied Mr. Li.

"Right, but that would change the nature of Green. It'd become a big Chinese superstore."

"Yes, and people all over London will come to buy things at the cheapest prices."

"But some of the units are already spoken for. We'd have to compensate the people who have already rented them. They've made an investment and we can't just kick them out."

"Do not worry. You won't have to compensate them. They will leave—they cannot compete with Chinese businesses."

"If you want the whole building you'll have to pay more—not much more but, still, more ... You understand that renting unit by unit is different from renting the entire building. And you'd have to take on all the general costs—lighting, security, cleaning, all those things."

"That is no problem. You tell me the total price for Green and I'll tell you if I can pay it or not."

"I'll have to do the math. Can you come tomorrow? I'll have your answer then."

"Ah yes, tomorrow! Think about it, Mr. Spencer. It is a good deal for both of us."

I told Mary to find Bennet and Hamilton and tell them I needed to see them immediately. They didn't play hard to get.

That same afternoon they received me at their office, where there were no employees other than the sad secretary who also had to open the door.

When I told Bennet and Hamilton what was happening they couldn't get over their shock.

"But this Mr. Li, is he trustworthy?" asked Hamilton.

"I don't know. I'll need reports from the bank and at least a year's deposit in advance. But renting the entire building means a sizable sum," I said.

"He'll have to pay our asking price," Hamilton cut me off.

"Mr. Li isn't stupid. The only reason he's prepared to rent any units at all is because the prices are cheap," I replied.

"But we're not going to just give away the shopping center," interrupted Bennet.

"That'd take the cake, if this Li gets all the benefits from our sacrifices and we don't even get a pound in rent for Green," insisted Hamilton.

"Gentlemen, until yesterday you had a mostly empty shopping center and were about to declare bankruptcy. Now you have the chance to make Green profitable and be accountable to the banks. You might not make huge profits, but at least it'll get you out of this jam, and in time the shopping center will start to make you money. If Li invests in Green and business goes well, they'll keep renting the units, and might even buy them. I don't know that, but I do know that if you rent the building to him then you'll at least have something in hand."

They hesitated. Greed made them think that I had pushed them to undervalue Green. I have to admit that I was eager for them to agree to do business with Li. It was hard enough for me to have managed to rent out the fifty units so far, and even though I had rid myself of Cathy, these two would soon realize that I was not much better than her.

"What is it you're proposing, Mr. Spencer?" Mr. Bennet asked me.

"Fix a price for the building and have Mr. Li sign a contract saying he will be responsible for all the expenses of maintaining the shopping center. All expenses means *all* expenses. In addition, you can profit from the parking. You can rent out the entire center to him apart from the parking garage. Customers going to Green will need somewhere to park. You'll still manage that. If Li does well with the business you'll get a slice of it with the parking garage."

This was something that had occurred to me on the way over and it seemed I'd had the right idea, because a hint of a smile appeared on Mr. Hamilton's face.

We talked for a while about the price of renting Green and in the end they gave me the authority to negotiate with Li. Taking advantage of the moment, I asked them for a commission from the amount that they were about to get.

"But you're our employee! None of this commission nonsense. Why should we pay you a penny more?" protested Bennet.

"For the simple reason that you hired me to do publicity. No more than that. My salary doesn't cover managing the rental or sale of your shopping center. I'm doing a job for which you have to pay me. Fifty thousand pounds in commission is a very low fee."

"We can negotiate with Li directly," Hamilton shot back.

"Yes, you could," I replied defiantly, as if I were keeping something up my sleeve.

"You're very ambitious, Mr. Spencer," stated Mr. Bennet.

"You think so? I'd say you're getting a pretty cheap deal. A couple of weeks ago you were about to be seized by the banks for that debt you're struggling to pay off. I'm offering you a solution to your problems and that, as you must know, comes at a price. My price is cheap, considering your serious financial difficulties."

They looked at each other, a look that was enough to tell me what their decision was.

"All right," said Hamilton, "but it'll be forty thousand

pounds. Twenty thousand on signing the agreement with Mr. Li and the other twenty within six months, once we know that this Chinese bloke can be trusted."

"No, Mr. Hamilton. You will pay me the fifty thousand pounds the day after we sign the contract. Then I will stop working for you since my services will no longer be necessary. The three of us will all be satisfied."

We argued for some time, but I knew that I was going to win this battle.

I thought about not calling Li for a few days, so he wouldn't think he was our only option, but I decided against it; the sooner I called him the less likely he'd back down.

This time I went to his office, located in a run-down building near the Thames. The building that housed his office also served as his warehouse. I was amazed to see so many Chinese people entering and leaving one building.

Mr. Li's secretary turned out to be his daughter. I was surprised by her nondescript appearance. Neither attractive nor ugly, short and very thin, with gap teeth and black hair cut in no particular style. She was well dressed in decent clothes, and spoke English with a distinct British accent.

Mr. Li offered me a cup of tea, which I declined, but from his expression I realized that my refusal had been a mistake. He signaled to his daughter and she left the office, only to return immediately with a tea service of English porcelain and several pastries, the kind sold in those enormous boxes at Harrods. Since the Chinese counterfeit everything I wondered whether these pastries were real or had been manufactured in some Chinese village. I corrected my previous mistake by saying that I had a serious sweet tooth, and that I could hardly turn down one of those exquisite Harrods pastries. This seemed to please Mr. Li.

As we had tea he sang the praises of his daughter, Tany. Apparently she was born in England and he had made every effort to ensure that she had received the best education. Tany had a degree in English from Oxford.

I was getting impatient, but decided I had no other choice but to let him be the one to set the pace of our conversation.

Some time passed before he asked me about the price to rent Green. When I told him his face remained unreadable but he took a few moments to respond.

"That is more than it would cost me to rent it shop by shop," he said, smiling.

"It is, but trust me that if you rent Green it would be like having your own shopping center. You can do or not do whatever you want without having to answer to anyone. The only thing Mr. Bennet and Mr. Hamilton require is that you meet the date we agree to for payments."

"Even so, the price is higher than expected," insisted Li.

"You know that it's barely a ten percent increase on prices that were already very low."

"The reason they were low is because you couldn't find a way to rent them out."

"You're not wrong—it's a commercial strategy to put Green on the map."

"You said that the car park does not enter into the agreement—may I know why?"

"Mr. Hamilton and Mr. Bennet want to keep it for themselves and run a public garage. It won't make a difference to you. Your customers will still be able to park there."

"Paying."

"Yes, of course, paying."

"I would prefer to rent all of Green."

"You never said anything to me about your interest in the garage. I'd have to talk to Mr. Hamilton and Mr. Bennet. And this would raise the price, which may not suit you."

"Perhaps I should meet with your bosses and deal with them directly. That is always better than negotiating through intermediaries, don't you agree, Mr. Spencer?"

"No, that won't happen. Mr. Bennet and Mr. Hamilton are waiting for the two of us to close this deal first, and then you will meet with them and their lawyers. In the meantime you will have to make do with dealing with me."

"And are you capable of deciding whether the rental of Green includes the car park?"

"I'd have to check."

"Then it would be better for me to deal directly with your bosses. It would save us all time."

"Mr. Li, if the deal does not include the garage, would you still be interested in renting Green? That is all I need to know."

"I would have to think about it."

"Great. Then think about it, and when you've made a decision give me a call."

I stood up, facing a stunned Mr. Li. I wasn't prepared to waste my time or lose him for the sake of subtlety.

Tany accompanied me to the door without even looking at me, and said goodbye with a murmur and a slight nod of her head.

I was frustrated. I'd have to call Bennet and Hamilton to convince them that my brilliant idea for them to be in charge of the parking garage could be a stumbling block in closing the deal with Li.

When I reached the office I told Mary what had happened and she seemed to relish my failure—as if she weren't aware that if they fired me then she'd also be out on the street.

"The Chinese are very ceremonial. You have to keep them entertained," she said, as if she were an expert on Asia.

"Right, and how do we keep them entertained?" I asked in annoyance.

"Don't seem impatient, or make it obvious that it's important for you to close the deal. Wait four or five days before you call him again, or even longer," Mary advised me.

"Right, and Bennet and Hamilton? I'll have to tell them we haven't closed the deal."

"If they've waited this long they can wait a few days more."

"And if they don't want to rent him the garage?"

"Then it'll all depend on Mr. Li. Don't worry, neither of us will be worse off than we were before we worked here."

To my surprise Mr. Bennet and Mr. Hamilton told me they weren't intending to rent out the parking garage. They had already calculated the profits they could get if Li turned Green into a major Chinese shopping center. They imagined huge lines of cars with avid shoppers looking for bargains.

I was unable to convince them to give in to Mr. Li's request.

"What is this Chinese bloke thinking? We can't let ourselves be pushed around by him. No, no way are we renting him the car park. You tell him loud and clear, our answer is no," said Mr. Hamilton angrily.

I followed Mary's advice and waited a few days before calling Li. His daughter told me to come over that same morning, because her father was about to leave on a trip and would be out of London for several weeks.

I went, intending to show that I wasn't anxious to reach an agreement. This time I accepted the tea that Mr. Li offered, which Tany brought to us minus the Harrods pastries. I thought that tea without pastries must be the prelude to failure.

"Mr. Li, I'm sorry to say that my bosses do not wish to rent out the garage. I understand your interest but at the moment they have no intention of doing so."

I fell silent, watching him. I tried to seek out some reaction in his face, but Li didn't move a muscle. He waited a few moments before replying, doing so only after finishing his tea.

"It is a pity we cannot reach a deal that suits both sides. Well, they must have their reasons."

Silence descended. I didn't know whether to stand up and leave, since Mr. Li no longer seemed interested in Green, or make one last attempt. I thought that Mary would have advised me to leave, and I hesitated.

"With or without the garage, it would be a good deal for you to rent Green. You won't find anywhere else with these features at this price. But your business is your business."

Mr. Li seemed to look at me with curiosity. I remained sitting there, not moving a muscle, just as unreadable as him. We returned to silence.

"The price would have to be lowered," he said suddenly.

"No, we're not going to lower it by a penny. We won't just give Green away."

"Do you work on commission?" he asked bluntly.

"That's a personal matter that concerns no one but myself," I replied stiffly.

"The parking has three stories, does it not? Very well, let me have the first. I need it for my employees and for storage. If I get it I will give you a good commission—how does twenty thousand pounds sound to you?"

If I had been a decent person I would have felt offended by the offer. I should have said something like, "You must be confused, Mr. Li. For me, loyalty is the guiding principle of my life. My duty is to represent the interests of my bosses, and not go behind their backs for your benefit."

But I didn't say that. I was neither honest nor decent—I wasn't then and am still not now—so I accepted. I was about to add another twenty thousand pounds to what I'd already asked for in commission from Bennet and Hamilton.

I don't know how I did it, but I managed to get my bosses to agree to Li's request. The truth is, I threatened them. I told them they had no choice, that Li had ordered credit checks on them. He knew they were broke and could ask for an even lower price. I also warned them that I was sick of tilting at windmills and even hinted that, since Li had made inquiries about them and knew their precarious financial situation, he could spread the word that their assets were about to be seized. So anyone who rented a unit could find themselves facing the unpleasant surprise of being thrown out on the street right after having invested money refurbishing their store.

They looked at me in horror and Bennet hurled a couple of insults at me, but eventually they concluded that I was right, so they gave their consent for me to close the deal with Li. They rented him the first story but at a higher price than Li had offered. The Chinese businessman accepted and three weeks later, accompanied by their respective lawyers, they signed the deal.

I demanded that Li as well as Hamilton and Bennet pay me with certified checks. I had earned seventy thousand pounds and felt satisfied.

I didn't give Bennet and Hamilton the chance to fire me. I told them they no longer needed me. I know that I should have been concerned about what might happen to Mary, but I wasn't. I had no intention of seeing her ever again, so I didn't care what happened to her.

"The Chinese will be moving into the building tomorrow," I told her by way of goodbye.

"And me?"

"You'll have to fend for yourself."

"Well, whatever you do, you'll need a secretary."

"Yes, but not one like you."

I don't think Mary was surprised by my reply. She saw through me and knew that she could expect nothing from me. Even so, I could have shown more kindness toward her. Perhaps I could have said something like, "Don't worry, I'll recommend you to Mr. Li. Even though his daughter Tany is his personal secretary he'll need someone who really knows Green."

Yes, I should not only have said this but also have gone through with it. Mary was no marvel, but she could be useful once just a little pressure was applied. And after all, she knew the mall well and could have solved a number of Li's problems.

I could even have said to her: "If I find another job I'll see if I can request you to be my secretary—trust me, I'll do all I can. In any case, if you have to find another job and need a reference don't hesitate to ask. In fact, I'll leave a letter of recommendation saying that you're an excellent and efficient secretary."

Mary was smart and would have understood that I wasn't planning to hire her in the future, but at least we could have had a decent goodbye. But as I said, I'm a scorpion—only an idiot would trust me.

Hamilton and Bennet insisted on taking me out to dinner. I accepted. I had no friends in London.

The Big Easy was in Chelsea and served some pretty decent barbecue ribs.

"You've saved us from bankruptcy," admitted Bennet.

"That's why tonight we ought to celebrate," said Hamilton, "and so . . . well, we have an appointment at a rather special place. A friend recommended it to us. Not everyone can go there, only the right sort, you know, with money."

I would never have guessed that they would take me to a whorehouse. But that was what the elegant South Kensington residence of Madame Agnès was.

Hamilton and Bennet looked at the girls with hunger in their eyes, but Madame Agnès made it clear that any inappropriate behavior would lead to expulsion from her house.

I had never been in a place like that. I'd always thought that sleeping with a whore was for old men, or guys who had no other options. That was never the case for me. But I had fun, and I got into it. And yes, from that night on there were many other nights on which I knocked discreetly at the door of Madame Agnès.

With seventy thousand pounds in my checking account I decided that I could easily rent an apartment and take my time looking for another job. That figure wasn't bad for the first time I'd ever worked in my life. But I didn't get drunk on my good fortune and decided to be cautious when it came to spending my money.

I found a small studio in an elegant and modest building near Kensington. I did not long for an apartment on the scale of my parents' in New York; what's more, I had become used to living in the few square feet of Mrs. Payne's house. My landlady said goodbye with tears in her eyes, telling me it would be hard to find another tenant like me.

Finding work turned out to be easier than I'd thought. There is nothing more attractive than success. Without me knowing it, the unusual advertising campaign to rent out a shopping center in a run-down neighborhood—and my having managed to rent it out in a matter of weeks—had not gone unnoticed in the City. Many thought that Li had been tricked, without realizing that renting Green had actually been a great deal for Li.

Mark Scott telephoned me a few months later at my new "quarters," as I dubbed the studio I was renting.

He took it for granted that I knew who he was and would be delighted to meet him, and he summoned me to his office the next morning at eight o'clock sharp.

I investigated, and was surprised to discover that he was the creative director of one of the City's largest marketing and advertising firms. It was said that he was an advertising genius capable of selling anything, and that his partner, Denis Roth, was the firm's financial genius.

I also read that the Scott & Roth Agency was considered one of the greatest in the world, with offices on five continents. There was nothing they wouldn't take on—the only requirement was that their clients could pay their steep fees.

The agency was located in a modern building of steel and glass, where the tall windows of Scott's office gave him the finest view of London.

His assistant was waiting for me impatiently because I had arrived three minutes late.

Scott welcomed me. I was surprised to see him dressed in jeans, a blue shirt, and no tie. He was around forty but looked younger, perhaps thanks to his outfit and personality. He seemed like the kind of guy that women liked: tall, blond, muscular, and with dark blue eyes, his face slightly tan, no doubt from some kind of outdoor exercise. His handshake was firm.

"Thomas, it's a pleasure to meet you. I'll let Denis know you're here. He'll be keen to meet you too."

Denis Roth turned out to be about the same age as Mark Scott, though he looked very different. He was dressed in a bespoke Savile Row suit, an Italian silk tie, and he was pale, as the English tend to be. The blue of his eyes was less brilliant than Scott's and he was going bald; he also kept his jacket buttoned up to hide a growing paunch. I imagined that women would still find him attractive because he radiated a sense of power.

They offered me tea but I asked for coffee instead. I was sick of drinking tea and coffee was better for the good shot of caffeine I've always needed to start the day.

Scott submitted me to a light grilling while Denis Roth watched me closely, as if he could see beyond my words. They wanted to know who I was and where I had worked in New York because, they told me, they hadn't been able to find any information about my professional activities. They were too smart for me to try to con them, so I laid all my cards on the table.

They asked about the Green operation and my relationship with Cathy Major. I told them that Cathy was good at advertising but that the Green business had been too big for her, as it dealt with something beyond just an ad campaign.

They pressed me for details about the operation, about Bennet and Hamilton's financial situation and how I had convinced Li to rent all of Green, but I frowned and told them that I wasn't going to discuss internal matters, or the persons involved or operations in which I might have participated. I knew they'd like this. Discretion is valuable in the City, where everybody has skeletons in their closet.

"Well then, Thomas, perhaps you'd like to work with us. You don't have experience, but your aptitude for business is evident," said Scott.

"Your ads for Green weren't great—pretty old-fashioned I'd say—but clearly they were effective when it came to getting results. Yes, you're still a bit of an amateur when it comes to creative work, but there's definitely something you could do," added Denis.

I looked at them without saying a word. If they had called me it was because I interested them, but they also did not want me to think that I held too much value for them.

"It's about expanding the business. We need growth, new clients. Once you've landed a client, we'll take over. You'd have to work in coordination with the sales and creative departments. You'd report directly to me." As Scott said this he looked into my eyes, trying to gauge what effect his proposal had on me.

"And this position wouldn't end up being a go-between for the two departments?" I asked.

"Yes, a little. Clients prefer to work with me or with Denis. The creative team doesn't take a step without consulting me and they'll continue to do so. I decide if a campaign works or not and I always put the finishing touches on their proposals. As for the sales department, sometimes they do their own thing a bit too much. We want to do what you did with Green: something beyond just offering an advertising campaign," Scott replied.

"Do you think you're capable of pulling off a repeat performance?" Denis wanted to know.

"What's the pay?" That question reassured them. In the City they don't trust anyone who doesn't have a price.

"A contract of three thousand pounds a month; if you work well, then after six months we'll increase it to five thousand," replied Denis.

"We should start at five thousand and then go up to twelve," I bluffed.

"Not so fast. We pay our people well, but only once we know they're worth what they believe and that they're what we need." Scott's voice had lost its friendly tone.

"All right. Let's give it a shot."

We shook hands and Denis left the office, saying that he'd have the contract drawn up in fifteen minutes, ready to sign. It was clear how certain they'd been that I wouldn't reject their offer.

Scott spent an hour with me explaining the ins and outs of my job. Then he walked me to what would be my office and called over a young guy named Richard, whom he introduced as my assistant.

"Richard will be your guide. He knows the company well; he's been here several years already. Oh yes, and he'll take you to HR to sign the contract."

"When do I start?" I said, for the sake of saying something.

"Right now." And he left the office, leaving me with Richard.

My assistant looked at me suspiciously. The truth was I had no idea where to begin, and decided that the best thing would be to dissect the guts of the company. I sat behind what was to be my desk and invited him to sit down opposite.

Richard was not overly talkative—or rather, he wasn't ready to reveal everything to a stranger. He told me nothing that was worth my time, just general details about the work routine at the company. He didn't seem particularly eager to help me beyond what was strictly required, so I decided to play hardball with him.

"You know, Richard, I understand your discretion. You don't know me and I don't know you, but I'll tell you one thing: I'm not going to give you long to decide if you're playing on my side or not. I want someone who's completely trustworthy, trustworthy to me; if that's not you then I'll find someone else."

He understood immediately, and even though it took him a few days to size me up, eventually he decided to risk it and work for me without holding back.

We were roughly the same age. Richard was no more than twenty-five, and had a master's in advertising from the best business school in London, after having graduated with a degree in history from Oxford. And he had that unmistakable air about him that rich kids always have.

A secretary, recommended by Richard himself, rounded out the team. "Maggie is pretty efficient," he told me. I accepted his suggestion immediately.

Maggie was old enough to be our mother and knew everything there was to know. She had seen plenty of young people like us pass through the agency, and we didn't impress her in the slightest. I was there because Scott thought I could bring some fresh ideas, but if I didn't have some immediate success he'd fire me without thinking twice. As for Richard, he had more opportunities than I did: his father was on the board at one of the largest banks in the City and his mother, Lady Veronica, was the daughter of an earl.

Scott and Roth seemed to wash their hands of me. I called a couple of meetings with the rest of the team. It was obvious that I was supposed to make the role they'd hired me for worthwhile, and was meant to bring in some lucrative deals for the company. Maggie had warned me that Scott & Roth was suffering due to the recent economic downturn and the company's revenues had shrunk. She knew this firsthand, as her last two years had been spent in the accounts department.

I didn't have a clue where to start. Nobody was going to commission me to design a campaign for one of their clients: the truth was that Scott had hired me in the hope that I'd be able to repeat the same miracle as I'd performed for Green.

It was Richard who suggested to me that the agency could open a department dedicated to teaching politicians the art of communication.

"What are you talking about?" I pressed him.

"In the past the agency has designed institutional campaigns—you know, keep your city clean, use the emergency services correctly, pay your taxes, that sort of thing. But we've never worked directly for political parties. Personally, I think we're missing out on opportunities."

"That's clear enough. But why?"

"Well, it seems that Denis Roth likes keeping friends on both sides—no one knows if he votes Labour or Conservative."

"And Mark Scott?"

"He votes Labour—he was actually a member of the party in his student years. He stopped being an activist when he became partners with Denis, but just as a formality."

"And what could we offer that would be different?" I asked curiously.

"I don't know, but there may be politicians who need someone to teach them how to interact with the media, or how to feel at home in a TV studio. It came to me this weekend when I was listening to Lord Elliot—he's a member of the House of Lords and a friend of my father's. He was complaining that he'd been interviewed on television and it was a mess because he didn't know which camera to look at, and he couldn't answer some of the presenter's trickier questions."

"But that already exists. Every party has communications experts," I snapped.

"Yes, but for the generals, not the troops. Perhaps we could convince the Conservative Party that some of their MPs need a training course in communication techniques, to avoid a lot of the problems that come from a lack of experience with the press. Remember that there'll be mayoral and council elections in six months. And politicians of a certain age often don't understand the ins and outs of communications."

I didn't think that this was a particularly groundbreaking idea, but frankly nothing else had come to me.

"And why would we want to offer our services to the Tories? I'd prefer Labour."

"It's all the same to me, but the Conservatives will pay more. But then again, we also don't have to limit ourselves to a single party."

"And what is it exactly that we're going to offer them?"

"A package. Audiovisual communication techniques. They'd

have someone to prep them for important debates, teach them how to avoid awkward questions, which tie looks best on television . . . How should I know?"

"All of that's already done by the parties' communication departments. And as far as I can tell, members of the Conservative Party already know which clothes to wear at what hour of the day. We'd have to offer something more. Go develop the proposal further. I'll get to work too. Tomorrow afternoon I want a report on my desk."

"Give me a couple of days."

"I'm giving you twenty-four hours, not an hour more."

"So, tomorrow afternoon."

"Exactly."

It wasn't a great idea, but Richard was right: the parties put communications teams at the disposal of their leaders but they forgot about their other members. And in the English electoral system, candidates for any post would embark on personal campaigns, sometimes without their party giving them the necessary means to form a communication policy.

The next day Richard handed me about a dozen pages developing the idea. All that remained to be written was the cover letter: a proposal in which we'd convince potential clients that improvisation wouldn't do in the communications era. We wouldn't offer them a full-time service, but would rather provide courses that would teach them how to handle themselves in front of a television camera or win a debate. It would be like a game.

This was nothing that other publicity agencies weren't offering. Richard waited for me to congratulate him on his work but I simply told him that he would have to continue developing the proposal. The kid had a well-ordered mind.

"Right, our first step should be to meet discreetly with the leader of the Conservatives. Can you take care of that?" I said.

"It's not that easy. And before we do anything we should check with Scott."

"You're wrong—before we check with Scott we should check if there's water in the well."

"Right, but we can't go to Westminster using the company's name."

"You want to cover your back."

"Actually, you're the one who should be covering your back. Scott and Roth will find out about the proposal immediately. They have friends in Westminster."

"Are you giving me advice?"

Richard shrugged. Even though he worked for me, there was a limit to his loyalty, and if there were any problems he wanted to be able to say *I told you so.*

Even so, I decided not to consult Scott. Richard's idea wasn't even all that brilliant. The truth was we were going to offer them the same thing that the other agencies did, but our particular brand of snake oil would be wrapped in a bow. If Scott and Roth didn't like my proposal the worst they could do was fire me, and that wasn't something that particularly concerned me. I suppose my recklessness stemmed from the fact that I had a safety net. I could always go home and ask my father and grandfather to turn to one of their influential friends to give me a job. I wasn't the type to worry about wounded pride—I have always been too practical for that.

One of the young creatives designed us a proposal that almost had me convinced. The glossy gray paper, the perfect font size, a couple of intriguing phrases . . . Yes, the nicely wrapped snake oil seemed almost real.

Richard resisted opening up his family's extensive contact book of political friends to me. But he did eventually agree to set up a meeting with a university friend of his, working with the local elections coordinator of the Conservative Party.

After putting further pressure on my assistant, I managed to get a meeting held at his club. I was beginning to understand the rules of hermetic London society, where the club one belongs to makes all the difference, and Richard's club was the best of the best.

Charles Graham was a lot like Richard, though he dressed more formally. While Richard liked to present a certain level of informality, Graham did not deviate from the prewritten script for someone working for the Conservative Party.

I had decided that it should be Richard who would sell our services to him, convinced he'd find it easier to persuade an old university friend. But Richard's lack of enthusiasm forced me to take the reins of the conversation.

I couldn't have done too badly, because Graham seemed to believe that we were offering something more than the other agencies. He promised to speak with his boss and get us a meeting.

He kept his word. Two days later Richard and I were seated in front of one of those gray politicians found in every party. He got straight to the point. The local elections would be in six months and there were a number of new candidates who could use some "fine-tuning." If our price was better than those of the other agencies, the job would be ours.

We hadn't managed to fool him. The man was practical. He knew that Richard was the son of Philip Craig, one of the most renowned bankers in the City, and that his mother, Lady Veronica, was famous for organizing some of the finest fox hunts in the country, even attended by members of the royal family on several occasions.

Richard had warned me that gentlemen didn't discuss money over lunch, but that same afternoon I sent a longer proposal to his friend's office detailing what we could offer their candidates and the total cost. He called me the next day to tell me the job was ours.

"We got it," I said excitedly to Richard.

"Great—but now comes the hard part. Frankly the quote you gave was way too low. I don't think Scott will like it."

"Quit worrying about Scott," I snapped.

But he had managed to sow doubt in my mind. So I went to Scott's office with confirmation of their acceptance of our proposal, and a meeting scheduled for the next day in which we'd sign the agreements.

Scott received me right away and invited me to sit, offering me a cup of tea. His smile turned sour as he listened to me and flicked through the file.

"How dare you make decisions without consulting me? Our agency does not work for political parties. Denis and I have always made that clear: we don't want to dirty our hands with cockfights, which is precisely what elections are. We have friends on all sides, from the Conservatives, Labour, the Lib Dems . . . Call Graham and tell him there's been a mistake—you were wrong, you're new here, you had no idea about the workings of our agency and that's why you didn't know that we don't work for political parties. Fix this shit and then . . . I'll talk to Denis. Kid, you've failed us."

"I'll tell Richard to call Graham. It's been a pleasure knowing you all."

I stood up, ready to leave the office. There was nothing else to talk about. I wasn't going to give them the chance to fire me, which was exactly what they were about to do.

"Stay there!" yelled Scott.

For a few moments I weighed whether to stay or go, and in the end opted to remain standing there, looking at him with indifference.

"Do you want to explain to me why you got us into this mess?"

"The agency's balance sheet has stagnated over the past three years. You haven't grown and it's costing you a lot to keep all your clients. In fact, you've even accepted a couple of minor political campaigns. Politicians are a gold mine that anyone would try to exploit. Their main concern is to convince citizens to vote for them. They're vain and know nothing about communication techniques, so they're prepared to buy any old snake oil as long as it comes in a nice package.

"I've been studying which sectors the agency could grow in, and politics is the quickest and easiest.

"I can't work miracles, Scott. You hired me to do something to get the agency out of this stagnation. So I did. You don't agree, fine, that's no problem for me. I'll leave."

"Sit down!"

"The conversation is over." I was relishing my own nonchalance.

Scott was calling Denis, asking him to come to his office. As we waited we regarded each other in silence. I realized that the macho appearance he liked to present actually concealed a fragile individual.

Denis Roth entered with an unworried expression. He smiled at me like someone expecting to hear good news.

Scott filled him in, and I watched as, barely perceptibly, one of Denis's facial muscles moved. A tic that appeared, much against his will, when he was nervous.

"You've really dropped us in it," said Denis.

"I don't see it like that. But then, this isn't my agency, so things stand pretty clear. I'll leave."

"What advantages are there in working for politicians?" asked Denis bad-temperedly.

"The money. They pay well. And it's the only sector where you can achieve growth right now. If it were my agency I'd try to do this, not just in the U.K. but in every Commonwealth country. I think that in a couple of years you could increase your earnings by thirty percent."

"You have overstepped," Denis interrupted me.

"Either I work with my hands untied or I don't work at all. I left school a long time ago. You asked me for results and I've placed a contract on the table," I replied brazenly.

"A piece-of-shit contract," spat Scott.

"Yes, the budget is small. But it was the only way of convinc-

ing our Conservative friends to switch horses—why else would
they? They trust this agency for its prestige, yes, but they know
we have no experience in political marketing. Offering reasonable prices is one way to start. We've offered them a basic package, but we can offer them much more, and each extra brings in
more money.

"Anyway, gentlemen, it's clear that we've all made a mistake.
Now if you'll excuse me, I'll go get my things."

I left the office without giving them a chance to respond.
Richard was waiting for me in the hallway.

"They sacked you?" he asked.

"I sacked myself."

"You're the shortest-lived boss I've ever had."

"Well, don't despair, there's always someone looking to break
another record."

I didn't have many things in the office they'd assigned me.
Nothing personal really, apart from a wallet I'd seen in a shop
near my new apartment, and had bought without even looking at the price, using the money I'd gotten from Green. I went
to say goodbye to Maggie but she didn't give me a chance to
speak.

"Go to Scott's office. They're waiting to speak with you
urgently."

I hesitated. I didn't like scenes, and I already considered my
time at Scott & Roth to be done. In the end, curiosity won me
over.

Scott seemed just as nervous as Denis. He was actually pacing
from one end of the office to the other as if he were dying to get
out of there.

"We don't like the way you've acted, but what's done is done.
Now the damage has to be minimized. You'll have to present the
same offer to the other parties, and above all guarantee complete
neutrality. We will teach communication methods, but we won't
get involved in the content. We won't invent any slogans or be

associated with candidates. We'll just teach them to communicate." Denis delivered his whole speech without taking a breath.

"All right?" asked Scott.

"I don't know. I don't know if after this I'll be able to feel comfortable at the agency. And I don't think you trust me either. I know that something's broken now and—"

Scott punched the desk, and from the way that he was looking at me it felt like he was ready to punch me too.

"Cut the bullshit, Thomas! You're just an amateur who thinks you're someone because you happened to do well with the Green business. So don't give us some speech about being the wounded gentleman. The role doesn't suit you." Scott looked at me with fury.

"What's done is done, Scott, and it's not our style to feel sorry for ourselves. We'll see if we can salvage something from this mess. Do you clearly understand what your boundaries are, Spencer? Scott and Roth will not take on electoral campaigns. We'll only be teaching communication techniques. And now we mustn't waste any more time. You have a lot of work ahead of you," concluded Denis.

I shrugged. I wasn't convinced I wanted to give up my role of the smart guy who didn't need anyone, but I thought it best not to be out of a job.

Richard was waiting by the office door, and made a gesture to show that they had also called him in.

"Did they sack you?" Maggie asked when she saw me.

"I was out for a while, now it seems like I'm back in. I don't know, but I also don't care much."

"Lucky you that you don't need a paycheck at the end of the month."

"That's what happens when you have rich parents," I replied, fully intending to irritate her.

"Yes, that must be it," she agreed.

Richard didn't say anything to me, but you didn't have to be a genius to work out that Scott and Denis had told him to keep an eye on me and inform them of anything I thought up. He must have agreed. He knew not to expect anything from me.

We spent a couple of weeks meeting with politicians from all sides to sell them our proposal. We offered them nothing new, except a good price on our services and the promise that their candidates would learn in record time how to communicate with the media. To my surprise, they swallowed it whole, and we managed to get them to put us in touch with their candidates so that anyone who wanted to could use our services. The party would pay half, the candidate the rest.

"We have thirty-odd Conservative candidates, around the same for Labour, but the Lib Dems are being a bit more resistant. Oh! And this morning someone named Roy Parker called. He says he'd like to talk to us. He represents a number of people from various parts of the county of Derbyshire. He says that they're sick of traditional parties and want to try their luck at the ballot boxes themselves. Apparently they're going to run in ten or twelve districts," Richard informed me.

"Where is this county?"

"More or less the center of England, near Manchester, in the Midlands. They live off milk and sheep."

"Right. Yeah, I don't think we're interested," I replied dismissively.

"If you say so." Nothing fazed Richard.

"It's not bad what we've achieved so far, don't you think?"

"Well, yes, but we're not exactly a huge success," he said disdainfully.

"Your friend Graham could get involved and find us more mayoral candidates, couldn't he?" This was my way of riling him.

"My friend Graham is not the leader of the Conservative Party. We should already be grateful to him that we have more than thirty of his candidates."

The next phase wasn't easy either. We needed someone who knew television to play the role of "professor" to our aspiring mayors. Someone who'd know how to teach them to look at the camera and show them which hand gestures they should or shouldn't make. Maggie suggested we find someone from a university.

"Professors don't charge much. There must be someone who'll want to collaborate."

She was right, and we found half a dozen supposed experts in television. In reality none of them had ever been in front of the camera—they had all once been hardworking students who, after finishing their degrees, remained at the same university to continue their academic careers, so they knew all the theory and nothing more. But since we found nothing better, we hired them.

"You and I will teach them how to dress, what sort of tie to wear, things like that," I suggested to Richard.

"And why us? Anyway, you were the one who said that Conservative candidates were born with their ties on."

"But not all of them—we also have some candidates whom the press are so fond of because they say they're self-made men. And remember that we have a number of Labour candidates as clients, and they haven't studied at Oxford like you. And you know why we will teach them? Because, as Maggie says, we're two little rich boys who have been taught from a young age not to pick our noses. We know what to wear to dinner and how to look polished even when dressed informally," I replied, puffed up and in a bad temper. Richard always added "buts" to my plans.

"You really think the candidates won't know what tie to choose?" he replied, his temper matching my own.

"So far we've met with a couple of hicks who want to be mayors of towns that aren't even on the map. But they have ambition, so they want someone to tell them not to wear a plaid tie to dinner."

"And what about Roy Parker? He's called half a dozen times. He wants to hire us," Richard reminded me.

"That hick? Forget him, he's small-fry."

The first tutor I hired was Janet McCarthy. I don't know why I did it. I suppose it was due to pressure from Richard.

Neither tall nor short, neither fat nor thin, neither blonde nor brunette, the only thing that made her stand out was the liveliness of her brown eyes.

She taught communication theory and had never set foot on a television set. Nor did she know what a radio studio was like. But she was willing to work extra hours, since her teaching salary was meager and she dreamed of vacationing in the Caribbean.

The second candidate was Philip Sullivan, an acquaintance of Richard's. He had been a professor of communications at the University of London, which had invited him to make a discreet exit as he liked to poke his nose where he shouldn't. To be frank, he was well known among hackers, although his appearance was the exact opposite of theirs. He was tall and thin with slicked-back hair and thick-framed glasses and always wore a ridiculous bow tie instead of a tie.

"So this friend of yours, they nearly convicted him of rummaging around where he shouldn't: in the private correspondence of the Prince of Wales, no less," I remarked to Richard while I considered whether to hire Sullivan.

"Actually, it wasn't Philip who was responsible, and that was proved during the trial."

"Tell me the whole story . . ."

"As you will have realized, Philip . . . well . . . you'll have noticed that . . ."

"That he's gay. Is that what you're trying to say?" I found Richard's political correctness exasperating.

"Two years ago he was living with a journalist. This guy was working as a freelancer without much success. He couldn't come up with a better idea than hacking the Bank of England's IT system to look for some little secret to sell to one of the London tabloids. But they caught him. The problem is that he was using Philip's computer, so then he had to testify, but his friend cleared him of all responsibility."

"And I suppose that after this honorable behavior Philip must have married him to repay the favor and since the marriage they've been living happily ever after." I couldn't resist a sarcastic comment.

"Not at all. Philip was extremely angry, and although he helped him out by paying for a decent lawyer, he threw the guy out of his house and they ended their relationship. That business was very damaging for Philip and the university decided they'd rather not renew his contract, and now he's unemployed."

I hired him. I had no aptitude for new technologies, but I knew that in this era of communications it was essential to have someone on the team for whom IT held no secrets. The politicians would love him.

In spite of Richard's insistence, I refused to hire more staff. An idea was buzzing around in my head. Cathy Major. No doubt she would not have forgiven me for what happened at Green, and she was right to think that I was an untrustworthy son of a bitch. But perhaps she would accept my offer, given that she still hadn't found a job in the City and was getting by on freelance work.

Cathy had talent. She was a genuine PR expert and she would dazzle the string of politicians who'd hired us. She was attractive, elegant, and knew how to move in high society. Yes, I needed Cathy.

Richard did not agree with my idea of bringing Cathy on board, and Maggie frowned when she found out.

"If you had problems with her once, you'll have them again," declared my experienced secretary.

"Truth be told, it was she who had problems with me. I stole her job and commission."

"She'll never forgive you and she'll try to get back at you," Maggie warned me.

"Yes, of course she'll try, but when the moment comes I'll get her out of the picture again."

"If you can," murmured Richard.

I found it amusing to call Cathy and I was surprised she didn't hang up on me.

"I've got a proposition for you. What do you say to a drink this evening? You choose the place."

"I'll see you at Le Gavroche, in Mayfair, at seven," she said, and hung up without asking me a single question.

I don't know whether Cathy set out to impress me that night, but in fact all the men in the restaurant stared at her as she made her way to the table where I was waiting.

A fitted black dress, Jimmy Choo shoes with skyscraper heels, and earrings with multicolored stones. I don't know quite what it was about her, but she looked spectacular.

I went to give her a kiss but she dodged me and sat down without giving me time to pull out her chair. She motioned the waiter over and ordered a cocktail, then turned to me and looked me in the eye.

"What's your proposition? Because I assume that if you've called me it's because you need me for something."

Her hard tone of voice made it clear that she still harbored a deep resentment but was willing to negotiate with me if this would get her out of the hole into which I'd thrown her.

I didn't waste time and I explained what I wanted from her. She listened to me in silence without interrupting until I finished my speech. Cathy was sipping leisurely from her drink, watching me as if she weren't interested in my proposition, but I knew that wasn't the case.

"Before you give me your answer, why did you agree to meet with me?"

"Because you work for Scott and Roth, which is one of the most respected PR agencies in the sector."

"Does that mean you'll accept my proposition?"

"We'll see. I may accept, with conditions."

I was about to reply that her circumstances meant that she was in no position to impose conditions on me, and the fact that she was there having a drink with me was proof of that. But I held my tongue. Once again it was I who needed her and, in spite of her precarious situation, Cathy was more than capable of leaving without accepting my offer.

Her main condition was an armor-plated contract with a generous payout in case of dismissal. And also that Mark Scott would mediate between us should any conflicts arise.

"Oh, so you want to play with a referee. I thought you had more faith in yourself."

"I've got plenty, Thomas. I've got plenty. The person I don't have faith in is you. I've known Mark Scott for years and he's a decent guy, so I'd prefer that he have the final say."

"He's the head of the agency, so he'll always have the final say," I replied, irritated.

"I would rather have this conversation with him present."

"You're in no position to—"

"Yes, I am in such a position. You're a son of a bitch, Thomas, and I'm not playing games with you again. If you've called me it's because you think I can do the job. If not you wouldn't have risked being turned down by me."

"I'm the head of the department and I don't want the people who work for me to have divided loyalties."

"I won't be loyal to you, Thomas. I will merely work in your department but in reality my boss will be Mark Scott and he is the person who will know exactly what I'm working on at all times."

"You're unemployed, Cathy, and as far as I know nobody's made you an offer worth your while. I'm the one offering a job and you're trying to get me to give the green light for you and Scott to go over my head."

"You're the one who called me."

"And if you're here it's because you need a good job."

"Thomas, I haven't come to argue with you. Give it some thought. You have my number. Oh, and thanks for the drink!"

Cathy stood up without giving me time to reply. She left the restaurant with a confident stride, ignoring the gazes that focused once again on her behind and her extremely long legs.

I decided to spend the rest of the night at Madame Agnès's. It was a place as good as any other to have a drink in the company of a beautiful woman. As beautiful as Cathy, or even more so. Madame Agnès's girls were renowned for their beauty.

I called Cathy the next morning after speaking to Scott, who seemed, for the moment, to have lost the enthusiasm he showed when hiring me.

"Of course I know who Cathy Major is and I heard she was left out in the cold on the Green deal. So she won't trust you . . . smart girl."

"She wants you to know exactly what she's working on at all times. Perhaps you could put her in her place and make it clear that I'm the department head and you are the overall boss and she can't go pestering you with trivial nonsense."

"I would be delighted to accept her conditions and meet with Ms. Major from time to time, so if you want to hire her, go ahead," Scott agreed, to annoy me.

I went ahead even though I knew that Cathy and Scott would become allies and screw me over if at all possible. If I continued working at the agency it was thanks to Denis Roth, who was clearly more concerned about the numbers adding up than Mark Scott's scruples.

Janet McCarthy, Philip Sullivan, and Cathy joined my team, which until this point had consisted of my assistant Richard Craig and Maggie.

Cathy immediately became friends with Janet, whom she in turn made her assistant. As for Philip Sullivan, I decided that we would use him to teach the candidates about new technology for contacting their voters. Mind you, this service wasn't part of the package and they would pay for it separately.

Things weren't as simple as I had expected. We had to travel the length and breadth of the United Kingdom to work with each and every one of the candidates who had engaged our services. Not one of them was prepared to come down to London given that the clock was ticking and they were spending every minute doing the rounds of their constituencies, greeting their neighbors and promising to turn their towns and cities into paradises if they were elected.

Cathy's presence was vital. As soon as a candidate saw her, he seemed to willingly accept all our recommendations. An attractive, well-dressed woman with such personality—she clearly knew what she was doing.

We had also hired a television crew and a radio crew who traveled with us and set up improvised studios wherever they could so that the candidates could receive special lessons in how to look at a camera and when to move their hands.

Janet would give them a talk, explaining all the academic theories on the subject. I realized that the candidates were benefiting from these sessions. They played at being actors for three or four days, which was the length of the little course. They let themselves be directed without resistance, eagerly accepting all our suggestions. "Your left side is your best side." "You've got lovely hands—move them; emphasize your message with your hands." "Always look for the red light below one of the cameras: that's the one that's on you." "Never get angry, no matter what they ask you." "Be gracious to your opponents. Don't even think of showing your superiority." These were some of the lines we would repeat to them, and, in addition, Cathy would advise them on how to consolidate their campaign messages, making them attractive to their potential voters. "Talk about what the people want to hear, not what you think is important." "These are local elections; your constituents need you to guarantee that the pothole right outside their front door is going to disappear, not explain how to resolve the problems in the Middle East."

Richard performed the role I had assigned him, advising some of the men on how to dress and even going with them to buy suitable clothes for their public appearances.

"Steer clear of brown. It's not a flattering color. Go for blues and grays." "If you want to be mayor of this town don't wear a tie. You're in the middle of the countryside and here a tie is considered over the top. Dress like you normally do."

I found it amusing that they would pay us for these snippets of advice culled from a few manuals.

The candidates for both Labour and the Conservatives spread word of what we were doing with their colleagues and we signed several more contracts, which prevented me from having the time to respond to the endless calls from Roy Parker. He didn't belong to any party and was desperate for us to take on his campaign. His calls to the office were constant, and Maggie was so fed up that she asked me to at least speak to him and tell him personally that we couldn't take on his candidates.

"What do I need you for if I still have to waste my time on this hick?" I replied grumpily.

On Fridays we would return to London. We normally held a meeting in the afternoon to plan for the following week and review what we had done so far.

Normally there weren't many people in the office, as the weekend is sacred for the British, although both Mark Scott and Denis Roth would sometimes surprise us by turning up in our meeting room to check on our progress. They didn't want to lose their grip on the venture we'd embarked upon, however much their friends from the Labour and Conservative Parties congratulated them on our efficient services.

Denis would repeatedly tell us to tread carefully, as working for both parties was an extremely difficult undertaking.

One of those afternoons Maggie interrupted us just as we were finishing our regular meeting.

"Mr. Parker would like to see you," she announced, holding back her laughter.

"He doesn't have an appointment."

"No, he doesn't, but it turns out he's come to London, and he says he won't leave without seeing you. You tell me what I should say to him."

"Tell him to go. I don't see anybody without an appointment."

The door opened and on the threshold appeared the figure of a tall, stocky man with ginger hair and shockingly intense blue eyes. He didn't seem to know what to do with his large worker's hands. At first he looked at us angrily, then he took a deep breath and began to speak.

"I apologize for interrupting you, but I've been trying to speak with you for two months, Mr. Spencer, and yet it seems that you've been unable to find the right moment to get to the telephone. Well, here I am, so let's talk. Is this your team? It's a pleasure to meet you. I'm Roy Parker."

To our astonishment, he went around shaking hands with each of us. His large hand enveloped each of ours, squeezing them in such a way that there was no way of disengaging until he decided to let go.

"Mr. Parker, I'm sorry I've been unable to respond to your calls, but we are very busy and, as my secretary has already told you, we don't have time to take on your campaign."

I gave it to him straight in the hope that he would leave me alone. But it was foolishness on my part to expect something like that. Roy Parker had turned up in London because he was one of those men who won't take no for an answer.

"We'll talk, Mr. Spencer, and after we've talked, then you can decide what to do. Do you keep secrets from your team? If not, I'll explain what I want in front of them," he said with such firmness that he completely threw me.

"We've already finished our meeting. Guys, we'll see each other Monday at the station," I told my team, adding, "I've got a few minutes to spare, but I've got plans and I need to get going."

Maggie looked at me, waiting for me to tell her she needn't stay in the office. It was Friday and she wanted to go home. I nodded that she should go, although I regretted it. That man was making me feel quite disconcerted and it suddenly struck me that it wasn't a good idea for me to be alone with him in the office.

"Well then, Mr. Parker?"

"Why didn't you want to talk to me? You've spent two months avoiding me."

"As you can see, we have a lot of work—more than we can handle. We respect our clients too much to take on jobs that we can't perform professionally and give the necessary time to."

"And what is your selection process? From what I've heard you have a fair number of Labour and Conservative clients who are campaigning to become mayors. In fact, it was our mayor who first mentioned your agency to me. He's Labour, and the man has decided to retire. He's over seventy and wants to relax."

"So you're Labour, then."

"No, I'm nothing. I'm fed up with both Labour and the Conservatives. I am, and so are a lot of others. I live in a region where we only see the big politicians on the television. We don't matter to anybody and nobody matters to us. We've gotten a group together and we're going to run in the elections."

"Okay, and who has formed this group?"

"Men like me from other small towns like mine. We're independents. We want to run our towns in accordance with the needs of the people. We don't promise anything we can't achieve and nobody is going to demand more of us than they know we can deliver. Our voters are our neighbors."

Listening to Parker I imagined remote towns where everyone knows one another and their only aspirations are for the local streets to be resurfaced or a new shelter to be built. I had to tell him that we weren't going to run a campaign for a group of rural peasants.

"Your goal seems laudable, but I'm afraid the services we offer are not ones that would be of interest to you."

"But yes, they do interest us. Those dandies in the mainstream parties think they know everything. They may not be as rural as us, but being members of the big parties has taught them a few things."

"I don't think it's likely that you'll be taking part in any televised debates."

"Of course we will. If they go on television, so will we. We'll do what has to be done. We just need you to teach us how to defend ourselves against them."

"There are other agencies better suited for what you're outlining. If you want, I could recommend one of the agencies that operates in your region. My secretary will call you on Monday. How does that sound?"

"No, Mr. Spencer, we want to hire Scott and Roth. We can pay you."

"I'm sorry, Mr. Parker, but I've already told you we don't have the time. We're a responsible company. We don't take on projects we can't do. I could send you one of my guys for a couple of days. He'd show you a few general points and then send you a bill that would send a shiver down your spine. Maybe other agencies would do that, but not us."

"I don't accept your refusal."

"Well, I don't understand your insistence that it should be Scott and Roth that takes on your campaign. There are plenty of other agencies in the city. Look for the one that suits you best." I was getting angry. I didn't understand this man's stubbornness.

"Yes, it's true, there are plenty of other agencies, but we want to hire yours. Our money is as good as the Labour and Conservative Parties' money. We won't pay you more, but we won't pay you less either."

"Mr. Parker, I realize that you're one of those men who are

not prepared for anyone to disagree with them. Even so, I must reiterate that we cannot take on your campaign, or those of your friends. Please, don't push this."

Roy Parker didn't bat an eye. He remained sitting in front of me, looking me over from top to bottom as if he were deciding what to do with me. I couldn't stand the man's stubbornness and I thought of calling security to remove him from my office once and for all.

"Of course you'll take on my campaign—this one and all my others. I'm going to take my first step in politics. Being mayor is a way of getting started. I won't be mayor for long. What I want is to make it here, to London, to sit in Parliament. But that won't be enough. A ministerial post is the least I aspire to."

"I'm glad to hear it, Mr. Parker, and given that the Queen already has an heir, it's best that you don't aspire to more."

"You can keep your sarcastic comments, little city boy. I know what I want and you're going to help me get it."

"Why me, Mr. Parker?"

"Because you are a man with no principles, but who is intelligent and cowardly. You take things right to the limit without stepping over the line. Your instinct for survival means you pull up just short when you reach the edge of the abyss."

For a few seconds I didn't know what to say. I was surprised at the precise description he had given of my personality. Not even I would have been able to define it so exactly. But it aggravated me that he had dared to do so. Furthermore, how did he know I was like that?

"You don't know me, but more importantly, it's not for you to make value judgments about me. This conversation is over, Mr. Parker. I'll call security to escort you to the door."

"I've studied everything that's been said about you with great care, Mr. Spencer: how you pulled a fast one at Green, how you got a certain Ms. Major out of the way and managed to get two broke rookie developers to sign a contract with a certain Mr. Li, whom you persuaded that Green was a great business opportunity. You convinced all of them that they didn't have another choice. The papers talk about you, Mr. Spencer. They say you're a promising public relations wunderkind. I've studied every step you've taken, how you've acted, in detail, and that's what convinced me. I've studied you in depth. I even know things about you that you can't imagine."

"That's enough, Mr. Parker. You've gone too far."

I picked up the phone to call security, but I didn't have time. Parker's hand closed over mine, forcing me to hang up.

"We will sign a contract, Mr. Spencer. I'm sure that we'll reach an understanding. We may even become friends."

"No."

"Of course you will. You've no reason to refuse."

"It's up to me who I work for."

"No, you work for the Scott and Roth agency, and it's your bosses who have the final say over who to accept as clients. Don't make me use my influence, Mr. Spencer. It's better that you accept my proposal and don't make me resort to that."

Roy Parker irritated me, but apart from his daring, I couldn't manage to dislike him. He had such an aura of strength and confidence in himself that I felt disarmed in front of him.

"Nobody can make me do what I don't want to do. I'm a free man, Mr. Parker. And since you seem to know a lot about me, you ought to know that I can leave this job. I don't need the money."

"I know. You're a rich boy from New York. Your father is a prestigious lawyer with the necessary contacts to find you a job immediately. But we will accomplish great things together, Mr. Spencer. You'll see. You'll end up enjoying yourself. And the sooner we get down to business, the better it will be for both of us. I've already told you my end goal and I'm forty, so there's no time to spare."

"So far, everything you've told me has confirmed that I shouldn't work for you," I persevered, tired of this duel.

"I'm inviting you to dinner, Mr. Spencer; we'll talk over some decent wine. Men get to know each other better when they share a good bottle. Diplomacy is not my strength and I say more than I should, but I'm not a bad sort. You won't lose anything by having dinner with me."

"I already have plans."

"I don't believe you. If that were the case you would have thrown me out a while ago. I think you've taken a shine to me, very much in spite of yourself. You don't know how to classify me and you're asking yourself why you've put up with all that stuff I said to you. I've been a bit clumsy, I realize that. Well, that's what I need you for."

"There are others who can help you. I'm not the best in this business, Mr. Parker."

"But I always surround myself with men who aren't like everyone else. That's why I've taken the trouble to hire you. You're from New York, you don't have class prejudices like the British do, and you're not bothered by how things work here. The Conservatives, the Liberal Democrats, and Labour, and what becomes of this damned country are all the same to you."

"Who did you say suggested you hire me?"

"Someone you don't know, but who'd heard that several aspiring mayors had chosen the services of Scott and Roth and that they'd put an American in charge of their political communications department. Based on that, I began some research to see whether you were the right man. You are. I've no doubt about it."

It was after seven and there wasn't anyone left in the building except security. I didn't have any plans for that evening other than to go back to my apartment, pour myself a whiskey, order a pizza or some Chinese, and put on a CD and listen to Sting or watch an old movie on TV.

I was hungry; perhaps having dinner with Roy Parker wasn't a bad idea. The man interested and irritated me in equal parts. A good dinner didn't commit me to anything.

"We'll eat at the Aubergine. They do decent food," I told him as I got up and put on my jacket.

"I assume they've got a good cellar. I can't stand bad wine."

"As always, Mr. Parker, it's just a question of having money in your wallet. But from what you've said I know that's not a problem for you. I'll call them en route."

Having dinner with Roy Parker was a good move. I have never regretted giving in to his insistence. We were almost inseparable for many years. We respected each other without being friends; we were never friends, nor did we seek to be. What has united us has been stronger—much deeper than friendship.

Roy Parker had married one of the richest women in the county of Derbyshire. His was a region that produced nothing but sheep's wool and his wife's parents were the owners of the largest flock in the area. Furthermore, they owned a factory that processed the wool, which they then sold wholesale.

His wife was an only child and the heiress to the rural empire that Roy now presided over, as his father-in-law had gradually delegated the running of the business to him.

"Suzi is an incredible woman," he told me of his wife. "She's clever and hardworking. She's the one who's encouraged me not to settle for what we've got. You'll meet her. You'll like her; you'll see that it's difficult to fool her. She's got good instincts and she's pretty too, the best-looking girl in the county. You might find her a little countrified, but she learns fast."

He showed me a photo in which he appeared beside a sassy-looking redhead and two equally redheaded children.

"That's Suzi with my two sons, Ernest and Jim. They're a couple of little devils but they're good boys, really."

That night we drank a couple of bottles of Château Margaux over dinner, in addition to two or three bourbons that were my contribution. Roy explained exactly what he wanted and what he was prepared to pay to get it, no beating around the bush. He even suggested that I leave Scott & Roth and work exclusively for him.

"It wouldn't be a good idea, at least not to start with. I'm a pretty new arrival; I don't know anyone relevant in London. I need the agency for a while. Doors open if you knock in the name of Scott and Roth and you're going to need a lot of doors to open."

Roy wanted to just get on with it. Managing his in-laws' businesses had taught him that if you have good relationships with those in power, life is much easier. He said that he was fed up with seeing how a local competitor gained advantages in his business dealings thanks to his relationships with mayors and local dignitaries. Furthermore, he wanted to become rich. He wasn't content with his wife's money.

"I could be content with being mayor, but I'm not going to settle for so little just yet. I'll take the next step as soon as possible: a seat in Parliament. I want to be the one who holds the reins of my destiny and the reins of other people's. I won't claim that I want power because I'm a caring soul. I want it for my own benefit and for the benefit of those I think deserve it, like I do.

"There's a lot of shamelessness in Parliament. Why shouldn't I get in there? They deceive the people by promising them a better life. I don't plan on deceiving anyone. I'll do what I promise to do, but, in addition, I'll always be seeking to benefit me and my friends. Suzi says I could end up as prime minister. I believe that too and you will help me achieve it. But I warn you, I'm not prepared to change. I won't become a dandy, none of that trying to get me to buy clothes in Savile Row or get my Suzi to wear one of those terrible hats like the Queen wears. We are what we are. You'll have to settle for that and for our money."

We finished the night at Madame Agnès's. When I suggested it he agreed without any resistance. I didn't ask whether he knew the place, but I have to admit that he acted like a regular.

I can't remember whether I was the one to take Roy back to

his hotel or whether it was he who took me back to my apartment. On Saturday I woke up on the sofa in the living room, fully dressed, glass of bourbon in hand and stinking of alcohol.

Why had I made a deal with this man? I asked myself while I tried to wake myself up with a cold shower. I couldn't find an answer right then, apart from telling myself that it had been impossible for me to say no to him. Such was the force that emanated from Roy Parker that he moved forward without any resistance. Later I understood that Roy represented a challenge. With him I was starting from scratch. I had to invent him. He didn't come from a good family, he wasn't a member of any party, and in reality he didn't seem to know anyone important in spite of the pretentious nonsense he spouted. And even so, he still aspired to be nothing less than prime minister. I told myself that we could try to even achieve it. It was a case of being able to fool not just a few but a lot of people. Ours wouldn't be a clumsy deceit of appearances, though, but something more subtle, because Roy had made it clear that he was not prepared to seem to be what he was not.

I thought Cathy would laugh at me. Every time we exchanged looks I could see deep disdain for me in her eyes. But she was too intelligent to show it beyond a few sarcastic comments and, of course, her undertaking to visit Mark Scott from time to time. But that had been the deal.

For Cathy I was just an incident along the way, and the same went for Richard Craig, my efficient assistant. They both wondered when I'd get bored or at what moment Mark Scott or Denis Roth would decide to get rid of me. They thought it was a question of time, and they were right. It was just that Roy had crossed my path and what he had proposed amused and stimulated me more than anything else that could have happened to me.

I had arranged to have breakfast with Roy at the Dorchester Hotel before he went back to his county. I had promised to bring a contract we would both sign. The only hitch was that I also needed the signature of the head of the finance department. I didn't hesitate to call Maggie and ask her to find someone to rubber-stamp the contract.

Maggie protested.

"It's Saturday," she reminded me. "Where does all this sudden interest in Mr. Parker come from? You didn't even want to come to the phone . . ."

I insisted and she agreed to try. Half an hour later she called me to tell me it was impossible. Nobody was prepared to go into the office on a Saturday. There was nothing that couldn't wait until Monday. I had to accept it.

Roy was waiting impatiently for me in the hallway of the Dorchester. He looked as bad as I did, the result of the copious alcohol we had drunk, but his mood was even worse than mine.

"Thomas"—we were now on a first-name basis—"don't arrange to meet me in a place like this again. There's no one here but sheikhs and people prepared to bow and scrape to them to get in on a deal. Can't we go somewhere else where they'll do us some decent sausages? I know a place where they do the best breakfast in London, a full English: eggs and bacon, sausages, tomatoes, fried bread, mushrooms, chips, and baked beans. The place is run by a family, the Pelliccis, and I guarantee you will never forget their breakfast."

I didn't give in. Roy's culinary tastes were very different from mine. I was not accustomed to big breakfasts. My mother's ethnic background and her battle against putting on the pounds had been deciding factors in certain customs at home. No eggs or sausages for breakfast for us, to the dismay of my father, who had to get used to having a cup of coffee with a couple of slices of toast with butter and jelly.

My mother said that eating eggs at seven in the morning made her queasy. As a result, my brother, Jaime, and I were the only boys at our school who had milk and cereal for breakfast, and a cup of coffee and the aforementioned toast when we were older.

Roy was upset that I didn't have the contract and he had to accept my word that I would have it signed and sent to him on Monday.

"You have to trust me," I told him.

"Of course I do! It's just that I don't like to waste time. I've never understood why things don't work as normal on weekends."

"Well, people have the right to rest."

He shrugged. Roy was the type who thought that if he was capable of something there was no reason why other people shouldn't be.

I accompanied him to the station and then I went back to my apartment. I had to come up with a strategy for Roy Parker and his friends' campaign. It wasn't going to be easy, and I also had to explain to Mark Scott that I had taken on a new client. But I was determined to keep my promise to Parker.

I arrived at the office at seven o'clock on Monday morning. I'd sent each member of my team a dossier with basic ideas for the Parker campaign and had summoned them to a meeting before they started their assigned tasks.

Maggie seemed to be in a bad mood and Cathy's wasn't much better.

"We're taking charge of Parker's campaign. I assume that you've had time to read the document I sent you yesterday. There are a number of ideas to get to work on. We're starting from zero. We need to come up with everything for them from scratch. Philip, I want you to make me an electoral map of the region: which party normally wins, what are the key economic issues in the area, what do the local papers say about this group that Parker's a part of. I want to know everything about them and, most of all, about the Labour and Conservative candidates they'll be facing.

"Cathy, you need to come up with a publicity campaign. We'll focus on these men's key virtue: they're people with close ties to the land, they were born there, just like their parents and their grandparents, and they invest everything they have, including their lives, in developing their region. They are what they are—a bit rough around the edges—so no transforming them to look like the candidates from the traditional parties. The voters need to believe that Roy Parker and his friends are transparent.

"Janet, find a team that can travel with us. This campaign takes priority."

"Are they going to pay more than the other clients we already have?" asked Richard with a hint of sarcasm.

"Not a pound more. But you'll agree with me that this is a challenge and I like challenges," I replied with more confidence than I felt.

"Have you spoken to Mark Scott yet?" Richard wanted to know.

"No. But I'll do it as soon as we finish this meeting."

"And what happens to the work we've already got under way? My plane to Birmingham leaves in a couple of hours . . . and Janet will need to come with me," Cathy reminded me.

"And you shall both go. We're not going to neglect any of our clients. We will honor all the contracts we've signed. I'll be the one who does most of the hard work, but I need your help. Oh, Maggie! Get the finance department to prepare a standard contract. I need it now. I'll take it with me to see Mark so he can sign it."

"This Roy Parker must be a very persuasive man," said the secretary.

"He is, Maggie, but however persuasive Parker may be, in the end this is a good deal for the agency, and I couldn't say no to that."

Mark Scott had never heard of Roy Parker, so he called Denis Roth to ask him if he knew anything about this group of rural guys who wanted to take over their county halls. Denis had heard a little but didn't know much either, and both he and Mark warned me not to sign any contracts until I had exact information about who Parker was. I tried to contain my impatience in front of them as I didn't want them to think I had any special interest. In truth, even I was surprised by how much I had committed myself to Roy Parker.

I had to call him to tell him that I wasn't able to go to his county that same day; I had to wait for the go-ahead from Scott and Roth.

"They can go to hell, I tell you. We don't need them," he told me angrily.

"I don't agree, Roy. It would be an error to lose the agency. Be patient."

"Patient! I thought you'd realized that patience is one of the many virtues I lack," he replied.

"I'll call you as soon as they give me the signed contract. They may even ask you to come back to London to sign it here. Mark Scott might want to meet you."

"Don't waste my time, Spencer. Our rivals already have the advantage."

"We'll catch them."

Denis took a couple of days to give the go-ahead. His friends in Westminster had told him about Parker and his friends. Inoffensive people with no political training: they were going to need a lot of luck to win a single mayoralty. It didn't matter to Denis's friends whether the agency provided them with any services; they wouldn't be able to compete with the Conservative or Labour party machinery anyway.

Mark told me all this when he gave me the contract, which was only lacking Roy Parker's signature.

"Don't waste time going yourself. Make him come to London. That way I can have a look at this guy. I like to know who we're working for."

———

Roy Parker complained when I asked him to come back to London. The only thing I could do to try to lift his bad mood was to meet him at the station.

To my surprise, he and Mark got along, but Denis couldn't help looking at him with a certain disgust. Roy had arrived at the agency dressed in a way that seemed more suited to herding cattle. But he felt comfortable in his outfit, even despite the contrast between his checked button-down shirt, worn sweater, and thick-soled rubber boots and Mark's Armani jacket and Denis's tailor-made Savile Row suit.

"Well, we've already signed. Now I hope that Spencer will get straight to work. I think we can win at least a dozen mayoralties," Roy declared.

During the following months I spent many hours on the old train that went to Roy's home county. There was a lot of work to do, and Mark and Denis had made it clear that the agency's priority was not "that bunch of bumpkins," as Denis described them. I was everywhere at once. I didn't want my assistant, Richard Craig, or Cathy telling Mark tales that I was spending more time on "that bunch of bumpkins" than I did on his friends in the Conservative or Labour parties.

Philip did a thorough job. He had presented me with a meticulous dossier, which included in-depth biographies of not just our candidates but also those standing against them. He didn't tell me how he'd done it and I didn't ask, but he had found out how much money was in the current accounts of not just Parker and his friends but also their opponents, and even whether they were unfaithful to their wives. I didn't want him to give me any details, but I suspected that Philip, who was a hacker when all was said and done, was capable of finding out all kinds of confidential information. Eventually I could no longer control my curiosity.

"How on earth did you manage to find out so much about Roy's opponents?"

"Well, you might not want to know. I . . . perhaps I've overstepped the mark." Philip trembled as he spoke.

"What have you done?" I asked, worried. I couldn't forget that Philip Sullivan had had problems with the law, even though he had eventually been cleared of any wrongdoing.

"I . . . you must see that I only want to do a good job, Thomas . . . It's not easy to find out certain things," he answered, stammering.

"Come on, Philip. I want to know. I hope you haven't done something stupid."

Philip fell apart. He seemed to be on the verge of tears, which immediately provoked a sense of revulsion in me. I have never been able to stand weak people, although I have used them. And in Philip's case, his weakness had made him my faithful dog. Whatever he may have done, it was clear that he did it to curry favor with me.

"I've got a friend who's a journalist."

"The one who tried to hack the Bank of England's IT system using your computer?" I asked.

"No, this is a different friend. He's got problems and he's out of work, but he's a good investigator and I thought he could be useful to us."

"What have you gotten us into? I warn you, I'm not going to take any crap from you."

"Please, Thomas! I'll introduce Neil Collins to you. He's a good guy. You don't need to worry."

"So you have a little friend named Neil, and my guess is that this is who you've been giving the research money to."

"You didn't ask me . . ."

"I didn't tell you to hire anybody!"

"I didn't hire Neil. I've just been paying him for his work."

"And what has this work consisted of?"

"Everything that's in the dossier that I gave you about Roy Parker's opponents. And, as you well know, there's material there that could put an end to their campaigns."

I had to make a decision: either fire Philip Sullivan or meet this Neil guy. I decided to take a risk and did the latter.

Neil was an unemployed journalist. Intelligent, brilliant, cultured, and also a drunk and a drug addict. It was difficult to believe that he could have compiled those dossiers: when he wasn't under the influence of alcohol he was under the influence of cocaine.

He had worked for the *Times* and the *Sunday Times* and also at the *International Herald Tribune* in Paris. He was a good investigator, able to find shit wherever it might be and on absolutely anybody, whoever they were. If someone had made a mistake, Neil would find out about it.

They had fired him from all his jobs, not only due to the alcohol and cocaine, but because he'd gone sniffing around the upper echelons and they had clipped his wings. He'd been down to his last penny when Philip called him, so he agreed to investigate the lives of Frank Wilson and Jimmy Doyle, the two politicians Roy wanted to beat at the ballot boxes.

Neil must have been around forty and he was a mess. In addition to the alcohol and drugs, he wasn't exactly pleasant or nice. But I liked him. He struck me as someone you could trust. And from what Philip told me, the Internet didn't have any secrets from Neil.

I told Philip that he shouldn't tell the rest of the team anything about Neil's existence or his background. Cathy and Richard would have run straight to Mark Scott and Denis Roth, and those two would have been more than capable of not just firing me but turning me in for bad practice too. Philip swore that he wouldn't say a word. I told him that he should continue to be the one who dealt with Neil but that he shouldn't tell or give me any compromising details.

"I'm giving you this job and it's up to you how you do it. If anything goes wrong . . ."

"Yes, you want to be able to say that it was entirely down to me, that you trusted me and I betrayed that trust."

"Smart guy. Oh, and I don't want to see your friend Neil Collins again."

Richard Craig didn't seem to be worried that I was making Philip Sullivan my right-hand man. He seemed to enjoy directing the conventional campaigns. I let him do it. I needed him to do this part of the job so that I could focus on Parker, but I tried to make sure that he didn't always have Cathy available to work with him. They made a good team and I knew that if I ever took my eye off the ball, they would ensure that Mark Scott and Denis Roth got rid of me. So, although Cathy put up resistance, I made her travel with me to Derbyshire, Parker's home county, on a regular basis.

We gave the group of "bumpkins" a name—the Rural Party—and we established the key points of their campaign: defending the interests of the county by electing people committed to fostering the community's well-being.

I found it hard to convince Roy that the group needed a female candidate.

"A party with no women is unacceptable." I laid it out for him.

"The women of standing in the county are our wives. They have power, but within the house. You won't find a single one who wants to leave her home to dedicate herself to becoming mayor."

"Well, one of them will have to do it," I replied.

It was Cathy who found a couple of possible candidates. One of them was a friend of Suzi, Roy's wife. She was named Victoria and was a teacher at one of the local schools. She was in her forties and seemed bored with children, her husband, and rural life. Cathy convinced Suzi that she should persuade Victoria and they all had a surprise when she agreed right away.

The second candidate was named Alberta and she was the daughter of a shepherd in a small, remote village. This good woman accepted the proposal, knowing that this would be the only adventure in her life. Her mother was in poor health with heart problems, and as soon as she died Alberta would have to take on her mother's role and help her father, which meant resigning herself to that inhospitable land forever.

Cathy designed a very bucolic poster: a stretch of green grass full of silhouettes of men and women. The slogan was simple and effective: WE KNOW OUR COMMUNITIES.

Roy thought it was great and Suzi loved it. In fact, Suzi felt genuine admiration for Cathy. They couldn't have been more different. Suzi was simple, direct, and fought to control her wild ginger mane, which was never properly styled. She carried a few extra pounds, but was attractive. Cathy wore her elegant slenderness wrapped in designer suits. When Suzi appeared in her best outfit she always looked badly dressed beside Cathy, even if the latter was in jeans and a sweater.

"So, Thomas, tell me how we're going to beat my opponents. I'm not worried about the Lib Dems; the liberals have never had a mayor here. But Frank Wilson is well known and his lot, the Conservatives, are in power in London. As for Jimmy Doyle . . . well, he's not a bad candidate, but he doesn't have the same charisma as the current Labour mayor, Robert, who's been in office these last ten years."

Yes, Jimmy Doyle and Frank Wilson had become a nightmare for me, but, thanks to Neil, Philip Sullivan had come to know all there was to know about them. Frank went to a discreet brothel twice a month. He'd taken care to visit one in another town, but he was methodical about his visits on the first and fifteenth of each month. The brothel was run by a widow who had three women working for her. They were good girls, Philip told us, married with children, and their husbands were out of work.

Apart from that, Frank Wilson was a good family man who attended church every Sunday. He had a shop that sold a bit of this and a bit of that, from ladies' tights to bath salts and hats.

What Philip had found on Jimmy Doyle was that he had a

number of debts. He liked to live beyond his means. Although he had inherited a hardware store from his parents, he didn't know how to run it properly and was unable to adapt to the times. He had mortgaged his house and the store itself to keep it going, and though the bank was putting pressure on him, he still kept spending money he didn't have. Furthermore, he had used money from a party account to cover one of the interest payments on his loans. As for his credit card, it was smoking; when he traveled outside the county he liked to go to good restaurants and surprise his wife with side trips and gifts.

Philip Sullivan and I met with Roy Parker to tell him his rivals' weak spots.

"How the hell do you know that Frank visits a brothel? Have you hired detectives?" Roy asked Sullivan directly.

"There's no need to hire a detective if you know where to look," Philip Sullivan replied, proud of his achievements.

"Outrageous. Everything you've found is outrageous." Roy seemed surprised.

"Let me remind you," I intervened, "that you wanted to know everything about your opponents so as to beat them soundly. But I agree with you: Wilson and Doyle are two good men."

"I don't like the idea of sinking a man who doesn't know how to swim," Roy said in his usual grumpy tone, "but if it's a case of my own survival . . . I'll do it." He avoided meeting our eyes.

"You've got the figures here: right now you don't have enough support to become mayor. It looks like Frank Wilson and the Conservatives are likely to win this time," I warned him.

"And what you're proposing is to let the whole world know that Frank plays away from home."

"No, I'm not proposing anything. You asked me to find out everything about them, and that's what we've done."

"The voters can't trust a man who deceives his family. As for Jimmy Doyle, that'll be easier; you can't put a man in town hall who can't even balance the books at his own business. Perhaps," declared a smiling Sullivan, "he wants to be mayor to save himself so the bank won't call in his debts."

"Well, no one's said you ought to use any weaknesses in your opponents as part of your campaign," I added.

"You're a swine, Thomas."

Roy's look told me that that was exactly what he thought of me. The insult didn't bother me, but the fact that he had used it alongside my first name and in front of Philip did.

"Well, that's why you hired me, Mr. Parker. Neither you nor your friends have any chance of winning a single mayoralty."

"We'll wipe the floor with them, Thomas, much as it pains me to destroy a man because he has trouble with the bank or likes to go to bed with other women."

"You certainly don't have any other weapons to beat them with."

I was disconcerted by Roy's attitude. He suddenly seemed to have scruples, and even a conscience. With time I became used to his changes of opinion. He was as likely to want to offer his opponents help in resolving their problems as he was to want to assassinate them once and for all.

"I hired you in order to win," he reminded me.

"You hired me to try to win. We don't trade in miracles," I replied sharply.

"And what you're proposing is that I should wipe out Frank and Jimmy . . . They're my neighbors; our families have been friends since before we were born. I don't like it, but we'll do it. It's what you advise."

I got to my feet. I wasn't prepared to fight against his bad conscience. It wasn't my problem.

"I'm the one who has no interest in sinking your friends. It doesn't make a difference to me who is mayor of this place. You asked us to find their weak spots. They have nothing more to hide than what we've already uncovered. Tell me what you want us to do, pay, and that's what we'll do."

"Don't get upset, Thomas. I wasn't criticizing you. It's just that I was wondering whether being in power is really worth it."

Suzi arrived just in time to hear her husband's last few words. She gave him a hard look and there was a hint of disdain in her eyes.

"Don't you have the guts for it, Roy? Politics is one great big cesspit. You either need to be prepared to swim in it or you stay at home and stick to managing the family businesses. But if you do that don't complain later, because I won't listen to you. You've been telling me for years that you want a seat in Westminster. Do you think they're going to give you one just because that's what you want? You'll have to earn it and to do that you can't feel pity for your opponents. It's them or you. You need a killer instinct to succeed in politics. If you don't have one, get out now and don't waste the family's money." Suzi said her piece without raising her voice, in a tone as icy as her gaze.

I thought that she should have been the one trying her luck in politics. She was a practical woman who didn't waste time on sentimentality. Her loyalty was limited to her own. Outside her family was the rest of the world, and no one there was capable of moving her.

"Darling, you shouldn't be so hotheaded," Roy reproached her.

"You're the hotheaded one. One day you want to conquer the world and the next you don't dare take a single step. Make up your mind, Roy, and don't waste any more time, not theirs"— she nodded at me and Sullivan—"nor mine, nor my family's."

Roy was too macho to accept a public telling-off from Suzi.

"Leave us, Suzi, we're working. We'll talk later."

I was surprised she left without a fight. It was clear she knew when to stop pushing things. They were a strange couple.

"Women meddle in everything, but they don't know anything," said Roy without hiding his disgust.

"So, what do you want to do?" I pressed him.

"Be prime minister."

"Then you'll have to start by getting your two beloved childhood friends out of the way," I decreed.

"Then let's do it. Tell me how."

"Sullivan will give you the details. Obviously we can't just call a press conference. We'll have to leak the information. First online. From there it will spread to the papers. There's a struggling local radio station, Radio East; they're on their last legs. We hadn't planned to place any advertisements for the Rural Party there—it's too small and irrelevant—but we will. We need to earn their confidence. The head of the radio station desperately needs advertising revenue. We'll ask him to follow our candidates' campaigns and we'll brief one of his reporters so that this information about Wilson and Doyle also spreads on the radio. There's nothing better than a struggling businessman. He'll be our best friend."

"You're going to buy journalists?" he asked, shocked.

"That would definitely be a serious error. But you and your friends will spend some time with the reporter from Radio East, while we work with the station owner to ensure he earns a decent sum from advertising. He'll know who to support and what information his guys should spread."

"And who cares what a little local station has to say?" asked Roy.

"We'll make sure that everything said by this station is picked up by the London papers. The *Times* will end up publishing the story that Frank Wilson has a relationship with a prostitute. You'll see. It's a case of creating a climate of opinion, and we know how to do that. I'm going to buy a number of advertising slots and tomorrow we'll have dinner with the head of the station. You're going to be his salvation, Roy. You'll see."

"I wasn't wrong about you, Thomas. You really are a dirtbag."

I shrugged. Roy's insults didn't offend me. In truth, I thought he described me quite accurately.

Why did I agree to sink those two men? In reality it was Roy, not me, who made the decision, although I was the one who put it in front of him.

Could I have acted differently? Of course:

When Philip Sullivan came to me with the information he and Neil had dug up, I could have told him off and said, "Forget what you've found, Philip. We're not going to use it. This is about helping Roy Parker win some elections, not making a couple of family men's weaknesses public. We won't do that. Find something else—I don't know, political disagreements, electoral irregularities, the usual."

Roy would never have found out his opponents' secrets. I could even have hinted to Roy that there was some dirt under the rug, but at the merest suggestion of pulling the rug aside I could have said no: "Don't expect me to destroy these two men. There are lines you just don't cross."

But I didn't say any of that, because I was as keen as Roy to take down Wilson and Doyle. I didn't have anything against them, and they didn't strike me as bad guys; it's just that we were playing with marked cards in order to win the game. Plus, why kid ourselves? There's not a single politician who would resist striking a mortal blow against his opponents, especially if in doing so he would stand out as a paragon of moral virtue.

Philip Sullivan asked me whether we were really going to do it. Sullivan had a hacker's heart, but it seemed he retained some scruples.

"It's part of the game," I said. "They'll do the same if they find any skeletons in Roy's closet. There are no innocent parties in the game of power."

At that moment, what I said was just a line and nothing more: a line that struck me as suitable to dismiss Sullivan's doubts.

With time I learned that it was also correct. As far as Philip Sullivan was concerned, he accepted that the game required us to bathe in the same shit as our clients. I asked him to say nothing to either Cathy or Richard. I had come to know them well enough to know that they would refuse to take part in anything underhanded.

"It'll be hard to stop them from finding out," Philip protested.

"They've got their job and we've got ours. Decide whether you're coming over to the dark side, Philip, because there's no going back."

Christopher Blake, the owner of Radio East, was a typical struggling businessman. He had too many debts and, aside from what we would present to him, no other option that would guarantee the radio station's survival.

Blake had inherited the business from his father, who had had the foresight forty years earlier to set up a small media empire. The senior Blake started a local paper dedicated to community news and then acquired a license for a local radio concession. The business was healthy if modest, but his son had squandered his inheritance and was on the verge of going under. What made Christopher Blake Jr. lose sleep was the thought of telling his retired father that the paper and radio station no longer belonged to the family because he had borrowed against them and the bank was calling in his debts.

Christopher Blake received me in his office, impatient and curious about the urgent call I had made to arrange this meeting.

I was as honest as possible given that it was a first meeting. I surprised him by saying that Roy Parker had decided to promote his campaign and that of the Rural Party on Radio East. We wanted advertising slots at all hours, and I also hinted that we were considering buying a few pages of advertising space in his paper. No, we weren't asking for a special price, I told him, we understood that we would have to pay the going rate, although we would be extremely grateful if his public affairs program covered our campaign.

"You can imagine what it's costing the Rural Party to edge in between the Conservatives and Labour. The big media outlets barely pay us any attention."

I invited him to dinner two days later with Roy and Suzi Parker.

"You'll like him, you'll see. Mr. Parker dreams of making this region's voice heard in London. He's a man of firm convictions."

Roy protested at having to cajole Blake.

"I pay you so I don't have to waste my time," he responded when I told him that I'd booked a table for dinner and that he should bring Suzi with him. Cathy would be in charge of taking her to buy something suitable. We weren't going to turn Suzi into something she wasn't, but we also didn't want her to turn up at dinner in rubber boots.

On the night of the dinner Suzi looked lovely. Cathy had chosen a simple outfit of black trousers and a white silk shirt. I was surprised that Cathy hadn't suggested she wear high heels and that she was wearing a pair of pumps that barely gave her an extra inch.

Cathy explained to me that Suzi walked like a duck when wearing high heels and it was better that she stuck to heels below two inches and avoided stilettos.

I have to acknowledge that Suzi looked really good; even her untamable mane was firmly tied back.

The dinner was a success. A scoundrel and a survivor is what Parker and Blake were. As for me, I focused on guiding the conversation and preventing Roy from telling Christopher Blake too much.

Two days later I got a call from a reporter at Radio East.

"Mr. Spencer? Thomas Spencer? My name is Evelyn Robinson. Mr. Blake has put me in charge of following the Rural

Party's campaign and Roy Parker's campaign in particular. Do you think you could arrange an interview with him? I'd also like you to send me a copy of the campaign schedule, where he'll be making appearances, what public events he'll take part in . . . I'll cover the campaign on the radio but Mr. Blake has also asked me to cover it for the paper."

I met her immediately, accompanied by Philip Sullivan. At the end of the day it was he who would have to guide her.

Evelyn was no older than twenty-four. Of average height, with straight brown hair and bulging, equally brown eyes, she would have seemed nondescript if it weren't for her very long legs. There was nothing about her that grabbed one's attention. But we didn't take long to realize that she was ambitious and was not prepared to spend the rest of her life in that remote region. She would do whatever was necessary to escape her dead-end job.

She interviewed Roy and became his shadow. Those were Blake's orders: she had to report exhaustively on the Rural Party's campaign. I don't know whether Blake had ordered that whatever she said or wrote should be favorable or whether she didn't need to be told. The fact is that she became a propagandist and was almost sickeningly sweet. Suzi adored her. I was surprised that a woman as smart as Suzi ended up believing what Evelyn said about Roy, whom she described as a kind of knight errant, prepared to sacrifice himself to make the region's voice heard in the halls of power in London. But time has taught me that we are all prepared to believe even our own lies when it suits us.

Philip Sullivan had built up solid relationships with the local journalists, and did a good job spreading suspicions about the Conservative and Labour candidates. Silken words, hints that were already bearing their first fruits. It was he who asked Evelyn what she thought about certain rumors about the Conservative candidate, Frank Wilson.

"I don't normally waste time on rumors" was Evelyn's response, "but if there's something that's caught your attention . . ."

"I don't know . . . judge for yourself. I was surprised to hear someone say that Frank Wilson isn't such a fond family man as he makes his voters believe. Perhaps it's a pack of lies. You'd know . . . I'm not from around here and I wouldn't know whether or not Wilson plays away from home from time to time. Anyway, if that were the case . . . I don't know, but I can't abide people with double standards, who make people think they are something other than what they really are."

"And do you think I ought to just repeat all the crap that's flying around here? That's not journalism," Evelyn replied mistrustfully.

"That's not what I said. I only asked you if you think what they're saying about Wilson might be true."

We had to turn to Blake to dismiss his reporter's doubts by ordering her not to ignore what was being said about Frank Wilson.

"I want us to prove that we're a serious business. We should report on everything. We need to make noise so that people talk about us. Check out whether there's proof that Wilson has a lover. If that's the case, he doesn't deserve to be elected mayor. Investigate. You said you wanted to become an investigative journalist."

Evelyn saw Christopher Blake's challenge for what it was: an order to spread all the shit at hand about Frank Wilson.

That night, when she got home, Evelyn found a piece of paper in her mailbox that listed an address and a day of the week. Thursday.

Thursday was the next day. It was clear that someone wanted her to prowl around that address, which was in a town not far away. She asked Blake for a photographer to come with her. He immediately agreed even though the paper had only one photographer.

"We can do without him for a few hours. Who knows what you might find?"

By that point Evelyn understood that whatever she might discover could be front-page news and get top billing on all the radio news updates.

Christopher Blake seemed to have recovered his good mood since the electoral campaign had begun, and from what was said in the editorial office, he had found a source of financing that was keeping the paper and Radio East afloat.

Evelyn didn't know it, but some of Roy Parker's friends had bought shares in the media company, injecting a considerable sum of money that was going to guarantee its survival. Roy had told Blake that while it wasn't ethical for him to have shares in media firms, he thought the region couldn't allow two local media outlets to die, and a group of his fellow businessmen wanted to buy shares in the business.

"We have to make our voice heard. No one will pay any attention to this damned region if we don't make London listen to us. That's why we need you, Christopher. I'm not asking you to only speak well of me, just that you keep the region's interests in mind. That's more important than anything else, including me."

Money was no longer a problem. Blake was even talking about taking on some young journalists.

Evelyn and the photographer arrived at the address on the anonymous note at first light. The house formed part of a row of identical buildings, each with two floors and a small front yard.

Bob, the photographer, had brought a sandwich, a bottle of water, and a couple of pouches of tobacco.

"You've certainly come prepared."

"That's the way these things are, we might have to spend the whole day waiting."

"Well, come midmorning we'll call Blake and he can tell us what to do."

"Look, when I worked for the *Sunday Times* and we were tailing celebrities I could spend whole days standing guard without anything happening. You have to be patient. Whoever sent you the anonymous message wants you to find something . . . and so does Blake."

Evelyn liked Bob. He wasn't far from retirement. He had returned to the area five years ago, having left when he was young and still had dreams of being a famous photographer.

He had worked in photojournalism for many years, traveling to conflict zones and then selling his photos and reports at bargain prices. The Middle East, the Horn of Africa, Southeast Asia . . . They were all places that had left numerous scars on his soul, but he had barely been able to scrape by on what he was earning. It didn't matter to the papers that he had risked his life to report on a war, a coup d'état, or a famine. So one day he returned to London in search of a stable job. He didn't imagine that the best he'd get was working for a tabloid photographing celebrities at compromising moments, with secret girlfriends and the like. His heart had hardened as he lost hope of fulfilling his dream. "A knicker-sniffer, that's what you are." That's what his wife had told him before leaving him. Yes, that is what he was, but he was good at his job, and when somebody left an anonymous tip, it was so you could discover something dirty that might make the front page the next day.

If there was one thing that he'd learned it was that there were two kinds of bosses: those who believed that a journalist's mission was to tell the truth no matter what it was, even if it was about those who paid their monthly salaries, and those who weren't squeamish about publishing the dirt as long as it wasn't about their friends or shareholders. It was obvious to Bob that Blake was the latter and was interested in finding a decent amount of shit somewhere nearby. They would find it. It didn't really matter to him whom it was about. He worked for Blake because he had grown tired of knicker-sniffing in London and had spent his life savings on a house in his hometown, where he planned to retire in three years, as soon as his pension kicked in. The only thing he regretted was not having children with whom to spend his final years. His wife hadn't wanted children, because, as she said, she would be embarrassed to have to tell them what their father did for a living. Ever since she'd left him a few years into their marriage, he hadn't spent two nights running with the same woman. If Evelyn weren't so young . . . But no, she wouldn't want to share her life with a man on the verge of retirement whose best offers were long walks in the countryside and a trip to the cinema a couple of times a month.

It wasn't until after three in the afternoon that Bob elbowed Evelyn and nodded at the taxi that had just stopped in front of the house they had spent hours watching. She was absorbed in her notebook and grumbled.

"Well, now we know why we're here. Look who just got out of the taxi," Bob told her.

Frank Wilson looked along the street in both directions before ringing the bell. They managed to see a well-groomed woman open the door and invite him to come in.

"And who could she be?" Evelyn asked, as much muttering to herself as expecting an answer from Bob.

"That's what you have to find out. I've been able to snap a couple of photos. They're not that great, but you can see him going into the house and greeting the woman who opened the door."

"I don't know where to start."

"Come on, Evelyn, this is basic journalism. Ask who lives in the house."

"Now?"

"Now, or when Frank Wilson comes out. But if you start now you'll have the job done. I'll stay here. If he comes out I'll snap him again."

"Right."

"I'd start by asking there," Bob told her, pointing at a shop on the corner of the street where newspapers were sold.

"That's what I was thinking of doing," Evelyn agreed, with a confidence she lacked.

She crossed the street with a determined stride and headed for the shop, where she dawdled, flicking through the papers on display while the owner took payment from a woman with a dog in her arms who was telling the man funny stories about her pet. When she finally left, Evelyn cleared her throat before deciding to ask, "Excuse me, but could you tell me who lives in that house? The fifth one, counting from this corner."

The man looked at her coldly and seemed to consider whether to answer.

"And why do you want to know? Why do you think I should tell you?"

"I . . . excuse me but . . . I'm a journalist. I'm carrying out an investigation and I know that that house . . . Well, it's not just any house. I imagine you know the owners."

"Sure, but I don't know anything and there's no reason I should tell you anything."

"I'm sorry to have disturbed you. I didn't think it would be such a big deal for you to tell me who lives there."

"Mrs. Hamilton. That's Mrs. Hamilton's house."

Evelyn turned upon hearing those words and found herself facing an older woman with white hair and a friendly smile.

"You should be more discreet, Mrs. Prince."

"What's wrong with telling this young lady that that's Mrs. Hamilton's house? Well, I've just come for my William's paper. He's had to stay in today because he's gotten a terrible cold and is running a fever."

"Does Mrs. Hamilton live alone?" asked Evelyn, interrupting the conversation.

"Yes, you might say she lives alone. Of course . . . well, she has two or three female friends who visit her every day. And then there are those gentlemen. Some of them are very distinguished-looking. They hurry in and leave quickly. Very discreet, they are," said Mrs. Prince maliciously.

"Are they relatives of Mrs. Hamilton's?" asked Evelyn.

"Friends—close, old friends. I live in Number Three and I've been seeing the same gentlemen for years," confirmed the old lady with a sickly sweet smile.

"Mrs. Prince, you shouldn't! And you, missy . . . why don't you leave? If you want to know something about Mrs. Hamilton, ask her directly. We don't need journalists poking around and causing problems."

"Are you a journalist, sweetheart? Do you work for the television? Perhaps you're even famous . . . I don't see very well and that's why I haven't recognized you."

"No, I'm not famous, madam, but I am a journalist and . . . well, we're investigating some things related to that house."

"Oh! It didn't occur to me that you might be investigating Mrs. Hamilton. She's a good woman. She was widowed a while ago and, well, she does what's necessary to survive. She's very discreet, and so are her lady friends and the gentlemen. Anyway, the gentlemen aren't from around here—we'd recognize them—but no. They're strangers. They say things around here."

"What sort of things?" Evelyn pressed her.

"There's always someone who talks for the sake of it!" interrupted the man behind the counter. "Please leave if you're not going to buy a paper."

"I'll buy all the papers necessary. Tell me, Mrs. Prince, what do they say about Mrs. Hamilton?"

"I don't want to be indiscreet; she's a good woman, a good neighbor, pleasant . . . No, I won't be the one to get her in trouble. Well, I've said too much. I always do. My William says I shouldn't get involved." And the woman turned away with a satisfied look.

Evelyn watched the old woman take her paper and set off toward her house. She was about to follow but decided not to.

The woman might get nervous and cause a fuss. She went back to rejoin Bob.

"Nothing. Wilson hasn't come out. Not him, nor anybody else. How about you? How did it go at the shop?"

She told him what the old lady had said and Bob started to laugh.

"What's so funny? You can save your breath if you're going to make fun of me for not getting more out of her."

"But she told you everything! For God's sake, Evelyn, you can't be that much of an idiot!"

"She didn't tell me anything useful. And I don't like being laughed at."

"You're very green. I don't know why Blake gave you this job."

"I assume it's because he knows what I'm capable of."

"Yes—doing whatever it takes to get ahead. You don't have many scruples but you lack experience."

"And in your opinion, what has this woman said that you seem to understand and I don't?"

"Well, this Mrs. Hamilton runs a brothel. A place where she and her three friends receive certain gentlemen, with the necessary discretion. Or rather, it's clear that Frank Wilson comes here to let off steam. It's an hour and a half by train from his local area, so he's not running the risk of bumping into his wife in the street. He does things the old-fashioned way."

Evelyn looked at him, discomfited. At first she thought that Bob either had his mind in the gutter or was very clever to draw such a conclusion from Mrs. Prince's words, but it didn't take more than a moment for her to accept that he was right.

"My God! Blake isn't going to believe it!"

"He's going to believe it. He sent us here to find this—to nail Frank Wilson. You realize that Parker's the real boss now, don't you? They say he and his friends bought shares in the radio station and the paper. We're small-fry but we serve his interests. Tomorrow we'll publish a story saying that Wilson is an adulterer and the day after the *Times* will pick it up. Frank Wilson's political career ends here."

"You're a cynic," said Evelyn, who at that moment was feeling rather uncomfortable with the situation.

"Come on, Evelyn. Lacking experience is one thing, but playing dumb is another. We all know that you'd do anything, including going to bed with Blake, if it would help you up the career ladder. It's just that he hasn't propositioned you. But I will proposition you. What do you think of spending the weekend together? I can give you a few lessons in journalism."

"You're a pig!"

Bob shrugged. He liked Evelyn. She was ambitious, but she hadn't completely lost her innocence yet.

"What do we do now?" she asked, trying to regain control of the conversation.

"I wait here for him to come out and snap another couple of photos of him. You try to find another source that confirms what that old lady told you. Ask in the other local shops."

"We could do something even better," Evelyn murmured.

"Like what?"

"We'll look up Mrs. Hamilton's phone number. Look, there's a pay phone over there. Perhaps we'll find her in the phone book. We have her address. And you'll call saying that a friend recommended her house. That you'd like to visit her and get together with one of her friends. Tell her that you're in the area and this afternoon would suit you."

"Look at you, little missy! Blake's chosen well. But no, I'm not going to do your job. You can do it yourself. If I was still working for the *Sunday Times* I'd do it. The salary there was worth it. But I won't do it for what Blake pays me. I wouldn't do it for you either, even if you promised to spend the weekend with me."

Evelyn hurried over to the phone booth. Right next to the telephone hung a phone book for the local area. It didn't take her long to find Mrs. Hamilton's number, insert a coin, and call from there.

"Mrs. Hamilton? Good afternoon. I'm sorry to disturb you but a mutual acquaintance told me you might be able to use my help. He's a gentleman who's paid you visits on occasion and . . . well, I need work. Perhaps you'd like to see me."

Evelyn waited, expecting an answer as the silence at the other end of the line grew longer. Then she heard a voice asking her which gentleman she meant.

"No, I can't give you the gentleman's name, at least not over the telephone. You know how these things are. Discretion is paramount. You don't need anybody? I assure you that I'm as discreet as I am accomplished and I need the work. I'm from a neighboring town and . . . well, I can't work there—everyone knows me—but I could here, and since you run such a well-regarded house, if you would give me a chance . . ."

The conversation lasted barely a few minutes longer before Evelyn hung up and returned to the car.

"What happened?" Bob wanted to know.

"She's very clever. She told me that she didn't have any work to offer, that I must have made a mistake because she's a widow and barely leaves the house. She said that she doesn't know any gentlemen outside her family and that if I couldn't give her a name then I must have the wrong number. You should have been the one to call her."

"You haven't done that badly. Look." Bob pointed toward one of the house's windows, and started clicking away with the camera at the same time.

Visible in the window were the silhouettes of a man and a woman, who seemed to be brushing her hair. They were difficult to make out.

"Is it him?"

Bob tried to visualize the photos he'd just taken and made an annoyed face.

"No, it isn't. It's another guy spending the afternoon at Mrs. Hamilton's house."

It didn't take long for the door to open, and this time it was Frank Wilson who hurriedly left the house, barely taking his leave of the woman, who quickly shut the door.

They followed him to the station, where Wilson caught a train.

"Now what?" Evelyn asked Bob.

"We can go back to the house and wait to see who comes out. If these friends of Mrs. Hamilton's don't live with her, they'll have to leave at some point."

"I'm exhausted and hungry. You've at least eaten the sandwich you brought with you."

"You'll soon learn that when you're following someone you have to go prepared."

Another man visited Mrs. Hamilton's house at four. And another at five. Just like Frank Wilson, they hurried up the steps, rang the bell, and the door opened a few seconds later. Someone they assumed must be Mrs. Hamilton invited them to come in and quickly shut the door.

The two men left, one at six and the other at seven, and it wasn't until eight, when Evelyn was exhausted and starving, that three women left the house. They were chatting in low voices and Evelyn felt they seemed a bit worried. Her call may have put Mrs. Hamilton on alert. If Bob was right and these women were running a discreet prostitution service, they would indeed be concerned.

"What now?" she asked Bob, who hadn't stopped taking photos.

"You follow one and I'll follow another; we'll see where they go."

"Should I talk to her?"

"Improvise, Evelyn. Journalism isn't an exact science. There isn't a protocol to follow. You react to the circumstances. You already know where I've parked the car. We'll meet here. Whoever gets here first will just wait."

Bob left her standing and walked briskly across the street so as not to lose one of the women, who had started to walk as if she were in a hurry.

Evelyn decided to follow the shorter of the two women who were still talking outside Mrs. Hamilton's house. She was a woman in her fifties with dyed blonde hair and the inoffensive appearance of a housewife. She was wearing a gray skirt, a black wool coat, and modest heels.

The woman walked calmly, as if she weren't in a rush in spite of the hour. She kept going for a good while until she reached a row of cheap houses, the kind built for workers in the seventies. She opened her bag and took out a key. She suddenly turned and looked at Evelyn, who was barely a few steps behind her.

"Why are you following me?" The woman's voice was nervous.

"I . . . well . . . I'm not following you. It's just that . . . Excuse me, but do you work for Mrs. Hamilton?"

"Who are you? What do you want?"

"I'm a journalist. My paper has put me in charge of an investigation and . . . Well, it's to do with Frank Wilson. He was at Mrs. Hamilton's house this afternoon."

"So you're after Mr. Wilson. You're ambitious for someone so young. What are you looking for?"

"It's very strange that Mr. Wilson should come to Mrs. Hamilton's house. What happens in that house? What do you do?"

"Seriously, what cheek! What makes you think you have the right to ask me?"

"You don't have to answer."

"Exactly, I can choose not to answer you. I can also report you for following and harassing me."

"But you won't, because . . . Well, it's obvious what goes on in Mrs. Hamilton's house."

"So it's obvious, but you ask just in case. And what's so obvious?"

Evelyn had the impression that the woman was making fun of her, in spite of her serious tone of voice and the tension in the lines of her face.

"Perhaps Mrs. Hamilton and . . . well, and her friends receive men there who are in search of a good time," Evelyn said hurriedly, with a flash of shame. Whatever she may have been doing, the woman had a dignity that disarmed Evelyn.

"I don't know where you get these ideas from, missy. But you ought to look around you. What do you see? There used to be work in this town, but now the men spend the day in the pub and the lucky ones find work from time to time. But life goes on. You have to pay the rent, send the kids to school. Food's expensive. You have to keep living as best you can. There's no work for the men and even less for the women. People around here try to get by on welfare payments, but it's not enough. Most of the families don't exactly live in harmony. You must know, when money's short, problems bloom. Men get desperate and the children . . . the children don't respect their fathers, who they see wasting their lives drinking beer and complaining about the lack of work. And we women . . . well, in addition to complaining, women have to put food on our children's plates every day. So we do what we can. But we don't steal and we don't swindle anyone. The fact is, the only damage is what we suffer to . . . That's life. We don't have a choice."

"And you earn money by going to Mrs. Hamilton's house where . . . where certain gentlemen visit."

"That's what you say. I see that you don't understand a word I've said. It doesn't really matter to me. What paper do you work for?"

"For Radio East and the *Eastern Daily.* I double up."

"A miserable little paper and a station no one listens to. But you're young and you want to get out of a rut and you don't mind what you have to do, so anything I might tell you is pointless. You have a goal, which is to get out of here. I don't blame you, and I assume you know that Frank Wilson is your passport to greatness. I'm sorry. I can't help you."

"Do you know Frank Wilson? He was at Mrs. Hamilton's house this afternoon and so were you. You must know him."

"Good night."

The woman crossed the threshold and smoothly closed the door. Evelyn didn't know what to do. In truth she didn't even know exactly where she was. She retraced her steps until she reached a road, where she asked a passerby how to get to the address where they'd parked the car. It took her twenty minutes to get there.

Bob was leaning against the car, smoking. He seemed tired. But it didn't matter to Evelyn how Bob was feeling. At least he's had a sandwich, she thought.

"Did you get anything?" she asked Bob as he got into the car.

"Not much. I followed the brunette to the suburbs, to a dump of a house. There were several teenagers who like to play at being badass in the street, smoking a joint. She told one of them to go into the house. He didn't even look at her. She hung her head and went in. End of story. This isn't a prosperous town. These women are just trying to feed their families, and the only thing they can do in a place like this is go to Mrs. Hamilton's house to entertain the Frank Wilsons of this world. It's a disgrace."

"People need to know about this."

"Do you know what will happen?" Bob asked, without looking at her as he accelerated, searching for the main road.

"Frank Wilson's political career will be over. What a hypocrite! The article will also bring attention to the situation in this area: the unemployment, the desperation. It'll be a good story."

"Take care writing it. You can't accuse Mrs. Hamilton without proof."

"You said yourself that it was obvious what's going on in that house."

"And it is. But you need proof or that woman will demand

compensation that will leave Blake quaking no matter how much money Parker's giving him."

"But—"

"You're dumber than you look. You'll have to write the story without statements, just questions. For example: 'What is candidate Mr. Wilson doing at Mrs. Hamilton's house?' or perhaps, 'Who is the mysterious Mrs. Hamilton whom Frank Wilson visits once a month?'"

"Fantastic!"

"You'll have to put it like that."

"You're a genius!" exclaimed Evelyn excitedly, giving Bob a grateful look. She wondered whether perhaps it wasn't such a bad idea to go to bed with Bob and learn a few things about journalism along the way. It wouldn't be easy, but she was starting to find him attractive. The guy really knew what he was doing.

"The damage you're going to do doesn't bother you?" Bob asked, more of a statement than a question.

"Damage?"

"These women's husbands will give them a good beating. It may be that they suspect that if there's food on the plate it's because their wives are up to something, but they prefer not to know what."

"I don't know their names—just Mrs. Hamilton's."

"Once you cast the first stone, there's no going back. Their names will come out alongside Mrs. Hamilton's. They won't just get a flogging from their husbands, but their children . . . in the end, those poor things will have to put up with people telling them their mothers are whores."

"Why are you trying to make me feel guilty? I'm not responsible for what happens. It's just an article."

"Go ahead, girly. You don't have a heart."

"Come on, Bob, don't wind me up."

Evelyn called Christopher Blake from a phone booth. It was late but she was sure he'd want to know what they'd found out.

Blake congratulated her, telling her to go straight to the editorial office and start writing. She would also have to take part in the radio news broadcast first thing in the morning, explaining how much they knew about the "Wilson case."

"Okay, so the boss sends his congratulations, and he likes your headlines."

"Yes, they're good. We'll cast the stone then hide our hands behind our backs."

"Tell me, Bob, why did you leave London to come to Derbyshire and work on a dying paper?"

"Because I didn't care anymore. Journalism used to be my great passion—getting the photo no one else could, pushing boundaries. I've played my part in ruining a number of reputations. And I don't regret it. Those guys deserved it. I can't stand those jumped-up little boys who spend public money giving lessons in morality to everyone else and think they can do whatever they like."

"But you don't seem very happy that we're going to tell people about Frank Wilson's little hobby."

"Well, I've never been interested in who sleeps with who. Our society is very hypocritical in that respect. The worst that'll happen to Frank Wilson is that he'll go through the humiliation of asking his wife and voters for forgiveness. I'm not worried about him. I feel sorry for those women who have to put up with guys like him to keep their families going. They're the ones who'll have the worst of it. They'll be singled out and their lives will become hell."

"I'm sorry, but I'm still going to write the article."

Bob shrugged and concentrated on driving. He didn't want to keep thinking about the women.

I was having dinner in London with a young female publicist when they told me there was a call for me. I was tempted not to answer but the municipal election campaign was under way and we had too many clients who might call, either because of something stupid or because of something important. So I smiled at my bubbly colleague and answered.

It was Christopher Blake and he was euphoric. He hurriedly told me that his team's investigations into Frank Wilson had unearthed a surprise that would be a real bombshell, and he summarized everything Evelyn had told him.

He ruined my dinner. I had to call Roy Parker immediately to tell him about the front page of the *Eastern Daily* and inform him that Evelyn was going to tell the "strange" story of the relationship between Frank Wilson and a certain Mrs. Hamilton live on the early morning news bulletin.

Philip was at home and came over to my place in twenty minutes. Nor did he complain about having to leave for Derbyshire that very night to be at Roy Parker's side and prevent him from saying a single word on the subject.

At ten in the morning the next day, all the county could talk about was Mr. Wilson's amorous adventures. The media agencies and other radio and television stations had been unable to do anything but repeat Evelyn's exclusive. She had called the Conservative candidate and insisted that he explain his bimonthly visits to Mrs. Hamilton's house.

In the middle of the afternoon Frank Wilson appeared at a press conference accompanied by his wife. He said that he was ashamed at the damage done to his family and his voters, and announced that he was withdrawing from the electoral race to spend time atoning for his mistake and taking care of his wife and children.

Roy called me that evening, delighted.

"One down! The Conservatives will have to field a substitute candidate now. You're a genius, Thomas. I knew I could trust you. Your boy Philip made me memorize what I had to say to the journalists—you know, things like it came as a great surprise to me because until now I had considered Frank Wilson one of the pillars of the community. Then I said that we politicians ought to be entirely transparent or pick another trade. Philip made me say that I was sorry for the difficult time the Wilson family was having."

"Good, Roy, that's good. Don't go off script. Don't improvise."

"Tomorrow Suzi's going to come with me to visit the market and the small local businesses. Philip says that the voters need to see that we're a happy family. They've also given Suzi a couple of crib sheets with what she should say if the journalists ask her questions. Don't worry, we'll do a good job."

No, I wasn't worried. I was sure that Roy and Suzi were more than capable of appearing upset by the Wilson case and bringing a few local voters on to their side at the same time. As for Evelyn Robinson, the girl was good and could be useful to us in the future.

A couple of days later I traveled to Derbyshire to meet first with Christopher Blake and then with Roy and Suzi.

Blake was bursting with enthusiasm. One of the heads of the Conservative Party had called him wanting to know how he had gotten the scoop. He also asked him why his paper and radio station seemed to be supporting those "novices" from the Rural Party. From what he told me, he too had done a good job playing his role of media impresario whose concern was only the prestige of his outlets and who just couldn't ignore a scandal like that. The man from the Conservative Party seemed conciliatory: "I'm sure we can come to an understanding. We admire your business, Mr. Blake. We know the difficulties you've overcome and you must know you can rely on our support for anything you might need." Blake seemed to have learned the words by heart because he recited them to me off the top of his head.

"Now they realize we exist! They've never invested in even one page of advertising in the paper or a single radio slot. Now they won't be able to avoid thinking of us. And I suppose Mr. Parker is satisfied with . . . with how his campaign is going."

"Yes, he is. I thank you on his behalf for the support of your station and paper. The Rural Party is a decent party that will know how to represent its citizens' interests. Mr. Parker is an upright man. And my congratulations; I hear that an investment group has bought shares in your company. They're betting on the future."

I said this last part to remind him that if he was doing well now it was because we had thrown him a life belt to cling to. Blake was more than capable of coming to believe that Evelyn really had discovered Frank Wilson's visits to Mrs. Hamilton's house all by herself.

That night I had dinner with Roy and Suzi. Philip joined us. I was surprised to see that Suzi had lost a few pounds and that her hair was perfectly styled. Both things detracted from her charm. She was also wearing some Jimmy Choo shoes in which she was struggling to remain upright.

"Who told you to go to the hairdresser and lose weight?" I asked her grumpily.

"Well, I think it's what's expected of a candidate's wife. I can't go about with my hair in a mess. And, to be honest, I envy Cathy's figure. Everything fits her as if she were a model."

"Mrs. Parker, you can't, nor should you, look like Cathy; she wouldn't get a single vote in this county. As you can imagine, the Rural Party is for the people from around here, people distanced from traditional politicians, people who can milk a cow or help a sheep give birth."

Roy fidgeted uncomfortably and looked at me with such anger I thought he was going to hit me.

"Don't overdo it, Thomas. It's not for you to decide how Suzi does her hair. It's one thing for us to accept your advice and another for us not to make our own decisions."

"You see, Roy, this is how things are: either you follow our advice to the letter, including how your wife wears her hair, or we pack our bags and leave. You decide."

I wasn't bluffing. I knew that either I made it clear who was in charge or it was better to go back to London that very night. Roy could throw out everything we had achieved as a result of his harebrained ideas, like letting Suzi appear as a caricature of the candidates' wives from the traditional parties.

"So no hair salons and no high heels," she intervened, aware that her husband's political career could end right there.

"You are what you are, a plump housewife with rebellious hair that you struggled to control with those clips you were wearing before. And no, Jimmy Choos don't suit you. Wear what Cathy advised you: low-heeled pumps, and only when you have to attend a serious event; the rest of the time, stick with the rubber boots. Be who you've always been, that's your greatest charm."

"All right. I'll do it. I thought I was better like this . . ."

"No, you're not. I promise you, like this you seem vulgar but you were attractive the way you were before."

Roy hadn't said a word while Suzi and I were talking. He seemed to be weighing what to do, whether to fire me or give in on this. He chose the latter option.

"Okay, when do we move on to the second part of the plan? There's still the Labour guy, Jimmy Doyle. I told your guy"— he nodded to Philip—"that it would suit us if the stuff about Doyle's economic problems was already leaking out. As soon as we get him out of the way I'll be the only one left."

"And Philip will have explained to you that we won't be doing anything before the final stages of the campaign. There will be no further scandals until that point. You will continue visiting little old ladies, going to see other landowners, meeting with unemployed workers . . . You will follow the plan that Philip has designed. Don't veer even a millimeter off the script. The rest is up to us."

"But that means giving Labour the advantage! Jimmy Doyle's got good support in the county."

"Yes, I already know that, and he will have up to the day I've told you. Roy, you have to know how to strike at the right moment. I'll bet you were one of those kids who beat the others up without a second thought. It doesn't work like that in politics. Anyway, the Frank Wilson case is already front-page news. Don't be impatient. You can't get rid of all your opponents at the same time, you'll attract attention. The journalists from other outlets are asking themselves how a young, unknown reporter like Evelyn Robinson was able to uncover Frank Wilson's amorous entanglements. They will think, they will speculate, and someone might tug on the thread and try and follow it back to you. I recommend you read *The Art of War,* it will do you good."

"Did Churchill write it?"

"No, it was written by someone who lived several centuries ago. I think it was the fourth century BC. He was named Sun Tzu and his book is studied in all the military academies."

"He was Chinese, right?"

"Yes, he was Chinese."

Roy didn't seem impressed by my recommendation, but Suzi made a note of the book's title. I was sure that she would read it and then summarize it for her husband.

I decided that it was best for Philip to remain with Roy until the campaign was over. We had hired a couple of publicists to organize its day-to-day running but they weren't able to make Roy do anything that he didn't want to do or prevent him from carrying out his own ideas.

"I have to go back to London tomorrow. I've got a mountain of other candidates and I need to coordinate various campaigns at the same time. Philip will stay with you and don't think I'm happy about that, but it's the only way to stop you from putting your foot in it and taking yourself out of the running. But I should warn you, Roy, we won't keep working with you unless you follow instructions from Philip or any other member of my team to the letter."

"Even that insipid woman Janet McCarthy?" asked Roy with a smile.

"As far as I can tell, her lessons on how to behave in front of a camera and how to come off well in a debate have served you very well so far."

"She's like a schoolteacher," Roy replied.

"She's a professor at the University of London, and you've been privileged that she's agreed to teach you some of the skills you need to succeed in becoming mayor."

"You seem tense, Thomas," Suzi intervened, trying to prevent us from getting embroiled in an argument.

"I'm tired. I've already told you that we're running campaigns for more than forty candidates; men and women who aspire to be mayors of their towns."

"Don't get angry, I'll be as obedient as can be," Roy promised.

He was exhausting. He personified the word "mercurial." He was as ready to turn sentimental as to act like a killer.

The Frank Wilson case didn't disappear overnight. The husband of one of the women who worked for Mrs. Hamilton gave her such a beating that she was left in a coma. They arrested the man and he had no qualms admitting he had wanted to kill her.

The other women didn't come out of it well either. Their husbands threw them out on the street after a few blows and the standard cries of "whore." As for Mrs. Hamilton, she put the house up for sale and disappeared. The neighbors claimed she hadn't even said goodbye to anyone.

"Isn't your conscience prickling?" Bob asked Evelyn while they smoked a cigarette. They were in bed reading the Sunday papers and Evelyn's editorial was in the *Eastern Daily*.

"I'm not responsible for what happened," she replied.

She liked Bob, going to bed with him was fun, but she was irritated by these moral embers he would let flare up every so often.

Evelyn refused to accept that she had anything to do with the misfortune that had befallen those women, although from time to time she couldn't help remembering the dignity of that woman on her doorstep, refusing to say a single word about Frank Wilson or Mrs. Hamilton, simply explaining to her that some things happen because there is no other option in life. If Bob went on about it too much she would get angry, because she didn't want to remember that the woman's son refused to have any more to do with her while his father took off his belt to make her pay for the public humiliation he'd been subjected to.

I agreed with Philip that we couldn't leak the documents we had on Jimmy Doyle's debts and late payments through Evelyn. Her colleagues on other papers would say that there was no way she could have so much luck in a single month. We even considered whether it might make sense to send them to a different media empire to avoid suspicions.

"How did your friend Neil get hold of those photocopies of extracts from Doyle's bank statements?" I asked Philip.

"I don't know, he never tells me how he gets the information. He hands it over and that's that."

"Yes, but are you sure the extracts are authentic?"

"I trust him. He's the best."

"Yes, he seems to have a particular talent for digging up shit. What do you think?"

"Let's send them to various outlets, including the *Eastern Daily* and Radio East. No addressees, just to the editorial teams. Blake will publish them, and if the others don't they won't be able to say it's because they didn't have the papers; it'll be because they didn't want to take the plunge."

"Blake won't like the fact we're depriving him of a scoop," I reflected aloud.

"But it would be very risky for him if his paper and radio station were the ones who ruined the other candidates' careers. People aren't stupid. The Conservatives and Labour will join forces to track down whoever's after them and the question they'll ask themselves is who stands to benefit from these scandals. They'll find the trail that leads back to him, back to us, and they'll crucify us."

"So let's go a step further. First we'll put it out online that Doyle has financial problems, that he wants to become mayor to put an end to these problems. That way there'll already be a bit of a hubbub. Then we'll send the papers to the media."

We were going to destroy another man. I admit that it didn't matter to me, nor did I hesitate for a minute. It was my job. They didn't just pay me to do it; I enjoyed pushing the boundaries, knowing I was cleverer than the others.

I could have told Philip I didn't have the stomach for it, that after the Frank Wilson thing I wasn't able to repeat a similar infamy with Doyle. But that's not how I felt. I wasn't struck with remorse for a single moment.

When the papers showing Jimmy Doyle's unpaid debts reached Radio East, Blake told Evelyn to follow up on the lead, even though I had subtly told him that if a case similar to Frank Wilson's were to crop up he shouldn't assign it to Evelyn. But Blake trusted her and was sure that if these papers were genuine his newspaper and radio station would have scored another bombshell.

The papers had been leaked several days earlier but they hadn't had the repercussions we'd been expecting. Philip said that it didn't matter, that sending the information in the mail anonymously acted as a firewall for us. We had to avoid anyone putting two and two together: everything that was happening was beneficial to Roy Parker.

"Blake wants me to publish all of Doyle's debts." Evelyn showed the papers to Bob, whom she was sleeping with every night.

"What are the odds?" Bob exclaimed.

"What are you trying to say?"

"That it's a real coincidence that another scandal should break just now involving the candidate with the greatest chance of winning, now that Frank Wilson's out of the running."

"I don't follow you."

"Yes, you do follow me, Evelyn. Of course you do. It's as clear as water. It's like Agatha Christie's *And Then There Were None*. They've already got the Conservative candidate out of the way. Now it's the Labour candidate's turn. There are two left—the one for the Lib Dems, good old Mr. Brown, and Roy Parker from the Rural Party. The Lib Dems have never won many votes in this town; their fielding a candidate is almost symbolic. That leaves us Roy Parker. He'll be the next mayor."

"You can't know that."

"Take it as given, Evelyn. I assume you've asked yourself about this period of prosperity our boss's businesses are going through. We've got advertising revenue, a group of investors who've bought shares . . . what a coincidence! Furthermore, Blake told you to follow Parker's campaign and suggested you give it favorable coverage. Do you want more proof?"

Evelyn got out of bed, feeling uneasy about what Bob had said. She knew he was right. She'd drawn the same conclusions, but didn't dare speak them aloud, not even to Bob.

"Let me remind you that we're not the first to hear of the Doyle case. The boss wants us to hold back. He told me to look and see if there's anything more. Anyway, you always have a conspiracy theory."

"You know I'm right. You ought to pay more attention to what I'm teaching you. A lot of stories reach newsrooms because someone wants to take revenge on someone or has a vested interest in something."

"You're saying that us journalists don't do the legwork?"

"Listen, darling, investigative journalism is a very serious thing and some of our colleagues put their lives on the line. But there are times someone provides a lead and one has to ask themselves if their interests are aligned with the general public's.

It can be for revenge, money, politics ... What's important is knowing how to tell the difference. You found an anonymous note in your mailbox that gave you Mrs. Hamilton's address. They put the fish on the line and we swallowed it."

"So we're someone's willing stooges, is that what you're trying to say?"

Bob shrugged and lit another cigarette as he watched Evelyn walk back and forth across the room. He observed that she seemed uncomfortable with herself. He stared at her legs, her best feature.

"No, of course not. Except in your case perhaps."

"You're a dick! How dare you tell me I'm just a stooge?"

"Because you are, Evelyn, and you know it."

"I am an investigative journalist," Evelyn replied, on the defensive.

"You? I don't think so, sweetheart. We have colleagues who go on the hunt without anybody telling them to, without being given a tip-off beforehand. When that's the case you usually find yourself facing a wall, which consists of the interests of the very paper you work for. Even so, they keep going. They press on and sometimes they jeopardize the 'system,' and other times their obsession ends up turning them into pariahs. Years ago I met one of the best in our field. You'll have heard of him. Neil Collins. He was freelance."

"Of course I know who Neil Collins is. His pieces were in so many of the major papers. He's famous."

"Yes, famous for his integrity, because he never made concessions to power, because he never gave in to threats, because he checked every single detail of what he published and nobody could deny that what he wrote was the truth."

"He doesn't publish anywhere anymore."

"They got rid of him for knowing too much. He was drinking too much. One night he met a guy in an underground casino whose tongue had been loosened by alcohol and cocaine. This guy worked for the Ministry of Defense and let slip that our beloved country was selling weapons to buyers it shouldn't. You know, those countries on the United Nations' blacklist. Neil took it upon himself to investigate and write the story, but none of the papers would buy it. The ramblings of a drunkard— that's what the editors of all the papers said. Who can trust a guy like Neil who always smells of alcohol and has a trace of white powder under his nose? But Neil didn't give up. He ended up publishing the story in a marginal magazine, but he published it. Since then no paper has bought a single article from him."

"What happened to him?"

"He's going through hell now. He's a pariah. Embittered. He can barely live with himself. That's how those in charge treat people; they ostracize those who get too close to their secrets."

"Like in the Watergate case?"

"That was pure journalism. Two guys found the story, followed the thread, and were able to unravel the whole thing. Bob Woodward and Carl Bernstein are two of the greats, proof that there are decent people in our line of work. But the world was a different place then, and although the newspaper magnates wanted to earn money, they also had what you might consider a romantic idea of journalism. They wanted to be loyal to their readers. Today the media is in the hands of investment groups for whom the truth is a mere inconvenience, especially if it could lose them money."

"You're too obsessed with the powers that be. You think everyone high up is full of shit."

"More than you know. That's the way things work. I've absolutely no doubt that this Roy Parker has something to do with what happened to Frank Wilson and what's currently happening to Jimmy Doyle."

"If things are as you say, why haven't they sent me another anonymous tip? I . . ."

"Yes, it would've been a real coup for you. Too risky. A young reporter who gets a lucky break once is believable, but twice in such a short span of time . . . They've been leaking the Doyle stuff to the competition."

"And now Blake is determined that I should play my part."

"You've got it easy. So far they've published a few documents supposedly leaked by an employee of the bank. We already know that Doyle spends what he doesn't have and that he's misappropriated party funds. It would appear that he likes to spoil his wife. Talk to the wife's friends, to local shopkeepers . . . You could write a piece with a more personal touch. Surely someone will tell you about Mr. and Mrs. Doyle's private life in lurid detail and how their standard of living was a surprise to their friends. Look at how the children live, what cars they drive, whether they get handouts from Daddy . . ."

"You're amazing!" Excited by Bob's suggestions, Evelyn had turned back to face the bed.

"You're very green, Evelyn."

"But I'm learning so much from you. Although I'd say that *you* have a very romanticized idea of journalism," Evelyn reproached him.

"Romanticized? You know, Evelyn, that article you wrote about those poor women has nothing to do with journalism."

"Of course it does! We fulfilled our duty to inform. The public has a right to know."

"Journalism is an obligation. We have a duty to the readers, to everyone who buys the paper each morning and has faith that we'll tell them the truth. But in order to fulfill that duty we have to steer clear of power, of the people in charge, to prevent them from manipulating us and protecting their interests. If even once you sell them your soul, you're no longer a journalist. I may romanticize journalism, but, you know, I do think it's worthwhile. I've known some of the best, journalists who haven't compromised, who've never betrayed their readers. Without journalists there would be no democracy, and the world would be a much worse place. We have colleagues who risk their lives because they believe in these principles, because their only mission is to tell people the truth. We've lost a lot of our own trying to bring the shit that goes on in the world to light—wars, weapons, drugs, corrupt politicians . . ."

"Stop giving me morality lessons."

"Calm down, girl. You'll go far."

Bob privately thought that she had more ambition than brains and that she lacked the raw talent to be a good journalist, and that there would always be a Blake to exploit her ambition. What Bob could never have imagined was that his hero Neil Collins was the one who had helped to dig up some of the dirt that had been essential for getting those candidates out of the picture.

Evelyn managed to get some of Mrs. Doyle's friends on the radio, who declared that they were devastated by the scandal, yet commented on the Doyles' expensive standard of living, especially given that they were Labour.

Jimmy Doyle appeared alone at a live press conference to announce that he was withdrawing from the race and that he understood the voters' anger. He admitted to having financial problems but swore he'd never swindled anyone.

Mrs. Doyle did not accompany him. Her friends told those who would listen that she was undergoing treatment for depression.

I was with my team watching the press conference on television. Philip could barely hide his satisfaction while Cathy, Janet, and Richard Craig remained silent.

"This whole thing stinks of foul play," Cathy declared.

"Foul play? What do you mean?" I asked.

"Come on, Thomas. You're not going to tell me it's a coincidence that two of the most important candidates in the county have had to withdraw from the race."

"Well, one of them was visiting prostitutes and the other was spending money he didn't have," Philip asserted.

"And who cares whether a candidate in a rural town uses prostitutes?" said my assistant, Richard.

"Well, since he's a Conservative . . ." Philip replied.

"I never imagined you to have such exacting moral standards."

"I'm not running for office, nor do I tell others how to live or what's right or wrong. It's not unreasonable for me to expect politicians to be what they claim to be," replied Philip angrily.

"We're not going to fight over this, are we?" Janet intervened.

Janet McCarthy couldn't bear arguments. She became nervous if any of us so much as raised our voice.

"What we need to do is keep working for our candidates. Roy and his guys have an opportunity here and they need to make the most of it. I wouldn't say that it was pure luck, but very nearly," I declared.

Cathy looked at me sideways. "Well, I doubt that those scandals were triggered by an innocent party."

"That's not our problem. Roy Parker hired us to make his campaign a success and things are going more and more in his favor. Cathy, I want you to give Suzi a media training refresher; she talks too much and could put her foot in it with the press. Janet, you need to prepare for Roy's television debate with Brown from the Lib Dems. Brown's an experienced man. He's at retirement age but it looks like he's set on becoming mayor. And Roy still isn't completely comfortable in front of the camera."

"But we've got several more important clients who need us during the last few days of campaigning," Cathy interrupted me.

"Realistically, the Rural Party is . . . well, it's not going to get anywhere," Richard declared, still on his high horse.

"Oh really? What makes you so sure?" I tried to appear unworried.

"You'll see, Thomas. They're outsiders, people from outside politics; they're not in the big leagues. I'm not saying that Roy won't be mayor, given the circumstances . . . and one or two of his friends might be successful too. But at this point both Labour and the Conservatives are wondering what happened in Derbyshire and I guarantee that both parties will go above and beyond to take the wind out of their sails. He's just too much of a bumpkin. He doesn't fit in," my assistant explained, very seriously.

"He doesn't fit in? What do you mean he doesn't fit in?" I asked, containing my anger.

"With the system. You'll see how the system swallows him up. It's a question of time," said Richard.

Richard was exasperating. In spite of his jeans, his deconstructed jackets, and his sneakers, which, admittedly, were Prada, he was still the little Conservative boy who had studied history at Oxford, but had finally settled on a career in PR because he thought it would be fun to do "something different."

A few days ago there had been photos of him in the papers, at a party where members of the royal family were also in attendance.

I decided not to argue with him. I wasn't inclined to be Roy's defender. It seemed unnecessary.

"Well, until the system swallows him up we have a contract with Parker. You're right, Cathy, we can't put more effort into the Rural Party's campaign. Anyway, the people we've assigned to them are doing a good job. I just ask that you take the time to speak to Suzi, even over the phone; you know how much she admires you. Really, you're the only one she listens to. Regarding the TV debate, I do need you to go, Janet. Find a train that leaves first thing and come back the same night. Roy will do fine with a few pointers."

Cathy looked at me in surprise. She clearly didn't understand me. Giving in without a fight didn't bother me. Only an idiot would have tried to stir up my team's suspicions any further. Janet was a simple soul, incapable of thinking ill of anyone, not even me, but it was clear that Cathy and Richard had an inkling about my part in the scandals.

As for Philip Sullivan, he maintained an uncomfortable silence, seemingly shocked by Cathy and Richard's suspicions.

Roy was elected mayor. We had considerable success. Of all the candidates whose campaigns we were running, only ten weren't elected.

We followed the election results from the office. I asked Maggie to arrange for some sandwiches and something a bit stronger than tea.

Even Mark Scott and Denis Roth dropped by our headquarters, the meeting room where we had several television screens set up and four or five interns listening to the radio coverage while following developments online.

"Well, things haven't turned out badly at all," Mark admitted.

"But we've winged it. Now that it's all over we'll have to think about setting up a more professional political and electoral publicity department," Denis announced.

I caught Mark looking at Cathy and I wondered whether they had already planned my exit and were about to tell me that Cathy would be the new department head. I didn't say anything, just in case, but let myself be congratulated by my team. At the moment we numbered more than twenty because we'd had to bring in external subcontractors.

Philip Sullivan was the most enthusiastic of us all. I guess he was worried about his future. He was friendly with Richard, but recently they had drifted apart, and he must have been wondering whether I had more of a past than a future at the Scott & Roth Agency.

"You have to come! Suzi wants to thank you in person for what you've done for us," Roy said on the telephone.

"I'll come as soon as I can. But I can't right now. I've got too much work."

"Then quit and come and work exclusively for me. We're on to phase two now. Remember that I want a seat in Parliament. We need to get to work immediately."

"Come on, Roy, you haven't even been sworn in as mayor yet. Don't be in such a hurry. The only way you'll make it to London is by doing a good job at the local level, and given the situation there it's not going to be easy for you. We'll see whether your stint as mayor doesn't prove the Peter principle."

"Peter? Who's Peter? Listen, don't tell me to read more weird stuff like that book, *The Art of War,* by the Chinese guy . . . Forget about Peter and come to Derbyshire. We need to celebrate and talk about the future."

"I can't, Roy. I'll call you as soon as possible."

I let a couple of days pass without answering Roy's calls. I didn't want to talk to him in front of Mark and Denis, or any of my team members. Despite the fact that my phone never stopped ringing and Maggie kept telling me that Roy had called to speak to me, I focused on dealing with other clients, the ones from "the system," as Richard would say. Roy could wait.

4

Over the next two years I settled into monotony. My department grew larger, always under Mark Scott's distrustful gaze.

It was about two in the morning on a Thursday. I'd been wandering around my apartment for a while and was on my second whiskey when the telephone made me jump. If it was Roy I'd tell him to go to hell, I thought, but it wasn't him. My father's number had come up on the screen. It was nine at night in New York, what could he want? I hadn't spoken to him for two or three months. I imagined him sitting in his office with a glass of cognac in hand, wondering how I was getting on. He didn't usually call me. Nor did I often call home. I didn't have anything to say to them and our conversations, although brief, struck me as absurd. I hesitated before picking up.

"Thomas." My father's tone of voice unnerved me.

"Yes?"

"Please excuse the time. I know it's very late in London. I must have woken you. But . . . you have to come. Your mother is dying."

I remained silent. Had he just said that my mother was dying?

"I'm sorry—I'm sorry to give you this bad news."

"What happened?" I asked. I felt strange, as if my father's words had nothing to do with me.

"Cancer. They diagnosed her with lung cancer a year ago. They've operated on her twice and she's been through chemo and radiotherapy . . . But none of it's worked. She's dying."

We remained silent. I needed to process my father's words and he was giving me the time to do so.

"So she fell sick a year ago," I murmured.

"Yes. She was the one who realized something wasn't right. She asked one of the doctors at the hospital to do a scan and the result was positive. Cancer in her left lung. Your mother's always been a heavy smoker, and so . . ."

I was aware of that, but what I had to take in was that she was dying. I wasn't really sure what I felt right then, but I realized that I didn't feel any pain, or at least that kind of pain that other people feel when they're about to lose their mothers.

"She didn't want us to tell you. She said that you needed to live your life, that it was unfair to clip your wings and make you come back. But now . . . She's been in the hospital for the last month but she's asked her doctor to let her come home. If you'd been able to hear that conversation . . . Your mother said, 'Dr. Cameron, you've done everything possible. Let me die in peace at home. They'll take care of me. All I ask is that you ensure I'm not in pain.' Your mother is a good nurse. She's seen a lot and nobody can lie to her about something like this."

"What do you want me to do?" I asked.

"She'd like to say goodbye to you. Things have never been easy between you two, but . . . well, she's your mother. She loves you and you love her."

"No. To be honest, I don't love her." The whiskey made me more honest than usual.

"Son! You can't say that. You're both strong characters and that's caused you to clash, but of course you love her! As she loves you, there's no doubt about it."

"You may not have doubts, but I do. And, honestly, nor do I care. I may have cared once, but, in any case, I don't care now."

"Thomas! I can't believe you're saying this. She's your mother. You're talking about your mother."

"Yes, I'm talking about her, and you know what, Dad? I have absolutely no desire to pretend that I'm distraught. I'm not. The last few days have been exhausting and it's two in the morning here. The only thing I need is to finish my drink and go to bed."

"You have to come." My father's voice was pleading.

"Why? She's going to die whether I'm there or not. She doesn't need me there to die."

"I'm going to forget you said that. You're a man now. Don't fly off the handle like you did when you were a little boy. You have a responsibility to her, to us. You can't let her go without having the chance to speak to you."

"I'm not promising anything. I'll call you later."

I hung up the phone. I couldn't stand the tone of supplication in my father's voice. I poured myself another generous measure of whiskey and downed it in one gulp.

I was honest with my father, but should I have been? If only for his sake, I should have seemed more caring, said something like, "Don't worry, Dad, I'll pack my suitcase and go to the airport. I'll take the next plane to New York. You should have called me sooner. If I'd known she had cancer, I would have come." But I didn't say any of that, nor did it cross my mind that I should have.

Not ten minutes later, my phone began to ring again. My grandfather James's number was on the screen. I didn't answer the call and chose to keep drinking.

How much did I drink that night? I don't know, but it was more than I could handle. I wasn't even able to put myself to bed. I collapsed on the sofa and that's where I stayed. It wasn't until ten in the morning that my phone's insistent ringing woke me.

"Have you died? No, of course you haven't. Take a shower and come in as soon as possible. Mark Scott's been expecting you in his office for two hours and you're not doing yourself any favors by keeping him waiting. Oh! And your father and your grandfather have called at least ten or twelve times. It seems . . . Well, have they told you that your mother isn't well? Thomas? Can you hear me?"

Maggie's voice was cutting a path through the thick fog the alcohol had left in my brain. But I was still drunk and the words seemed reluctant to leave my mouth.

"Thomas! Listen, stop this nonsense and get going. I've reserved you a seat on the flight that leaves for New York at six. You've just about got time to come in and speak to Scott and get to the airport, so you'd best bring your suitcase with you."

I looked around and found myself lying on the living-room floor next to a couple of empty whiskey bottles and a broken glass. The ice bucket was on the floor too, and there were splashes of water and whiskey everywhere. My right hand felt sticky and as my senses returned I became aware that I smelled of sweat, vomit, and stale alcohol. I needed to get up but my head hurt too much and my arms and legs didn't want to obey me. In the end I dragged myself to the bathroom and managed to get myself into the shower.

My phone rang incessantly, and this helped me remember that Maggie had called me and told me something important, but what could it have been?

When I got out of the shower things still weren't entirely clear to me, nor did I feel better, but it seemed that I could walk without my legs giving way. I fell onto the bed wrapped in a towel, trying to get my mind in order.

I made an effort and found a couple of aspirin, which I swallowed with a gulp of water. I don't know how I did it, but I succeeded in making myself some strong coffee and putting a slice of bread in the toaster. It was half past one when I left the apartment with the worst hangover of my life.

Mark Scott hadn't yet come back from lunch. Maggie warned

me that he was angry and had seemed to calm down only when she told him that my mother was sick and I needed to fly to New York.

"Tell the team I want to see them," I instructed Maggie.

Cathy and Richard were the first to arrive. I was surprised to see Cathy looking as fresh as if she had just stepped out of the shower. Nor did Richard show any signs of fatigue. Only Janet McCarthy and Philip Sullivan, who arrived soon after, seemed to have any trace of tiredness on their faces.

"Right. Tell me how things are going. I assume you spoke nice and calmly to some of the head honchos this morning. I don't remember whether it was Mark or Denis who called me yesterday to say that it was necessary to restructure the electoral department and that we would talk today. This is a sign that we haven't been doing at all badly."

They listened to me without much interest, as if they weren't really present. In spite of the hangover I realized that I was the one who was missing something.

"Is there something I should know? You're quieter than usual."

"Haven't you spoken to Mark yet?" Cathy asked with a smile that surprised me.

"I just arrived . . . Last night . . . Well, I spent last night drinking."

"Right . . . Well, it would be best if you spoke with Mark as soon as possible," said Richard.

"Why don't you tell me what's going on? You seem very content, Cathy. Have you managed to coax Mark into making you head of the electoral department? I've always said there's nothing a good pair of legs and a nice set of tits won't get you."

I thought Cathy was going to hit me because she got up and stood right in front of me, but she didn't. She smiled before speaking.

"You're disgusting, Thomas. You look terrible and your

breath . . . phew! You stink. But you're not just disgusting because of that, but because you're made of shit and there's not a single centimeter of you that's not made of the worst kind of shit. You're an opportunist; you've got no talent to offer other people. The good thing is that this is something that quickly becomes obvious. All it takes is a couple of conversations with you to work out that you're a miserable bastard. Didn't your parents love you when you were little, Thomas? Is that why you're a son of a bitch?"

"Come on, Cathy, leave it." Richard took her by the arm and pulled her back into her seat.

Janet was pale. And Philip Sullivan looked at me in shock.

"Ooh, rebellion among the ranks." I didn't have time to say more because Maggie came in to tell me that Mark was back from his lunch break and was waiting for me.

"And I've booked a taxi for four o'clock. It will give you time to get to the airport and catch that plane to New York. I promised your grandfather, such a charming gentleman."

Mark Scott had a sour look on his face when I entered his office. I was uncomfortable.

"It's not very professional to turn up to work and . . . well, to turn up to work in this state. You look a mess."

"Yes, I got drunk. I drank until I collapsed to the floor senseless," I replied in a challenging tone.

"Denis and I have been thinking about making some changes. We think Cathy is the right person to head the electoral department. She's got class, she's discerning, and she'd never bend the rules of the game. Do you understand?"

"I don't know what you're talking about, Mark, all I understand is that you're giving me a kick up the backside. Is that right?"

"Denis spoke to a couple of his friends in Westminster. I won't say we didn't hear the rumors two years ago but . . . in the end we weren't diligent. We should have moved you out of the electoral department and not let . . ."

"What, Mark? What shouldn't you have let happen?"

"You used highly unorthodox methods to ensure that your friend Roy won in his constituency."

"Really? Who says that?"

"No one can prove anything, but . . . it's difficult to believe that Roy's opponents just happened to be struck by scandals right before the elections."

"Oh come on! You're telling me this two years later. So it seems I'm responsible for the fact that Frank Wilson was a hypocrite, one of those men who preach one thing and practice quite another. He was the one visiting a brothel, not me. And Jimmy Doyle, the honorable Labour candidate who liked to charge gifts for his wife to the party donors and spend money he didn't have on extravagant fripperies. Was that my fault too? Roy Parker won because he didn't have skeletons in his closet. It was that simple. But your friends from the Conservative Party and the Labour Party can't stand people from outside the system taking their seats. So they've dug around in the past and decided to ask you for my head, and you're going to give it to them. How brave you two are!"

Mark seemed to hesitate. I'd defended myself well and he was a decent man, so perhaps he was wondering whether he might be treating me unfairly.

"We're not going to sack you, Thomas. We're just going to give you a different role. Cathy knows the ins and outs of British politics better than you—when all's said and done, you're American. But we want to keep you on board. Maggie's told me that you need to go to New York, that your mother . . . well, she told me that she's dying. You go and see her and don't worry about anything else but her. Work can wait. You take all the time you need."

"I'll do that, Mark, I'll do that."

I didn't want to go to New York, but I couldn't come up with a better option just then; it was preferable for me to absent myself for a few days. In the meanwhile, I would come up with something, either to get rid of Cathy or to get myself a new job if I didn't like what Mark and Denis had to offer.

"You haven't brought a suitcase." Maggie scolded me when I got back from Mark's office.

"Yes, I know, but it doesn't matter. I've got clothes in New York. I don't need to take anything with me," I said without conviction.

"Rich kid. The taxi's waiting. Will you come back?"

"Why wouldn't I? Don't assume I'm done for," I replied grumpily.

"Right. Give my regards to your father and grandfather. They really did seem like lovely gentlemen."

"That's got nothing to do with me."

"Yes, I can believe that."

I left the agency like a robot. I could still feel the effects of the alcohol. My head hurt and I couldn't think clearly. "I don't think I'll go to New York," I said to myself, but the doorman opened the door of the taxi and I found myself on the way to the airport.

"They told me you need to catch a plane at six. I'll do my best to get you there in time," said the taxi driver.

I was about to protest, to tell him to take me to my apartment, that I had no intention of boarding a flight. But I didn't because at that point I felt so tired that I didn't care about anything.

I fell asleep and the taxi driver woke me when we got to Heathrow.

"If you hurry you'll catch that plane."

I was suddenly aware that if I went into the airport I would end up flying to New York. I didn't want to have a debate with myself or even to think. I was tired, my stomach was heaving, and the only thing I wanted was to sit down and go to sleep.

I went to the British Airways business check-in. They gave me my boarding pass and urged me to hurry. "All the passengers are already on board except you. We'll let them know that you're going to board, sir," an airline employee told me with all the friendliness she could muster, though obviously my lateness annoyed her. But I didn't bother running. I didn't care whether I caught the plane or not.

I fell asleep as soon as I sat down and gave no sign of life for seven hours. The flight attendant shook me gently to tell me we had landed.

I didn't have a single dollar on me, just some pounds sterling and my credit cards. I had to change some money to pay the taxi driver for the ride to my parents' apartment. That was when I got angry about being there, for letting myself be carried along and boarding a plane I didn't want to take due to a strange inertia caused by the alcohol.

I was exhausted and the last thing I wanted to do was see my mother. But that's what I was there for.

María, the old nanny, opened the door and made an exclamation that wasn't exactly one of joy.

"You've come! For the love of God . . . I'll let your father know. The doctor is with your mother. They're giving her oxygen."

She left me alone in the hall. I felt strange being in the home that had once been mine. If Jaime hadn't appeared at that very moment I think I would have left.

"Thomas! Thank God you're here! Come on, come on, it would be best for you to see Mama as soon as possible. She never stops asking for you. We had to call the doctor because she was drowning for lack of oxygen. Dad's with her. He must have told you there's nothing they can do . . ." Seeking consolation, Jaime threw his arms around me.

"I should take a shower first . . . I'm not exactly presentable."

"No, no, you need to see her right away. She's worried about dying without saying goodbye to you. She'll feel better when she knows you're here. Dad said that you might not be able to come because of work, but I told him you'd never forgive yourself if you let Mama die without hugging her first."

That's how Jaime was. He thought that the rest of humanity

shared his goodwill. He seemed determined to ignore how much of a dick I was.

"Where's your suitcase?" María had reappeared.

"I didn't bring a suitcase."

"Right. Well then . . . ?"

"I assume there're still some clothes in my wardrobe. Or don't I have a bedroom or a wardrobe anymore?"

"Your mother never let us do anything to your room. It's just how you left it," María replied grumpily.

That day, when Jaime opened the door to my parents' room, I learned that the arrival of death is preceded by a special odor.

My father was talking to the doctor in a low voice by the window. My mother had her eyes closed and behind the oxygen mask I could see how hard it was for her to breathe. A nurse was standing beside her.

Jaime pushed me toward the head of the bed without giving me time to greet my father. My brother wasn't prepared to wait a single minute to fulfill our mother's wishes.

I didn't know what to do. I didn't recognize my mother in that thin body with the hair shot through with gray and skin like old leather. It seemed to me that my mother wasn't in that lump of flesh.

She opened her eyes, and just then I saw a spark of what she had once been in her gaze. She didn't smile at me, but gave me a slight nod of recognition.

"Take her hand," Jaime told me in such a low voice I could barely hear him.

But I didn't. I didn't want to have her hand, which at that moment seemed unknown to me, between my own. It seemed like her fingers had grown thinner and her nails were so short it was difficult for me to believe they were the hands of my mother, whose hands were always neat, with painted nails.

I felt her eyes studying me. I held her gaze. Jaime pushed me again and I almost fell onto the bed. I felt one of her hands on my arm.

"How are you?" I asked, for something to say.

She made a move to take off her oxygen mask but the nurse stopped her.

"Please, Mrs. Spencer! Wait awhile; I'll take the mask off for you as soon as your breathing's back to normal."

The doctor had left the room and my father was behind me.

"It's a relief to have you here. Thank you, Thomas. It'll do both your mother and us good to know that you're here."

We stayed by her bed for some time, looking at her without saying anything, which made me nervous. I was tired, I needed a shower, and I didn't like the role of prodigal son.

My mother seemed to have fallen asleep and the nurse suggested we let her rest.

"Her most recent morphine injection is taking effect. She'll sleep peacefully knowing that her eldest son is here."

My father gestured that we should go to his office. Up to then he'd made no move to embrace me; he had barely spoken to me.

"Well, it seems like you still have a tiny bit of conscience left" were his first words.

My father had never spoken to me with such anger, although perhaps there was more disappointment than anything else in his voice. He finally seemed to have realized and accepted what a bad person I was.

I shrugged my shoulders. My brother intervened, ready to avoid any confrontations.

"Dad, the main thing is that Thomas is here and that will help Mama. This is not the moment for recriminations."

"Your grandfather and I had to beg your secretary to convince you to come," my father complained, paying no attention to Jaime.

"Yes, you must have been very convincing because she practically put me on the plane herself. The truth is, I don't understand why my mother's so anxious to see me. We've never got along well and . . . I don't know if we've ever loved each other."

"How dare you say that?" My father had stood up. He was shaking and he seemed on the verge of hitting me.

"Dad! Thomas! Please! Mama is dying. The only thing that's important is that she dies in peace. That's the only thing we can do for her. She's always been aware of everything. If we get embroiled in arguments she'll know it. Can't you make her happy in her last few hours?" begged my brother.

"You sound like a priest," I told him disdainfully.

"I don't care what you think of me, Thomas. Say what you like, but I am going to ask that you don't make Mama suffer. The doctor says it's a matter of days or even hours."

"I'll take the first shift tonight. I'll wake you at four," my father said to Jaime and left the office.

"We divide the time between us so that one of us is always with her. Grandma Stella and Grandpa Ramón come first thing in the morning. They spend all day here, but they're old and Dad insists they go home to sleep. Uncle Oswaldo comes as soon as he gets out of work. He's very upset. I imagine that you'll want to take your turn to be with Mama."

"Right now I'm going to sleep. I'm tired. And we'll talk tomorrow. I assume María's got my room ready."

"Knowing her, that seems likely," Jaime replied.

If they hoped to see me sad, they were mistaken. I still didn't know why I was there and I wasn't yet sure I wouldn't decide to return to London tomorrow, as soon as I'd gotten my head together after sleeping.

I woke early, at six o'clock. Plagued with nightmares, I hadn't slept well. After taking a bath I went to the kitchen, where María was making breakfast.

"There's toast and coffee," she told me without enthusiasm.

"And who's this tray for?" I asked, watching María put a coffeepot, a creamer, and several slices of toast on a tray.

"It's for Jaime. He's been with your mother since four. He needs to eat breakfast."

I poured myself some coffee and ate two slices of toast with butter and bitter orange marmalade while I thought about whether to go to my parents' room or busy myself doing something else. I had no desire to act as nurse.

"What about the nurse?" I asked María.

"The one who works nights just left, but the day nurse is here."

"And where does my father sleep?"

"In the guest room. They've arranged your parents' room so that your mother could receive the same care as in the hospital."

The doorbell rang and I decided to open the door. To my disgust I found myself face-to-face with my grandmother Stella and my grandfather Ramón, who tried to kiss me as they thanked God I was there.

"I knew you would come. A son never abandons his mother. I've always told my daughter, 'Your Thomas loves you, he'll come, you'll see,' and here you are. See, Ramón, wasn't I right?" said Grandma Stella, punctuating her speech with her arms.

I got away as soon as I could. I never could stand those two old fogies, let alone just then, when it seemed that my grandfather's indigenous features had become more prominent, which reminded me that destiny had dealt me a bum hand when it came to DNA. My brother clearly had predominantly Spencer DNA: pale skin, blond hair, tall and elegant.

Returning to my room, I considered leaving. My mother wanted to see me, and she did. She couldn't ask more of me than that. She knew better than anyone else that I wouldn't play the part of the prodigal son returned to make good, settling myself at her bedside to hold her hand or help her drink. I was dialing the number for British Airways when Jaime entered without knocking.

"I didn't invite you in."

"I don't care. Come see Mama. She's worse. I've just woken

Dad and called Dr. Cameron. I've also called Grandma Dorothy and Grandpa James and Uncle Oswaldo."

"What about Aunt Emma? Haven't you called her?" I asked sarcastically.

"She's already on her way over. But you're the one Mama wants to have near her. She asked for you as soon as she opened her eyes."

I saw then that Jaime was something more than the little angelic blond boy I'd assumed him to be. There was a determination in him that surprised me. I followed him to my mother's room, where the nurse was struggling to keep Grandma Stella quiet.

"Please, don't overwhelm her. She knows you're here. She doesn't need to open her eyes to know that much."

But my mother seemed to have sensed my presence, because at that very moment she opened her eyes and gestured me toward her with her hand. I went unwillingly. I was shocked to hear her voice.

"I'm dying," she said in a whisper.

"Yes," I replied.

My brother elbowed me in the ribs. There was deep anger in his eyes. But I wasn't going to take part in this macabre game of telling a dying person that she still had life ahead of her. And especially not my mother. I felt no compassion toward her.

The nurse asked us to leave the room while she tidied my mother up and looked at me with aversion.

"You can stay if you want to help me lift her, ma'am," she told Grandma Stella.

"I'll tell María to come," Jaime offered.

"There's no need. Let me help her," my grandmother insisted.

We went into the hallway. My father came over, his eyes red. He seemed exhausted. He couldn't have had more than three hours of sleep. If I'd harbored any good feelings I would have felt pain upon seeing him like that, facing my mother's imminent death.

Grandma Dorothy and Grandpa James and Aunt Emma arrived at the same time as the doctor. He seemed as tired as the others. He went in to examine my mother and when he came out he told my father that there was only one solution: to increase the dosage of morphine, although that, he added, "means accelerating her passing, but . . . well, it's up to you to decide. If I increase her dose she'll fall asleep and there'll be nothing to do but wait for the end. Give it some thought."

Jaime told María to serve everyone coffee in the living room while he and I spoke with our father.

"It's a decision we need to think about and make between us, whatever happens," he told the others.

"She's my daughter, I have a say in it too," protested Grandpa Ramón, upset.

"You're right. You come too; María, tell Grandma Stella."

We went to the study. My father seemed dazed. He sat down in his old leather chair without looking at us.

"We need to think about Mama—just her, not ourselves," Jaime told us.

"And does that mean we should let them end her life?" Grandpa Ramón raised his voice angrily.

"I won't let them kill my daughter!" shouted Grandma Stella.

"Please! Don't say such things! How can you think that any of us want Mama to die? It's a case of . . . The morphine will shorten her life by a few hours. It's a case of letting her go in the most comfortable way possible, without the anxiety of being unable to breathe." Jaime tried to hold back his tears as he spoke.

"No, no, and no! I will not let you kill my daughter. God alone is the master of our lives and He will decide exactly when He wants to take her to Him." Now it was Grandpa Ramón who was shouting.

My father continued to stare into space, uninvolved in the discussion. I felt like a distant spectator, although I was irritated by my grandparents' histrionics.

The study door opened and María announced that Uncle Oswaldo had arrived.

My mother's brother had never managed to feel comfortable in our home, in spite of my father's and my brother's friendliness.

"May I come in?" asked Uncle Oswaldo in a trembling voice.

"Go ahead, Uncle. Perhaps you can help me convince my grandparents that we need to prevent Mama from suffering any further," said Jaime.

"Yes . . . yes . . . Hello, Thomas, I'm glad to see you," he babbled.

I didn't move from my seat. I nodded to him and continued sitting there, ready to see how this standoff between my brother and our grandparents would end.

Jaime explained to Uncle Oswaldo what the doctor had said and how the spasms were making Mama feel as though she were drowning.

"I don't know what to say . . . To think that if she has the injection she won't wake up again . . . No, no, it's not for us to make that decision. It doesn't seem right to me. The doctor should decide what's best for my sister. I couldn't live with myself knowing that I'd decided to cut her life short, even if it were for her benefit," Uncle Oswaldo eventually said.

"And you, Thomas, what do you think we should do?" asked my father in a barely audible voice.

"You're talking about euthanasia. It's up to you to decide. I've never gotten along with Mama, so I wouldn't be objective making a decision for her."

My reply shocked them. My father seemed to shrink, sinking into his chair. Jaime looked stunned. As for my grandparents, my words left them dazed. Only Uncle Oswaldo confronted me.

"She's your mother, Thomas. She hasn't been a bad mother. She's always worried about you. You can't wash your hands of this as if it has nothing to do with you. We need to make a decision . . . I don't feel able to make it because I love my sister Carmela so much that ... but you ... you can't keep your distance from all this just because you two have had your differences."

"Yes, yes, I can. Don't count on me to play the part of the sorrowful son or, more importantly, to make a decision about something I don't feel concerns me: whether or not she lives a few hours more or how she dies."

I didn't realize my father had gotten up until I felt his hand collide with my cheek. It was the first time he'd ever hit me. Until then my father had never laid a finger on me, no matter what I'd done. It wasn't so much the pain as the surprise that left me motionless. When I did react I got up and was going to leave the study when my brother, Jaime, stepped in front of me and took hold of my arm.

"Stop being such a dick. We know you're good at it, but we're not going to let you make one of your scenes right now. You're going to participate in this decision whether you like it or not."

Jaime was squeezing my forearm. I had never imagined my brother to be so strong. I thought he might punch me.

"You're a coward. You don't want to take responsibility. You're trying to clear your conscience and put this onto the rest of us. Do what you think best, it's all the same to me. But don't hide behind the grown-ups' legs like you did when you were little. And now, would you kindly let go of me?" I said to him disdainfully.

"You will stay here until we reach a decision," Jaime said, pushing me toward the armchair.

"All right, I'll stay here watching while you fight with one another."

María suddenly came in without knocking; she was very nervous.

"The doctor says that Mrs. Spencer wants to speak with you all."

My father got up so quickly that by the time we began following him he had already entered my mother's room.

"Carmela, are you all right?"

"Juan, my darling, I'm dying," she said in Spanish.

"No . . . No . . . I won't allow it . . ."

"I've seen a lot of people in the state I'm in now. I've asked the doctor to . . . I don't want to suffer, Juan. I know that there's nothing left for me now. I recognize the signs of the end. Let me decide."

My father collapsed to his knees by the bed, desperately clinging to my mother's hands, kissing them.

"No. No, I won't let this happen. I won't let you go. Hold on. You have to hold on. You're strong. You've always been the strongest one in this family. We'll go to the hospital . . . Yes, yes, right now. Doctor, call an ambulance. They'll look after her there, they'll be able to do something . . ."

"Juan . . . Juan . . . Don't move me. Don't make me die in a hospital room . . . I'd rather my last view be of this room, our room, Juan . . . please . . ."

The doctor came over and helped my father to his feet. He looked at the nurse and she left the room to prepare the morphine injection.

"She's capable of making this decision," the doctor told us, lowering his voice.

"Juan, darling, tell my parents to come here . . . I want to say goodbye to everyone. Is Thomas here? You know I need to talk to him, that I can't go without telling him . . ."

"No! Let it go, Carmela."

"Please!" begged my mother.

My paternal grandparents were the first to go to her. Grandpa James and Grandma Dorothy smiled at my mother as if they were merely saying goodbye for the day and expecting to see her tomorrow.

"Dearest Carmela . . . we love you . . . You know that, right?

You've been a joy to us," said my grandfather as he squeezed her hand. Grandma Dorothy gave her a kiss on the cheek and stroked her hair.

"Thank you . . . Take care of Juan, your John . . . although it sounds better in Spanish, don't you think, Dorothy? In the beginning you always used to frown when you heard me call him Juan."

"Of course, darling, Juan sounds better . . . We'll always call him that."

"Thank you . . . thank you for . . . You were always very good to me and Thomas. Thank you."

At that moment it became clear that something was going on concerning me, but I couldn't work out what it was. Why was it strange that Grandma Dorothy and Grandpa James had been good to me? I thought quickly, but I couldn't figure it out.

Grandma Dorothy and Grandpa James moved away from the bed, giving way to Aunt Emma. Always so confident and calm, she seemed unable to control her weeping.

"Carmela . . . Carmela . . ."

"Emma, will you take care of Juan and my sons? If anyone can, you can. You're so strong. They're going to need you. Especially Juan. It'll take him the most time to get used to the idea . . . Will you do it?"

My aunt seized my mother's hands and kissed them impulsively, as if she were a saint.

"Don't say anything, Carmela. Of course I will . . . I'll do what you want. Don't worry about Juan, or Jaime or Thomas, they'll get through this. You'll see . . ."

My mother closed her eyes as she tried to hold back a coughing fit. The doctor came over to put the oxygen mask on her.

"You need to give her a few minutes. She needs oxygen."

"Should we leave the room?" asked Jaime.

"Move away from the bed . . . Give her some air," the doctor instructed.

I didn't want my mother to die, not at that moment. She had told my father that she had something to say to me and he had begged her not to do it. Whatever it was, I wanted to know. I went over to the bed.

"Can I speak to my mother?" I asked the doctor.

"Not right now. I've just told you. You need to let her rest for at least a few minutes."

"Have they given her the injection?" My question was a blow to the ears of everyone present. Jaime came over and dragged me out of the room.

"You're plain wicked! How dare you say something like that in front of her?"

"Leave me alone! Anyway, she knows she's dying, she's saying goodbye, or haven't you realized?"

"You're the one who doesn't realize what's going on . . . If you say something like that again, I swear, I'll crack your head open!"

I went back into the room thinking that Jaime might follow through on his threat at any moment.

My mother was very agitated when we entered the room. She seemed to calm down when she saw Jaime and me again. She smiled at Jaime and shot me one of those severe looks I had grown used to during my childhood.

Grandpa James grabbed me by the arm, forcing me to stay by the door.

"Don't you move from this spot until the doctor tells you to go over. And for once in your life, try to rise to the occasion. She might not matter to you, but the rest of us here love her and we will do whatever's necessary for her to pass in peace. She deserves that," my grandfather declared.

It suddenly seemed to me that my grandfather was talking to me as if I were a stranger. There wasn't a single drop of affection in his voice. I felt unsettled. They weren't going to let me dodge the duty my mother seemed to have established for me.

Uncle Oswaldo, crying, went over to my mother. My mother began speaking Spanish again.

"Oswaldo, my brother, what are these tears? Listen, don't come to me crying. It makes it harder for me."

"Juan's right, we should get you to the hospital," my uncle babbled.

"Why don't you want me to die in my home?"

"You don't have to die!" he shouted with a great sob.

"I'm already more on the other side than I am here. There's nothing that can be done to cure this. One day, perhaps, but not yet. I have never fooled myself since the day they diagnosed me. There you have it, little brother, this is what happens when you smoke . . . You should learn from my example and quit. You could do that for me . . . Do you know how much I love you?"

"Carmela! Carmela! Don't do this." Oswaldo was crying like a little boy, bent over the bed while she stroked his hair.

"Be good, hey! Don't go upsetting our parents. Maybe you'll stay in this job awhile and get married."

My uncle was crying and sniffling. The doctor went over and led him away from the bed. My mother was having trouble breathing again.

It was her parents' turn and I feared the worst. Grandma Stella had already been crying for a while and so noisily that we could barely hear what my mother was saying to the others.

"My daughter! Oh, my daughter! Oh, darling of my heart! Don't go! We're not going to let you go!"

"Mama . . . Mama . . . please, don't cry . . . Darling Mama, don't break my heart . . . Please don't cry . . . You tell her, Papa, tell her not to cry . . ."

Grandpa Ramón was weeping in silence. You could barely see his clouded eyes through his tears. He was trying to hold my grandmother back so she didn't throw herself onto my mother. He had his arm wrapped tightly around her, but Grandma Stella paid no attention to anything but her desolation.

I felt there was something morbid about this scene, my mother saying goodbye to us all, one by one. It seemed like a piece of theater where she was the principal character and the rest of us just had bit parts.

The doctor had difficulty moving my grandparents away from the bedside. They would barely have taken a step back when Grandma Stella would move forward to embrace my mother again. This scene lasted several minutes, which seemed in keeping with the histrionics typical of their people.

My mother had the strength to lift her hand toward Jaime. There was no doubt that he was the one she was waiting for, because she smiled as if she were seeing an archangel.

Jaime went over, smiling back at her, and kissed her several times, gently stroking her face and hair.

"I love you, Mama. You're the best mother in the world."

"And you're the best son I could ever have dreamed of. You've made me so happy!" she murmured.

I felt the old envy roiling in my stomach once more. There were the two of them, displaying a love that was above what either of them could show any other person. Jaime was my mother's darling boy and, for him, she was the perfect mother, someone who had always offered him a refuge. They were united as neither would ever be with anyone else.

My mother held him to her for some time, whispering something in his ear. Jaime squeezed her hands while listening to her with a rapt expression. Not even the doctor dared interrupt, despite her needing the oxygen mask at one point. But as soon as she was feeling better, she hugged Jaime again and continued whispering who knows what to him.

After a while, holding back his tears, Jaime moved away from the bed, indicating that I should go over. My brother asked everyone else to leave the room.

"We'll come back in a bit, but right now Mama wants to talk to Thomas alone."

For a moment I felt unable to go over to the bed. I became

aware of the sweat running down my back. I hesitated. Jaime took me by the arm and tugged me over until I was in front of my mother. Then he left, along with the rest of the family. So did the doctor and the nurse.

"If she looks like she's having trouble breathing, put the mask on her and give her a few minutes to recover. She's making a huge effort . . . Let us know if she needs us," the doctor said.

I nodded while trying not to crumble under the intensity of my mother's gaze. My eyes were stinging.

"Thomas . . ." She found it difficult to speak. She was exhausted.

"Yes."

"Thank you for coming from London. I had to talk to you before . . . before leaving. I couldn't die in peace without telling you something."

I wanted to leave the room. Right then I wasn't sure I wanted to hear whatever it was she was about to say. But I said nothing and waited. I didn't take her hand, nor did she move to give it to me like she had done with the others, fearing I might reject her.

"You've been my biggest nightmare . . . I assume I've been yours too."

Her statement left me speechless. My mother had just put what we'd been to each other into words.

"You've paid for a mistake . . . My mistake . . . Yes, you're the one who's paid for it. Without bearing any responsibility. And I understand if you can't forgive me for that." She closed her eyes for a few seconds.

"I don't know what you're talking about," I replied curtly.

"It was during my first year at college. The Hispanic students had a party. You know what those college parties are like . . . Alcohol and drugs . . . I drank too much. I won't give you the details, but . . . well, I was a virgin before that night. I was drunk and . . . there was a moment when the alcohol meant I didn't know what I was doing or what others were doing to me . . . Several boys . . . well, they raped me. I resisted but I couldn't do anything, I was so drunk . . . When I came to I found myself in the hospital. Someone had taken me, given my state . . . an alcoholic coma . . . The next month my period didn't come. I was worried but my friends told me that nobody gets pregnant the first time. They and I both knew that wasn't really the case, that it could happen. It happened to me. I didn't know whose it was. I didn't know how many boys had . . . I didn't know. My friends didn't know either; they'd had as much to drink as I had. I couldn't identify anyone. Yes, they might have been some of the boys who laughed when they saw me, but I didn't have any proof. I wondered whether to have an abortion. My mother realized what was going on. She's always been a good Catholic, so she made it clear that she would not let me go through with it. My father . . . well, I can still feel the sting of the slap he gave me when he found out. But I continued with the pregnancy and you don't know what it cost me. I wasn't sure, I hadn't chosen to become a mother and, furthermore, I didn't know who your father might be. But all this changed the day you were born and the nurse put you in my arms. My parents loved you from the very first, and although I hadn't chosen to be a mother, I was proud of you and thought you were the most beautiful baby in the world. You and I were irreversibly linked and I no longer felt you were a burden I couldn't bear.

"My mother told me I should continue my studies and become a nurse as I had always wanted; she would take care of you. And so it was during the first year of your life. I studied, worked whatever jobs I could get, and even had a few nights out with my friends since my parents were looking after you."

She closed her eyes again. Each word she said cut her life shorter. She could barely speak.

"Sometimes I spent ages looking at you, trying to work out which of the boys on campus could be your father. But I couldn't see anything that marked you out. You could have been anyone's son.

"Then I met John . . . We fell in love. I think he's always loved me more. I didn't tell him I had a son until he asked me to marry him. Then I told him no, I couldn't, I had a son. I told him the whole truth. I thought he would leave once he found out what happened to me, that he wouldn't be interested in a girl who drank so much she passed out and was passed around . . . But John, my Juan, isn't like other people, he's a special man. He insisted on marrying me and told me he wanted to adopt you. 'Thomas will be my son too. From now on I don't want anyone to be able to think otherwise. He's our son, Carmela, ours,' he told me."

She started to cough. I knew she couldn't carry on. I put the oxygen mask on her like the doctor had told me to and wondered whether to call him or to wait. I wanted to know, I needed to know. After a few seconds my mother gestured to me to take the mask off and continued talking, although her voice was fainter and fainter.

"John has always treated you like a son. He's never treated you any differently from Jaime, who is his true son, or if he has, it's been to favor you. And he loves you, Thomas; your father, the only father you've ever had, truly loves you. When you started to grow up, I don't know why, but I seemed to irritate you . . . You wouldn't let me be close to you . . . I became depressed; I didn't understand your rejection. John insisted on sending me to a psychiatrist who specialized in these things; he said it was a way for us to understand what was happening. I went to therapy for two years, but it was a failure. I blamed myself for being unable to make you love me, for dreaming that you would be waiting to play with me when I got home, or for me to help you with your homework, but none of that ever happened.

"So, you see, I loved you but you didn't love me. I'm still surprised by your father's immense love in trying to understand, to help me. Another man would have been unable to live with my emotional highs and lows. I have to acknowledge that

I improved for a while when Jaime was born. That was when I felt the maternal instinct that you had never let me show explode inside of me. I couldn't stop smiling at my little one, couldn't stop wanting to hold him in my arms day and night. Nothing and no one were more important to me than him.

"I guess you realized my happiness at having Jaime right from the get-go . . . I didn't know what to do to get you to let me love you and you were determined to gain my attention. You needed me to pay attention to you, but when I tried, you would reject me.

"Yes, you can criticize me for throwing in the towel for a while, because I was spending hours with Jaime but almost didn't dare kiss you or try to hug you. I carry the lack of love you've shown me like an unbearable weight on my conscience, because I feel responsible. It's as though you somehow knew that . . . deep down, you were not a wanted child. I don't want your forgiveness because I know you can't forgive me. But I owe you an explanation and I beg one thing of you: I need to know the cause of the distance between us. I don't know if I'm doing you any good by telling you all this . . . Your father . . . Juan thinks I shouldn't be telling you, but you have the right to know. I don't want to die a coward for having been unable to tell you the truth."

My mother closed her eyes, I don't know whether it was because her effort had exhausted her or because she couldn't hold my gaze. I was so quiet that I could hear my breathing. I was trying to process everything my mother had told me. I had entered that room with one life and identity and I was going to leave with another.

I was unable to move. I could only contemplate my mother's agony. I asked myself what she was expecting me to do right then: to move closer and take her hand? Tell her I forgave her? I couldn't do it, so I stood motionless for some time. Then she opened her eyes and I thought I saw a tear run down her cheek.

"I'm sorry. It wasn't your fault but I made you pay the price for that damned night. If God exists, He'll send me to hell for that night."

She was finding it difficult to breathe and her voice was different. I remained in a state of shock, without speaking or moving, and I watched her, trying to find an answer inside myself.

I don't know how long we remained silent. I know I didn't do what I should have done. I should have reached out to her, given her a kiss, taken her hand, and said:

"Don't worry, Mama, I'm the one who should apologize for everything I've put you through. My behavior toward you has been appalling. You've been the best mother anyone could ever dream of; I wouldn't have wanted anyone else but you. Will you forgive me? I know I've made life very difficult for you, but you don't have anything to reproach yourself for. This is just the way I am. I'd like to be a better person, but . . . The only thing I regret is making you unhappy. I must thank you for giving me John as a father. I couldn't have had any better. I can't and I don't want to imagine any other father who isn't him.

"You've given me a good life, Mama; you've given me a family. It pains me so much that I wasn't able to show you how much I love you! Please don't worry; I'll take care of Dad and Jaime, but that won't be soon, because you have to get better. You have to fight to come out of this. I'll be here. I'll stay with you. I'll help you with your battle . . . You'll be able to get up soon . . . You'll see."

Then I would have embraced her and covered her face with kisses, trying to make up for lost time.

But I didn't do or say any of this. I won't say I wasn't tempted to. I hesitated. But it seemed as if I'd been nailed to the floor, there, at the foot of her bed. I felt sorry for her and for myself, but at the same time I didn't want to change direction, I couldn't, I didn't know how. I listened to her agitated breath and watched as she suffered. If she'd hoped for a word of comfort, she didn't hear it from me.

After a few minutes she opened her eyes and her gaze was filled with desolation. Once again she had failed in her attempt to be closer to me. Even on her deathbed, she had failed.

"Call the doctor. I can't take it anymore . . . Thank you, Thomas. Thank you for coming, for listening to me. I hope what I've said helps you find yourself, find the peace I've never had."

I walked out of the room and nearly collided with my father, who was glued to the door. He didn't even look at me but pushed me aside, went in and stood at the head of my mother's bed. The others followed.

"Carmela, darling, look at me," my father begged her.

"I can't take it anymore, Juan . . . I can't take it anymore. I need to sleep. Tell the doctor to give me the morphine."

"No, no, no! You've got to hold on. Carmela, for God's sake, don't do this to me!"

Jaime wrapped his arm around my father's shoulders, trying to lead him away from the bed.

"Dad, let Mama sleep . . . It'll be all right. She'll wake up in a little while. Let's not make her suffer, please."

Grandpa Ramón was crying like a baby in the arms of Uncle Oswaldo, and Grandma Stella was kissing my mother's face, soaking her in tears while putting a picture card of Saint Patrick on her pillow. Meanwhile, Grandpa James, Grandma Dorothy, and Aunt Emma waited in silence at the doorway.

It was Jaime who took care of everything.

"Please, could you step outside for a moment? Dad, give Mama a kiss and wait outside. Come on, Grandma, let her breathe . . . Uncle Oswaldo, would you mind taking Grandma and Grandpa out? As soon as Mama gets her injection and oxygen mask you can come back in. Thomas, can you stay here with me?"

My mother looked at Jaime gratefully. Her dear son was there by her side, watching over the last minutes of her life as gently as if he were handing her a bouquet. They smiled at each other. There was so much love and understanding between them. I felt an envy so violent it made me want to go up to the bed, grab my mother, and shake her. I didn't move. Grandpa James and Grandma Dorothy were the first to step out of the room while Uncle Oswaldo clung to his mother and tugged at her, and Aunt Emma looked after Grandpa Ramón.

My father was hugging my mother and she was stroking his hair. I didn't catch what she whispered in his ear, but whatever it was, it brought tears to my father's eyes.

The doctor glanced impatiently at Jaime and my brother approached my father, gently forcing him to let go of my mother's embrace.

"Juan . . . stay . . . Give me your hand . . ." my mother asked.

"Don't worry, Carmela," the doctor, who was an old friend, reassured her. "The pain will go away. You'll be better soon," he added, giving her a smile.

"Well, I hope it's true, no one has come back to say whether the afterlife is better than this one."

"You're not going anywhere, Mama. Just try to rest. You don't need to withstand this pain," Jaime intervened.

"It's the best thing, I know . . . But . . . it's hard, you know? It's hard knowing that . . . Give me your hand too, Jaime."

The doctor injected the morphine into the IV bag and the liquid started to flow along the transparent tube until it reached the vein and entered my mother's body.

My brother caressed her face and my father her hair, both squeezing her hands. I was there but I was like a ghost. They seemed not to notice my presence. But my mother's last glance was for me. Her eyes were closing when, suddenly, she opened them again and with her clouded gaze she looked for me. Then she closed her eyes forever.

My father and Jaime remained by her side for at least a couple of hours. They didn't talk, just stroked her and held her hands tight. The rest of the family came in one by one, but Jaime gestured for them to keep quiet. When at last my brother decided we should do so, we all stepped out into the hallway.

"The doctor said Mama has a strong heart. She is asleep and . . . it could be a few hours, a day, two . . . We don't know. But at least she's not suffering. You can be in the room but be silent, like you've been until now. No crying, Grandma," he said to Grandma Stella. "She probably can't hear anything, but just in case. We have to allow her to go in peace. Dad, you're wiped out, you should rest for a while."

"No. I'm not moving from her side."

"All right, me neither, but at least we need to eat something. Let's go to the kitchen. We'll ask María to make us some coffee. Aunt Emma, make sure nobody says a word in there until I'm back."

Grandpa James and Grandma Dorothy joined my father and brother while Aunt Emma looked after Grandpa Ramón, Grandma Stella, and Uncle Oswaldo. I was still at the foot of my mother's bed, but nobody seemed to worry about me. It was as if I'd become transparent.

After a long time, Aunt Emma came to tell me, "You should go with your father and your brother. You don't look too good. Some coffee will make you feel better."

I went out of the room, not because my aunt had said so, but because my bladder was about to burst. I lay on the bed in my room for a while. María knocked once on the door.

"What do you want?" I asked, in a bad mood.

"Your brother says you should come to the kitchen."

"Tell them to leave me alone."

I listened to María's footsteps as she walked away mumbling

that I hadn't changed and was as insufferable as I'd been before I left.

I needed to gather my thoughts. I didn't want to accept it, but I was stunned by my mother's confession.

I suddenly had to assume I didn't have a father, that the man who had performed that role bore no relation to me. The Spencers were not my grandparents and Aunt Emma wasn't my aunt. Jaime was my half brother.

I should have realized a long time ago that I was not a Spencer, that my father could not have been anything other than a short Hispanic man with olive skin. I'm a mutt, I thought, trying to think of it as funny.

Now my mother was about to die and I had no place in that house. There was nothing of mine there. Not that I had planned on staying, but suddenly everything that had once been certain in my life had vanished. Despite how badly I had gotten along with my mother, I'd always thought I could count on my father, that he'd lend a hand, that he'd get me out of any kind of trouble, and that Grandpa James could always pull strings to get me a good job.

But I'd been living a lie. Everyone had lied to me. My mother, my father, my grandparents on both sides . . . No, I had to stop thinking of the Spencers as my grandparents and John as my father. They were not. They had patronized me. I was about to feel sorry for myself but caught myself in time. I wasn't going to carry my mother's guilt, much less beg forgiveness for existing. Nor was I planning to fawn gratefully over this family of white, blond, liberal, wealthy lawyers. Let them deal with it. What they'd done was only for my mother: they'd never done anything for me. I wondered if Jaime knew we were only half brothers. I didn't care anymore, but I wasn't going to tolerate any sympathy.

I don't know how long I stayed in my room. Maybe three or four hours. Evening had fallen when Aunt Emma opened the door and came in, oblivious to how angry I was.

"Your mother is sleeping peacefully, although she's still on the oxygen. The doctor just went in to see how she's doing. He says he doesn't know how long she'll hold on . . . that in these cases we never know . . . He offered to take her to the hospital, but your father said no. She would want to die here."

"My father? You know I don't have a father. Not even my mother knew who he was."

"So, she told you . . . and now you're licking your wounds. What's important is for you to know that . . . you don't have anything to lament, Thomas. Your father—yes, your father, the only one you've known and had—loves you, like we all do. And God knows you've been difficult, but even so, we've all loved you."

"How kind! How hypocritical! What a sacrifice you've had to make for the Hispanic bastard! Did you have to explain to your friends why you had a nephew with olive skin? Of course it was enough to see my mother . . . I guess people might have said behind my back how unlucky it was to have a child who, instead of looking like the father, inherited the mother's genes. They'd look at Jaime and think: At least *he* took after the Spencers."

"I don't know what your mother told you, Thomas, nor do I want to know. What matters now is that you remain by your father's side, that you help him when the moment comes. I'm not as worried about Jaime, he's strong and well-adjusted, but John . . . He loved your mother madly, he won't know what to do without her."

"He has Jaime, he has you. He's a prestigious lawyer . . . He knows everyone. Don't worry, he'll survive without her," I replied, with more bitterness than I'd meant to reveal.

"I haven't come here to argue with you. I understand that today you've suffered a shock. Your mother was very brave to tell you the truth despite your father not wanting you to know."

"Stop saying 'your father' . . . Whoever my father is, it's clear he's not John Spencer. You also have nothing to do with me."

"How can you say that? Of course I've got something to do

with you. I changed your diapers, I taught you to sail, I covered up for your mischief when you came to Newport . . . I spent afternoons reading you stories, taking you to the movies . . . Come on, stop feeling sorry for yourself! I thought you were stronger than that."

"I am, Emma. It's not every day that your mother tells you that she doesn't know who your father is, that any dark-skinned guy from her college campus could be your dad . . . Minor details! Nothing I didn't already know, except for the part about me not having a known father."

"Carmela has always been sincere. She wasn't capable of hiding the tremendous suffering it caused her to get pregnant after what happened to her."

"You women flatter yourselves. My mother was drunk out of her mind and it was all the same to her if she spread her legs for one or for twenty-seven. She wasn't sorry until she found out she was pregnant. She herself told me so: 'You know what those college parties are like . . . Alcohol and drugs . . .' That's what she said."

"If you don't forgive her you will be lost to yourself."

"So *I* should forgive, should I? Did you ever ask her to forgive herself? Why do I have to pay for her wild drinking spree? No, I won't forgive her, Emma."

"I see, now you're going to call me Emma instead of Aunt Emma . . ."

"Don't you think we should stop pretending now? My mother is no longer here."

"She's not dead yet."

"How long will it take? One hour, two days? Her beloved son has decided that it's best if she dies. Yes, he's arranged for a peaceful death for our mother. Grandma Stella is right, someone here has behaved like God, deciding the moment when my mother should die."

"Your mother is terminally ill. The doctors were very clear: a matter of days. The only options were to let her die in pain, or to make sure the last hours are peaceful. Carmela chose this. She has seen many people suffering because their relatives refused to give them morphine. And she didn't want to go through that.

"Don't blame Jaime. Your mother asked the doctor to bring her home, to allow her to say goodbye to all of us and then take morphine so she could be asleep when she met her death, which is already at her door. So stop blaming your brother. One thing is true, though—she insisted on not taking the morphine until she spoke to you."

"She needed to confess, so that I would absolve her."

"Knowing you, I doubt very much that she was expecting your absolution. I suppose she believed that she owed you the truth," my aunt replied, upset.

"She could have told me years ago."

"Your father, John, never allowed her to. And I always advised her against it. You have too much anger inside of you."

"Tell me, Emma, do you think I have any reason to be angry?"

She looked at me directly as she weighed her answer.

"No, you don't have any reason to be angry. I understand that this rift between your mother and you has done you a lot of harm, but you caused it. She was never able to understand why you rejected her. But now it's about avoiding more damage. You need to help your father face the loss of your mother. It's the least you can do."

"You mean I owe him? And you're calling in the debt?"

Emma went out at that, slamming the door. I could call a taxi to the airport and take any flight to London. The other option was to stay and continue to endure this drama. If I hadn't been so tired, I would have left—or was there a reason to stay that I didn't comprehend? My father used to quote Pascal, the French philosopher: "The heart has its reasons which reason knows nothing of." Perhaps that's precisely what was happening to me. I washed my face with cold water before returning to the room where the family was waiting for my mother's heart to stop.

Emma didn't even look at me when I went in. My father and Jaime were sitting next to each other by the bed, while Grandpa Ramón and Grandma Stella were at the foot of the bed, sobbing quietly.

Grandpa James came and patted me on the back. This gesture annoyed me. Until that day he, along with my father, had been the family member I had loved the most, but now I had to accept that this man had nothing to do with me.

"Shall we go to the kitchen and have some coffee?"

I followed him. I couldn't stand the ritual of waiting in my mother's room.

María was making some sandwiches and barely noticed us.

"Who are those sandwiches for? Are we throwing a party?" I asked sarcastically.

"You can't go all day without eating. Your brother asked me to prepare some sandwiches and coffee for everyone."

"My brother, always so thoughtful," I replied, sarcastically.

"Well, you're right, he is," María said, with her usual curtness.

Grandpa James sat at the table and María served him a cup of coffee.

"Thomas, we're all having a very hard time. Carmela . . . your mother . . . We all love her very much."

"Sure."

"Your father is devastated. He's going to need you and Jaime by his side. I don't want to think what it would mean to him for your mother not to be here . . . His whole world will collapse."

"My mother told me that John is not my father."

I spoke without regard for María's presence, and when she heard these words, she dropped one of the trays she was carrying to the table. She looked at me as if I had gone crazy. She looked as though she were about to scold me for saying that I was not my father's son.

"María, if you could leave me alone with my grandson . . . As you can see he is very upset," Grandpa James apologized on my behalf.

"Yes . . . I'm going to the ironing room. I have things to do, but before I do . . . I'm sorry, I'm sorry, I dropped the tray . . ."

We had to wait a few minutes as she picked up the sandwiches from the floor. After she left my grandfather looked at me resentfully.

"I never want to hear you say that John is not your father ever again. He has been your father since the day he met you and that was many years ago. You can never accuse him of not treating you with the same affection he showed Jaime. He never played favorites."

"You're right, neither my mother nor John played favorites. The problem is that I was different. I used to have trouble accepting the fact that I didn't look like you or John, did you know?"

"Can't you try to be a bit more understanding? She always tried to do the best for you. And things weren't easy. You have to take into account what it was like for her to become pregnant without knowing who the father was. Without intending it, you were a reminder of a fact that . . . well, she was ashamed of, but even so, she always loved you and tried to show it. She was very young when that tragic incident happened. She never got over it. You have to try to understand her."

"What about me? Does anyone care about how much I've suffered?"

"I told you already that occasionally I suggested to your father that we should do more to try to make you not behave with that . . . with that disregard for your mother. She went to therapy."

"Unsuccessfully."

"The problem lay in you, not in her. Thomas, nothing needs to change. We are your family, we love you. Don't torture yourself."

"I'm sorry, but things have changed. I don't see you as my grandfather anymore, but as John's father, and I can no longer see him as my father."

"That's ridiculous. You can't erase the love, neither the love we feel toward you nor the love you feel toward us."

"You said it, 'us.'"

"I don't understand . . ."

"Yes, that 'us' contains the difference. You accepted me but I am not part of that 'us.'"

"If anyone claimed you weren't my grandson they'd get a good punch in the face."

"Come on! Look, it's better if we let it be. Things are what they are. I've always wondered why I looked so different from you and John. I'm only five foot seven, I have dark skin and black eyes, and my features reflect who I am. It's obvious—it always has been."

"I understand that you're hurting right now, but don't punish yourself for long. That would be foolish. Nothing will change except what you want to change."

Grandpa James stood up and left the kitchen without looking at me. I poured myself another cup of coffee and ate four sandwiches. They were very good and I was hungry.

The doctor returned around nine and, after examining my mother, recommended that we get some rest.

"It could take some time. You never know . . . Don't expend all your energy the first day. Take turns. But make sure you get some rest."

Everyone protested. It seemed nobody was willing to leave, not until my mother's heart failed.

Jaime again made a decision. Nobody, not even my brother, consulted me on anything.

"Dad, I know it will be hard to sleep, but at least lie down on the bed and stretch your legs. Grandpa Ramón and Grandma Stella can rest in my room. Uncle Oswaldo, take the couch in the living room. And you," he said, addressing the Spencers and Aunt Emma, "I think it's best if you go home. If anything happens we'll give you a call."

They were reluctant. Nobody wanted to leave that room and

it seemed to me like they were vultures, eager to see my mother's body turn into a cadaver. But Jaime was unyielding and practically kicked everyone out of the room except for me and the night nurse, who was there to monitor my mother's vital signs.

"Thanks for staying here with me," said Jaime.

"With you? Interesting that you'd thank me for staying with her. Remember, she's my mother. So thank *you* for staying."

"I'm sorry, you misunderstood me," Jaime whispered, alarmed at how the rage began to surface on my face.

"I understood you perfectly. Here I am, little more than a guest at this spectacle that you've organized around my mother's death. I would never have imagined you asking to expedite her death. I thought you were the sort who'd beg people to fight till the end."

"As you know, it was she who asked to be put to sleep. I only carried out her wishes."

"Aren't you a good Catholic? As far as I know, Catholics are against euthanasia."

"And what does this have to do with euthanasia? Nobody's given Mama an injection for her to die."

"They've given her an injection to put her to sleep, supposedly to keep her from suffering, the end result of which is that she will never wake up again and it's now a matter of hours until her heart stops. Can you tell me what the difference is?"

"Thomas, I understand what you're going through. I . . . I didn't know anything. I had no idea what Mama wanted to tell you."

"And how do you know now?"

"Dad told me. He's sorry that Mama . . . well, that she revealed some things to you. He asked her not to, but she needed to explain herself to you."

"She needed to clear her conscience."

"Don't be so miserable! You're a man. You can handle what Mama told you."

"Easy, just like that?"

"No, I'm not saying it's easy for you. It wouldn't be for me. But you're not a child anymore, so there are certain things you can understand."

"Well, you see, the only thing I understand is that when she was at college she went on a drinking binge so bad that she let any passerby do what he wanted with her and she got knocked up. She must have been disgusted with herself for putting herself in a position where she could be abused. She should have shot herself if she couldn't handle it, and not brought an innocent child into the world, because I was innocent."

"I'm sorry, Thomas. I really am sorry about all of this. But she has always loved you. She's your mother."

"Maybe."

"She always tried to show it, but you wouldn't let her."

"I can't stand clichéd phrases, much less getting little pats on the back. You're the one who received what little good there could have been in her."

My mother stirred despite being sunk in deep sleep. She seemed unable to breathe even with the oxygen mask.

The nurse took her pulse and checked the machine monitoring her heartbeat.

"She's getting weaker," she whispered.

"Is she suffering?" asked Jaime, alarmed.

"No . . . no . . . The morphine prevents her from feeling any pain. You shouldn't worry about that. But she's agitated . . . I don't know why. I'll call the doctor."

We listened to the brief conversation with the doctor, who recommended another injection.

"You'll finish her off at that rate," I said.

"Don't say that!" Jaime reproached me.

"She should face death with her eyes open," I fumed.

"We all deserve to die in the best way possible. I've never agreed that a human should have to die suffering. Drowning . . . in a huge amount of pain . . ."

"Ask your God why He delights in watching us suffer."

"That's something I've asked Him many times."

"And has He responded?"

"No, I've never found the answer." Jaime glanced at me, devastated.

My mother died a little before dawn. At five in the morning her heart stopped. My father was holding one of her hands while Jaime caressed the other. I was at the foot of the bed. There we were, the four of us and the nurse.

Half an hour before, she had stirred again. The nurse said she thought the end was near. Jaime didn't want to tell our grandparents or Uncle Oswaldo, who were still resting. He preferred for our mother to go when it was just us.

When my mother passed, Jaime continued caressing her hand for a long time. He made a gesture at my father to indicate what was almost an order: he was not to cry, at least not there, at that moment.

I don't know how John was able to control himself but he did. He didn't let out one whimper of emotion but the tears were falling silently.

I wondered what he felt; I searched within myself for some emotion, but I couldn't feel a thing and for a moment I thought the dead person was me. I was surprised at not being able to feel while the pain was so visible in the eyes of my brother and John.

I didn't even feel able to say anything, or move. I wondered whether I was really there. But I must have been, because one hour later, my brother gently let go of my mother's hand. He kissed her and hugged her and whispered something into her ear. I wondered what could be said to a dead woman.

My father kissed her several times. What did he feel as he put his lips on that pale, lifeless face?

Jaime looked at me as though inviting me to do the same. But I didn't move from my spot. I only put my hand on the blanket and felt her cold legs.

"Come on, they have to prepare her." Jaime signaled for John and me to step out of the room.

"You go ahead," said John. "Arrange everything, I'll stay with her. I need to be alone with her, please . . ." A plea and an order were mixed in his voice.

My brother nodded and, putting his hand on my arm, nudged me gently out of the room. The nurse also left.

"In an hour I'll call the funeral director. Mama wanted her body to be prepared here too. She was horrified at the thought of them taking her anywhere else. So the wake will take place at home."

"You're not crying?" I asked, surprised at how calm he was keeping, knowing how close he and our mother had been.

"Not yet. Mama needs me to do all the things I've promised. And they must be done properly. She'll have the best funeral. A Mass at Saint Patrick's. If you want to help me, there's a lot to do."

"Aren't you going to wake our grandparents up?"

"Not yet. Dad needs to be alone with Mama. If we wake them you know what will happen. I'm going to have another coffee, will you come with me?"

María was just getting up. She'd slept barely a few hours. She was tired and moved clumsily.

"Call Fanny," said Jaime after saying that our mother had died.

María started crying. My brother again insisted that she should phone Fanny.

"Why? I can manage by myself."

"Please, call her. There'll be a lot of people and lots to do," Jaime urged.

"My brother's right," I chimed in, seeing that María was inconsolable.

Fanny used to come two or three times a week to help María with the more difficult household chores. She was a young woman of Chinese descent who barely ever spoke.

We drank the coffee in silence. It felt strange to sit next to my brother, each of us lost in his own thoughts, not even looking at each other. I glanced at him out of the corner of my eye and noticed the tension in his face. He was making an effort not to fall apart. He knew it was up to him to assume the responsibility of organizing our mother's funeral. John was worn out and couldn't help with anything. As for me—Jaime knew exactly what to expect from me.

Then everything happened quite fast. Two men from the funeral home came and took a couple of hours to prepare my mother's body, aided by María.

My father shut himself up in his room while my maternal grandparents cried in the study with Uncle Oswaldo. Grandma and Grandpa Spencer and Aunt Emma didn't take long to come. They looked better than us; you could tell that at least they had gotten some rest.

Friends of the family and my mother's work colleagues started arriving midmorning. Her nurse friends said it had been a miracle that she had held on for so long, considering how aggressive the lung cancer had been.

Jaime had arranged for the coffin to be placed in the study, and my father received condolences there from all the people who arrived.

For a few hours, I received condolences from people I didn't at all care about, who patted me on the back with one hand while holding a canapé or a cup of tea in the other. Man is a social being when faced with death.

It was already four when María told me that a "young lady" was asking for me, but she hadn't wanted to come in.

I was surprised to see Esther. Yes, that Italian girl who had been my classmate at Paul Hard's School of Advertising, and whom Lisa had hated so much.

"I . . . I don't want to disturb you, but I just wanted to say I'm sorry for your loss."

"Come in . . . Please, come in." Suddenly I was happy to see someone who was there just to see me.

"No, no . . . I only came here because you wouldn't answer your phone. I had to ask Paul Hard for your address. It was actually he who told me about your mother. Apparently it was in the society news."

"So you're still in touch with Paul?"

"I teach at his academy a couple days a week."

"I see, so you've found something to do that's not related to your family's restaurant."

"I also work for an ad agency. I've worked on several campaigns now. But I couldn't say no to Paul. One of his teachers left and he needed someone to fill in but didn't want to have to pay too much, so he called me."

"A good girl, as always. You seem . . ."

Yes, Esther seemed different. The ugly duckling had not become a swan but her appearance had improved. She wore her hair in a way that conveyed style. She was wearing a blazer that was not bad although it was cheap, and she even had makeup on. Yes, she'd improved noticeably.

"Come in and have a drink."

"No, I don't want to disturb you . . ."

"Stay awhile, since you're here."

I went with her to the kitchen, where María and Fanny busied themselves with putting canapés on trays.

"Do you need a hand?" Esther offered.

"A little help would be great . . . There are more people than we were expecting," whispered María.

Esther smiled at me and started helping Fanny make the canapés.

"I've had a lot of practice. I've been helping at my parents' restaurant for years."

"Yes, but you've come here to express your condolences, not to make sandwiches," I protested.

"You know I'm incapable of being idle."

María and Fanny were grateful for the unexpected help from Esther. While Esther and Fanny filled the trays, María went in and out of the kitchen and passed the trays around for the guests at the wake. Aunt Emma also assisted with that task and, although she was surprised at the presence of a stranger in the kitchen, she didn't say anything.

Jaime came looking for me. He seemed annoyed, but if he was planning on reproaching me for anything he held his tongue when he saw Esther.

"Thomas, I've been looking for you. There are lots of people here and they're asking after you. Everyone wants to express their condolences. And . . . well, Lisa's parents have just arrived. Mr. and Mrs. Ferguson. Of course it's you they want to see."

"The Fergusons? Look, I'm not in the mood to keep listening to people's drivel. Everyone keeps saying the same things. 'Your mother was so good.' 'What a great loss.' And then they want me to tell them about me, what I do for a living and why I don't live in New York."

"Our obligation is to welcome all these people who've kindly come to be with us," Jaime insisted while glancing uncomfortably at Esther, whom he didn't recognize.

"Your brother is right," she said, as she put another coffeepot and some cups on a tray.

"You are . . . ?"

"Esther Sabatti. You won't remember me. Actually, I'm almost glad you don't. We met at your brother's graduation."

"Oh, I remember now! Sorry, Esther, but there have been so many people that I no longer know who I recognize and who I don't," my brother explained, although I was sure he didn't remember her.

"Esther is helping María and Fanny; she's been making sandwiches and canapés for an hour," I said as if I were proud that someone I knew was capable of doing something useful.

"Oh, well! I'm grateful. I'm sure María and Fanny are too, although . . . Thomas, I don't think it's a good idea for your friend to be here in the kitchen."

"Don't worry. I'm fine and I'd rather be here. I don't know all those people and I don't mind lending a hand. But, Thomas, you should go and be with your friends."

"I'm not going to leave you here," I replied, feeling awkward.

"I'll stay awhile longer to help and then I'll go. Don't worry."

"Yes, that would be best," said my brother.

"Go see the Fergusons, I'll come in a minute," I said to Jaime, who left the kitchen in a huff. Then, to Esther, I said, "Give me your phone number and address. We could have dinner tomorrow, if you like?"

"Tomorrow is your mother's funeral and burial," replied Esther, aghast.

"But by midafternoon it will all be over. I hope so, at least. I've never understood why after a funeral everyone has to go back to the dead person's house to continue eating and drinking."

"Come on, Thomas, now's not the time to say those things. And I live where I used to live, and my phone number's the same as when we were studying at Paul's academy."

"Okay, but I don't have it anymore. Write it down for me before you go, okay?"

I didn't enjoy seeing the Fergusons. I didn't actually want to be reminded of Lisa. I'd put her out of my mind. She was a thing of the past. I barely paid attention to them. I slunk away as soon as I could.

The house was full of people until eight. I remember I had an intense headache. I'd barely eaten, had had too much coffee to keep myself awake, and the repetitive conversations were getting on my nerves. I sighed in relief when María closed the door behind the last stragglers to leave.

Jaime took the lead again and almost ordered our maternal grandparents and uncle to go home.

"Uncle Oswaldo, it's best if you go and rest. Tomorrow will be even harder than today. The funeral Mass is at nine. The burial is at eleven, and then we'll come back here for some refreshments."

Our grandparents protested. They wanted to stay and keep vigil over their daughter, but Jaime was unyielding, so they left at the same time as Grandpa and Grandma Spencer and Aunt Emma.

My brother ordered María to go to bed and asked Fanny to come back early the next day.

Suddenly Jaime, John, and I were alone in the study, the three of us sitting next to my mother's coffin. John didn't seem aware of anything, not even our presence. His gaze was fixed on my mother's lifeless face.

"Dad," whispered Jaime, "you need rest too. Get some sleep, I'll stay with her; then Thomas can take over. I promise I'll wake you up soon."

"Thomas? Thomas is going to stay with your mother?" John asked Jaime, but looked at me as if he were unable to conceive of such an idea.

"Yes, of course, just like you and me. She won't be alone tonight. There will always be one of the three of us," Jaime assured him.

"No, no. I'm staying with her, you can do what you like."

"Don't be stubborn, you're exhausted. You'll make yourself ill if you don't sleep a little." Jaime was wasting his patience on him.

"Leave me alone, I said I'm not moving from this spot."

We stayed silent for a long time. I think it was midnight when I got up and left them alone with her. I was too tired to keep sitting motionless, staring at a dead body, even if it was my own mother's.

In the morning, my father and brother were exhausted. Jaime had not wanted to leave my dad alone and they'd stayed with my mother the whole night. I'd be lying if I said that at that moment I felt worried about John's health. I thought he was stupid for not getting some sleep, and my brother was even more stupid for following his lead.

Would I have done the same now? I should say no. I know I should have stayed with them and even tried to comfort John. I imagine things could have been thus:

"Dad, Mama wouldn't have liked to see you this way. You need to listen to Jaime and get some sleep. We'll take turns."

And when he protested, I could have taken him gently by the arm, making him get up. But first I would have hugged him, and Jaime would have joined that embrace.

"The past doesn't matter, what matters now is that we give my mother a good farewell. I loved her even though I was not able to show it, and I love you. You are my only family."

But none of this happened and that night I slept like a log, although I awoke just as the sun was rising. I was cold.

The day went by more quickly than the previous one. I suppose having to go to Saint Patrick's and then to the cemetery and back home made the hours pass swiftly.

I was surprised to see Esther sitting in a pew at the back of the cathedral. She was hearing Mass as if it were the most natural thing to her.

She left without giving me time to say anything, and I was annoyed. I didn't know why but suddenly I seemed to feel the need to be with her.

That afternoon, when we were alone again, Jaime wanted the three of us to have dinner, John, him, and me. But I said no.

"I'm planning to go back to London in two or three days."

"That's fine by me, but that shouldn't stop you from having dinner with us tonight."

"We've had the funeral already, we've buried her. There's no point in continuing to lament. She's not here. She's gone forever. That's that."

My brother looked furious. I thought he was considering whether to punch me, but in the end he shrugged.

"Do what you like. I think the least you owe Dad is to have dinner with him tonight. He's devastated and needs our support."

"I see, another one who talks about duty. Your aunt Emma also told me I'm indebted to John."

"Yes, you're indebted to your father, as am I—because he's our father, the only one we've had, and you know full well how much he has loved us and loves us still."

"Speak for yourself."

"I speak for myself and for you. You'd be a bastard if you said Dad didn't love you."

"Effectively, I am a bastard, but you knew that already. The only one who didn't know was me."

"What you are is an idiot. You know what your problem is? Your problem is not other people, your problem is you, the way you are. You should get yourself checked."

"Enjoy your meal."

I left the house, slamming the door behind me. I knew I was being churlish, that Jaime was right and the least I owed John was to offer him consolation. But I was running away from a scene that I would have found too unbearable. John, Jaime, and me sitting at the table while María served a consommé and then a piece of roast. My brother would retell stories about my mother that involved the three of us, and he would even do the impossible and get my father to smile at some memory he was especially fond of.

I may well have chimed in with a mea culpa, saying I'd been

an overly active child and my mother was always on edge, and then I'd admit that I had loved her very much and I'd been fortunate to be able to tell her so before she died. I could have even added that I was lucky to have them.

But instead, what I did was take a taxi and go find Esther. I dialed her number, as I gave the taxi driver her address.

On the phone, she told me it wasn't the right evening for us to go out for dinner, but I insisted.

"Look, I need to be with someone who isn't family or I'll end up going crazy. If you don't want to have dinner with me then I'll dine alone."

In the end she accepted. I took her to dinner at what used to be my favorite Chinese restaurant in Chinatown, Joe's Shanghai.

I discovered I felt great when she was around, better than with any other person I'd ever met. And that very night, after dinner, as we strolled back to her house, I asked her to marry me. I myself was surprised at the proposal.

"Are you asking seriously?"

"Yes. Will you marry me?"

"No, we don't know each other well enough. Besides, you just told me you're planning to go back to London. It seems to me you're not very sure what you want. And . . . well, nobody decides to get married just like that, out of the blue."

"Why?"

"Because getting married is a serious matter. It's a lifelong project together, but above all, it requires a very important element: love."

I didn't know how to reply. I couldn't lie and say I was in love with her because she wouldn't have believed me. I actually didn't have any logical explanation except that it seemed a good idea to be with her. And that's what I said.

"Okay, that's a reason but it's not enough."

"And what's your reason to say no?"

"I'm not in love with you. I've always liked you but that's it."

"That's something at least. I didn't know you liked me."

"It was obvious."

"So . . ."

"So you asked me to marry you and I don't think it's a good idea. Don't you think that's enough?"

"No. But I think we should try it."

"Try . . . what? Look, Thomas, I can't afford not to take life seriously."

"I'm serious. I want to be with you."

"We'll see."

Esther's serenity was disconcerting. She seemed to know who she was and, above all, what she expected from life. I decided that whatever her hesitations, I would not give up.

But I had to make a decision. If I wanted to be with her I'd have to stay in New York and I wasn't sure I wanted to give up what seemed like a promising career in London. Roy kept calling me, asking me to come back. He had big plans and he said he needed me for them.

I didn't actually have to make the decision myself because Mark Scott and Denis Roth made it for me.

When I phoned Maggie to ask how things were going, my efficient secretary said things were going very well and that Cathy was a very agreeable boss. I pretended not to hear that and asked her to put me through to Philip Sullivan instead of Richard Craig, my assistant. I knew that Sullivan would tell me what was going on.

"Thomas, I sent you a few e-mails and called you, but you haven't returned any of my calls," he complained when he heard my voice.

"My mother died. Now tell me what's been happening."

"You're out. Mark and Denis decided to hire Cathy to oversee everything, in addition to the electoral department. Mark told us your methods aren't exactly orthodox, and concern has been raised about . . . well, you know, about what happened to Roy's opposition. And Denis says that the agency's morality and ethics must not be put into question. At first there were rumors that they were searching for another mission for you, but it seems they've decided they don't need you. They are going to sack you. Maggie has actually already packed all your things in a box. Are you planning on coming?"

"I don't know . . . The thing is, I'm not surprised Cathy got her way. She wanted revenge. But I'll have to come back. I have an apartment, a car, a bank account, and Roy Parker, who keeps calling me."

"Thomas . . . I don't know what you're planning on doing, but whatever it is, you can count on me."

I was surprised at Sullivan's loyalty. The computer guy, the IT genius, had a heart too. And I knew I wasn't his type. He liked men who were tall, blond, and muscular, none of which described me.

So I had to start thinking about what to do with my life, but I was glad this allowed me to be with Esther. I was in no rush to go anywhere.

I didn't tell my brother or John until a few days later.

"I've been fired from Scott and Roth and I want to marry Esther Sabatti, that Italian girl who was in the kitchen the other day," I announced at breakfast.

John lifted his gaze from his cup of coffee and looked at me like I was a lunatic.

After a pause, my brother said plainly what was on his mind: "Poor girl, she seems like a nice person. Why does she want to marry you?"

"She doesn't want to yet, but I suppose I'll convince her."

"Is she that desperate?" asked John, trying to find an explanation as to why a woman would accept me as a husband.

"Her parents own an Italian restaurant. She works at an advertising agency and also teaches a couple of classes a week at Paul Hard's academy, where we both studied."

"That girl . . . Isn't that the girl . . . ?"

"Yes, the one Lisa tried to hit the day I graduated. She's always been a good friend."

"Well, I didn't realize you'd kept in touch." Jaime seemed surprised.

"Yes, and we always got along. I don't know why but she's the only person I feel at ease with, and who I don't want to piss off," I admitted.

"Coming from you, that's like saying you're madly in love," said Jaime.

"Yes, that's what I think."

"But what I don't understand is why she . . . well, why she wants to marry you," John insisted.

"Maybe she doesn't altogether hate me," I replied ironically.

"I imagine you'll wait an appropriate amount of time before getting married. We just buried Mama and the family isn't ready for celebrations," my brother advised.

"Like I said, I still need to convince her. Also, I need to decide whether to return to London or stay in New York. Can't say either of you seems surprised that I've been fired, by the way."

"So you need to decide what to do with the rest of your life," John replied.

"Something like that."

"Well, let us know when you clear that up. But you need to wait at least six months because of Mama," Jaime insisted.

"I didn't say that there's going to be a celebration, just that I want to get married. But before I do, I need to find a job."

"I guess Dad can help you find one, or Grandpa James," said Jaime, looking at John.

"As soon as you've decided whether you're staying in New York I'll make a few calls," John said.

"I'll let you know soon."

They didn't seem much affected by the news that I had lost my job.

I looked at them and felt the same rage I'd felt as a child.

Jaime and John were like two peas in a pod: same hair color, same build, same way of holding a cup of coffee and of putting their index finger on their nose when lost in thought.

I asked Esther to come with me to London. The idea was to spend a week there and get my things sorted out, then come back to New York. As the Christmas holidays were coming up, she accepted, because she could take a few days off from both the advertising agency and Paul's academy.

I must admit that not even I understood my determination to marry Esther. I looked at her and didn't find her physically attractive. She wasn't, she'd never been, but the fact is I couldn't leave her side, nor did I want to.

When I arrived at the agency in London I was met with my first surprise. My access card had been canceled, so although the security guard knew me, he didn't allow me into the elevator until Maggie gave the go-ahead. In the lobby of what had been my office, the woman who had been my secretary was waiting for me with the box in her arms.

"Here are your things, Thomas. Go to Mark's office. He and Denis are waiting for you."

"Well, aren't you efficient?"

"It's nothing personal, you know that. It's the rules. I do what I'm told."

"That's why you'll always do well, Maggie, although your life will be boring."

"To each his own."

Mark and Denis received me without enthusiasm. They had to get over the hurdle of firing me and they seemed worried about my reaction.

Denis gave a spiel about ethics as an added value to the agency's work, and Mark pointed out that I didn't match the professional profile they were looking for.

"Of course, we've transferred all the money you're due."

I didn't grant them the pleasure of looking offended or worried. I shrugged, shook their hands, and walked out of there forever.

That same night Esther and I went out to dinner with Roy and Suzi. Roy had insisted on coming to London to convince me that my place was by his side.

Esther and Suzi seemed to get along, which Roy was excited about, so he winked at me and said, "If the girls understand each other, things will work out better between us."

He went straight to the point during the second course. I must admit I was surprised.

"Well, I'm mayor now. But the goal is to get to London—to Parliament."

"And then you'll try to become prime minister," I joked.

"All in good time. What I want now is for you to work exclusively for me. I have some friends interested in helping. They've got plenty of contacts."

"And they want to become MPs as well? Now that's ambition!" I replied, laughing.

"Stop being absurd, Thomas; this is serious. I need someone I can trust and . . . well, someone who has no relation to any specific power bloc and who can do what needs to be done. We'll pay you well. Very well."

"You're speaking in the plural . . . Are you plotting to make the Queen abdicate?" I continued in the same obnoxious tone.

"My goal is to get a seat at Westminster, and for that, we need publicity and proper handling of the press. You've demonstrated you're very skillful at both, but above all that you don't have stupid scruples like your old bosses, who go around begging forgiveness from the Labour Party and the Conservatives because I was selected instead of their candidates. They are worthless."

I didn't contradict him. I couldn't care less what Scott and Roth might think. Esther looked at him in surprise. Roy didn't seem like her kind of person.

"Who are your friends?" I asked.

"Businessmen, bankers . . . They keep a low profile. They're not in the papers."

"And what do they want of you?"

"Sometimes the defense of their interests requires that public opinion is not against them. In order for that to happen, it is necessary to utilize the media, to do certain things. You can do those things."

"But exactly what are those interests you need to defend?" I insisted.

"We'll go through that over lunch at the Dorchester, if that's okay with you."

"I thought you didn't like the Dorchester."

"I don't, but you do."

"Will any of those friends of yours be there?"

"No, you and I need to talk first. Plenty of time for you to meet them. But let's leave serious things aside. Shall we go and have a drink after dinner? I've been recommended a place which I think you'll like."

When we returned to my apartment I asked Esther what she thought of Roy.

"Dangerous."

"So you liked him," I rejoined.

"And what's more: he has no scruples. If push comes to shove, he'll throw you to the wolves. He's one of those who never lose."

"You mean you don't think he's too . . . rustic?"

"He's much more than that. His appearance is just that. He may not have gone to an elite university, but he's intelligent, he has a calculating and quick mind, he knows what he wants and is willing to do anything to achieve it. He likes you, but he'll give you up in a heartbeat if that benefits him."

"I thought you were a PR expert. Who knew that you were a practicing psychoanalyst?"

"You know I'm right. You like Roy because he represents a challenge. He is dangerous and you like to walk on the edge. You are made for each other. Until the time comes when survival instincts kick in and one of you decides to throw the other one overboard. If you are going to do business with him you need someone to watch your back."

"Are you suggesting I should hire a bodyguard?" I couldn't stop laughing.

"It wouldn't do you any harm, but that's not what I mean. In your team you'll need people you can trust, who are incorruptible, who won't betray you. It won't be easy."

"You're assuming I'm going to accept his offer."

"Yes, of course you will. You don't have anything else to do and whatever he proposes will be a challenge for you."

"I propose that you be the one who watches my back." I was speaking seriously.

"Me you can trust, but I'm not sure I want to have anything to do with Roy Parker or his wife."

"I thought you liked Suzi."

"Neither like nor dislike her—she simply doesn't interest me. But she's also not to be trusted. Those two will never be able to separate because they'll have too many skeletons in the closet."

"Very perceptive! Suzi is Roy's stalwart."

"Yes, it seems to me he has met his match."

"Marry me, Esther. You said so yourself, I need you."

"That's not a reason for me to marry you."

"Are you still not in love with me?"

"Are you in love with me?"

"I'm not going to lie to you. I don't really know what I feel for you, except that you are the only woman I want to be with. I can't get enough of looking at you, of being with you. You make me see things in a different light, and I feel like I can talk to you about almost anything."

"But you don't feel an overwhelming passion for me." This time, she was the one to burst out laughing.

"Details!"

"These things aren't insignificant. There are ways in which we don't excite each other."

"But that shouldn't be an obstacle. You know that lust fades away."

"Sure, but it's great while it lasts."

"And then what? I think our relationship is more solid than if right now we were too eager to get into bed together."

"But that's important too."

"For the relationship to last there has to be something more, and I mean something that isn't resignation or the children or the financial situation. That something more is what we have, what there is between us, and that's what lasts forever."

Esther looked pensive. She resisted giving up on the romantic and passionate love that people usually feel at least once in their lives. She could have felt it for me, but it hadn't worked out that way.

We got into bed and made love. It was nice but not passionate. But for me, Esther was more important than good sex.

I arrived at the Dorchester before Roy and ordered coffee and toast. I wasn't hungry but I knew it bothered Roy to have to eat alone. He arrived late, blaming Suzi for the delay.

"And where is she?"

"She insisted that the taxi drop her off at Harrods. Anyway, there are things she doesn't need to know."

Then he got right to it.

"You know what I want: work only for me. My friends, actually they're two lawyers, can give you a job. You can choose your own people, like that IT guy, Sullivan, who you worked with on my campaign. Look for people like that. You'll make plenty of money, more than you can imagine."

"You're still talking in the plural. Stop beating around the bush and tell me what you and those mysterious friends of yours want," I demanded.

"What we want is very simple, I'll give you an example: imagine that a company wishes to obtain some land to extract natural gas via fracking. The local environmentalists, the people living in the nearby village, some well-intentioned journalists, and even some local politicians may oppose it, saying it will have negative effects on the environment, that it will cause a natural disaster, that the gas emissions can endanger public health: you know, the same old nonsense. What you would have to do is change public opinion. We'll take care of the politicians; although should the need arise, you'd also have to step in and change the minds of those who are reluctant to see it our way. Do you get my drift?"

Suddenly I realized it was Roy who had manipulated me, and that his determination to gain control over one of the main districts of the county had nothing to do with his political ambitions. It was all about business.

"Is that what's under the grass where your in-laws keep their sheep? Gas? Is that why you needed to be mayor and why you're aspiring to a seat at Westminster? So that they reassess those lands and God knows what else?"

"I thought you knew that already." He looked at me, surprised and slightly disappointed.

"You were saying?" I prompted him, to avoid admitting that he had used me.

"There are people I've made promises to . . . Suzi doesn't know any of this."

"You mean, you've even lied to her."

"My in-laws would never consent to drilling on their land and neither would Suzi. But they won't be a problem. I want you to be prepared to help me. My friends are going to hire you at one of the agencies they manage. We'll have to buy media, bribe them; they're looking for the dirt on our opposition . . . But all this has to be done discreetly, under the guise of respectability. I'm not going to tell you how to do the job; you know how to do it and you've got balls. The sooner you get down to business, the better for everyone."

Either Roy had changed and was now showing his true colors, which Esther had picked up on, or today was not his day and that's why he seemed so unpleasant.

"You know something, Roy? I don't like being bossed around. Don't get confused, I don't need to be your employee, or anybody's. Besides, I'm not looking for a job. If I want to start my own agency I will, I don't need your money. Watch your tone or I'll leave you to finish your breakfast solo."

"I see! It seems you've got amour propre."

"Don't underestimate me, Roy."

"I'm sorry if I've offended you," he replied, aware that I might leave him sitting there.

"I may be interested in what you're proposing, but if I do accept it will be for my own amusement. I don't need your money or that of your friends. I like a challenge. I very much enjoyed getting you elected. And if I accept, Roy, it will be me who sets the terms, not you. Oh, and before agreeing to anything, I want to meet your friends. I want to know who I'm doing business with."

Roy gave me a cold look, trying to determine whether he had misjudged me.

"All right. We'll arrange a few meetings with people."

"Make it quick, Roy. We're leaving for New York in four days."

"That girl, Esther. She seems smart. Is she your girlfriend?"

"I've asked her to marry me and she still hasn't given me an answer."

"Can you trust her?"

"She's the only person I trust, aside from my family."

"Would she work with you? She said she does advertising, publicity . . ."

"I can't speak for her. Anyway, I haven't yet said whether I am going to do business with you and your friends."

"I hope you will."

"What you want me to do . . . there are many others who could do it. Manipulating public opinion is what publicists do."

"But I trust you and . . . I'm new here, Thomas. I need to have my own cards. Marked cards. You are part of the deck. Actually, there's something else you should know. My friends want you to work with someone, a first-class guy. He worked for them on other equally . . . delicate matters."

"I see, another surprise. But I don't need partners."

"Actually, it's me who wants you to work with us on a permanent basis. You'd be like another partner, someone who takes a slice of the earnings, who shares the same interests. My friends don't see it that way, but I've been given the green light. Although they have one condition: that Bernard Schmidt is part of the business."

"And who is Bernard Schmidt?"

"The guy I was just talking about—a German guy who knows more about propaganda and media hype than anyone else in the world."

"If you've already got your man, what do you need me for?"

"Because he's *their* man. I want mine."

"You know what, Roy? You're going to have to tell me a few more things before I meet up with your friends and decide whether or not I want anything to do with you all."

"Fair enough. Just ask and I'll tell you anything you want to know."

"For now, start by telling me what this is all about."

"I've told you already."

"No, you've told me about some friends, about your wanting to influence public opinion in your county so that a fracking company can search for gas. And that there is one Bernard

Schmidt who wants to work with me. In other words, you've told me almost nothing."

Roy seemed to hesitate. He was riled up, almost furious. He thought he'd had me eating out of the palm of his hand; that if he proposed something I would do it without thinking. The servant was turning out to be impudent. In reality, although I didn't like to admit it, he had played me like a fiddle; still, he had underestimated me.

"All right, I'll tell you what this is all about. I'm associated with a group of businessmen. They represent companies that are looking for new energy sources; they're also invested in the arms trade. And yes, there is gas under my father-in-law's land. My in-laws don't even want to hear about the possibility of digging up their land. They don't have ambitions: they have more than enough money to survive thanks to their sheep. They have plenty of land, though some of it isn't worth anything, and they hire it out for hunting during the season.

"Years ago my friends' partners tried to set up a research company for microbiological and other high-tech weapons in the region. One of my in-laws' properties met the specifications they needed. They spoke to me. They didn't need to waste their breath to persuade me, but my in-laws refused. They said that it would upset the tranquillity of the region, that it would destroy the environment, that the birds would flee because of the noise, that biological weapons are a danger to humanity ... A whole load of nonsense. There was no way they could be persuaded, but I was unwilling to let those men go elsewhere. I pressured my in-laws to the point that I threatened to stop managing their lands. They were worried I might be capable of leaving Suzi and the kids, but they wouldn't budge. Suzi and I argued and it was she who threatened to leave me.

"Nothing could stop me. You know that, in addition to the family business, I also manage the estates of some other landowners in the county. Because it couldn't be my in-laws' land, it needed to be someone else's, and it wasn't hard for me to decide which property would be convenient for these people to use. The estate belonged to a family who hadn't set foot on the land in three years except during hunting season. Even so, they didn't want to sell, much less to support a company that would experiment with weapons.

"These friends told me that if we managed to ruin the land, the owners would be forced to sell. I offered to help them. A few days later some men arrived with barrels. I gave them access to the estate. I don't know what they did, and don't ask me what was in the barrels because I don't know that either, but two days later a disease destroyed the flora of the place and many of the animals died. That land was suddenly worth nothing and became a burden to its owners. They were willing to sell it at whatever price they were offered. I partnered with these friends of mine to buy an estate that is apparently wasteland but where, it seems, there are gas pockets. Nobody knows this, not even Suzi. Of course, the county's environmentalists will be up in arms on the day we start fracking. I've also carried out other operations for these associates. I need you for when the exploratory drilling starts. People will be against it, there will be protests, and they won't want fracking on land that's adjacent to theirs. As mayor, I will have to make it seem like I'm mediating, that I myself am debating between protecting the environment and encouraging progress. I need you to take care of everything."

"And you think these men are your friends? Come on, Roy, you're a useless fool, nothing more!"

"You have a very low opinion of me, Thomas. You see me as uncultured. I may not have been educated in good schools, but I'm nobody's fool. They need people like me and I need people like them. As long as we are useful to each other, things will tick along. I've managed to make changes in the region."

"And now they want the gas from your in-laws' land. What about Suzi? Your wife isn't stupid. I'm surprised she hasn't realized that you're hatching this kind of plan."

"She doesn't know. She thinks I like politics and that I want to become prime minister. She can see herself having tea with the Queen."

"So she isn't aware of your business dealings?"

"No, she would never turn against her parents. Nor would she do anything to alter the English countryside. She's been hunting since she was a child: she likes animals and doesn't understand that progress happens only when you make certain sacrifices. The world cannot stop for the sheep."

"She'll catch you red-handed."

"She hasn't yet."

"We'll see."

"I'm not lying to her, I'm just not sharing a few things with her."

"Why do you need a seat in Westminster? I'm sure your partners already have a bunch of good friends in Parliament, government ministers too."

"That's right. But I don't want to depend on just them. I need to cover my back. To be someone, not just a pawn they can use according to the circumstances. But the next step is to get that damned seat in Parliament. Being mayor is making me popular."

"You're a piece of work."

"That's why I knew I needed your help. When I read in the press what you'd done with Green, the shopping mall nobody wanted, how you sold it to the Chinese and got Cathy Major off your case, I was sure you were the man for me. You have no scruples, just like me."

"Those people . . . I don't know who they are but I doubt they consider you anything more than their pawn. When they don't need you anymore they'll get rid of you," I insisted.

"That's why I want to be at their level. But for now, I'm mayor and the next step is to win a seat in London. I'm not a worthless man of the prairies."

"You need me more than you imagine."

"So, do you accept?"

"No, as I said, I want to meet your partners. As for that Bernard Schmidt character, we'll talk later. I like to work on my own."

"All right, we'll talk about the German when you meet my partners."

I told Esther about the conversation with Roy, omitting nothing. If I was sure of anything I was sure that I could trust her.

"He's proved to be smarter than you. He made you believe he was a simple country man putting on airs and it turns out he is a shark. He manipulated you as he pleased," Esther declared.

She was right. During his electoral campaign, Roy had played me. Now I was deeply annoyed not to have realized this. I fancied myself a man of the world, but I actually had a lot to learn.

"You were and still are very young," Esther reminded me, "so it should come as no surprise that Roy took you for a ride."

"He deceived me," I complained.

"You were too clever by half. You're too full of yourself in your role as the bad boy. Also, when Roy called you, after the Green operation, you'd become arrogant. You thought you were the king of the world. You'd cashed out on two bankrupt real estate developers and a rich bystander; and to top it off, you'd been hired by a prestigious PR agency."

"Mark Scott didn't like Roy . . . nor did Cathy . . . I don't know why I let Roy convince me to work on his campaign."

"Because he knew what he wanted and played hardball. He won. He had you. Maybe another agency wouldn't have wanted to take charge of the campaign. He was going to lose all those votes, he needed to find someone like you to do the dirty work. It was essential that his election had the necessary guise of respectability."

"But his partners could have helped him."

"What for? They preferred to keep Roy as their messenger boy in that region. They don't need him in Westminster. Of course, they don't need you either, but since Roy is starting to get out of hand, they've decided it's better to get someone to rein him in."

"And what would you do?"

"I'm not in your place. I'm not like you, I don't have the same ambitions; my answer isn't useful."

"But you could give me your opinion."

"I could, but you don't need it."

"Don't you want to help me?"

"Of course I do, but you're the one who has to decide. I think you're dying of curiosity to meet Roy's partners. And . . . you'll accept."

"I haven't made the decision yet!"

"Of course you have. It's just that you're feeling insecure; you're worried Roy might manipulate you again. That scares you. You thought you were in control, and now you see that Roy was pulling the strings all along."

"Will you marry me?" I asked, worried.

"I don't know . . . I still don't know. I enjoy spending time with you, but is it enough? I don't think so. I aspire to love, Thomas, and with you, I'll never have it. We might share other things, and I'm not saying we can't be happy, but I dream of more than that. We already discussed this last night."

"You're very important to me, I wouldn't want to live with any woman but you. Our marriage would be more solid than if we were infatuated with each other; that stuff has a sell-by date."

"Yes, but once it's over something remains. There's something else . . . There are the embers of love and those embers maintain the union forever. I see my parents smiling at each other when they think we're not looking. My father holds my mother's hand, and when he does, we realize how important she is to him, how much he's loved her. And because he has loved her, he continues to love her. I don't know if you understand what I'm saying."

"Marry me, Esther, you won't regret it. We'll always be together."

"I need to think about it. I need to be sure that I care for you enough to renounce the kind of love I was hoping for. Anyway, now that you're staying in London you might find someone else, or I might meet someone else in New York. Let's not make plans, Thomas, not yet."

"I'm not staying in London. I'm coming back to New York with you."

Esther laughed.

5

She was right: I stayed in London. When I dropped her off at the airport I promised we'd meet in New York in a couple of days. I didn't keep my promise. She didn't expect me to either. Anyway, I missed my visits to Madame Agnès's house. The truth is I didn't want to be bothered; I preferred sleeping with any one of Madame Agnès's girls to spending nights with girls who smile at you and look at you all starry-eyed, like they care about you. Likewise, I hated having to make conversation with women I didn't know as a necessary step to ending up at my apartment.

Roy was very secretive about the people we were going to see and the place where we'd meet them. He insisted on picking me up at my apartment.

The place was as ordinary as could be, if "ordinary" is a word that can be used to describe a glass-and-iron building where you have to go through several security screenings to enter. The building was occupied by various companies and businesses. They were waiting for us on the twentieth floor, where a secretary greeted us at the elevator.

"Good morning, Mr. Parker, Mr. Spencer . . . They're expecting you."

We followed her to a door that she opened without knocking. It looked like a meeting room; it wasn't big. A round table with six chairs around it, a leather sofa and a couple of armchairs, a polished wooden bookcase, two or three pictures. Nothing that stood out.

Two men, whose appearance was as bland as the building, were waiting there for us. They were both in their fifties. One in a dark blue suit, the other in gray, both with discreet silk ties and good shoes. They seemed like classic executive types, as likely to be selling detergent or missiles.

"How are you doing, Roy? Mr. Spencer, I'm Brian Jones and this is Mr. Edward Brown. Please, take a seat."

Brian Jones shook my hand and I liked that his handshake was firm. Edward Brown seemed to hesitate, but in the end he shook my hand as well.

"I'll be clear, Spencer. We represent a conglomerate of businesses with different interests. Our clients demand discretion and efficiency, and that is what we give them. There's a very high price to pay for indiscretions in certain situations," Brian Jones said, looking at me directly.

I didn't bother to respond. I kept looking at him, waiting for him to say something else, as if that slight threat he'd slipped through his words did not affect me.

"Mr. Parker is very satisfied with the electoral campaign that you conducted. He insists on having you work for us. We have excellent PR and communications experts at hand, whose results have been more than satisfactory and whom we have put at his disposal. But Mr. Parker wishes you to be in charge of his affairs. Given that we hold interests with Mr. Parker, we wouldn't want the discretion which distinguishes us to be jeopardized. So we're not willing to work with any communications expert if we do not have full control. Our clients are people whose businesses have great standing and social prestige and they don't want anything to tarnish that reputation," Brian Jones continued.

While he was speaking, he tried to catch any expression on my face that might give away what I was thinking. But I remained impassive.

"Our dear friend Roy wants to fly high," Brown put in. "That's fine, it's good to be ambitious, as long as he doesn't do anything that threatens our business."

"Yes, Roy has his own ideas about how to do things, but it's easy to make a mistake," Brian Jones remarked.

"From what we understand, you insisted on meeting us. Well, our concern is doing things as they should be done. We believe that the best thing is for you to join one of the agencies that work under our supervision. You will, of course, have to sign a strict confidentiality agreement. Our clients pay us to ensure that they can operate with peace of mind," Brown added.

I glanced at Roy, fuming.

"I assured them they can trust you," said Roy, oblivious to my anger, waiting for me to confirm my trustworthiness to these men.

"Gentlemen, I am grateful for this meeting. I insisted to Mr. Parker that I meet you because it's important to know if we share the same interests; otherwise there's nothing more to talk about. However, I have not yet made a decision about whether I want to tie my fate to yours or to the people you represent. I don't know who they are or what they do, and as a matter of principle, I don't trust anyone, no matter their credentials.

"I suppose you researched my background prior to this meeting, so it won't be necessary for me to tell you that I don't need your money or your permission to start my own business if that is my ambition. In any case, if I decide to work with Mr. Parker I will mark out my own boundaries and decide what I will and will not do, whom I will work with and how. It should be clear to you that I am not looking for a job. I don't need one."

They looked at me, their poker faces not reflecting anything—not surprise, not annoyance, not interest, nothing.

"If you are here it's because Mr. Parker insisted on it. These days we need another way of doing things . . . Fresh ideas. You are very young. But you should understand that it's we who set the terms," said one of the lawyers.

"No, Mr. Brown, that is not the correct equation. If *I* decide to accept *you* as my clients, would be more precise."

I detected a flash of indignation in Brown's gaze. I knew he was thinking that I was nothing but a stuck-up brat and that as soon as I left the room they'd tell Roy they weren't going to support his decision to hire me.

"If we decide to work *together*, does that sound better? Naturally, you would need to adjust to our way of doing things. We have guidelines, norms, which are nonnegotiable. If you decide to work for . . . with us, we thought you might join GCP, Media and PR Management; it's a good agency, you may have heard of it. Mr. Lerman, Leopold Lerman, their director, is a prestigious professional. GCP, like other agencies that work for us, is under the supervision of a gentleman who has our total confidence, Bernard Schmidt. There is no one better than him at . . . the media business. If you decided to join GCP we would ask Mr. Lerman to allow you to put together a small team, perhaps your own secretary and a couple of assistants," Brown concluded.

"I may decide to help Parker with the fracking business that he and you want to carry out in Derbyshire county, but I'm not sure I want to be involved in anything else. You don't trust me but I don't trust you either. You don't seem to understand that I am not looking for a job," I replied, defiantly.

"Well, you'll have to make up your mind, Mr. Spencer. The exploratory drilling for fracking should begin in a couple of months. It's all the same to us if you decide to come on board or stay where you are." Brian Jones's tone was mild and indifferent.

"Come on, Thomas, don't pretend to be so peevish, it doesn't suit you. What's the problem with working for GCP?" Roy cut in.

"An agency where I will be just another employee," I responded, with more arrogance than was good for me.

"You were also an employee at Scott and Roth," Roy reminded me. "Why don't you try it out? If you're not convinced, you can go. I told the lawyers that I want you to dedicate yourself to me as you did when you were working at Scott and Roth. And as you can see, they agree."

"I don't know if I want to work for someone else again, to be given orders, to have to report on what I do and how, and consider whether there are red lines that can't be crossed."

"Mr. Spencer, you should draw your own red lines. If you do something you shouldn't, it will be your problem, never ours, because we'll never—remember this—we will never ask you to do anything that shouldn't be done."

"I see. This is beginning to sound like an espionage movie. The boss instructs the employee to risk his life and get rid of a few select targets for the good of the country, but if he is caught, the boss will say he doesn't know him, that he's never seen him before. That's what you're saying to me, isn't it?"

Brown and Jones both scowled. They didn't approve of my tone, and they didn't like that I was spelling out what was already implied. They needed someone else to dirty his hands, but they covered their backs so that, if anything went wrong, they could say they had never sanctioned any illegal activity.

I didn't like men like that. I preferred Roy, even though he had manipulated me. He was a liar capable of selling out his own mother if he could benefit from a situation.

"Mr. Spencer, you're very young and impulsive. I think it's going to be difficult for you to work with us. What you're saying is very far from what we want and, of course, from what our clients want." Brian Jones spoke slowly, but it was obvious he wanted to dismiss me.

Roy seemed furious. The way he looked at me made me think he would have punched me if he could. I had a split second to decide what to do. I didn't like those men and they'd made it clear that if I ran into any trouble they would abandon me to my fate.

"When can I meet your man?" I asked.

They seemed disconcerted by the question.

"What did you say?" Brown asked.

"You want me to work with somebody you trust. I want to meet him and speak to him before I make a decision."

"You can meet Mr. Lerman tomorrow. We'll call him to arrange a meeting. As for our general supervisor, Mr. Schmidt, he is not in London, but he'll be back in a couple of days. Perhaps we could arrange a meeting then," Jones said.

"I'd rather see Mr. Schmidt alone, without any of you present. If Mr. Schmidt doesn't object, I could take him to lunch. Ask him."

"Well . . . I don't know if that's the best idea. You'd be meeting Mr. Schmidt, nothing more. The correct thing to do would be for you to first meet with Mr. Lerman as soon as possible." Brown didn't like my proposal.

"Ask him. I insist on inviting Mr. Schmidt to lunch, since he's your man. Roy will tell me if Schmidt accepts, if that's all right?"

No, it wasn't all right, but Roy decided it would be done the way I asked. He wasn't prepared to lose ground beforehand and, if there was a possibility I might continue to work for him, he wanted at least to give it a try.

I left the building with a bitter taste in my mouth.

Those two men had given me indigestion. It had been naïve of me to think I would sit down with the people who truly ran the show. Brown and Jones were their representatives. I would never meet anyone other than these lawyers. Those who were really in charge were out of my reach.

I realized I still had a lot to learn, that I was a puppet to men like them, even Roy. I needed to think about whether I should move forward or get off a train I wasn't driving and whose final destination was unknown to me. But one thing I was sure about: I was no one to those two men and if they had to get rid of me they would do it, by hook or by crook—of course they would never stain their own hands.

I needed Esther to watch my back, to help me think, to keep my feet on the ground. I laughed at myself. I'd believed I was smarter than them, but I still had a ways to go if I wanted to measure up to men like them.

I called Esther and told her about the meeting. She listened to me without interrupting.

"Well, what do you think?"

"Roy's been playing you since the day he showed up at your office at Scott and Roth. What I don't know is whether he's as smart as he thinks or is just an ambitious opportunist. We also don't know whether those men you met intend to continue working with Roy after those fracking companies drill up the county. It might be that once they get what they want, they'll get rid of him."

"That's what Roy must think, that's why he wants to stack his deck."

"Of course, but because those men don't trust Roy, they've told him that if he wants to do business with them they'll have to keep tabs on everything he does. They won't let him work with you if it's not under their supervision."

"Would you accept?"

"Me? No, of course not. I like advertising—I enjoy designing a campaign to sell diapers or perfume, but a press office is something else entirely. It's about convincing the public of . . . well, more subtle things. Personally, I'd be scared of those men."

"You mean, you wouldn't work with me?"

"Don't ask me to, Thomas."

"Is there any chance that you'll say yes?"

"I don't think so. I'd prefer to continue living in New York. And in case you were wondering, I'm against fracking. Besides, you don't really need me. Call that Philip Sullivan guy you introduced me to. He'll do whatever you ask. He admires you."

"All right. And what do you think about Janet McCarthy?"

"The television communications professor? She seems like a

nice woman, so I don't know if she'll run for the hills as soon as you propose something that she considers not right. You're running a risk."

"Esther, I need you."

"Maybe you do."

"If you don't want to work with me, at least accept my first proposal. Let's get married."

"You want to have someone at home you can talk to about everything that's happening and who will give you good advice. But that's not love."

"For God's sake, don't keep repeating that! I don't know what love is, at least not the way you understand it, but I do know that I don't want to be with anyone else but you for the rest of my life. Is that not enough?"

"I'm afraid not. Call me any time you want. I'll listen to you and give you my honest opinion."

"I still haven't said yes to Roy and I don't know if I want to keep living in London either."

"Of course you do, that's why you stayed in London. You'll say yes."

"I want you to marry me."

"We'll talk about that later. We have time to make that decision."

I had to accept her answer. At the time it was the most I could get from her. But I started to realize that Esther was becoming an obsession. I thought that she was the only one who would be loyal and would help me, come what may. It would be difficult to convince her to work for me, but at least if we got married I would have her by my side. I was surprised at her romantic streak, but if I wanted to get her to accept my marriage proposal I needed to behave like an idiotic person in love. That same day I went to a flower shop with branch offices in New York and arranged for them to deliver a dozen red roses every day. It was a start. I'd think of something else later.

Roy took me to dinner to tell me he was annoyed with me.

"You're a brat. You nearly ruined everything."

"You know, Roy? I'm sick of your games. Either you tell me the whole truth or I'm out. I don't like being taken for a fool."

"I've told you everything you wanted to know and I introduced you to my partners, what more do you want?" he snapped.

"Those are not your partners, Roy. Those men represent a conglomerate of different interests. You are a pawn. Nothing more. Don't be mistaken. Of course you'll reap some benefit, but if you think they consider you to be one of them, then the joke's on you."

"I've done well until now. I'm a lot richer than when I met them and now I'm mayor."

"They'll clip your wings when they don't need you anymore. You're not one of them," I insisted.

"No, I don't go skiing in Switzerland, nor do I get invited to dinner parties where men do business over a glass of champagne. I don't rub shoulders with the 'big boys' yet, but I'll get there soon. Give me time and you'll see."

"What are you after, money or power?"

"Aren't they one and the same?"

"Not exactly. There are men who have fought for power without caring about money."

"I don't believe that; in the end, money and power always converge."

I didn't argue. I could have given him a few examples of men who fought for the power to change things, but never cared about money or simply enjoyed the thrill of imposing their will on others. But there was no way I could persuade him, so it wasn't worth trying.

"Are you going to work at GCP with Lerman?"

"Roy, I have a problem with you: I don't trust you anymore."

"Come on, Thomas, I can't always show you all my cards. I needed to make sure I could trust you, to see whether you really are worth what you think you are. Nobody in their right mind would have told a stranger everything you now know."

"And you're not worried about what I know?"

"Were you worried about ruining Frank Wilson and Jimmy Doyle? One of them you presented as an adulterer and the other almost as a thief. Not only did you manage to get them out of the election, but you also ruined their lives. Now we both know what kind of shit we're made of."

"Touché."

"It's surprising that you, being so young, could be so evil. I'm no saint myself. That doesn't mean we don't love our families. I love Suzi and the children and you love your family, but that does not make us good people."

I was about to retort that I doubted he loved Suzi; he didn't seem to give her much thought when we went to see Madame Agnès. And he couldn't imagine how little I cared about my family. But I kept my mouth shut.

"Get that appointment with their man, Bernard Schmidt, and I'll see what I decide. But my advice is that you shouldn't try to fly too high, or they'll clip—"

"My wings. You said that already," he cut in with a smirk.

"All they need is your in-laws' land, they don't need you," I said.

"You think I don't know that? I've hopped onto the wagon and I'm not going to let them push me off when they don't need me. Don't worry, I know how to look after my interests, and I will also know how to look after yours."

"Make no mistake, Roy, our interests are different. It may be that I work at GCP for a while, but I won't be your slave or theirs."

Esther was right. I stayed in London because I planned to accept Roy's offer. I didn't know why. Still, it all depended on the interview with Schmidt.

I'd started to think about whom I could hire among those who had already worked for me. One thing I was sure of: Philip Sullivan would be the first person I'd turn to.

Philip kept calling me to ask what my plans were and whether I intended to stay in London. But neither Janet nor my former assistant, Richard Craig, had called me after I'd returned to London. I had been someone of no importance who had passed through their lives. Neither ever entertained the possibility of having me as a friend. Janet, because she was a prude who spent her life fussing over her cat and the minutiae of university life. As for Richard, he didn't see me as an equal. He was an aristocrat who thought I was nothing but an American rich kid with no class. And he was right. Richard was always horrified by my clothes, which usually displayed brand logos. He considered this to be in bad taste. He never told me so, but he didn't need to: the look on his face was enough.

In addition to Philip Sullivan, I planned to make Maggie an offer. She was a good secretary. A skeptic, and efficient. And she needed money. If I offered her a good salary perhaps she would consider leaving Scott & Roth. And of course Neil would be key. He'd proven himself to be an exceptional researcher who didn't mind sticking his nose where it shouldn't be. I didn't care about his alcohol and drug problems. That was his business as long as he did the work I asked of him.

For a couple of days, I had nothing to do. I was waiting for Roy to call me to confirm my appointments, first with Leopold Lerman, then with Bernard Schmidt. The inactivity was making me anxious, so I decided to go to New York to see Esther. If Roy called me, I'd tell him that both Lerman and Schmidt would have to wait.

It was snowing in New York. But that wasn't a surprise. When I arrived home only María was there. My father was at the office and my brother, Jaime, had returned to Harvard, where he was now attending law school while combining his studies with work at a prestigious firm in Boston.

María wasn't happy to see me, nor I her. She said my room was ready. "Your father instructed me to keep your room ready, in case you turned up," she said. I didn't reply. I unpacked, took a shower, and phoned Esther, who didn't seem surprised that I was in town. She was at the agency and in the afternoon she had to go and teach at Paul's academy, so we arranged for me to pick her up there and go out for dinner.

I had a few hours to kill so I got into bed and fell asleep. It was around four when María entered my room. It infuriated me that she did so without knocking.

"Your father just arrived. He says he'll see you in the study and that I should make you a bite to eat."

"No need, I'll be going out for dinner."

"Sure, but you need to eat something, you haven't had anything all day."

"I've been asleep," I reminded her.

"That's what I mean." She left, slamming the door.

John was sitting in his old armchair reviewing some papers with a whiskey in his hand. When he saw me he got up and tried to give me a hug, which I avoided by extending my hand for a handshake.

"I'm happy to see you," he said.

"I'm only here for a couple of days," I replied.

"This is your home, you can stay as long as you want."

"Just two days, then I'll be back in London."

"I thought you'd decided to set up camp in New York, find work here."

"I've received a job offer. If we reach an agreement I'll stay there."

"What about that girl, Esther? You said you wanted to marry her."

"Yes. But we still haven't decided on it. Getting married is a decision that requires two people, you know. Anyway, I'm going to get ready. I'm going out to dinner with her."

"It's still a few hours till dinner and María told me you haven't even had coffee."

"I'm not hungry."

At that moment, María entered with a tray. I was tempted to say I didn't want anything, but I couldn't resist the warm ham and cheese sandwich.

"I'd like to speak with you. We have a few things to discuss," said John.

"There's not much to be said, don't you think?"

"Who are you angry at, Thomas? Me? Your brother? What have we done to you?"

"You've made me live a lie."

"Jaime didn't know anything."

"Maybe he didn't."

"As for Carmela . . . Your mother and I agreed that the best thing would be for you to live a normal life. I accepted you as my son, I've loved you and still love you like a son. There was no reason to tell you . . . that I was not your biological father. Do you really think it matters? I don't think so, Thomas."

"Well, it does. So much so that my mother didn't want to die without telling me."

"Your mother suffered a lot, yes; she never forgave herself for what happened to her when she was young, but she never regretted bringing you into the world. She didn't understand the reason for your attitude. The more she tried to be near you the more you rejected her. That led her to believe that she had to wash away her sins, and that if you only knew you'd be able to forgive and even love her."

"Well, she didn't achieve that."

"Why are you so cruel to everyone and to yourself? You have no right. We've always loved you: your mother, your grandparents, your brother, me. You'll never be able to say you weren't loved."

"It was all a huge lie."

"No, no, it wasn't. That's where you've got it wrong. There hasn't been one shred of a lie in the love we all feel for you. Whether you like it or not, to me you are my son; that's how I feel, that's what I want. My parents and Aunt Emma feel the same way. You are their grandson, her nephew. They can't think of you any other way. Grandma Dorothy is devastated because of your attitude. You didn't even let her give you a kiss. And Emma . . . You were always her favorite nephew, and you know it."

"Do you want me to thank you all for your pity?"

I noticed John was struggling to hold back a tear. He'd grown old and his face bared his desolation. If I was another kind of person I would have felt moved.

Yes, I should have reached out and hugged him, made him feel like I loved him. The scene could have been like this:

"I'm sorry, Dad, I never intended to make you suffer. It's just that Mama's confession was so painful . . . But I love you, and I loved her too. I love you all—you, my brother, my grandparents, Aunt Emma. You're my family and you always will be. I would never be able to love another father who isn't you. You are the best in the world. Thank you for accepting me as your son."

I could have said this. I could have made him aware of how important he had been to me, and still was. But I didn't; I didn't say any of those words because the resentment that I held within was a thick fog that kept any other feeling from emerging. I couldn't even feel pity for that man who loved me so sincerely.

I finished eating my sandwich, completely ignoring his pain. I was tempted to say that I would take all my things out of the apartment and that they would never see me again. But I thought it was better to be practical. I didn't know what the future might have in store and it was better to keep one foot here . . . making him and the rest of the family, of course, feel like they owed me something for their deceit.

"What do you want me to do, Thomas? Tell me. If I have to ask for your forgiveness, I will." I heard John's voice falter.

"Why don't we leave it be? There's nothing that can be done. Things are what they are."

And I went out of the study, leaving him alone with his despair. I thought I heard a whimper and I picked up my pace to get to my room as quickly as I could. I had another shower and went out with no destination in mind. I needed to kill time until I picked Esther up. I don't know why I ended up in front of Tiffany. I looked in the shop window, remembering the movie *Breakfast at Tiffany's.* I didn't think that Esther could remain indifferent if presented with one of those Tiffany rings.

I'd earned enough money to be able to spend a good amount on the gift. But it had to be a discreet ring: Esther was discreet, and she would never wear a big, flashy stone. I spent an hour with a nice saleslady whom I got to try on an endless number of rings to see what they'd look like when worn. In the end, I went for the most modest one, an engagement ring with diminutive diamonds. Esther would be able to wear it without fearing that it would draw too much attention.

I asked the saleslady what kinds of things a girl might like on the day she is proposed to. She gave me a few ideas. Thankfully, with a cell phone and a credit card you can make miracles happen. I went into a café and made a few phone calls. Then I went to Paul's academy. I was early. Esther was still in class, but Paul welcomed me, delighted.

"Wow, it's good to see you. I've been told that you've triumphed in Europe. I never doubted you'd make it. You have some survival instinct. Tell me all about your adventures."

I told him about the Green operation and Paul laughed heartily.

"So you deceived a few villagers and a Chinese guy. Well done."

"Well, I didn't really deceive them. Everyone won in the end."

"Especially you."

I didn't say anything, but I thought that if one day I had my own business I'd hire Paul. He was a washout, but had talent. Of course, I didn't know whether he was unscrupulous enough to be able to do certain things. Maybe he was. Paul was always short of money and the academy made barely enough for him to survive. His teachers were always leaving because he paid them too late. Esther was owed her last two months' pay.

"Brands are advertising less and keep asking for lower prices. Even the big agencies lay off people from time to time. You don't know how many old colleagues have knocked on these doors begging me to let them teach a couple of classes," Paul told me.

Esther came out of class. She smiled when she saw Paul and me chatting like old friends. She barely brushed my cheek when she kissed me.

Paul insisted on the three of us having a drink, but I refused.

"Another day. Today I need to talk to Esther about something important."

"Are you going to propose?" he asked, curious.

"If I were I wouldn't tell you before her."

We found a taxi two blocks away from the academy. I'd booked a table at one of the trendy restaurants in SoHo, which I thought Esther would like. I couldn't wait to give her the ring.

We had dinner and laughed, talking about all sorts of things. I insisted on ordering soufflé for dessert.

"But you don't usually eat sweet things," she remembered.

"But this is a special evening."

She looked at me, intrigued, and was surprised when I took

the box wrapped in Tiffany paper out of my jacket pocket. I had asked the saleslady not to give me a bag so as not to spoil the surprise.

"And what is this?" she asked, staring at the little package.

"Open it."

"But . . . I don't know . . ."

"Please!"

She tore the paper off and looked at the box before opening it. Her eyes shone with astonishment when she saw that symphony of tiny diamonds. She wouldn't dare take the ring or even try it on. It was me who took it out and put it on her finger.

"I'd like this to be the engagement ring, but if you are determined not to marry me I hope at least you never take it off and remember me always."

Esther looked at the ring and then at me without knowing what to do, but I realized she'd been moved; not so much by the diamonds as by what I'd said.

"I don't think I'll ever be able to forget you," she whispered.

"Then I won't give up on the hope that you won't need to forget me simply because we'll be together. I feel . . . Well, I wish I could be more romantic, but I am what I am and I can't deceive you. If it's any use to you, I'll say these days I've thought about you so much my head hurts, and you know what? I think you're the most adorable woman in the world."

She started to laugh with joy. She knew how hard I was finding it to say all that palaver.

"I don't know what to say . . . I don't know if I can accept this ring."

"Yes, you can and must accept it. I meant it when I said that even if you reject me I'd like you to keep it always. I don't want you to forget me."

She reached out her hand and I took it in mine; I didn't know what else to do. Then I signaled the waiter and he presented her with a rose. I'd wanted them to give her an entire bouquet, but when I phoned the restaurant they said they'd see what they could do at that hour of the evening. Apparently they'd managed to find only one rose.

For a second I thought Esther would burst into tears. She wasn't expecting me to pull out all the stops. And there was one more thing to come. An accordionist played us a few romantic tunes: "Lara's Theme," "Strangers in the Night," and "Only You."

When we were alone again she clasped my hand.

"Thank you, Thomas, this is the nicest evening I've ever had. I know this kind of thing . . . well, is not your style."

"Do you see now that I love you?"

"Yes, I think so."

"Will you marry me?"

I barely heard her say yes, but from her expression there was no doubt.

When we went out of the restaurant a limousine awaited us at the door. Esther started laughing. She was happy.

"The night of surprises!"

"The night when you finally decided to marry me."

"And what if I'd said no?"

"Well, I didn't really have a plan B."

The chauffeur knew what he had to do, so he drove us around New York for a couple of hours while we drank champagne and kissed. If I'd tried anything else Esther would have ditched me. She wanted romance and I was willing to give her plenty, at least for the night.

Esther's parents weren't pleased to hear their daughter had decided to marry me, but they knew that trying to oppose the match would have been pointless. As for John and Jaime, they seemed satisfied by the news.

John had phoned Jaime at Harvard to tell him, and my brother turned up in New York to congratulate me.

"Well, I'm glad you're marrying that girl. She seems like a trustworthy person with common sense."

"I thought you wanted me to wait before getting married."

"Yes, that's what I asked you to do, to wait at least six months. But Dad and I talked about it . . . Well, it's pointless to expect you to follow social conventions. You are the way you are. If you've got your mind set on getting married, that's what you'll do, and it's best if we're supportive and lend a hand."

Jaime's condescending attitude irritated me. My brother was treating me as if I were an impulsive teenager he had to put up with to avoid disaster.

"I don't need your support. I'm merely notifying you that I'm getting married," I said.

"Yes, you do need us even if you can't stand that fact." Jaime was upset.

"I'm not going to turn my wedding into a social occasion," I warned him.

"Does Esther want to get married without her family there? I doubt it. I doubt very much that she'll be content going to City Hall, getting the license, and considering herself married. She'll want a proper wedding—the way it should be."

Jaime went back to Harvard that same day and I stayed at home, where John was still trying to get me to speak to him. But I kept avoiding him. I tried not to get up until he left for the office, and I came back late, when he was already in bed. I did this to put him out. I needed to hurt him.

Jaime was right. Esther wanted a wedding she could invite her family and friends to, and assumed I wanted the same thing.

"I'd like a small wedding, if possible, with no one but you and me," I nearly pleaded with her.

"What will your father think? And your grandparents and brother? No, Thomas, we're not going to elope. We're going to have a wedding where we can share our joy with everyone we love."

I realized that I still hadn't explained my family problems or told her that I wasn't really John's son.

When I did tell her about it, Esther looked at me without

flinching. I even thought that in light of my family circumstances, she might decide to cancel the wedding.

"I'm surprised at you. You say you can't stand your father and you talk about your brother with such contempt," she said, worried.

"I just told you, he's not my father."

"Of course he is. And the least you owe him is to treat him with affection and consideration. John Spencer has proved to be a great person."

"You think I owe him."

"We all owe something to someone. Yes, in life we are perpetually indebted to others, to the people who generously give us their love, whether they're our parents, our friends, or our children. We have to do things because it's the right thing to do, but on some level we always expect a reward; with affection, we at least expect to get back what we've given."

At that point I started to wonder whether I had made a mistake by insisting on marrying Esther. We couldn't be more different. She had some principles that I was lacking.

I decided not to change direction. I knew I needed a woman like her to help me, so that she would think for me, even if I then decided to take a plunge into the abyss.

Besides, marrying her had now become a matter of stubbornness, so I let her organize the wedding as it suited her.

Aunt Emma—I still hadn't managed to stop thinking of her as my aunt—phoned me to offer help with the wedding arrangements; she even suggested we get married at her home in Newport.

"Spring is a nice season of the year. Esther is Catholic. She'll want to be married in a church, of course, and there's one in Newport that's very special. It's where Jackie married John F. Kennedy. We could organize a reception in our garden. Why don't you suggest it to Esther?"

I was tempted to say no, but I preferred to speak to Esther about it. She had been complaining for a couple of weeks about how expensive it was to organize a proper reception, especially considering our many relatives. When I insisted that money was not a problem, she would get impatient.

"We shouldn't overspend without good reason. You may have been born into a rich family, but even rich people go bankrupt if they don't know how to handle their money."

At first she wasn't sure if we should get married in Newport.

"I've never even been there. All I know is that it's where rich people from New York and Boston have their vacation homes, and precisely because of that I don't know if that's where I want to get married," she said, uneasily.

"I'll take you for a visit and if you don't like it then there's nothing more to discuss," I said, without trying to convince her.

Esther and Aunt Emma seemed to get along, at least on the phone. For Esther, it was a relief to be able to count on somebody to help organize the wedding. She worked from dawn to dusk and her mother spent all day at the family's restaurant. Aunt Emma seemed enthusiastic too. She didn't have anything else to do and organizing a wedding would keep her entertained for a while. When Emma invited John and Jaime to what she called an improvised family reunion, they agreed immediately.

So the following weekend we went to Newport. Before arriving at Aunt Emma's house, I showed Esther around the area. She looked at everything with wide-open eyes, like a child.

"Oh my God, those mansions! This place is beautiful! And the people . . . they seem so happy and carefree. You can tell people here are different."

"Don't be silly. This is just a place like any other," I replied, amused.

"Of course it's not! Neither my family nor I would be able to afford to come to a place like this. You're used to it because the Spencers have money."

I shrugged. Yes, the Spencers had always had enough money

to live comfortably but that didn't mean they were rich, at least not in the way Esther was thinking.

We strolled for a good while longer around the port. We sat down for coffee and watched the boats. The scent of the sea filled the air; that always improved your mood. We walked past St. Mary's Church.

"It seems so unassuming on the outside . . . And to think this is where Jackie married the president . . ." she said, gazing at the church in awe.

"When they were married he wasn't president," I reminded her.

"Of course, but he was rich enough for his family to have a vacation home here."

Esther was nervous about seeing the Spencers.

She had met them only a couple of times: the day of our graduation, when Lisa insulted her, and then briefly during my mother's wake.

She looked in amazement out the car window and wouldn't stop talking about what she was seeing.

"You can tell people who come here are rich. They go around looking disheveled but look at them, they wear only designer clothes," she said.

"You think?"

"Yes, they're exactly like you. You wear T-shirts but yours aren't like the ones the rest of us wear, that's why they look so good," she proclaimed.

"I'll give you a few." I chuckled.

When we arrived at Emma's house, she met us at the door. Esther wasn't able to contain herself. She exclaimed, "My God, what a mansion!"

"You like it? You have no idea how happy that makes me, but wait till Thomas shows you the real mansions on Bellevue

Avenue. When you visit the palace of the Vanderbilts, Marble House, or The Elms, you'll see that my house isn't a mansion. But we've all been very happy in this house. Thomas used to love spending the summers here. We went sailing, played tennis, held tea parties with our friends' children . . . I hope you have children and come visit." Aunt Emma beamed as she showed Esther the garden.

I didn't comment, but suddenly I felt good in that house full of big windows that gave way to the horizon, with the sea drawing a line against the sky. The scent of the ocean and the flowers in the garden took me back to my childhood. I wasn't going to admit it, but the closest I'd ever come to being a happy child had been in that place.

They took some time to come back to the living room, and when they did, they looked like the best friends in the world. They spoke about how they would decorate the garden, whether it was necessary to set up a gazebo, which caterers to hire . . .

"It's been decided, we'll get married here. Your aunt is right, we'll do it in the spring. Imagine how beautiful the place will look . . . And of course, I want to get married at the same church where Jackie and John F. Kennedy were married. God, my mother won't believe it! It's a dream!"

Breakfast went better than I'd expected. John didn't speak much but Jaime and Aunt Emma chattered away, and Esther kept pace. I simply observed them, as if everything were happening without me. Even so, it was going to be an uphill battle to spend the entire weekend there with the others . . . If they had vanished and left Esther and me alone, I would have been happy.

John proposed a tennis match in the afternoon. I was going to say no but Esther went ahead and agreed on my behalf.

"What a good idea! We can play tennis, you against Thomas and me against Emma or Jaime."

"Well, I'd rather not play tennis today, it's cold. I'll wait by the fire," said Aunt Emma.

I was saved by the bell. My cell started ringing insistently and Roy's number appeared on the screen. I excused myself from the table and went to my room.

"Everything's been arranged. You'll have lunch with Bernard Schmidt on Monday at the Savoy. Then you'll meet Lerman."

"I'm in New York."

"Fantastic, you have plenty of time to come back to London. You're the one who insisted on that lunch, so don't start inventing excuses like being in New York."

"I didn't say I wasn't coming. Tell Schmidt I'll be at the Savoy at noon. And remember I want to have lunch with him alone. By the way, he must be a very busy man, I've been waiting a couple of weeks for your call."

"Don't try my patience, okay? Things aren't as easy as you think. Schmidt is a very important man. He couldn't come to London sooner. I imagine you've been thinking about who you're going to hire for your team. Decided on any names?"

"I'll be honest with you, Roy. I haven't thought about anything. I've been wandering around New York for two weeks. I'm getting married."

I don't know why I thought he'd be glad to hear the news, but he was quiet for a few seconds before congratulating me.

"I hope that doesn't delay our plans."

"Your plans, Roy. I still haven't decided if we're going to share them."

"Don't start! Grow up, Thomas, and stop playing hard to get. I don't know why I trust you . . . You're still wet behind the ears."

I didn't like what he said and I hung up. Actually, I was beginning to like Roy less and less. My cell rang again. I answered.

"You seem very susceptible right now, pal. Getting married is clouding your judgment. Suzi will be very happy to hear you're marrying Esther—I assume that's who you're marrying. Suzi liked her. They'll become friends, you'll see."

"Forget about it. We'll talk later." And I hung up again.

Roy's phone call had saved me not only from playing tennis with John, but, even better, from spending the rest of the weekend with a family that I didn't feel was mine. I found it absurd that Esther should refer to John as my father and Emma as my aunt.

I returned to the dining room and announced that I had to depart for London immediately.

"I have an important business meeting on Monday; a lot of things depend on that meeting."

Esther was upset that I would cut the weekend short. She felt at ease in that house and seemed to be enjoying spending time with the people who had been my family.

"We don't need to go back to New York now. You can fly tomorrow," she entreated.

But I didn't accept. She'd seen Aunt Emma's house, and she'd had lunch with my father and brother. That was enough for her to get a feel for the place and for those people.

"I'm sorry, but I need to go now. I'm hoping to find a flight tonight. I have to prepare for that meeting and the papers I need are in London."

"You don't need to go. Stay with us. You can return to New York tomorrow with John," Aunt Emma said to Esther.

"No, no, I appreciate it but it's best if I go too."

"Are you worried I might beat you at tennis?" Jaime joked with Esther.

"I know I'll win. But that match will have to wait," Esther replied with a smile, though I could tell she was upset.

John seemed devastated that I was leaving and insisted on returning to New York too. But Aunt Emma wouldn't allow it, saying she'd invited a few friends to dinner that night to meet Esther and, since Esther and I were leaving, she couldn't disappoint them even more by canceling the dinner party.

During the return to New York, Esther was very quiet.

"I'm sorry the weekend was ruined, but you know I was waiting for Roy's call."

"Yes, I know. But you don't need to make me believe you're sorry he called you precisely today. You wanted to leave. You're an idiot, Thomas, a tremendous idiot. Only an idiot wouldn't appreciate everything you have. Your family adores you, and they would do anything to make you happy."

"You don't understand." I found it infuriating that she would burden me with her opinion when I didn't want it.

"It's not possible to understand something that doesn't have an explanation. You're hurt, deeply hurt because your mother gave birth to you. You would like to have been like Jaime because he looks like John, and you, like all kids, loved your father and wanted to look like him. But it turns out you're dark and barely over five foot seven, and you have a complex about that. Actually, you must have always known something was up . . . That's why you had that tense relationship with your mother. You were never able to enjoy her love, or your father's, or the rest of your family's. It seems ridiculous that someone like you would believe that what matters in life are our blood ties. If that's what you think, you're wrong; what matters are the ties of affection that are woven each day. You love John, not because he's your father, but because you received his love, so much so that you couldn't remain indifferent. The same happened with your aunt Emma. As for Jaime, it's obvious that you're jealous. Even so, he loves you."

"You should have been a psychiatrist, as I told you before," I replied, curtly.

"Do yourself and the rest of us a favor: stop hurting yourself. You have a beautiful family, enjoy it."

I nearly ordered her to get out of the car, telling her that I couldn't stand her and that there was no way I was going to marry her. I almost did. I didn't want a woman by my side who'd try to rip my soul to pieces.

"What we are going to do is never speak about all this again. I won't stand for being accused of being jealous of my brother, or any of those things you said. If that's what you think of me maybe you shouldn't marry me."

Esther wasn't expecting that answer. She kept quiet for a long time, as if she were making a decision.

"You're right. We shouldn't get married. At least not before you've made amends with yourself and with everyone else. Until then, you won't be happy, and you won't be able to make anyone else happy either."

I didn't know what to say. Esther had given me a taste of my own medicine. We remained silent until we arrived in New York. I dropped her off at her home. She said goodbye with a kiss so light I barely felt it.

The scene could have been different. It should have been thus:

I should have told Esther that at least I'd make an effort, yes, I'd try to make amends with John and with Jaime, and I'd send some flowers to Aunt Emma to thank her for offering to help us with the wedding. I should even have promised to introduce Esther to Grandpa and Grandma Spencer as soon as possible. She'd like them. Grandma Dorothy would be a bit aloof at first, but as soon as she decided that Esther was the right girl for me she'd give her her full attention.

Yes, I should have promised her that I'd try, that I wouldn't go back to London before making things right with her. But I didn't. I remained silent, watching her walk through the door. She didn't even turn back to look at me.

During the flight to London, I tried to visualize how I should have behaved. How Esther would have reacted, John's joy if I'd hugged him—but there was no turning back. I was already on a plane and I wouldn't regret not doing what I could have done. I was simply the way I was and Esther would be fighting a losing battle if she tried to change me.

I arrived at the Savoy a few minutes early. Bernard Schmidt was already waiting at the table, which annoyed me, but annoyance soon gave way to surprise. He wasn't what I was expecting. I don't know why I'd visualized Schmidt as bearing a physical resemblance to Mark Scott. Instead, I met a man who was already in his sixties, with white hair, barely taller than me, wearing a boring navy-blue suit. The only thing that stood out about him were his icy gray eyes.

He shook my hand firmly, so firmly I had to pull away immediately.

"Well, I'm glad we're meeting at last," I said, as I sat down.

He looked at me and just nodded. He seemed to expect me to start the talking. I gave a drink order to the waiter and began.

"As you know, Roy Parker has a special interest in having me take care of his affairs again. I was responsible for his electoral campaign and he was pleased with the results."

Schmidt continued regarding me with interest, without flinching. I was starting to get nervous.

"Mr. Parker's partners suggested the possibility of my joining one of Mr. Lerman's agencies, GCP, which, as far as I know, you supervise. I'm sure you understand that before making any decisions I thought it absolutely necessary for us to meet and see if we could work together."

I paused. It was his turn. I wasn't planning to say another word until he did, so I occupied myself by taking a sip of the Campari that the waiter had brought me.

He took his time to speak. He allowed the silence to settle between us while he brought a glass of white wine to his lips.

"That's a fantastic Chardonnay," he said, moving the glass on the table. "Well, it's best if we begin by clarifying a few con-

cepts. You work for Mr. Parker, and I've been collaborating with
the law firm of Mr. Jones and Mr. Brown, whom you recently
met. Mr. Parker was so insistent on working with you that we've
gone on to consider the option of you joining GCP, where you
will primarily look after Parker's affairs."

"A good option for you to consider; Roy wants to work with
me," I replied with a smirk.

"Mr. Jones and Mr. Brown represent several consortia and
cannot afford to leave their clients' interests outside of their
control. Outside their full control."

"So I've been told. But, at least for now, Roy is indispensable
for advancing the interests of some of those clients, so you are
going to be tolerant in allowing me to continue to work for him.
These are the facts at hand, Mr. Schmidt. Now let's move on to
the important part," I countered, impatiently.

"Brian Jones has asked me to explain to you how we work.
The agencies we collaborate with receive my assessment regard-
ing issues concerning our clients. I give the final go-ahead, and
not one piece of paperwork is handled without my knowledge.
Any action taken, whatever it is, must meet with my approval.
If you join GCP, you will be in charge of everything related to
Mr. Parker. You will be able to design strategies, appoint your
team members; you'll have a certain degree of autonomy, but the
penultimate decision is Mr. Lerman's, and the final one is mine.
If this is clear between us, there won't be any problems. There's
a lot of money at stake and Mr. Jones and Mr. Brown don't want
to take any risks. I am in charge of ensuring that GCP does what
it has to do, and overseeing the way in which things are done."

"I'm sorry, Mr. Schmidt, but if I decide to join GCP, I will
not be answering to anyone or anything except my own criteria.
Nobody will be above me on matters concerning Mr. Parker. I
don't work for anyone."

"Of course you do, Mr. Spencer, you actually haven't stopped
doing so since you left Paul Hard's academy. Who is, by the
way, a good publicist though with very bad luck."

He was right. First I had worked for Cathy, then for Mr. Bennet and Mr. Hamilton, both of them apprentice developers. Later for Scott & Roth. I'd actually never been independent, but I had acted as if I were. However, I was sure that if I joined GCP, Bernard Schmidt would never allow me to forget that he had the final say.

"You are very young, Mr. Spencer. You still have a lot to learn. The clients of the solicitors of Jones and Brown do not allow for beginner's mistakes. They won't put one pound at stake without being certain they will win. They never even consider the possibility of losing. My role is that of a consultant, although as I said before, on certain issues I have the last word. Take it or leave it."

"You mean you are not another partner of GCP. Are you a partner of the solicitors?"

"Listen, Mr. Spencer: I am invisible. I am not here, I am not speaking to you, I don't exist."

"I don't understand . . ."

"There's nothing for you to understand. If you decide to accept Roy Parker's offer, let me know. I will tell you what to do and how to do it. All you have to do is follow my instructions. If you do, everything will run smoothly. Of course, you'll be able to put a sign on your office door that says 'associate director' if that soothes your ego." Bernard Schmidt spoke in a monotone. Maybe his words were offensive, but his way of saying them seemed to take away the harshness. However, it was obvious that he was used to being the boss and having no one argue with his orders. I realized that if I had been so naïve as to think I could take the reins by meeting him, I'd been wrong. As things stood, I was going to get into something I didn't quite understand. The word "consortium" was starting to sound strange to me.

"You're telling me I'll only be a straw man," I said.

"I'm saying that there are some rules in this game, which you have just joined. The truth is that you can only be a pawn. Take it or leave it. It's all the same to us. Mr. Parker wants you, but you are not indispensable, not even to him."

We'd barely touched our food, though I was hungry. I didn't want anything to distract me from this conversation, which Schmidt was dominating. He had barely touched the sole meunière that the maître d' had so highly recommended, although it was too buttery for my taste.

"I need to think about it."

"Do. I don't think you know what you're getting yourself into."

"I have a few clues," I retorted.

"I don't believe you do. You would do well to think carefully about this. I'll tell you one thing: once you get into this you won't be able to come out unless they want to throw you out, and that will be either because you did your job badly or because they don't trust you, which will have dire consequences for you."

"I believe you underestimate me." I wanted him to know I was offended.

"Hardly. I know you better than you know yourself, that's all. You're enjoying your role as the bad boy, living on the edge. Because you know that there's a safety net underneath, which is your family. Also, you believe you're worth more than you really are because up until now you've managed to avoid stumbling."

The coldness of his monotone didn't preclude my feelings of surprise and irritation. I found his references to my family particularly presumptuous. I didn't know how to respond. I would have liked to have said something hurtful but I couldn't think of anything.

"I have nothing against you personally, Spencer. I limit myself to doing my job, and if I have to supervise your work at GCP that's what I'll do. But when one works for certain clients one must know what the rules are, and whether one is treading on firm ground or heading into a swamp."

"You've made things very clear, Mr. Schmidt. I'll tell Mr. Parker whether I accept the offer or not, and under what conditions. If you don't mind, I won't be staying for coffee."

I didn't shake his hand goodbye. I left him there at the table. And I didn't bother paying the bill, even though it was me who'd said I'd take him to lunch. Let the consortia or the lawyers pay.

On my way to my apartment, I had to fight the temptation to phone Esther. She would have analyzed the situation with the distance with which she considered everything related to work and daily life. I needed her advice. I felt more alone than I'd ever felt. I was aware that I had no one I could trust, and no one to go to. Even if my relationship with John had been good, I wouldn't have been able to tell him about a conversation like the one I'd just had with Bernard Schmidt. John was too honest a man to accept that there was a hidden world of shadows where history was written.

I phoned Roy's cell, but Suzi picked up.

"He's in the office at a party meeting."

I nearly burst out laughing. Suzi talked about the party as if it were something important, and not something invented by Roy to become mayor, as a necessary step toward getting a seat in London. He had done so not to defend the farmers or the miners in the area, but for his own benefit, and that of his supposed partners, Jones and Brown.

"Their meetings are at your home?"

"Well, it's just the most important people. I'll tell him to call you."

"Yes, tell him, it's urgent."

"When will you drop by for a visit?"

"I have a lot of work, but I'll find the time."

"We could always come to London instead. How's your girlfriend? She seems like a nice girl."

"Tell Roy to call me." And I hung up. The last thing I needed was for Suzi to try to get me to talk about Esther.

If I wasn't able to speak to Roy, then there was only one other person whom I could talk to with a certain degree of trust: Philip Sullivan. He had helped me to set up the smear campaign against Roy's political rivals. His hands were as dirty as mine, so he wouldn't get all panicky even if he was shocked by what I had to tell him.

Philip was eager when I invited him to my apartment for a drink and to talk about our professional futures. At least there was someone who would listen to me.

I didn't go into much detail, but I told him enough to give him the idea that on this occasion what Roy was proposing was not as innocent as before.

"So Roy wants you to work for him alone. He's a dark horse, isn't he? I thought he was just some sheep farmer," Sullivan said, worriedly.

"Well, now you see that he's not. But his partners have made it clear that if Roy wants me with him, there would be strings attached. I'd have to join GCP, Leopold Lerman's agency. His partners are lawyers who represent all kinds of special interests— guns, energy, cement, you name it. Anything that makes money. I don't think Roy means much to them. When they get what they want from him, they'll get rid of him."

"And that's what Roy is trying to avoid."

"Exactly. He thinks he can sit at the big boys' table."

"He's too ambitious."

"Yes, and that could ruin him."

"Have you decided what you're going to do?"

Philip Sullivan looked at me expectantly. I decided to be honest with him.

"I haven't, and that's why I'm talking to you. I'm not going to hide it from you, the chance to work with Roy again is tempting, but there are a lot of risks attached. If the election campaign two years ago was dirty, just think what could happen from here on out."

"Also, his partners have made it clear that they're washing their hands of him. And if you do something you shouldn't . . ." Philip said.

"Exactly. What would you do?"

He was silent for a while, and his silence made me nervous.

"Come on, make up your mind," I insisted.

"It's a tough one. There are risks in working for an agency and being an employee. Another option would be to set up your own agency, communications or PR, and to have Roy as one of your clients. You'd have control and you wouldn't have to do anything you didn't want to."

I thought for a few moments. Philip Sullivan had just given me an idea: striking out on my own.

"But that's not what Jones and Brown want. They want to have absolute control. There are other firms that work for them and they don't need a new one, much less one to handle difficult cases," I said.

"Well, forget about Roy and his partners and go out on your own. You made a name for yourself in London thanks to the Green deal and the Rural Party campaign, and you haven't lost that reputation."

"Don't be so innocent. No one here will give me any of the big jobs. I'm still a foreigner."

"So you think you've got no options but to accept Roy's offer or go back to New York . . . I don't see it like that, but you'll have to decide for yourself."

I was annoyed that Philip Sullivan wouldn't come down on one side or the other. Suddenly he seemed to me like one of those prissy English types who get all nervous at the first sign of change.

"You're right; I have to decide. Would you work with me?"

Philip was silent again. It was hard for him to give me a straight "no."

"It depends," he said after a pause. "I'd have to know more about these partners of Roy's, and more than that I'd have to know what role I would be expected to play. What we did in Roy's campaign . . . Well, you know it wasn't good. I don't know if I want to carry on taking part in . . . things like that."

"And your friend Neil?"

"I suppose he'd be up for it, he's got nothing to lose. He always needs money. Alcohol is expensive in England."

"I'd like to be able to count on you," I insisted.

"Thank you. You know that I've always worked well alongside you. I trust you. But this may be too much for me. Why don't you get Neil to sniff around a bit and try to find out more about these lawyers, Brian Jones and Edward Brown?"

"And Bernard Schmidt. Ultimately, Schmidt would be in charge. Yes, you're right. Could you ask Neil to look into it?"

"You know it'll cost you."

"I'm willing to pay."

I gave Philip an envelope with two thousand pounds in it, for Neil to get to work.

I was left alone, and in a foul mood. I had hoped that Philip Sullivan would unconditionally offer to throw in his lot with mine, but he'd suddenly become cautious. I guess he was scared of going too far. The first time he'd crossed the line was when he was dealing with that guy who hacked into the Bank of England. The second had been during Roy's campaign. He was scared that the third time his luck would turn.

I poured myself a whiskey with a single ice cube and downed it. I didn't have anything better to do than drink. I didn't really have any friends in London. I didn't know anyone apart from some wannabe models who would be happy to have dinner with a man like me, who would take them to a fashionable restaurant where they could be seen and who would then get a little extra present from me in bed. There were also Madame Agnès's girls and the people I'd worked with. But not even Philip Sullivan was my friend.

I dialed Esther's number, but hung up before she could answer. I couldn't tell her that I was going to change and reconcile myself with John and the rest of the family, and she had made it very clear that she didn't want to have anything to do with me unless that happened.

I wondered if I could ever find anyone else like her. A woman with whom I didn't have to pretend to be someone I was not. Yes, there had to be another Esther in the world. It was just a matter of finding her.

I thought of Cathy. She might agree to have dinner with me. I called her.

"What do you want?" she asked drily when she heard my voice.

"To sign a peace treaty. How about we have dinner this evening?"

"A terrible idea. You're the last person on earth I'd have dinner with. Anything else?"

"Yeah. How often did you have to fuck Mark to get my job?" I retorted.

She hung up without saying anything. I can't say I was surprised. I kicked a chair and hurt my foot and then my cell phone rang. It was Roy. I was pleased to hear from him.

"All this party wrangling is nonsense" was the first thing he said. "I've spent the whole afternoon listening to nonsense. Did you and Schmidt eat?"

I told him about the meeting with Schmidt in detail and he didn't seem to like what I had to say.

"Hey, Thomas, don't waste my time. I want you but if you don't want to come aboard then tell me. Jones and Brown have made things clear: you have to work for GCP and Schmidt is part of the deal. They don't know you and they don't trust you. There's a lot of money at stake, and they can't take any risks. That's fair enough, don't you think?"

"I thought it was you who decided who ran your business," I said angrily.

"That's what I want, but they've got the whip hand here, and it's their way or the highway. I'm going with them. I need them: when I'm stronger I'll be able to do without them."

"And they'll be able to do without you." I laughed.

"They'll try."

"You'll never be in their organization. They won't even let you come in through a side door."

"Yes, I guess they'll play their hand and I'll play mine. You need to decide if you're going to deal yourself in, or pass."

"I still haven't decided, Roy. All I can see at the moment are the drawbacks. These lawyer friends of yours seem dangerous."

"They are, Thomas. There's no one who represents the electricity companies, the gas companies, cement, the arms industry, who isn't dangerous. If they were nuns they'd be in a convent."

"Well, we agree on that."

"I'm going to insist, Thomas. Give me a yes or a no."

"I need to think about it."

"Okay, I'll give you two days. If you don't call me within two days then I'll take it that you're opting out. But if you're in, then I don't want you to come to me with bullshit. You'll have to work for GCP and get on with Leopold Lerman, and you'll have to keep Schmidt informed of every step you take."

"I need a week."

"A week? You need a week to decide if you're going to work with me?" Roy was getting ever more agitated.

"This is the most difficult decision I've ever had to make. I need to go over the pros and cons carefully."

"I don't believe you."

"All right, don't believe me, but give me a week."

Roy fell silent. I could hear his breathing on the other end of the telephone. Knowing him as I did, I imagined that he was considering whether to end our relationship, maybe even hang up on me.

"I don't trust you, Thomas. I don't know what you're playing at," he said.

"I don't trust you either, Roy, but I need a week. If you don't want to accept that, it's no problem—we'll each go our own way."

"A week, not a day more."

After talking to Roy I decided to get drunk. I think I must have finished a whole bottle of whiskey. I woke up on the living-room floor. It was cold, but I was so drunk that I didn't think I could stand, so I stayed where I had fallen. That's how the maid found me the next morning. I had forgotten that she was due to come.

"Mr. Spencer! Are you all right? Goodness!"

I held on to the edge of a table and pulled myself to my feet as best I could.

"I'm fine. Do what you need to do. Do it quickly and get out," I managed to say in a drunken nasal voice. Then I spent a long time in the shower. My head hurt and I wanted to throw up.

When I left my room, shaved and dressed, the maid had already gone. She had only straightened up the living room. The right thing to do. Drunks are unpredictable.

I called Philip Sullivan to find out if Neil had taken the job. He had, but he didn't know how long it would take for him to discover information about Roy's partners. I insisted to Philip that I needed to know in under a week.

"What you want isn't easy to do. Neil will get the information, but it'll take time."

"Roy's given me a week to make up my mind."

"You've got a lot to lose. You could set up your own agency and not have to work for anyone," he insisted.

"I could go back to New York as well."

"Yes, you could go back to New York. That wouldn't be a bad idea either. Ah, and Cathy's told everyone that you rang her up last night and invited her to dinner. They've had a good laugh at your expense."

"I just wanted to screw her."

"That's not a good idea, given that she'll never forgive you for the Green business."

"It's thanks to me that she's working for Scott and Roth now," I reminded him.

"She's a practical girl," Sullivan said, with mild irony.

I felt alone. I had nothing to do. I didn't want to go to museums. I decided to leave. It was a Tuesday. I had a week before I had to give Roy an answer, so I bought a ticket to Madrid. I don't know why I chose that city. I guess I thought it wouldn't be a bad idea to visit the city my mother's forebears had once left. That is, if there was a drop of Spanish blood left in her body, because given the color of her skin, and mine, it was clear that her ancestors had bred with blacks and Indians.

Madrid surprised me. I don't know why, but I thought it would be small and backward, and I instead came to a large city that swallowed travelers whole.

As he was driving me to my hotel the taxi driver gave me endless recommendations, from restaurants to fashionable bars, and he even mentioned a couple of places that, he said, had stunning girls.

The hotel was in the city center, near a mildly bohemian district called the Barrio de las Letras. I thought it would be something like the Latin Quarter in Paris.

The concierge added a few suggestions to the taxi driver's. I asked him when the bars closed and he smiled.

"Madrid never sleeps."

"But it's nine o'clock already," I said, dubious.

"That's early for here—too early. It's even too early to eat dinner. Younger people go out later, at around midnight."

I left the hotel ready to discover a city that I didn't know if I would like.

I fell in love. Yes. I fell in love with Madrid. I had been born in New York, I had lived in London, and I had seen the world. Berlin, Paris, Vienna . . . All of them are doubtless more attractive, but Madrid has something that they lack: it is an open city, where nobody cares where you come from, who you are, what you want, or where you're going, and where people talk to you without knowing you, and welcome you into their lives.

I went to a bar that was rowdy enough for me to pass unnoticed. I sat at the bar and ordered a whiskey. The bartender looked at me strangely but he served me at once.

"You surprised him," I heard someone say.

I turned around and found myself face-to-face with a young woman who was looking at me with a smile. She was with a group and no one seemed to think it odd that she had spoken to me.

"Surprised? All I did was order a whiskey."

"That's why. Almost nobody drinks whiskey. Well, older people."

"What do people drink here, then?"

"Gin, cocktails, beer, wine . . . Where are you from?"

"I've just gotten here from London," I replied.

"But you're not a Londoner . . ."

"I'm from New York."

She looked me up and down until she seemed satisfied that I might be from New York.

"Are you alone?"

"Yes."

"Do you know Madrid?"

"No, it's my first time here."

"I'm Ivonne."

"Thomas."

She introduced me to her friends. A varied group. Ivonne explained to me that she was Parisian and that she lived in Madrid and taught French at a language school, as did two of her friends. The others all did other things. They were celebrating the fact that one of them had just gotten a job.

"José works for a car company, Pablo teaches Spanish to foreigners, Matthew teaches English, Ana just got a job as a secretary at a multinational corporation, Blanca's a piano teacher."

There were a lot of people in the group and I lost interest in finding out what all of them did. I don't know how it happened, but I quickly found myself caught up in their conversation.

I remember that they were talking about the advantages and drawbacks of globalization. I started to have fun. This was a new situation for me. And I was even more surprised when they said that they were going to another bar. Ivonne invited me to go with them. I accepted immediately.

I don't know how much I drank that night. All I know is that it was the most enjoyable night I can remember. I decided to imitate them, ordering beer at one bar and wine at the next. At the third bar, José, the one who bought and sold cars, said to me sotto voce: "Hey, you should eat something or you're going to get drunk. The key to drinking is to keep a full stomach."

I followed his recommendation, although I admit that by the end of the night the alcohol had gotten to me a little. Ivonne and José offered to take me back to my hotel.

The next morning I was woken by the insistent beeping of my cell phone. It was Ivonne. I didn't remember giving her my number, but I must have done so.

"Does your head hurt?" she said by way of greeting.

"A little," I replied.

"Who drinks like that? You drank a lot, and that's compared to us, who aren't lightweights. What are you going to do today? If you want, Blanca and I could come and give you a tour of Madrid. She finishes her classes at one and I don't have any classes until five. What do you think?"

Blanca drove a Mini Cooper. They gave me a tour of Madrid and then took me to a bar to eat. They got me to order what they were having, paella, and a bottle of red wine that the three of us drank.

"Well, I've got to get to class, see you tomorrow," Ivonne said as she got up to leave.

They had already asked for the bill and refused to let me pay it, for all that I insisted, so we split it.

I needed another coffee to shake off the wine, and Blanca ordered another as well.

"What do you want to do now?" she asked.

"I don't know ... I don't know anything about the city, or Spain in general, for that matter."

"And why did you come here?"

I told her that I had a free week before I had to decide whether to take a job, and that without knowing exactly why, I'd decided to spend it in Madrid.

"Well, you're a New Yorker with Spanish ancestry, aren't you? Where are your parents from?"

The question upset me but I couldn't get angry because Blanca had asked it so naturally. I paused for a few seconds. I didn't know her at all, so I changed my official version a little.

"My mother is Hispanic and my father is a typical American WASP. I'm a mixture."

"Well, it's clear that your mother's genes are stronger than your father's."

"Yes, it looks that way," I said, holding back my anger.

"I was born in Paris, but I'm Spanish. My parents were emigrants. They went to work in France and it went okay for them, and they saved until they had enough money to come home. Now they run a little supermarket in Salamanca. That's where we're from."

"Salamanca?"

"Don't you know where Salamanca is? It's a wonderful city! It's less than two hours from Madrid. It's got one of the most important universities in Europe."

"I'm sorry, I don't know anything about Spain."

"It's always seemed odd to me that the education system in the U.S. is so ... I don't know ... apart from the elites, normal people don't seem to know all that much. We complain about our education system here a lot, but any child knows where New York is."

"And how come you ended up studying music?" I asked, a little annoyed by her opinions about Americans' supposed lack of culture.

"It's my passion. My mother loves singing and she insisted that I take piano lessons. I studied the violin as well, in Paris. Ivonne and I met each other at the conservatory there. She was studying the piano but she dropped it. Her parents had insisted, but she didn't like it enough. We've been friends since we were ten years old."

"And Ivonne prefers living in Madrid to living in Paris?" I asked with surprise. Madrid was like the end of the world to me, a spot lost on the edge of the map of Europe.

"Of course! Paris is wonderful, a unique city, but it doesn't have enough sun. When we were younger Ivonne would sometimes come with us to Spain during the summer holidays. And now that she's graduated with a degree in translation and interpretation she's come to Madrid. She's lucky to have a job at a language school, but the best thing would be if she got a job at the French consulate. I hope she manages it."

"And you live here alone?"

"Now I do. I used to share an apartment with Ivonne, but she and Pablo are together now. We're having dinner together on Saturday, okay? You should come. You'll meet the rest of the group that way."

"How long have you been teaching piano?"

"I don't just teach piano. I compose as well. I have very good hours at the conservatory—nine to one. The rest of the day is for me. I have some friends who work in theater: I've composed music for their plays. Experimental theater. There's a rehearsal this afternoon. If you want, I'll take you to see it. It's a small theater, in the older part of Madrid. You'll like it."

I did like it. As a matter of fact, I liked everything; everything surprised me. Blanca introduced me to her friends, who accepted me as though they'd known me all their lives. No one seemed to care who I was or what I did. They treated me like just another member of the group. That would have been impossible in London or New York. Of course, I was in Madrid partially because I had not been able to find anyone to have a drink with in London despite having lived and worked there for several years. I had been in Madrid for a little under two days and already I knew more people than I had ever known in London. We left the theater, having promised to come back on Friday for the premiere.

It was as if everything that was happening to me was unreal. Either I had fallen in with a group of eccentrics who rubbed shoulders with anyone they happened to run into, or else Spanish people were very unusual.

I spent the rest of the week making my way into the soul of this city, led by Blanca and Ivonne who, luckily for me, did not leave me alone for any length of time. I almost forgot about Roy. But a call from Philip Sullivan brought me back to reality.

"Our friend has found out some things. It's not a lot, but it'll be enough for you."

He couldn't tell me more over the phone. It was as if he were afraid of something, and he refused to name names or to say anything that might get him in too deep. We agreed to meet at my apartment on Monday afternoon. He would come, he said, with "our mutual friend," meaning Neil.

The call annoyed me. I didn't want to go back to reality. I liked Madrid more with every day that passed. Or rather, I liked the people who lived there. I've never met more accepting people than the Madrileños.

"Will you come back?" Blanca asked me when I said goodbye to her after the dinner at her apartment.

"I'd like to, but I don't know. I told you that I've got a job lined up."

"You can always get away. London is two hours away from Madrid."

"And Madrid is two hours away from London," I answered with a laugh.

"All right, we'll come to see you. Is there room in your apartment?"

"I've got a guest room. It's not big, but it's not bad."

"Excellent, I haven't been to London for a couple of years."

I knew she would come. Spanish people are like that. They don't have the same sense of shame that we Anglo-Saxons have. Yes, I'm calling myself an Anglo-Saxon here. In spite of my mother's genes, I was brought up in New York, where people rarely invite you back to their house for no reason. And they do so even less in London.

The dinner at Blanca's apartment was enjoyable. No formalities. No one felt like a guest, but rather as if they were in their own house.

On that trip to Madrid I almost managed to reconcile myself with my Hispanic origins, but couldn't because I sensed a subtle difference between being Spanish and coming from a Latin American country. There, it was the same as in New York: the Latin Americans I saw in Madrid worked as bartenders or cab-drivers, cleaned people's houses, or looked after children and the elderly. The maid who tidied my room, the porter who helped me with my suitcase, the street sweepers I saw on the way back from Blanca's house . . . they were all Latin American.

I asked myself whether Ivonne and her friends would have welcomed me in the same way if I had been a Latin American immigrant. I said to myself that yes, they would have, that Ivonne had known nothing about me when she spoke to me. But I didn't want to deceive myself either. There are differences that are obvious to anyone. I don't look like I earn my living with my hands. Blanca herself had said to me: "You can see that you're posh. When Ivonne started talking to you I said that you looked like you were a rich Mexican or Colombian." And so, despite what Spanish people say, appearances can be deceptive.

I liked Blanca. I thought about her on the flight back to London. I asked myself if she could ever be a substitute for Esther. I wasn't going to fool myself. There was no way I could confide in Blanca the things I had told Esther. She would have been shocked and would have told Ivonne and the rest of the group about me. So there was only one possibility left: to have some fun with her. Yes, we could share a bed and go out at night, go to the theater or a concert, but I would never be able to reveal to her my true self.

London seemed grayer than ever. The sky was covered in clouds and it was raining heavily. It was barely three o'clock in the afternoon and it was as if the day were drawing to an end. Blanca was right, it's the light that makes Spain special. I had left Madrid under a perfect blue sky.

The maid must have come back to my apartment because everything was in its place. Thank goodness.

Philip Sullivan and Neil Collins arrived at five o'clock. I had decided to offer them coffee or tea instead of a drink.

"If you don't mind, you could pour me a drink." Neil ordered me rather than asked.

I did so. Without asking, I poured Philip a cup of coffee, which was what I served myself.

"Brian Jones and Edward Brown are two lawyers who work as a front for various companies," Neil started to explain.

"I know that already," I said impatiently.

"They are retained whenever there's a problem, anything that needs to be sorted out outside of legal or official channels. They look for the necessary people, even though they never show their faces. If, say, a waste management company wants to set up in a forested area, they'll do a study of the economic and political implications and the media landscape. That's the first thing they'll do. Then they hire two or three of the PR firms that work for them. These firms do the same thing that you did for Roy.

And once the land is taken over, their employers have the green light to do whatever they want. They've got subtle methods. No unnecessary violence."

"What do you mean?" I asked in surprise.

"Well, in the case of the waste management firm, they ran a clever campaign about the jobs they were going to create. They sometimes try to buy favorable coverage in the media. If they have to defend the installation of a residue incinerator that will contaminate a huge area, they'll do so by claiming that the jobs it creates are essential, and then they'll publish a large number of opinions from select experts to the effect that there is no danger to the forests or the rivers from the installation in question, because today's technology has built-in safeguards."

"Basically they're just doing what we did in Roy's campaign. Nothing new," Philip Sullivan added.

"There's something else. It's not just about factories that destroy the environment. Their main work is for arms and pharmaceutical companies. Wherever there's a conflict you'll find Brian Jones and Edward Brown," Neil continued, ignoring Philip.

"You said they work behind the scenes?"

"Yes, but I found them. Right now they're working to convince people that a small-scale, low-intensity war in the Horn of Africa is necessary. A few weeks ago people from one tribe killed people from another tribe, the same old story. The American government washed its hands of the situation; for them this part of the world is a long ways away. But the arms factories now have a chance to fill the warehouses of both governments over there. And so if you read the newspapers you'll find hundreds of hand-wringing editorials shocked at the West's inaction in the face of what's happening in the Horn of Africa. There'll be a war."

"I don't think the U.S. is going to send in the marines," I said with a laugh.

"No, they won't. The U.S. learned from Vietnam. They won't send soldiers, but they'll send weapons and subcontract armies, mercenaries—nobody cares whether they live or die. But the money for these wars, which the marines no longer fight, comes from the pockets of Americans. In Washington they know that public opinion won't support the sight of more bodies coming back in black bags and people will start to question just what the U.S. needs from the Horn of Africa. But then there'll be reports on CNN showing the horrors of what's going on there, so there will always be someone saying that someone has to do something."

"They know how to manipulate public opinion to justify any war," Philip Sullivan added.

"That's right," said Neil.

"So, these companies profit from wars," I said.

"Yes, they always have one aim: to confuse public opinion. They always win. They manage to protect their own interests by muddying the waters. Divide and conquer, right?"

"Right."

"So, if one of their clients wants, for example, to get his hands on oil anywhere in the world, or gas, or tantalite, and the local governments aren't all that keen, then they create a conflict. They'll run a campaign to emphasize the facts that everyone already knew, that the country is a dictatorship or that the people there suffer because their rulers are corrupt. It's all true, of course, except no one cared up until that point whether the people were starving. If they need to cause a war, they'll cause one. It's easy to get public opinion on your side when it's a question of getting rid of a dictator."

"Dictators who were their friends and allies until they stopped serving their interests," Philip Sullivan added.

"That's the theory, but what else?" I said.

"There are Western governments that hire them to do their dirty work for them."

"You're exaggerating," I said, wondering if he'd gone off the deep end.

"I promise you, I've managed to get the gist of it over the last few days," Neil said, unmoved.

"How can you know something like that?"

Neil shrugged before answering.

"It's not that hard. If you read the newspapers carefully you can come to the same conclusions."

"And Schmidt?"

"He was born in Berlin. He studied sociology and modern languages at the university there. He's a polyglot: he speaks English, French, and Spanish like a native, and knows Russian as well. When he was a professor in Berlin he had great influence over his students. He was like the Pied Piper; they did everything he told them to. He gave classes at the Sorbonne, which confirmed his reputation. He taught at Oxford as well."

"And why would such a prestigious man go to work for a couple of shady lawyers?"

"For the cash. His mother died in childbirth. His father was a construction worker. Schmidt got scholarships and had to work hard to pay for his studies. Someone realized that he was exceptionally intelligent and suggested that he put his talent to use for the 'dark side,' which always pays better. And he seems to have been hit pretty hard by his father's illness. When his father had a stroke and couldn't work anymore, Schmidt didn't have the money to pay anyone to look after him. And then one day Schmidt came home and found his father dead, from another stroke. The old man died alone."

"So he's bitter," said Philip Sullivan.

"No, don't get it wrong, Philip. I don't think that Schmidt is bitter. He's a cold man, who hasn't ever been given anything, who can adapt to any circumstance. Even his own personal circumstances. And that's what he's done."

"It's almost as if you admire the man," I said, irritated.

"If you're going to work with him, or for him, or near him, you'd better not try to pull any tricks or you'll end up floating in the Thames," Neil said.

"So Schmidt is a genius," I muttered.

"An expert in mass behavior. His job is to think, influence, manipulate, strategize . . . He has worked for governments, for security agencies, for large multinational corporations . . . He's protected by the richest men in the Western world. Untouchable."

"You have to be careful, Thomas," Philip said. He seemed to be truly worried.

"And what about Roy? What do you think of his desire for me to work for him via these lawyers and their PR firm?" I asked Neil.

"Roy's shooting too high. He wants respect, but Jones and Brown are stringing him along. They'll leave him high and dry," Neil replied.

Neil seemed tired and looked at the whiskey bottle. I got up and filled his glass in spite of Philip's recriminatory gaze.

"What would you do in my position? Would you work for GCP?" I asked Neil.

"If you don't think you're cleverer than Schmidt and if you don't go off the course he sets for you by even a millimeter, then maybe you can risk it. But you have to understand that your boss is not Roy but Schmidt, which is to say Jones and Brown, which means the weapons manufacturers, the oil companies, the banks, the pharmaceutical companies . . . You wouldn't be going to work for some sheep farmer, like you did with Green, if that's what you thought."

"You're not giving me much hope." His coldness made me uneasy.

"You could thank me for giving you free advice," Neil said as he sipped his whiskey.

"Think about it, Thomas. If you take the job you could end up in a pretty sticky situation." Philip made his uneasiness clear.

"Would you work with me?" I asked them.

"If you give me a specific job, I'll tell you if I'll do it or not, and how much it'll cost. That's as far as I can go" was Neil's reply.

"I . . . I'm sorry, Thomas, but I don't think I can. It's too risky. I'd like to help you but . . ."

"You're scared, Philip." I spoke angrily, trying to offend him.

"Yes, I'm scared. Neil's already told you: these people aren't like the others. They spend millions of dollars, millions of pounds, millions of euros, and people like us are nothing to them. A little excitement is good, but not too much." Philip sounded sincerely upset that he wouldn't be able to follow me if I decided to take the job.

"So you'll keep working for Scott and Roth," I said, an affirmation more than a question.

"Yes, they've asked me to sign another contract with them," Philip revealed.

When they had left I pushed my coffee cup away and poured myself a whiskey. I had to call Roy and tell him whether I would work for GCP. I was worried about what I'd be getting into if I said yes, but at the same time I thought I might be losing something if I said no. I called Esther.

"I'm working, I'll call you later." And she hung up.

I felt very alone. Actually, I had realized what loneliness meant only a week ago. Until then I had never felt I needed someone else to rely on. But I had never been in a situation like this one and I felt the need to speak to someone, to hear some advice even if I wasn't going to follow it. To feel that I had people on my side, sharing in the situation, worrying alongside me.

I couldn't call Blanca. We barely knew each other, but even if we had been friends for years she couldn't have understood anything about this. It was outside of her experience.

I was tempted to call John. I couldn't. I didn't want to think of him as my father, but I know he would have listened to me and given me good advice.

I hesitated. I hesitated for a long while. I know it's what I should have done, but I didn't do it.

If I had dialed John's number I know he would have been pleased. The conversation might have gone something like:

"Dad?"

"Thomas? Good to hear from you, son. How are things?"

"Not bad, but I need to make a decision and I'm conflicted."

"If there's any way I can help you . . . You know you can count on me. What's bothering you?"

I would have explained the situation to him. John would have listened to me without interrupting, thinking about how he would reply as I relayed the facts.

"What do you think? What do you think I should do?"

"Thomas, in my opinion, you shouldn't get involved. These people . . . well, their hands aren't clean and you know that. You'll end up in trouble sooner or later. You don't owe this Roy Parker anything, you've done enough for him already. If you want your own PR agency, come back to New York. You know I'll help you set it up. We have friends here, you'd have good clients, and you'd be able to rely on Esther. How are things with her, by the way? She seems like a good kid, and I don't want to get involved in your personal life, but you were very taken with her and if you stay in London . . . well, I suppose it would be difficult to keep your relationship going. The sensible thing is for you to come back. I don't like what you've told me about these people."

"All right, Dad. I'll think about it."

Yes, I'm sure that John would have advised me to give Roy a firm no. It was the most reasonable thing to do.

I poured myself another whiskey. I drank too much, but back then this didn't worry me.

It was already dark when my phone rang and woke me up. I had fallen asleep without realizing it. I suppose the drink knocked me out. I saw Roy's number flashing on the screen. I looked at the time. It was past nine.

"Weren't you going to call me?" Roy sounded angry.

"Yes, I was just going to."

"I can smell your breath from here. Even your voice is drunk," Roy said.

"Stop pissing around."

"I'm starting to get tired of you," he said in a low voice, as if he were talking to himself.

"I'm tired of you too," I said.

"So you've made a decision."

"Yes, I have."

"Well, tell me what you decided, you prick!"

"I accept. I'll work for GCP, but I'll do it my own way."

"Don't forget that your job is to look after me. You'll have Schmidt in charge of you, so take care."

"Yes, I know the deal, but I'll be running things on a day-to-day basis."

"Schmidt runs things. He chooses everything, even the type of paper you use to wipe your ass," he said with a laugh.

"I'll try it out."

"Okay, well, get to work."

"Oh, and I reserve the right to leave whenever I want. If I don't like how things are going or if Lerman or Schmidt are too much for me, then I'm off."

"Not so fast. The lawyers have drawn up a document. You'll have to sign it. Confidentiality clauses and so on. It's a good salary."

"Right," I said, annoyed.

"And a couple of other things besides. That's what they've decided. They're calling the shots and you've got to follow their lead."

"Hey, Roy, I don't like the sound of this. Either we work as we've been doing till now, or there's no deal." I made one last effort to bring him over to my side.

"No deal, then. I'm sorry, Thomas, but I don't make the rules."

"Is this you talking? Are you an employee of Jones and Brown now?" I asked him, just to annoy him.

"Don't get on my case, all right? I've got my interests, they've got theirs, and we're on the same page for the time being. If you want to come with me then that's fine; if you don't then I'll find someone else."

"If that's what you want . . ." I said.

"No, it's not what I want. What I want is for you to sign the damned contract and get to work. I trusted you, damn it!"

"I'll do it, Roy," I said, lowering my voice.

"All right. I'll be in London tomorrow, I'll meet you at the lawyers' office at eleven o'clock."

Why did I accept? I still don't know, but that decision changed the rest of my life. No, I wouldn't turn back; I don't regret it. I don't have enough scruples to regret anything.

Brian Jones and Edward Brown were indifferent to my decision to join GCP. They introduced me to Leopold Lerman, the agency's director, who treated me with cool friendliness. I said that I wanted to be able to employ two or three people I could rely on and he made no objection. "As long as it's within budget, Mr. Spencer," he said, with a hint of warning.

When we left the offices of Jones and Brown I invited Leopold Lerman for a drink but he refused.

"Maybe you could come to the agency tomorrow. I hope you find the office you've been assigned comfortable."

I didn't like Lerman. Not then and not now. Too German. His father was German, his mother was English, and he had been educated at a Swiss boarding school. I suppose his parents must have chosen neutral ground because, as I found out later, they had split up shortly after Leopold was born. I found this out through Maggie, who knew everything.

Yes, I managed to get Maggie to come and work for me. She couldn't reject the salary I offered. I knew that I would be able to get my hands on Cathy's secretary only if I put an exorbitant quantity of money on the table, a quantity that Scott & Roth couldn't even approach. Leopold Lerman protested, but I was inflexible where Maggie was concerned.

I wanted Maggie by my side not simply because she was an efficient secretary, but also because she always spoke the truth, regardless of whom she might annoy. I signed up someone else whom I was satisfied with: Evelyn Robinson, the journalist we had manipulated in order to get rid of Roy's rivals. I knew that she wouldn't be able to resist the temptation of leaving Radio East and slamming the door on Christopher Blake to come live in London. Evelyn was aware that although Blake's company had been refloated thanks to the money from Roy and his friends, she was still working for a local radio station and newspaper, and she wanted much more. Also, I wanted someone on my team who had unlimited ambition and who would be willing to do anything to achieve her goals.

I gave Evelyn an envelope containing a few hundred pounds and told her to buy some clothes.

"I want you dressed in the latest style, elegant but modern. And go to the salon and get something done to your hair. You look like a country schoolteacher."

Philip Sullivan took control of Evelyn's transformation. Despite his refusal to be employed by me, he was not opposed to carrying out certain tasks, although he always charged me for them. Sullivan was the son of a well-off family whose father was a part of the establishment, so he knew the rules for making one's way in the City. Also, he had good taste when it came to advising a woman on how to dress.

In just twenty-four hours he managed to transform Evelyn. A haircut and a few blonde highlights that lit up her chestnut hair, Jimmy Choo shoes, Stella McCartney dresses, Armani jackets . . . She didn't look like the same person at all. Philip had transformed the hayseed reporter from Radio East into one of those women who stride through the City's corridors.

Evelyn was surprised when it turned out that Neil Collins would be working with us. She admired his work and now she would be working with this old, broken-down legend.

GCP was in one of those Thames-side glass-and-steel buildings that held the offices of companies from all over the world and where we would blend in. There were two working groups at GCP, one of them made up of copywriters and communications graduates who did what I called "white work," whether that was a campaign to sell detergent or revamp some company's image. For "black work" there was another group, which I was a part of. Along with Maggie and Evelyn I needed to recruit a team, but it was not easy. I didn't know enough people to whom I could offer a job as dirty as this one. Once again it was Sullivan who helped me by recommending one of his friends, Jim Cooper, who was also a hacker.

My first day at GCP I received an unexpected visit from Bernard Schmidt. I was irked that he would come to see me without warning, and all the more so because he came and sat in my chair, behind my desk.

"It's urgent for you to prepare a campaign in the county so that Roy can start to change people's opinions about fracking. We must have everything done in a month." Schmidt didn't make suggestions; he gave orders.

"That will take time. I'll sit down with Evelyn tomorrow and plan the campaign. She's from there and knows her peers."

"Tomorrow is too late. Get down to it now. We won't get the license unless public opinion is sufficiently softened up. The environmental activists will make a lot of noise. You will have to counteract them. Here, read this. It'll tell you where to start," he said, and held out a folder that contained about thirty pages with no identifying letterhead.

"And what's this?" I asked after looking through them.

"What you need to do. How to neutralize these young people. There are several arguments there."

"I thought that finding arguments was my job."

"Well, then you're lucky that someone's already done it for you. All you have to do is follow the path these documents set out. It'll be easy."

"You don't like me," I said, and immediately regretted it.

Schmidt looked at me indifferently, but he must have been surprised at my statement.

"Look, Mr. Spencer, this is business. Nothing more. Don't behave like an immature little boy wondering whether I like you or don't like you. All you have to do is what is expected of you. If you're looking for applause or a pat on the back, then you've come to the wrong place."

"You would not have chosen me to do this job."

I saw that he was weighing whether to answer, and eventually decided not to. He shrugged and stood up.

"I'll see you again in a week. By then I expect to have seen articles along the right lines appear in the press."

He left my office without saying goodbye, but he did share a word with Maggie.

"Ha, he's getting to you and you don't like it one bit," Maggie said with a laugh.

"I'm getting to him as well," I said grumpily. "Tell Evelyn to come to my office. We've got work to do. And we'll need you as well. You'll have to stay after five o'clock."

"I'll put the meter on. You know that my overtime rate is in my contract. As long as you pay there's no problem."

I read the papers Schmidt had given me very carefully. They described, step by step, what I had to do, and the first thing was to call Christopher Blake, whose radio station and newspaper were now the major media players in the region. I invited him to come to London and have dinner with me and he accepted eagerly. He didn't even complain that the invitation was for the following day.

The papers Schmidt had given me contained a detailed investigation of the lives of the leaders of the environmental groups. Most were young enthusiasts; only two had Achilles' heels. We had to smear those who had done something incriminating in the past. It's not that these things were particularly bad, but if the material were presented in the right way then these activists could be neutralized.

I explained the plan to Evelyn and she looked at me in amusement.

"So it was you who sent me all that information about Roy Parker's opponents, and I followed your lead like an innocent child."

"You didn't publish anything that wasn't true," I added.

"And now you want us to sink two of these people. One of them because he had a drug problem when he was a teenager, and the other because he worked for a fracking company and now, after being fired, works for a renewable energy firm. That's not a lot to go on."

"If it's in the papers it will have an effect. All we need is for Blake's paper to publish an article about who's who in the movement against fracking. Once the shit is stirred then the smell will stick to everyone. We'll shift people's attention from the main issue. We want people talking not about fracking but about the crap that all the people opposed to it are involved in, especially when the firm will bring definite benefits to the county and create jobs where they're most needed. Which of your old colleagues could use this information? Oh, and we need it on the Internet as well."

"A shame that Philip Sullivan doesn't work with us. He's a wizard with Internet stuff."

"Jim Cooper is too. And Sullivan himself recommended him to us," I said.

Cooper, as he preferred to be called, was an excellent hacker.

He had been Philip's friend when Philip was sharing his apartment and computer, and his love, with the guy who cheated him. When the case went to court, Cooper gave a statement in Philip's favor, claiming that he was more gullible than anything else. But Cooper himself wasn't at all gullible, and he was always short on cash. He had to support his parents; his mother had never worked and his father had been fired from his job at a mattress factory. Cooper also had two younger brothers. The whole family relied on him. His bills kept building up, so for a good salary he was more than happy to be our Trojan horse into the Internet.

The aim was clear: to smear the names of the two activists and prompt the media to focus more on their shameful pasts than on what was really at stake: the fact that the county was about to be changed by fracking.

Evelyn suggested pseudonyms for the two people we were out to destroy: we called one Donald, for Donald Duck, and the other Mouse, after Mickey.

"So no one will know who we're talking about," she said, pleased with her idea.

I asked her to come with me to the dinner I was having with her former boss. It took Christopher Blake a certain amount of effort even to recognize her. The girl with the buggy eyes and the stringy hair, dressed in ragged jeans, was now in a black Armani dress and six-inch heels that drew the attention of all eyes in the room.

"Well, well, well, my favorite journalist is now quite the executive," Blake said admiringly as he pulled out Evelyn's chair.

We explained what we needed from him. Thankfully, Blake was no coward.

"These kids have no idea how important gas is to the county; it would bring us money and jobs. There are always people who are set against progress," Evelyn explained.

"What we would like you to do is publish opinion pieces both in favor of and against fracking," I interjected. "Do some vox pops, especially with unemployed people in the region. The activist who had drug problems ... I don't know ... Perhaps he's a bit unstable. As for the other one, don't you think it's immoral when working for a renewable energy firm to lead a campaign against a competitor? There's a conflict of interest there," I added.

"I know what you mean ... Don't worry. But you should know that there are lots of people in the county who are opposed to fracking. Ours is a county of shepherds. Our wool is famous. To break up the ground in this way ... Well, people are scared of what might happen, especially if it might bring their traditional way of life to an end. What does Roy Parker say? His father-in-law has huge tracts of land in the county and the fracking will affect them," Christopher Blake said.

"Parker will serve the interests of the county," I replied.

"And what does that mean?" Blake seemed worried.

"That if they show that fracking won't harm the environment and that it will create jobs, then he will support it even if it means causing conflict in his family," Evelyn said.

"I don't even want to think about what Suzi will say ... Parker's wife is very strong-willed and she loves the land." Blake said this as though it were a warning.

"Suzi knows that her husband is dedicated to the progress of the county and, however much it hurts him, he needs to put the interests of the many above the complaints of the few," I declared.

It was a conversation among cynics, and the subtext was evident enough for us all to understand the unspoken. When we said goodbye it was clear that we would have his enthusiastic cooperation with our campaign. A campaign in which the most crucial factor was the invisibility of our influence.

Evelyn did a good job. She knew the county well and, moreover, she knew who was who at her old company, so that she was able to carefully brief some of them about how and when to release the information that was most important to us. In less than a week we had organized a grand polemic in which the supporters and detractors of fracking threw all sorts of mud at one another. One of our featured events was Roy Parker's press conference. We prepared his part down to the last detail and, I must admit, he gave an Oscar-worthy performance.

Parker was extremely serious, stating that he would do whatever it took to make sure that no fracking company set up shop in the county, and that he would rethink his opposition only if he were presented with at least three positive reports drawn up by independent scientists on the consequences of using this method for extracting gas. And he reminded the public of the personal conflict that would be caused by his having to support a project of this scale, given that his family owned a large tract of land adjacent to the area where the proposed fracking was to be carried out. But, he added, the interests of the citizens would be put above all other considerations. If the reports showed that there was no risk, then he would be ready to reconsider his initial opposition.

He had made Suzi come with him. This reinforced his credibility because everyone in the entire county knew that his wife's family was dead set against fracking, or anything that might alter nature's balance in the area.

His performance was impeccable, and the journalists left the press conference convinced that Roy Parker was an honorable man.

I congratulated him. Roy thanked me. Once we were alone, he and Suzi didn't bother to hide how furious they were with each other.

"Why do you get my husband involved in this shit?" Suzi snapped at me.

"I don't know what you're talking about. If he's involved then it's because he's concerned. This isn't an easy topic and for that reason I think it's the right thing for Roy not to decide on anything without sufficient guarantees."

"Do you think I'm an idiot? Don't underestimate me,

Thomas. Fracking is a business, and there will be people who will pocket a lot of money. And others will lose it. What will happen to my parents' sheep? And the wool works?"

"Don't get ahead of yourself, it's still not guaranteed that anything will happen. You heard what your husband had to say. If there aren't guarantees that the environment will remain unharmed then he won't support the project," I said.

"Fuck that. I know my husband and I know how much he lies," Suzi replied, avoiding her husband's angry glare. "If he supports this project it's because he thinks he can get something out of it. The worst of it is that this is all done in the name of progress. What progress? Lots of people are going to lose their jobs. People will lose their fields, their sheep. It will be a tragedy for the farmers."

"Look, I don't care how people make a living, whether it's with sheep or gas. But it's not true that jobs will be lost; actually, jobs are going to be created. A gas plant needs a lot of workers," I insisted.

"Yeah, and of course they're going to employ shepherds. You're still underestimating me, Thomas. Don't do it or you'll really find out what I'm made of."

"That's enough, Suzi!" Roy said, making his exasperation quite clear. "I've already told you that I can't oppose the gas plant simply because your parents own sheep. I don't like fracking either, but if the reports show that it doesn't cause damage to the land, or the animals, then it will be difficult for me to stand against it. They'll accuse me of defending my family's interests."

"I wanted you to be a politician. I liked the idea. But now I realize that all you really want is power and money," she said regretfully. "My money wasn't enough for you; you needed your own. And that's why you've sold off these lands. You convinced the owners that their land had no value. And in certain cases . . . well, strange things happened that 'encouraged' people to sell. And you've been behind it all. I see it clearly now. I've been a fool." She seemed to be on the verge of tears.

Roy's press conference was even picked up by the national press. Some opinion pieces praised his principles. On the same day the papers started to publish articles both in favor of and against fracking. We had found so-called experts who were willing to swallow the lies. When the public reads an article, they don't know who is behind it. If you add a university degree and an impressive-sounding position to the credit line, then people will think that the person in question is trustworthy. Sometimes this is not the case. You can always find someone to defend your interests, especially when there's money in the equation.

On his newspaper's front page Christopher Blake published a report about the leaders of the anti-fracking movement in the county. Most of the biographies were uninteresting, but the disclosures about Donald Duck and Mickey Mouse led to an endless stream of articles in other newspapers as well as commentary on the radio and television.

Donald had been to rehab, which was where he had learned to love the land. When he got out, he started to work with an environmental group. Soon radicalized, he had participated in certain campaigns, such as one to convince people to stop eating meat and an antinuclear initiative in which he'd chained himself to fences outside nuclear power plants to demand their closure. We had nothing serious on him, but we were able to present him as a paranoid and a radical who hated society, which he blamed for driving him to drugs. He wasn't to be trusted. As for Mickey Mouse, it was far easier to destroy him. This young man, an engineer at a company developing renewable energy sources, was protecting the interests of his employer. He didn't want the gas works to be built because his company wanted to expand into the county. An open-and-shut case. It didn't make any difference that Mickey Mouse's company stated that it had no intention of expanding into the county. The seeds of doubt had been sown, and many people didn't even bother to read the report in which the company said it had nothing to do with the conflict that was taking place in the county.

We raised a fine fuss. Even the London newspapers reported the controversy in the county, which helped to polarize public opinion even more.

Local Labour Party members stood up against fracking, but it wasn't hard to oppose them, given that they had allowed great assaults on the environment to take place in other regions of the country for years.

We won. Roy was sent three technical reports signed by independent experts, one of them a professor who regularly appeared on television and in the papers.

The time had come. I left London just as dawn was breaking. Jim Cooper came with me up to the county to organize a press conference in which Roy would say that he would not oppose the gas company.

It was a little before ten when I called Roy to tell him that we had arrived. He asked me to come to his house and I sent Cooper to work with Roy's people to organize the press conference. When I got there I found him arguing with Suzi. I said I would come back later, but Suzi stopped me.

"You're here right on time. You'll be the first to know that I want a divorce. He's deceived me. And you too," she said, looking at me with hatred.

"I'm sorry, but I don't know what's going on here. In any event I don't think it's my business," I said, eager to leave.

"Sit down." Roy's voice filled the room.

I stopped, expectant. I didn't want to have any part in this battle.

"I'm going to ask for a divorce and I'm going to take our children. And don't try to stop me or I'll tell the whole world what you are," Suzi threatened.

"If I've done things that weren't . . . pure, then you got a lot out of them," Roy said, his voice equally angry.

Suzi bit her lower lip as she considered her response. I tried again to leave, but Roy's hand closed on my arm.

"When do you want us to do this damned press conference?" he asked.

"Tomorrow morning. Nine o'clock. It'll be broadcast on all the television and radio news networks. I've brought you a script. It will be fine. You've done your part. No one can blame you for anything," I said, with as much conviction as I could manage.

"I'll announce something myself tomorrow. I'll come with my lawyer and hand you the divorce papers," Suzi said with a bitter smile.

Roy walked toward her with his face twisted. For a moment I was scared that he would hit her. Suzi looked straight at him, daring him to do it. I walked over and pulled at Roy's arm.

"You're old enough to solve your problems in a civilized manner. You've got two children; you should think about them." I didn't enjoy my role as mediator, but I had no other choice.

"You're right," said Roy. "I'll sort this out later. Now tell me what we're going to do tomorrow."

Suzi left the room and Roy seemed relieved, though he was frowning. He seemed unsure of what to do.

"Call your press spokesman; get him to call the media for tomorrow. You'll make a statement. Here it is. All you have to do is read it. Then you take five or six questions. We've chosen which journalists will get to speak. So you can stick to what you need to say without fear of making mistakes. There won't be any follow-up questions. The important thing is for you to repeat the same message: You want to make good on your promise of a few days before. In view of the reports, even though this affects your family interests, you find no justification to oppose fracking. You don't like it, but you can't stand against it. At the same time, you should make it clear that the opinions of the experts have calmed you down a little, and that they've assured you that the environmental effects will be minimal and that the small-scale shepherds will not be impacted. The sheep will still be able to graze safely. Say that you want to highlight the advantages that the gas works will bring to employment in the area. You will insist that you understand the desire among some people to keep things the way they are, but you'll remind them that there is no progress without change, and that you also need to take risks to move forward." I gave him some sheets of paper that summarized what I had just said.

"All right, I'll learn the speech," said Roy.

"The important thing is for you to really interiorize it, so that it is believable. Tell me, is this trouble with Suzi affecting you?"

Roy sighed. He really didn't need to say anything. It was clear that he was beside himself because of the argument.

"Maybe you'll think what I'm about to say is ridiculous. We've been together all our lives. We met when I was just a kid. She's always believed in me. She stood up to her parents because I was a nobody," Roy admitted, growing more upset.

"What exactly happened?"

"Suzi is no fool. There was a time when she preferred to look the other way and let me get on with what I did. But it's her parents' land that's going to be affected. Her father won't sell. When the offer reached them, just as I'd arranged, he didn't even read it. He threw the papers on the ground and stamped on them. He accused me of being the instigator of the whole thing. I defended myself, saying it wasn't like that, that I was looking out for his interests, and that the gas plant would be installed there in any case. Better to sell the land before it became completely useless. He got so furious that he had a heart attack. Suzi blames me. The worst of it is that if she had to choose between her parents and me then it's obvious, she'd go for her parents every time."

"And has the old man recovered, or is there no hope?"

"The doctors aren't keen on making any long-term predictions, but it looks like he's getting better."

"Well then, I think it'll pass, that Suzi will get over it as soon as her father gets out of the hospital," I said, trying to cheer him up.

"She took advantage of the fact that I was out a few days ago visiting villages around the county and she shut herself up in my office. She read all the papers that I've kept about this thing. The e-mails I sent to the gas company, to you . . . She says I've betrayed her, that I've manipulated her. I think she's started to hate me. My children are confused. They don't understand the conflict between us, but they're clear about one thing: if they have to choose, they'll choose their mother."

"Roy, there's too much at stake here. You have to concentrate on the press conference tomorrow. You have to give the go-ahead for them to start the exploratory drilling. Your friends, Jones and Brown, aren't going to let there be any mistakes. You know that better than me. You can't fold at the last moment. There are lots of people who believe in you and who will do what you say. There are lots of hicks ready to sell their grazing land without knowing that their sheep are sitting on top of a sea of gas and that they're being offered a tenth of what the land is worth. If you flake out now, then everything will fall apart."

"I know, but I can't take my mind off it. Suzi is prepared to give me the divorce papers tomorrow."

"Ask her to wait a couple of days."

"She won't. She's made it clear, she wants to finish me, she wants the whole world to know I'm a son of a bitch."

"I'll tell Evelyn to get here as soon as possible. She may be able to make Suzi change her mind."

"I don't think so. She doesn't trust you and she doesn't trust Evelyn. Even now she's saying that she regrets having allowed us to ruin Wilson and Doyle to get me to the mayor's house."

I made him learn the statement by heart. And we tried out the questions and answers that would come up in the press conference. I said goodbye at midday. I didn't want to accept his invitation to lunch. Roy was looking for an excuse to leave his house for a while, and I didn't want to share a table with someone as depressed as he was. Also, I just didn't care about his family problems.

I had decided to walk back to the hotel when my cell rang. I didn't recognize the number, but I did recognize Bernard Schmidt's deep voice.

"What's going on over there?" he asked me without even saying hello.

"Everything's going well. Roy knows the statement by heart. There won't be any problems."

"I'm asking you what's going on over there, not about tomorrow's press conference."

"What do you mean? I'm telling you, everything's going well."

"No, it's not going well at all. Roy called the lawyer, Brian Jones, and Jones called me just now in a state of alarm. Roy told him that his wife wants a divorce and is ready to kick up a fuss with the drilling."

"A married couple's squabbles. They don't affect the general plan," I said.

"What do you mean? Am I hearing you correctly? Either you're stupid, or else you're not at the level required if you're going to work for an agency like GCP. If Parker's wife opposes the drilling, if she gives the slightest hint of her suspicions about this business, if her lack of agreement with her husband is so significant as to lead her to petition for divorce, what do you think will happen? We'll be right back at square one, but in a far worse situation than we are at the moment. Don't you realize?" There was no emotion in Schmidt's voice. He spoke in a low register. However, he was so blunt that I felt a shudder down my spine.

"We'll try to counter whatever Suzi Parker says," I said, just to say something.

"And how are you going to do that?"

"I don't know. Perhaps I can speak to her and convince her to keep quiet. Evelyn Robinson is on her way. They get along well;

perhaps she'll listen to her. I don't think that Suzi really wants to hurt her husband."

"What you think means nothing to me. I want guarantees."

"I can't guarantee anything."

"In that case, tell me what you're going to do to stop the main story tomorrow from being Suzi Parker's announcement instead of her husband's press conference."

I didn't say anything. I wasn't sure where he was trying to lead me, but in any event I had no way to prevent Suzi from demanding a divorce. I could try to dissuade her, but nothing more.

"As I've said, I'll try to talk to her."

"Let's imagine that she is still keen on causing trouble."

"I can't guarantee anything," I said angrily.

"You are wrong. We pay you to guarantee that our clients are not presented with any unpleasant surprises or forced to wrestle with any last-minute problems. Either you sort it out or we will sort it out for you. But if I have to fix things then you'd better start working out a severance package. I'll give you an hour. Call me and tell me if you're going to fix this disaster or if you're incapable."

Bernard Schmidt hung up before I could reply. I walked quickly back to the hotel, hoping to find Cooper there. I was pleased that there was someone to talk to.

"Evelyn called me. She's coming up by car, with Neil. She said that you sounded very worried. She told me that Suzi Parker has had an argument with her husband and that . . ."

"I know the story. I was the one who told Evelyn. We have a problem. We have to stop Suzi from serving him the divorce papers tomorrow. If we don't then we'll end up out of a job."

Cooper's right eyebrow started to twitch. It was a nervous tic of his.

"If Suzi Parker asks for a divorce we're going to get the sack? But what can we do about it?"

"Well, someone's expecting us to do something about it. If

Suzi explains why she wants a divorce, and mentions her father's heart attack, then we can give up on the fracking project, and Roy's friends aren't going to like that at all."

"Unless we kidnap her, or spike her drink, or slip her a laxative so she can't leave the bathroom . . ."

"You want to stop talking bullshit?"

"There's nothing we can do. Roy has to convince her, not us."

"Roy can't do it. She doesn't even want to see him."

The steaks they gave us at the hotel restaurant were hard. We ate scarcely a mouthful. When we had finished, I called Suzi, worried that she wouldn't want to speak to me. She told me that Evelyn had called her asking her not to do anything until she'd spoken to her, but Suzi had made it perfectly clear that there was no one who could stop her from asking for the divorce. Roy, she told me, was going to sleep on the sofa in the living room. She had thrown him out of their room. She wanted her husband to pack his bags and leave as soon as possible. I listened to her without interrupting. She needed to let herself go, to get all her bitterness out into the world. When she finally stopped talking I started to speak calmly, weighing each word with care.

"Suzi," I said. "I understand how upset you are. You've had a big shock with your father's heart attack. But you can't blame Roy for what has happened. Your father's an old man who must find it difficult to accept that the world is changing. Older people are always worried about change, wanting nothing to happen to the world they're used to. It's normal, it'll happen to all of us when we reach a certain age."

"You're all sons of bitches!" Suzi shouted.

"No, we're not. Roy isn't. He hasn't done anything to be ashamed of, and neither have we."

"No? Well, what do you call what you did to the other two candidates in the mayoral election? You tried to find anything, any old thing that could sink Wilson and Doyle. And you destroyed them. One because he sowed a few wild oats, and the other because he owed money. Or don't you remember?" Suzi's voice was growing stronger.

"No, it wasn't like that. You always look for your opponents' weak spots in politics, and any skeletons in the closet must be brought to light. The electorate has a right to know everything about public figures. We didn't invent anything. Everything that was published was true. You remember how you said we shouldn't have pity on them? You wanted your husband to become the mayor. You dreamed about having tea with the Queen. Or are you the one forgetting things?"

"Don't try to blame your dirty tricks on me! I was naïve, but I'm not going to allow you to destroy this land. My husband will do anything to get his way. He signed a secret deal with this gas company; he's made it easy for them to take over all the land in this county. But he won't get our land. I can swear to you that I will not allow it."

"You're not thinking straight, and you can't see things for how they really are. Roy hasn't signed any deals with the gas company."

"Do you want to see the papers? There's a whole file filled with documents that would be very interesting to the press. I've made photocopies of everything. You'll see."

I was scared now. It seemed as if Suzi were truly willing to stick the knife into Roy. She was out of control. I had no idea what was in those papers, but I guessed that they could probably ruin Roy and drag us down at the same time.

"I can't believe that you hate Roy, that you're willing not only to hurt him but to damage your children's future. They'll point at them in school, whisper that they're the children of a disgraced man. And that wouldn't be fair, not for the children, and not for Roy."

Suzi didn't say anything. I realized that this last argument had struck a nerve. She didn't care about hurting Roy; in fact, that was what she wanted to do most of all, but there was no way she would hurt her children. She took a while to reply.

"My children have nothing to do with this."

"They're his children too. If you humiliate their father, do you think it won't affect them? You should consider what you're going to unleash. It's not just Roy who'll face the consequences, but your children as well."

"I want a divorce. I won't stay with a man like Roy, not for anything in the world. He fooled me. Yes, I'm in a bad place at the moment. My parents warned me that there was nothing to Roy apart from ambition, that he married me in order to get ahead. They were right."

"No, they weren't right. Only a couple of hours ago your husband told me, in despair, just how much he loves you. He can't imagine living without you." I added a touch of melo-drama to my voice.

"He only loves himself. I've been a means to an end for him, a way for him to achieve what he wants. I will try to keep my children out of this, but I will do what I have to do. I'm meeting my lawyer at eight o'clock tomorrow morning. He will have the papers ready and all I have to do is sign."

"You won't do that, Suzi. Give yourself a bit more time; think about it some more. You are angry and you are refusing to understand why Roy does things the way he does. You're judging him too harshly. He wouldn't do anything to steer the county in the wrong direction. It's his land, his people. Do you really think he'd be so soulless as to allow anything that would put his people in danger?"

"A few years ago I would have slapped anyone who said that Roy had no morals, that he was capable of anything. The truth is, I never knew the man until a few months ago. This is the real Roy—a ruthless and dishonest man. He'll do anything to get what he wants. If he had to destroy the county, he would, as long as it was to his advantage. But that's not a surprise to you. You're his perfect match. You're a son of a bitch, just like him."

I didn't defend myself from her insults. There was no point, and it would have just made her more angry. I swallowed, and contained myself, trying not to insult her in turn. The way she was setting herself up as a victim pissed me off. Suzi had been perfectly happy with the idea of sacrificing Wilson and Doyle, but she had decided to forget about her complicity and pretend she had never been involved in such a plot.

"Well, do what you want. I don't think you've thought this through. Perhaps your children won't be able to forgive you for marking them as the sons of a pariah. Let your conscience be your guide."

I hung up. Cooper was looking at me worriedly. He had been able to follow the conversation: he was sitting right next to me, and Suzi had been shouting.

"She's going to ruin everything. What shall we do?"

"Well, what you said: either someone slips some sleeping pills or a laxative into a glass of water and knocks her out, or we kidnap her," I said grumpily.

"The best idea is the sleeping pills. We can earn some time if she's fast asleep."

I looked at him, not believing that he was really considering this possibility. But Jim Cooper was a naïf, innocent in some things and entirely amoral as far as his profession was concerned.

"Would you give her the drugs?" I asked, following this crazy train of thought.

"It would have to be Roy. We can't get involved in this."

"Are you serious?" He was driving me mad.

"Of course." Cooper seemed surprised at my doubt.

"Forget about it, it's ridiculous. I'll have to call Schmidt. We can consider ourselves fired."

It took Bernard Schmidt a while to pick up the telephone. I told him about my conversation with Suzi and said that I didn't think I could find a solution. She was determined to take Roy down.

"This is too much for you to handle. I'll call the lawyers." He hung up.

"And now what?" Cooper asked.

"Now we wait for Evelyn and Neil. Maybe they'll come up with something. We'll turn up at Roy's house at seven tomorrow to take him to the press conference. Start thinking about how you're going to fight the bombs that Suzi's going to drop. Roy's going down, but that's not the problem. There'll be such a scandal that no one will dare give permission for the fracking. They'll cut our balls off."

"We have to do something," Cooper insisted.

"You've only come up with crap so far," I replied.

"Well, you haven't even gotten that far. And I can't lose this job, I need the money."

"Forget about it. You heard Suzi. She wants to hurt Roy, and she will."

"Call Roy."

"Why?" I didn't want to speak to anyone, and especially not Roy.

"We'll go to his house. We'll think about it—we're bound to come up with something. But we can't just sit here as though nothing were going on."

"I'm sorry, Cooper, but that's the way things are."

"I'm telling you, call Roy. He must be taking it really badly if he's been thrown out of his own bedroom."

I didn't need to call Roy Parker. My cell whistled and it was him.

"Hey, Thomas, you need to get over here. We have to change the press conference tomorrow. I'm thinking about standing down. I'm not just going to lose Suzi and the children, but also the respect of my constituents. I don't want to be seen as some dick in the gas company's pocket. It would finish me. I'd never be able to show my face again."

"Calm down, Roy. I'm coming over now with Cooper."

Roy met us with a glass of whiskey in his hand. He stank of alcohol.

"Drinking isn't going to solve our problems," I scolded him.

"The problems are all solved. I've given in to Suzi. There's not going to be any fracking in the county," he said. He seemed relieved to have come to the decision.

"If you pull out you're not going to be able to live here. Sooner or later people will find out why you resigned. They'll feel betrayed. Also, you'll lose Suzi whatever happens. When something like this happens in a marriage there's no way back."

Roy threw his glass against the wall. He looked at me with hatred, a deep and savage hatred. He came toward me and grabbed me by the lapel.

"So, you're an expert on marriages as well!" he said as he let me drop, pushing me away disdainfully.

"You know what, Roy? You tried to fly high, but you don't have the guts for it. You can't control your wife and you can't even control yourself. You don't have the heart or the determination to do what you said you could do. You should have been satisfied with Suzi's money, and kept sheep, tricking your neighbors a little every now and then. You don't have what it takes to play with the big boys. You're nothing but a shepherd."

Jim Cooper looked at us fearfully. He couldn't understand how I dared say such things to Roy, who stood in front of me with violence in his eyes.

"Come on! Calm down! We're not going to get anywhere fighting amongst ourselves," Cooper said as he tried to separate us.

"Get out of here! I called you to tell you that it's all over. Get out!" Roy's voice dripped hatred.

"Yes, that's exactly what I'd like to do. But you're putting us in a tricky situation. Yourself too. I don't think that your friends Brian Jones and Edward Brown will let you walk away from the game. You'll have to finish your job before you leave."

"I've told you, I'm not doing anything!" Roy shouted.

"Yes, you've said what you want to do," I replied, raising my voice as well. "But now the three of us are going to sit down and analyze, calmly, what you can and cannot do. It's clear that sooner or later these lawyers will give you the boot, but they're not going to let you get away with causing a scandal just because your wife found out what kind of a jerk you are and decided to dump you. Although, yes, her holier-than-thou behavior's a bit surprising too. She didn't blink an eye when it came to taking the other mayoral candidates down. All her scruples today are nothing but pure hypocrisy. She's behaving like a schoolgirl whose father has caught her cheating on a paper. You know what, Roy? What I don't understand is how people as clever as Jones and Brown thought they could do business with you."

"That's enough!" Cooper said. He was trembling and seemed like he was about to cry.

Roy sat down on a chair, broken. I sat down on the sofa next to him.

"Evelyn and Neil are about to arrive. We'll see if they've thought of anything. In any case, we have to stop Suzi. Your wife can't hand you divorce papers tomorrow. She'll have to wait until the business is complete. And that means waiting for months," I said firmly.

My cell started to ring. Evelyn's number appeared on the screen. They had arrived in the county. I didn't ask Roy's advice. I ordered Evelyn to come at once to Roy's house, and to bring Neil.

When they arrived, I brought them up to speed. Roy listened as if I were speaking about someone who wasn't him. Before I finished, Neil interrupted me: "I got a phone call. They gave me a lead and I think it could help to neutralize Suzi, if Roy agrees."

We said nothing. Who had called Neil? What sort of a lead had he been given?

"Who called you?" I asked.

"He didn't give his name. He just told me to investigate an old story about Suzi's father. I had to make a few calls, call in a few favors. An old friend who works for the police helped me find what I was told to look for. I spent the whole trip over on the phone." Neil looked at us, knowing we were all on tenterhooks. But that's how he was; he liked to create dramatic tension.

"That's right, he didn't speak to me the whole way. He was on the phone the whole time," Evelyn said.

"Are you going to tell us this story about Suzi's father?" I asked.

"Many years ago, Charles Stone, Suzi's father, killed a man." Neil savored our reaction.

"What's this rubbish?" Roy said, in shock.

"He was very young. He liked to show off to his friends because he had a hunting rifle. It was during the years of rationing. England was trying to recover from the Second World War. Apparently someone who had nothing to eat rustled a couple of sheep. Old man Stone, Suzi's grandfather, used to curse the people who came onto his lands to steal sheep. 'One day I'll put a bullet in their heads,' he used to say. And his son decided to surprise his father—make the old man proud—and be the fellow who caught the criminals. One night he sat watch on the hill where the sheep were penned at night. It was sometime before dawn when a man came and jumped over the fence. The dogs started to bark but the thief wasn't scared. He picked up a sheep, and as he tried to escape he fell to the ground. Charles, Suzi's father, had put a bullet in his back. He didn't try to hush it up, but even went over to the man to gloat about his victory. He insulted him and threatened that if he moved he'd shoot him again. But by then the man was already dead.

"They arrested Charles and held him for a few days before he was tried. His family, one of the richest in the county, managed to cover it up. The police changed their preliminary report, and ended up saying that the man who'd fired the bullet could have been a poacher. The family of the dead man didn't have enough money to pursue the case and have a proper investigation. Suzi's grandfather bribed them as well. He bought them a house in another county and gave them enough money to keep their mouths shut. The man's widow accepted the terms. But they also had children. The youngest boy barely knew his father. If we gave him a bit of a push we could get him to ask for the case to be reopened."

"Is all this true?" Roy looked stunned.

"Every single word," Neil insisted.

"Imagine the news reports: 'Charles Stone killed a man for stealing a sheep, and years later he's willing to hold the whole county back just to keep his wool business going.' Imagine the headlines." Evelyn seemed excited about the story she could write about this.

"Yes, we could present it as the story of a man capable of doing anything as long as it's in his own interest, putting himself ahead of human life and the good of the county," Neil added.

"Well, now you've got some leverage against Suzi," I said.

"You're mad! If I use this against her she'll never forgive me," Roy protested, almost frightened.

"Whatever you do, she's not going to forgive you. You have to give up on Suzi." Cooper spoke as though he didn't care about the disgusted look on Roy's face.

"Tell her to come in. I'll tell her how things are. I won't make you do all the work," I promised.

"I don't know. All this is ... well ... unexpected." Roy couldn't think straight.

"This is the only card we have, Roy, and we have to play it. You wanted to be in this world. There are rules. It's better for us to solve our problems now, before your lawyer friends have to get involved. That would be worse for Suzi."

Evelyn didn't wait for Roy to react. She went off to look for Suzi herself. We heard shouting even before she came into Roy's office.

"If you think you're going to change my mind, you're mistaken! I'm not going to stick by Roy, not for anything on earth."

"You have to hear us out. Listen and then decide," Evelyn tried to convince her.

Roy didn't dare look at his wife. He sat in the armchair and looked down at the floor. Suzi barely glanced at him.

"So, here you are in your little cabal. I wouldn't waste your breath trying to make me back off now," Suzi said with disdain.

"It's not about us and it's not about Roy. It's about your father. You have to decide if you're going to save him or hang him out to dry," I said, with all the coldness and indifference I could muster.

"My father? Don't you dare bring my father into this," she said, coming in close to my face.

"You and Roy should have thought a bit more when you first got into this business. Once you're in, it's not all that easy to get out again. You know what happened to those two upstanding fellows who both wanted to become mayor." I hadn't moved an inch. I could smell her breath.

"What are you threatening me with now?" Suzi asked, and there was a spark of worry in her eyes.

"Your father is a killer. He was arrested for murder years ago. The victim's family may be interested in reopening the case," I said, spitting out every word.

Suzi slapped me so hard that the marks of her fingers were visible on my cheek.

"You motherfucker! How dare you insult my father? I'll bring you all down, I'll tell people what you do, I'll drag you through the mud! And you first of all, you cocksucker." And she turned to slap Roy.

He didn't move. He didn't even blink when Suzi's palm smacked his face. Roy seemed resigned to accept everything that his wife threw at him.

Evelyn moved across the room to try to calm her down, but

Suzi pushed her away. She was like a wild animal, ready to sink her claws into anything that came near her.

"You have to accept the truth. Your father is a murderer and there's nothing you can do about it. Although whether or not this story resurfaces depends on you," I said, without looking at her.

She came back toward me and I thought she was going to slap me again, but she held herself back. This time she sat on the sofa and started to cry as she continued to insult us.

"Cocksuckers! You're all a bunch of cocksuckers!" Suzi repeated these words like a mantra.

I made a gesture to Neil, who laid out, step by step, what he had learned. He even went a little further, stating that it was a matter of money whether or not the son of the man in question would ask to reopen the case. Suzi had her head in her hands and seemed to be somewhere else, distant from what Neil was telling her, but when he finished, she straightened up, her eyes filled with tears.

"Roy in exchange for your father. That's the deal." I took pleasure in her despair as I spoke.

"Suzi . . . darling . . . I . . ." Roy couldn't put a sentence together.

"Roy has nothing to do with this. He just found out, same as you. But I've told you already. You've put forces in motion that you can't control. You wanted to have tea with the Queen of England. All right, well, this is part of the price. You don't get a free ride if you want to become part of the establishment." This time it was me who stood up straight in front of Suzi, and I looked at her as she seemed to shrink.

"What do I have to do?" Suzi asked between sobs.

"Nothing. You don't have to do anything. You'll go with Roy tomorrow, just as you always do whenever there's anything important to announce. You'll keep living together as you have until now. There won't be a divorce. Or at least, not while we think it could do harm to Roy," I said.

"My father . . . my father will die if I support this gas company. He'll never forgive me," Suzi said, without talking to anyone in particular.

"At least he'll die with honor," I said. "I don't think he'd like the newspapers picking up on the fact that he's a murderer, a man who's willing to kill over something as little as a sheep. That will destroy him, and make his neighbors despise him too. A rich family that buys out a poor family in order to save their headstrong son from prison. It's a story the papers would love to run with."

"I don't want to live with Roy . . . I can't, not now . . ." Suzi whimpered.

"Well, you'll have to. The house is large; there are enough rooms. You can still live under the same roof. And yes, try not to give the maids any reason to gossip. Oh, and you'll have to continue appearing in public with Roy as often as is necessary. You do a good job of being the supportive wife." My words were an order.

"Call your lawyer, Suzi. Tell him that you don't want to divorce Roy, that you had a fight about nothing and that you've made your peace now," Evelyn suggested.

"Yes, I'll do it," Suzi murmured.

"You'll do it now. We want to hear you," I instructed. "You understand that we don't trust you."

"You think I'd ruin my father's life and let him be painted as a killer?" Suzi's voice broke with anger and despair.

"If you didn't care about the pain you were going to cause your children by ruining their father's life, then I don't need to believe that you'd care any more about your own father. You have to prove it. And there are other things, Suzi. Other things that could destroy your family, could destroy you. We still have some ammo." I threw out this bluff, knowing that at this moment she had given up.

"You disgust me, Thomas."

"Well, it's not like I have a very high opinion of you or your family. At least none of *us* are murderers. I'm ahead of you there."

"That's enough, stop it!" Roy looked at me, ready to hit me.

"That's how things are, Roy. Go on, Suzi, make the call. I want to hear you talk to your lawyer."

She made the call. She played the part of the contrite wife perfectly. When she hung up the phone she stood up.

"If you don't mind, I have things to do. I'll fulfill my role."

She left Roy's office with all the dignity she was capable of. But she was beaten and she knew it. Roy watched her, sadly. I was surprised that after everything he still loved her.

"Problem solved," I said. "Now we can get to work on the important things."

"We've already prepared my speech for tomorrow," Roy protested.

"Yes, but there are other things we need to talk about."

Roy accepted without further argument. After all, he was relieved, even though he knew his relationship with Suzi was effectively over. She would not forgive him for capitulating when we'd blackmailed her.

I slept badly that night. I woke up at dawn, soaked in sweat. A bad conscience? I don't think so. I've never allowed my conscience to grow, and I didn't think twice about putting the screws on Suzi.

But the passing of the years has not changed the fact that, despite feeling no need for repentance, I could have done things another way. What would have happened if I had behaved differently?

When Neil appeared with Evelyn and explained that Suzi's father had a man's blood on his hands, perhaps I could have refused to pressure her with that:

"No, Neil, there's no way we're using that. It wouldn't be right. Suzi's father is in the hospital recovering from a heart attack . . .

The old man could die if we raise this scandal. It's water under the bridge; he was just a kid back then. Also, if we try to blackmail Suzi then her marriage to Roy is through. We'll have to find something else. Come on, guys, let's think."

But I said nothing of the sort. I didn't doubt for a moment that we had to blackmail Suzi, and that her father's checkered past was our best bargaining chip. If we hadn't used it perhaps we could have saved Roy's marriage. But I didn't care about that so much. I felt something akin to affection for Suzi and for Roy, but not enough for me to shirk my responsibilities.

Yes, if I had acted differently, then the gas company wouldn't have set itself up in the county and Suzi might have ended up forgiving Roy. But I didn't do it. Quite the contrary. When we got back to London I invited Evelyn and Cooper to a first-class dinner. Neil didn't want to join us. Although he got his hands dirty doing the tasks I sent his way, he thought that I was a bastard, and so he came to my table only when I had work to give him.

Three days later, Bernard Schmidt called me. His voice was slightly more friendly than usual.

"Well, in spite of everything, you've been able to solve this gas situation. Our clients seem relieved."

"It wasn't easy."

"Of course it wasn't. That's why we're expensive. But I didn't call to massage your ego. We have business in Spain and we thought you could deal with it."

"I thought I was just working for Roy Parker," I said uncertainly.

"There will be exceptions."

"What's it about?" I asked, without much enthusiasm.

"Oil."

"Wow."

"Apparently there's a significant deposit of oil in the south, in a tourist area. Near a nature reserve, Doñana. Have you heard of it?"

"No."

"Well, you have to get up to speed. It's not going to be easy to convince the authorities or the public that the park will be left undamaged. Our client won't invest unless he has full guarantees that he'll be able to act in whatever way is convenient for his interests."

"A Spanish company?"

"An American company that will work alongside a Spanish one for this purpose, not because it needs to, but simply to avoid the bureaucracy. Spaniards are difficult. It's better for a Spanish company to be the figurehead and the one that negotiates with the authorities."

"And what do we have to do?"

"Soften up public opinion. It's what we do. Or hadn't you realized?"

"When will I get the details?"

"Your boss, Leopold Lerman, will give them to you. I sent them over to him while you were in Derbyshire. Get to work. And reserve a ticket for Madrid."

Lerman came to my office two minutes later with a large folder. He didn't give me any details.

"Look at these papers," he ordered.

I couldn't help asking myself why Lerman and Schmidt had chosen me for this job. I wasn't one of them, or at least I didn't feel like one of them.

I spent the rest of the day reading the papers. I asked Cooper to look at them as well. I was growing more reliant on him. He was as clever as he was weird, or maybe he was just as odd as hackers usually are, but he could be trusted.

I asked him to draw up a plan I could discuss the next day with Evelyn Robinson. She had been a good choice on my part. She was game for anything, no matter how murky, so she was a perfect addition to a firm that dedicated itself, in Schmidt's words, to "softening up" public opinion by any means necessary.

I still felt lonely. London for me was no more than an office, a place to work. I have never managed to enjoy the city, and enjoyed it far less back then. My life was reduced to work and Madame Agnès's house. I asked myself how it was possible that I had become such a frequenter of prostitutes. I missed Esther although I knew that it would be difficult for us to take a step back and find each other again. Even so, I called her, not caring what time it was or what she might be doing. Most often, she was working. When she heard my voice she seemed to cheer up. She was interested in my work. I explained in detail what we had done.

"You're a real son of a bitch, aren't you?" she said, but there was no condemnation in her voice. It was just a statement of fact.

"Will you marry me?" I asked, knowing that she wasn't expecting me to ask her again.

"I think we did the right thing breaking the engagement. It wouldn't have turned out well."

"I don't agree."

"I think you do, deep down."

"I miss you. Do you believe me?"

"I believe you, Thomas. Of course I believe that you could miss me. You're alone over there, you don't have any friends, you don't have anyone to support you. You have to play the role of the bad guy twenty-four hours a day and that must be very tiring, even for someone who isn't a very good person."

"But you were ready to marry me."

"Yes, I was. I dodged a bullet there. Hey, you know I bumped into your brother the other day? He's charming."

I felt sick. Physically sick. I couldn't bear the thought of Esther being close to Jaime.

"And where did you 'bump into' him?" I asked, trying not to show how affected I was by what she'd said.

"On the street. I was waiting for a taxi in front of the office and then I heard a horn and saw Jaime waving at me to get in his car. He offered to drive me home. Your brother is quite the gentleman."

"Nothing else?"

"What do you mean, 'nothing else'?"

"He drove you home and that was that?"

"We talked about how much fun we'd had the day of our failed engagement, you remember, at your aunt's house in Newport, and he invited me to come back there whenever I wanted. He was very friendly."

"Will you go back?"

"To Newport?"

"Yes."

"I don't think so. It wouldn't make sense. You're not there and I don't think it would be appropriate to accept the invitation, although I must say I was tempted. Your father and your aunt are wonderful, just like Jaime. Ah, I forgot! We agreed to meet up and play tennis one of these days. I don't get to do it that often and your brother invited me. I couldn't resist."

"So now you're making a play for my brother," I said angrily.

Esther was silent for a moment or two. I imagined her biting her lower lip as she looked for the right words to reply.

"I could go for him, Thomas. I don't owe you anything. But neither Jaime nor I would allow ourselves to do it. Your brother has a highly developed sense of honor and he wouldn't do anything that could upset you. For you I'm a ship that has passed in the night, but even so he wouldn't allow himself to start anything with me. You should know him better."

"My perfect brother!" I said angrily.

"Look, you're right, he's a wonderful person. Educated, intelligent, a gentleman, and handsome too. He's got it all." Esther had gotten angry.

"And when's the wedding?" I was still trying to rile her up.

"You're an idiot, Thomas. You don't deserve Jaime's support, or mine."

She hung up on me. I dialed her number again but she didn't pick up. I kicked the sofa and cried out because I nearly broke a toe. I was jealous, very. I couldn't bear to think that Esther and Jaime . . . But at the same time I realized that my brother would be much more able than I was to appreciate Esther's qualities. Yes, they deserved each other. I didn't know anyone better than the two of them apart from John, and merely recognizing this made me so angry I could hardly breathe.

I got drunk. I drank a bottle of whiskey on an empty stomach. The maid found me stretched out on the floor the next morning. She wasn't surprised. Not anymore.

I couldn't get up until the afternoon. I spent a good part of the morning throwing up, and my head throbbed so hard that I thought it was going to explode. But I made an effort and went in to the office. Jim Cooper offered me a detailed plan of what we could do in Spain. It wasn't bad, but it needed a little more spice, a little more wickedness. I decided to send him and Evelyn to get the lay of the land while I took a trip back to New York. I couldn't bear the idea that Esther and Jaime might become friends.

6

John was pleased to see me, as always. I dodged his hug and shook his hand. He put up with it.

He had just gotten back from the office. He was about to have lunch by himself and he asked me to join him. I accepted. I needed him to tell me what he knew about the recent friendship between Jaime and Esther. So I had a quick shower and went to the dining room, where María was waiting impatiently by the soup tureen. She looked coldly at me. I looked coldly back at her. María was very old now, but she seemed not to have forgotten my childhood exploits. We didn't like each other. Perhaps she knew me a lot better than the rest of the family did. Also, she hadn't ever forgiven me for the way I had treated my mother. María had loved her deeply. María thought of me in much the same way that Roy did: I was a wretch, a scoundrel.

John said nothing to me about Jaime and Esther; he must not have known that they had seen each other.

"You made a mistake breaking up with that girl. She's a good kid and she seemed to love you. Maybe you could try again."

"Yes, perhaps, except that your son Jaime's getting in the way," I said suddenly, disconcerting him.

"Jaime? I don't know what you're talking about."

"He 'bumped into' Esther. He invited her to visit Newport and to play tennis with him."

He said nothing. He seemed to be digesting my words. María watched us both as she served the roast. I could see the dislike in her eyes. It pained her that I was not more affectionate with John. María pursed her lips and served me a very small portion of meat. It was her way of punishing me.

"I don't think that your brother would have orchestrated the meeting. It's not the kind of thing Jaime would do. But . . . well, you shouldn't have left. She won't wait for you for the rest of her life. She's a good kid, like I said, and sooner or later someone's going to realize just how good she is and marry her. If you love her you still have time to try again, but if you don't, then don't get involved in her life . . . Or in anyone else's." John looked straight at me and I could see the hurt in his eyes.

"So, you think it's good that Jaime's getting my girl," I said, angrily.

"Jaime couldn't play a mean trick if he tried. If he said he met Esther by chance then he met her by chance. I don't think there's anything wrong with being nice to her. Esther and Jaime got along when they first met, and getting along with someone doesn't have to mean anything more than just that."

"There's no going back. I'm not going to marry her," I said, with a conviction I did not feel.

"So why are you worried?"

"I think Jaime's being disloyal, sticking his nose into my life. Esther is a part of my personal network."

"And you've come all this way to tell him that? You've traveled for nothing. It's clear that you don't know your brother very well. Listen to me. Don't fool yourself. Esther doesn't belong to you, she can do whatever she wants. She's free and she owes you nothing. You left New York and abandoned her, remember. And don't let yourself be carried away by jealousy. Neither Esther nor Jaime deserve it."

I don't know whether my father had intended to return to the office that day, but he did, probably to avoid me. I'm sure the conversation had left a bitter taste in his mouth.

I stayed in the study thinking about what to do. My brother was at Harvard and wouldn't be back until the weekend. It was Wednesday, so I would have to wait to confront him.

I was pouring myself a glass of my father's whiskey when María came into the study. She stood in front of me. She wasn't very tall or particularly broad, but she seemed to have grown, such was the anger she had to master in order to look at me.

"Why don't you leave him alone? Your father is sick. Do you know that he had a heart attack a week ago? He fainted in his office."

"So what? Does that stop us from talking to each other?" I said, angry at her interference.

"Talk? You don't talk, Thomas, you radiate evil. You hurt everyone who loves you. The surprising thing is that there are still people who are able to love you. You behaved toward her like . . . like . . ."

"Like a pig?" I knew she was referring to my mother.

"Yes. You behaved wretchedly and now you've come back to hurt your father. Why? You owe him so much, and he loves you. He's always looked out for you. He's moved mountains to make you happy. He's given you everything. You owe your father respect, at least."

"He's not my father."

"Really? He's really not your father? I thought that your father was the person who wiped your nose, watched over you when you were sick, put you up on his shoulders, played basketball with you, helped you with your homework . . . He never lifted a hand against you, though maybe he should have. He's always been kind to you, excusing your faults, finding explanations for your rage. Don't you dare say that John is not your father, because you are lucky that he's behaved like the best and most generous of fathers in giving you his love."

"When did you get a new job? Have you stopped being a maid and switched to family counseling? You have no right to meddle in our lives. And don't you ever scold me again, or I swear I'll get John to fire you."

"You know what, Thomas, I don't know anyone worse than you. You are a bad person. And you don't need to remind me that I am the maid, although neither your father nor your mother have ever treated me like a servant; they've always made me feel like a part of the family."

"Well, you're not a part of my family, so don't get on my case. Stop telling me what you think, I don't care. You're a nobody, you're nothing!"

María turned around and left the study. I thought I heard a sob. I didn't care that she might be crying. She thought she could interfere in my business because, having known me since I was a child, she believed she could talk to me as an equal.

If I had obeyed the basic norms of decent behavior, if I had felt even a single spark of affection or pity, then I would not have treated María like this. I could have listened to her and agreed. That would have been enough:

"Did my father really have a heart attack? What happened?" I would have asked.

María would have gone into detail and I would have listened patiently.

"What did the doctor say? He must have given him something . . . You know what? I'm going to call the doctor. I want to know exactly what's happening with my father. And don't worry; I'll try not to upset him. You're right, he doesn't deserve it."

But I didn't say any of this. All I did was say out loud just how much her very presence irritated me. She knew me as I truly was. She had seen me grow, get older, watched this motiveless malignity build its nest in me, this hatred for my mother that I felt without knowing why, this unease because I had not found my proper place in the world.

Yes, I should have pretended to listen and borne her reproaches with my lips tightly sealed, even if only out of respect for her age. But I didn't have it in me to behave like that.

I called Jaime. He didn't pick up. I was surprised, because I didn't think he'd be in class, although I wasn't sure. I didn't know if he'd be on campus or at his office. I thought enviously about how my brother was on the verge of getting his degree. Soon he would be working for the same firm as John, and as my grandfather James before him. I couldn't stop thinking about James Spencer as my grandfather, for all that I tried to force the idea out of my mind. I knew that I only had two acknowledged and authentic grandparents, my mother's parents, Ramón and Stella, and my only other direct relative was Uncle Oswaldo, that simple man who made me feel ashamed. That was why I rejected my maternal grandparents. Stella liked to say that I was identical to Oswaldo: "Just look at him, like two peas in a pod, the same eyes, the same hands," she would say to my mother when she came to visit us. I would run away. I didn't want to hear it. The notion that I resembled my uncle Oswaldo was insulting to me. But my grandmother Stella was a simple woman who couldn't understand why I rejected her. "He's a very unfriendly little boy. You spoil him and you'll ruin him," she used to say to my mother. And my mother would nod, nervously, aware of the rage that filled me and afraid I would do something I shouldn't, which would confirm what my grandmother had said.

I had not seen my maternal grandparents since the day we buried my mother. From time to time they would call me, but I would not pick up the phone. Whenever I saw their number on my phone screen I would refuse to answer. I had nothing to say to them, and there was nothing they could say that would interest me. It was all ancient history. People I had never felt close to, whom I did not love. I won't say that my behavior toward them weighed on me. It wouldn't be true. Now that my grandparents are dead and my uncle Oswaldo is withering away, suffering from dementia in a nursing home, I still don't regret it. What did I have to do with them? I hadn't chosen them.

But to return to that day in New York, I felt, once again, furious with the world and with myself. Because I couldn't speak with Jaime I started to call Esther, then thought better of it and decided to go look for her.

She would be about to leave her office. I caught a taxi and arrived just as she stepped out of the building.

She didn't seem surprised to see me. But she didn't make any attempt to give me a kiss, and received mine without enthusiasm.

"I wanted to see you," I said, and I took her arm and adjusted my pace to hers.

"I knew you'd come," she said peevishly.

"But you're not happy to see me."

"Sometimes you tire me. Everything with you is always complicated. You're not even an amusing friend."

"I don't want to be your friend. I want to marry you. I came here to ask you to marry me."

"I would have liked that once, but now I don't think it's a good idea. In fact I think it was a stroke of luck that you left and that we didn't go ahead with the wedding. It would have been a disaster."

"You're wrong. I love you and you loved me even before I loved you. I haven't done well by you, but I'm here to sort that out. You are the only woman I can live with."

"Yes, I'm sure. But you aren't in love with me. You trust me, and that's more important for you than love."

"I don't understand you."

"Yes, you do, and you know I'm right. I don't judge you. Ever since we first met I've accepted you for who you are. You have never had to pretend in front of me, to try to be something you're not. That's why you want to live with me, because you know you can tell me anything without shocking me; you also know I'll give you good advice, and try to help you. But love, as

I told you before, is something different. I thought you might learn to feel something for me, but you can't love anyone, not even yourself."

"I love you, Esther. I swear that I love you."

"No, although you might think you do. In fact, all you need is for someone to give herself up to you unconditionally. Someone who will not blame you for being who you are, someone you can trust, whom you can tell everything that you do or think. And you think that the only person you know who wouldn't betray you is me. You're wrong. Your father and your brother wouldn't betray you, and your aunt Emma wouldn't, and your grandparents, the Spencers, wouldn't either. And although I don't know them, I'm positive that your mother's parents wouldn't betray you. There are lots of people who love you. The problem is that you don't love them, and that's why you feel so alone."

"You're right, the only person I love is you."

"No, you don't love me either."

We walked hurriedly, but not in any particular direction. Esther was speaking with a degree of agitation, and every one of her words went straight to its target. She was right. Everything she said was right. That's why I needed to have her by my side. That's why I had gone to look for her in New York and why I was ready to do anything to make her agree to marry me, to be with me. With her I would stop feeling so alone.

We were silent for a long time. It was comforting to have her near me. Her mere presence calmed me down, gave me strength. With her by my side I felt capable of anything.

"Where do you want to go for dinner?" I asked her, sure that she would abandon anything she had planned for me. I was right.

"I need to call my mother; I told her that I'd give her a hand at the restaurant tonight. The whole place is reserved for a birthday party."

I gave her arm a thankful squeeze, and then I stopped and gave her a kiss, which this time she did not reject.

"Come on. We can go to any old Chinese restaurant."

"I'd rather go to a nice restaurant. It's a special occasion. We have to celebrate finding each other again."

"We're not going to celebrate anything. I'm not wearing the proper clothes and you aren't either. I just got out of work and I've been in the office since eight o'clock this morning. Look at me."

"You look wonderful," I said, sincerely.

Esther had learned to dress well. Stylishly. She was not wearing expensive clothes because she could not afford them, but she knew how to combine the various elements of her wardrobe and she carried off her look. I thought she was attractive, in her black jeans, high-heeled boots, and long, unstructured jacket, which she might have bought just as easily at some couture house as at a secondhand shop. She looked Parisian.

She led me to a French restaurant in Tribeca. I didn't know it, but it seemed to be fashionable. There were lots of admen there, and artists, and musicians . . . There weren't any tables available, but I slipped the maître d' a sizable tip and, after ten minutes and a series of protests from people who actually had reservations, he led us to a corner table. It wasn't the best, but we would at least eat. The only thing I wanted to do was please Esther, to convince her once again that the best thing for both of us would be to share our present and our future. But I decided not to be a bore about it. I knew that in order to find a way through her suspicions I would have to make her laugh. Women grow more relaxed when they laugh, they become more trusting, and it's easier to get to the heart of their emotions. I spent some time telling her about my life in London, but I did so in a comic style, so that she would laugh at me. She asked me about Roy and Suzi and I explained what had happened. I hesitated before doing so, but in the end I did it. She appreciated my sincerity.

"You behaved like little shits," she said, without showing any sign of anger.

"Yes, you're right. But Suzi made it very difficult for us. She was about to throw the whole operation into the garbage. They would have fired me. Plus, it wasn't me who dug up all this crap about her father's past. Bernard Schmidt served it to us on a plate. And Neil's very good at pulling strings, seeing what he can uncover."

"But you've ended their marriage. Suzi is never going to forgive Roy. As soon as she can, she'll leave him."

"She can't do it."

"The day her father dies she'll do it. You'll see," she spoke with certainty.

I was always surprised by her capacity to understand the human condition. While I was busy with the present moment, she always went further, and did so by analyzing the ins and outs of people's personalities.

We dined together peacefully. I even made her laugh by telling her how scared the maid was every time she came into my apartment and found me lying on the floor with whiskey spilled all over the carpet.

"You shouldn't drink so much. Alcohol is not the cure for loneliness. You should make some friends."

"It's not easy. Or at least for me it's not easy."

"Ask Cooper to invite you out with his friends," she suggested.

"Cooper's gay and I think that most of his friends are too, so I don't think I'd have all that much fun going out with them," I said.

"The important thing is getting to know people. Who cares what they do in bed? I'm sure you'd end up becoming friends with some of them at least."

She was serious. Esther did not have any prejudices. That was one of the things I liked about her. We went over the people I knew in London and she decided that I should have an informal dinner at my apartment and invite some of them.

"Invite your boss as well, Leopold Lerman. You might even be able to invite the mysterious Mr. Schmidt," she said, enthusiastically.

"Things don't work like that in London. The English are very formal, especially people of a certain social class."

"Yes, but you don't rub shoulders with that elite social class, you work with people from the PR world. I'm sure they go out over the weekend and drink at those pubs they like so much. And what about girls? Aren't there any you like?"

"I haven't even noticed the ones who work in the office."

"Well, maybe it's time you did." She was like a schoolteacher giving her student instructions.

"Let's do something. Come to London with me and help me organize this dinner."

"I can't, Thomas. I have to work, my life is here."

"You were going to leave it to marry me and move to London," I reminded her.

"Yes, things were going to be like that and now they're not. I've gone back to my reality. You know, the agency, the classes at Paul Hard's school, my family's restaurant . . . I'm fine like this. I don't want to change my situation."

"And Jaime, right? You've got Jaime now as well."

"Your brother is charming. If I hadn't been close to marrying you then I would think about going out with him. But neither he nor I would feel comfortable about it; you would always be there, standing between us. We haven't spoken about it, there's no need, both of us know it. And although there might be a certain degree of attraction between us we're not going to get carried away by it. Happy?"

"So you admit you like my brother." I wanted to hit her.

"Yes, I like him. But you knew that already. Any girl could be interested in Jaime, including me. But there's you, and I've said it already, that means things will never go further than playing tennis or going out for a meal every now and then."

"What sacrifices you make!"

"It may be difficult for you to understand, but there are certain codes of behavior in the world. And loyalty is a part of it. Jaime wouldn't take a step beyond simply offering me his friendship. He loves you very much and he knows that you would never forgive him if he made a play for me."

"So I have to be grateful to him now. That's icing on the cake!"

"No, no one is asking you to be grateful for anything. All I'm doing is explaining how things are."

"I'll do whatever you want, but marry me. Don't leave me again."

"You'll remember that it wasn't really me who left you . . . But in any event, I think it was the right thing to do. I want a kind of life that isn't the one you've opted for."

"In that case, fine. Let's do what you want."

"Are you really prepared to spend weekends in Newport with your father, your aunt, your brother, your grandparents? To share Thanksgiving dinner with them? To lend a hand washing dishes at my parents' restaurant? To have children, bring them up with love and affection? I don't think so, Thomas, I really don't think so."

"My real family is just my mother's parents, and her brother, my horrible uncle Oswaldo. I can't stand them. As for John and Jaime . . . I can't feel anything for them. My life with the Spencers has been a sham."

"You see? You're stating precisely why things can't be as you want them to be. Our realities are different. I think your father is charming and your aunt Emma is a wonderful lady. I like them. A lot. To me they are your family. They are the family your mother chose for you. You should be happy; she couldn't have made a better choice. And as for your mother's parents . . . poor things! Your grandfather Ramón had to make his way in a society as classist and racist as ours, in which only the people with the most money are respected. If he had been a million-aire . . . But he's an immigrant, a worthy person who has earned the right to be here through his work. You should be proud of him. His hands are the hands that have fought to make a place in the world for you."

"That's a fine speech. Come on, Esther, don't pull my leg. You're not going to make me believe that if I promise to go and visit my family then you'd rethink the idea of marrying me. I am offering you a life together. Just you and me. Everyone else is superfluous."

"Not to me. I love my parents, my brother, my nephews and nieces . . . And I might even have come to love yours. Let's not argue and let's leave it at that. I will always be a good friend to you. You can call me; I'll come be with you if you need me, but nothing more. That's what you really want."

"You're being vindictive! You haven't forgiven me for going back to London. You knew how much was riding on that meeting with Schmidt . . . I couldn't back out just because we had planned to spend the weekend in Newport. If you like it so much, we'll buy a house there."

"Yes, I like Newport, but above all I like the atmosphere at your aunt's house. Warm, familial. I would really have enjoyed spending weekends at that house with you and with them."

"It's as if you like the Spencers more than you like me," I said angrily.

"No, Thomas. I loved you. I believed that I loved you. And after dreaming of you for so long, you finally looked at me for a moment, and even decided you wanted to marry me. I was not convinced, because I saw that for you love is not the same as it is for me. I'm a romantic. I felt a knot in my stomach every time you looked at me, but it was clear that you felt nothing of the kind. You don't love me, Thomas. You just think that you need me, that you need my loyalty, my love for you, but in fact I don't do anything for you. And if I can't provoke any emotions in you, then obviously you can't feel love for me."

"Answer me. Do you love me?"

"I'm not going to answer that."

I did not know how to convince her that any emotion I felt for her was far stronger than any fleeting attraction would be. But neither could I understand how a woman who was so intelligent and rational could have this infantile romantic streak.

I promised her that I would not leave New York without her and that if things had to be that way, then I would stay there forever. She laughed at me. She knew me too well. She knew that when my phone rang and they asked for me in London I would be off to the airport like a shot.

Sometimes it's the hardest thing in the world to find an empty taxi in New York, so we walked for quite some way before we found one to take her home.

I decided to try to win Esther back. So, first thing next morning, I called Maggie, my secretary, to tell her that I would be spending several days in New York on family business. She could call me or forward my mail. I also spoke to Jim Cooper and Evelyn Robinson, who were in Spain laying the groundwork. I even called Leopold Lerman, my boss, whom I imagined frowning when I told him I was in New York and wouldn't be back for nine or ten days.

Lerman scolded me for leaving without giving him any explanation, reminding me that there was work waiting for me and that I was the one who should be in Spain, not Cooper and Evelyn. I didn't bother arguing with him. Things were what they were and I warned him not to waste time calling Bernard Schmidt and asking him to call me in his place. I had resolved the course of action I would take. And I decided as I spoke that I was going to stay in New York, at least until Esther agreed to come back with me to London, and that was not going to be an easy task.

I had breakfast with John. The previous day I hadn't paid any attention to his pallor, the bags under his eyes, his tired movements. Neither of us referred to the conversation of the day before. John was too well-mannered and loved me too much to bring up subjects that might alter the tricky balance we maintained in our relationship. It was difficult for him to understand why I would address him by his name and refuse to call him Dad. He was hurt by this cold treatment, as though it were a punishment for his not being my real father.

He was surprised when I asked him to call his sister Emma and arrange for us to be invited to spend the weekend in Newport.

"You want to go to Newport? You don't need me to arrange it. Call your aunt, she'll be pleased that you're going."

"I don't want to go alone. I'd like you and Jaime to come as well. I'll be coming with Esther."

"Right."

"She likes Aunt Emma's house. She still would like to enjoy a weekend there," I explained reluctantly.

"You want to pick things up where you left off?"

"What do you mean?" I asked, prepared to get angry.

"I suppose you want to go back to the day when you took her away in a hurry because you'd gotten the call to go back to London. Are you sure that this is what she wants?"

"How about you don't meddle in my business? All I asked was for you to arrange a weekend in Newport. Is it too much trouble for you to do that one thing?" There was such annoyance in my voice that John swallowed my words with a bitter grin.

"Of course I'll do it, if that's what you want," he said as he got up. And with a nod goodbye he left the dining room.

María looked at me with hatred. She had the coffeepot in her hand and was preparing to pour me a cup, but she paused. I could see in her eyes the desire to pour the coffee over my head or strike me. She was breathing heavily. But she was unable to hold herself back when it came to defending the Spencers.

"Do you want to kill him? I told you he had a heart attack. Can't you see what he looks like? How come you can't feel any pity for him?"

"Leave me alone. Don't tell me what I can or can't do."

"Poor woman, to have had a son like you . . . You're the shame of everyone who knows you," she said, as she put the coffeepot back on the burner and left the dining room, slamming the door.

Esther refused to come to Newport and I got mad at her. I thought that she would like it, that she would understand that my intention was to start again from where we had left off, and that this trip would be like a new declaration of love.

We had an argument. I said that she didn't give my gesture the respect it deserved, and I accused her of trying to make a play for Jaime. She hung up on me.

I unloaded all my anger onto John that evening when he said that Emma would be delighted for us to go and stay in her house that weekend.

"Well, you can call her again and tell her I'm not coming."

I didn't give him any further explanation, and he didn't ask. There was no need. It was clear that the cause was Esther. He didn't even suggest that we eat together. He said that he was tired and was going to bed. María would bring a glass of milk to his room.

I didn't reply. We were in the living room and I had the television on and pretended to be deeply absorbed in the news. Before he left the room he seemed to want to say something, or at least he tried.

"I know that lots of things aren't how you want them to be. I'd do anything to make you happy," he murmured.

I sat in front of the television for a long time without even thinking about what I should do. Esther had hung up on me again and I realized that I had no friends in New York. I had no friends anywhere at all, for that matter. No one I could call for a drink. For my two years at the Paul Hard School, I had stayed on the margins. I had made friends only with Esther, and that was simply because Lisa had thought we could use her for our benefit. Lisa had been my whole world then.

I felt a stab of discontent. Was I the only person in the world who had no friends? Why did no one invite me to dinner, or to spend a weekend with them? People make friends with the people they work with. Everyone did except me. No one seemed to think of me.

This realization was like a kick in the gut. I was alone. Completely alone. The only two people who had ever accompanied me for any part of the way through life were Lisa and Esther. And I had let go of Lisa without a second thought. I didn't even feel compassion when I saw her destroying herself with drugs. I let her do it. Now I realized that in my own way I had loved her. Not like I thought I loved Esther, but at least with Lisa I had not felt alone. She had filled some aspect of my life.

And as for Esther, I was aware that I wanted her in some egotistical fashion. She was right: more than love, what I wanted was the security of knowing that I could count on her, unconditionally. She did not blame people for things.

I felt impotent in the face of the knowledge that I could not convince her to give our relationship another chance. I had been stupid to go back to London without realizing that if I really wanted her by my side, I would have to confirm our relationship by getting married. But I had been impatient, and curious to meet Bernard Schmidt. Now I knew him, but on the way I had lost Esther.

I was at a dead end and didn't know what to do, didn't know how to overcome her resistance.

My cell rang and pulled me out of my thoughts. It was Evelyn.

"Hello, boss. Are you still in New York?"

"Yes, for the time being."

"Here's what we've got. The Spanish government would like the prospecting for oil to go ahead. They want to increase their tax revenue and reduce unemployment, and if they strike oil then they're not going to be skittish about killing a few fish. The problem is where it always is, with the locals. The environmental groups have been mobilized. All the coastal villages are filled with posters calling for the defense of the ecosystem. Of course, there are people in favor of the prospecting—they think that if there's oil, they'll get some kind of benefit out of it. But it won't be easy to carry out a campaign in favor of the oil business, especially because all the prospecting is to be paid for by the Spanish government, or rather the taxpayer. You know, the rich never lose."

"Don't come to me with speeches, Evelyn. They've hired us to do a job and you have to tell me if it's possible or not," I replied.

"We'll do it. But we need firsthand information, or else we'll lose a lot of time. I'm not an expert on Spanish politics. We need to know who's who and who's against whom before we spring into action."

"Read the newspapers," I said curtly.

Evelyn said nothing for a few seconds. I suppose she was trying to work out whether to tell me where I could stick it and hang up, or if it was better for her to carry on earning two thousand pounds a month plus expenses. She opted for the second choice.

"I don't know if you're in a bad mood or if you've got problems, but if you think about it you'll see that I'm right. Call me when you can. We'll continue working here, we'll get what information we can, but we need someone to lay out the situation for us. I think we'll need to find a Spanish agency and work with them on this one. We should call Neil as well; perhaps he's got a Spanish colleague who can give us some lessons on Spanish politics over a good dinner."

"Call Neil. I pay you too well for you not to be able to deal with this yourselves."

I hung up. I wasn't in the mood to spend time on a bunch of long-haired Spanish environmentalists.

I went back to thinking about myself. About my loneliness. I felt a flash of rage. I was in New York, it was my city, and I couldn't call anyone to go out for a drink because I had no friends or even acquaintances. I had to ask myself why, had to analyze why I was alone. But I have never been the kind of person to blame myself for anything. If I were to be sincere, and not fool myself, then I really should have realized that the fault lay somewhere in my personality, as the rest of the world didn't seem to have any problems making friends.

I dialed Esther's number again. I needed to speak to her, for her to explain what I knew but did not want to admit. She picked up, but there was a note of weariness in her voice. She didn't want to talk to me. I bored her.

"What's wrong with me? Tell me the truth. I need you to tell me why I'm alone, why I don't have any friends. I want to know why, if you said you loved me a month ago, you don't love me now. Is it my fault?"

She replied quickly and bluntly. So quickly and so bluntly that I jumped.

"Yes. You are your own worst problem. But there's no solution," she said coldly.

"What about other people? Is it really just me who's the guilty party?"

"Yes. Everyone else sees you for what you are. And you aren't trustworthy. You'd sell out your own mother. You show no emotion. You don't give any signs that you have feelings. You make people feel repulsed, Thomas. People spend time with you because of work, because they don't have better options, but they don't love you because they know that you'd never love them back, and that if you had to sacrifice them then you'd do so without pity."

"I'm a bad person? Is that what you're saying?"

"You're not a good person. No one knows that better than you."

"But I love you."

"Not really, although I would have been happy if you had loved me. I wanted to love you and wanted you to respond."

"Do you think that if I didn't love you I'd want you to marry me?"

"Yes, because it's in your interest. I've told you already: being with me makes you feel calm. You don't feel any more passion for me than you might feel for someone you meet one night and take to your bed and whose name you don't remember in the morning. Everything you do, even making love, you do with immense coldness, as if nothing gives you any pleasure. Do you know why? You have no emotions. And that's why I don't want to get back together with you."

"You don't love me?"

"I don't know, Thomas, I don't know anymore. But I do know for sure that what I think of as love is something I will never experience with you, and that this is an experience I don't want to renounce. Sooner or later I'll meet someone . . . And as for you, well, I'm already reconciled to the idea that with you nothing's going to happen."

"You don't even want to give me a chance. Let me show you how important you are to me."

"I know I'm important, that you need me. But I'm talking about love, Thomas, not need."

"You're so stubborn! Why won't you believe me? I love you, Esther. I've never loved anyone else. No one. I swear it."

I heard her sigh over the telephone. I thought that I might have managed to move her and waited impatiently for her reply.

"You love me, yes, but not how I need to be loved. That's the problem, Thomas. You can't give any more and I need a lot more; I need a type of love that you will never be able to feel, a love that even if you wanted to you would not be able to give me. I would feel unsatisfied. I would never be able to stop thinking that I was missing something. I don't want to resign myself to that kind of life, Thomas, not yet. Maybe I will never find what I'm looking for, what I think love must be, but at least I want to be prepared for it when it comes. If I'm with you, then I will be giving up on that possibility. This conversation is over. Let it go."

"No one will ever love you like I love you." I spoke sincerely; this was how I felt.

"But maybe someone will love me like I want to be loved. Or at least, that's my hope."

"No, Esther, I can't stand here with my hands in my pockets and let you go. Tell me what I can do, anything, that will show you that it might be worth the trouble to give me another chance. Don't deny me this, please, let me try to show you that I can give you what you want. Maybe I haven't yet managed to express the intensity with which I love you, but if you just give me a chance, you'll realize that this love, this love filled with emotion, is something that you and I can find together. I don't think that there's a man on earth who will ask for your love as I'm asking for it now."

"Please, don't talk about asking for love."

"Esther, let me try. If I fail, then I understand if you close the door on me forever. But not now, not like this. Don't ask me to give in. If I'm fated to lose, let me at least die fighting."

Her silence made me think that she was vacillating. I was nervous. I felt something like despair.

"We'll talk, Thomas. I'm tired now. I've had a difficult day. I presented a campaign for a diaper account and I'm not sure if they liked it or not. They won't tell me until tomorrow."

"I'm sorry. They're idiots, and you're the best," I replied, sincerely.

"Thank you, but not even I am certain that it was my best campaign," she said with a laugh.

"I won't bother you anymore. I'll call you tomorrow and maybe we can have lunch or dinner together. I don't want to pressure you."

"When are you going back to London?"

"I'm not going until I get an answer from you. Work can wait. If I lose my job, what can I do? I'll start again from the beginning."

"Talk to you tomorrow, Thomas."

I noted that my last words had flattered her, even though she surely didn't believe me. But I was sincere, on this occasion at least. My boss, Leopold Lerman, could call me, or Bernard Schmidt himself, or the impassive lawyers, but I had no intention of leaving New York. Not this time.

I looked at the television again. A river had burst its banks somewhere in Asia, I don't remember where; famine in Africa was leaving a trail of death; the defense ministers of all the NATO countries were meeting in Brussels; the U.S. president was on a trip to the Middle East . . . Same old, same old. The news kept repeating itself. There was nothing that particularly caught my attention.

I poured myself a glass of whiskey. I didn't have anything better to do. Alcohol helped me forget myself, and that was an invaluable achievement.

I don't know when I fell onto the floor, but I woke up at dawn with the cold running through my bones. The last embers had died out in the fireplace. The television was still on. CNN was like a dragon that instead of fire threw out news items one after another.

I was cold but my body refused to respond to me; it took a huge effort to sit up and my headache was unbearable. I retched, and the taste of whiskey was disgusting. I sat myself on the floor as best I could and my eyes adjusted to the half-light. The sun was coming up and dawn was about to break.

I stayed sitting on the floor for a few minutes, with my back against an armchair. If it hadn't been there I would have fallen over. I said to myself that I should go to my room and sleep until the effects of the alcohol had worn off. It had hit me particularly hard this time. I was dizzier than usual. I felt a pressure in my chest and my gut was turbulent. It crossed my mind that I would hate to die drunk and not in control of my faculties.

The silence was ominous. John would be asleep, and so would María, although she usually got up early to prepare our breakfast. What time was it? I couldn't focus on the hands of my wristwatch.

It annoyed me to think that María might find me in this state. I didn't care if my maid in London had found me drunk on the floor on several occasions, but I did not want to see disdain appear again in María's eyes. I didn't care, I told myself, what she might think, but I didn't want to leave myself open to attack.

It took forever, but in the end, holding on to the edge of the chair, I managed to gradually pull myself up until I was standing upright. And then I fell over again. I tried once more, although my back hurt terribly, as did one knee, which I had hit on the way down. I had twisted my wrist as well.

When I finally left the living room I walked along leaning against the walls. It was getting lighter and that helped me find the way to my room. I threw myself down on my bed and although the room spun I ended up falling asleep.

I was woken by María's screams. It took me a while to understand what she was saying. I could barely see her through my drunken haze.

"Your father! Your father is sick! He can't speak! Help me!" she shouted as she shook me to get me up.

I don't know how I did it, but I followed her to John's room. He was laid out on the floor of the bathroom, trembling, with his eyes rolled back. María helped me to stretch him out on the bed.

"Call an ambulance," I said in a thick voice. It was hard for me to talk.

María ran out of my father's room. When she came back I was sitting on the bed, looking at John, not knowing what to do or how to help. I couldn't pull myself together. The damn whiskey had done its job, though I was sure I hadn't drunk more than on other occasions.

"I'll stay with him. You go and . . . at least wash your face, you stink." María ordered me around as though I were still a little boy.

She didn't bother to hide her disdain. Making an effort to

keep myself upright, I left my father's room and walked toward mine. I got into the shower just as I was, fully clothed, and when the cold water started to wake me up I took my clothes off. I heard María knocking on the door and came out wrapped in a robe.

"It's the ambulance, they're taking him. They're asking for you. You have to give them the insurance details."

"I'll go right away, tell them to go ahead. I'll follow them with the papers. Call me a taxi."

I was lucky. I reached the hospital only a few minutes after the ambulance did. My father was in a terrible state, they said, he'd suffered a stroke. They hadn't yet been able to evaluate the damage. The doctor would speak to me as soon as possible. I filled out all the forms they gave me. We were lucky enough to have a policy that covered any possible circumstance.

I dialed Jaime's number, although I guessed that María would have called him already. She trusted my brother, especially in moments like this. She didn't think I was capable or worthy of taking control of the situation.

My brother answered at once. He was on his way.

"How's Dad?" he wanted to know.

"I still don't know, I'm waiting for the doctor to come out and tell us. Are you coming by train?"

"I'm in the car. I wanted to get going as soon as possible. Call me as soon as you hear something. Thomas . . . I'm glad you're here. Dad will need us."

I hung up. I didn't have an answer to what he had said because not for a moment did I think that I could be of use to John.

My head hurt. My hangover had still not disappeared and I hadn't had time to have coffee. I asked the nurse where I could find a coffee machine and she pointed toward the hallway.

After two cups of coffee I started to feel better, or at least that's what I thought, but I suddenly felt the urge to vomit and had to lock myself in the bathroom. When I came out the doctor was waiting for me.

"I'm Dr. Patterson. Your father is in critical condition, but he will survive because he was brought here in time. Strokes require treatment right away. He may have lost some of his functionality; we still can't tell. His speech appears to be affected, as does the movement on his left side, but it's too early to know if this will be permanent. We can hope that he will fully recover. We'll know in the next few hours. Now you can go in for a couple of minutes to see him if you like. But don't talk to him too much. He's agitated, he needs to rest."

"What caused the stroke?" I asked out of curiosity.

The doctor shrugged as though my question were irrelevant.

"It's a cardiovascular accident. High blood pressure, high cholesterol, a shock . . . There are lots of possible causes. We're trying to work out what might have caused it. We'll tell you when we find out. Go and see him. Five minutes, I have to get back to work."

I followed him to the room where John was being kept under observation. There was another doctor, a black man, who to me looked very young, and there were a couple of nurses standing by the bed, looking at a screen that showed John's vital signs. I heard Dr. Patterson give his colleague, the young doctor, a few instructions. Then he left without saying anything.

"You can come closer," one of the nurses said.

I did so, with a certain degree of apprehension. I have always avoided being around sick people, then and now. Sickness repels me.

John opened his eyes and looked at me with such intensity it was as if he were speaking to me. But I could not interpret that silent gaze.

I didn't take his hand or kiss him. I stood a couple of paces away from the bed, far enough for me to escape physical contact with him. He closed his eyes and I saw a grimace of pain on his face.

"You can speak to him," the nurse suggested.

She must have thought that I didn't move or do anything

because I was in a state of shock. The truth is I felt nothing. Neither surprise nor pain. No emotion.

"How are you?" I asked, confronted with the nurse's expectant gaze.

John opened his eyes again. He seemed to want to say something. I think he tried, but his voice was unable to convert it into sound. The nurse nudged me closer to the bed. I suppose she must have thought that I was shy, or that I didn't dare approach him. I bent my head down to John's and managed to hear a few distinct words. "I'm sorry ... I ... I want ... have ... your mother ..." Incoherent words that made sense only in his head. I stood up and looked at him for a few seconds, mainly to stop the nurse from telling me what to do.

The young doctor asked me to leave. I was in the way.

"I'm Dr. Payne. It's better if you leave now. I don't want your father to get agitated trying to talk. As soon as his condition has been completely stabilized we'll call you again and you can come in."

I nodded and didn't object, because I had no intention of staying there. My stomach was churning, I felt a creeping nausea in my throat, and my head was aching fiercely. I was more worried about myself than about what might happen to John.

"Stay outside, I don't think we'll be long," Dr. Payne added.

I went to the nurses' station and went up to the woman who seemed the friendliest. An elderly, fat woman, who looked like she'd seen it all.

"Do you think you could give me something? My stomach's churning and my head's going to explode."

"That's what happens when you drink too much. Throw up, it'll help, and drink a lot of water. The best thing is to sleep. In fact, the best remedy is to wait till tomorrow, you'll see how everything looks better then."

I looked daggers at her. I thought that she was laughing at me, although she hadn't moved a muscle. She did not seem to have any pity for my suffering.

I didn't say thank you, and I went away from the counter. It was still only ten o'clock in the morning and it would take Jaime at least another two hours to arrive. I thought about leaving. I needed to sleep. The fat nurse was right. I don't know why I didn't. I'm still asking myself that question, even now. I had already abandoned John. I refused to treat him as my father, although sometimes I couldn't stop myself from thinking of him as such, nor did I think it odd when people referred to him and me as father and son.

I needed aspirin, urgently, and as I could see that no one here would offer me any, I decided to call Esther. I didn't even think how ridiculous such a request might sound.

I explained to her what had happened and I heard a sigh from her end of the telephone. It seemed that Esther had been sighing rather a lot lately, though I didn't care much about that either.

"I'll try to find an excuse. I don't think I'll be too long in getting there."

She kept her word. I felt relieved when I saw her coming down the hospital corridor, where I was still waiting while the doctors decided what to do with John. She had a bottle of water in one hand and a cup of what turned out to be coffee in the other. She held them out to me at the same time.

"Drink, and I'll give you the aspirin."

"Thank you, you're always there for me."

"So it seems. What happened?"

Esther listened to me carefully. She seemed worried.

"Have you told your aunt Emma?" she asked.

"No . . . it didn't occur to me."

"Well, call her, although Jaime might have called already, or María."

I saw Dr. Payne coming toward us.

"Your father is being taken into the ICU. He needs to be under observation for at least another few days."

"But why aren't you taking him to a room?" I protested.

"It's not the right time. He might have another stroke, and if that happens then we'll need to take immediate action. It's for his safety," Dr. Payne said, and looked at his watch.

"What should we do?" I asked, disoriented.

"Whatever you want. There's a room here where you can wait, or if you go make sure to leave a phone number so we can call you if anything happens."

Dr. Payne seemed to be impatient for us to make a decision, because he kept looking at his watch. In the end Esther decided for me.

"We'll stay here," she said. "The rest of the family will arrive soon, and maybe one of them could be allowed into the ICU," Esther suggested.

"Maybe in a while. Not now."

Esther took me by the hand and led me toward the waiting room. She had taken control of the situation and I was happy that she had done so. It reaffirmed my belief that I needed her in my life. She always knew the right thing to do.

We sat down next to each other. I finished the coffee and waited impatiently for the aspirin to take effect.

"Call your aunt, then you can shut your eyes for a bit. It's going to be a long day. You look terrible, you know. You're too young to drink like that. You don't have any reason to. You should be capable of coping with yourself instead of running away via alcohol. If you can't bear to be alone with yourself, why should others?" she said.

"Do you have a whole speech prepared? I'm not in the mood to be scolded," I complained.

"No, no scolding. All I want is for you, when you have a moment, to think about how you behave. It's pathetic for someone your age to become a drunk."

"I'll call Aunt Emma," I said, so as not to fight with her.

Emma did not take long to arrive. Jaime and María had already told her, as Esther had guessed. She gave Esther a hug, and didn't even try to do the same with me.

"As far as I can tell, you've been upsetting your father ever since you got here," she said, reproachfully.

I had not a single doubt that María had told her all about the conversations I had had with John. I didn't reply. I didn't want to have to face up to her either.

"I don't suppose you want to blame me for John's state. María said he'd been having heart problems lately, and so what happened was more or less inevitable," I said.

"There are things that are avoidable. You could stop behaving like an idiot, for example. Don't call your father John again, I forbid it. Do you hear me? You don't have any right to hurt him. You should feel thankful for how much he has always loved you, for how much he still loves you, even though you don't deserve it. He thinks of you as his son and he feels that you're his son. I will not allow you—listen to me—I will not allow you to call him John one more time, or refuse to treat him with the respect and affection he deserves. I am the executor of his will and I promise you that I will make sure you don't see even a single dollar of inheritance if you dare cause him any more pain."

"Do I have to call you Auntie?" I asked ironically.

"No. You're not important to me anymore. I never could have imagined, not even in my worst nightmares, that you would turn out to be such a despicable person."

"Leave me alone," I answered, and walked out of the room.

Esther followed me; I saw her make a gesture to Emma that seemed to indicate she would look after me.

She stood next to me without saying a word. I felt the heat of her arm next to my body. I didn't look at her. I got into the elevator and headed toward the door of the hospital, fully set on leaving. John was nothing to me. Let his real son, Jaime, and his sister, Emma, look after him, I thought, without any sense of remorse.

"You shouldn't go," I heard Esther say, and she grabbed my hand to stop me.

"Why not? I can't stand them."

"You owe them. They can make you as angry as you want, but you have a debt to your family, one that can't be paid off. I hope you're not going to be so miserly as to refuse to try."

"So you're one of those people who thinks you have to pay for everything in this life. In that case, where's the glory in giving? Do you give something in order to receive?"

"Don't simplify things, Thomas. With me especially, don't get caught up in your cheap philosophizing. Giving and receiving are the essence of relationships between people. Some people act disinterestedly, yes, but the love that you get from your parents, your brothers and sisters, from certain other people whom you meet over the course of your life, is a love that deserves an answer. You can't remain indifferent to it simply because it wasn't something you sought. This love flourishes on its own. The mother who has just given birth feels love for the little innocent creature in her lap. Without any prompting, she gives the child infinite love, spontaneously. Does she expect something in return? Of course, she expects a response to this love, not out of selfishness, but because the love you receive is the necessary complement to the love you give."

"Now it's you with the cheap philosophizing," I retorted.

But Esther did not shrink away from me. I never managed to make her lose her cool. She was always in control of our relationship, whatever form it took as the years went by.

"Your aunt Emma is right. Ever since your mother died you haven't stopped upsetting your father. You need to hurt him to take revenge for the fact that he isn't your biological father. You would have given your life to be like him, and as that isn't the case you're making him pay for things that aren't his fault. Things that nobody should have to pay for. Especially not John, but not yourself either."

"Philosopher, psychologist. What else?" I was trying to mock her, and laugh at her words.

"Don't make it harder, Thomas. You make it impossible for all the people who love you. If we stop loving you, imagine what you could expect from the rest of the world. You've got a pretty good dose of sadism in you, which you like to deploy on yourself as well. You have a death wish. You know that what you do will destroy you, but you still carry on. You are the scorpion who asks the frog to carry him across the river, and who can't resist stinging him even though he knows it'll mean his own death."

"My star sign is Scorpio," I said, laughing.

"I've made a decision, Thomas, and listen to me, because what I am about to say is irreversible."

We were at the door of the hospital. It was cold. I don't know why I was so worried. I suggested that we go to the cafeteria. I didn't want to stay outside.

We sat down at a table apart from everyone else and ordered a couple more coffees. My head was still aching and I begged Esther to give me another aspirin. She seemed to hesitate, but she gave me one.

"If you can't make peace with yourself, if you can't make peace with the people who have given you so much, your father and the rest of your family, then I don't want to hear from you again."

"Right, the Good Samaritan wants me to be a good little boy with what you call my family."

"What I want is for you to stop destroying yourself. I want you to stop, right now. I want you to face up to your life with no resentment, I want you to accept who you are, to enjoy what you have, above all to appreciate the people who love you. If you can't live with yourself, then there's no room in your life for anyone else. All your relationships will be contaminated."

"Are you trying to break up with me?"

"You understand what I mean. I'm not even considering the possibility of marrying you, just the possibility of being your friend. You are, the way you are at the moment, too harmful for anyone who comes close to you. Think about it, Thomas. Take all the time you want, but face up to yourself without any tricks or foolery. And when you've done so, and have come to a decision, then call me, if you still want to."

"I can't stand it when women want to make men change."

"It's not about making you change. It's about accepting yourself as you are. I think you need help. Maybe you should see a psychiatrist. A psychiatrist would help you put your mind in order."

"Leave me, Esther, I don't need you." I got up and turned away without looking at her. I didn't pay for the coffee.

I bumped into Jaime on the way out of the hospital. I couldn't stop him from giving me a hug. There were traces of tears on his cheeks. The idiot must have been crying as he drove.

Jaime thanked me, I don't know for what, and said that it was a great help for him that I was there. He put his arm around my shoulders and pulled me toward the elevator without giving me any time to react, to tell him that all I wanted to do was to leave, to go have a good long sleep.

Aunt Emma was still sitting in the waiting room. Her face lit up when she saw Jaime. He hugged her and I saw that his mere presence calmed her down.

My brother insisted to the fat nurse that he wanted to speak to the doctor. His insistence was almost a plea, and it seemed to move the woman, so first Dr. Patterson appeared, then Dr. Payne. Neither of them said much more than what they'd already told us. John was in serious condition, but this was something he could perhaps recover from. It would be necessary to wait a few hours to see how much damage the stroke had caused. There was nothing to do but wait. Meanwhile, Dr. Payne repeated, John would have to stay in the ICU, but he told Jaime and Emma that he would let them in to see him for a few minutes.

When they came out of the ICU, Emma's face was distraught. She wasn't ready to lose her only sibling.

Jaime seemed calmer and, more than anything else, resolved to be the one who would take control of the situation.

"We'll take turns. We don't know how much time we'll have to be here and it's useless for us to tire ourselves out on the first day. The best thing would be for Thomas to go home, he's been here since early this morning. Aunt Emma, you stay until seven, then you go and take a break."

"What about you?" Aunt Emma asked.

"I'll stay here for a while. Then I'll go home, have something to eat and come back. Then you can go. I want to spend the night here in case something happens. Tomorrow Thomas can come at eight o'clock. I'll stay here until the doctors give us their morning report and then I'll go and rest until midday. Thomas can stay the night tomorrow and you can be with both of us for a part of our shifts. How does that sound?"

I didn't intend to spend any time sitting in a chair in that hospital waiting room or sitting next to a hospital bed. I was going to do whatever the hell I wanted, but I didn't want to fight either, especially as Jaime was offering me the opportunity to go home, which was the only thing I wanted at that moment.

María seemed to have gotten even older. She must have been watching from a window, because she opened the door just as I was putting my key into the lock.

"How is he?" she asked anxiously.

"Bad." I enjoyed saying that.

"But he'll get better? He is going to live, isn't he?"

"They don't know yet, maybe not." I enjoyed watching her suffer.

Her arms fell to her sides, weak, as though she were surrendering herself to this news.

"The doctors can't do anything?" she asked in a faint voice.

I shrugged and asked her to bring a tray to my room with

something to eat. I was famished and exhausted. I needed to lie down for a while and sleep in order to feel like myself again. And that's what I did.

I went to sleep immediately. I heard Jaime's voice in the distance. It was difficult for me to wake up, and when I made an effort and opened my eyes I saw my brother's figure taking shape before me. He was sitting on the edge of the bed, waiting patiently for me to wake up.

"I'm sorry to have woken you, but there's some good news. Dad is speaking and moving his leg. Dr. Patterson says he's going to make it. But I'm afraid he's going to have to stop working, at least for a while. Oh, and our grandparents are about to arrive. Their plane gets here at nine. They were lucky to get tickets. Could you go and pick them up at LaGuardia?"

"Our grandparents?" I asked, still half asleep.

"Yes, James and Dorothy. They're very old and a little slow. You know they've been in Florida for most of the year. Come on, Thomas, wake up."

"Why don't you send the driver from the office?" I asked. The last thing I wanted was to go all the way to the airport.

"Because it's after six and his shift is over. Take my car, it won't take long."

"What about you?"

"I'm on at the hospital, and I'll go back there. I'll be there all night. Grandma Dorothy will insist on seeing Dad, so you should bring them to the hospital and then take them home."

"Yes, boss," I replied, with obvious annoyance, just to let him know that I didn't like him giving me orders.

But Jaime skated over my grumpiness. He left my room sure that I would do what he had told me to do.

I got up and got into the shower. I noticed, as the water ran over me, that the effects of last night's alcohol had evaporated. Although I had eaten a good slice of roast beef, I was still hungry. But I couldn't delay if the Spencers' airplane was landing at nine; in fact, I scarcely had time to get to the airport. And so

I went. I was surprised to see them so fragile, so old. Grandma Dorothy's mind seemed to be wandering a little.

I did everything that Jaime had asked of me. I took the Spencers to the hospital and waited for them to see John. Jaime had convinced Dr. Patterson that my grandparents would not be able to rest until they had seen their son, and the doctor had accepted this. Jaime had the curious ability to make people do what he wanted them to do. I suppose it must have been his good manners, his wheedling tone, the fact that he looked like a polite, well-brought-up kid. Anyway, everyone always did whatever he wanted.

The Spencers had a maid who lived permanently in their New York town house. She was as old as they were. She had helped them for so many years that she was almost part of the furniture. Although they lived for six months of the year in Florida and didn't need her in New York, it would never have occurred to them to fire her. When we arrived, the woman was waiting for them with a light meal. They insisted that I stay for a while and share their food. I did so. Although I was no longer hungry, I would've liked to have eaten something more substantial than a ham and cheese sandwich and a salad.

I had always respected my Spencer grandfather. I would never have dared call him James, or my grandmother Dorothy. But I didn't want to call them my grandparents, so I tried to find a way to talk to them without using this title either. It was not easy and on many occasions I failed in the attempt.

Grandfather James asked me how I was enjoying my life in London. He wanted to know about my work in detail, but did not seem satisfied when I explained to him everything I had been doing. As for my grandmother Dorothy, her only interest was in whether or not I would marry Esther. "The girl suits you," she said, then added, "In spite of being Italian, but maybe that's not such a disadvantage." I was surprised that she said this. What was it about Italians that rankled my grandmother? She was quintessentially white, Anglo-Saxon, and Protestant, but

Grandmother Dorothy had always been a liberal, just like my grandfather and John.

I didn't get home until midnight. I stayed up to watch television for a while. I tried to avoid thinking about what Esther had said to me. I knew that she'd been serious and that if I didn't exhibit a substantial change in my behavior then I would have to accept that our relationship was over. Change? No, I wasn't going to put on an act for anyone. I was who I was and I felt how I felt; I wouldn't behave differently, even for her. I would miss her, and it would be hard for me not to have her to rely on, but I would have to get used to it. I couldn't betray Esther; I didn't want to, I didn't know how. So I had to overcome the temptation I felt to call her, for all that I wanted to talk to her. I would have to get used to the idea that she was not going to marry me, and that she would never be at the other end of the telephone line.

I was going to pour myself a whiskey, but I didn't, because I could still feel the memory of my debauchery last night in my mouth and my gut.

Bernard Schmidt called me a few days later. He insisted that I carry out my project in Spain as soon as possible. I wasn't upset by his lack of interest in John's health. The only reason he had called was to get me to go back to work. He seemed impatient.

"Evelyn and Jim Cooper are more than capable of handling it themselves. I can manage them from here," I said, knowing that he would say no.

"You have a contract," he reminded me.

"Yes, but I'm not leaving New York for the moment. I've already told you that my father is in critical condition. Also, I work for Roy, he's my major client for the agency."

"But not your only one."

"That's not what Roy wanted. If you're not okay with that

then we can break the contract whenever you want and your hands will be free to employ someone else."

"That's an excellent idea. We'll do that. There won't be another job, but finish this one. I'll talk to the lawyers, or I'll get them to get in touch with you to work out the details of the cancellation."

"I'll talk to Roy."

I felt somehow free after this conversation with Schmidt. Up until that point I hadn't realized just how stressed I felt working with him or for him, even if it was only as an intermediary. He riled me, that man did, as much as I riled him. I liked the job, but not enough to put up with Schmidt—or anyone—breathing down my neck. I would work, yes, but I would be my own boss. The problem was that I had to do the work in Spain before terminating my contract. But I wasn't going to drop everything and head over immediately. I wasn't ready to be their errand boy. Also, I didn't want to leave New York. It wasn't that I cared about John's health, but I needed to think about myself, to decide what I wanted to do with the rest of my life. I felt an intimate satisfaction just being in the city. I felt like I was a part of New York, as if I were in some way an extension of the streets, the people, the air we breathed.

I called Cooper to explain the situation to him. He sounded scared when he asked me what it would mean if I broke the contract with the lawyers, whether he and Evelyn would be fired.

"I don't know, Cooper. Schmidt wants to get rid of me and I want to be free. They may decide to keep you on, but I can't guarantee anything."

"You should come and clear things up," he said, almost begging me.

"Not just yet. You and Evelyn will have to sort things out without me. I don't think it will be a problem for you to organize a campaign to convince the Spaniards of the advantages of having oil just off their coast."

"It's not as easy as all that. This is a strange country," Cooper protested.

"You have Neil."

"Yes, but we need you here," he insisted.

"Keep working. I'll come as soon as I can."

It took me two weeks to get back. I would go and visit John in the mornings, not because I thought it was my duty but because I needed some kind of routine to dispel my unease. When I left the hospital I would take long, aimless walks. I liked walking in Central Park, letting my legs guide me wherever they wanted. I would sometimes go to see a movie, and once or twice I even met up with Paul Hard.

I liked talking to Paul, because he was a man whom nothing could surprise. He liked drinking as much as I did, so it was easy to spend time with him.

Paul advised me to go to Madrid and finish the work.

"You won't be free until you do. Schmidt will make you fulfill the contract," he said.

He was right.

We also talked about Esther.

"She's the best student to have passed through the academy. She should have gone to a good university; it's a shame she didn't have the money. But she'll go far, you'll see. She's done a few campaigns that have made people take notice of her."

When I asked him what I could do to get her back, Paul shrugged.

"You don't have anything to offer her, Thomas, nothing she wants. Esther is how she is. You've got different interests. You need her, she doesn't need you. Also, you're not even in love with her."

I protested. I insisted that I loved her a great deal, but Paul laughed and replied that it was not love that made me want her.

"Esther is like your mother's womb, a place where you feel safe."

Paul introduced me to a couple of his friends, middle-aged women. We went out three or four times together. I slept with the oldest one. She treated me like I was her son, but I didn't care. It wasn't the first time that I had gone to bed with a woman old enough to be my mother. Even so, I preferred to seek my own entanglements, and I told Paul I'd rather see him alone. I didn't need to explain why.

I realized that something was happening with Paul that was similar to what had happened with Esther. I didn't need to play a role. It would have been useless to try to fool him.

I called Esther on several occasions, but hung up before the phone connected. What could I say to her? I knew from Jaime that she called the hospital from time to time to ask after John. My brother said that one night, after leaving work, Esther came by the hospital. John was pleased to see her. Jaime too.

If I didn't exist, I thought, Jaime and Esther would surely fall in love. But I was a shadow too ominous for them to ignore, and I was not prepared to allow them to be happy.

Bernard Schmidt didn't call me again, but Roy Parker did.

"Are you dead?" he asked in irritation.

"I'm still alive, what about you?"

"Stop dicking around. I was with the lawyers yesterday. Brian Jones and Edward Brown are both furious with you. Schmidt has convinced them that you're a fool and untrustworthy. They want to sack you, Thomas."

"Good for them."

"Are you joking? I went through a lot of trouble to persuade them to take you on at the damn PR agency, so you have to come back to London. Talk to them, tell them you've had to be at your dying father's bedside and swear that you're able to do the job, whatever it is."

"No."

"What?"

"No, I won't do it. Look, Roy, I'm not going to work for anyone ever again. I'm going to do things my way. I'm sick of London; I'm going to set myself up in New York. I'll come to Europe when I need to, but I'm going to live here."

"You owe me," he said.

"No, I don't owe you anything. You contracted me, paid me, and I did your job. We don't owe each other anything. Also, I didn't say that I don't want to work for you, only that I'll do it on a case-by-case basis, if you're okay with that, but I won't be your lapdog. I won't be anybody's lapdog. I don't like your lawyer friends, and I don't like Schmidt. And I don't really like you all that much."

"Son of a bitch." Roy's voice blazed with anger.

"Fair enough."

"I'll ruin you, Thomas," Roy threatened.

"No, I don't think so. I'm the one who can ruin you. Of course, with the friends you've got, I'll look twice before I step into the road. But I warn you that if you decide to come after me . . . I have papers and films that could get into the wrong hands. Or do I mean the right ones? There are lots of decent journalists out there, Roy, far more than you could imagine."

"Finish the job in Spain, Thomas. Then come back to London and we'll talk."

"Maybe, Roy."

I hung up. There was a bitter taste in the back of my throat. It came up right from my gut.

I had made things quite clear, but I knew that Roy was right, that I had to close the contract and do the Spain job. I don't know why, but I didn't like what I was supposed to do. It wasn't logical that Schmidt should trust me with something when it was clear that I didn't have the necessary resources.

I spoke to Jaime. I told him that I had to go to Madrid, that I didn't know when I would be back. My brother didn't blame me for leaving. John seemed to be out of any immediate danger and Dr. Patterson seemed more or less optimistic about his recovery. He still had to spend a few weeks in the hospital. Fifteen, twenty days, he couldn't say exactly.

Jaime, with the help of the Spencers and Aunt Emma, would probably be support enough.

It wouldn't be right to say that Jaime surprised me. Jaime was looking after John, taking control of everything, but he still managed to do his schoolwork. He was finishing up his studies at Harvard. His academic record was extraordinary.

He spent his time next to John's bed, and when John slept he studied. He spent the nights at the hospital studying as well. Grandpa James encouraged him. John would not be able to work for a long while, maybe ever again, so it was a matter of urgency for Jaime to take control of the firm as soon as he got his degree. The firm that my great-grandfather Spencer had started. It was still prestigious, and now had a couple of partners, but there had always been a Spencer in charge.

I said goodbye to John, taking advantage of the schedule that Jaime had organized to pick a time when he was alone.

"I have to go to Madrid. I left some work half done."

"Of course, I understand. You've done a lot for me. I don't want your work to suffer on my behalf." John spoke very low, without much strength.

"When I'm done, I'll be back."

"Aren't things going well in London?" he asked worriedly.

"Well enough, but I prefer to work for myself and not for others."

"You know I can help you . . . You can rely on me if you need to."

"I'm not a lawyer, I can't work at your firm," I replied bitterly, thinking of Jaime.

"But if you want to set up your own advertising agency I . . . I could help you."

"I can sort things out for myself."

I didn't kiss him goodbye. I still wanted to punish him. I couldn't help feeling a little satisfaction, knowing that he was suffering.

I know he didn't deserve to be treated like that. I should have taken him by the hand and told him how grateful I was that I was always in his thoughts:

"Thank you, Dad, I know that I can count on you. But I have to try to make it on my own. Although if things go badly, I will of course come to you."

John would have smiled at me. My words would have made him happy.

"You know that your grandfather and I know a lot of people. Don't hold back in asking for help, at least not at the start. You'll need clients and maybe we could convince some of our friends to give you a chance, commission a campaign from you. Do you remember Robert Hardy? Your mother took care of him in the hospital when he had his heart operation. I'm sure he'd commission a campaign for one of his food lines. I don't know, canned tomatoes, mayonnaise, something."

"I'm sure he would, Dad, but don't worry about that now. I'll be back soon and if I need help I'll ask you and Grandpa to lend me a hand. But I'll feel a lot better about leaving if I know you'll take care of yourself. Don't push yourself to go back to work. Do you promise?"

"Of course, of course."

Then I would have leaned over to kiss him on the cheek and he would have been overjoyed.

But I didn't say any of those words or make any of those gestures. I left the hospital room without even looking at him.

———

Evelyn was waiting for me at Barajas Airport. In Madrid that morning the sun lit up the city even though the cold made its way through the seams of my coat. The light—I was reminded that the magical thing about the city was its light.

Jim Cooper was with Neil Collins and a couple of newspapermen he'd met on his trips through Spain. But they weren't going to bring me up to date on the situation until later that afternoon, so I went to the hotel to relax.

I slept until the telephone rang. Evelyn said that they were waiting for me at reception to go and have lunch.

"It's three o'clock," I replied. "It's no time to have lunch."

"Remember we're in Spain. Now is when they eat. There's a restaurant nearby, and the food is amazing. Hurry up."

Yes, we were in Spain. For a moment I had forgotten that Spanish time is very different from American or English time. I was surprised by these people, so able to live and to work at all hours. The light, I said to myself again, it's the light that makes them like this.

Cooper gave me a rundown of the situation. It was not easy for them to design the campaign. The environmental organizations and the political parties and the newspapers were far too powerful as opponents. Even though unemployment in the south of Spain was high, and oil could help to counteract the economic downturn, none of this affected those who viewed oil companies as the enemy.

Spanish society was more ideologically rigid than in the U.K. and especially the U.S., where the only form of militancy was a fundamental belief in the free market.

"Where do we start?" I asked.

"We've already set up cooperative links with another agency. It's owned by a man named Pedro López. We need someone who understands the terrain, who knows who's who and how to deal with them. The owner of the agency is an odd guy. I'd say that he was an out-and-out bastard, but he's clever enough to move between the Left and the Right without being caught.

He gets good write-ups in the press. He's never been involved in politics; all his agency does is market studies for various brands," Cooper said.

"Why are you making such a fuss about left- and right-wing politics?" I asked.

"Because this is a country that is divided down the middle; you're either on one side or the other, and it's enough for you to say A to make your opponent say B. It's surprising, but no one listens to anyone here. People's positions are based on being opposed to what their opponents say, not on thinking for themselves and reaching their own conclusions," Evelyn said.

"All right, let's get a detective to look into the private lives of the people against this project, all of these environmentalists and journalists and influencers," I suggested.

"Dangerous. There are no secrets in this country. We'd end up being denounced in the papers ourselves. We'd have to do the work with tremendous patience, gathering information from all over the place, but without letting anyone know what we're looking for. Although I suppose that Bernard Schmidt might already have a dossier about these people, or at least information that could give us something to go on." Neil looked at me expectantly.

"If that were the case he'd have sent it to us already. I think that if he's hired us to do the job, then it's because he doesn't have anyone better to do it."

"Perhaps . . . It is odd that he hired you for this job. You don't know Spain, your experience is limited to Roy and those kinds of dirty tricks, and now we're trying to make room for an oil company to make a multimillion-dollar investment. There's something here I don't like." Neil looked me straight in the eye.

"And what is that?" I asked uncomfortably.

"I'll tell you. An old friend of mine, when I raised the subject of oil with him, said that a few months ago this company was spending loads of money inviting journalists out to visit oil rigs. A few of them had already been to the North Sea and to

Texas . . . Here things are complicated and simple at the same time. The journalists who support the government defend the government's interests shamelessly. The journalists who support the opposition are against the proposals. And there are people in the area itself who are mistrustful of the project and fearful, with good reason, that a nature reserve as special as Doñana might get contaminated," Neil continued.

"Right, but all the same, it's nothing more than a question of shifting the rhetoric a little one way or another. That's the battle we have to win," I said.

"It's your battle, not mine. All I'm doing is telling you a few things."

"There must be journalists we can influence."

"I don't buy journalists," Neil said bluntly.

"I didn't tell you to buy anyone," I replied.

"I don't cheat them either. I don't try to change their minds. You know what, Thomas? Although it might be hard for you to believe, I have a great deal of respect for what used to be my profession and for the people in it who are not like me, and who, as they say here, tilt against windmills without giving up. You know how I work: I carry out investigations and I tell you what I've found out, nothing more. What happens next is up to you."

"I didn't ask you to do anything else."

Neil shrugged and Cooper cleared his throat uncomfortably, while Evelyn looked at us with wide eyes, wondering if she should say anything.

"I also don't feel quite right. I don't trust Schmidt either," I admitted.

"So what are we going to do?" Cooper asked.

"What do you suggest?" I said, no longer pretending that I was completely calm.

"We need to carry on, but carefully," Evelyn suggested, and didn't blink when we all looked at her in exasperation for saying something so obvious.

"I'll carry on doing what I've been doing up until now," Neil said. "Having breakfast and lunch and dinner and getting drunk with anyone who might be able to tell me anything. In this country, everything is sorted out over a table, a plate of food, and a drink."

"It's true, he's doing most of the hard work," Cooper said.

"And what about this guy you mentioned to me, the one with the agency?"

"López Consultants. We told them that we had been given the task of finding out how receptive the public might be toward drilling. Just that. Nothing at all about how to twist people's arms and get them in line. But the information he's giving us is useful enough. Although I think he knows more than he lets on," Cooper said.

"Does he think that we work for an oil company?" I asked.

"More or less. It's what we suggested, saying that our client is a little worried and is not willing to take any risks in a country where he won't be accepted, even though that means perhaps losing some clear financial opportunities," Evelyn said.

"And he really thought that an oil company would stop drilling on land or out at sea because of the complaints of a few activists? Don't insult his intelligence!" I said angrily.

"We're not doing that, but this way we stay within acceptable limits for him. He doesn't want to know more and he doesn't need to," Evelyn insisted, annoyed at my tone of voice.

"All right, then it's clear that you can carry on without me. I'll go to London tomorrow. I need to see Roy and the lawyers."

"What's your plan?" Cooper asked.

"I'd be lying if I said I had a plan. All I know is that I want to move back to New York and set up shop there. I've been thinking about setting up an agency with a branch in London as well; I hope I'd be able to rely on you. But I still haven't decided yet. I have to do research on the investment required, to think about who might be our clients. What I really want to do is concentrate on election campaigns. They pay well and are easy. I don't like jobs like this. They cause all kinds of complications. This is too dirty, even for me."

"Is this your conscience speaking?" Evelyn asked, a tone of concern in her voice.

"No, it's nothing like that. I may be bad, but I'm not stupid. I don't want problems, or at least ones I can't control. Brian Jones and Edward Brown have a business. Dirty work for people who want to keep their hands clean. They pay well, it's true, but if you work in the sewers your whole life then you end up smelling like shit. And that's a smell that lingers. Doing the dirty work for an oil company is not the same as doing the dirty work for Roy. I still don't understand why Schmidt gave us this job. We don't have the experience to deal with something this big."

"Do you really think something's up?" Cooper asked in alarm.

"I think so. The sooner we get out of this, the better. We'll do the job, but without getting in too deep. I don't know this country and I don't know its rules, so we have to be aware that we're likely to misstep. Don't do anything that could compromise us, and don't do anything that's not strictly reasonable. If Schmidt isn't happy with the work, that's his problem. But we're not going to dirty our hands any more than is absolutely necessary. Got it?"

"You're a true lawyer," Cooper said with admiration.

"Don't get me wrong, I'm not that. What I don't want to do is fall into a cesspool, and if you fall then I fall."

"After London, are you going to New York, or will you come back to Madrid?" Neil asked.

"I'll come back here. I'm not going to leave you hanging, but I want this tied up in the next two weeks."

"Impossible," Neil said.

"We'll see. We'll do what's necessary. Maybe we don't need

to do anything more than write a clever report for Schmidt. We'll show him the way, but we don't have to guide him by the hand."

I think they all felt relieved. Evelyn and Cooper were both ambitious, but they needed someone to lead the way. As for Neil, he was a clever enough survivor to know when to abandon a sinking ship. He had lived too long to put his neck on the line for anyone. And although it was hard for me to admit it, Neil still had a code of ethics that went beyond being willing to do anything to make money for booze.

"Ah, and Neil will be in charge while I'm gone."

"No," Neil replied, to Cooper and Evelyn's bewilderment.

"You know the lay of the land better than any of us," I said, trying to persuade him.

"Look, Thomas, I'm not on your payroll. You hire me to do a job, and if I can do it, then I do it. But I'm free; I'm not going to accept responsibilities or get involved any further than I need to. I'll give Cooper and Evelyn all the information I come across, but you need to decide what you do with it. I don't care. Plus, there's something fishy about this job."

That's the kind of person Neil was. He refused to commit to anything, let alone go to bat for causes that weren't his own. He didn't give a shit about me. He had made it clear from the start that he wasn't going to risk anything for me. And so, though I wanted him to become more involved in these projects, he always kept his distance.

"All right. But I need a report with all the information you have about this other company that's already working for the oilmen. Write it down for me. And you do the same," I said, turning to Cooper and Evelyn. "I need, in writing, everything that you've done and that you think there is left to do. Leave it in an envelope at reception at the hotel. I want to take the first flight to London tomorrow morning."

———

I had no intention of spending the rest of the day with them. They bored me. And I was due to meet Blanca. I had called her from the airport and she had invited me to have dinner with her. "Alone," she had said.

I liked Blanca; I wasn't going to lose my head over her, but I had fun when I was with her. I don't think she expected more from me than the time we might spend together.

I got to her place at nine o'clock, just as she had said. She opened the door and I was surprised because she gave me a hug as if she were exceptionally pleased to see me. That kind of greeting made me uncomfortable. I have never liked effusive people.

"Come in, I'm making supper. I hope you like fish. I'm just about to put the bass into the oven. I've got something to eat while we're waiting as well. I've just opened a Ribera. You'll like it."

I liked it. I didn't know much about Spanish wine, but I found that it lost nothing in comparison with the French varieties.

While the bass was cooking slowly in the oven Blanca decided to play the piano.

"Do you like Chopin?" she asked expectantly.

"My father loved opera, and when we were old enough he took my brother and me to the Met every now and then to see productions. And he took us to classical music concerts, but I can't tell Chopin from Mozart."

Blanca laughed, not believing what I was saying. But it was true. I remembered with annoyance the times when John had tried to get the whole family to go with him to the Met. Jaime listened attentively. My mother was very still and appeared to be listening, but I, who knew her well, could see that she was bored. And as for me, I would always fall asleep as a way of expressing my disapproval.

But I liked listening to Blanca play. She shut her eyes and slid her fingers over the keys, pulling out notes that filled the room with sound. She didn't look at me; she seemed caught up in the music, separated from anything that was not her or the piano.

"Well, I think the bass will be ready by now," she suddenly said, coming back to reality.

We drank the bottle of wine as well as a couple of gin and tonics that I made.

Blanca was different. Free. She radiated freedom.

I couldn't help comparing her with Esther, and Esther came out badly. She's soppy and predictable, I thought. Quite the opposite of Blanca, who looked at you with a smile that seemed to be telling you to get ready for the next surprise.

I missed the plane to London. We had only gone to sleep at dawn. I woke up as Blanca shook my arm.

"It's nine o'clock! I have to go to class, I'll be late. Close the door when you leave."

And she left the room without a single gesture of affection, as though the night that had just passed had dissolved into the cold of the morning. She was a practical girl. She didn't ask for more than she gave.

My head didn't hurt all that much. I went to the kitchen for some coffee. The pot was still warm and I poured myself what Blanca had left. Then I went to the hotel. The concierge gave me an envelope with the reports that I had asked for from my team. I asked him to find me a seat on the next flight to London.

I was lucky. I would have time to make it to the meeting with Roy and the lawyers, which was arranged for the afternoon.

When the secretary showed me into Brian Jones's office, the first thing I saw was Roy and the other lawyer, Edward Brown, sitting at a little circular table a few feet away from Jones's table. Bernard Schmidt was there as well.

"So, here we all are," I said in greeting.

They all looked at me. There was contempt in Schmidt's eyes, and anger in Roy's. Jones and Brown looked aggressive.

"Sit down, Mr. Spencer," Brian Jones said.

The informal "Thomas" had been replaced by a formal "Mr. Spencer." It was clear that this would be a tough meeting.

I sat down next to Roy in the only empty chair.

There was a tea set on the table. Schmidt had a cup in his hands, and so did Edward Brown.

"I'd love a coffee," I said, knowing that it would annoy them.

Jones didn't even look at me. He pressed a button on the intercom and asked his secretary to bring some coffee.

"Well, tell us what's happening," Brian Jones asked.

"I'm not your man. I can work with you and for you on various projects, but I can't be your employee. Mr. Schmidt has shown his disapproval of me from the get-go, and I think he's right. I don't serve you well here." I'm sure they understood the literal meaning of "serve" as well: I was refusing to be their servant.

Edward Brown spread his hands in a gesture that looked like a question and Brian Jones sat still, waiting for me to say something else. Roy took charge of the situation.

"You're going through a bad time because of your father. I understand that. But as far as I know he's out of danger now, so you can come back to work."

"Yes, I'll come back to work, but to the work I choose. I don't want to be an employee. You said that I was ambitious," I replied coldly.

"What do you want, Spencer?" Schmidt spoke even more coldly than I did.

"To leave. I don't want to work for you, not like this. I'm going to set up my own agency and of course I'll always be open to any interesting jobs you might send my way."

"We thought you were someone a little more . . ." Edward Brown didn't finish the sentence.

"More serious? You know that I refuse to work like this, to be ordered around. Mr. Parker wanted me to keep working for him, but you didn't want to lose control of Roy. You defend your interests. I understand that. But I have my own interests and I'm not happy working for GCP. I want out. You don't need me and I don't need you either. And as for Spain . . . you've given me a very strange job."

Bernard Schmidt didn't move a muscle, as though my words had no effect on him whatsoever. Brian Jones looked at me in surprise and Edward Brown looked off into the distance. It was Roy who asked the question:

"What do you mean?"

"There's already a Spanish agency working for the oil company that wants to drill off the coast. A well-known agency. Owned by someone close to the current government. It's not the first time they've done this kind of thing. And they do a clean job. They've taken some journalists to look at oil rigs in the North Sea, to show them that extracting oil doesn't have to mean an assault on the environment or any of the nonsense that the activists say. There have been articles and even reports on television in favor of the drilling in Andalusia. There are discussion programs on television and the radio in Spain where journalists on both sides of the political spectrum appear. They fight among themselves in the name of the politicians, defending each party's position."

"How interesting," said Brian Jones. "And are there no independent voices?"

"There are always a few independent voices that nobody likes."

"You still haven't explained yourself," Roy said.

"You get it, Roy, just as Schmidt and the lawyers do: you've hired me to do a job that someone else is already doing. Why?" I asked, looking at Schmidt.

"We haven't hired you to do the same job. You have to overcome resistance. I told you to take care of the journalists and environmentalists who are causing problems. To finish them." Bernard Schmidt did not get angry, but there was something in his tone of voice that indicated just how much he disliked me.

"The dirty work. Yes, that's what you hired me to do. Reckless of you, I think. You know that I don't know Spain very well. I visited for the first time only recently, and I haven't been there for more than a week at a time. I speak Spanish, yes, but that's it. What you're asking me to do is difficult for someone who has to start from zero. A single false step could cause a scandal that would damage the interests of your clients. Or hadn't you thought of that?"

"You don't have any contract with the company, there's no way they could connect the two things," Brian Jones said.

"Of course they could. If rumors are being spread about the people opposed to the project, do you really think no one will ask why? Or that the people under attack will do nothing? Don't underestimate your adversaries. Also, Spanish people work according to a different logic; they're unpredictable."

"They're like the others. Not any more valuable," Schmidt said.

"If you say so . . . In any case, I'm not going to risk my neck in a country I don't know and where the penalties for an error would be extremely great. Let someone else do it."

"What are you saying?" Schmidt seemed on the verge of losing patience.

"That I'm not going to do the job you hired me to do. It's that easy. I can do exactly what this Spanish agency that the oil company already hired is doing, but I won't take a single step further. I can give you a list of the people who oppose the project, who they are, what they do, but it will have to be you who finishes them off. I cannot work in an environment I do not know. This job needs local people."

"Well, find those people," Schmidt said.

"I'm not going to improvise. I don't know how to conquer ground I'm unfamiliar with. I'm brave, daring, I can break the rules, as I showed in Roy's campaign, but I'm not suicidal. I'm not prepared to do what you want me to do in Spain."

There was a long silence. They seemed to be digesting my

words. Even Roy looked thoughtful. I sat back, pleased with myself, but Bernard Schmidt wasn't going to allow me my moment of glory.

"You can't be so simple," Schmidt said, not with irony, but with scorn.

I didn't know what to say. I didn't understand. Roy raised an eyebrow, waiting for the next attack, and the lawyers sat back expectantly.

"You signed a contract, Mr. Spencer. You are obliged to work for us for the next five years. You can go, but you will have to compensate us," Schmidt said.

"You're wrong. I didn't sign that," I said with more certainty than I felt.

"Of course you did. Your contract has several clauses in it which it seems you did not bother to read," Schmidt continued.

"The five years and the compensation were a safeguard for both parties. Don't try to play hardball with me, Schmidt, or it won't be pretty. You want to stop me from going? How are you going to do it? You two are lawyers." Here I looked at Jones and Brown. "You know there's no such thing as an unbreakable contract. If you want us to take this to court, we can do that. You'll play your cards and I'll play mine."

"What are you suggesting, Thomas?" Roy asked worriedly.

"I'm leaving the agency, without asking for anything and without anyone asking anything from me. I'll keep the confidentiality clause and we'll all be friends."

"You've got a good job here." Roy seemed desperate.

"I don't think so. You want me to work with you and they . . ." I looked at Jones and Brown again. "They want you on a short leash, even if they have to crush me to get that. Mr. Schmidt was never okay with my involvement, but you pressured them and, because they still need you, they came up with this arrangement, one that really doesn't satisfy either party. This doesn't mean that I can't work with you or with these gentlemen as far as you are concerned or on other issues. We can do it the easy way or the hard way, you decide."

Silence fell once again. Schmidt looked ready to jump at my throat, but Edward Brown made a gesture with his hand to say that he shouldn't do anything. He was going to answer me.

"Mr. Schmidt is right; we can make things difficult. Contracts are there to be fulfilled, Mr. Spencer. But we would all lose out if we got caught up in a fight. We don't like useless battles. But before we talk about tearing up the contract, you have to do the Spain job."

"I don't have the capacity to do it, I've told you already. You'll have to find someone else."

"You are very obstinate," Brian Jones said.

"Nothing more than cautious. You haven't given me a single explanation as to why there has been another agency working for the oil company for months already."

"You gave us the reason yourself earlier. They do the clean work and you have to do the dirty work. It's your specialty." Bernard Schmidt seemed to be spitting each word he said.

"I don't have any scruples, but I do have a survival instinct. I'm not accepting the job."

"You have to accept it, Thomas. These oil people . . . well, they supported me, they gave me money for the campaign. They gave me more than that . . . They're expecting a lot from me. You're my boy, I put you where you are today."

"No, Roy, I'm not your boy. You found me and I did your job. It worked out for you and you paid me. We're even."

"You have to do me this favor." Roy seemed to be begging.

"I don't mean shit to these friends of yours, and maybe I don't mean shit to you, but I mean a great deal to my friends and I'm not going to put my head on the line."

"Give us a way out at least . . . Improvise, but do what's expected of you," Roy insisted.

"I want to leave this office with a piece of paper in my hands that says I'm leaving the company amicably, that I'm not asking anything of anyone and no one's asking anything of me. Then you can look for whoever you want or whoever can do this job you're so desperate to get done. But I'm not going to be caught up in this. I'm going to be in the background. I'll pull strings just enough to avoid being visible. If there's the slightest suspicion that I'm being toyed with, then I will leave immediately. I will disappear and leave a time bomb waiting to blow."

Brian Jones and Edward Brown looked at each other and I saw smiles of relief cross their faces. I had just promised to carry on with the job. In my fashion, but I was going to carry on. I wouldn't put myself on the line for them, but neither would I abandon ship.

"All right, Mr. Spencer. We'll do it like you want it done. We'll sign the document of annulment tomorrow. Is that all right with you?" Brown asked.

"I'd prefer to do it now. It shouldn't be difficult for you to draw up. Shall I do it myself?" I asked defiantly.

"Well, it's past six already . . . There's no reason for us not to draw up the document carefully and study it well," Brian Jones said.

"I'm in a hurry, Mr. Jones. If you want me to give you a hand in Spain, then it would be better for all of us if I got back there as soon as possible," I insisted.

Jones and Brown looked at Schmidt. They seemed to be looking for some kind of a signal before they accepted my arguments. Schmidt made a sign I didn't know how to interpret.

"Mr. Spencer, you'll have to wait until tomorrow. We need a few hours to speak and clear things up amongst ourselves. You owe us this time."

Bernard Schmidt would not allow me to have everything my own way. I had to accept; they gave me no other option. They made an appointment for the next day at five p.m., fairly late by London standards.

I left without shaking hands. Roy followed me. He seemed

like an angry buffalo, breathing hard while we waited for the elevator. We didn't speak until we were down in the street.

He grasped me firmly by the arm and forced me to stop. I felt his fingers on my forearm and almost gave him a kick in the shin to make him relax his grasp.

"Would you like me to invite you out for dinner?" I asked, ironically.

"We can go anywhere. It'd be better to go back to your flat, where we can speak calmly."

"All right, we can get some pizza or Chinese. All I've got there is whiskey."

We walked in silence back to my place. It was raining, but neither of us was in a hurry, and so we got wet and didn't complain.

While Roy dried himself off in the bathroom I called a nearby pizzeria. I would have preferred to eat at a good restaurant, but it was clear that Roy wanted to speak. I poured a couple of whiskeys with water. The night was going to be a long one and I didn't want to be knocked out by my first drink.

Roy took a long swig then nearly threw the glass in my face.

"What bullshit is this? Since when do you drink whiskey and water?"

"We'll speak first, then we'll drink."

"Thomas, I don't drink water."

"I don't like it either, but we've got to start somewhere."

I didn't relax. I didn't want us to end up drunk before we'd even started talking. Roy was a compulsive drinker, like me. We couldn't keep a full glass in our hands for all that long. The liquid would rapidly drain away and once we had started neither of us knew how to stop.

I tried to make small talk by asking him about how things were with Suzi. I didn't want us to get into an argument before the pizza arrived. Only on a few occasions had I taken note of the advice that it's a bad idea to drink on an empty stomach. This was one of those occasions.

"We're separated. We live together, but I have to sleep in the guest bedroom. She says that she'll leave me when the kids are older. She may try to leave me earlier. If her father dies, then she won't care anymore what people might say about him. And so I threaten her with taking the children if she thinks about trying to divorce me. I've lost everything, Thomas."

"You've lost Suzi, nothing else."

"I've lost her and I've lost my life. I'm like a guest in my own home. I'm lonely. I don't have anyone to talk to about what I'm going through. Suzi was always near me, ready to give me advice, to take part in everything I needed her for. I feel a huge void without her there."

"Come on, Roy, you weren't ever faithful to her. I know several girls who passed through your bed. We went to Madame Agnès's house together, and there were several willing girls there."

"Yes, but here in London, never in the county, never with anyone she might know. Those girls were whores: expensive whores but whores nonetheless. They didn't mean anything to me."

"You seemed to like the redhead," I said, just to keep the conversation going until the food arrived.

"I don't even remember her name. These girls meant nothing to me, Thomas, they were pleasantly shaped pieces of meat. You spend a while with them and then bye-bye. You don't expect anything from them; they don't expect anything from you. Did they mean the same to you as Esther did? No, of course not, but you're not going to miss the chance for a good fuck."

"Maybe things will sort themselves out. Give Suzi some time."

"You know her. She'll never forgive me. And she hates you. She'd turn you into mincemeat if she could. She'll never forget the blackmail."

"You blackmailed her, Roy. It was a question of your interests, not mine."

The pizza arrived, finally. We sat down at the table, but I didn't even lay a cloth.

"Don't you have a bottle of wine? No one can eat this, it's horrible," Roy protested.

He was right. It had gotten cold on the way over, the cheese was like chewing gum, and the pepperoni tasted like horsemeat. Even so, we ate it. I grudgingly opened a bottle of Cabernet Sauvignon.

When we had finished I poured two glasses of whiskey, this time with no water and no ice.

"Okay, Roy, what do you want to tell me?"

"We've sold our souls to these guys," he said heavily.

"To the lawyers? No, not me, Roy. *You* sold your soul. In order to get where you wanted they offered a price, which you accepted. Better not to look back. All you can do now is go forward."

"You think they'll let us leave? Don't be naïve." Roy spoke as though he were relieved to have someone to share his worries with.

"They don't care about me, I'm nothing but a pawn they can get rid of at any time. You are the one they helped make mayor, the one who sold them land at laughably low prices, the one who made it possible for a company they represent to drill holes all over the county. They can still get a lot out of you, Roy. These people like to have friends in Parliament, and they'll support you if you want a seat. You're one of them now. Me, not so much."

"You know too much." He was angry that I insisted on my freedom.

"Yes, I know too much, and that's going to save me. I'm a son of a bitch, you know that, and so do they. And that's why I've covered my back. If I have an accident . . . if anything happens to me . . . well, they'll have a number of problems. But I don't think it'll happen, Roy. I'm not a major part of their organization. It's convenient for all of us to work together, but I want to be independent. I've made mistakes as well. I should have followed my instincts and refused to work for them or for GCP. They gave me an office, allowed me to hire Maggie as my secretary, and Cooper and Evelyn as well, and keep working to save your ass. And I agreed to do other work as well. I was completely mistaken. And that's why I want to go, because they have control now, Roy, and I don't."

"You can't leave them, Thomas."

"We'll see."

"And if you did go, what would happen between you and me?"

"I'd still keep working for you, Roy. You could still be my client. What I don't want to do is get mixed up in things I can't control. I don't like the Spain business, there's something strange going on there. Maybe Schmidt got me into it to get rid of me."

"Schmidt hates you."

"Yes, that's crystal clear. I wouldn't piss on him if he were on fire either."

"And what if they trick you?" he asked.

"Stop worrying. I'll sign tomorrow and be free. I'll fulfill my part of the bargain. I'll go to Spain and do what I can without getting too involved. Period."

"It's what they want . . . Well, you'll have to do it."

"I'll think of something."

"You said that you were going to go back to New York. Why?"

"Hmm. I don't really know why myself. I suppose it's because I want to marry Esther. I won't manage to do that from here. I don't like London very much either, at least not enough for me to stay here for good. I'll try to maintain a little organization here. Cooper and Evelyn will keep working for me, if we have any clients. You could be our main client, Roy. But I want to think about working in New York as well. I'm from there; it's my city. You can't understand, but when I arrive in New York it's as if I'm wrapping myself in a blanket: everything is familiar there, the streets, the people, the way people behave . . . It all makes me feel secure and relaxed."

"Did your father ask you to move back?"

"No, no, he didn't, he wouldn't dare. He's too respectful to tell me what I have to do."

"But you're moving back for him, because he's ill?"

"No, of course not! My family would be the very last reason for me to move back. I have to go back, and that's it. I want to have control over my life and here I feel that I don't. In fact, I lost control the very day I listened to you and signed up to work for your lawyer friends."

"I don't know if they'll let me keep you on," Roy whispered, as if he were talking to himself.

"That depends on you. Tell them I know where the bodies are buried and that it's better if we stay on the same side."

"You know what, Thomas? Ever since I met you I've asked myself what life has done to you to make you . . . like you are."

"An evil bastard? You can say it, Roy, say it loud and say it proud, I'm an evil bastard. Well, Roy, it was a choice, my very own choice."

"But so young . . ."

"Yes, I'm not yet thirty, but I'll get there. It's all a question of time." I said all this with a chuckle, as I found his apparent shock amusing. He still didn't understand my reasons.

"Anyway, being how you are . . . I'm surprised that you're so obsessed with Esther. She's a good kid, but she's no beauty. She's clever, yes, but at first sight there's nothing so extraordinary about her that would make you so keen on marrying her."

"But she is extraordinary, Roy, I swear she is."

We agreed that we would go and have a final drink at Madame Agnès's house. For some time I hadn't allowed him to come with me. If I had been able to bring down Frank Wilson because of his brothel visits, then someone could do the same to Roy. But Madame Agnès's house was one of the most exquisite and discreet brothels in London, and in my many lonely nights in the city I had become one of her best clients.

The girls changed frequently, but they were all beautiful, well-mannered, and discreet. They dressed elegantly. I liked the way the place looked above all, a house where men met to discuss business and politics. It wasn't an odd sight to see people sitting in a corner discussing important issues without anyone bothering them. The place was a favorite of the Russian oligarchs, although Madame Agnès didn't seem to like this kind of client all that much. "Too noisy," she whispered to me one day. I suppose she thought that they did not know how to behave as properly as the stuck-up hypocrites who were her usual clients.

I liked to experiment, so I always chose a different girl; Roy, on the other hand, on the few occasions when he came along, always sought the company of a young redhead who reminded him of how Suzi had been twenty years before.

None of these women was in the slightest bit vulgar. They spoke about politics and economics. They knew how the market fluctuated and they were capable of talking about art. Once I asked Madame Agnès just how it was possible for these women to dedicate themselves to entertaining men like the ones who came to her house.

"All of my guests are gentlemen like you. And they are very generous. They appreciate beauty, delicacy, good conversation . . . and we appreciate your generosity, and gentlemanliness."

That evening Roy was thwarted. The redhead was chatting with a politician and the rules of Madame Agnès's house were strict. Nobody was to interrupt other people's conversations. I decided on a young Anglo-Japanese girl. She was new. Another rule of the house was that we weren't allowed to ask questions. The girls weren't allowed to ask about the clients and the clients weren't allowed to ask about the girls. Even so I broke the rules and asked her how she had ended up there.

Yoko (she said her name was Yoko) replied, quite naturally, that she was studying English at London University. But she wouldn't let me ask anything else. She started telling me about a Rubens exhibition at the National Gallery, and enthusiastically advised me not to miss it.

I invited her to come with me, breaking another rule. Madame Agnès did not allow the girls to see clients outside the house: if they did, they could not come back to work there.

Yoko shook her head and smiled gently. I realized that this girl was affecting me and I hadn't even slept with her yet. I thought about Esther, believing that doing so would help me regain a sense of perspective. Yoko was a prostitute: high-class but a prostitute nonetheless. Roy would laugh at me if he saw how keen I was on her. I knew what he would say: no man should lose his head over any of these girls.

Despite the years that have gone by, I remember my first time with Yoko. It was a voyage of discovery into sensations I did not know existed. She became Esther's alter ego. I needed Yoko's body and Esther's brain. I promised myself that I could have both, and regretted that it was impossible to combine that body and that brain into a single organism.

Roy called me the next day. He woke me up. I was in a good mood and suggested that we eat together. He begged off and apologized. He was going to eat with the Conservative chief whip.

I already knew that Roy was not the only puppet of those two lawyers. He was just one of many. Jones and Brown represented clients whose fortunes were as large as the GDP of certain countries. That was why they needed to buy politicians, journalists, and businessmen, and to blackmail anyone who got in the way of their clients' interests. Behind their façade of good manners were two entirely unapologetic men. I was not certain if there was anything human left in them. Well, some people had found it difficult to discern humanity in me as well.

At five on the dot I was at the lawyers' office, but it was Schmidt who was waiting for me.

"And the lawyers?" I asked disdainfully.

"They're busy. We'll sort this out ourselves."

"I don't think you want to sort this out," I said bluntly.

Schmidt didn't reply. He didn't think that I was important enough for him to reply to my provocation.

"Here's the document for you to sign. You will cease to be an employee of GCP, but you will continue to be bound by the confidentiality agreements relating to the work carried out for the firm. You also promise to work with us when needed, even as an independent contractor, at least for the next five years. For the time being, that is the only way in which you can continue working with Roy Parker. This means that even if you set up your own agency, you will have to do everything connected to Roy Parker through us. You can't make decisions on your own. Ah, and you won't be able to work for other agencies either."

"That's not what we agreed," I protested, standing up and getting ready to leave.

"You can't act on your whims. Either you accept this or we will activate the clause by which you have to compensate the firm for not fulfilling the terms of your contract. The sum would be two hundred thousand pounds."

I still ask myself how I could have been so stupid to have signed that contract. I suppose that I can't have been as intelligent or as mature as I thought I was back then. I was still a young kid who put on airs. I had gone into the lion's den by myself. And the lion wasn't ready to let me go without giving me a good bite on my way out.

Those were the cards I'd been dealt. I couldn't leave the game. I would get some of my freedom back, but I would have to pay the price they demanded.

"What exactly do I have to do, Schmidt?"

"You know. Look for dirt about the people who oppose the drilling. Filter it to the press and that's it. We'll deal with the rest ourselves."

"You know that I'm not the right person to do this work in Spain. I can do it in England, in the U.S., but not in Spain. There are other rules at work there, rules I don't know. If something goes wrong you'll pay the price," I warned.

"If something goes wrong, it will be you who pays the price. This is the office of two well-respected lawyers who advise their clients on how to deal with certain crises. It has nothing to do with the work you carry out."

"But they employ me to do it."

"Do you have any proof?" he said with a twisted smile.

"I could have a hidden microphone." This was a bluff.

"Mr. Spencer, although you do not know it, to get to this office you have had to pass through several X-ray machines. Shall I tell you the color of your underwear?"

I didn't ask. He could have been bluffing as well, or maybe he was telling the truth.

I signed the document and when I handed it over he didn't give any sign of satisfaction. He had never doubted that I would sign.

"I'll do what I can but nothing more."

He didn't say goodbye. He merely called the secretary on the intercom and asked her to accompany me to the elevator.

I could have gone back to Spain that very night, but I didn't. I was eager to get back to Madame Agnès's house and see Yoko. I had spent the best night of my life with her and I wanted to repeat the experience.

It was early when I arrived at the house in South Kensington. There couldn't have been more than three or four clients there, all peacefully having a drink. They were chatting among themselves and there was no sign of the girls. I asked Madame Agnès for Yoko. She looked at me in annoyance. She didn't like clients getting too fixated on a particular girl. She said that this was just another source of problems.

"She won't be here this evening. She only comes to see us occasionally. Would you like a glass of champagne, or maybe something a little stronger?" she asked impatiently.

I asked for whiskey, a double. I felt a nearly uncontrollable urge to destroy this room, which suddenly, without Yoko there, seemed exceedingly vulgar.

"When will she be back?"

"I don't know, Mr. Spencer. Yoko is not one of the regulars, she calls when she wants to come in. And, from what I've heard, you were very generous last night. Not just to the house, but to Yoko herself. As you know very well, that is against the rules."

I was disturbed that Yoko would tell Madame Agnès that I had left the thousand dollars I had on me in her room, as well as the pounds. It wasn't permitted to pay the girls. The rule was to ask for a bill when you left. The bill included the champagne and the rest of the drinks, as well as a separate entry for "extras." This was always the largest part, never less than four hundred pounds.

I apologized to Madame Agnès. I didn't want to cease being welcome in her house. I had seen her telling clients to leave and never come back. And she must have been very persuasive, because they never did come back. Or maybe she had some way of stopping them?

"Please don't worry. If I ask you about Yoko it is merely because she seemed a very agreeable young lady, but no more so than the others who . . . who accompany us."

"As you know very well, my friends are all charming, none of them is better than the rest. I am sure that tonight you will find a charming companion to talk with and share a glass of champagne."

She made a discreet signal to a girl who had just arrived. Tall, blonde, thin, dressed in a simple yet elegant black dress and with huge green eyes. She came over to us.

"My dear, I don't know if you know my good friend Mr. Spencer. We were talking about the weather, about how it always rains in London at this time of year. I think we could do with a little food. I'll ask the maid to serve some of the crepes the cook has been preparing."

She left us alone, sure that we would continue talking. There was no reason why not: the girl was very attractive, and I would gladly have spent any other night with her, but I had come in search of Yoko.

I drank my whiskey too quickly and left before the night got too lively. Madame Agnès said goodbye with a disapproving look. She knew that I was leaving because Yoko was not there, and that this kind of behavior affected the smooth running of her business.

I went back to my apartment, ready to keep on drinking. I had three or four bottles of whiskey in the cupboard. There wasn't even a carton of milk in the fridge. I wasn't hungry. Along with the seafood crepes, I had had some smoked salmon. Enough not to have an empty stomach and to be able to drink for a while before the alcohol caught up with me.

I poured myself a glass up to the brim. I was in a bad mood. I had promised myself a night with Yoko, and here I was, alone, in front of the television.

I called Esther. She picked up the phone, which I took as a good sign.

"Do you know what time it is in New York?" she asked.

"It's eight o'clock here. It must be three there, right?"

"I'm working. We can't talk now."

"Call me when you get out of the agency," I almost begged.

"I have to go to Paul's academy. I'm teaching a class."

"Call me when you get home, then."

"It'll be late for you."

"It doesn't matter. Wake me up. Will you do that?"

"I will. Are you all right?"

"More or less."

"What happened?" she asked, mildly preoccupied.

"I think I'm nearly free. The lawyers are willing to cancel my contract if I do the work in Spain."

"And if you don't?"

"It'll be sticky. And I'll have to compensate them to the tune of two hundred thousand pounds."

"Wow."

"So I'm leaving for Madrid tomorrow. I'll try to do the things they ask of me. I hope I don't get my fingers caught and that I can forget about these people for good."

"And Roy?"

"He's a busted flush. Suzi won't forgive him. As soon as his father-in-law dies or his children grow up she'll leave him. She's making him sleep in the guest bedroom."

"He deserves it."

"Well, she can't play the innocent. She didn't think it was a bad idea when we brought down Roy's opponents."

"But now it's her father, about making him abandon his land, his business, his way of life."

"Selfishness."

"It's only logical that she's reacting like this. For Suzi, the family is a line in the sand."

"Roy is her family, he's married to her," I replied, irritated not so much by what she said as by the fact that I was still thinking about Yoko.

"He's her husband, but that's not the same as being her family. Your family is your parents, your brothers and sisters, your children, but a husband . . . a husband or a wife is something else, you can always find another one. But your parents are your parents, it's something you can never change even if you wanted to."

"You don't need to tell me that. We'll talk later." I hung up.

I got drunk. I didn't want to do anything else. I was drinking and remembering last night with Yoko; then I lost consciousness. Once again, I woke up on the floor. My cell was ringing insistently, but I couldn't move. My whole body hurt and I wanted to throw up. And that's what I did, all over the carpet. I didn't have the strength to get up and make it to the bathroom, and so I curled up, covering my mouth so that the smell of vomit didn't make me throw up again.

The maid found me on the floor. She wasn't surprised. She opened the window and rudely asked me to get out of her way.

"Go to bed or somewhere where you're not in my way, but I'm telling you, this is the last time I'm going to pick up your vomit. It's more than my job's worth."

Because I didn't move, she bent down to help me. I couldn't stay upright. She got me to my feet somehow and bundled me to my room. I don't know how, but she helped me into bed. I lay there for a few more hours. I could hear the noise of the vacuum cleaner and her complaints at the state of the carpet. She said goodbye as she left, but I didn't reply. I couldn't find the strength.

It took me a couple more hours to be able to stand up straight. It was nearly midday. I had missed my flight to Madrid. I took a cold shower to wake myself up. I came out shivering, but the water had brought me back to my senses. I made myself coffee in order to charge my batteries with a good dose of caffeine. I wasn't ready until a little before two.

I was lucky. There was a flight to Madrid at six that evening. I called Jim Cooper to tell him when I would arrive. He was with Evelyn in Seville. Neil was still in Madrid. When the plane landed I called Blanca. She said that she was playing the piano that night in a café with a string quartet. "Come along, we can go out for a drink afterward." I accepted. I was starting to get used to the Spanish way of life. I was surprised by how they were able to work and enjoy life at the same time.

Blanca had told me that Madrid was a city that never slept. She didn't lie.

I woke up at her apartment. I hadn't drunk too much, so my head barely ached. I had agreed to meet Neil at eight for breakfast at the hotel. I tried to get dressed without making any noise, but Blanca woke up anyway.

"Are you leaving already?"

"I've got a breakfast meeting."

"Okay. Will we see each other later?"

"Maybe, it depends on how the meetings go. I'll call you."

She shrugged and turned over in the bed. She seemed not to care if I saw her again or not.

Neil brought me up to speed. There wasn't much to tell me.

"Local opinion in Andalusia is divided. They are aware of the advantages, but also that environmental degradation will be inevitable. There are newspapers that are in favor, newspapers that are against . . . They're having a proper brawl. The PR agency that the oil company hired is doing a good job. Because that's what they need to do, cause a split in public opinion, make it seem that no one's in the right."

"And what about the opposition?"

"More than anything else, it's the environmentally minded political parties. There are no arguments that sway them. Despite the promise to limit unemployment in the region, they're still strongly against it."

"What have we got on their leaders?"

"Things don't work like that here." Neil was talking to me as if I were a child who needed to be taught very basic facts about the world.

"If we can smear two or three of their leaders then the problem will be solved."

"No, Thomas, not in Spain. We can maybe get the newspapers to publish some dirt, but that won't take any strength away from the opposition. This is an ideological country, and public opinion doesn't shift along the same lines as it does in England or the U.S. A political party can have a good handful of corrupt leaders and nothing happens. They are put on trial, they are sent to prison, they are set free, but the voters still trust the party itself. And something like this is above what the parties say anyway. People don't want an oil rig to screw up the environment."

"But we must be able to do something."

"I think it would be useless to try to smear anyone because this won't change opinions. All we can do is push along in the same direction as the Spanish PR company."

"Schmidt and the lawyers want blood."

"Well, I don't think they need it in this case. The most practical thing we can do is to get some experts on the environment, selected by us, naturally, and with some bright shiny university degrees, to write in the newspapers, take part in debates, give interviews . . . You could fill the media with reports that tell you that drilling for oil actually helps the environment, or whatever . . ."

"But in the material you gave me there was some solid dirt about some of the big names here."

"Send it to the papers if you want, but it really won't make all that much of a difference," Neil insisted.

"Schmidt doesn't see it like that."

"Schmidt doesn't know Spain, or if he does know it, then he doesn't understand it. The people here are very passionate, they support their party even if rationally they shouldn't. There is a huge silent mass in the middle, a group that pushes the balance in one direction or another: these are the people we need to talk to. The environmentalists are scaring people and saying that drilling a few miles off the coast could trigger an ecological catastrophe. The fishermen are afraid for their future, and the tourism companies think their businesses will suffer. They are the critical mass that will support the environmental movement because their interests are the same. These are the ones we have to convince, and we don't need to destroy anyone to do so. It's better to run a positive campaign. That's how I'd do it."

"What do you suggest?"

"Up until now they've invited journalists to come to the oil rigs. I'd invite some tourism companies, get a couple of Nobel Prize winners to come and give speeches, and spread a little money to the people who run the fishing fleets. I'd try to get the women to change their minds too. There are associations of housewives, of working mothers, all kinds of things. You have to convince them that their children's futures aren't going to be affected by this drilling, that it might even be a way for them to earn their living."

"All right, we'll do it as you say. Neil, you're a genius."

"I'm no genius. There are things that are evident; you don't send an army to change people's minds, it would be counter-productive."

"Could you put down what you've just told me in writing?"

"I've got it here. I knew you'd ask. Hey, I've got nothing more to do here. I've had some good wine, I've eaten like a king, and I've even had time to get a good quiet look at the Prado and the Thyssen-Bornemisza museums, but I don't have any proper work to do. I could stay. But while I'm here the meter's running and you know I'm expensive. You tell me."

"Stay a couple of days more, and give Evelyn and Cooper a hand organizing everything you've said."

"I think you should talk to Pedro López, the head of the Spanish agency. He knows how to get things done."

Cooper and Evelyn got to work looking for experts who'd make the claim that oil prospecting would be a boon for any area. And I, albeit unwillingly, finally met Pedro López, whose agency had been feeding us useful information.

López's agency was located in Chamberí, a wealthy part of town.

From the moment we shook hands López reminded me of my former boss Mark Scott. Same age, same clothes—jeans, blue shirt with no tie, cashmere jacket, shiny lace-up shoes—and an overly friendly smile. He even gleamed with that tan belonging to men who use outdoor exercise as a chance to do business and maintain their meticulous appearance at the same time.

"I've been looking forward to meeting you, Mr. Spencer. It's a pleasure working with your agency. Cooper and Evelyn have discussed with me what's needed ... It's not easy to convince the public of the benefits of oil prospecting, but we'll do what we can."

"That's just what it comes down to, convincing people. And there's no better way to convince than by presenting things in a positive light. We don't want to fight with anyone, we don't want any hostile confrontations with opponents of the project. The ideal way for citizens to have an opinion is to provide them with the tools to reach that opinion on their own. That is what my clients expect from us," I said, satisfied with myself.

"How do you intend to do that?" asked López curiously.

"I'd like you to draw up a list of all the civic organizations in the region: housewives, tourism groups, fishermen ... Essentially, representatives of all areas of society. We'll invite their leaders to visit a couple of oil rigs, just like with the journalists, but this way they will see for themselves the security measures in place on these rigs and how they work. Then we want to promote a series of conferences and debates among experts—maybe we'll bring along a Nobel Prize winner."

"And politicians? The Andalusian politicians will want to see too."

"No, absolutely not. Our mission is to convince society. If society is convinced then politicians will have to act accordingly. We've got no interest in journalists either."

"Very wise. Good, we'll draw up a plan and as soon as you approve it we'll get started straightaway."

"We need the plan tomorrow so we can get to work on it the day after."

"Too soon."

"We don't have much time."

López promised nothing. He couldn't master time, but he did invite me to play tennis with him that weekend.

"You're invited to lunch at my house, but bring your racket, we'll play a game first. A couple of other friends are coming, so we can play doubles—sound good to you? And of course if you want to bring someone that's no problem. My wife loves to have the house filled with people."

I made my excuses. I didn't have the slightest desire to spend the weekend listening to conversations I didn't care about between executives about whom I cared even less.

I preferred to keep waking up at Blanca's. I was having a good time with her, even though I would have preferred to be waking up next to Yoko. I couldn't stop thinking about her. But Blanca was a good substitute, not least for the carefree and cheerful attitude she brought to everything she did.

I sent Schmidt a report with the strategy we were going to execute and sent a copy to the lawyers. I received no response, which I took to mean that they were giving me free rein to get this right or wrong. Whatever happened, I would be the one responsible.

López proposed we set ourselves up at his company, and gave us a small office. "It's best if we're in touch at all times, working side by side." He was right. Cooper and Evelyn also found it easier.

Blanca suggested that I stay at her apartment while I was in Madrid, which I guessed would be a couple of months. I was tempted to say yes but I preferred to keep my room at the hotel. I didn't want to create any kind of tie that would complicate the relationship, nor did I want to feel obligated to share every night with her. I was willing to do that only with Yoko or with Esther—or both at once, if that were possible.

Those were the best months of my life, even without Yoko and Esther. I started to reconcile myself with my Hispanic origins, and while the Spanish didn't exactly remind me of Latinos in the United States, they shared a willingness to confront life head-on, even when luck had turned its back on them.

I was surprised to see how people were always open to spending time together. They shared a beer—a *caña*—at the bar, and many spent their time going out for a stroll along the streets, as if the mere act of breathing were sufficient, in spite of the ups and downs of the economy.

"The light, it's the light," I heard again and again, and I still believe that it is the light that defines the character of a country, as well as its people.

I don't think there was a single night when I went to bed before the wee hours. Even when I wasn't sleeping with Blanca. Some days, when we left López's agency late, he insisted that we go out for a beer. And so we would, and there were few occasions when we couldn't still be seen out at two or three in the morning, savoring a drink at some bar.

"Your wife doesn't get mad when you come home late?" Cooper asked López on one of these nights.

"Why should she get mad? She knows that if I come home late it's because I'm working."

"Sure, but right now you're not working, we're drinking," replied Cooper.

"Yeah, but you've hired my agency to get a job done. You're not from around here, I can't leave you on your own." He laughed.

His logic didn't make sense to us. Leaving work, going to a bar, getting tapas or going for dinner, continuing the conversation in a café or a cocktail bar—this wasn't exactly what Cooper, Evelyn, and I called work. Sure, that could be justified for one night, but there were altogether too many nights when we shared wine and laughter with López and his coworkers. The surprising thing was that the next morning they would all arrive at work on time. It also confused us that there were no strict working hours.

"The Spanish work more than we do," admitted Cooper.

"They do put in the hours," added Evelyn, "but they don't seem to care about that."

"It's because they spend so much time eating. At midday people disappear from work and they don't come back until four or five," I tried to explain to them.

"Which is right when we would be having tea and finishing up the workday. They do it all the other way around," Evelyn said admiringly.

Two months later we had achieved all our objectives. A group of astonished housewives had visited the oil rigs in the North Sea. Two Nobel Prize winners had spoken in the heart of Huelva on the subject of oil, as a provider not just of energy but also of jobs. UN environmental experts debated with local conservationists. Society remained divided, but the idea of oil as a force of evil had been warded off. I couldn't say that public opinion had made a U-turn, but we had softened the positions of "civil society"—common people, by any other name.

I sent a detailed report to Schmidt, filling him in on what I considered to be our achievements. I received an e-mail a week later, summoning me to a meeting with the lawyers. I resented having to go to London, but I had to get used to the idea that my Spanish adventure was over.

This time, Brian Jones and Edward Brown were at the meeting as well as Schmidt. As I went over the results with them I could see in their eyes that they weren't satisfied.

"You've spent several thousand pounds without any results," said Schmidt.

"I can't do any more than I have," I assured them, ready to face another uphill battle with Schmidt.

"It's not much, what you've achieved," said Brian Jones.

"I've done what you've asked, but without bloodshed. The outcome is the same. I'll be honest—this would have been far more difficult without Pedro López's agency. Their work has been essential to us. They could be useful in the future." I didn't want to miss the chance to show my gratitude to the Spaniard.

"Bernard, what do you say?" Edward Brown asked Schmidt.

"The work isn't bad, but the problem has not yet been solved," ruled the German.

"This is what you get when you do things properly, without killing your opponents," I remarked sarcastically.

"This morning I spoke with the directors at the oil company. It's up to them now to apply full pressure on the Spanish and local governments to allow them to go ahead with the drilling. If they can't manage that they'll have to withdraw," Schmidt said to Brown, ignoring my comment.

"Well, then they should start thinking about drilling elsewhere," I concluded.

They looked at me with something akin to scorn.

"Very well, Mr. Spencer. From today the modification to your previous contract takes effect. We've ordered your secretary—Maggie, isn't it?—to pack up your things and have them ready to be removed from the building. You will tell them where to send it all. Mr. Lerman already has the settlement prepared." Edward Brown's tone was as cold as ice.

"Case closed. Oh, and you should send the invoices with the latest fees as soon as possible." Brian Jones prevented us from getting tangled up in an argument.

"I'm intending to continue handling Parker's matters," I warned them.

"Well, Mr. Parker will have to stick to his commitments. There may be issues that you might take on, or we may recommend another adviser. In any case Mr. Parker knows he must fulfill certain commitments made to some of our clients," emphasized Edward Brown.

It was clear that whether or not Roy permitted it—and sooner or later he would have no say in the matter—they would get rid of me. Roy might have considered me trustworthy, but they didn't. Those were the rules. As well I knew.

We nodded our goodbyes. We didn't shake hands. Schmidt ignored me, not even bothering to go through the motions. He remained seated, looking through me as if I were transparent, as if I didn't exist.

I returned to Madrid. Some of my clothes were at my hotel, the rest in Blanca's closet. I wanted to have a goodbye dinner with Pedro López. I'd gotten along well with the guy in the end. I'd invite Cooper and Evelyn too. They were worried because I hadn't wanted to make any commitment about their futures. I couldn't do so before I'd first considered what I wanted to do with my own future, although I already knew what that was. I'd been mulling it over during the two months I'd spent in Madrid.

The farewell dinner was crowded. People from the agency, Blanca and her friends, Cooper with a somewhat feminine-looking young man, and Evelyn, who surprised me by introducing one of the publicists from López's agency as her "Spanish boyfriend."

It was a memorable night. Sunrise found us at Blanca's apartment, where we'd gone for one last drink. We said goodbye with the sorrow of those who know that their time together has ended.

When everyone had left Blanca started to make coffee. I was still standing, in spite of how drunk I was.

Blanca had been concerned all night about not forgetting to eat. "You have to soak up the alcohol with something," she insisted, and I did as she said.

She prepared a tray with a pot of coffee and a plate of toast, butter, and jam. We breakfasted almost in silence. We were exhausted.

"I have to get to class. If you want you can stay and sleep awhile."

"No, I'll go back to the hotel. Then I'll have lunch with the others. We need to talk about the future."

"You think today's the best day to do that? You can't decide your future when you're tired."

"And why not?" I asked, surprised by her assertion.

"Because you're all on edge, you want to sleep, your head hurts . . . Your brain will be telling you to rest but since you can't, you'll be irritable. You might even end up getting angry. I'd put off the conversation until you're back in London. When are you leaving?"

"Today," I replied, ashamed for not having said so earlier.

"Then you'd better rest for a few hours at your hotel."

"Huh. I didn't know you were so eager to get rid of me."

Blanca looked at me very seriously and took a bite of her toast, putting the words she'd prepared to say to me in order.

"We've had fun, Thomas. But I've always known that you were just passing through. If I'm perfectly honest with you I'd have liked it if that weren't the case, if you had fallen a little bit in love with me as I have with you. But you've been honest with me. You've never led me to believe that I mean anything more to you than the good times we've shared together. I won't say it doesn't hurt. Of course it does. But things are how they are. You were only in Madrid temporarily and at some point you were going to have to leave. And that point is now—today is the day. Period. Like the corny cliché goes, it was good while it lasted."

She stood up and went into the bathroom. I listened as she shut the bolt and then the shower water began to run. I got dressed. The coffee had helped to clear away some of the dull fog in my brain from the alcohol.

I left without saying goodbye. Blanca didn't want goodbyes. I didn't want to spoil what we had had with a tearful scene. I preferred to remember her good side.

I realized that I knew hardly anything about Blanca. During the time we had shared we'd barely talked about ourselves; we had joined our naked bodies together but not our feelings, not our emotions. From her, however, I would always have a love for Chopin's piano sonatas.

On the way to the hotel I saw a florist. I should have gone inside, bought two dozen red roses and sent them to Blanca. But I didn't. I don't know if she would have expected me to do something like that. Maybe she would have liked it.

I imagine her surprise upon opening the door and finding the boy from the florist handing her a bouquet. No card. Not that that would have fooled her. She'd have known it was from me.

But I didn't do that. I sent no roses. Blanca was already out of my life. She meant nothing to me. Why waste my time on some useless gesture? Now I know that I should have done it. She deserved it. She was the only woman who asked nothing from me, whom I didn't deceive precisely because she expected nothing from me. Or did she? Roses might have taken the edge off her sadness.

Midmorning I went to López's agency. He was in the office, working with the rest of the team as if he hadn't spent the previous night drinking. We had lunch together. It was a professional goodbye. Then I went back to the hotel to pack my suitcase and, following Blanca's advice, told Cooper and Evelyn that we'd talk in London. It was Friday. We'd have the whole weekend to think. It would do us good.

When I got back to London I went to Madame Agnès's that same Friday night. Yoko was talking to an older man. Or rather, he was talking and she was listening with a smile, as if whatever he was saying was the most important thing in the world to her.

I watched her for some time as I drank a glass of champagne. I listened to Madame Agnès prattling on, complaining about my absence.

When the gentleman talking to Yoko stood up, I took advantage of the moment to approach her. Her smile didn't change. It seemed frozen on her face.

"I'm pleased to see you," I said, extending my hand.

Yoko shook it briefly. She didn't seem uncomfortable, just indifferent.

"What days do you come to Madame Agnès's house? I've asked about you before, but they told me they don't know when you come."

"Yes, I usually only say so on the day itself. I don't like to make commitments. I come when I need to. Sometimes I go weeks without being here."

"And today you needed to."

"I'm sorry, but you know personal conversations aren't allowed here. And that's something I fully agree with. Please don't ask questions, Mr. . . . ."

"Spencer. I see you've already forgotten who I am."

"Mr. Spencer, this is a very pleasant place. Everyone's a gentleman here. The conversations are interesting most of the time, although sometimes there's a tendency toward small talk."

The old man approached us. He didn't seem concerned to see Yoko talking to another man. Everyone obeyed the rules here, so there couldn't be any conflict. Madame Agnès came over immediately. I imagine she wasn't concerned about the old man's manners, but she was about mine.

"My dear, I'd like to introduce you to someone. Will you excuse us?"

And taking my arm, she dragged me to the other end of the room. A man was there talking to two young women. One of them I had never seen before. She couldn't have been any older than twenty. She wasn't wearing any makeup, and didn't need it. She had incredibly long black eyelashes, as black as the long hair she wore loose. She was wearing a plain pink dress and no jewelry. She didn't need that either. She was truly beautiful.

"Nataly, I'd like to introduce you to a dear friend of mine, Mr. Spencer. Anne you already know, and I think Mr. Smith too. Oh, but your glasses are empty! Let me get you some champagne."

I joined the conversation. There was nothing else to do, unless I wanted to make a fool of myself and have Madame Agnès instruct me to leave and never come back. Even so, I stood in such a way that I could watch Yoko.

The group was having some insipid conversation about horses. Mr. Smith (clearly not his real name—his face reminded me of someone I'd seen on television during a session of Parliament) was prattling on about a Thoroughbred's form. Nataly and Anne listened intently, as if they really cared about the correct distance between a racehorse's knee and hoof. I knew nothing about horses and simply listened and nodded like the girls did.

When "Smith" took a sip of his champagne, Nataly seized the moment to ask me to accompany her to the buffet. The girl wanted to get away from that bore. She must have thought that if she had to spend the rest of the night with him he'd treat her like one of his mares.

We served ourselves some salmon and sat close to Yoko and the old man.

"You like her, don't you?" she asked me, looking at Yoko.

"What do you mean?" I replied in surprise.

"Everyone who's with her always comes back to find her again. She must have some exceptional skills. She drives them crazy," she said brazenly.

"Well, I don't know—"

"Of course you do. I'm certain you've been with her—you can't stop looking at her. Careful now, because Madame Agnès won't let you out of her sight. You know how strict she is with the rules."

"And you've got a mouth on you," I replied.

"It's the third time I've come here. It's not bad. And yeah, I have a hard time following the rules. You can't say who you are, you can't go on dates outside the house, you can't have personal conversations . . . I guess that's how she keeps all this working without any problems."

"Since neither of us cares for the rules, what do you do?"

"I study at the University of London. It's my first term and I'm saving up for the admission fees to Oxford. I'm very good at quantum physics. But not everyone can afford to study at Oxford, as you can imagine. It's not just paying for admission, the rest of the course is expensive too, and so is living there."

"And your parents?"

"Immigrants. They've lived here thirty years. I was born in London. As you can imagine they can't afford to pay for me to study at Oxford. They've done enough to get me this far."

"Where are they from?"

"My father's Mexican, my mother Indian. I'm a real mix."

"Did they meet here?"

"Yes. My father came here to earn a living and got a job in construction. He met my mother at the dry cleaner where she was working. They had nothing in common, but they got on, and even though my mothers' parents were against it, they decided to get married. My mother is an untouchable."

"That's some story."

"Like so many others. There's nothing that special to it. London is full of people like me, don't you think? And where are you from? You look South American, but you're rich, that's clear to see."

Nataly had the gift of spontaneity. I enjoyed talking with her, but that didn't mean I stopped watching Yoko. I tensed up when I saw her leave the room accompanied by that geriatric. I knew where they were going. They would go upstairs to one of those soberly decorated, elegant suites. A lounge with a table on which there was always champagne and canapés, and a door that led to a bedroom.

"You really like her?" Nataly asked, as she in turn watched me.

"Don't pry," I admonished her.

"I'm not, but if you don't want Madame Agnès to get angry at you then you ought to hide it better. Are you going to spend the night with me?"

"I don't know."

"You mean you don't want to. I get it—you came here looking for Yoko. In that case, I can't stay here with you much longer. I have to work."

"We don't need to go to a room. I'll pay all the same."

"But that's not in the house rules. Madame Agnès won't like it."

"How long do you think that old guy will take?" I asked, referring to Yoko's companion.

"However long Yoko wants. She's a miracle worker, or so I've heard around here. Never less than an hour, of course. This is a respectable house; it would be vulgar for a gentleman to be with a girl for any less than an hour. That's what Madame Agnès says."

"Well then, we're going to break the rules. We'll go upstairs to a room and come down in half an hour."

"I'm not sure . . ."

"That's what we're going to do."

I grabbed her hand and pulled her along rather roughly. Madame Agnès was watching and frowned. She required her girls to be treated with care. Before we could leave the room she planted herself in front of us.

"Everything all right, Nataly?"

"Of course, Madame."

"Would you like to eat something more substantial and relax awhile, or would you prefer to stay here and have another glass of champagne?" she asked Nataly, not looking at me.

"Mr. Spencer and I thought we might like to talk somewhere a little less noisy," Nataly replied determinedly.

"Perfect. I'll send up a nice chilled bottle of champagne."

We went up to a suite. Nataly went to the bathroom and I waited for the champagne to arrive. The waiter took only a couple of minutes.

Nataly returned barefoot to the room and sat on the sofa. I handed her a glass, which she sipped unwillingly.

"Honestly, I don't really like champagne. I'd prefer a Coke. But they don't have it here."

I let out a loud burst of laughter. If Yoko didn't exist, I could end up liking this girl. She was unabashedly candid.

"You don't like alcohol?"

"Not at all, but I can't turn down champagne. It's a house rule. What are we going to do?"

"What are you talking about?"

"Well, if you really don't want Yoko to slip past you we shouldn't be here longer than forty-five minutes. Will that be enough time?"

"For me to sleep with you?"

"Of course."

"Yes. Come on, leave the champagne and let's go to the bedroom. You're right, we haven't got time to lose."

She stood up reluctantly. I guess she was hoping that, since I was so interested in Yoko, she would be free from the obligation of another sex session. I could have let her off, but I didn't. That champagne and that room were going to cost me a great deal, so I thought I'd get my money's worth.

Nataly mechanically went through the motions. She didn't even bother to pretend. She must have thought that since I liked someone else it wasn't worth going through all the effort to make me believe that I was Tarzan himself.

She slipped away from me gently, saying that it surely must be time. She got up and went to the bathroom, and when she came out she had an air of freshness and innocence about her, as if she hadn't just got out of bed.

"Do you know where Yoko lives?"

"No, she doesn't talk much. And Madame Agnès doesn't like us to make friends. We come here, we do our job, and then we leave. You know that we aren't all alike. Yoko is the quietest— she ignores us even, as if she thinks she's special."

"You don't like her?"

"I don't care about her. I imagine she's here for the same reasons we all are. She needs to be. It's a quick way of making money. You come twice a week and you take home eight hundred pounds. Not bad, don't you think?"

"She's a student too. You've never crossed paths with her at the university?"

"No, I've never seen her. What does she study?"

"It doesn't matter; I thought you might know more than you're letting on. I'm prepared to pay well for any information about Yoko: where she lives, if she has parents . . . things like that."

"And if she has a boyfriend, of course. I'm guessing that's what you're most interested in." She laughed.

"Don't get smart."

"I am smart, and it's obvious that you're smitten with her. Okay, I'll try and find out everything I can, but it won't be easy. Five hundred pounds for the information."

"I'll pay if it's worth my time."

"Then no deal. I don't want to find something out only for you to decide that it wasn't worth the effort. You'll have to pay me."

"All right."

"I come Tuesdays and Fridays."

When we went downstairs I looked around the room but Yoko wasn't there. I had another glass of champagne with Nataly and decided to leave.

Madame Agnès came over to say goodbye. Her sickly sweet smile concealed her distrust of me.

"How early! It's not even ten. Didn't you find our little Nataly charming?"

"Of course, Madame, and I'll be back very soon in the hope of seeing her. It's always a pleasure visiting your house."

"You're always welcome here, Mr. Spencer."

I decided to wait at the corner until Yoko left and then follow her home. I was sure that Nataly would do whatever she could to earn that five hundred pounds I'd promised her, but I wasn't certain she'd be able to discover anything.

Yoko didn't leave until midnight. I recognized her slim figure wrapped up in a black coat. A taxi stopped outside the door of the house and she got inside. I cursed myself for not having foreseen that something like this might happen. Now I couldn't follow her. The taxi passed by me and I could see her through the window. Our eyes met, though she showed no sign of recognition.

It was cold and I felt nostalgic for the Madrid night—at this time of year, late March, the air would have been warm.

Even so, I decided to walk back to my apartment. It wasn't far, just over half an hour if I walked quickly.

Once again, I felt overwhelmed by loneliness. The weekend felt too long. I'd said to Evelyn and Cooper that we'd see one another on Monday, but on Saturday morning I called to invite them to lunch. They accepted, anxious for me to unveil my future plans to them. I was as honest with them as I could be.

"I'm not part of the GCP group anymore, but I'll still be working for them occasionally on certain things, especially with Roy."

"And what difference will that make?" Cooper asked worriedly.

"It means I can also work for myself and have my own clients, though I won't be allowed to work for any other agency."

"Right, okay . . . That's a little odd, isn't it?" said Evelyn.

"I've decided to set up an agency. I have an agreement with GCP, but my agency could get other clients as long as their interests don't conflict with GCP's. And I don't want to leave Roy hanging. I'd also like to have both of you start right away. We'd find a small office, big enough for the two of you and for Maggie to carry on as secretary and office manager. We'd have to find clients. We'd send a letter to all those mayors we did the campaigns for, reminding them that I was the one to help get them where they are. We'll also introduce ourselves to all the largest companies to offer our services. Maybe someone might hire us for something."

"And how are you going to explain to the press that you don't work for GCP anymore? First you worked for Cathy Major until you screwed her over with the Green business, then Scott and Roth, then GCP—and all this in just five years. They'll think that there's something not right since all these companies are kicking you out," said Evelyn.

"You're right. That's why we should move fast. We'll set up a dinner with a handful of journalists and tell them a half-truth—that I'm sick of having a boss and I've decided to fly solo, together with your help. And we'll also explain that I'm maintaining my relationship with GCP for Roy's business. Let them think I'm ambitious and arrogant. But I want your opinion. Is it worth the effort? Guys, you're not in any way committed to me, nor am I to you. I don't think you'd have any problem finding work here in London, and neither would I in New York."

Evelyn seemed hesitant, but Cooper was too introverted to want a new boss.

"You starting up a small agency seems like a good idea to me. Will you have partners? I have some money I could invest . . ." Cooper proposed.

"Well . . . that is a surprise. But I don't have a penny to spare.

I'm saving up to buy a house," said Evelyn, taken aback by Cooper's offer.

"I don't want partners yet, but it would suit me to have someone else get involved in the business. Then I wouldn't have to worry about spending as much time as I need to in New York. It'll make the whole project run smoother. And as for you, Evelyn, don't worry—you're still irreplaceable. The best support that Cooper could have. But before we start anything I have to talk to Roy. I'll see if I can meet him tomorrow."

"If you're going up to the county I'll take you. I was thinking about going this afternoon after lunch. I haven't seen my parents for a while," Evelyn suggested to me.

"Perfect, I'll call Roy right away."

Evelyn was a good driver, though her car was hardly built for speed. It was small, comfortable, and practical, decent enough to get us to the county in good time. Roy had insisted we have dinner together. Suzi had left with the children to spend the weekend at her parents' estate, where he wasn't welcome. They wouldn't be back until Sunday night. The kids liked to enjoy the countryside and ride horses.

Roy was waiting for me at the hotel and barely gave me time to take my bag up to my room. He seemed eager to have somebody to talk to.

He took me to the best restaurant in the county on the outskirts of the city, an old windmill converted into a Michelin star restaurant.

"I'm bored of being alone, Thomas. It doesn't matter so much during the week, but I don't know what to do with myself on the weekend. I insist on the party having meetings, but they aren't always willing—they all have families and their wives complain if they're left alone on Saturdays."

"You have to try to rebuild your life with Suzi."

"There's no point. She hardly speaks to me. Only the bare minimum so that the kids don't feel too uncomfortable. The other day Ernest—my eldest—he told me how worried he was getting, seeing us like that."

"You can't separate—it would be a disaster for your political career."

"I know that. But how much can I put up with?" asked Roy, as if I had the answer.

"She won't leave you, at least while her father's still alive. She knows that we'd leak the story about him."

"The old man's in bad health and he's really been affected by the gas plant. The fracking is already wreaking havoc on their land."

"We always knew that was going to happen. That's not news."

"We did, but some of the landowners are starting to complain. They're saying they feel cheated."

"Why didn't you tell me this? We have to counteract whatever these men are saying."

"I called the lawyers a couple of days ago. They told me that Schmidt would send someone to deal with it." Roy lowered his head. He knew that I would feel betrayed.

"So that means you're going to keep on working with GCP, and that means you won't need another adviser. I don't understand where this is coming from, Roy—I don't know why you've decided to get rid of me. You're leaving me out in the cold."

"It's not my decision. You know that without Jones or Brown I never would have gotten this far."

"I don't understand those goddamn lawyers, or that lackey Schmidt. The only reason I'm forced to remain tied to GCP seems to be to deal with you. Why is that?"

"I don't know. I asked, and they told me that from now on you won't always be the one taking care of matters in this county. They didn't want to give me any explanations. And I swear I insisted."

"You know you wouldn't have gotten where you are today without me. I was the one who got the other candidates out of your way."

"But Schmidt and the lawyers were the ones behind you. That's how things are. I can't go against them, Thomas, not even for you. I want my seat in Parliament. I don't understand why they don't want to put you in charge either."

"I'm going to set up an agency here, just a small one. Cooper and Evelyn will still be working with us. I've also thought about expanding the business to New York, dividing my job between the two cities. And I was counting on you, Roy."

"I don't know what to tell you, Thomas . . . I'd like to say that you can count on me, but it's up to the lawyers," Roy said regretfully.

"You know something? I thought you had them in their place. I thought that you weren't the kind of guy who lets himself get pushed around by just anyone, much less become some kind of grateful slave," I said with contempt.

Roy looked at me, hurt. He wasn't expecting such a low blow. I held his gaze. He lowered his eyes, looking at the tablecloth as he searched for the words to respond. He waited a few moments before looking at me again.

"I was the one who insisted that you work for GCP. I pushed for it, in spite of what Bernard Schmidt thought. He didn't see the need to have you around."

"Oh, so you think you did me a favor? You and I have always talked about setting up an agency to handle your business outside the lawyers. You were the reason I ended up agreeing to join GCP. And then your friend Schmidt treated me badly by sending me to Spain. I did that goddamn job to regain my freedom, because your friends wouldn't let me break my contract if I didn't. Make no mistake, Roy. Meeting those lawyers and Schmidt was not a good move for me—quite the opposite. You've sold yourself to them to achieve your ambitions. I'm not judging you—that's your business—but you should at least keep some independence and not just get dragged along. Otherwise they'll look down on you and will wash their hands of you as soon as they can. Pieces of shit are always disposable."

Roy was an open book, and an expression of disgust had been creeping over his face, until he suddenly burst.

"We're even. We don't owe each other anything. At no point did you do anything that you didn't want to do. The truth is you love living on the edge and you were dying to meet the men who pull the bloody strings of this world."

"Those two lawyers are worthless. They're underlings, just like you."

"Enough, Thomas! You think you're better than me? You aren't—you're made of the same old shit."

We fell silent, each looking at the other. I think we were both weighing what more we could say.

I asked the waiter to bring me a whiskey. Roy ordered another. We waited a few minutes before either of us spoke another word.

"At least keep Evelyn," I asked, unconvincingly.

He sighed. He seemed tired, not so much from talking to me but from all the changes to his life he'd had to deal with since dedicating himself to politics. The break with Suzi had left him bereft.

"I'll talk to the lawyers. I'll tell them that we'll go back to square one. That I want you in charge of my campaigns and my business. I'll take on this fight for you. I hope you won't object to keeping them in the loop about how you're going to handle my affairs. That's the agreement. They'll know what you're doing, but you'll take the reins."

"I'm sick of these people. I don't know why I should have to tell them what I'm going to do when I'm acting in your interest."

"They're your interests too. I can't fight them too hard, Thomas, you know that. If I do they'll drop me. Suzi is lying in wait to tear me to shreds. If she figures out there's nobody behind me she'll finish me off. What I'm suggesting here is a good deal for both of us."

"But I don't want Schmidt hovering over me. When you need my services I can tell them what I'm planning to do, but I won't ask their permission to go ahead with it."

"When are you going to New York?"

"It'll still be a couple of days—I have to take care of a few things. Evelyn will handle you exclusively. She knows the county as well as you do, and she knows which buttons to push and when. You'll be in safe hands with her. I think the best thing is for her to move back here."

"The party does have a communications team . . ."

"And she knows them all, there won't be any problem there. You're our main client, Roy, so Evelyn will always be at your disposal. I don't want her to leave your side. You've got to start gearing up to win the seat. They say the prime minster might hold early elections."

"All right."

"Evelyn is intelligent and ambitious. You can trust her as much as you trust me."

"And you?"

"I'll come back to England once a month. I'll meet with her, meet with you, we'll analyze the situation, decide what to do . . . And if there are any problems, any crises, I'll come right away. You're my priority, Roy, I promise you."

I was lying. I don't know if he knew it, but if he did he didn't show it—he seemed to believe me. Perhaps it's what he wanted. I wouldn't have.

He shrugged. He seemed suddenly older to me. I examined him carefully and noticed the many wrinkles around his eyes, his reddish hair spotted with white strands. He'd gained weight. He was getting a double chin. He'd lost that aura of strength and stability from when we'd first met. There was no trace of that stubborn, overpowering man who had practically forced me to work for him.

"You have to face up to the situation," I told him. "Life doesn't end with Suzi."

"You can't understand, Thomas. Suzi is the only person in the world who I can be myself with, who I don't have to pretend with. I can tell her anything, talk about my dreams, know that she'll always be there . . ."

"But you were wrong about that, Roy. Everyone has their limits, their personal boundaries. Suzi's limits are her family and those fields, the ones with the flocks of sheep that don't seem to be giving birth or producing milk anymore because of the fracking."

"It wasn't worth it. That's the worst part of all, that the price I've paid to be mayor absolutely was not worth it."

"Tell her that, and beg forgiveness."

"She doesn't want to talk to me. She refuses."

I was beginning to get bored. I had gotten what I was looking for—keeping Roy as a client—and his marital woes weren't of particular interest to me. But I knew that the only way he'd feel connected to me was for me to listen to him. And that's what I did for another hour, until we were the only people left in the restaurant and I volunteered to walk him back home. When we got there he invited me in for a nightcap. I was forced to accept and continue listening to how much he loved Suzi.

On Monday morning Cooper called me. A friend had rented us a place near Piccadilly. One hundred square meters at a decent price.

I had a hard time convincing Maggie to keep working with us. She didn't trust me and didn't seem to have much faith in Cooper either.

"The thing is, Thomas, I just don't trust you."

"I'll pay you a little extra if you come with us."

"And what guarantee do I have that you're going to behave? I've spent many years in the ad industry, and you do hear things . . . You've made a name for yourself, but not for your skills as much for your to-ing and fro-ing. First you messed Cathy around with Green. Then Scott and Roth invited you to pack your bags. Now you've left GCP with no explanation . . . Too many changes, even for an industry like ours."

"Two hundred more per month than you were earning at GCP. Agreed?"

"The rich boy always getting his wallet out," she remarked, as greed flashed in her eyes.

"Agreed?"

"Only with a guarantee. A five-year contract. If you shut down the agency you pay me the time remaining. Down to the last penny."

"Anything else?"

"Maybe. I'll think about it."

I hired her. There was no question I would. I knew that when it came to Maggie it was only ever a question of money. But she was worth it. She was more than a personal assistant. Only she could handle the management side properly and had the skills to put my business in order. She knew it all.

We bought the office furniture from Ikea. I didn't want to invest too much in the agency, which we simply named Global Communication.

Schmidt called me, and even though I could tell he was in a bad mood, he didn't let it show during our conversation.

"Mr. Parker has expressed his wish that you be put in charge of appeasing the people clamoring against the gas company in Derbyshire. He was very insistent, and the lawyers eventually gave in."

"Against your better judgment, I suppose. Why did you want to separate me from Roy?"

He didn't bother to answer my question.

"You will inform Mr. Lerman how you plan to proceed with this task."

"I don't work at GCP anymore and Lerman is no longer my boss. Why should I?"

"Do us all a favor, Spencer, and try not to provoke anyone.

You know that you're still tied to GCP, we've only modified the contract."

"I'm starting up my own agency." I told him this as if it would come as a surprise to him.

"You know what you've signed. You'll have to consult with us on what steps you're going to take and for which clients. If there's no conflict of interest then we don't care. You just have to keep us informed. Try to get campaigns selling colognes or toys, and leave the sensitive work to us. That's in everyone's best interest."

"Roy will still be my client."

"We'll decide who is best equipped to handle his issues as they occur. Get used to the idea that it won't always be you."

"But you've already had to give in once."

I thought I heard the distant sound of Schmidt's laughter before he spoke again.

"Lerman is waiting to hear your action plan. Don't delay. We have to cut off these dissident voices as soon as possible."

I was annoyed that I couldn't go back to New York as I'd planned. But I was the one who'd compelled myself to take on more work for Roy. Cooper seemed delighted when I told him.

"I'm pleased you're staying. It'll be better for the agency that you're here, at least at the beginning. It was too soon for you to be going to New York."

Evelyn wasn't particularly enthusiastic about being assigned exclusively to Roy. She didn't want to go back to the county. I convinced her by explaining that she could keep her apartment in London. We still had several months to go before the elections and if Roy got his seat he would have to travel regularly to the capital, and she'd go with him.

"But I want to work on other things . . . I'll go crazy if I have to be with Roy all the time, listening to him whine about Suzi."

We agreed that she'd be allowed to look into other matters.

It was a way of pacifying her. I didn't want her to quit. I needed someone whom Roy and I could trust to stay with him. There was no one better than Evelyn.

Getting the agency set up kept me busy the rest of the week. Arranging the furniture, buying filing cabinets, and lunching with five journalists—selected by Cooper—to announce that we had set out on our own, but still had a working agreement with GCP. The aim was to get them to publish a line or two about us in the papers. We got that. By Friday the space we had rented was nearly ready, allowing us to get to work the following week. Cooper had drawn up a list of potential clients to whom Maggie sent a letter offering our services. As for Evelyn, even though we hadn't even installed our computers yet, she started work at her apartment on the campaign.

"Thank goodness it's the weekend. I'm sick of hanging paintings and rearranging furniture," complained Maggie.

"Well, you can rest until Monday. I'm going to the country, to stay with some friends," remarked Cooper.

On hearing them make their plans for the weekend I felt another wave of loneliness. What could I do until Monday? Suddenly I remembered that little Nataly had promised to give me information on Yoko. Nataly went to Madame Agnès's on Tuesdays and Fridays, so I now had something to do that night. This cheered me up.

When I arrived there were already a number of men present, talking away. Only one of the girls was talking, with a guy who looked Eastern European—I thought he must be one of those Russian millionaires.

Madame Agnès welcomed me with the same deference as on previous occasions, offering me the usual glass of champagne that I'd later have to pay for. It was part of the game.

"My dear friend, how wonderful of you to visit us! Champagne? Of course, there's no better way to begin the evening than a glass of champagne and some good conversation. I'll introduce you to one of the gentlemen who is with us this evening. He asked me to let him know if you came. He read in the papers that you've started your own agency and he's interested in meeting you."

I followed Madame Agnès to a group of men. At that particular moment they were discussing whether Europe could maintain its current growth rates, or if it was instead on the verge of a new recession. Madame Agnès motioned to a man whom I guessed to be between forty-five and fifty years old. He stood up and held out his hand, introducing himself: "Anthony Tyler, I've been keen to meet you. You're a very promising young man. Have you met these gentlemen?" Tyler proceeded to introduce me to the other three men in the group and brought me into their conversation. I had to force myself to get involved. Their opinions about what Her Majesty's government might or might not do didn't interest me in the slightest. I was concerned. Nataly still hadn't made an appearance and I didn't want to get distracted. If any of Madame Agnès's clients got to her first I wouldn't be able to talk to her. Yoko wasn't there either.

After a while, once the room had gotten much more crowded, Tyler asked that we step aside.

"You know, I've heard talk about you."

"Bad enough to pique your interest?" I remarked, prompting a laugh.

"Of course, young man—you've made yourself some enemies already."

"Important ones, I hope."

"Very clever. I don't know if you think this is the right time, but I'd like you to work for me."

"Well, I work for myself."

"Yes, obviously—I meant hiring you for an ad campaign."

"What do you want to sell?" I asked with interest.

"I work in the import business. I want to introduce a new product to the market and I need a campaign to get people's attention."

"What kind of product?"

"Underwear, made in China. The costs are very low there. There's a company in Shanghai that's started to make women's underwear to cater to Western tastes. They actually just copy famous brands."

I couldn't help but laugh. The last thing I'd imagined doing was running a campaign to sell panties. Because honestly that's all this was.

Tyler stiffened when I laughed. He looked at me in disgust. He found no humor in selling panties.

"It sounds like a tempting offer. I hope I'm of the same quality as the product you wish to sell."

"I see you find it funny . . . Do you know how much money the lingerie trade moves? I can give you the numbers and you'll be amazed. I want to introduce these products to England and the rest of Europe. Cheap items that are well designed and competitively priced. The factory in Shanghai makes them with a material similar to silk—it has almost the same texture. There are thousands of women who can't afford to buy underwear at La Perla, but would love to have a bra or knickers that at least make them look like they can."

"Understood. I assure you that this campaign will be a great challenge for me."

"Well then, I'll give you my card." Tyler seemed uncomfortable. He must have been wondering if he'd made a mistake with me. "If you want you can call me on Monday. We'll set up an interview and if we come to an agreement the campaign will be yours."

"I'll call you. It's a very tempting job, I assure you."

He left me alone in the middle of the room and returned to talk with the group of men, who had just been joined by two of Madame Agnès's girls: the redhead whom Roy liked so much, and a Brazilian who was one of the house regulars. I was going to ask for another drink when I saw Nataly, who had been waiting for me to finish speaking with Tyler.

"I hadn't seen you," I said in greeting.

"I saw you. I've been circling for a while trying to make sure no one noticed me so I could talk to you."

"You're hard not to notice," I said to flatter her.

"Thank you. Now, how about we go upstairs and I'll tell you everything I've found out about Yoko."

"Do we have to go upstairs?"

"Yes . . . Well, no, actually, but this way I won't have to go upstairs with someone else later. I'm tired."

"All right."

I asked Madame Agnès to send dinner up to one of the suites. She gave a grateful smile. She liked nothing more than when clients dined in the suites, because that increased the bill. She charged as if her chef had three Michelin stars.

"Oh! And send us up a couple of Cokes."

"This girl . . . Champagne is the drink of love," she whispered in my ear.

"Naturally we'll drink champagne, but I want Coke too," I replied firmly.

When we reached the suite Nataly took off her shoes and sat in an armchair. Her face lit up when the waiter appeared with an ice bucket containing a bottle of champagne and a couple of Cokes.

"You're amazing! Huh, looks like tonight is going my way."

She waited until we were alone again before telling me what she had found out about Yoko:

"Her father is English and her mother Japanese. She was born in Kyoto, but she's lived in London since she was five. Apparently her father worked in sales and he traveled a lot to Tokyo, where he met Yoko's mother. They got married, and though they lived in Japan at first they eventually moved to London. When Yoko was twelve, they separated. Until recently she was living with her mother. Her father remarried, this time to an Englishwoman. They see each other once in a while. She adores him—even though he split up with her mother—and he thinks she's a perfect daughter.

"Yoko studies English literature, she's still got a couple of years to go. Until a year ago her mother was paying for her fees but now she can't anymore. Apparently she lost her job and decided to go back to Japan. Yoko didn't want to go with her. She lives on her own, and with the money she makes here she's paying for university and her flat. She's going out with a guy studying medicine. His name's Dave, he's English. His father's a famous doctor, they have a house in Richmond and a mansion in the countryside. Dave's taken her back home a couple of times and his parents have liked her. They like that she's a good girl who's trying to get ahead. That's it."

Nataly looked at me, satisfied that she'd found the information that was going to net her no less than five hundred pounds.

"Does she live with this guy?" I asked distractedly.

"Not exactly, but they do spend a lot of time together."

"Does he know that she comes here?"

"Of course not! This isn't something you talk about at home, not even with your best friend, let alone a boyfriend."

"Do you have the address of Yoko's apartment?"

"Yes, but it'll cost you more."

"Well, aren't you the businesswoman! All right, two hundred pounds extra."

"That's not very much."

"Don't push your luck, Nataly," I warned her.

From the tone of my voice she realized that I could get angry. She was smart, and knew when to back off.

"No harm in trying . . . All right, five hundred pounds is fine."

"I said two hundred."

"Two hundred?" She made a face, hoping I'd accept her price.

"How did you find all this out?" I asked.

"At university. I have a friend who works in the admin department and she found her file for me. From there it wasn't difficult to find people who knew her. I even talked with her myself."

"About what?"

"One day I pretended to bump into her at university—she was surprised to see me there. We'd never met there before. She was startled, and thought I would say something that would give the two of us away. I didn't even say hello to her—she was with a group of people and I just walked by. But on Tuesday we were both here and she was the one who approached me.

"She told me she was grateful that I hadn't given any sign that I recognized her in front of her friends so she didn't have to explain how we knew each other. I told her that she didn't have to worry, that I prefer discretion just like she does. She looked relieved."

"Is she coming tonight?"

"I don't know. She told me that she had an exam on Monday and needed to study all weekend, but that doesn't mean she won't still come here for a little while. It depends on whether she has bills to pay. She often comes Fridays, same as me, so you might be in luck."

"How much more do you need for admission to Oxford?" I asked out of curiosity.

"Less and less, but I still need to come here a couple more nights. But hey, what can you do?"

"You could find another job." I said this without the slightest hint of judgment.

"But I wouldn't earn what I do here and I'd have to work all day. This job isn't particularly pleasant, there are some really ugly guys—but they do pay well."

"Are you going to do this for the rest of your life?"

"One day I'll be a world-renowned scientist, but until then . . ."

"And do your parents know?"

"Of course not! They think I work in the coatroom of a respectable club where men go to play bridge or drink malt whiskey while they doze off in their armchairs. They would never suspect I was capable of doing something like this."

"And what if one day your father decides to come to work with you?"

"That wouldn't happen. Anyway, my father gets up early to go to work—when he comes back in the evening he's exhausted. I'm a model daughter. I've always had good grades and now I'm working to pay for Oxford. They couldn't ask for more."

We had dinner, chatting about this and that. And we laughed together. Nataly was very witty and loved to imitate people.

After dinner she stretched out on the sofa. She knew I wanted my pound of her flesh for the money I'd paid for dinner. And I did.

When we returned to the main room it was buzzing. Conversations, laughter, the indefatigable waiters serving clients, Madame Agnès insisting that the men drink champagne, the girls sussing out the highest bidders. And Yoko. There she was, talking to the same geriatric from the other night. She was listening distractedly and her smile looked like a mask. I told Nataly I wanted to be alone for a while. She shrugged and said quietly to me: "Be careful. Madame Agnès doesn't want her clients falling in love with any of us. And she doesn't let us be with more than one client per night. You know the rules." I knew them, yes, but I didn't care if I broke them.

I stood in a corner where I could observe Yoko without her being aware of my presence. I was fascinated by the delicacy of her movements, her sphinxlike face, her strange beauty. I don't know how long I spent watching her, but she suddenly seemed to sense my gaze because she located me in the room and fixed her eyes on mine. I read nothing in them, and recognized no emotion; she simply looked at me.

I approached her and the old man and greeted them. The man shook my hand reluctantly while Yoko nodded her head slightly.

"Will you permit me to share a glass of champagne with the two of you? It's too noisy tonight and I'm in need of some quiet conversation."

The old man looked at me in shock at my flagrant violation of Madame Agnès's house rules. No gentleman was to interfere when another was with a girl.

"We were about to retire upstairs," replied the man, annoyed.

At that moment Madame Agnès appeared, and from her expression I could see that she was displeased by my behavior.

"My dear Duke, we've prepared pheasant with grapes for your dinner, just how you like it, and a little foie gras for our darling girl. The waiter is ready to serve you dinner."

The duke took Yoko gently by the arm and, with a slight nod, headed to the hallway to go up to one of the suites. I was left alone with an unimpressed Madame Agnès.

"Mr. Spencer, it wasn't very considerate of you to interrupt the conversation between the duke and the young lady. You put them in an awkward situation. I think you know the rules of this house well enough. A gentleman never steps in when one of the young ladies is with another gentleman. You also know it's a house rule that the gentlemen who honor me with their presence do not become infatuated with any of my girls, far less show it. We are all adults here."

"I'm sorry to offend you, Madame Agnès, that wasn't my intention. And you must know that my time with Nataly has been extremely satisfying—she's a charming young lady. So I really wasn't looking for the attentions of any of the other ladies. I only wanted to talk awhile, though perhaps I didn't choose my conversation partners well enough."

Madame Agnès knew that I was lying. But she had no other option than to accept my apology. She knew that Yoko was becoming an obsession for me. She'd seen cases like mine before.

I was tempted to leave, but I didn't feel like going back to my apartment to drink alone. At least here I could take part in some meaningless conversation to help while away the hours. I also wanted to try my luck and attempt to follow Yoko after she had finished with the duke. And luck smiled upon me.

I had been starting to get impatient, wondering what this old fogy could possibly be doing with Yoko. Two hours had passed since Madame Agnès had told them their dinner was ready.

I was about to leave when I saw them reappear in the room. The man said goodbye to her with a kiss on the hand. Yoko nodded her head slightly before disappearing into the hallway in search of her coat. I didn't waste a minute and left the young girl I'd been talking to without even saying goodbye.

Yoko had left the house. It seemed to take ages for the maid to bring me my coat.

I saw Yoko just as she was about to get in a taxi, and I ran toward her, calling her name, not caring if anybody noticed me. She turned around, surprised. She stood immobile next to the car. When I reached her I gently pushed her into the cab and then got in myself.

"I'll take you home, but first let's have a drink somewhere. There's a place in Soho that's very trendy, I think you'll like it."

She didn't reply. She didn't even look at me. I gave the taxi driver the address and we didn't speak until we reached the bar.

I asked the maître d' to find us a quiet table, which was a lot to ask because the place was so full you could barely move, but he managed it. Of course I had greased his palm generously.

"What would you like to drink?"

"Water," she said calmly.

I ordered a whiskey for myself and for her a bottle of that very expensive mineral water that snobs drink. Yoko seemed absent. She was next to me but she wasn't with me.

"I'm glad you agreed to go for a drink. You know something? I haven't stopped thinking about you."

"You forced me to come."

"You didn't say no either."

"What could I have done? Screamed? Madame Agnès would have heard. She doesn't want any scandals."

"I haven't stopped thinking about you," I insisted.

"But you shouldn't do that."

"Why not?"

"As soon as I can I'm going to stop going to Madame Agnès's. So you won't see me anymore."

Her words surprised me. They were stern, but her soft and even tone made it sound as if they were wrapped in cellophane.

"I'm not interested in what you do at Madame Agnès's. I'm interested in you."

"Thomas . . . Yes, you said your name was Thomas or maybe someone told me, I don't remember. You see, Thomas, you're not part of my world, and I don't want you in it. We met in a certain place and under certain circumstances, but that doesn't mean we're going to become friends, or that we'll have any relationship beyond the walls of that house. I have my life and you have yours. And as I said, I don't want you in mine. And now I'm begging you to let me leave."

I didn't let her. I grabbed her arm so hard she could not stand up. I played my hand. Thanks to Nataly, I had an ace up my sleeve.

"We'll have a drink and then we'll go to your flat. I'll stay as long as I want, and that will be how it always is from now on."

Yoko looked at me in shock, as if she didn't understand what I had just said.

"I don't like women who drink water," I added, "so start thinking about what you want—whiskey, champagne, gin . . . whatever you prefer."

She remained silent, but looked at me fearfully. The waiter arrived with what we'd asked for and I asked him to bring a gin and tonic as well. I'd decided that was what she would drink.

"I want to leave, Thomas. You can't keep me here," she said in a voice so quiet it was practically a whisper.

"But I can, Yoko. I don't think you'd like your boyfriend, Dave, to know that you're a whore. Much less his parents."

I could see her trembling. Her body seemed to grow weaker as she sunk into her seat. She looked at me in horror, as if I had turned into a monster.

"I don't understand . . ."

"It's very simple. I want to sleep with you: I don't know for how long, it could be a day, two weeks, or three years. When I get tired I'll let you know. You have no other option. If you say no, Dave and his parents will find out what you do. Your father too, and even your mother—even though she's in Japan, she'll get the news."

"No . . . You can't . . . I'll go and talk to Madame Agnès right now . . . She won't let you back in her house."

"It's in Madame Agnès's interests to keep this quiet. She won't want the newspapers hearing about the kind of business she runs and the names of the gentlemen who go there every night to sleep with her whores."

"I've done nothing to you to make you want to harm me," she said, her voice shaking.

"You're very good in bed. That's all it is, nothing more."

"You can see me at Madame Agnès's . . ." she said, as if it were a plea.

"No, I don't want to see you there. I'll see you when and where I want. You will be at my disposal whenever it pleases me. It's that simple. Accept it. If you do, then neither Dave nor his parents nor yours will find out you're a whore. If you decline I'll make sure they know."

"But . . ."

"Your only other option is throwing yourself in the Thames. Imagine, not just your family and your boyfriend but all of your classmates and professors knowing that you're a whore."

She stayed silent. Immobile. Her eyes glazed over. A trance-like expression had fallen across her face. I savored my whiskey as I watched her. I was savoring my power over her too. I was the master of her fate. Her destiny depended on me and that gave me such satisfaction that it made me laugh. She looked at me, not understanding the reason behind my laughter.

"That night I was with you . . . I knew you weren't a good person. There was something evil in you," she managed to say.

"Wonderful. That means you're safe in the knowledge that

I'm capable of going through with my threat. Now drink your gin and tonic and we'll go to your place."

I gave her the glass and she took barely a sip. I wouldn't let her put the glass back down. I kept holding on to her arm, knowing I was hurting her.

"Drink it all," I ordered her.

She did so. She drained it down to the last drop. Then we went to her place. It was a tiny apartment. A single room that served as bedroom, living room, and open kitchen, with a door that led to the bathroom. Everything perfectly ordered and clean. There was barely any furniture.

"Where's the bed?" I asked, puzzled.

"I don't have a bed, I sleep on a futon," she replied.

"We'll see if I like it or not—if not you'll have to buy a bed."

She took the futon out of the cupboard and spread it on the floor. For a moment I thought there were tears in her eyes, but that didn't concern me.

From then on I was in charge. I could do with her whatever I pleased.

Many years have passed since then. I know that I possessed her body, but not Yoko herself. Yoko wasn't there. It didn't matter what I ordered her to do; the truth was that she was a statue of flesh, not a woman. She showed no emotion, not even a grimace of pain on her face when I insisted on grabbing at her, just so she would make a sound so I'd know she was there.

I abused her for some time. I don't regret it. I've never regretted that.

I could have gotten Yoko without any violence, just by making her believe I had fallen in love with her. Vanity is infinite, and women are vulnerable to men who say they love them and are ready to die for them. Their egos get puffed up.

That first night I could have told her that I had fallen in love with her, that I couldn't live without her by my side. I could have given her something for dramatic effect, I don't know what, maybe a ring, or some earrings that were expensive but discreet enough that she could appreciate them and accept them without her boyfriend asking where she'd gotten them. If they were discreet she could always say they were a present from her father.

I could have sent her a bouquet of flowers every day, and lain in wait to be the first to talk to her on the evenings she went to Madame Agnès's.

Yes, I could have played the role of the man in love, willing to wait as long as was needed to win over the object of his affections. A sensitive woman like Yoko may have ended up softening.

But I didn't. I never gave her a single flower, or piece of jewelry, or any caress that carried affection. I never treated her like someone who was special to me. If I had, I would have overcome her resistance, perhaps have sown doubt about her love for Dave. If I had made her laugh . . . But I did none of that. I didn't even consider it.

Yoko was a whore: that was how I'd met her, and I never believed she had any right to be treated differently. If she earned her living selling her body it was because she had no compunction. She couldn't expect us clients to treat her any better than a choice cut of meat, there for our consumption.

I never paid her to be with me. Even that I enjoyed. I could have her without paying a penny for her. Enjoy her body and her time as I pleased without her receiving a single benefit, save for my silence. Sometimes she would ask me to let her have her life back. I would just laugh.

I didn't make her break up with Dave. I preferred her to keep sleeping with him—it increased the terror she felt at the chance he could find out that she was involved in prostitution. Every so often she asked me permission to go with Dave to spend the weekend at his parents' country house. I usually agreed. The tighter the links she had with Dave's parents, the less she'd want them to find out that their son had a whore for a girlfriend.

Her distress never moved me. I didn't even falter when she started to lose weight, which the doctor diagnosed as anorexia. That day I slapped her and dragged her to a restaurant, forcing her to eat a steak. She gagged. I threatened her if she did not eat. When we got home I gave her an ultimatum: she had one month to get back to her previous weight, or I would tell everyone that she was a whore. I wasn't willing to sleep with a slab of cold meat with sharp edges.

It wasn't as easy as I thought it would be. She did everything she could not to vomit back up what she ate, but it took a lot of time for her to recover.

When she fell ill I could have softened and given her her life back. Told her that I was the one who had driven her to madness and I was prepared to disappear forever. I could even have offered to pay for medical treatment. But I didn't. I pressured her to eat, and bought a scale on which I forced her to weigh herself naked whenever I went to visit her. If she had lost a single ounce I would hit her and warn her that I would call Dave the next day to tell him who she really was. Then she would sit on the floor and, with superhuman effort, slowly eat whatever was in the fridge. She held herself back so as not to vomit, and then bore the weight of my body on top of hers, emaciated to the point where I found her unpleasant. But I still wouldn't give her her life back.

Yes, I could have freed her from me. But I didn't, and neither then nor now do my actions trouble my conscience. I did what I wanted to do.

As my relationship with Yoko was secured I had time to focus on business.

When I explained to Cooper that a businessman wanted to hire us for an underwear campaign he seemed nonplussed.

"Underwear, and made in China to boot?"

"Yes. The guy's named Anthony Tyler, and he wants all the working-class and middle-class English ladies who can't buy their silk panties at La Perla to buy the next best thing. He wants us to invent that brand."

It seemed like a good idea to Maggie. I imagine she hadn't thought me capable of finding a client who wasn't Roy Parker. As for Evelyn, it was she who gave us one of the best ideas for the campaign.

We went to see Anthony Tyler at his office. He was on the first floor of a building that overlooked the Thames. Not the best part of town, but at least he could say that it was fashionable. His job was buying and selling. He imported electronic products from China and made a good profit selling them to London chains. He was also in the clothing trade. The Chinese company he had found made knockoffs of La Perla and Victoria's Secret underwear, selling them at bargain prices.

Tyler wanted lingerie stores to purchase these Chinese bras and panties, but for that to happen he needed to create demand for them. That was why he needed an ad campaign.

Evelyn suggested a television campaign whose high cost made Cooper certain that Tyler would reject it.

"I know, but this is the only way to get all the lingerie shops and major retailers in the country to buy these," argued Evelyn.

"And how would we convince them?" I inquired.

"Simple. The ad should star a beautiful young woman, a model—if she's famous all the better, but just a pretty girl is fine too. We see her come home, take off her shoes, her dress, and she'll just be in her underwear as she enters the bathroom and turns on the shower. Some suggestive music, and then words on the screen: 'Exquisite Lingerie, coming soon to all good retailers.' This will make the lingerie shops wonder who distributes this underwear, because as soon as their customers see it on TV they'll start asking about it. No retailer will want to be without this brand, mark my words."

Cooper and I had no objection; it was a good idea. Evelyn

said that once the commercial began to run on TV, we would also have to place some print ads. The same model, in Chinese lingerie, not looking directly at the camera.

"It has to be sexy but subtle," explained Evelyn, "so that every kind of woman will want this underwear."

We presented the idea to Anthony Tyler. He said he'd think about it, as the proposed cost was higher than he'd expected. Evelyn made him see that our campaign would get him results fast.

"In a couple of weeks your phone will be ringing off the hook with requests," she assured him boldly.

A few weeks went by with no news of Tyler, and because I didn't want to call him I went to Madame Agnès's. I knew that he would be there every Friday, and one could always find time to get a bit of business done at that house. By that point I was spending most of my nights with Yoko, but just as I obliged her to continue seeing Dave, I also forced her to keep going to Madame Agnès's house. It didn't suit me for her to stop being a whore. After all, she had no other means of income, and I wasn't prepared to spend a single pound on her.

Indeed, that very Friday Yoko was there, talking with a group of men, Anthony Tyler among them. I approached the group. Yoko tensed up, but the other men didn't notice. As for Tyler, I could see that my presence annoyed him.

They were talking about Russia—a couple of the men had business there. I listened to them and asked a couple of questions, not out of interest but in order to integrate myself into the group. I didn't even look at Yoko when one of the men signaled her and the two of them went upstairs.

I don't know how, but I could suddenly feel someone's gaze burning into the back of my neck. Madame Agnès was watching me. I had in fact noticed her doing that over the last couple of weeks, as if she found my indifference to Yoko strange. I smiled at her. She smiled back and lifted her glass of champagne in welcome.

After a long time, once the men had almost all left the group so that each could dine with one of the girls, Tyler seemed to make his mind up to talk to me.

"How about we swap this champagne for a decent whiskey?" he suggested, aware that my presence that night was because of him.

We settled down in the library, the only place where there was no one else. A couple of waiters followed us, one with a tray of salmon, cheese, and cucumber canapés. When we were alone Tyler wasted no time getting to the matter at hand.

"I was planning to call you, Spencer, but since we're here . . ."

"I suppose you've made up your mind."

"I have. The campaign you presented me is good. Effective."

"But . . ." I added, awaiting his response.

"But too expensive. We'd have to sell millions of knickers to pay for it, let alone make a profit."

"And you will sell them," I assured him.

"Well, it's not that simple. The Chinese themselves bring over a lot of their wares to the West and they manage to sell them without spending a pound on publicity."

"But you're not a Chinese trader—you're a British trader with a reputation who moves in certain financial circles. The kind of circles that expect something more from you than low-quality merchandise. That's why you need our publicity. I won't deny that it'll cost money to go forward with the campaign, but publicity—good publicity—is expensive."

"Maybe we could lower the price," he suggested unconvincingly.

"I don't think so, Mr. Tyler. The campaign costs what it costs because it is extraordinary, and it's designed for you to make a serious profit."

"So you're not prepared to lower the cost of the campaign?" he said with surprise.

"No. If you want an effective campaign this is what it costs. If you want to spend your money placing a handful of ads where people won't even see them, go ahead, but you won't get results."

"You're very sure of yourself," he said rather disdainfully.

"Mr. Tyler, you're trying to fool millions of women. You want them to buy poor-quality underwear. The same underwear they could buy in some dollar store, but that you want to place in regular stores, in big department stores, so the price will be higher. To create demand from these women you need a story; you need to convince them that they could have something special, something that will soon be in stores. You can only reach them through a massive campaign—on TV, in women's magazines, in newspapers. They have to see the ads for weeks, at all hours of the day. This will work. Sure, someone might offer you a cheaper campaign, but you'd be throwing your money away."

"That's a pretty arrogant approach." There was irritation in Tyler's voice.

"No, it's not. It's a genuine plan. Well, in any case, it's been a pleasure working with you, Tyler, and I really wish you all the best." I said this as I stood and held out my hand, assuming the conversation was over.

Anthony Tyler seemed to hesitate. A look of confusion came over his face. He stood up and held out his hand.

"We'll talk on Monday at my office—does eight work for you?"

"Of course," I agreed, as he nodded slightly to me.

We left the library and Tyler looked for one of the girls he usually spent his time with during his evenings at Madame Agnès's. I went to the bar and sat down to finish savoring the whiskey in my glass. Madame Agnès came up to me.

"A young man like you shouldn't be alone. Is there no lady you'd like to go up to dinner with?"

"Of course, Madame, but I also appreciate the comfort your house offers to have a quiet drink."

"Nataly will be here soon, would you like to dine with her?"

"That would be a pleasure, Madame."

Nataly arrived a few minutes later. She carried the chill of the autumn evening on her. Madame Agnès pointed her to where I was sitting and she came straight toward me.

"Well, long time no see," she joked.

"You're always busy."

"Seems you are too."

"I haven't come here much lately."

"I can guess. How's it going with her?" she asked.

"Who are you talking about?" I laughed.

"Come on, Thomas! You can tell me."

"How about we go up for dinner, I'm hungry."

After the waiter left dinner on the table we started to feel more comfortable. Nataly took off her shoes, and sat down hungrily to eat.

"The food's great here. I love this lobster terrine."

"You should try it with champagne instead of Coke."

"At least with you I can drink what I like—even if Madame does charge you as much for Coke as champagne."

I always welcomed those dinners with Nataly. Beyond the sex, I enjoyed talking with her. She was naturally guileless and shameless.

"Yoko is suffering," she told me.

"How do you know that?" I asked curiously.

"She's thinner every time I see her. She looks miserable and she hardly talks with the other girls. Her nerves have been frayed for months and I've heard some of her clients saying that she doesn't seem the same. Madame is worried and has asked her over and over again what's going on, but she says that everything's fine. Obviously Madame doesn't think so."

"You know everything," I remarked in admiration.

"You just have to pay attention and listen."

"And what conclusion has Madame come to?"

"That Yoko has been put under a lot of pressure."

"And what do you think?"

"That it's your fault. You've forced your way into her life and you're making her spend time with you. That's what's destroying her. Am I right?"

"Am I that unpleasant?" I wanted to know.

"Not on the surface—the problem is how you are deep down."

"How do you think I am?"

"Oh, you're a nasty piece of work: unfeeling, capable of doing whatever you can to get your own way. Women mean less than objects to you. Yoko included. I imagine she's praying for you to get tired of her."

"You don't think very highly of me," I said, feigning anger.

"You'd be worried if I did."

I couldn't help but laugh. Nataly always disarmed me with her sincerity.

Tyler agreed to our campaign. He made one last attempt to get us to reduce the price, but I remained inflexible.

"Maybe we could have lowered the cost," said Cooper once we'd left Tyler's office.

"Impossible."

Aside from Roy, Tyler was our only client, which was starting to worry me. It wasn't that the cost of running the office was high, but without other clients we wouldn't be able to survive. It irritated me, as I wanted to get back to New York and this was the only reason I was delaying my departure.

It took us three weeks to launch the underwear campaign. It was a hit. Tyler's orders mounted up. There wasn't a single store in the country that didn't want to have synthetic silk lingerie.

"You've nearly convinced me to buy a pair of those knick-ers," Maggie told us, in her peculiar form of congratulations.

Even Tyler couldn't help but admit that it had been worth the cost. He invited Cooper, Evelyn, and me for dinner at his home with his wife and his gangly daughters.

Mrs. Tyler was the typical middle-class housewife, support-ing her husband as he climbed the social ladder rung by rung, while she tried to stretch every penny at home so they could keep paying their three daughters' school tuition.

One of the girls seemed taken by Cooper, unaware that he was more interested in looking at the waiter they'd hired for the occasion.

Tyler was so grateful that he promised to remember us for future campaigns.

"We're so pleased—and we'd be even more so if you recom-mended us to some of your friends," said Evelyn.

"Naturally I will. In fact, I have a friend who's thinking of importing olive oil to England. He might be interested, since your agency works wonders."

"Olive oil is a difficult product to sell. It's expensive. Only the upper classes can afford it," said Cooper, unenthused.

Evelyn cut him off. "It'll be a challenge."

After dinner I went to Yoko's apartment. It was the best way to end a night. I'd called her in advance to stop her from invit-ing her boyfriend over to sleep with her. Dave was only for the times when I left her alone. She would make excuses, telling him she needed more time to study. Sometimes they argued. Her boyfriend couldn't understand the change in Yoko's behavior and was pressuring her to move in with him. But she ruled this out, making him believe that it was her father who was paying for her studies and her apartment, so she had to finish her degree before they could start a life together.

I was about to put the key in the door when I heard Yoko's broken voice begging someone to leave. I guessed it was Dave, refusing to leave her alone. I couldn't resist the impulse to ring the bell. It was Dave who opened the door and looked at me in shock.

"I think you've got the wrong address," he said testily.

"I don't think so. This is where Yoko lives, isn't it? I study with her at the university and . . . Well, I was passing by and I decided to come up because she seemed upset today. We have an exam in a couple of days and I know that she's worried. I thought I might be able to help her out."

Dave looked at me, not knowing what to say. I took advantage of his confusion to push open the door and go inside. Yoko was sitting on the futon, her eyes reflecting her horror. She barely managed to stand before running to the bathroom. We heard her vomiting.

"This is terrible," said Dave. "Literature will be the death of her. She hasn't been eating or sleeping for so long now, she's on edge . . . I don't know what to do. What did you say your name was?"

"Thomas. I'm Thomas, and I've noticed something's not right with Yoko too. I'm worried about her."

"She's never mentioned your name to me before . . ."

"Well, we haven't been friends long. I came to the university after the course had already started."

"And where are you from?"

"I'm American. My parents forced me to study something practical, you know how it is, but in the end I rebelled and I'm here trying to study what I love, even though I'm frankly a little old for it."

He eyed me with suspicion.

"It's pretty late, don't you think? Yoko's exhausted. I'm trying to convince her to go to bed and sleep. I'll stay here, I've got plenty to study."

Just then Yoko came out of the bathroom. Her face was tense. She was trembling and could hardly walk.

"I've told your friend you need to rest. I won't let you

study tonight." The firmness in Dave's voice left no room for doubt.

I fixed my eyes on Yoko, trying to make her even more nervous. I enjoyed watching her run back to the bathroom.

"I'm a med student and . . . well, I think what's going on is psychological. My father thinks the same. This weekend I'm taking her to our house in the country. She needs to rest."

"Good idea. Is their house very far from London?"

"Near Bath."

"What a coincidence! I'll be right around there, some friends have invited me to stay."

"If you wanted to visit us, we'd be happy to have you. Do you like classical music? My mother's organized a concert. I think she's going to surprise us with a new string quartet."

"That would be wonderful—if it's no trouble."

Yoko was listening to us, propping herself up on the bathroom door. She was terrified. Her face looked like a madwoman's.

"Now if you don't mind . . . I think it's best if you leave." Dave took me by the arm and led me to the door.

I didn't resist. I followed him without protest. I was already looking forward to the weekend at Dave's house. Nothing could horrify Yoko more.

During my last visit, Nataly had asked me why I enjoyed making Yoko suffer. I'd laughed at her question, but didn't answer it. I hadn't known what to say. But now I realized that it was true. I felt infinite pleasure in watching her suffer. Her physical deterioration was proof of my power over her. I wanted to destroy her and I didn't know why.

I arrived in Bath midafternoon on Saturday. Dave's parents' house was one of those grand houses of the minor nobility. A landscaped garden led up to an ivy-covered façade with a huge wooden door where a butler was waiting. A few steps behind were Dave's parents, Mr. and Mrs. Gibs. He a doctor, she an amateur musician. They were the embodiment of the wealthy British bourgeoisie. Besides Dave, the Gibses had another son, who was under the age of fifteen and therefore could not attend the party. The British are merciless toward their children.

Dave introduced me to his parents as a good friend of Yoko's, and they accepted my presence without any further questions.

"Yoko told me off for inviting you. She says you're very busy and that you probably only accepted so as not to offend me," said Dave.

"She's very considerate, but I was already going to spend the weekend here in Bath, and it's an honor for me to be invited to your house. Your parents are charming."

"Yes, they certainly are. They adore Yoko and they're concerned about her. Do you think it's anything more than her worrying about passing her exams? I've talked to some of her friends, but they say they don't know anything, except that she's been acting very strange for a while now."

So Dave had invited me there in the hope that I'd reveal what was going on with Yoko. He was after information.

"I don't know many people at the university—as I said, I only enrolled a little while ago. And I don't know what Yoko was like before. In my opinion she's a very levelheaded person. She studies a lot and I think she has a real sense of responsibility."

"Yes, it could be that . . . Yoko's over there talking with some friends. Come on, she'll be pleased to see you."

Yoko went pale. Her hands began to tremble and the glass she was holding smashed into pieces on the floor.

"Darling!" Dave couldn't understand Yoko's reaction.

"I'm so pleased to see you. This place is beautiful. I'm so grateful to Dave for inviting me."

"Why don't you show him the garden before it gets dark?" suggested Dave, who was being called by his mother to attend to other guests.

I calmly walked up to Yoko and took her arm, gripping it tightly.

"What an excellent idea. Let's go to the garden."

We left the house and I led her to the leafiest part of the garden.

When we got there I stood in front of her and couldn't help but laugh.

"Oh, don't make that face. Aren't you pleased to see me?"

"What do you want, Thomas? How have I wronged you?"

"Don't be stupid, Yoko. You haven't done anything because there's nothing you could do to me. We'll do it here."

"What do you want to do?" she asked, her voice wavering.

"There's nothing more delightful than cheating on your lover right under his nose, don't you think? Good old Dave could never imagine you're a whore, and he's so innocent that he's invited me here not knowing anything about me. He handed me this on a silver platter. Come."

I pushed her to a bench and forced her to lie down on the marble; then I lay on top of her. She didn't say a word. She closed her eyes. The only pleasure I felt was thinking that someone might catch us, and how stupid Dave's face would look.

I wasn't that fortunate. No one saw us. So we went back to the house. Me, with the euphoria of having made her surrender to me; her, with her face smeared, her hair a mess, and her skirt stained. She wrenched away from me and ran up the stairs, presumably to her room or a bathroom, to try to erase the traces of my assault.

Mrs. Gibs's evening of music promised to be a long one. I preferred to go back to London and spend the rest of the night at Madame Agnès's. I made my apologies to Dave, who insisted I stay.

"Thank you for the invitation, but I'm due for dinner with some friends nearby. It's been wonderful to be here. The quartet is delightful."

"You'll have to come another time. Yoko would like that."

"Of course, and you should know that if you think I can help her you only have to ask."

Back in London I couldn't have felt more satisfied with how the day had gone. Although I remembered that I had caught Dave's mother, Mrs. Gibs, looking at me worriedly. She didn't like me. She didn't know why, but she couldn't hide her disapproval.

Perhaps I could have let myself be moved by Yoko's condition. I had spent months harassing her and abusing her. That day I could have pitied her and given her back her freedom. Told her that Dave was a great guy, that the Gibs family really loved her, and that she should have the chance to have a better life. Shortly after proposing to Yoko, Dave would marry her and the Gibses would have no problem helping them both pay for their studies.

Dave was a nice guy, but too innocent; I still don't understand how he didn't suspect anything about my relationship with Yoko. But there are people like that, people who don't have a bad bone in their body. Those who believe that life is nothing more than what they can see. Incapable of base thoughts.

Yes, I could have let Yoko go:

"You know something? These people are wonderful and Dave loves you. You should stop working at Madame Agnès's."

Yoko would have looked at me in shock, trembling, not knowing what would come next.

"I don't want to do you harm. I've done a lot to you, I know, but it's over. I won't say I'm sorry—what's done is done—but I'm not going to harass you anymore. Believe me, it's over."

I imagine her look of suspicion, thinking I was tricking her. But I would look into her eyes with all the sincerity I was capable of, assuring her that I was serious, that I would get out of her life. Her suspicion would turn into gratitude.

"Now I'm going, Yoko. It doesn't make sense for me to be here. Say goodbye to Dave for me. He's a good guy. He doesn't deserve to be lied to. Don't even think about returning to

Madame Agnès's. If I see you there, then I will be the one to tell him what you're doing."

"No ... I won't go back ... I promise you," she'd say in a faint voice, fearing she'd wake up from this dream.

"Goodbye, Yoko, and good luck."

"Goodbye, Thomas."

But this conversation didn't exist. I never said those words. I wouldn't give up having my own slave.

I arrived in London too late to go to Madame Agnès's, so I resigned myself to drinking at my apartment. I wasn't yet completely drunk when the beeping of my cell phone brought me back to reality. Jaime's number flashed on my screen.

"Thomas, you have to come. Dad's had another heart attack. The doctor isn't optimistic. He says Dad's heart can't take any more."

I was pleased to get Jaime's call. It was the excuse I needed to go back to New York. If I've had any virtues in life—and it's one I still have—it would be my sense of responsibility to my work, a sense of responsibility that has sometimes prevented me from doing what I wanted. But John's heart offered me the chance to leave London without having to reproach myself for unfinished work.

I called the airline and found a ticket for an early morning flight. I just had time to take a shower and throw some clothes into a suitcase. On the way to the airport I called Maggie.

"It's almost two in the morning on a Saturday. The only excuse for you to call me at this hour is to tell me you've died."

"Not yet. I'm going to New York, my father's had a heart attack. Tell Evelyn and Cooper."

"Poor thing. Anything else?"

"No, not at the moment. I'll call you when I can."

ADULTHOOD

7

It was snowing. I'd left London in the rain and found New York in the snow. I've always liked snow, even though I can't stand the cold.

I went to the house to drop off my suitcase and change my clothes before going to the hospital. María greeted me without ceremony. It had been a long time since she'd made any effort to be kind to me.

"Your father is dying. I hope you're not going to do anything to anger him—just let him go in peace," she warned me.

"The first thing I'll do when he dies is fire you," I threatened.

"That'll be up to Jaime," she said, turning her back on me.

"Make me coffee and a sandwich," I ordered her.

These confrontations with María were part of my daily life in New York. I stood under hot water in the shower. I was tired and was tempted to sleep for a while, but when I got out of the shower my cell phone was ringing nonstop.

"Where are you?" Jaime's voice was urgent.

"Just got here. I'm getting out of the shower—what's going on?"

"Dad had another heart attack. It's the second one in two days . . . Come as soon as you can."

I dressed hurriedly while eating a sandwich and calling a car company. I arrived at the hospital just as the doctor was explaining that John's only chance of survival would be from trying a new surgery.

"If you operate, will that save him?" my brother asked fearfully.

"I can't guarantee it. His heart is very weak, it might not be able to take it. But if we don't . . . then it's a matter of hours. I'm sorry," said the doctor, checking the clock out of the corner of his eye.

"That doesn't give us a lot of options," said a voice. I had trouble recognizing it as Aunt Emma's.

Emma had aged so suddenly she was almost unrecognizable. She had cut her hair and now wore it in a short bob; it had lost its golden color and was now gray, almost white. Her shoulders were slumped, her mouth a grimace. There was nothing left of the woman I'd once known.

The doctor responded after thinking for a few moments.

"I'm sorry, but I'd sooner tell you the truth. I can't guarantee that the surgery will save him, and he could die during the procedure. But if we don't operate . . . I'm sorry, I'm truly sorry."

Jaime looked at Emma, hoping she'd say something. Then he looked at me. We hadn't even greeted each other.

"I'm in favor of fighting. I don't know what you two think, but I think it's worth the risk for Dad to have the operation."

"If they don't operate he'll die within a few hours, if they do operate he still could . . . I don't know. Sometimes I think John is tired of living and would like us to leave him in peace," replied Emma.

"Yes, he's tired, but my father's not the type to retreat from battle. And I can't just let him die without doing anything," replied Jaime.

The two looked to me for my opinion. I held their gaze before replying.

"Do what you want. I won't be the one to make the decision."

Emma glared and I saw one of her hands rise up, ready to slap me. Jaime grabbed her hand and held it with the same force with which he was gritting his teeth, the effort apparent in the tension in his cheeks.

"Operate, Doctor. We'll hope for the best," he said to the doctor, who was waiting expectantly.

"Very well. If you want you can go in and talk to him for a few minutes. Then we'll operate immediately."

We went into John's room. He was lying on the bed with his body hooked up to several monitors. A nurse was attaching another electrode.

John opened his eyes and seemed to smile. Jaime went up to him and stroked his face, as Emma took his hand and held it between hers. I stayed away from the bed, standing next to the door. I felt like an observer, as if I weren't meant to be in this scene and had walked onstage at the wrong moment.

"Thomas." He spoke my name in barely a whisper.

Jaime came over and pushed me toward the bed until I was standing at its head.

"I'm so happy you're here . . ." John murmured. It was hard for him to speak.

I nodded. I had nothing to say to him. I didn't feel the need to tell him anything. This man, who seemed to have shrunk in stature from his illness and whose emaciation allowed his bones and veins to show through, was closer to death than life. I saw the effort it took for him to fix his eyes on me and speak again.

"I have always loved you, Thomas. Always." His voice barely made it out of his exhausted body.

"Dad, Thomas knows how much you love him, and he loves you too." Jaime grabbed me by the arm, forcing me to bend over John.

My brother wanted me to kiss that white cheek. He wouldn't let go of my arm, squeezing until it hurt. But I wouldn't give in, and jerked up hard until I was standing again. Emma looked at me with such hatred it almost made me laugh.

"You'll be okay, John. The doctor says they have to operate, and it'll go well, you'll see," said Emma as she stroked his face.

"Yes . . . yes . . ." whispered John, closing his eyes.

"I love you so much, Dad. Keep fighting, we all need you." Jaime's voice was firm and decisive.

John opened his eyes again and looked at us one by one. I thought he was trying to tell each of us something through that look. When he turned to me I saw the profound hurt he felt at my coldness, and his desire to communicate how much I meant to him.

They came to take him to the OR, and Jaime and Aunt Emma walked beside the bed as it was wheeled to the elevator. I followed them wordlessly. When the elevator doors opened, I saw that I was the last person John looked at.

"It'll be a long operation. We should go get coffee and something to eat," suggested Jaime, ignoring my indifference.

"Yes, coffee will do us good," agreed Emma.

We went to the hospital cafeteria and found a table. Jaime ordered coffee and some sandwiches.

The wait was unbearable to me. I was starting to feel my jet lag. I fell asleep there, sitting up, not part of Jaime and Aunt Emma's insipid conversation. I slept for a long time until Jaime's hands gripped my shoulders, urging me back to reality.

"They've just paged us. Let's go."

We went to the floor above, where the doctor who had operated on John was waiting. The moment I saw him I knew he was going to tell us that John had died. He hadn't been strong enough, and his heart had failed.

"I'm sorry . . . It wasn't possible . . ." the doctor managed to say.

Aunt Emma began to cry. She did so silently, without hysterics. I saw how Jaime was trying hard to stay standing, to hold back his tears and play the role of the strong man, the man who could bear even the death of his father because he now had to be head of the family. A family that, aside from the Spencer grandparents, now consisted only of him, Emma, and me.

Just as I was thinking about these grandparents, they appeared in the doorway. My grandfather James and grandmother Dorothy were looking at us in silence, realizing what had happened.

Jaime took charge of everything. As was to be expected of him. He asked Aunt Emma to go with the grandparents so they could all change into their mourning clothes. We went back home to wait for the body to be delivered so we could hold a wake, as we had done for my mother. Jaime wouldn't agree to a wake in an impersonal funeral home. María would prepare everything with the help of two hired assistants. The Spencer grandparents and Aunt Emma arrived before John's body did. They wore uniforms of black.

I didn't have a black suit, or so I thought. María came to my room with one, saying it was the suit I had worn for my mother's funeral. It didn't fit me well because I had lost weight, but it would do.

"These wakes are absurd," I protested as I watched María brushing down the suit.

Over the years I've relived that memory of how John died without me saying goodbye to him. I should have kissed him or held his hand before they took him to the operating room. Maybe I could have told him that I wanted with all my heart for the operation to go well, that I was there for him. But I let him die with no kind farewell, not a single reassuring gesture.

I could have said something like:

"Dad, I'm here because I want to be with you. Don't worry, you'll pull through this." Or maybe, *"Dad, I need you. Don't*

*leave me alone. I've done a lot of stupid things, but you know I
love you."*

But not one of these words came from my mouth. I said nothing
to ease his pain, or honor his wish that I show him some shred
of affection.

His last look had been for me and all he saw was nothing-
ness. Do I regret it? No, I don't regret it, even though I know
he deserved at least a glimpse of kindness from me. He never let
me down, he loved me all his life. But that wasn't something I
thought about, because the anger that courses through me has
always been far stronger.

Jaime called the family's closest friends. He'd also asked Miss
Turner, John's secretary, to tell John's most important clients
and associates. The wake would begin at three in the afternoon.

Esther was the first to arrive. María welcomed her warmly,
telling her the wake would be held in the main living room.
Esther hugged Jaime first, and I was filled with hatred as I
watched them lose themselves in each other's arms. When she
came over to me I stopped her from touching me. She didn't
seem to mind, just shrugged her shoulders. My bad mood was
met only with her indifference, which just increased my anger.

At that moment Aunt Emma entered the room, and on seeing
Esther embraced her.

"So kind of you . . . Thank you for being with us."

After Esther came the partners from John's office. My grandfather James stood in the hall to welcome all the family friends. I
noticed how old he was. He was supporting himself with a cane.
His fragility was unmistakable.

When there were enough people that my absence could pass
unnoticed, I went to my room. I was tired and needed to sleep

for a couple of hours. I locked my door. In my sleep, I thought I heard Jaime's voice calling me, and even my grandmother Dorothy's. But I paid no attention. I couldn't open my eyes. It was around eight when I woke up.

I'd fallen asleep on top of the covers, so I took a shower and changed my clothes before going to the kitchen in search of a cup of tea. Esther was there helping the two girls we'd hired to work with María. They were arranging canapés on trays.

It irritated me that the wake had to be held at our home.

Esther didn't even look at me. She was absorbed in making sure that everything went well. The two girls were asking her what to do and how to do it, and she showed them which canapés to prepare, how to distribute the sandwiches, and where to put the trays with coffee. Every so often she left the kitchen, then quickly returned with an empty tray or to fulfill a request to make another pot of coffee.

Jaime came into the kitchen but didn't see me. I watched as he went to Esther and took both her hands in his, looking at her with such intensity that I thought he was about to cry.

"Thank you. You're helping us so much. Aunt Emma can't cope, my grandmother doesn't even know what she's doing here, and my grandfather . . . But if you have to go—well, I don't want you to feel obligated."

"Let me feel useful. And don't worry, there's nowhere more important for me to be right now than with your family. There are so many people that it's difficult to see to them all properly. You should convince your grandfather to rest awhile. He's worn out."

"You're right. You know something, Esther? You're . . . you really are wonderful. Thank you."

As soon as Jaime left the kitchen I went straight to her.

"You're *so* wonderful . . . You have my brother wrapped around your little finger. When's the wedding?"

Esther left the tray she'd been preparing on the counter and looked me up and down. A grimace of contempt spread across her lips.

"What are you doing here, Thomas? Why did you come?"

"I don't understand—"

"Of course you understand. Your presence here is unnecessary. You didn't love John, you don't feel like you belong to this family. Nobody matters to you and you've stopped mattering to anybody else. I mean it: your presence here is unnecessary."

She spoke so harshly that I found it hard to recognize the Esther I'd always known.

"This is my house. Or have you forgotten that?"

"This was John's and your mother's home, and your brother's too. None of them matter to you. You've never loved them and you don't want them. You couldn't even take John's hand at the hospital, even though you knew his life was at stake."

"Did Jaime tell you that?"

"What does it matter who told me? That's not the issue, Thomas: the issue is this evil that lives in you. I've always known you weren't a nice person, but I thought that somewhere in all the shadow in you there was still some ray of light, and that over time you would make peace with yourself and appreciate those who have loved you."

"You loved me, Esther."

"Yes, Thomas, I loved you very much. You know that."

"And now?"

"Now we've all chosen our own path."

"Are you in love with Jaime?" I asked irritably.

"If I gave in to my feelings . . . then yes, I know that Jaime and I could be happy together. But you're you, Thomas, and that will stop Jaime from doing anything."

"Would it stop you?"

"Not anymore."

"Get out, Esther—you're not needed here." I grabbed her hand and pulled her into the hall, ready to throw her out.

My grandfather saw us and, in spite of his clumsy movements, came up to us angrily, incensed by my behavior.

"Let her go! What are you doing?"

"I want her to leave."

"How could you say that? Esther is someone we all love. Don't you dare tell her to leave," he said.

"It's my home!"

"It's the Spencers' home. First it was mine, then your father's, and now it will be Jaime's," he said, holding my gaze.

His words wounded me deeply. James Spencer had put me in my place. I saw the pain in his eyes, but at the same time his determination.

Esther looked at us, distraught. She hesitated, not knowing what to do, but my grandfather didn't give her a choice.

"If you don't mind, Esther, please go back to helping María. And thank you for allowing us to rely on you," my grandfather said to her.

When Esther returned to the kitchen we remained alone in the hall, face-to-face. Some of the people who had witnessed our argument had tactfully returned to the living room.

"I never thought I'd have to say this to you, but the time has come for you to make a decision: either you're in or you're out of this family. I'm not going to allow you to keep hurting the people who've given you nothing but love. We don't owe you anything, Thomas, absolutely nothing, so we're not going to put up with you anymore. You decide—take it or leave it. But if you do decide to stay, there will be conditions, the kind your mother and John never dared impose on you. You will change. You will behave like the best brother in the world to Jaime, you will show affection to your aunt Emma, and you will treat your grandmother and me with respect. If you cannot or you will not do that, then don't bother staying here a minute longer. Get your things and go. The sooner the better. I've already told you, we don't need you."

"I'm not one of you," I responded with a sneer.

"That's something you yourself decided a long time ago." My grandfather's voice was so harsh, it seemed at odds with the kind man he had always been.

I didn't know what to do. Out of pride, perhaps for the sake of dignity, I should have left right then and there. But I didn't. I was aware of how empty my life would be if I allowed myself to be kicked out of the only family I had known. Everything I'd done up to that moment I had done only because I knew there were people behind me. The Spencers were like a safety net above which I could walk a tightrope, knowing that if I fell they would catch me. They had endured my insults, the hostility I had shown them, all the cruelty I was capable of mustering. And the only reason they had endured any of that was because John wouldn't let them cut me out of their lives. John had protected me, even from myself.

I hadn't understood this until that moment. I realized that the net had been pulled out from under me and I had to tread carefully, because if I fell there would be no one to help me.

My grandfather continued looking at me, motionless, waiting for me to be the one to make the next move. He could barely stand. His age manifested itself in every pore of his skin.

"Understood," I agreed.

"Then I have nothing more to say to you." He turned his back on me and returned to the living room, just as Jaime was walking out to say goodbye to one of John's friends.

Jaime seemed to ignore me. His eyes wouldn't meet mine. He treated me like someone who wasn't worth the effort to consider. This set off all my alarm bells. Aunt Emma had given me up for lost a long time ago. Now I knew the Spencer grandparents had as well. Jaime had followed them. I was becoming a stranger in the very home I had called my own. We had reached a point where it would cost them nothing to get rid of me. They'd even welcome my absence, since my presence warped their peaceful lives.

My brother went back into the living room. I was stuck where I was, unable to react. And then I saw her. Yes, Esther was still there. She hadn't returned to the kitchen, just stepped back a couple of paces to let us talk. She came up to me and hugged me, and I let her.

"Come on, let's go to the kitchen and have a cup of coffee. It'll do you good."

"Thank you for the invitation. As you've heard, this is no longer my home."

"Thomas, your grandfather is right. You all can't go on like this. It makes no sense. No human should have to endure being hurt by another. They have given you so much love."

"You loved me too."

"Yes, Thomas, I did too. And I would have liked to keep doing so, but you wouldn't let me. The truth is you won't allow anyone to love you—it's as if it scares you to receive someone else's love."

I felt lost. I could never have admitted this to anyone, but I was never capable of pretending with Esther. I let her take me to the kitchen, sat where she told me to and drank a cup of coffee. Esther watched me. There was no compassion in her expression, but neither was there sorrow.

"What do you think I should do now?" I asked, eager for her answer.

"It's tough . . . They've had enough. They have good reason. You've cut the cord, Thomas."

"So today I cut the cord by trying to throw you out of here." By placing the blame on her I'd make her the one responsible for my situation.

"I hope I'm not the one to blame . . . I think that cord was cut a long time ago, but John stopped them from letting it show. He loved you and wouldn't let anyone go against you."

"There was no reason for him to love me," I replied angrily, as if John's love had been a burden.

"Nobody can control their feelings or emotions. He loved

you and that's that. To John you were always his first son, the son of his beloved Carmela. The mere fact that he loved her made him love you too. You know what, Thomas? Life has been generous to you, but you haven't been generous to the ones who gave you everything."

I broke down in tears. It was the only time I've ever cried in my life. I don't know why I cried, but I did. Esther embraced me and cried with me.

María came into the kitchen and was surprised to see us hugging, fighting back the tears. She said nothing. She picked up a tray and returned to the living room, gesturing to the two servers to do their work and leave us alone.

We hugged each other for a long time. Long enough for Jaime to see us. He came into the kitchen for ice and stood there for a minute, not moving. His face showed something like pain and betrayal, but he said nothing. He turned around and left the kitchen.

"I don't know what to do," I said to Esther quietly.

"I think you should go back to the living room and go to your grandfather. Give him a hug. You don't need to say anything, that will be enough."

"I don't know if I can do that. I . . . I feel nothing. That's the way I am. The truth is you're the only one I love, the only one I can count on." I started to sob again and Esther held me tightly.

Over the years, I have learned that women are capable of the greatest sacrifices if they think them necessary. They can give up everything, even happiness, to act as heroines in the theater of their own lives. My tears brought me back to Esther, they were what joined her to me forever. No word, no other gesture could have convinced her to come back to me. My tears were the only argument needed to break down her determination.

She came with me to the living room and waited in the doorway as I went up to my grandfather, but he just waved me away.

Jaime, meanwhile, continued to ignore me. I looked at Esther; I needed her to bear witness to these snubs. I went back to her.

"It's over," I said, trying to solicit her pity.

"You've brought it upon yourself, Thomas. But . . . well, now's not the time for reprimands. Look after your father's friends, try to be discreet, and we'll hope that they all leave soon so you can talk to your family," advised Esther.

I decided not to defy her. I did as she told me, though I was starting to feel vertigo from the emptiness the Spencers had opened up beneath me. It was around ten when the last guest left. My grandfather sat in an armchair and buried his head in his hands. My grandmother caressed his neck. Her mind had gone, and she didn't understand what was happening.

"Dad, you have to rest. María has set up the guest room for you both," said Emma.

"Are you going home?" asked my grandfather.

"No, I'll stay here. I'll keep vigil over John."

"I'll do it with you," said my grandfather, looking at his daughter.

"We'll take turns," Jaime interrupted. "You can stay awhile, no more than a couple of hours, then you have to sleep. Aunt Emma and I will stay the rest of the night."

"I also want to keep vigil for . . . for John," I said, taking a step toward Jaime. Esther had actually been the one to suggest I do this.

"That won't be necessary. No need to concern yourself," replied Jaime, his voice tense.

"I want to do it," I insisted.

"John would have preferred you to show a little more love when he was alive—it's too late now," Emma said scornfully, looking me up and down.

I was about to throw some insult at her but I decided against it. Esther was watching us and I didn't want to make a misstep in case I lost her again. I took a deep breath before replying.

"Now's not the time for reprimands, least of all with John's body here, don't you think? If you'll let me, I'd like to spend some time with him."

"We'd prefer to be alone," declared my grandfather.

My grandmother looked at us in amazement; she didn't seem to understand what was going on.

"S-so . . ." I stammered.

"The burial will be tomorrow at ten. We won't stop you from coming if you want to, but until then we don't want you here." My grandfather stood up, indicating that I should leave.

Esther came up and took my hand. We left the living room, feeling Jaime's eyes upon us.

"Pack some things in a suitcase right now," Esther ordered me.

"A suitcase?" I asked in surprise.

"You can't stay here anymore, Thomas, it's over. I thought there was still a chance, but there isn't. Maybe with time, but not now."

She came to my room with me and helped me to put all the clothes I thought I'd need in my suitcase. I let her do it. I was more upset than I wanted to admit. They'd kicked me out. They were getting rid of me.

We left what had been my home with me not fully comprehending what was happening to me.

It was cold outside. We walked a long time. I threw down my suitcase as I began to feel a wave of fury come over me. I started to turn around to head back and yell that I wouldn't let them throw me out, but then a taxi appeared. Esther flagged it down.

We got into the car and she gave the driver an address in Nolita. I only then realized that I hadn't asked her where we were going.

"We're going to my place."

"But you don't live in Nolita," I replied, confused.

"I've lived there for a couple of weeks now."

"But what about your parents?" It seemed incredible to me that Esther would have moved out of her family home.

"Well, they encouraged me. At some point I had to start living my own life. I earn enough to look after myself. The apartment is small but the area isn't bad."

The apartment wasn't as small as she'd said. At least it was bigger than Yoko's. Esther had decorated it tastefully. She'd painted the walls beige and the furniture was modern and functional. The main room was big enough to be divided into three spaces. On one side there was a sofa behind a coffee table, on another was a dining table with four chairs, and in a corner next to the window stood a desk. As well as the bedroom there was a bathroom and a kitchen with a couple of barstools behind the counter.

"It's perfect," I said, and meant it.

"I did it up myself. Well, my brother helped. I like it."

"I like it too. Thank you for letting me stay, at least for tonight . . ."

"You can stay as long as you want."

We slept together. Esther didn't feel she could turn me down after I'd planted the idea in her mind that she'd been the catalyst for my grandfather kicking me out of the family home.

She woke me up at six with a cup of coffee. She had dark circles under her eyes. I didn't look great either.

"You have to go back home and go with them to the church and the cemetery."

"I won't be welcome."

"Even so, you should do it. They'll appreciate the gesture."

"Will you come with me?" I tried to make my request sound like a plea.

"Of course. I told the agency yesterday that I wouldn't be in this morning. But as soon as the service is over at the cemetery I'll have to leave. I have a meeting with some clients at three."

When we reached West Seventy-Second Street we found some friends of John's at the apartment; my mother's parents, Stella and Ramón, and my uncle, Oswaldo, were also there. My grandfather James wouldn't even look at me. I swallowed his indifference with a twinge of uneasiness in my stomach. My grandmother Dorothy gave me a kiss, light as a breeze and lightning fast, as if she feared angering my grandfather.

My brother was standing in front of John's casket. He looked exhausted. He seemed lost in his grief. Esther came up to him and gave him a kiss that he didn't reject. Then they sat in front of the casket. They were speaking too low for me to hear, but I could feel them looking at me every so often. It bothered me that Esther would talk about me with Jaime.

I sat in a corner and accepted the condolences of all those arriving. As far as those people were concerned I was the son of John Spencer.

Emma, with the help of María and the two servers, went back and forth across the room, making sure that everyone had coffee and cake.

I was distractedly listening to one of John's partners telling me what good friends they had been and how they enjoyed playing golf together when I felt Jaime's hand on my shoulder. He asked me to come with him and I followed him to his room.

"I'm grateful that you came, though I imagine this was Esther's doing."

I couldn't be bothered to lie to him, so I didn't reply and remained silent.

"Last night I was talking to Grandpa and Aunt Emma. They think that the way you've behaved, it's not right. It wasn't right when Mama got sick and it wasn't right with Dad. Your indifference hurts, you know that? But even so, Mama always loved you and Dad did too—he'd never allow you to be thrown out of here. If you want to come back . . . I wouldn't object."

That was how Jaime was. I was tempted to say I'd come back, but I didn't. I had the chance to conquer Esther, to take her away forever. It would be a relief to her if the Spencers were to welcome me back, but that didn't suit my plans.

"Yes, I suppose that John wouldn't have allowed you all to throw me out like a dog," I said bitterly.

"Don't say that . . . Grandpa got angry when he saw how you were treating Esther. We've kept quiet about a lot of things all this time. We've put up with you treating us as if we were less than nothing, keeping your distance, making us see that you don't consider us your family. Grandpa snapped. That's understandable. He's very upset about Dad's death."

"And what about me?"

"You didn't love Dad, or at least you did everything possible not to love him. You offended him so many times . . . He never understood your heartlessness and always hoped that you would change, that the anger eating you up inside would eventually disappear. You know something? When he saw that Esther and I—well, that we got along, he asked me to give her up. He even told me he wouldn't forgive me if I hurt you. He was always looking for some display of affection from you, but you wouldn't even give him that, even when he was on his deathbed. You were the last person he looked at. He would have wanted you so badly to be near him and to give him a kiss."

I was surprised that Jaime had also noticed what was obvious to me—that when John was looking at me he was begging for affection. I was also irritated by what Jaime was saying about giving up Esther to please his father.

"Esther's old enough to decide who she wants to be with, don't you think? You didn't give anything up—she was the one who decided," I insisted, not feeling as much certainty as my words seemed to indicate.

"We're not going to argue—I just wanted to tell you that you can come home."

"But I'm not going to. I don't owe you people anything. I imagine that John left this place to you since it belonged to the grandparents. It's the Spencer home."

"It is, and that's why it's always been your home too. I don't know what's in Dad's will. We've got an appointment with the lawyer tomorrow and you should be there, obviously. Think about it. I don't mind if you live here."

"Stop being the good little boy. I don't need your charity."

"It's up to you. Now let's go back to the living room. We have to be at the church in half an hour for the funeral and then we have to go to the cemetery."

We went through all the prescribed rituals. I stood next to Esther, away from the family. She took my arm out of some desire to protect me. When we left the cemetery I didn't even say goodbye to my grandparents or Jaime. Aunt Emma watched me go but also made no move to say goodbye.

"You should go kiss your aunt and your grandparents," Esther suggested.

"They've put me through too much humiliation. Don't ask me to do things I don't want to."

It was midday and I suggested that we have lunch before she went back to work. I could tell she was impatient, so I made do with buying a couple of hot dogs from a street vendor and we ate them as we walked to the ad agency where she worked.

"I'll try not to be home too late," she said by way of goodbye.

I went to buy flowers, candy, and fruit to kill time until it was dinner.

I thought about unpacking my suitcase and hanging my clothes up in the closet, but I decided to be cautious. I should let Esther be the one to ask me to do that. I shouldn't pressure her, no matter how certain I was that I needed to convince her to marry me.

Maggie phoned me to fill me in on the calls I'd received and to pass on some admin issues, then she put Cooper on.

"I've had an interview with the olive oil company. They want us to present a campaign strategy to them in a week. I've got this young friend who's just finished his studies in advertising—I was thinking about hiring him. We need someone to help out."

"Absolutely not! We can't allow ourselves to have employees. We'll have to do the work ourselves."

"But you're in New York, Evelyn's spending the week with Roy, and I can't do it all," protested Cooper.

"The most I can allow is for you to hire him specifically for this campaign. If you really need ideas for the olive oil campaign then bring him in, but for that project only. I don't want to have to pay him a salary at the end of the month."

He accepted, relieved. That was the good thing about Cooper—he wouldn't defy me.

He also told me that Evelyn had been arguing with the Rural Party's communications team. They had wanted Roy and Suzi to spend their weekend visiting voters for a report to be broadcast on television. The idea was to present Roy as a man in touch with his constituents. But Suzi had refused and Evelyn knew that it was useless to try to force her. So she had faced the head of the party's communications team and ordered him not to organize any kind of event unless she gave the go-ahead. The guy ended up agreeing after Roy openly supported Evelyn.

None of that particularly interested me. All routine, though it would be good for us to win the olive oil campaign; at least then we'd have another source of income.

I was getting impatient waiting for Esther to come home. It occurred to me that I could take her out to dinner, but then I thought she might be tired, so I decided to add smoked salmon and French foie gras to the candy and flowers I'd already bought.

I set the table and then looked for the right music in Esther's CD collection. Leonard Cohen would be perfect for the occasion.

When I heard her key in the lock I hurried to the door. She seemed tired, and surprised to see the table set.

"Wow, so you made dinner . . ."

"I just bought a couple of things. I thought you'd be too tired to eat out," I replied, trying to display a sincere smile.

"I have to work. The client isn't convinced by the campaign I showed him," she said brusquely.

"I can help you. Though not much—the little about advertising I did learn was at Paul Hard's school . . ."

"I'm going to take a shower. Then we'll eat something and I'll get to work. You should rest too, you've got to go see the lawyer tomorrow."

She went into the bathroom as I swallowed and counted to ten so as not to say anything that could make her angry.

As we had dinner she relaxed, and even complimented the salmon.

"You spent a fortune on this salmon."

"Don't exaggerate, it's not bad but it's not the best either."

She showed me the washing machine campaign. It looked good to me, but apparently the manufacturer hadn't liked that Esther had opted to show a man extolling the washer's great qualities and ease of use.

"The idiot doesn't realize that women like to believe that their husbands are willing to lend a hand, and that men will feel useful just by seeing an ad," she complained.

"Go for broke. Tell him you have no intention of changing it, that he's making a mistake if he rejects it."

"What world are you living in? I'd be fired. You know how it is, the customer's always right."

"Then send them packing and work with me. You know I've started my own agency in London and I want to have an office in New York. You could run it."

She looked at me in surprise, as if she could not understand my determination to keep her close.

"That wouldn't be a good idea. And it isn't that easy to get clients."

I was about to tell her that the Spencers would help me, but I stopped myself. I had to accept the fact that I could no longer count on them. In the past, my grandfather could have handed me any number of clients, but I could no longer ask him to do that. I was the one who had removed myself from the family. Esther knew that. I don't know what she read in my expression, but she took my hand and held it as if she were trying to give me strength.

"Your offer is tempting but impossible; nobody's ever going to award a campaign to an unknown agency."

"We could try. If I made it happen in London there's no reason it should fail here."

We talked late into the night. I don't know how it happened, but Esther did agree to get on board with my proposal. Together we decided that we could also do with Paul Hard's help; at the end of the day he knew the business better than both of us.

Luck was on my side. John had been generous to me in his will.

He'd left me a decent sum of money and stocks. As was to be imagined, however, the residence went to Jaime, although the will stipulated that I could live there for as long as I needed to get myself organized.

My brother and I barely talked as the lawyer read us the will. When we'd arrived we had nodded to each other, and once he'd finished reading us the terms of the will I didn't stay in the office a moment longer than I needed to.

"Your father always relied on our advice for his investments. In fact, you have a fund that he set up when you were a child, which has seen excellent earnings. I hope you will grant us your confidence and allow us to continue managing your inheritance," explained the lawyer, satisfied with his good judgment in investing the money.

"For now I'll leave things as they are," I agreed, not making any further promises.

Thanks to John I was rich. Not very rich, but rich enough that, if I didn't waste it, I could live comfortably for the rest of my life. I could even splurge a little bit, I told myself.

I couldn't let Esther see that I was practically feeling happy. The next few weeks went by very quickly. Esther resigned from her agency, and while she took charge of looking for an office in SoHo, I convinced Paul Hard to join us. He no longer had any prestige, but he knew which doors to knock on and he still had a decent amount of talent, despite his alcoholism. As for Esther, she felt obliged to make things up to me after the loss of the Spencers. She became protective of me because she thought I was lost, and I acted as if I truly were defenseless.

Things couldn't have been going better for me. Cooper called to say that we'd gotten the olive oil campaign.

Paul Hard guided us with his advice. He was an old fox who knew the ad world like the back of his hand.

I believed that the pieces of my new life were starting to come together. I had what I wanted: Esther, who by now had made space for me in her bed. Sex with her never really did it for me, and I have to be honest and admit that I didn't do it for her either. But she mattered to me too much for this to be an obstacle.

We didn't satisfy each other, we never did, and to this day I still haven't figured out why. Perhaps that is why I wasn't surprised when one day I happened to see Esther crossing the street with Jaime.

I hadn't seen my brother since the reading of the will. Neither of us had called the other. I didn't know anything about my grandparents or Aunt Emma either. I hadn't even given in to the temptation of going to my parents' home to find the rest of my things. Esther said that perhaps, deep down, I didn't want to break all the ties that connected me with my family. She was wrong. The truth was there was nothing there that felt like my own. As for the clothes, I didn't really need the things I'd left in the closet; I substituted new ones for them. And there was nothing in my room that held any special value for me.

Esther ran the agency, and it wasn't unusual for her to have meetings with clients away from the office. But that afternoon she had seemed strange, evasive.

"I have to meet a potential client, I'll be home late for dinner," she said by way of apology.

Perhaps it was her tone of voice, or that she wouldn't look

me in the eye and barely gave me a chance to ask about the client she was referring to. As I had predicted, the business wasn't doing too badly. We'd won a bid for the account of a new chain of burger joints. Paul Hard was a genius when it came to figuring out what companies needed from a campaign. We were also running a TV campaign to advertise thermal T-shirts. It wasn't much, but it was better than nothing, and we could say that we were part of the game in the Big Apple.

I decided to follow her. She didn't notice. It didn't even occur to her that I would be capable of doing something like that. But I did it.

She was walking quickly, impatiently. She met Jaime three blocks from our office. My blood ran cold when I saw them embrace so intensely it seemed that time had frozen. He took her hand and led her to a nearby bar where they sat down inside. They had their backs to the window, which allowed me to watch them without them seeing me.

Esther gestured with her hands, agitated, and Jaime put his hand on her shoulder and pulled her toward him. She didn't resist.

I don't know what they talked about, but Esther cried. I know because I saw her look for a Kleenex in her bag, and dab her eyes with it as Jaime stroked her hair.

They loved each other. Even watching them from behind, it was obvious to me. I felt anger run down my spine, and a bitter taste filled my throat.

They were there for two hours, two hours in which I watched them, pacing from one end of the street to the other to avoid them noticing me. I felt numb. Every so often the waitress approached them and I imagined that they would order something to drink to appease her. First coffee, then whiskey, followed by a second round of whiskey. It was past seven thirty when they stood up. I had to speed up and find another spot from where I could watch them. They walked on, unaware of my presence. Jaime hailed a taxi for Esther and they said good-bye with a light kiss on the lips.

I saw my brother walk away with his shoulders sunk and his face drained of all color. The face of a loser. If Esther had given him any hope, Jaime would have been smiling.

I didn't hurry home. I wanted her to wonder where I was, to get worried. When I opened the door she was sitting at the computer. She seemed absorbed in her work.

"How did it go?" I asked.

She shrugged; then she bit her bottom lip and, after hesitating for a few seconds, she spoke.

"I've been with Jaime." And as she said that she looked at me with an expression that was midway between fearful and defiant.

I stayed silent. I hadn't expected her confession and I didn't want to say anything I'd regret.

"We had coffee. He's good and so are your grandparents. Your aunt Emma went to Europe with a friend of hers, another widow. I think they're in France right now," she continued, not looking at me.

"I'm pleased they're doing well," I said curtly.

"In spite of it all . . . Anyway, they keep wondering how you're doing."

"They kicked me out, remember?"

"That happened in a moment of stress. It's tough for parents—parents who are already old themselves—to have to bury their child, and your grandparents were devastated. As for Jaime . . . He was so hurt by your aloofness."

Esther's words alarmed me; if I were to forgive my family, this could be the prelude to her changing her mind about our relationship. I tried hard not to allow room for excuses.

"Things haven't been easy for me either. You know that better than anybody. My mother's lie really affected me—it threw my whole existence into question. I was left not knowing who I was, without a place in the world." I said this with conviction, trying to appeal to her. It worked.

Esther stood up and came over to me. She looked at me sadly before hugging me. Her embrace was maternal—there was no trace of the passion with which she'd embraced Jaime. I didn't move and she, noting my coldness, went back to sit in front of the computer.

"I have work to do. Tomorrow we have a meeting with that dog food company. It's the first time we're meeting with them, but I want to present them some ideas. Can you help me?"

I agreed. We worked for a couple of hours, which served to create some emotional distance between the two of us. When we went to bed I noticed that Esther was trying not to touch me. She must have still felt Jaime's lips against her own. If she had been any other woman I would have reveled in forcing her to have sex with me, but I had no power over Esther and I didn't want to give her any motive to go running to my brother. I could only hope that the shadow of Jaime was fading.

If I had been a different kind of person I would have packed up my things in a suitcase that night and left forever. Yes, I could have allowed her to be happy. But I didn't. Even today I can imagine the amazement and gratitude that would have spread over her face if I had shown such generosity. The scene could have happened like this:

"You know something, Esther? I love you too much to stop you from being truly happy. You love Jaime and he loves you—well, you two should make a go of it. You don't have to worry about me. I know that John made Jaime promise that he wouldn't come between you and me, and my brother is the type who'd sooner die than break his word. But it's the twenty-first century, and there's no place for that sense of honor. I'm leaving. I want you to be happy, at least to try, and if things don't work out . . . well, you know what Lauren Bacall said to Humphrey Bogart: Just whistle."

Esther would have embraced me with gratitude.

"I love you too, Thomas, it's just that . . . I don't know what's happened between us, but the truth is I don't love you in the same way anymore. Jaime . . . well, you know your brother, he's suffering, but he won't break the promise he made to your father. There's only one way of convincing him. Perhaps if you were the one to release him from this burden . . ."

If I had loved Esther as she deserved, I would have dialed my brother's number. Jaime would have been startled to hear my voice at that time of night and his stomach would have dropped as he heard me say that I'd never forgive him if he didn't make Esther happy.

But I didn't do that. I spent the rest of the night feeling the warmth of her body near mine, knowing that her sleep was racked by suffering.

I let a few days go by before I asked her to marry me. She listened to me in silence, not showing any emotion.

"Let's leave things as they are. I don't want to get married," she replied.

"I love you, you know that. I'm lost without you."

"I know you love me, but we don't need to get married. I'd prefer to continue as we are." The flaring of her nostrils revealed her discomfort.

"Well, we could at least move into a bigger apartment in a better part of Manhattan. What do you think?"

"I'm fine here. This is my first home, which I've been paying for through my own work. You're used to nicer places. I won't get mad if you decide to leave."

"No, Esther, I don't want to leave. I like this place too, but I thought it would be better for us to have someplace where we could host our best clients—you know, do the social side of business—but if that doesn't matter to you then it doesn't matter to me either."

I was lying, of course. I didn't enjoy living in Nolita. I wanted us to move somewhere around Madison or Fifth Avenue . . . I'd seen a couple of apartments on the Upper East Side with enough space not only to host clients, but also for Esther and I not to be always in each other's way. Sometimes I missed not having my own space to work. But it was clear that I had to pay a price to be with her and that any mistake I made could be decisive, so I didn't ask her to move again.

I wondered why I was this dependent on Esther, whom I never wanted to defy. Paul Hard gave me the key to understanding the matter one day at lunch, over a good bottle of Burgundy, though at the time his idea seemed crazy to me. Only with the passage of time have I come to see that good old Hard was right.

Paul knew the two of us well. He thought particularly highly of Esther, who, in addition to running our advertising agency, had helped give his school a veneer of respectability. She made him invest some of the money he'd earned at our agency into fixing up the academy and hiring a couple more instructors better qualified than the ones who had taught us. She even designed an ad page that made Paul's school look like an academically acceptable place.

"Esther calls the shots for both of us," he said to me as he finished off his glass of wine.

"You think so?"

"What I don't understand is why she's with you—or you with her."

I didn't like what he was saying.

"Hey, just because you've been divorced three times doesn't mean we all have to screw up our relationships. We love each other and that's that."

"You love each other? I mean, I wouldn't say you two behave like a couple in love."

"Well, we are," I said, annoyed.

"No, I don't think so. Esther acts like your mother and you let yourself go along with it. Even if there are times you could push back against her, you don't, as if you're afraid she'd get mad."

"You don't know what you're talking about," I protested through forced laughter. "I assure you, when I look at Esther I don't exactly see my mother. I don't like to make big speeches, but I will say that she's the woman for me."

"You know something? I don't know much about your life, but I still remember the day you all graduated. Your mother was a very beautiful woman and she seemed to be devoted to you, hoping you would pay her some attention. It seemed that you were bothered by her being there. And then that girl, Lisa . . . She was a real piece of work. She hated Esther. She was jealous of her."

"Jealous? How dumb. What bothered Lisa about Esther was that she was at the top of the class. Both Lisa and I knew we weren't exactly great students."

"You're wrong. What bothered Lisa was that you seemed to respect and confide in Esther more than anybody else. It was clear that you didn't get along with your family, especially your mother. But we all need a mother and Esther seemed to fill that role for you. She's still doing it. The truth is she's the person you can always turn to. Protective, loyal, generous. Just like a mother. There are women who are actually playing the role of mother to the men they live with and have children with. They end up confusing love with the maternal instinct. That's the way they are."

"I didn't know you were a fan of dime-store psychology. If that's your conclusion, you couldn't be more wrong. I adore Esther."

That conversation with Paul made me reflect on my relationship with Esther. But I completely rejected everything he'd said to me. I flat-out refused to accept his opinion. If I had gone to any of those overpriced psychiatrists on Fifth Avenue I'm sure they would have diagnosed me along the same lines that Paul did: I didn't get along well with my mother but I still needed one—someone whom I could confide in, who would accept my faults, who would sacrifice herself for me, renounce her own life so that I could be happy. That woman was Esther. That's why I needed her so desperately. Even though I didn't want to admit it, deep down I'd always feared that the maternal instinct that Paul talked about wouldn't last forever. Many years have passed since that conversation with Paul, and from this side of history I have to admit that he was right. That, I've come to realize, was the reason behind the permanent lack of sexual tension between Esther and me. But back then I couldn't even consider the possibility.

If reality didn't agree with me, too bad for reality.

The truth is that I was compensating for the sexual dissatisfaction I felt with Esther with countless other obliging girls whom I'd promised a shot in the Big Apple.

Paul was very familiar with the agencies that provided models for commercials. They had everyone, from charming grandmas to babies, not to mention statuesque young girls who dreamed of being supermodels.

Some of these girls, ambitious to a fault, couldn't achieve their dreams, so they ended up becoming occasional companions to men like me.

The only problem was that I had to meet these girls in hotels, and I was worried that someone I knew might see me and mention it to Esther.

We took on an ad campaign for laundry detergent, and in the lineup of models there was one who caught my eye. She was Japanese and I was quite taken with her for a couple of months. Her name was Misaki and she was around forty years old. It was actually Esther who chose her.

Misaki was surprisingly tall. Slim and angular, with hair as black as night and pearl-like skin. When I saw her during the filming of the detergent commercial I made up my mind to sleep with her. She didn't look like Yoko, but even so she reminded me of her. I longed for Yoko, so much so that at times I was tempted to call her to hear the alarm and terror in her voice. I imagined that my absence would have helped her to gain back some of her health, and that annoyed me greatly. But I couldn't leave New York until I was certain that my relationship with Esther wouldn't change. So for almost a year I didn't leave Esther's side, apart from my jaunts with the girls from the ads.

There was one modeling agency in particular, Zafiro, that managed to get some of the most gorgeous models in the city. I usually insisted on using their girls for our ads.

Sometimes I would see one of those girls in gossip magazines, hanging off the arm of some actor or some businessman freshly arrived in the city. I smiled, thinking about how they had been in my bed just as they were now in the beds of their new companions.

I became most taken with Olivia. Slim, with white skin and immense green eyes, she caught people's attention. The daughter of an Italian mother and a Swiss father, she had moved to New York because she was desperate to be an actress. When I met her she had appeared in only a couple of TV spots and played a small role in one film, and she still hadn't managed to distinguish herself from the hundreds of beauties like her who were fighting tooth and nail to get to the top of their profession. In her case, her handicap was her height.

She was no more than five foot five, too short to be on the runways, and she had no particular talent for acting either. But she never gave in, so besides the ads she made her living providing company to old guys or lost souls like myself. Five hundred dollars for an hour of company was good pay for someone whose only merit was her ephemeral beauty.

I met Olivia thanks to Esther; she picked her for the ad that would help us make our name in New York. Our success was assured when it won Commercial of the Year at the Effie Awards. The ad had been Esther and Paul's work—a small insurance company that wanted to go big had hired us for it.

I focused on negotiating contracts and handling the management side of the business, while Esther and Paul concentrated on the creative work.

Esther was looking for two women for the ad, one representing the American Midwest, and another with a more ambiguously ethnic look. Olivia attended the casting call, and neither Esther nor Paul hesitated in choosing her.

If I hadn't gotten there first, Paul would have been the one who ended up enjoying Olivia.

Olivia would also benefit from the award we received for the commercial, though this was more because guys wanted to sleep with her than because it did anything to advance her dream of becoming the next top model.

Esther was anxious as the Effie gala approached. We knew through Paul that the jury had liked our ad, but the world doesn't work fairly—the award doesn't normally go to the best, but to whoever did the best job gaining the goodwill of others.

Paul assured us that we had every chance, and for several weeks he had been immersed in a flurry of activity for which we received barely any explanation. But the bills he was running up for lunches and dinners at high-end restaurants gave me a shock. So much so that I had to talk to him.

"You know, I wouldn't mind having lunch several times a week at Balthazar or Cipriani either, not to mention champagne at the Plaza," I said, handing him the bills that had been piling up on my desk.

"I'm sure you wouldn't, but you don't have an excuse and I do. You think they're going to give us the award just because Esther made a great ad? Of course not. The members like it, they say it's the best of the year, but that doesn't mean we're going to win. You're old enough to know how these things work."

I resigned myself to his explanation, though I did order him to find less pricey places to entertain the members of the jury who he thought would be best disposed toward our cause.

On the night of the gala Esther was extremely nervous. The day before I practically had to force her to agree to buy an Armani dress. She resisted, saying the dress was too tight, and she couldn't see herself perched on those stilettos that she'd surely trip over. But she ended up putting them on, and her eyes lit up when Paul came to find us and whistled when he saw her.

"I've never seen you looking so gorgeous. You look like a model," he said, giving her a kiss.

She really did. The dress was a midnight-blue sheath, its only adornment an embroidered neckline with discreet gemstones that sparkled in the light. She was the picture of restraint and elegance. At the salon her chestnut-brown hair had been gathered in a low bun. I was sure that this very restraint and elegance would make her stand out from all the other women at the gala.

Barbara and Olivia, the two girls from our commercial, sat at our table. Barbara was the typical all-American mom, whose image had been called on for countless other ads—washing machines, laxatives, things like that.

I've always hated how these galas, whatever the occasion, invariably feature hosts who insist on telling a string of jokes that everyone roars with laughter at. That night was no exception. I was nervous too, wondering whether the money Paul had thrown around had done anything for us other than allowing him and his friends to dine lavishly at my expense.

When the host revealed that the big award of the night was going to Global Communication, for the commercial "An Assured Life," Esther broke down in tears. I made her stand up, and indicated that Paul should stay in his seat. I wanted that moment of triumph to be savored by her alone. I knew she'd appreciate the gesture and would think I was truly generous.

"Please come with me," she whispered nervously.

"It's your ad, go get your award," I said, hugging her.

She went up to the podium amid deafening applause, as the commercial played on-screen.

"Thank you to everyone who voted for us. I'm so happy, and for me this award is real encouragement to keep going forward. I want to tell you that this award isn't just for me; it's for all of us who work at Global Communication. Without the drive and the confidence of Thomas Spencer and the advice of Paul Hard this dream wouldn't have been possible. Thank you . . . thank you . . ."

As Esther spoke I slid my hand over Olivia's thigh. She didn't stop me. Real encouragement.

That night Esther truly made an effort in bed. She'd had a couple of glasses of champagne, but more importantly, she had won the praise of the sacred cows of advertising, and had even received job offers from two of the biggest agencies. Finally the advertising gurus had discovered her talent, which pleased and worried me in equal measure.

The morning crept up on us between our chatter and embraces, and I decided to go all in so as not to lose her.

"I want to make you an offer," I said, pouring myself another glass of the champagne we had beside the bed.

She tensed up, thinking that I was going to propose to her again. It vexed me that the mere idea that I was going to ask her to marry me made her nervous.

"This is a perfect night, Thomas. Let's enjoy it without getting all serious."

"I think you'll like my proposal. It's not what you think it is."

I saw the curiosity in her eyes. I hugged her and whispered in her ear: "I want you to be my business partner. Global Communication will be ours, equally. Do you accept?"

She pulled away from my arms, looking at me in surprise. She seemed hesitant, as if she didn't fully comprehend what I had just said.

"But . . . well, that would be amazing. But I don't have the money to buy half your company."

"Who said you'd have to put in a single dollar? I want us to go straight to the lawyers today. I'll give you half the business. That's it."

"I can't accept."

"Of course you can! I don't pay you a monthly salary. You deserve much more—the agency would be nothing without you."

"You've risked your money and I—"

"You're risking your talent. You risked it by leaving a safe job to come to Global Communication. I owe you, Esther. The truth is that I owe you so much I'd need a thousand lifetimes to pay you back for everything you've given me."

She cried. She couldn't help the tears from flowing, and she hugged me so tightly I couldn't breathe.

"You're so generous!"

"Generous, me? Hardly! What I don't want is for those Manhattan vultures to swoop in and steal the best creative in the city from me. It's sheer selfishness," I said, laughing. There was some truth behind my words.

"Partners? But how would it work?" she asked excitedly.

"Come eight o'clock I'll call my lawyers' office and get them to draw up a transfer document for half the company. I want us to sign it today."

"That simple?"

"That simple."

She got out of bed and started to pace back and forth across the room.

"Come back to bed, you'll get cold."

"I'm just so nervous . . . Imagine, me having my own ad agency! It should have taken years for me to get this far . . ."

"Sure, but you have it now. Come back to bed, I don't want my partner to start missing work because she's caught a cold."

She came back to bed and sought refuge in my arms. But she didn't thank me as I'd hoped, instead falling fast asleep.

As Esther slept, I thought more about my move: risky, yes, but unavoidable if I wanted to keep her tied to me. I had only two options, marriage or work, and I knew she couldn't resist the latter.

Paul Hard wasn't surprised when we told him.

"Clever boy. You've made a great investment making Esther a partner."

Our life changed. Esther became obsessed with the business. If she was a workaholic before, from then on it became her sole priority; I even worried she'd work herself sick. But her obsession also allowed me greater freedom, and the chance to enjoy some of the girls who had recently arrived in New York in search of opportunity. But above all I dedicated myself eagerly to Olivia, who as well as being attractive turned out to be an excellent cook.

Two months after Esther had become my partner, I received a call from Maggie.

"You're going to lose Roy if you don't come back," she said by way of greeting.

"What's happened?"

"Roy is too much for Evelyn and Cooper. And you've spent too long in New York. You can't run a business long distance."

"Well, Global Communication is in New York too. We're working wonders here."

"Well, not so much over here. Or don't you bother to check the London accounts?"

"We're covering our costs and we're making money."

"Less and less. The clients want you. You're the monster that made us famous. Cooper's a good guy and Evelyn's a clever girl, but that's not enough, Thomas. You should take a trip back here. And it wouldn't hurt for you to bring along our new boss. If you have a partner the least you could do is let us have a look at her."

I talked to Esther. I asked her to come with me to London and she agreed immediately.

"Maggie's right. New York is going well for us, but we're letting the other side of the business slide. We could go to London for a week. The sooner the better, because at the end of the month we have to present the Department of Defense our military recruitment campaign."

"All right, we'll go tomorrow."

Why was it always raining when I arrived in London? I have no idea why, but it's been a constant in my life. Even when I've traveled there in the summer, the city has always greeted me with rain.

Cooper was waiting for us at the airport. He hugged me as if he were actually fond of me.

"About time! We were starting to worry you'd decided to stay in New York for good."

"And close the business here," I added, spelling out his fears.

"Yes, frankly. Evelyn and I had started to think that. The agency belongs to you and . . . well, you haven't exactly been too concerned about what's been going on over here."

He took us to my apartment. The maid had been looking after it during my absence. I told Cooper we'd see him in the afternoon at the agency. I wanted to introduce them formally to Esther and have an initial meeting with him and Evelyn.

"Roy's here in London. I think that . . . well, I think he wants to break his contract with us. He says that you avoid him when he calls—that you put him off and he gets the feeling you're not listening to him. You should have dinner with him tonight."

"We're tired, Cooper. I'll see Roy in the morning. I'll call and invite him to lunch."

"I think it'd be better if you two see him tonight," insisted Cooper.

We slept for a couple of hours. It was almost midday when Esther woke up. She made coffee while I took a shower.

"Cooper is right, you have to see Roy. We can't lose him," she said.

"It can wait till tomorrow," I replied.

"Roy isn't the type to wait. It's incredible that he's put up with this so far, all those months when you weren't here."

"Which means that Evelyn hasn't been handling things too badly."

"I don't doubt that. But Roy is like a big self-centered kid, he needs everyone's attention. Call him, tell him you're dying to see him, that you have a surprise for him."

"What surprise?" I asked.

"Me. I'll be the surprise. Now I'm your partner, so Roy's problems concern me too."

"It would only be a surprise to Roy if I told him that we've gotten married and that's why I delayed my return to London."

"He'll have to make do with me being your business partner."

"For now," I said, picking up her hand and kissing it.

At three we arrived at the office. Maggie was waiting for us with fresh coffee. She remembered that I didn't care for tea.

Esther charmed Maggie and Evelyn, but she also didn't waste a minute in asking Maggie to show her the books.

Over the past months Cooper had brought in a couple of small accounts. Nothing important; just enough, as Maggie said, to cover costs.

"But the agency is dying. If you don't do something we can't go on much longer," my secretary concluded sharply.

Evelyn and Cooper couldn't help but agree, which worried Esther.

"You're right. We've neglected this side of the business. We'll remedy that right away," she said, so firmly that it surprised even me.

Evelyn gave us a detailed report on Roy Parker. The girl was valuable. Pacifying Roy wouldn't be easy. He was a tricky one to manage.

"The worst part is that I've had to fight his electoral committee nearly every single day. I'll be honest, Thomas, it's thanks to Bernard Schmidt that Roy hasn't made any more mistakes than he can afford to. Schmidt and the lawyers know how to put the brakes on him, but they're insisting that he get rid of you. I think the only reason Roy hasn't done it is because he likes to feel independent from Jones and Brown, but if they keep pushing, I don't know . . ."

"And Suzi?" asked Esther.

"Ugh. A real headache. She does everything she can to annoy Roy. She won't go anywhere with him. I had to explain to the media that Mrs. Parker prefers a quiet life, and that she has the right to a certain degree of privacy, even if she is the wife of a politician. I told them that Suzi Parker wants her children to have a normal life, to have distance from their father's work."

"Good explanation," I congratulated Evelyn.

"Not that good, but it was the only one possible. The rumors are unstoppable and the Parkers' cleaning ladies have taken it upon themselves to spread the word that the couple are sleeping in separate bedrooms and barely speak to each other."

"Sleeping in separate bedrooms isn't that unusual," said Maggie, "but not talking to each other at home . . ."

"Their family problems could harm his chances of getting a seat in London. You know how that county is, total hypocrites. Married couples stay together to save face with their neighbors, and they want the same from their political representatives," added Evelyn.

"We'll go to the county. I'll talk to Suzi," said Esther.

"Okay, first we have to talk to Roy," I added.

"Have you called to ask to see him tonight?" asked Cooper.

"Not yet."

"Do it. He's furious. I told him you're arriving today and

he'll never forgive you if you don't call him." Worry filled Evelyn's voice.

We skimmed over the contracts that had been signed. Cooper told us we had two potential clients: one wanted to promote rain boots and the other a new brand of tea. Esther told Cooper to set up meetings with them for the same week. She would meet them in person, and could even give them a couple of ideas for the campaign presentation.

Meanwhile, Maggie reserved a table at one of the most expensive restaurants in London, Pied à Terre in Fitzrovia. When we arrived Roy was waiting for us, and from his expression I guessed he'd already had at least a couple of whiskeys. He frowned when he saw Esther, even seemed irritated by her presence, though he kissed her twice and paid her a few compliments.

Esther asked after Suzi and told him that she was thinking of going to the county to talk to her, if he thought it was a good idea.

"I don't know what to tell you. I don't think it'd help. And . . . well, since you're Thomas's partner now what I've got to say concerns you too. I think the time has come for a change, for other people to be in charge of my campaign. At the end of the day, Thomas isn't here anymore. It's not that I'm unhappy with Evelyn but . . . Well, that's how things stand."

I'd been expecting him to say something like that, so I showed no surprise. Esther didn't move a muscle either, waiting for me to reply.

"I understand, Roy. If you don't need us anymore you'll be making the right choice in getting rid of us," I said, so decisively that even Esther couldn't help but look at me out of the corner of her eye.

"I'm glad you're taking it well. I hope we can stay friends."

"So who will take care of your business?" I asked, as if it didn't mean that much to me.

"Schmidt convinced me that I'm a sucker to pay for a service that Brian Jones and Edward Brown give me for free."

"Well, I wouldn't say your communications agency does anything for you for free. Though I understand why it suits them better to have you fully under their control. You're not an easy guy, so this way they'll make sure you don't go off the rails. Smart move. Congratulate them for me."

I knew that my words would get on Roy's nerves, even if he wouldn't admit it—at least not yet.

"I don't think they'd be interested in anything you have to say. The lawyers have gotten sick of you. So has Schmidt."

"The feeling's mutual. But let's leave that there and you tell me how things are going. You matter to me outside of work, you know."

Roy spent the rest of dinner droning on about his difficulties getting a seat in Parliament.

"The London papers don't usually pay me any attention. Of course that doesn't matter to the lawyers. Their main concern is that I keep defending to the county any matters that have to do with their interests or their friends' interests," he concluded, as if this were news to me.

"Of course, that's why they backed you. Have you forgotten? They move you about as they please, and when you're no good to them anymore, checkmate. That's how politics is. That's why I advise you to firm up the structure of the Rural Party, and work to win more councils in the next election. I'm guessing your party will put other candidates forward for the general elections. That would be a huge step ahead, it would secure your positions."

"Yes, we have the candidates already. Schmidt has given instructions to the electoral committee about how to run the campaign."

"Great, so things couldn't be going better for you. My friend, I'm so satisfied to see that you no longer need me."

Esther was listening to all this; she had barely said a word. She was aware that this game had only two players: Roy and myself.

"I'm surprised you're taking this so well, me letting you go . . . The last time we saw each other you practically begged me not to break with you," he said sullenly.

"Of course we'd prefer to keep you as a client, but there's a beginning and an end to everything. It's obvious that you don't need us, nor do we need you. I'll be honest—thanks to Esther things couldn't be going better in New York. We'll keep the office in London, but our business is over there, so it actually suits me that you're letting us go. You cost us more than you pay us."

"Well, that is a surprise! Do I owe you something, Thomas? How could you have the nerve to say I'm costing you money?"

"That's how it is, Roy. You had exclusive use of Evelyn, and that girl is very good. If she no longer has to be dedicated to you she can focus on other clients, ones who will be more profitable for us and won't take up all of her time. It comes down to math."

"She does know the county well . . . She even gets on all right with Suzi," admitted Roy.

"Yes, that's true. But let's leave work talk for now, Roy. Esther and I are exhausted. Like I told you over the phone, we got into London first thing this morning and we've only had time to rest for a couple of hours. We need to sleep. We have a lot to do over the next few days. Cooper isn't dumb and he's managed to line us up a few prospective clients."

Roy insisted we stay for another drink, but I remained firm. It was my way of showing him that he was no longer important to us. If Esther hadn't been there, Roy would have thrown some insult at me. I kept up my indifference, but I was starting to feel it in the pit of my stomach. I was waiting for Roy to make his move. He did it as we were saying goodbye.

"Perhaps it would be a good idea for you to come up to the county for a couple of days. Suzi has always gotten on with Esther . . ."

"Yes, that would be wonderful, but we won't have the chance. Some other time," I said.

"Is it that easy to break with a friend?" he asked me bad-temperedly.

"Break with a friend? I don't know what you're talking about, Roy. As far as I know we haven't broken our friendship, we've only decided to stop working together. That's what you wanted to tell me this evening, wasn't it? Well then, now it's said."

"You're a real bastard, Thomas!" yelled Roy.

"I don't understand. Where is this coming from?" I replied, looking at my watch and stifling a yawn.

"You're going to leave me alone in the lion's den," he said sadly.

"No doubt you'll be in good company. The lawyers are your mentors, listen to them."

"That's what they want!"

"Come on, Roy, don't get upset. You've always known what Brian Jones and Edward Brown are like. Of course they want to control you. But you're old enough to know how much you'll let them get away with."

"Evelyn used to draw the line. She warned me about the dangers when they tried to insist on me doing certain things . . ."

"Yes, that was what you paid us for. But you can figure all that out without us. Come on, Roy, we'll talk another time, maybe on our next trip. But now we're really exhausted and we have other clients to see tomorrow."

We said goodbye, leaving him desolate. Roy had expected me to battle to keep him as a client. He wasn't anticipating my agreement.

"You've made him think he doesn't matter to you." Esther was amazed by my behavior.

"Yes, it's our only option to make him change his mind."

"You're such a cynic!"

"What would you have done? If we'd asked him to reconsider his decision to leave our agency, he'd have strutted around like a peacock. Roy likes to think that he's in charge. Showing him that we don't care is our best bet to win him over."

"Do you think he'll call?"

"In a couple of days, no later than that I would think."

"I hope you're right, or the London accounts won't stack up. Cooper doesn't seem to have achieved many great things in your absence."

"He's a good boy, decent, but he needs someone to guide him," I admitted.

"We'll have to find someone else if we want London to work out—especially if Roy doesn't call. You know something? You almost had me convinced that we don't need him."

"It's a game of poker. He was the one who wanted to cheat but in the end we were the ones who cheated him."

"You've got the balls for poker. If the advertising gig doesn't work out for us you could always turn to the casinos." She laughed.

It didn't take Roy a couple of days to call. He called first thing the next morning. I was shaving when Esther came into the bathroom with my cell phone in her hand.

"We'll have dinner tonight, but alone. My treat," he said, without even saying good morning.

"It's six thirty in the morning. I've got a meeting at eight, another at ten, a lunch and—"

"Cut the bullshit! Are you really going to say no to dinner with me?"

"Come on, Roy, as soon as I get to the office I'll tell Maggie to draw up a new document. Then the lawyers can cut me loose once and for all. I won't charge a penny for that, so don't you worry." I knew that my words would further frustrate him.

"Oh, how generous! Do you really think they were going to pay you to be sacked?"

"Could be. But now you know I have no intention of claiming anything. I don't have time to talk about what a nice morning it is. We'll speak soon, Roy." I hung up the phone.

"You play hardball," said Esther, looking at me with admiration.

"I hope I haven't gambled away the rest of our chances," I said, very aware that Roy might not react exactly how I wanted him to.

The cell phone rang again. This time I answered.

"Seven at Madame Agnès's. It's the only place in London where we can talk without anyone bothering us. And don't tell me no, or I'll come looking for you if I have to."

"I can't, Roy. I can't leave Esther alone for a—"

"Of course you can! You don't want to come with me to the best whorehouse in London? At seven, Thomas—you owe me."

"What exactly do I owe you, Roy?"

"Wouldn't you say we're friends? Well then, nobody would turn down a drink with a friend."

I sighed resignedly, and stayed quiet a few moments before replying.

"All right, Roy. One drink, just one drink. I'll be there at seven."

I hung up the phone, relieved. Roy was full of surprises.

"Game, set, and match," said Esther with a smile of satisfaction.

"Told you so," I agreed, bluffing confidence.

"Don't jump to conclusions—just because you're in the game doesn't mean you'll win it. Though I admit you've handled this situation masterfully."

"You couldn't have done it better yourself. Is there coffee?"

"A full pot."

"I'll have to go out to dinner with him . . ."

"Of course, don't worry about me. I'll bring work home. I want to go over the accounts thoroughly."

"Maggie's a good secretary, I trust her."

"So do I, but I prefer to know all the expenses in detail. And we have a number of things that need dealing with on the New

York side, so it'd be good for me to have a quiet night to work while you have dinner with Roy."

It was great to have Esther at the helm of Global Communication. She was meticulous in her work and not even a misplaced comma could get past her. I saw that Maggie was getting impatient at Esther's endless questions, but that she also respected her—more, in fact, than she had ever respected me.

Esther accompanied Cooper to the meeting with the rain boot manufacturers and came out with a signed contract. In the afternoon they also met with the tea importer. He was impressed by the ideas Esther sketched out. He didn't commit to anything, but Cooper and Esther thought we had a good chance of getting the campaign. We weren't exactly going to make a fortune, but at least it would mean that we could keep our heads above water.

I felt anxious as the evening came around. The meeting with Roy was making me nervous, but more than that I wanted to know if Yoko would be working at Madame Agnès's.

At seven on the dot I rang the bell at Madame's house. The old butler opened the door and seemed pleased to see me.

"Mr. Spencer! Come in, Madame will be so surprised. She was wondering when you would come to see us again."

I was pleased to be there too. I felt the comfort of arriving at a familiar place where there are no surprises.

Madame Agnès came over to greet me. I kissed her hand, as she liked her clients to do.

"My friend, I was wondering about your absence. But I'm pleased to see you among us again."

"Business, Madame, it's just business that's kept me from your house. Have you seen Mr. Parker?"

"He's just arrived, he's waiting for you in the small library. I'll make sure nobody disturbs you. And I'll send over some champagne."

"I think Mr. Parker would prefer whiskey," I suggested.

"Naturally, but you will drink champagne as always, no?"

Roy Parker was pacing compulsively in the room that Madame called "the small library." It was a circular room, not very large, with floor-to-ceiling shelves on which stood, among other books, the complete Encyclopædia Britannica.

A waiter entered behind me carrying a tray with a bottle of Roy's favorite whiskey and another bottle of champagne. Madame Agnès was going to wring a lot of money out of the moment of privacy we needed.

"You came," said Roy, as if he'd doubted I would.

I shrugged in reply, watching as the waiter first served Roy a double whiskey, then opened the bottle of champagne and, after pouring me a glass, placed it back in the ice bucket.

When we were alone Roy seemed to relax.

"Well then?" I asked straight out.

"You're not going to break the contract," said Roy, looking at me with resentment.

"Aren't I? I sent the document to your lawyers this morning. I'm waiting for them to sign it, and then both of us are free of any obligation. You'll agree that I'm being generous by not claiming any compensation, since you're initiating the termination of our contract. So I don't understand what the problem is."

"The problem is that I'm sick of you, that you're a bloody manipulator, you're unscrupulous, you're a—"

"Enough, Roy! Do you think I came here to be insulted?"

"We're not going to end it, Thomas. I won't give Schmidt and the lawyers the pleasure."

"I don't understand, Roy . . . They want me away from you. And you know what? I don't think they're wrong. They have their own way of doing things, and they're your safety net. Without them you wouldn't survive in politics. So it's not much they're asking from you in return, only that you get rid of me. Well, now the time has come. Anyway, I'm going to be spending more time in New York, so I won't be able to properly deal with London business. Not even yours."

"That's where you're wrong. I demand that you continue handling my business, Thomas, that's the trade-off."

"You're not hearing me, Roy. I'm not negotiating another type of contract—"

"Enough bullshit! You're going to stay with me, Thomas, end of discussion."

"You don't need me anymore, Roy."

As I said this I watched him. I knew that I couldn't push him too far. In the end, my goal was to maintain the contract.

Roy sat down. I hadn't realized until then that we'd both been standing, staring at each other so closely that I could smell the whiskey on his breath. I sat down too.

"I'm sick of this, Thomas. Sometimes I regret ever getting involved in this shit. I was happy before. I was running my in-laws' business, and I had Suzi."

"It was your decision, Roy."

"My ambition. Yes, it was my ambition that brought me here."

"You can't go back now. You can't get your life back. If you continue in politics you still have a chance to save yourself and get Suzi back, but if you let it all go, then what's left? If you don't have any power Suzi will end it with you."

"My kids don't understand anything. It hurts them to see their parents hardly talking," lamented Roy.

"You want to become prime minister. I don't know if it'll happen, but if you want to try you have to pay a price."

"I never thought it would be so high . . ."

We drank in silence, letting our eyes wander for a while to the fire that was crackling in the fireplace.

"All right, Roy . . . we won't break the contract." I said this with resignation, like someone being forced to make a decision he didn't want to make.

"Evelyn is really good at her job," muttered Roy.

"I know, that's why I put her in charge of you. And that's how it'll continue," I assured him.

"And you?" Roy's question was loaded with worry.

"We'll go over how things stand—I'll meet with your people, with your electoral committee, and if possible with Suzi. We'll draw up a new action plan, which Evelyn will be in charge of carrying out. Then I'll have to go back to New York."

"Have you married Esther?"

"No."

"Why not?"

"We live together. It's good like that, and she's my business partner too—half the company is hers."

"Will you come to the county?"

"Yes. How long are you staying in London?"

"A few more days, till Friday. I came down for some business at the Treasury. You can spend the weekend in the county."

"We'll have to do that. I'll tell Evelyn to coordinate all the meetings with your people. Esther wants to go back to New York on Monday."

"You can't stay longer?"

"We'll see. In any case my visits to this country won't be long."

Roy seemed calmer knowing that he could still count on me. I was surprised how easy it had been to trick him and win the game. The truth was, the man I had in front of me hardly resembled the one I had once known.

"Let's go celebrate with the girls. There are a couple of new ones," said Roy, trying to cheer himself up.

We went back into the main room, where there were already a number of men talking to Madame Agnès's girls. Then I saw her. Unmistakable in her black dress, which made her look even slimmer. Yoko was talking to a couple of men.

I went up to her and grabbed her hand, bowing exaggeratedly before her. One of the men greeted me warmly. It was Tyler, the Chinese underwear importer.

"What a surprise, Mr. Spencer. They told me you'd moved to New York . . ."

"I have business on both sides of the Atlantic, Mr. Tyler, but here you find me."

Yoko's face was filled with such horror that the two men looked surprised. We watched her run to the hallway. I knew she was going to throw up.

"Hey, what's going on with her?" one of the clients asked loudly.

"She must be unwell. She's an old friend, so if you'll allow me . . . Well, I'd like to talk to her awhile."

The two men seemed to be weighing whether to let me go ahead. Tyler decided in my favor.

"Well, sure . . ."

I waited by the bathroom door until Yoko came out. When she opened the door and saw me she broke down in tears. Her face showed such desperation that any other person would have been moved.

If I'd been a decent type I would've told her to calm down, that I didn't mean to do anything more than say hello to her: "You don't need to worry. Look, I don't want to hurt you, the past is the past. And I have no intention of getting together with you again. You have a right to your own life."

Yoko would have looked at me, incredulous, and she might even have thanked me for giving her back her freedom.

But I didn't say any of that, I grabbed her tightly by the wrists instead and forced her to look me in the face.

"We'll have dinner together. I'll tell Madame Agnès to send us up some champagne."

I pulled her toward the stairs while asking the butler to give the order for us to be served dinner in one of the suites on the second floor. He looked at Yoko with concern, but he didn't say anything. The customer is always right, and if I had chosen Yoko, the establishment could raise no objections.

Once we'd entered the room I pushed her hard. She tripped and fell to the floor. I didn't bother to help her. She got to her feet and I watched how her expression blossomed into one of terror until her face became a mask of desperation and madness.

"Why?" she stammered.

"Why? I don't know what you're talking about."

"Why have you come back? Why do you hate me? Why do you want to destroy me?"

"You're a whore, Yoko, just a whore. This is your job. I'm your best client. This is the way things work. Girls like you have to please their clients, you don't get to choose."

"We do here . . . We do at Madame Agnès's . . . We don't have to go with anyone we don't want to go with . . ."

"But you want to be with me, Yoko, of course you do. Now we'll have dinner and then we'll go back to your place. We'll spend the rest of the night there."

"No . . . No . . . No, that's not possible. My boyfriend . . . He's at the flat, he's waiting for me . . ."

"Really? Does he know where you are right now?"

"He doesn't know anything . . . Please, give me my life back!" she shouted with such desperation that I was afraid someone might hear her.

"Shut up! Don't make a scene, Yoko, or you'll make things worse for yourself. Call your boyfriend and tell him to leave, tell him not to wait for you, that you won't be spending tonight with him."

"But I can't tell Dave that!"

"Then I'll tell him. I'll tell him what he ought to know, that you're a whore and you've been deceiving him for years. And that I pay you extra so I can go to your apartment, and so he needs to leave."

"Don't do this to me!" Her cry was like a wounded animal's.

The waiter arrived with our dinner. He placed it unhurriedly on the table while looking sidelong at Yoko, who had sat down and was covering her face with her hands. When the waiter left, I went over and hit her.

"Are you trying to cause trouble? Do you want the waiter to tell Madame Agnès that you're crying? If that's the case, you'll pay dearly for it."

A few gentle knocks at the door warned me to lower my voice. I opened it. The waiter handed me a bottle, a second bottle of champagne "on the house." I could make out the figure of Madame Agnès behind him.

"Excellent, we'll soon finish this off. Reunions are always so emotional."

I didn't let him come in and I closed the door immediately. I looked at Yoko with such fury that all she could do was tremble. She knew that if she made another sound there would be very unpleasant consequences for her.

We ate in silence. When we finished I told her what I expected of her.

"Call Dave. Tell him to go, it will be best for everyone."

"But we're here . . . Why do we need to go to my flat?" she said, crying again.

I took out my cell phone and started to dial the landline for Yoko's apartment. She looked at me with such fear that her face became the embodiment of pain. She got up and came toward me so fast that she managed to get the phone out of my hands.

I pushed her hard and threw her to the floor again.

"I don't like this game, Yoko. You're going to end up hurting yourself."

She suddenly stopped crying. She got up with difficulty and looked at me with determination.

"Okay, let's go."

"Smart girl."

We went down to the hall and a maid handed us our coats. We went out into the cold of the London night. Yoko was walking fast. I started to think that she had tricked me, that the reason she had suddenly agreed to go to her place was because Dave wasn't there. She had used him to try to dissuade me, but seeing my determination, she had given in to reality. I couldn't have been more satisfied.

I don't know how it happened. Yoko suddenly began to run. She took me by surprise and I ran after her, but I couldn't catch her. She reached the intersection of two roads, which several cars were crossing. She threw herself under the wheels of a car that was moving fast. The man braked, but not in time to prevent Yoko's body from being thrown to the ground and the wheels from going over her, breaking all the bones in her skull and thorax.

I remained motionless. I didn't approach. I watched the scene from a distance. Several cars stopped and the man who had hit her swore that the woman had thrown herself into the street, that he had been unable to avoid the collision. He was a young guy, not much more than twenty or twenty-two years old. He had been driving faster than the speed limit, but that wasn't the cause of the accident.

An ambulance and a couple of police cars arrived a few minutes later. I continued watching without moving any closer. Nobody had seen me with her.

I walked quickly back to Madame Agnès's. She seemed concerned to see me.

"I need to speak to you, Madame."

I followed her into her office and she closed the door to make sure nobody bothered us.

"Something unbelievable has happened, Madame . . . I left your establishment a few minutes ago; I offered to go with Yoko to find a taxi. She was in a very strange mood tonight . . . In fact, she was walking so fast I couldn't even keep up with her.

She suddenly started running and I lost sight of her. I sped up and . . . well, something terrible has happened . . . She's been hit by a car. I didn't get too close, you must understand why. I've come to tell you what happened."

"Oh my God! Oh my God!"

"Calm down, Madame."

"Calm down? One of my girls has an accident and you ask me to calm down . . . Is she badly hurt?"

"I don't know, Madame, but I fear the worst."

"What are we going to do?"

"I assume you've considered the possibility that accidents like this might happen . . ."

"Accidents! No, no, I've never planned for the possibility that any of the young women who work here would ever end up under the wheels of a car! And so close to my establishment . . . Someone might have seen her leaving . . . It will be a scandal . . ."

"You have friends in high places, Madame, I'm sure that you'll be able to deal with the problem."

"But what about you? What happened tonight? The waiter who served your dinner told me that Yoko was crying, that she seemed very upset . . ."

"And so she was, Madame. She didn't tell me why."

"She seemed perfectly fine until you arrived . . ."

"That was not the case. She told me that she was fed up with this job, that she couldn't do it anymore . . . It seems she has a boyfriend and he was starting to suspect something. She seemed so sad that . . . well, it didn't seem appropriate to have any kind of amorous relations with a woman who was so upset."

"That was very chivalrous of you," replied Madame Agnès with no conviction whatsoever.

I was thinking about how not having slept with Yoko would keep me safe from any ensuing investigation. If she was dead, as I believed she was, and they performed an autopsy, they would find no trace of my semen. This would be in my favor.

"We'll have to wait and see . . . I can't publicly appear to know about what happened."

"Sooner or later the police will come. I'm counting on you to be discreet . . . I came to your establishment tonight to meet with Mr. Parker. It would be terrible if he found himself negatively affected by this awful event. I hope that your staff are worthy of the trust we put in them."

"Of course, Mr. Spencer. But . . . in the end . . . I hope we can avoid any trouble. If Yoko survives the accident, it would be best for everyone."

"Of course. She's a lovely young woman with a promising future."

"Is there anything else I should know, Mr. Spencer?" As she was speaking, Madame Agnès seemed to scrutinize the most remote corners of my mind.

"Everything happened just as I've told you. It was all so fast . . . She seemed anxious to get home, and as I said, I offered to go with her to find a taxi."

"And in doing so you broke one of our rules. You know that we don't want our guests to have any contact with our girls outside of the establishment."

"I was only going with her to find a taxi, Madame, and I offered to do so precisely because seeing her so upset worried me. As you may imagine, especially given the circumstances, I'm sorry for breaking that rule."

"Yes, I suppose so. In fact, there's a person among our guests tonight who might be able to advise us. He's a gentleman who works in Whitehall."

"There's no doubt that it would be very useful for you to ask his advice, Madame. In any case, I want to request that you try to keep my name from coming up."

Madame Agnès didn't make me any promises because she couldn't. Neither of us knew what might happen from that point forward.

I decided to take a walk. I needed to process what had happened. I cursed Yoko. I was furious that the night's events might be damaging for me. If anyone connected me to her not only would I have to close the agency, but I might lose Esther forever.

Yes, I cursed Yoko without pity, hoping that she was dead. That outcome would be most convenient for me. If she was alive and the police questioned her to try to find out what had happened, the fool might break down and end up telling them about her job at Madame Agnès's and my relationship with her. Dead she might cause me problems, but alive and badly injured she would cause me a whole lot more.

I didn't think for a moment that I should have run to help her. Yes, I could have. I could have gone to where she was lying and held her as the ambulance arrived. The police would have questioned me and I would have had to tell them that I was just a friend, and to show how distressed I was by the accident.

I would have had to go with her in the ambulance to the hospital and wait until the doctors came out to give their verdict: alive or dead.

But I didn't. I didn't feel the need to. I was apathetic to Yoko's fate except for how it might affect mine.

When I arrived at my apartment I found Esther speaking to someone on the phone.

"I'm talking to Paul Hard. Do you want me to pass on any messages?"

"That he should take care of our agency. That's if he knows how," I replied moodily.

When Esther finished her conversation with Paul she focused on me. She had picked up on my tension.

"What happened? Didn't Roy take the bait?"

"Yes, of course he did. We'll keep the contract and Friday we'll go with him to Derbyshire."

"I can't say I'm looking forward to it. Still, we came here to work and it wouldn't be good for us to lose Roy. But why are you in such a bad mood?"

Esther was too smart for me to trick her. I had taken a gamble on her. The reason I needed her was because I was sure that she would never abandon me. I decided to tell her the truth. My version of the truth.

"Roy arranged to meet me in a rather special place. It's a discreet establishment in South Kensington. A kind of club where businessmen often meet to discuss their affairs and . . ."

"Have a drink in pleasant company, is that it?"

"Yes. Madame Agnès is a woman of the world whose girls are high-class: university students, models, aspiring actresses, even a few titled ladies who've come down in the world. They're not prostitutes. Or at least, they don't seem like prostitutes. They're able to discuss movements in the stock market, the latest auction at Sotheby's, or British geopolitics in Asia."

"How very clever." Esther's tone of voice suggested a certain disdain.

"I don't want to deceive you—I'll never do that. It's not the first time I've been to Madame Agnès's. I've met up with Roy there on various occasions. He loves that place, he even used to go when things were going well with Suzi."

"I'm not surprised. Roy is one of those guys who loves his wife but has no problem sleeping with other women."

"At Madame Agnès's everything is . . . well, everything is elegant, there are certain understandings . . . There's nothing vulgar. Roy arranged to meet me there."

"Why didn't you tell me?"

"I didn't mean to hide it from you," I declared firmly.

"So what happened to make you so worried?"

"An accident, a terrible accident."

Esther tensed up. She got up and came and stood in front of me. I saw the worry in her eyes and she saw the fear in mine.

"Sit down and tell me everything."

I sat down on the sofa while she got me a whiskey.

"After talking to Roy I chatted with a couple of people,

Mr. Tyler, the underwear importer, and some other men. Then . . . well, I had dinner with one of the girls who works there. Yoko, a Japanese girl."

"With whom you've had a relationship, or am I mistaken?"

"I used to, Esther. She was a girl I had dinner with and went to bed with occasionally. Yoko was studying literature, she's a cultured, educated woman. When I saw her tonight I had dinner with her there. Madame Agnès doesn't permit relationships outside her establishment. When we finished dinner and were saying goodbye, she told me that she was done working for the evening; that she had to go home, that her boyfriend was waiting for her."

"You only had dinner together?" Esther asked very seriously.

"We only had dinner, I give you my word of honor. But Madame Agnès charges a considerable sum for dinner, even if nothing happens afterward. So by having dinner with me Yoko had earned her night's wages. Madame Agnès doesn't let her girls spend time alone with more than one gentleman per night."

"How considerate," she commented sarcastically.

"It's one of the keys to her business's success."

"Why don't you just go ahead and tell me what happened?" said Esther, urging me to get to the end of the story.

"Yoko seemed worried. I don't know, she was upset. When we left Madame Agnès's I offered to go with her to find a taxi."

Esther interrupted me again.

"So her boyfriend was waiting for her. And does he know what she does for a living?"

"No, of course not. I've already told you that she's not a professional; she's a student who pays her tuition by going to Madame Agnès's a couple of nights a week."

"There are other ways to earn a living," Esther replied severely.

"I don't know exactly how it happened . . . When we were getting close to the main road she suddenly started running. She took me completely by surprise; I didn't know what to do. I didn't know whether to follow her or not; I sped up and . . . I don't really know what happened, but she was under the wheels of car. I froze. I . . . I think that she was badly hurt, perhaps killed . . ."

"How awful! And what did you do?"

"Nothing, I couldn't do anything. I went back to Madame Agnès's to tell her what had happened. I assume there'll be an investigation and I don't want to find myself implicated in any scandal that could also affect Roy. Imagine the headlines in the papers if they could connect the accident with me, and with Roy by association. We'd both be finished!"

"And you just left her lying there?" Esther reproached me.

"There was nothing I could do, nothing. You have to understand that," I replied, repressing the urge to shout at her.

"So now we're in a fix."

In spite of her anger, Esther was on my side. She didn't say "you're in a fix" but "we're in a fix." That's how she was, she'd never abandon a ship in a storm.

"Nobody saw me."

"Or that's what you think. Anyway, there will be people who saw you with the girl at Madame Agnès's. We need to be prepared for what may come. They could call on you to testify, to give an account of the girl's final hours, who knows."

"You're right . . . What do you think we should do?"

"I don't know, Thomas, but the thing is . . . Well, it's not the first time that you've been the last one to see a girl alive. Remember . . . Lisa was with you shortly before she died . . ."

Hearing Lisa's name made my stomach lurch. Esther was right. If some smartass journalist started to dig around in my past they'd come across Lisa's death in Newport. I realized once again how important it was for me to have Esther to rely on.

"Do you trust Madame Agnès?" Esther asked with a worried expression.

"She's not eager for the papers to take an interest in her. Her business is based on discretion. Important men visit her establishment, including politicians like Roy, bankers, civil servants . . . She'll do anything to keep herself out of the spotlight, so she'll try to keep me as far away from it as she can. Or that's what I hope."

We barely slept that night. When we got into bed, Esther embraced me as if I were a defenseless child. I felt a great relief in her arms, as if nothing could happen to me because she was there, prepared to face off with anyone who tried to harm me. She didn't reproach me at all. She accepted me as I was, just as she had in the past.

She got up just before six. She was in the shower for a long time; I suppose she was trying to rid herself of the night's ghosts. When I got up she was already in the kitchen, sitting with a cup of coffee in front of her and a newspaper in her hand.

"I've read the paper, there's no mention of the accident. You have to go to Madame Agnès's," she said, without even saying good morning.

"Now? No, that's impossible; Madame doesn't open before six in the evening."

"You'll go at six, then."

"I don't think that's a good idea."

"We have to know how the girl is, whether anyone's made a connection between her and Madame Agnès or you . . . You have to go."

"But if that were the case . . . Well, I guess we'll find out."

We arrived at the office early. Even Maggie wasn't in yet.

Esther began reviewing some paperwork and I started trying to work out how to solve Roy's problems. I had said I'd go to Derbyshire and I would have to do it.

Evelyn arrived a few minutes after Maggie and I decided to talk to her about Roy's issues.

"We need to give Roy's political career another boost."

"Yeah, but it's not that easy. The Rural Party only has ten mayors. It's difficult to get the London press to take an interest in them unless they become embroiled in a scandal."

"What about the local press?"

"There's no problem there, the local media give them coverage. The problem is London. Roy wants to be featured in the *Times,* with a photo on the front page if possible," Evelyn said sarcastically.

Esther joined us after a while. She listened attentively to Evelyn and then sat lost in thought for a few minutes. Then she surprised us with one of her ideas.

"Roy needs to do something special, and there's nothing better than telling his voters that he wants to learn about their problems firsthand, not through them recounting them, but by experiencing them himself in person."

"And how will that work?"

"It's very simple. I assume that we have a profile of his voters. Roy will work in the mine for a week. He'll spend another week as a cashier in a small business, in a bread factory, sweeping streets . . . Basically, he'll step into his voters' shoes. That will get the attention of the London papers. We'll have to get a TV crew to follow him for a couple of weeks and then show a full report on everything Roy's done. Oh! He could also try a new way of listening to his voters. He could hold an open meeting once a month, as if it were a parliamentary session, where the voters ask him questions, debate among themselves, and tell him what their priorities are, what they want him to fight for in London if he manages to secure a seat."

"And you just came up with that on the spot?" exclaimed Evelyn with admiration.

"More or less."

"You're amazing." I gave her a round of applause.

"Will Roy agree to it?" asked Esther.

"He'll make a fuss, but he'll do it," Evelyn replied. "But we still have a problem with Suzi. It's more and more obvious that

their marriage isn't working and that could cost Roy supporters. His future as a politician is hopeless if he can't maintain the
semblance of a happy family life."

"Well, there are only two options: either they divorce or they
reconcile."

"A divorce is unthinkable. People will want to know why
and it will come out that Roy deceived Suzi and her family, as
well as all his voters. That would completely finish his political
career," Evelyn declared.

We spent the rest of the day in meetings: Esther sat down
with new clients and I went with Evelyn to talk to Roy. We had
to explain Esther's plan to him.

Roy was in the Rural Party's small London office and when
we arrived he was shouting at a young woman who, according
to what Evelyn whispered to me, was his assistant.

"I was thinking of calling you. We need to talk," he said.

"That's why I've come, Roy," I replied.

"Good. As for you, gorgeous, it would be best if you went
shopping or whatever for a while," he told Evelyn.

"I'm sorry, Roy, but I have a role in what we want to propose
to you." Evelyn didn't seem bothered by Roy's attitude.

"Get out of here. When I want to talk to you, I'll call you. Go
on, leave us in peace."

Evelyn looked at me, waiting for me to intervene. I decided to
ask her to go back to the office.

"Get to work on what we discussed. I'll explain it to Roy."

We were left alone. Roy still hadn't invited me to sit down,
but I took a seat anyway.

"What happened last night?" he asked me with no preamble.

"What do you mean?"

"Madame Agnès got me out of bed, which I happened to be
sharing with a very pretty girl, urging me to leave her premises
immediately. She told me that you'd gotten us into a fix and that
the police could turn up at any moment. She barely gave me time
to put my trousers on."

"What else did she say?"

"Nothing. She didn't say a single word more. She wanted her clients to leave as soon as possible. I met a couple of guys who work for the government in the hallway. You owe me an explanation."

I was almost honest. I told him the same version I'd told Esther, which more or less matched the truth, though I omitted to tell them that I had known Yoko better than I was implying.

"Was she running away from you?"

"Absolutely not! There was no explanation. I think she had some kind of problem . . . Who knows what . . . The fact is, she just suddenly started running and . . . well, perhaps she tripped and that's why she fell. The driver was going too fast. If Madame Agnès wants to keep her business, her only option is to be discreet. A scandal in the papers would spell the end for some of her clients, but also for her," I said with little conviction.

"Well, in reality, what happened is no one's fault. The girl started running, she tripped and she had an accident. I hope she survived, but if she's copped it, the police will investigate and they will find out about Madame Agnès," Roy declared.

"But they can't accuse her of anything. She wasn't even there when the accident took place," I replied. A shiver ran down my back.

"Of course not, but they'll want to know everything about the girl: her family, where she works . . . Someone will end up pointing out Madame Agnès's, and there might also be someone who remembers that you two left her establishment together."

"It would be an inconvenience, but nothing more," I reassured him with a confidence I didn't feel.

"And what will Esther say?"

"I've told her what happened. I've no reason to hide anything from her. I'm not responsible for the accident."

Roy was surprised that I'd dared tell Esther that I'd visited a brothel and had dinner with one of the whores, who'd ended up under the wheels of a car. But, most of all, he didn't understand how Esther could have accepted all this without breaking up with me.

"Damn, you're lucky! If Suzi caught me doing something like that . . ."

I convinced him that we should call Evelyn. I wanted her to help persuade him of the advantages of Esther's plan, and, more importantly, we needed to call an urgent meeting of the electoral committee in Derbyshire, where we would spend the weekend.

When we got back to the office Esther was about to head back to the apartment.

"I've had an exhausting day, but it's been worth it. With a bit of luck the London agency will be a success. I've spoken to Jim Cooper. You're right, he's a good guy, but he's too laid-back. He needs someone to keep an eye on him. We can trust him because he's honorable, and the same goes for Maggie and Evelyn, but you'll have to come over here regularly, for at least a week per month."

"By myself? What about you?"

"I'll come too, but less often. You know the British market better, and I'm better off handling things in New York."

"That's not necessarily true; in one hour you've managed to come up with a whole publicity plan for Roy, which, by the way, he's agreed to. He complained for a while because it's going to require a lot of hours on his part, but he's aware that his career is stalling."

"It's our business, Thomas. I'm not going to ignore what's going on in London, but we have to divide up the work."

It was almost five and Maggie told us she was leaving. Cooper also said goodbye as, according to him, he'd arranged to meet a friend. As for Evelyn, she'd gone home to her apartment after we'd said goodbye to Roy.

I went home with Esther. I would have liked her to come to Madame Agnès's with me, as this would have given me a sense of security that I didn't feel without her. But I couldn't suggest that she set foot in a brothel.

I hailed a taxi and asked the driver to drop me near Kensington. I needed to walk, and without realizing, or perhaps I did, I made my way to the corner where I had watched Yoko throw herself into the street.

I tried to calm myself down, telling myself that it would have been difficult for anyone to see me the previous night. Not just due to the darkness, but because from that corner I could see but not be seen. Or that's what I wanted to believe.

Walking quickly, I arrived at Madame Agnès's, wondering what I was going to find there.

The butler opened the door with a guarded expression and invited me to come in.

"You're here early, Mr. Spencer. Will you have a drink in the library or would you prefer to go into the lounge?"

"It's six o'clock," I said as if in apology.

"Indeed."

"Could you let Madame know I'm here? I'll wait for her in the small library."

I went to the library, where a minute later a waiter appeared with a bottle of whiskey.

"Would sir prefer whiskey or shall I bring some champagne?"

"Whiskey today, just whiskey."

Madame appeared immediately. She closed the door and we found ourselves alone.

"It looks like we'll be able to weather the storm," she told me very seriously.

"What do you know about Yoko?"

"She's dead. She died at the scene. The car crushed her head and chest."

I knew it, of course. I had witnessed the car drive over Yoko's fragile body.

"Has anyone come asking about her?"

"Aren't you at all affected by what I've just told you? Yoko's dead. She was already dead when the ambulance arrived."

"As you must know, I'm upset by the news, but, even so, I need to know if an investigation is under way that . . . well, that could affect us both," I said, looking at her closely.

"No, there's been nothing so far. A friend told me that the authorities are considering it just another accident: a careless girl who was running and must have tripped and fallen into the street, and an irresponsible young man who may have had one drink too many. And that's what happened—you told me that yourself."

"Yes, Madame. But . . . does anyone know she was working here?"

Madame Agnès seemed uncomfortable at the question. She didn't think it fitting that I should say that the girls who visited her establishment worked there.

"All the girls who join us here know that the sole condition of employment is their discretion. In the thirty years that . . . that I've been receiving guests, not one has committed a single indiscretion. You know that our dear friends are good people, students, ladies with financial problems . . . It is they who benefit most from maintaining such strict discretion," she insisted.

"It's best that way."

"But you . . . I think you owe me an explanation. The waiter insists that Yoko was crying when he served you dinner."

"I didn't claim otherwise. She didn't tell me why, but it was obvious that she had some kind of problem."

"And you don't know what it was . . ."

"Exactly."

"It's all so strange . . ."

"Yes, it is, Madame. You'll understand that I'm the most surprised of all."

"I hope we don't find ourselves impacted by what's happened. In the end it was a tragedy. The only thing I regret is being unable to attend the funeral; I couldn't explain how I knew her."

We remained in silence for a few seconds, each absorbed in our own thoughts.

"We shouldn't feel guilty, Madame; it was an accident."

"But she . . . The waiter said she was crying."

"I've already told you I don't know why. In any case, whatever the reason may have been, I don't think it can be linked to the fact that a young man had too much to drink, put his foot down too hard on the accelerator, and crashed into her."

"But why was she running? Why did she leave you behind?" Her voice was reproachful.

"I don't know, Madame. I only offered to go with her to find a taxi and she suddenly sped up. Perhaps she saw one in the distance, perhaps she regretted letting me go with her, given that your rules are strict about prohibiting contact outside the walls of your establishment. We'll end up going crazy if we try to find an explanation. It was a terrible accident and we have to get over it," I insisted.

"Her colleagues are very upset, and so are the rest of the staff here. Yoko was reserved, but kind and helpful."

I poured myself another whiskey from the bottle the waiter had left on a low table next to the ice bucket.

"We ought to forget," I murmured.

"Will you dine with us tonight? I think Nataly will be here this evening . . ."

"Ah, Nataly! Nothing would please me more than having dinner with her."

"I'll go and see whether she's arrived yet and I'll let her know that you're here. What time would you like us to serve dinner?"

I looked at my watch. It was almost seven. Esther would be at the apartment, working. I could call her and tell her that I was going to be late. That's what I did. She didn't ask me why or how late I was going to be, she just murmured a quiet "All right, I'll be working for some time."

Nataly came into the library wearing a vibrant pink dress and black ballet flats. She looked even younger than she was. The pink suited her.

"I'm pleased to see you," she said coldly, holding out her hand to me. It was forbidden to kiss as a greeting at Madame Agnès's.

"I'm pleased to see you too," I replied without much conviction.

To be honest, I had no desire for her that night. I wanted to get out of that place. I could feel how uncomfortable Madame Agnès was to have me there. I felt the same. I realized that this could be my last visit to her establishment. We needed time to forget, or at least to relegate everything that had happened to some forgotten corner of our minds.

"Madame has told me that we'll be having dinner together. I don't really fancy seeing anyone I don't know tonight. We're all very upset about Yoko. The university is organizing a memorial service."

As on previous occasions, Nataly was the best source of information on Yoko.

We went up to a private room and this time Nataly didn't take her shoes off. I looked at her expectantly.

"I'm not wearing heels today. I twisted my ankle a week ago. Look, it's still swollen," she explained without my asking.

"Tell me everything you know about . . . well, about what happened to Yoko."

Some gentle knocks at the door announced the waiter, who arrived with two trays on which were arranged smoked salmon, roast turkey, and the obligatory bottle of champagne. I ordered a Coca-Cola for Nataly.

"So tell me . . ."

"You know something, don't you? She was with you last night. It seems that a waiter saw her crying when he brought your dinner up. Then you left together and, it would appear, Yoko was hit by a car on her way home."

"So that's what they're saying here."

"Well, you can't deny that you were with Yoko last night, when she had the accident. Everyone saw you. I wasn't here, but the girls told me. They said that Yoko was fine, that she didn't seem sad, that they don't understand what could have made her cry, except that you . . . sometimes you're a bit rough. But you couldn't have had time because she was already crying before dinner . . ."

"I didn't sleep with her, she told me she wasn't feeling well. She didn't tell me why she was crying either. I offered to go with her to find a taxi. Since she'd gone up to a private room and earned the fee for dinner, there was no reason for her to stay any longer."

"That's all? Are you sure you didn't insist on going home with her?" she asked mistrustfully.

"Hey, what are you suggesting?" I asked, alarmed.

"You seemed so obsessed with her before you went to New York . . . Well, in truth, I was the only one who knew about that. You asked me for her address, her boyfriend's name . . . You wanted to know everything about Yoko. And I knew you were seeing each other away from Madame Agnès's."

"What would you know?" I replied, irritated.

"I . . . I don't think Yoko liked you. Her face would cloud over when she saw you arrive here. She would go and throw up. Maybe the others didn't notice, but I did. I used to watch you two. Just seeing you made her suffer and she started to lose weight. She looked like a ghost. Madame told her off; she'd say that she looked so starved she was going to scare away the gentlemen guests. Even so, none of them complained. Yoko's regulars remained her regulars. Then you left and Yoko gradually started getting better. She even smiled from time to time."

"You've crossed the line, Nataly, and you're jumping to the wrong conclusions. Perhaps things weren't going well between Yoko and her boyfriend, or maybe she had problems with her parents. You yourself told me that her mother had gone back to Japan and was pressuring Yoko to join her," I replied angrily.

"Or perhaps someone threatened to tell Dave, Yoko's boyfriend, how she earned her living." Her words were an accusation.

"And who would want to do a thing like that?" I asked defiantly.

"Perhaps you. At the end of the day, you were obsessed with her. Perhaps you threatened to tell her boyfriend if she didn't do what you wanted. That could easily have been the case."

"I thought you were going to study quantum physics, but maybe you should become a novelist instead. You have such an imagination! Be careful, Nataly, don't go saying things you might regret," I said with a threat in my voice.

"Do you think I'm stupid? I'm talking to you, saying aloud what I think. I haven't spoken to Madame Agnès about this, and she's asked me what kind of man you are on several occasions and whether you might have done anything to harm Yoko."

"What an old hag!"

"Well, it makes sense that she would want to know what kind of men frequent her establishment. Here at Madame Agnès's the girls are guaranteed that they won't have to put up with any strange fantasies on the part of the men who come here, that there are lines that the gentlemen can't cross."

"And what have you told her?"

"That you're not delightful but you are acceptable. You've got a lot of anger inside you but you control it. You know you can't go too far, at least not at this establishment. As for other places . . . I pity the girl who falls into your hands!"

"You don't have a very good opinion of me," I protested.

"Nor you of me. To you I'm a whore and to me you're a guy who needs to solve his problems by sleeping with whores. We're even."

"You've got some nerve."

Nataly shrugged and looked anxiously at the plate of salmon. I wasn't hungry but I told her to eat. She didn't hesitate and served herself a generous helping.

"Salmon with Coca-Cola." I smiled.

"You should try some, it's really good."

"And what do they say at the university?"

"The people in her department think it was an accident. Yoko's father has explained that a drunk driver hit her when she was trying to cross the road.

"I think they're going to do an autopsy and then they'll cremate her in a few days' time. Her family is waiting for her mother to arrive from Japan. I know that her classmates want to hold a memorial service for her in addition to the funeral her father's arranging and that they'll all attend."

"What about her boyfriend?"

"He's distraught. He was waiting for her at the flat. When the police arrived and told him that Yoko had died I think he had a nervous breakdown. They were very much in love. I don't know if you knew, but they were planning their wedding. They were going to get married within a month. Yoko had bought her dress and they'd sent out the invitations."

Nataly set her cutlery on the table and looked at me so intensely it felt like she was scrutinizing my mind.

"Was it an accident?" she asked me in a low voice.

"Yes, of course it was an accident. When we left Madame Agnès's, I offered to help her find a taxi, but she was in a hurry and was going so fast it was difficult to keep up with her. She was almost running, she left me behind and . . . well, what happened happened, the car hit her. That's all. I'm not responsible for any of it," I declared firmly.

"Well, one thing's for sure, she's dead and we'll never know why."

"It was an accident," I insisted.

"Yes, perhaps it was . . ."

"Will you find out the results of the autopsy?"

"Perhaps. You know I know a couple of people in her department. They might know something."

"I'd like to know the results."

"I suppose you would."

"Will you be here tomorrow?"

"I won't be here again until Friday."

"Then change your shift or give me your phone number so I can call you."

"I'd rather keep you out of my life. I have no intention of giving you my number."

"If you come tomorrow and tell me what you know, I'll make it worth your while."

"All right. It's a fair trade, but don't you think Madame will find out the results of the autopsy? She has friends in high places who will let her know everything to do with Yoko's death."

"You do what I've asked. I'll pay you well for it. I want to know whatever's said about Yoko."

"All right, tomorrow at six."

When she had finished eating she looked at me lazily, without hiding her lack of interest in having sex. On another occasion I would have forced her to, but Esther was waiting for me, so I let her go without laying a finger on her. I saw that she was relieved.

I didn't say goodbye to Madame Agnès. After all, I would be back the next day.

Esther was making a sandwich when I got home. I asked her to make another for me as I told her what I had found out.

"We'll have to wait until tomorrow. The worst that could happen is that they find traces of your DNA on that girl."

"I told you, I didn't go to bed with her. They won't find anything."

"That would be best."

We slept better that night. We were exhausted and soon succumbed to sleep, mine full of nightmares and Esther's calm and deep.

———

The next day we had a meeting at the office with the whole team. Global Communication could survive. Esther was sure of it, and she had even convinced the ever-skeptical Maggie.

"You're lucky to have your partner," she told me after Esther had given her a list of things that needed to be done.

"I know," I agreed, proud of Esther.

"What I don't understand is why she's agreed to be your partner, she doesn't really need you."

Maggie's comment annoyed me. Was my dependence on Esther so obvious? It looked like it, at least for intelligent people who kept asking themselves why a woman like her put up with a guy like me. To be honest, I couldn't explain it either. She wasn't in love with me; her love for me was in the past. She had more creative talent than I could ever have. She was meticulous and a perfectionist at work, while I got bored if I had to work on something for more than an hour at a time. And since we'd been earning money her appearance had improved. She had never been pretty, but some good Italian shoes, a few designer pantsuits, and a collection of natural silk shirts worked miracles. Oh, and her hair—her new hairstyle suited her. She no longer wore her brown hair long and curly; the hairdresser had managed to tame her mane into a gently wavy midlength style. She wouldn't grab people's attention as she passed, but if you gave her a second glance, she was clearly an attractive woman.

I found the day interminable. At Esther's suggestion, I invited Maggie, Evelyn, and Cooper to lunch at a fashionable restaurant where the food is terrible but people go to be seen. Maggie was delighted because a model and a famous soccer player were sitting at the table opposite ours, and a well-known BBC journalist and a government minister were sitting at another.

"So this is what it's like where the rich and famous eat," she said, amused.

The shrimp cocktail didn't agree with me. I threw up after we'd barely finished eating.

"I'll sue them," I told the others as we walked back to the office.

My head started to hurt and I felt nauseated, but I pushed through. I had already decided to go to Madame Agnès's to see Nataly.

Esther was worried to see me so pale and running to the bathroom every few minutes to throw up.

"I think you've gotten food poisoning and it would be best if you saw a doctor. Let's go."

It was four o'clock so I let myself be taken. The doctor told me the obvious, that it must be a food-borne illness.

"You have to expel everything that's poisoned you," he confirmed while he jotted down a prescription for several medicines. "Go to a hospital if you experience any further symptoms, but I think that you'll feel better by tomorrow with what I've prescribed. For now, you need to rest."

Esther insisted that we go home, but I knew that I wouldn't be able to rest easy until I knew the results of Yoko's autopsy. So Esther decided to come with me to Madame Agnès's.

"You can't come, they won't even let you come in."

"I'll wait for you on the street or in a nearby café, but I won't even consider leaving you alone in this state."

I couldn't convince her. I felt so sick that I let her have her way.

At six on the dot I rang Madame Agnès's doorbell with Esther watching from a short distance away. The butler let me in and told me that Madame had said that if he were to see me he should let her know immediately.

Madame Agnès was waiting for me in the library. She was speaking to a gentleman I'd seen there on previous occasions but with whom I'd never exchanged a word.

"Ah, Mr. Spencer. Come in. Would you like a glass of champagne or would you prefer a whiskey?" Madame Agnès offered.

"I'm going to surprise you today, Madame, I'd like a chamomile tea. Lunch did not agree with my stomach."

"Chamomile tea? Well, if that's what you'd like . . . Oh!
Allow me to introduce Mr. Stewart, a dear friend who happens
to be passing through the city. But please take a seat, Mr. Spencer. Mr. Stewart was just leaving, isn't that right, my dear?"

Mr. Stewart nodded to me and stepped out of the room. The
waiter brought the chamomile tea to the serving table. We were
left alone. Madame handed me the tea.

"I've got news about Yoko."

"And Mr. Stewart . . ."

"Is a civil servant with good connections. They found nothing
that might be damaging to us during the autopsy. They found no
traces of semen on her. Nor should they have . . . all my gentlemen use condoms, isn't that right?"

"I've already told you that she was out of sorts and I decided
to give up the night as a lost cause. What kind of man do you
take me for, Madame?"

"She died instantly. One of the wheels crushed her head. It
was a terrible accident. They're going to cremate her first thing
in the morning the day after tomorrow. It's a relief for everyone
that it will be over."

"There won't be any further investigation?"

"No. Yoko was a good student. Her boyfriend has said that
he thought her parents were supporting her and they haven't
contradicted him. I think that her mother . . . well, I think her
mother may have known that her daughter was coming here,
but obviously she hasn't wanted to share that information in a
situation like this. When all is said and done, Yoko is gone and
nothing will bring her back."

I finished drinking my tea, which would naturally cost me
the same as champagne. My head was spinning and I was feeling
nauseated again. I steadied myself when I saw Nataly's silhouette through the glass pane in the door.

"But, darling, it's Thursday today!" Madame Agnès exclaimed in surprise.

"I hope you don't mind that I've come today. I'll come again tomorrow, of course," Nataly said with a half-smile.

"You're always welcome. I think some of our friends are in the lounge . . ."

"If you don't mind, Madame, I'd like Nataly to join me for a light dinner," I interrupted her. "I can't stay long, but if she doesn't mind . . ."

"Of course! I'll tell them to serve you dinner immediately in the Blue Room. How does that sound?"

"Lovely, thank you, Madame."

I clutched Nataly's arm because my head was spinning so fast I was afraid of falling over. Once we entered the private room I made for the bathroom, where I spent quite a while vomiting.

Nataly waited patiently in the small lounge, enjoying a Coca-Cola the waiter had brought along with the champagne.

I collapsed onto the sofa. Sweat was running down my face and neck, soaking my whole body. Perhaps I should have gone to a hospital, but I would let Esther make that decision as soon as I left Madame Agnès's.

"You look terrible, what's wrong?" asked Nataly, without a hint of compassion in her voice.

"I've been knocked out by shrimp."

"You should go home."

"That's exactly what I'll do as soon as you tell me everything you've found out."

"Dave, Yoko's boyfriend, is distraught. His friends at the university say that he doesn't understand what happened, that Yoko went through a bad patch a while ago, but that she'd been better recently. They say that Yoko . . . well, that she was a nervous girl, especially given the anorexia. She ate very little and was constantly throwing up." Nataly conveyed an element of reproach in her words.

"What else?"

"Yoko's mother would like to take her ashes to Japan. Her father doesn't have any objections, but there's so much red tape that they eventually agreed to lay her to rest in London. And that's all."

"There's nothing more?" I asked mistrustfully.

"Nothing more. It's better that way, isn't it? If there were more to know you probably wouldn't like it."

"You've been very impertinent, Nataly."

"You know what, Thomas? Before I didn't think you were such a bad guy. It's not that I liked you, none of that, but at least there's no need for pretense with you. You've never worried about what a girl might feel, so you only expected them to please you. That's fine, faking it is very boring. But . . ."

"But what?"

"I regret having given you information about Yoko. I was wrong to do it, I think I harmed her. Ever since I told you what I found out about her, things changed. Yoko started to lose weight, she threw up every time she saw you here . . . She was nervous, she was afraid of something. She was afraid of you."

"You're crossing the line. Yoko had no reason to be afraid of me. I didn't want anything special from her. Of all the girls here she was the one who pleased me the most, nothing more."

"Well, I think there was much more to it, Thomas."

I didn't like what Nataly was suggesting. Her inquisitive stance and her implication that I had something to do with Yoko's death annoyed me.

"I'm going back to the U.S. in a few days. Tell me how much I owe you for this information."

"Five hundred pounds."

"You haven't told me anything that's worth five hundred pounds."

"It's a fair price, Thomas." She looked at me, defying me.

I gave her the money. I didn't want to argue with her. I was starting to feel nauseated again and I wanted to get out of there.

We left the private room and I leaned on her arm again to go down the stairs. The butler was waiting at the entrance with our coats and I placed the envelope with the money to cover my visit on the silver tray. Like all Madame Agnès's clients, I knew the rates. When I went out onto the street and into the cool evening air, I felt better. Nataly didn't even say goodbye to me and walked quickly until she disappeared among the first shadows of the night. I looked around until I spotted Esther, who was waiting a few steps from Madame Agnès's. Her nose was red from the cold.

"Who was that girl?"

"A friend of Yoko's."

She didn't let me tell her anything until we got back to the apartment. She made me undress and get into bed and take some of the medication, which made me vomit even more. I had a hellish night.

On Friday morning the vomiting and nausea had passed, but I felt so weak that I couldn't get up.

"I won't be able to go to Derbyshire and Roy's expecting us for dinner tonight," I reminded her.

"I'll call him and we'll go tomorrow. You shouldn't worry. You've had food poisoning; it can happen to anyone and Roy will understand."

I spent the rest of the day in bed. I got up only so that the maid could clean our room, which after a night of sweating and vomiting was like a battleground.

On Saturday morning we went to Derbyshire. I felt better, although not well enough to face the intensely emotional situation waiting for us. We not only needed to see Roy but to confront Suzi too.

Roy was waiting for us at the Rural Party headquarters with his fellow mayors. They had prepared a small room with tables of sandwiches and drinks, ready to spend most of the day there.

Esther explained the change of strategy. Roy needed to fit in with his voters, so he would do what they were doing. The electoral committee should arrange things so that over the next few weeks Roy could balance his time at the town hall with working as a baker, mechanic, office worker, farmer, sheep shearer . . . whatever the men in that county did. Furthermore, once a month Roy and the rest of the Rural Party mayors would hold an open meeting with all the county voters who wanted to raise any issues.

I listened to them discuss Esther's proposals for some time. I remained silent; I didn't have the energy to convince them of anything. I still wasn't feeling great and I didn't give a damn what those men thought.

Esther handled them well. She listened to them patiently, she let them speak, she didn't disagree with any of the ideas they suggested, but in the end she made sure that her ideas won out. Roy had the last word: "We'll do what Esther has suggested." Evelyn smiled in relief.

Then we went to Roy's house. He had insisted on inviting us over for dinner. Evelyn seemed worried about what Suzi might say.

"She knows you're here. I told her this morning and I warned her that I don't want any trouble. She'll join us for dinner."

Roy poured us some drinks in the lounge while we waited for Suzi, who was late in appearing. When she came into the lounge I couldn't help looking her up and down in astonishment. She was thin, so thin that she was unrecognizable.

"She barely eats," said Roy when he saw me looking.

Esther hugged her and Suzi didn't reject her, but she didn't return the hug either. I went over to her but I didn't dare kiss her, or even offer her my hand. Evelyn did. Suzi didn't respond to her either.

"Darling, you look terrible and this is ridiculous," Esther began, having sat down next to her.

"What do you know?" Suzi murmured.

"I know very well what's happened and you're stupid if you destroy yourself over it. You've got no reason to. Yours won't be the first marriage of convenience—take advantage of the situation."

"And how do you take advantage of living with someone you detest and no longer respect?"

Roy took Suzi's declaration with a gulp of whiskey from his glass.

"Come on, Suzi. Roy hasn't done anything so terrible. He acted in good faith. He thought he was doing the best thing for the county," said Evelyn, sticking up for Roy.

"My husband isn't an innocent little lamb, of course he knew what he was doing. He stabbed my family in the back. He stabbed me in the back. He betrayed us," Suzi replied without even looking at Evelyn.

"You've closed your eyes and you don't want to see beyond your version of what's happened. Do you think that Roy wanted to ruin you? Would he be so stupid as to ruin your father and leave your children without an inheritance? Please, Suzi, you're an intelligent woman!" Esther intervened.

"And so are you, so find another argument. He hoped to get a lot out of his betrayal, more than they've given him."

"Things haven't gone so badly, Suzi. Your parents still have a lot of land, they're not ruined and they've received a good payout for the damage caused," I chimed in.

"My father didn't need more money, he just wanted them to leave his sheep in peace."

"I can't believe that you've stopped loving Roy . . ." Evelyn intervened again.

"Would you love a man who doesn't mind blackmailing you? That's what Roy's done with your help, blackmailed me by preventing me from asking for a divorce and defending my parents. But once my father's no longer with us . . . on that day . . ."

"You have two children, Suzi. Do you want to punish them?" I asked, dispensing with tact.

"On that day we'll get out of here. My children won't have to live in this county or put up with the stench their father leaves in his wake."

"I can't reason with her," Roy declared, clenching his fists.

Esther looked at me and I read in her eyes that she agreed with Roy, that there was no hope.

"Perhaps it would be best for you to divorce amicably. Agree on the terms so as not to do damage to yourselves. You could even go and live elsewhere for a while," Esther suggested, looking at Suzi.

"I'm not leaving while my father's alive. I can't leave him alone here."

"Suzi, your attitude isn't getting you anywhere. You're hurting yourself. Only yourself," Esther stated.

"Would you let your husband screw your parents over and make a mockery of you, then?" Suzi barely contained her rage as she spoke.

"That's not what's happened. There've been a range of circumstances that make Roy look like the villain, but that's not the case. Were you stupid enough to marry and live with a bastard? Wouldn't you have realized sooner if that were the case? Or do you think that Roy is such a dirtbag that he managed to deceive you for all those years? Stop feeling sorry for yourself, Suzi. You've succumbed to unreasonable bitterness. I'm not saying that Roy's done everything right, but who doesn't make mistakes? However, he never wanted to hurt your father at any point and he certainly never wanted to lose you. You're the one who seems to want to get rid of him, it's as if you've been waiting for an excuse to put an end to your marriage. You should be honest with yourself and with him. No, I don't believe that Roy is the problem; the problem stems from you."

Esther's speech sounded like a verdict. Suzi remained silent, looking at Esther in astonishment. Roy shifted uncomfortably in his armchair, and neither Evelyn nor I dared move. Esther had taken a gamble.

"We sometimes make excuses to do things that we want but don't dare to do . . . Perhaps the only thing that happened to you is that you didn't know how to end your marriage," Esther insisted, holding Suzi's incredulous gaze.

Silence fell once more in the lounge. We could hear one another's breathing. I had to repress the urge to vomit. My stomach still wasn't quite right.

"And what do you have to say to me about the blackmail? You've threatened me with making public what . . . what happened to my father when he was a child. That terrible accident."

"Which ended the life of another man," I said. "It wasn't our idea, it was Schmidt and the lawyers'. We did what they told us to. We didn't enjoy coming here and making threats about making what your father did public . . . I swear we didn't. But you didn't leave the lawyers any other option. I'm not happy about what we did. But we couldn't refuse. Schmidt would have had our balls." I spoke with all the conviction I could muster. I thought I could again taste the flavor of shrimp rising from my stomach to my mouth.

"You're not trying to present yourself as the victim, are you? That really would be rich," Suzi replied angrily.

"Money has its own rules," I replied, "and some of them are very dirty. The lawyers have invested a lot in creating the Rural Party and making Roy a leader."

"Roy needs to establish himself," Esther intervened, "for the Rural Party to grow, to make a name for himself in London . . . Only then will he be free and be able to put an end to his relationship with those lawyers. But until then . . . Well, in reality he's had no choice but to do some things that have left their mark on him. You're not being fair to him on that count. You should have been by his side, supporting him through the bad times that he had to go through precisely because he didn't want to harm your father. Roy's gone to Calvary and you've made it even worse. But I know that's not the issue, Suzi. The real issue is that you've fallen out of love with Roy. What's happened has provided you with an excuse—not just one to offer him, but for you to justify this to yourself as well," she concluded in a monotone, yet bolstered with such certainty that Suzi hesitated to reply.

"Are you trying to make me feel guilty?" she finally asked, surprised.

"I'm not trying to do anything, Suzi; I'm analyzing reality. Sometimes we look for excuses to escape situations that make us uncomfortable. Nothing that Roy has done deserves your disapproval, let alone the threat of divorce. I think that when a woman makes a decision like that she doesn't do it quickly, especially because you have two children, boys to whom you would have to explain why you're separating from their father. And you don't feel able to tell them the truth: 'I don't feel anything for him anymore.' These children of yours would never forgive you, so you've preferred to play up Roy's errors to make him the guilty one and justify your split from him."

Esther spoke so firmly that even I began to think that this was what had really happened.

We were silent again. Suzi was disconcerted. She seemed to be asking herself whether what she was hearing were true, if she might really be the guilty one for not loving Roy enough.

I didn't know whether Esther had said all that because she truly believed it or because she was an arch-manipulator.

"You've just said that we should get a divorce," Suzi said, bringing us back to reality.

"Yes, I did say that," Esther confirmed. "I think it's what you want, Suzi, and it would be best for both of you. But do it without playing tricks, without trying to justify yourself. The love is gone, Suzi, it's better to admit it, but there's no need to convince yourself or others that your husband is a monster. It's better to recognize the situation, speak about it honestly and seek an agreement. It would make the most sense. Roy shouldn't try to harm you, nor should you try to harm him, and neither of you have the right to harm your children. An amicable divorce is better than continuing to live in this hell," she declared, trying to catch Suzi's eye.

"I'll think about it. Yes, I'll think about it. That could be the solution," Suzi admitted.

Roy's face fell. He looked angrily at Esther. I felt the need to intervene before we lost control of the situation, although, in my opinion, Esther had been amazing; she had calmed Suzi right down.

"I think we should eat, it's getting a bit late," I said to break the tension.

We went to the dining room and, surprisingly, Suzi seemed livelier. Evelyn embarked upon some small talk, and Suzi didn't refuse to take part in the conversation. We told her about the plan we had to advance Roy's career and she listened attentively, and even couldn't help laughing when she learned that her husband was going to spend several weeks doing the same jobs as the other men in the county. Roy was the one who proved taciturn; he barely spoke.

I didn't eat a single mouthful; I limited myself to a couple of cups of chamomile tea. I wanted to go to the hotel.

When we got to our room I congratulated Esther on having managed to appease Suzi and asked her whether she believed anything she'd said.

"But of course I believe what I said. I'm not a cynic like you. I'm convinced that Suzi has gotten tired of Roy but doesn't dare admit it, not even to herself. Perhaps politics has come between them. For Roy politics has become his principal preoccupation and pastime. He travels to London regularly, she must have grown impatient. It may even be that he's stopped treating her with the same kind of devotion as he did when he was just the husband of the richest woman in the county. Marriages often fail without there being a specific cause. But splitting up is difficult and spouses often want to feel like they have explanations before they take the fatal step. Anything will do. And Roy gave all the trump cards to Suzi. He gave her the perfect excuse when he made his father-in-law sell his land to the gas company."

"Have you always thought that was what had happened?" I asked in astonishment.

"No, in truth, I came to that conclusion along the way, once I saw Suzi and saw how uncomfortable Roy was. I don't know, but I think that things can't have been going well between them, however much he swears that she is the only woman for him. In reality men find it very hard to upset the status quo. It's easier to live with your wife and your children, even if you don't feel the same way about your wife as you used to."

"Do you think Suzi has . . . well . . . that there's someone else?"

"No, I don't think so. But since Roy got involved with politics, he's been enjoying a freedom that he never had before, and it may be that Roy hasn't been behaving like the loving husband he would have us believe he is. It may also be that she's met someone she secretly likes . . . Who knows. But I think that their problems go back a long way. Sometimes women don't know how to rid themselves of their husbands; we need a good reason to present to the rest of society and even to ourselves. It's the result of decades of education intended to make us into model wives and mothers, and breaking out of that role is not within everyone's reach."

Esther has always been able to surprise me. Then and now. Paul Hard is adamant that she is the only person I've ever admired. I suppose he's right. That night I went to bed fascinated by the way that she had handled, and almost resolved, the situation.

I didn't feel well. My stomach was still dancing inside my body. I was exhausted and the only thing I wanted was to go back to London and my apartment. But we still needed to earn the salary Roy paid us.

It was four in the morning when the trilling of my cell phone woke us up. Roy's voice broke the silence of the night.

"You screwed me over," he said in a thick voice. The voice of a drunken man.

"Listen, Roy, it's four in the morning. Why don't you go to bed?" I protested.

"Suzi is delighted with your girl's idea that we should divorce. She told me that she's prepared to reach an agreement satisfactory to both of us. Silence in exchange for her liberty and a significant amount of money. She wants the shirt off my back. She's made it clear that she's not going to let me benefit from the money I gained from her father's suffering. She's demanding everything I have, including the house, which I have to leave at the earliest opportunity."

"It doesn't seem like a bad deal to me. We'll talk about it in the morning."

"You're a bastard! Of course it's a bad deal, you've played me right into her hands."

"You were already there, Roy," I replied.

"She was the one in my hands," he shot back crossly.

"You know that's not the case. Suzi was a time bomb, and now at least you can deactivate her."

Esther, who was listening to the conversation, took the phone from me, gesturing that I should let her speak to Roy. "All yours," I whispered, wishing I could go back to sleep.

"Roy, the way things stand, the best outcome is a divorce by mutual agreement. I'll come up with a draft of the terms Suzi has to agree to so that she doesn't break her word in the future. You should call your lawyer first thing in the morning. He needs to compose a document outlining the conditions of the divorce that you will both sign. Then we'll meet with Suzi and, if she signs, job done."

"It's that easy . . . You've ended my marriage. I'll never forgive you." Roy spoke so loudly that I could hear him through the phone.

"I'm convinced that you will and that you will soon recover. I'm sure you'll find consolation at that Madame's place, what was her name?"

"You're a walking disaster!" shouted Roy.

"I work for you, I defend your interests; trust me. Call your lawyer. How about we meet at his office at eight?" said Esther, not giving in to Roy's pressure.

"It's Sunday, or had you forgotten that?"

"This is a small town, Roy, I don't think you'll have much trouble convincing him how urgent it is that you see him. Make it worth his while. He'll say yes, you'll see. Call us at seven to give us the address. Good night, Roy; try to rest awhile."

I had sat up in astonishment at what Esther had said to Roy.

"Are you planning to dictate the divorce agreement?" I asked her.

"No, just to give some directions. It seems fair to me that Suzi should take him for all he's got, but with conditions. For example, she should promise that under no circumstances will she give interviews to the press, nor reveal anything that took place during the years of their marriage or the cause of their separation. If she does otherwise, she'll have to return every last penny to Roy, with interest."

"Where's all this come from? You're worse than Machiavelli."

"Let's go to sleep for a while, tomorrow is going to be a trying day."

Esther kissed me on the cheek and then went to sleep. I couldn't stop thinking about what awaited us in a few hours' time.

I called Roy at seven. He had fallen asleep drunk and didn't remember that he'd called us a few hours earlier. I told him to contact his lawyer and it took him some time to understand why. He protested and fired off a few curses before hanging up on me.

Esther was taking a shower so I asked them to bring breakfast up to the room. Chamomile tea for me and toast, orange juice, and strong coffee for Esther. Roy called us to say that his lawyer would expect us at nine, after he'd promised to pay him four times his regular fee.

When we left the hotel, the first breath of fresh air made me feel better. My stomach had accepted the morning's chamomile tea calmly and had even tolerated half a slice of toast.

Roy's lawyer was in a bad mood when he greeted us. Even so, he listened patiently to Esther's instructions regarding the terms of the divorce.

"Wow, I didn't realize things were going so badly between you . . . I'd heard rumors, but I assumed you were going through a crisis . . . In short, I'm sorry. Is Suzi in agreement?"

Roy nodded and I practically offered up a silent prayer that Suzi hadn't changed her mind. You never knew what to expect with that woman.

We left the lawyer to work things out with Esther and waited for the document to be written up. They took almost two hours, or rather, Esther wasn't happy with the first drafts and made the lawyer redo them until the text of the document said word for word what she thought was best. It was midday when we finished and set off for Roy's house.

"Does Suzi know we're coming?" I asked, fearing that she might not.

"Yes, she's expecting us," Roy assured me.

It was true. Suzi was expecting us, and she wasn't alone. There was a man with her. Her father's lawyer. An old man who'd known her since she was a little girl. Roy frowned. She hadn't told him that she was thinking of calling her own lawyer, but Esther seemed delighted.

The elderly lawyer read the document through at least three or four times. Then he handed it to Suzi.

"Economically you come out the winner, but it's for you to say whether you're prepared to do what they ask of you."

Suzi read the papers and her frown grew as she did so. She

would have liked to enjoy an absolute victory, to finish Roy off. She asked her lawyer to go with her into another room. She wanted to speak with him in private. The time started to pass agonizingly slowly. I began to feel hungry. A good sign that I was recovering, but I was mainly worried that Suzi might reject the agreement. When they came back, it was her lawyer who spoke first: "Suzi does not agree that it's necessary to announce the divorce to the media."

"But it's essential," said Esther, "you have to do these things properly. It's a case of both parties appearing before the press to say that they have, by mutual agreement, decided to put an end to their marriage, that neither of them deserves any blame because they've spent many happy years together, that they love and respect each other and want to maintain a good relationship for the benefit of their children, and that there is no other cause for the separation than the passage of time. They need to ask the press to respect their private lives and warn them that from this point on, neither of them will say anything further regarding their decision to divorce, and that they trust the media to understand this. Roy will declare that he owed his voters this explanation, and Suzi will add that Roy is the best of men and a politician who can be trusted, and will ask that all those who supported him in the polling booths continue to do so."

"Indeed. That's exactly what Suzi doesn't want to say," explained her lawyer in annoyance.

"It's necessary that she do so, not just for Roy's good, but also for Suzi's, and, most importantly, for the children's," Esther insisted.

"And if I don't?"

"We'll go back to square one. There will be no divorce," Esther said, fixing her gaze on Suzi.

"I don't want to say that Roy's a good man. He isn't!" Suzi exclaimed.

"He is the father of your children. You should think of them.

It would be terrible if you destroyed their lives purely for your own personal satisfaction and your children grew up traumatized. Yes, their parents have separated, not because either of them is a monster, but because the love faded, ended." Esther spoke with such conviction that I wanted to applaud her.

Silence reigned for several seconds. Suzi seemed to be mulling over Esther's words and her lawyer was watching her expectantly. For his part, Roy barely managed to contain the rage that was welling up inside him.

I felt like a spectator. I could allow myself this role because Esther was taking the lead. I told myself that I ought to try to persuade her once again to marry me. I couldn't let myself lose her.

Suzi's lawyer began to clear his throat, then he looked at her timidly and finally decided to speak: "You have to make a decision."

"Yes . . . I need to do it. My children don't deserve to have to live with the evidence that their father is a bastard, but that means I have to keep it quiet from others too . . ." Suzi murmured without looking at anyone.

"You come out of this the winner, Suzi," Esther encouraged her. "You'll end up with everything. Roy will give up all your shared belongings and will also have to give you his own money, which he earned independently, outside of the family business."

"Thanks to his corrupt ways," Suzi spat.

I looked at Roy out of the corner of my eye. He was red in the face and a vein in his neck was pulsing so hard it looked like it was about to burst. Esther took hold of his arm soothingly.

"All right. We'll sign the divorce agreement. I'll agree to make the announcement at a press conference and say what needs to be said, but in my own way," Suzi said.

"No, not in your own way, Suzi, in the way that is stipulated in the document you are about to sign." Esther's voice was solid as a rock.

We agreed that Suzi and Roy would sign the divorce papers and the appending agreements first thing Monday morning and then go on to the headquarters of the Rural Party, where they would inform the media of their decision to bring their shared life to an end. This meant that we would have to stay in Derbyshire an extra day, even though Esther had a ticket booked to go back to New York.

We spent the rest of the afternoon at the hotel, listening to Roy's complaints. Esther and Evelyn were trying to convince him of the advantages of the divorce, but he was like a sailor whose ship was sinking.

"You'll need to remarry once a suitable period of time has passed," Esther advised him.

"Marry? Are you mad? I'm never doing that again," Roy declared.

"You'll have to if you want to remain in politics and be anything more than a mayor. You'd do well to find a woman who makes you look good. There must be some divorcée or widow of good family and limited means who would find marriage to you beneficial. It won't be easy to find her—you're not exactly a catch," said Esther, unconcerned at Roy's frown.

"I don't want to get tangled up with a woman again, you only cause problems," he insisted.

"Well, you'd better quit politics then," Esther declared. "People don't trust politicians who aren't like everyone else. They want them to have a wife and children and be part of a happy family. In your case nobody's asking you to fall in love, a marriage of convenience would be best," Esther continued.

"I'll make a list of possible candidates," said Evelyn, laughing.

"You've gone completely mad! Do you think I need you to set me up with a woman? I'm perfectly happy going out with who I choose," protested an agitated Roy.

"Now, ladies, first the divorce, then a few months of bachelorhood. Letting himself be seen with his children each week, so that nobody can say that he isn't an extremely loving father.

And later on we'll see whether he ought to get married or not," I intervened, taking pity on Roy.

"You're right," Evelyn joined in, "but we still need to get to work on a list of possible candidates so he can get to know them. Time waits for no man."

She seemed delighted at the chance to tease Roy, but he thumped his fist on the table, making it clear that nobody should say anything further on the subject. He was not able to take a joke just then, so I signaled to Evelyn not to push it.

We arrived at Roy's lawyer's office at eight o'clock on Monday morning, where Suzi and her lawyer were already waiting. All that was left to do was present the petition for divorce by mutual agreement to the courts. The lawyers assured us they would take care of it that very morning.

When we arrived at the Rural Party headquarters there were more journalists than usual. They had been summoned with the information that Roy was going to make a surprise announcement.

Roy and Suzi, with very serious expressions, entered the room where the press was waiting. Standing in front of a microphone, Roy made the announcement: "I am sorry to inform you that our lawyers have submitted a joint petition for divorce this morning. It's a painful decision which was the subject of lengthy consideration. We ask you to respect our private lives given that we don't want this news to affect our darling children, Ernest and Jim, any more than is necessary.

"I owe a duty to my constituents and that is why I am sharing this particularly painful moment with them. Suzi is the best wife a man could dream of and I hope that life brings her great happiness, all the happiness she deserves, because her happiness is also mine and our children's."

Roy passed the microphone to Suzi while the journalists started to raise their hands, anxious to ask questions. Suzi took the microphone, ready to play her part: "I would like to ask you to respect our privacy at this time. We have made this decision by mutual agreement. Neither party is to blame. As happens to so many couples, our relationship has reached an end, but this does not mean that we have stopped respecting each other and maintaining the consideration and affection that we each deserve as individuals. I hope that Roy's voters will continue to recognize his worth. Thank you very much."

Suzi and Roy left the room in spite of the journalists' protests. Evelyn took the microphone and asked for calm.

"You need to understand that Mr. Parker and his wife have the right to a certain level of privacy. They have informed you of a difficult and painful decision, but from this point on neither of them will make any further reference to their private lives. We ask for your consideration and respect for them and their children, two great kids who don't deserve to see their parents' divorce become a public spectacle. Thank you very much."

Evelyn sounded very convincing, although I doubted the journalists would just accept this and not go digging for more information about the Parkers' divorce.

We went back to London that afternoon and Esther took a flight back to New York that night. I would have liked to go with her, but she insisted that I stay a few days more to keep an eye on Roy and take care of our own interests at the agency. She was right.

The news of the divorce was even featured in one of the London papers, although not the *Times,* which was the only one that would have consoled Roy.

The routine of the London office bored me, and although I had promised myself not to go back to Madame Agnès's, I started to go every evening. I didn't have anything better to do. My only acquaintances other than my colleagues were the men I spoke with in her reception rooms.

Madame was not happy to see me, but she tried to disguise her dismay at my visits.

For the first few days I insisted on being with Nataly, but neither she nor I managed to feel comfortable with each other. The shadow of Yoko hovered between us, although neither of us referred to her.

Nataly's behavior was that of an unwilling partner and she barely spoke to me, which irritated me because her spontaneity and sass were the very things that had most amused me about her in the past. So I decided to spend each evening with a different girl.

I was late getting back to my apartment, but not a single night did I skip calling Esther. I don't know whether she began to suspect that I was still visiting Madame Agnès's, but she never asked me where I'd been, she just asked how things had gone at the office and, most of all, wanted to know whether there were any new developments regarding Suzi and Roy.

As for Madame Agnès, early one evening when I arrived before her other guests, she felt obliged to offer me a glass of champagne and chat with me.

We spoke of banalities to begin with, but I couldn't resist asking her if there was any news about Yoko's death. I knew that Nataly wouldn't have told me if there had been.

"Case closed, my dear friend. We've been lucky. In truth, we worried too much. You know that I have friends in high places, and, from what they told me, not only did the autopsy confirm that Yoko died as a result of the accident, the driver also did us the favor of admitting that he had crashed into her. He couldn't have said anything else, but you never know. The investigators found a couple of witnesses who had seen her running and falling under the wheels of the car.

"The questions of where she was coming from and why she was running remain unanswered, but it seems that there's nothing strange in a young woman hurrying, momentarily losing her concentration, and trying to cross where she shouldn't. Accidents like this are quite common. Or so they tell me."

"And none of the girls have said anything? I don't know . . ."

"What would they say? There's nothing to say. We all depend upon discretion, and they most of all. You know that most of them visit this establishment on a temporary basis. They have other ambitions. A few days ago I saw photographs of one girl's wedding to a distinguished aristocrat in the marriage pages of the *Times*. I was very happy for her."

My visits to Madame Agnès's earned me a couple of accounts. The director of a multinational toy manufacturer with whom I chatted from time to time suggested that I take charge of a television campaign for his toys in the run-up to Christmas. I also signed with an outdoor footwear manufacturer.

Jim Cooper got to work on the campaigns but insisted that he couldn't do it all by himself, and since Roy took up almost all of Evelyn's time, he urged us once more to take on as a subcontractor his friend, who was unemployed but, according to him, was an ace. I agreed, in spite of Maggie's protests, but I also asked Evelyn to help him out. It was a relief for her as she was getting tired of babysitting Roy.

I would see Roy from time to time at Madame Agnès's. It was the best place for us to talk. And although I would see him laughing and enjoying the girls' company, as soon as we were alone he would start to complain about losing Suzi.

"I feel lonely, Thomas. Damn you all for convincing me to agree to the divorce."

"It was the right thing to do, Roy. Suzi had no option but to accept your conditions. She had no other way out. Sooner or later she would have ended up exploding: your ex-wife has a lot of character."

"And what about my kids? I have to settle for seeing them one day a week and a couple of weekends a month."

"It's the same for other divorced fathers. Don't complain. It's good for you to be seen around the county with the boys; take them to see a rugby match, to eat burgers, I don't know . . . Do the things that single fathers normally do when it's their turn to see the kids."

Roy had rented a small apartment in the area, but he wasn't enjoying his life as a bachelor.

"Esther was right, I'm going to have to get married," Roy admitted, "and not just because it'll keep the voters happy, but because I don't like living alone. I thought regaining my liberty would be fun, but I feel depressed when I get back to my flat. And in London, well, you can see . . . My only distraction is visiting Madame Agnès's. That's not a life, Thomas, I'm telling you."

He was right. I had also begun to value my shared life with Esther. That was why I was eager to go back to New York. I found it comforting to find someone there when I got home from work, to have someone to talk to, to feel a hand on my forehead when I felt sick, to not have to worry about restocking the refrigerator and to no longer find, to my surprise, that there was nothing at home to eat.

Yes, I understood Roy, and I advised him to start looking for a wife.

"She shouldn't be too clever, Roy, or she'll make your life complicated. You need a calm, well-mannered woman for whom you are the main occupation."

"They don't exist, Thomas. Look at you. Esther's so clever that she doesn't want to marry you."

"Marriage isn't essential for us," I claimed, annoyed by his comment.

"You can't fool me, my friend, she's the one who doesn't want to get married. She's right, she's worth much more than you are. What does she need you for?"

I returned to New York three weeks later. I went straight to the agency from the airport. I found Esther and Paul Hard arguing about whether to take on a campaign for a new brand of detergent. Paul was saying it wasn't worth it, that the manufacturer's budget was too small to afford an advertising campaign that would make an impact. Esther thought that this was the very thing that made it a challenge and that we should try. I supported Esther. She looked at me gratefully. In reality I wasn't worked up about the detergent campaign but I did want Esther to feel like I was always on her side.

I got back into my routine. We often got up early. Esther would go out for a run at six thirty in the morning and I would go to a gym near the agency at seven. The idea of going out for a run whether it was hot or cold did not appeal to me. The truth is that I've never liked sports, but I needed to follow Esther's lead and she insisted that exercise led to good health.

The gym I had found offered one advantage: all kinds of executives used it. There were some who were obsessed with their physiques and some who did just enough. After speaking with both kinds, I realized that for many of them, going to the gym was an issue of status. It was good for extremely busy Wall Street executives to be seen spending at least an hour a day keeping in shape. The gym had a room where coffee and fruit juice were served all morning, along with whole wheat toast, organic butter and spreads, boiled eggs, and a whole range of guilt-free cuisines.

There were days when the only thing I did was have breakfast and then go to the agency. I was not the only one.

Neither Paul nor I were fooling ourselves. The work came in because of Esther. She was the rising star, the one who was sought out for her original ideas, the one who could make an advertisement for dog food into a work of art.

I took care of the finances and personnel and administered the business. She and Paul did the creative work, along with three young people they'd recruited.

I made a new attempt to persuade Esther to move to a different area, but she proved reluctant. She was proud of the apartment in Nolita, even though she was beginning to admit that we could do with more space.

"At least think about it," I asked her. "I'm not suggesting we move uptown. I know you like downtown or Brooklyn, and there are reasonably priced places there."

"Do you want to buy yourself a place?" she asked me.

"I want to buy us a place, partner, for both of us."

"But . . . No, no, that wouldn't be a good idea."

"Why not?"

She didn't answer me. I knew the answer: because she still dreamed that I might free her from the duty of being with me. An unwritten commitment, but one by which she felt bound to me. Leaving things as they were meant there was still an air of the provisional about our personal relationship, but letting me buy us a place to live was to further tighten the bond between us.

"I don't have the money to buy anything in Greenwich Village or Brooklyn," she said eventually.

"But I do," I replied, watching her closely.

"Yeah, but you can't buy a place in both our names—it wouldn't be fair."

"I'm going to do something different, Esther. I'm going to go see my lawyer and ask him to prepare a document stating that all my worldly possessions are also yours. What I have, we will share."

I regretted it as soon as I said it. It was the stupidest thing I could have done, but, on the other hand, I savored the drama of the moment, passing myself off as a man so deeply in love that he was prepared to put his life, or rather his money, in the hands of a woman.

Esther began to cry. She covered her face with her hands and began to shake. I knew what she was feeling: like a bad person for not loving me as I appeared to love her, for still longing to escape from me.

I was acting like an innocent child who was placing himself entirely in her hands: whatever her personal wishes were, she couldn't abandon me.

I hugged her, trying to get her to calm down and stop crying. Then I called my lawyer, who asked me several times if I was sure about what I was planning to do. I told him yes in a serious voice and said I wanted the document written up that afternoon. Esther said she would come with me but with the intention of dissuading me.

"Wouldn't it make more sense for you to marry?" suggested the lawyer.

I didn't reply. But I urged him to call my bank so that the manager could take charge of the new situation.

"I can't accept this," Esther murmured, raising her hand to ask me to bring the conversation with the lawyer to an end.

"I'm going to do it whether you like it or not. Nothing and nobody will prevent me from sharing what I have with you, not even you. If you don't want it, give it away, or take the money and throw it out the window. It's as much yours as it is mine," I said when I'd hung up the phone.

She looked at me and I saw fear reflected in her eyes. She knew that if I took this step she would never be free again.

She started to cry again, perhaps out of even greater desperation. This time I didn't go over to her but sat down to watch her. I felt like a fool. Only a fool is capable of giving away his fortune. But I didn't want to back down. If I had done so Esther would have been relieved.

Yes, I could have taken it back:

"Don't cry . . . I realize that you're worried about this because you think I'm tying you to me irreversibly. You're right, that's my intention, this is my way of holding on to you. Look, don't worry, I'll call the lawyer right now and tell him not to do anything. It wasn't a good idea. Forgive me, it's just that . . . well, you know that I would do anything to keep you in my life forever. But I can't force you to accept me. Let's leave things as they

are except . . . Well, perhaps you could let me twist your arm and agree to rent a place in the Village with a little more room . . ."

I could have been generous, given her back her freedom, but I didn't. If I had, Esther would have regained her smile, and then she would have agreed that we should rent a place with a few more square feet of floor space. You can always escape from a rented home, but it's much harder to escape from the home you own.

But I didn't give her this opportunity. I didn't say a single word that would be an open door to her freedom. I kept silent, watching her, hoping for her unconditional surrender. She was too decent to snub me, to offend me by rejecting my generous offer. You wouldn't even give a wife as much as I was prepared to give her.

"Why are you doing this to me, Thomas?" she managed to say in a whisper.

"Because I love you, Esther; I can't imagine life without you. If you're not by my side I'll stop breathing, I'll become nothing. I need you to understand that."

Once she'd stopped crying she ended up giving in. I was soldering her to me irreversibly.

I knew that Esther was too honorable to screw me over, but even so I didn't stop telling myself that I was an idiot.

That very afternoon I signed the documents in which I made her co-owner of all my possessions. My lawyer made the good decision to introduce a safeguard that Esther accepted immediately: she couldn't make use of my funds above a certain figure without my consent.

"That's not what I asked you for," I protested.

"We have always administered your family's funds, and so we see ourselves as obliged to insist you accept the necessity of this clause . . ." said the lawyer who was in charge of administering the money I'd inherited from my father.

Esther was in a state of shock and only managed to whisper, "He's right," but I acted as if I hadn't heard her. I was determined that she should belong to me forever.

I felt my hands trembling as I signed. There was no doubt about it, I was paying a high price to have her by my side.

"We should celebrate," I suggested as we left my lawyer's office.

I took her to the best restaurant in the city and, in spite of my efforts to make her laugh, all I got were serious looks. She seemed to be witnessing her own funeral rather than being happy at having become a rich woman.

A week later she surprised me by telling me that she knew of an apartment for sale in Brooklyn that might suit us. We went to see it. I liked it. It needed some work, but it was perfect for us. There was a large bedroom with a dressing room with two en suite bathrooms. By taking down a couple of walls we could create a reception room of considerable size where we could get together with at least thirty or so friends. It also had a separate kitchen and a couple of bedrooms that we would convert into our own offices, another room with its own little bathroom that could serve as a guest bedroom, and a utility room. In sum, more than three thousand well-appointed square feet.

The best thing was that we would no longer live in Nolita. The price was no bargain: a million dollars, which I paid without complaint.

"I think you're mad," Paul told me when he found out that we had bought a place in Brooklyn and that I had decided to share my entire fortune with Esther.

"Yes, I am," I admitted.

"Do you think you're going to hold on to her like that?"

"I'm not trying to hold on to her, Paul, just love her," I replied, making Paul chuckle.

"Man, that's a great line for an advertisement. Come on, Thomas, it's me you're talking to. You're terrified at the possibility of losing Esther."

"Is it so hard for you to accept that we're a happy couple? I'm going to share the rest of my life with Esther, so all that's mine is hers."

"Right . . . How romantic! The role of lovestruck fool doesn't suit you, Thomas, it doesn't ring true. In reality you need her so much, so desperately, that you're terrified that she might dump you for someone else and so you blackmail her emotionally. Even so, adding her name to your bank accounts is more than I imagined you were capable of. If I were you I would find myself a good shrink. New York is full of shrinks who'll explain what's happening to you."

Two months later we were settled in our new home and gave a cocktail party for our friends. Unlike London, in New York we knew a fair number of people in the advertising world with whom we had good relations, in addition to the friends Esther and even Paul invited. So fifty people attended and for a moment I even thought we'd have to put guests in the bathroom. You couldn't squeeze another person in.

Esther seemed almost happy. She would have preferred to continue living in Nolita, but even so she had begun to admit that it was good for us to have more amenities and enough room to each have our own space.

"You've got the cream of the industry here," Paul told me, satisfied to see that most of the fashionable creatives had accepted our invitation.

"It's all thanks to you and Esther. You were the ones in charge of the guest list," I replied sincerely.

The party was a success. Everyone ate and drank without stopping, they made jokes, some of them smoked without anyone telling them off, and, most of all, they bad-mouthed the people who weren't there, all those in the industry who hadn't been invited.

The last guest—Paul—left at midnight. When we were alone, Esther sat down on a sofa and stretched her legs.

"Phew! I thought they'd never leave!"

"They had a great time. Would you like a drink?"

"That would be lovely, I haven't had anything to drink all night. I wanted everything to go perfectly."

I opened a bottle of pink champagne.

"I've always noticed that the things that matter are celebrated with champagne."

"And you think that's a bad thing?"

"In truth, I've never been able to afford it, it's too expensive."

"Well, you've been earning enough money to be able to drink champagne for a while now," I joked.

"But it still seems expensive to me."

"Well, it's something that we're not going to go without," I added, laughing.

That was one of the nights when we pleased each other more than we normally did. This usually happened when she'd had a drink too many and we had something to celebrate. The rest of the time our intimate relations remained marked by monotony. It didn't bother me. I was still seeing Olivia, the short model with green eyes.

To begin with, we saw each other a couple of times a week at her apartment. An apartment whose rent I helped pay.

The truth was that Olivia couldn't get much work, and I knew that her earnings were the fruit of various nights when she was called upon to accompany some foreign businessman or other who was passing through the city. But I decided that I would prefer that she dedicate herself to me alone.

Nonetheless, I did manage to get Esther to hire her for a few advertisements.

When did Esther find out that Olivia was part of my life? I've sometimes asked myself this, and I haven't been able to determine the answer. In any case, it didn't bother her, neither in the past nor in the present. I think that she was relieved that I fulfilled my sexual fantasies with another woman. Esther didn't want anything else and I knew that I couldn't ask more of her, although I didn't give up on my attempts to persuade her that we should marry. She owed it to me. No man puts his entire fortune in the hands of a woman without her paying a certain price for it. There's no doubt that Esther would pay me with her loyalty, a bond more solid than any piece of paper she could sign, but even so, it wasn't enough for me because if I had my secrets, Esther had hers too.

My trysts with Olivia led me to invent commitments, meetings with imaginary clients. Esther accepted anything I told her in good faith. She didn't fight with me or complain when I came home in the wee hours smelling of alcohol, my clothes impregnated with a woman's perfume.

Paying Olivia's expenses was no problem for me. It was worth it because this way she was always available to me. Furthermore, I had taken a liking to the dishes she cooked me. She was a fantastic cook who liked to give free rein to her imagination. I even paid for her to attend a cooking class run by one of the best chefs in New York. From that point on she began to surprise me with ever more sophisticated dishes.

Yes, Olivia was my secret, but my brother, Jaime, was Esther's secret.

I found out shortly after we moved into our new home.

It was one of those evenings when I'd lied to Esther, telling her that I had to have dinner with a potential client and that she shouldn't wait up for me. She nodded indifferently, as she usually did.

That same night Olivia demanded that I take her out to dinner before going back to her apartment, and insisted on going to a fashionable New York restaurant with two Michelin stars. I refused. It was one thing to deceive Esther, but quite another to make a fool of her, which is what would have happened had anyone seen us together. I convinced Olivia that we should go to Chinatown, to a small Chinese restaurant where the food wasn't bad. She protested but agreed; she didn't have any choice.

We arrived at eight and they seated us in a small booth. Halfway through the dinner, Olivia got up to use the restroom. I stayed where I was, bored, waiting for her, wishing dinner would end. When she got back she was trying not to laugh.

"Who do you think is having dinner here?" she said, with a mocking expression.

"Who?" I asked, mistrustfully.

"Your darling Esther. Did you know? Did you know that she would be having dinner here tonight? The guy she's with is very attractive. You must know him, he's probably a friend of yours . . . Tall, blond, blue eyes, muscular . . . Very classy; yes, sir, very classy. If you were to see them . . . anyone would say they were in love."

"Shut up!" I told her, repressing my rage.

There was no need for her to offer further details. The guy in question could only be my brother.

"Come on, don't get mad, these things happen. Your Esther looks like butter wouldn't melt in her mouth, but you have to be wary of girls like that," she continued, with glee.

"You're an idiot. Esther's having dinner with my brother. So quit inventing romantic scenarios."

"Your brother? How strange! You don't look anything alike . . . He's so blond . . ."

"So what? My father was blond and my mother was dark," I replied angrily. I couldn't stand explaining myself to Olivia, whom I considered to be nothing more than a whore I paid to entertain me.

"Well, your girlfriend and your brother seem to get along very well," Olivia commented again, knowing she was upsetting me.

"Don't even think of making insinuations like that or you'll pay the price," I threatened.

I don't know if it was the tone of my voice or a twist of cruelty showing on my face, but Olivia realized that if she continued provoking me, she'd pay, really pay.

"They didn't see me," she said, lowering her voice.

"That's good. I can't justify having dinner with you," I said, looking at her scornfully.

"Well, I'm a model. We could be discussing you hiring me for some campaign or other," she suggested in a small voice.

"Do you think Esther's stupid? She's already wondering why she let herself be convinced to give you the role in the beer advertisement. You weren't the right fit. If she sees me with you . . ."

"Well, she's with your brother."

"Exactly, she's with my brother. She's his shoulder to cry on."

"Then what shall we do?"

"They're by the entrance? We'll have to stay here until they leave."

And that's what we did. I know that Olivia would have liked to erase that night from her life. I used her to vent all the fury I felt at the thought of Esther in Jaime's company. It's not that I thought they were sleeping together. Esther's loyalty and Jaime's sense of honor would have held them both back, but the fact that they were still seeing each other and that Olivia had been able to guess that they were in love from a single glance hurt me so much my blood ran cold.

When I got home Esther had already arrived. She seemed to be sleeping soundly.

She spoke to me about Jaime the next day. I don't know if it was because she had seen us at the restaurant in spite of our efforts or if she'd simply guessed that the anger I was trying to control was an indication that I had seen them. It was lunchtime, and we were eating sandwiches in my office.

"I had dinner with Jaime last night."

She said it without anything special in her tone of voice. I started at her confession.

"Really? You didn't tell me you'd planned to meet." I tried to keep my voice as neutral as hers.

"It was something we decided on in the spur of the moment . . . It wasn't planned. Well, anyway, we had dinner. He wanted to tell me something. He's getting married."

I didn't know how to reply, but I did feel relieved. If Jaime was getting married, Esther would belong to me even more. I began to smile.

"Do you think it's funny?" Esther asked, rather irritated.

"So he's getting married . . . Good boy. He graduated with a good degree, he's inherited his father's office, and obviously the next step was to get married. Who is she?"

"A classmate from college. The daughter of one of your family's lawyer friends; I think her name is Eleanor Hudson. Jaime told me that you know her."

"Eleanor! Of course, she's perfect for Jaime," I said. "Her father has a practice that deals with divorces and inheritances. He's made a lot of money. He's handled the divorces of some of the richest people in New York. Aunt Emma used to invite them to spend the odd weekend in Newport. No doubt John would have been pleased at his son marrying a Hudson. Yes, that's perfect. The perfect couple. She studied law like Jaime too. They've got a lot in common," I added, watching Esther's face.

I could tell that she was uncomfortable, but she had great self-control so she didn't move a muscle.

"I've told him he should invite you." She tried to move the conversation in a direction where I'd feel less comfortable.

"There's no reason for him to do that, and you shouldn't have asked him to. I'm done with the Spencers forever."

"Thomas, you carry their name. You are a Spencer; it's what your mother wanted, so don't reject who you are."

"Do I have to remind you that they were the ones who rejected me?" I asked, upset.

"You did everything possible to arrive at an unsustainable situation," she reproached me.

"Great, so now you're on their side!"

"No, no, I'm not taking their side. You know I'm speaking the truth."

"What truth? Their version? Yours?" I exclaimed.

"Let's not fight, Thomas. In any case, I think you should go if they invite you. It would be an opportunity to normalize your relationship with your family. Jaime's told me that your grandparents and your aunt Emma still regret that things got so out of hand."

"They were the ones who threw me out," I insisted.

"If they invite you, will you go?"

"I don't like hypocritical scenes, Esther, you should already know that. I don't think the Spencer family misses me. Nor do I miss them."

"I don't understand you, Thomas. We all need a family. You don't even want to have anything to do with your maternal grandparents or your uncle Oswaldo. And you have to agree with me that you have nothing to hold against them. You haven't seen them since your father's funeral."

"I don't have anything in common with my mother's family. I've never felt comfortable with them. What brought all this on, Esther?" I asked angrily.

"Your brother is getting married, Thomas. I don't know whether or not he'll invite you, but if he does I think you ought to accept. I'm just giving you my opinion."

"What else did he tell you? If you had dinner with him you must have had time to talk about something other than his wedding."

"Mainly he wanted me to know that he had made that decision, nothing more."

"And why did he want you to know?" I asked, wary of her response.

"Because . . . Do you want the truth, Thomas? I'll tell you. You already know that Jaime and I . . . Well, at one point there could have been something more between us . . ."

"But there isn't," I asserted harshly.

"No, there isn't, nor has there been, but even so . . . Forget it, you can't understand. I hope that girl, Eleanor, makes him very happy."

Paul Hard came into the office and we put an end to the conversation. Paul brought a proposal. A New York man hoping to win a seat in Congress wanted to hire us to run his campaign. Having worked as an assistant to a senator who had recently passed away, he had decided that this was his moment to take the plunge into electoral politics. He had made a name for himself as a lawyer, spending one day a week providing free counsel on civil cases for residents in marginalized areas; in particular, he had tried to help immigrants gain legal status . . . Nothing compromising.

"Very astute, what else?" I asked Paul.

"I still don't know much about him. Give me a day and I'll give you the lowdown. He's come on the recommendation of an old friend."

"Why us?" asked Esther.

"I assume because we already have a reputation but we're not very expensive. If he had a lot of money he would have found himself a firm with experience running political campaigns."

"Global Communication has experience with political campaigns, Paul. May I remind you that in the U.K. I ran the campaign of a new political party, the Rural Party, and directed those of other candidates," I stated proudly.

"Well then, he must have read about that in the press and that's why he's come to us," Paul responded sarcastically.

"I'm not sure I want us to get involved in politics here. I'd prefer to continue with product advertisement," Esther intervened.

"We can't miss this boat. If it works out, it will bring in work," Paul declared.

"Have you accepted the contract?" Esther turned to Paul.

"You guys are the bosses, it's up to you; I'm just an esteemed employee. All I've done is arrange for him to come in for a meeting tomorrow afternoon. At five, when the office is quietest. Is that okay?"

It was all right with me, but not so much with Esther. She thought that politicians were too much hard work and caused major headaches. Roy Parker was a prime example.

"They're different from mere mortals . . . Ambitious, egomaniacal, selfish, with the spirit of artists . . ." Esther complained.

"But they're not all the same," Paul parried.

"They're worse than artists. In truth, they are artists; if they weren't, they wouldn't be able to transform themselves when they step onto a stage. The worst is that they end up thinking that they are essential. They even believe their own hype," Esther argued.

In spite of her reluctance, we met with Ralph Morgan.

Ralph had experience in politics, so he did what politicians do when they spring into action. He arrived accompanied by his campaign manager, Nicholas Carter.

"Esther . . . Thomas . . . I'm pleased to meet you. I've heard a lot about you, and all good," Ralph said after shaking hands, offering his most genuine smile.

I realized it right away. Esther liked Ralph. Yes, I could feel the tension that's so hard to disguise when a woman finds a man attractive or vice versa.

It was Carter who got the conversation started, making clear what he expected of us: "Ralph has the possibility of winning a seat in Congress. It won't be easy but it's not unreachable. First he needs to win the Democratic primary, and then he'll have to duke it out against the Republican candidate, a guy who's been in Congress his whole life and has enough money to run a strong campaign."

Esther held up a hand, interrupting Carter, who frowned; he was used to being in charge.

"Before you continue, Mr. Carter, we want to make it clear that we have no intention of getting involved in political campaigns beyond what is purely formal; you know, the paraphernalia: organizing appearances, ordering balloons and T-shirts, designing flyers, candidate photo shoots . . . But we don't want to get involved on the political side. By that I mean that we will not take part in the development of your slogans or strategies to beat your adversaries."

"Well, you do speak plainly," Carter replied, annoyed.

"We prefer to clarify things before you tell us anything more than we need to know in case you do decide you might want us to work with you," Esther replied.

Paul Hard and I looked at each other uncomfortably. Esther was sidelining us. It seemed like she alone would decide whether we would take the job.

"Thank you for your honesty, Ms. Sabatti," Ralph said, looking her firmly in the eye.

Esther barely held Ralph's gaze and then looked at me, waiting for me to say something. It was clear that she was doing everything possible to put Morgan and Carter off.

"We have experience in political campaigns," I said, looking at Carter. "In fact, we have a number of politicians among the clients of our London office, so perhaps we might be able to help you."

"We don't have a big budget, at least not at the moment, so we need whoever works with us to give it their all—and for that it's essential to get to know Ralph, to believe in him. Only by believing in someone can you convince other people to do the same," Carter replied, looking at his watch and thinking that they were wasting their time.

"Come on, Nicholas, these guys don't need to believe in me . . . They're professionals, we're hiring them to do a job and, well . . . well, I agree with Ms. Sabatti: it's up to us to take care of the politics and they can deal with everything else, which is equally important. There's no reason for them to get involved in our battle against the other candidates." Ralph Morgan left no room for doubt: he had decided that he wanted us to work for him.

Carter held him back. "Perhaps they need to think about it, Ralph."

"Bearing in mind what Ms. Sabatti has said, I think it would be best for us to explain what we need and for them to present us with a plan and a quote to determine whether we can afford it. If so, we'll come to an agreement, but if it's too much for us . . . well, it will have been a pleasure to have met you, in any case," Ralph Morgan declared.

"Yes, that's a good idea," Esther agreed.

"Well then . . ." Carter seemed uncomfortable.

"Well then, show them the plan you've come up with for how we want to launch the campaign, these guys will work out an estimate, send it to us and we'll make a decision and draw up the framework for our collaboration based on that. I don't think it needs to be any more complicated. What do you think?"

"Sounds great," replied Paul.

Nicholas Carter looked at Ralph Morgan with displeasure, but he didn't say anything. Esther seemed uncomfortable too.

"Great, then let's get to work and take a look at those papers," Paul said cheerfully, as if we were all in agreement.

We humored him. We spent a couple of hours examining the campaign plan and Esther outlined what they could expect from us.

"If you give us three or four days, we'll send you an estimate," I proposed.

"My, you do work fast," Carter commented.

"We don't want to waste your time or our own. It will be a rough estimate, but sufficiently detailed that there won't be any unpleasant surprises," I assured him.

When they left Paul poured three whiskeys without asking us. He drank one of them down in a single gulp and I would have done the same if Esther hadn't been there.

"Don't you like Ralph Morgan?" I asked Esther.

"Why wouldn't I like him? It's just that I don't want us to get involved in any problems and politicians are always a source of conflict. They ask you to design a poster and you end up facing off with their adversaries as if they were your own."

"If they agree that we do half the work and they pay us for it, then it's a good deal," Paul observed.

"Yes, it would be a stroke of luck; it seems like Morgan likes us." I looked at Esther while I was talking.

"He seems like a good guy and he's got a sad backstory to sell which could earn him a few votes," Paul interrupted me.

"What backstory?" Esther asked with curiosity.

"He's got a seven-year-old daughter with heart disease. His wife had to give up her job to take care of her full-time."

"While Morgan busies himself working toward his own ambitions. You men are all the same," Esther replied grumpily.

"Well, someone has to support the pair of them," Paul said, amusing himself by provoking her.

"And why doesn't he stay at home taking care of his daughter?" Esther looked at Paul defiantly.

"Would you do that?" Paul asked her.

"Do what?"

"Would you stop caring for your sick daughter in order to work?"

"Don't try and trick me, Paul." Esther raised her voice. She was really on edge.

"I'm not playing tricks, I just asked you a question. Mothers usually prefer to care for their sick children. Naturally we men could also do it, but in the end it's your instinct that makes you decide to stay with your child."

"That sounds awfully antiquated, Paul. Why not share the responsibility between them? Why don't they both give up stellar careers and settle for working to support the family and being with their daughter? Why is it just Morgan's wife who has to make a sacrifice? Is she somehow worth less than him?"

"She's got you there, Paul; admit that Esther's beaten you," I intervened, trying to mediate.

"It's the feminist century, I realize that. Even so, I admire Mrs. Morgan for being able to sacrifice her ambitions to take care of her daughter and support her husband in running for Congress." Paul didn't seem to want to surrender.

"Of course, you men admire women who are prepared to sacrifice themselves on the altar of your ambitions."

There was no point in prolonging that stupid fight, so I told Paul that it was time for us to leave. We would get to work on the estimate for Morgan the next day.

We left the office in silence. I knew that Esther's mind was in turmoil. First we had argued about Jaime's wedding, then I had agreed to take on part of Morgan's campaign. We barely spoke until we got home. She surprised me as she always did: "You know what, Thomas? I don't understand why my feelings don't matter to you."

I repressed my response. I didn't want to give her the opportunity to break up with me. It was obvious that she was referring to her feelings toward my brother, which I ignored as though they had never existed in the past and didn't exist right then.

"You can yell at me all you want, Esther, for anything, and you'd be right, except for not caring about your feelings. Do I have to tell you again how much I care about you? What do I have to do to prove it to you? I don't know what to do anymore, Esther . . . Tell me what you want, and I'll do it, I'll even disappear forever."

She fell silent and I read a certain fear in her expression. Yes, she wanted to run, to free herself from me, but doing that would mean going back to square one, because she was too honorable to keep my money. Furthermore, we had signed an agreement according to which she couldn't access sums of money above a certain figure without my signature. So she would have to go back to being an employee at an advertising agency, to counting every dollar because she couldn't afford to overspend; she would give up the home that she currently enjoyed, and the car and chauffeur that we had hired for the agency but was really for her to use, and being able to go into any shop without worrying about the price of a pair of shoes or a skirt. And she'd be giving up her family's admiration. The Sabattis were proud of her. Esther was the one in the family who had succeeded. Her brother worked in the family restaurant; he would spend the rest of his life there.

Going back to square one is difficult. And Esther was human, so she weighed in her heart what she had and what it would mean to lose it.

She could have left me broke if she had wanted to. After all, I had been stupid enough to authorize her signature on all my accounts and I had transferred quite a number of stocks and dividends to her, in addition to making a will favorable to her.

She was too decent to ruin me, but she had also experienced a different reality, the one where you don't have to worry about the electricity bill.

My statement had been a trap to make her feel indebted to me. So I remained quiet, staring at her and waiting for her response.

"I'm having a bad day today, Thomas, let's not fight."

She shut herself in the bathroom for a long time. When she came out she went straight to bed. She didn't even ask me if we were going to have dinner. I was tempted to go see Olivia, but I made myself a sandwich and sat down to watch television. I didn't go to bed until I thought she was asleep. She was curled up on one edge of the bed, so I knew that she was pretending to be asleep.

In fact, Esther was hoping for a supreme act of generosity from me. She would have renounced everything I had to offer in exchange for her freedom, but she needed me to give it back to her.

That night I could have sat down at the edge of the bed and taken hold of her hand.

"Open your eyes, I know you're awake."

She would have opened them slowly, letting me see the depth of her suffering.

"Forgive me, you're right. I try to ignore your feelings because I'm scared of losing you. Call Jaime; tell him not to get married, that you love him. You two have the right to make a go of things. You don't owe me anything, Esther; my generosity to you was just selfishness, my way of holding on to you. Go. You and my brother can't act as though you were Romeo and Juliet and your love was impossible. It's ridiculous that you should renounce being with each other. We'll go to my lawyer's office tomorrow; I don't want to leave you with nothing, but ... well, you won't lack for anything with Jaime. We'll rewrite the will and I'll instruct them to remove your name from my accounts. Simple as that."

Esther would have thrown her arms around my neck and drenched me with her tears.

"You're so good! I don't deserve you! But I can't ... I can't leave you. I can't call Jaime. That girl, Eleanor ... They've made a commitment to each other, they're getting married in a couple of weeks ..."

"Do you want me to call him? I'm prepared to humble myself in front of my brother. I'll tell him that I'll punch him if he doesn't come and get you right now and take you away with him. You're in love, nobody in the world has the right to interfere with your love. Go on, Esther, do it; keeping you at my side without you loving me is harder than losing you."

Esther would have hesitated. I would have picked up my cell and dialed Jaime's number.

"Were you asleep? Come and get Esther and stop acting like an idiot. You're behaving like little kids. This doesn't make sense. How can you think of marrying Eleanor Hudson? She's not the girl for you. She's just the spoiled daughter of an arrogant father."

I didn't free her because I didn't want to. I preferred for her to suffer at my side rather than for her to be happy away from me. I loved her, but I loved myself more and I wasn't prepared to endure the loss of her.

Neither of us slept. We got up early. Esther went for a run as she did every morning and I went to the gym, where I didn't lift a single weight but spent the time breakfasting on whole-grain toast with butter and reduced-sugar jelly, and coffee. Everyone has their own way of letting off steam.

When we saw each other in the office later, Esther seemed in a better mood. She shut herself away with Paul to prepare the estimate for Ralph Morgan. They were driving one of the secretaries crazy with requests to send e-mails to our providers asking them to assess the costs of each strand of the campaign.

I saw a couple of clients and at midday, since she and Paul were still wrapped up in their work, I called Olivia. She was my best option to pass the rest of the day with. Olivia told me that she was making a salad with flowers, one of those dishes she had learned in her cooking class.

When I arrived at her apartment I found her in a bad mood.

"I want to work, Thomas; I want to be on-screen, on the stage."

"I'll do what I can, Olivia, but it's not my fault if your beauty doesn't come with any extraordinary talent."

"You're a pig, Thomas!"

"I'm telling you the truth, beautiful. If you had special talents you wouldn't have to earn a living off of guys like me. But so far you haven't convinced anyone you have a talent for performing, except in bed."

Her anger didn't bother me. I was too lazy to look for someone else like her.

"I'll help you, Olivia, I promise. I'll come up with a way to get you a job."

We reached an agreement. She didn't have a particular gift for acting, but she wasn't stupid and she didn't want to depend exclusively on me. She wanted to keep trying to make her way in movies or television. She wanted to earn her own money, even if it wasn't enough to pay for the apartment and buy herself designer clothes. What she earned for herself would be her insurance for the future, for the moment when the light in her green eyes was overshadowed by wrinkles. She was a smart girl.

Had I become monogamous? I was happy with Olivia; yes, as long as I had Esther with me. I didn't want more, but I was worried that, in spite of everything, Esther might someday break her ties with me, because of Jaime or someone else.

It didn't take me long to confirm what I had already guessed during our first meeting with Ralph Morgan. Esther was attracted to him. Ralph also liked her because of the confidence she exuded. I understood why when we met Constance, Ralph Morgan's wife.

The day we signed the contract, the aspiring congressman came in with his wife and daughter, Ellen, as well as Nicholas Carter.

I liked Constance. Blonde, of average height, fragile-looking, and with huge blue eyes, she was like a porcelain doll. Everything about her was harmonious, including her tone of voice, and I noticed the coolness of her skin when we shook hands.

Yes, I really liked her. I decided that I needed to have her. Surely a woman like her would feel lonely, given that her husband was dedicated heart and soul to carving out a niche in politics. And if the responsibility of caring for her sick child also fell to her, it seemed to me that it would be easy to seduce her.

She didn't speak but seemed interested in everything we had to say. And when Ralph Morgan asked for her opinion, she simply agreed that no doubt everything would work out well.

"Mrs. Morgan doesn't have much free time, but she'll do her utmost to support her husband," Nicholas Carter explained. "As you know, little Ellen has a heart condition and needs all her mother's care and attention."

"Does she go to school?" Esther wanted to know.

"Of course. We try to give our daughter as normal a life as possible, but unfortunately she can't cope with a full school day. Sometimes she has episodes and it's necessary to take her to the hospital immediately," Ralph Morgan explained.

"I'll do everything in my power to help my husband," Constance added.

"No doubt you'll be a great asset to his campaign, Mrs. Morgan. The public values nothing more highly than family, and you, your daughter, and your husband are a beautiful family," Paul Hard declared.

Esther got along well with Constance. In truth, you couldn't help getting along with her: she had such an aura of sweetness and serenity that she made the whole world want to protect her.

As for little Ellen, the girl looked more like her father: she had inherited his brown hair and dark eyes, and was extremely thin. Though seven years old, she was very quiet and didn't disturb us so we almost forgot she was there.

"Will Ellen be able to go to any rallies with her father?" I asked, conscious of the effect this would have on the voters.

"Our intention is to keep our daughter away from her father's political activity, but she might want to go and watch her father onstage, isn't that right, darling?" Constance said.

"That is none of our business, Thomas," Esther reminded me.

"But good advice is always appreciated," Ralph commented with a smile.

So Carter and the Morgans became a part of our lives in the same way that Roy Parker and Suzi had been part of mine in the past. They started to become integral to our routine, an important element in our conversations and concerns. We had signed a valuable contract so we couldn't let them down.

Esther decided that Paul would be responsible for communicating with Carter, warning him not to put even a toe over the boundaries established in the contract.

"You like Morgan, Paul, but I don't want us to end up tripping up his opponents. No politics. Our job is just to make sure that when he meets his supporters the microphones work, the stage is well lit, and the same goes for preparing for his television appearances. But we will not advise him on what he should say or how he should challenge his rivals," she stressed, looking at us both.

"His wife and daughter have great potential . . . They could win him a lot of votes," said Paul, ignoring Esther's recommendation.

"Listen to me, Paul. I don't want us getting involved any further than is stipulated in the contract we signed."

I decided to remain neutral. My main priority was to reestablish my relationship with Esther. Since the day she told me that my brother was getting married she had avoided me in bed. If she had been anyone else I would have forced her, but had I done that to her she would have left me.

That night I suggested that we go out for dinner and she agreed without enthusiasm. We spent a good part of the meal talking about the Morgans and it wasn't until dessert that I openly stated my disquiet: "Are you angry with me?"

"No, don't be stupid."

"Come on, Esther, you always tell the truth; or at least I think you do."

"No, I'm not angry, Thomas, although I am rather upset."

"Just because I don't want to go to Jaime's wedding? For a start, my dear brother hasn't invited me. You'd like things to be different, Esther, but they are what they are. You are very close with your family. I never have been with mine. You have to accept that."

"Yes, I suppose I don't have a choice."

She said it in such a way that she seemed to have given in. The shadow of unhappiness fell between us again. She had loved me when we were very young, but that love had evaporated; and yet she was bound to me, I had bound her, and she didn't know how to release herself without hurting me.

At least that conversation managed to relax the tension for the next few days, so we went back to normal.

We didn't mention Jaime again until the Sunday morning when the papers published news of his marriage to Eleanor Hudson in the society pages.

"He's gotten married," Esther murmured while we were eating breakfast. We had gotten up a bit later than usual and I had just made coffee.

I didn't need to ask whom she was talking about. The pain gradually transformed her expression until it dominated her face. I saw that she was trying not to cry, but her nerves betrayed her and she dropped her cup of coffee.

While she got up to pick up the cup I glanced at the paper. There was a photo of the couple. Eleanor looked stunning and wore a happy smile, but my brother's expression was as serious as if they'd dragged him to the altar.

When we finished breakfast, Esther gave me the surprise of my life.

"Do you still want to marry me?" she asked.

I was left speechless. I was about to tell her no, to take revenge for needing her, because that made me weak. I hated her, yes, for a second I hated her.

"Yes," I said without adding a word more.

"Then let's do it. We can get married this week."

"We can't organize a wedding in a week."

"It's a matter of you and me getting married, not of putting on a show. I have absolutely no intention of wearing a white dress or of organizing a reception."

"Your parents won't be happy."

"They'll be angry, I know that. But I'm not going to have an Italian wedding surrounded by relatives. I haven't been to a church in years. It would be ridiculous. Do you want a religious ceremony?"

"No, I'm fine with going to City Hall."

I said it with apathy, as if getting married to her was no longer a priority for me. I wanted her to feel vulnerable, to feel disoriented. She had lost Jaime and she could lose me. I reveled in the role of the man who's no longer enthusiastic about getting married. She was shocked. I read it in her eyes. She suddenly felt lost.

"Perhaps we could have a party here, invite our closest friends. What do you think?"

"If that's what you want, then fine by me."

I looked down at the paper and began to read as if it were the most important thing for me to do. She got up and left the kitchen. She came back in a few minutes wearing a tracksuit.

"I'm going for a run. Are you coming?"

"No, I'd rather stay here and read the paper and enjoy some quiet time. We've had an exhausting week."

"We could go out to celebrate that we're getting married."

"Not today, I'd rather stay home."

She looked at me with concern and came over to kiss me goodbye on the cheek. I noticed she was upset because her upper lip was trembling.

We got married two weeks later, the amount of time it took us to get a license and organize a cocktail party at home, to which we invited a number of friends as well as Esther's parents and brother.

Paul Hard and Miriam, one of Esther's childhood friends, were our witnesses. When the judge declared us man and wife we had to steel ourselves to kiss each other.

"I never imagined I'd attend your wedding," Paul told us when we left City Hall.

"Well, I always thought they'd end up getting married," Miriam asserted.

Neither Esther nor I replied. We both knew why we'd gotten

married, and it had nothing to do with what other people might think.

Although I didn't appear to be happy, in reality I was. I had achieved my goal. Esther was even more mine and that was what I wanted. It didn't bother me that she didn't love me in the way I knew she could love. It was enough for me to know that she would always be there, that I could count on her, that she would watch my back. That as long as she existed, I wouldn't be alone, that her maternal instinct would make her protect me, even from myself.

I had wished for this moment and I savored it privately because I didn't want her to enjoy it. She had agreed to marry me only because Jaime had married Eleanor. In truth I hadn't given them a choice. Jaime had promised his father that he wouldn't come between me and Esther, and, very much in spite of himself, the fool had kept his promise. As for Esther, she had become more and more entangled in my web and she had lost all hope of escape some time ago.

Jaime needed someone by his side and had chosen Eleanor Hudson. The Spencer family approved of their union. Aunt Emma had organized a big wedding up in Newport. Esther would have liked a wedding like that, but she punished herself by insisting on a nondescript ceremony that had lasted barely a few minutes. I didn't care either way. The important thing was that I had achieved my goal: Esther Sabatti had become Mrs. Spencer.

Esther's parents protested at how hurriedly we had organized the wedding and at their daughter's refusal to celebrate it in accordance with Catholic ritual.

During the cocktail party that we gave at home, her mother approached me and politely complained: "This isn't what I'd expected my daughter's wedding to be like. We have a mountain of relatives who don't understand why she didn't invite them and I don't know what to say to them."

"I'm sorry, Mrs. Sabatti. All I want to do is make Esther happy. This is what she wanted."

"But at City Hall it seemed so sad . . . You didn't even know the judge so he wasn't able to say a few words about you both, something more personal than declaring you husband and wife."

I avoided her as much as I could. Her disappointed-mother complaints bored me.

The party lasted well into the night. I had given in on everything except the catering. I ordered lobster, oysters, roast beef, and French champagne. There wasn't a single bottle left over.

Esther and I barely spoke all evening, but she surprised me once the last guests had left. That night she was the one who took the initiative. I knew that she was exorcising all the rage she felt because it was me and not Jaime, because he had married another woman, because she was with me and felt nothing for me.

We woke up late in the morning. Esther seemed uncomfortable about what had happened, but I made no mention of it. I know she was grateful to me.

On Monday we were back at work. Paul said that we seemed content. We almost were. We went back to the routine that protected us from ourselves.

As soon as I could slip away from Esther I went to see Olivia. Our agreement was working well for both of us. I had her at my disposal whenever I wanted and she had stopped worrying about how expensive the stores on Fifth and Madison Avenues were.

"So you and Esther are married . . . I would have liked to be at your wedding."

"I wouldn't have minded, but Esther was in charge of the guest list."

"And you forgot about me."

"Well, she just wanted our closest friends there, darling, and you are not on that list, or at least not on Esther's."

"Do you plan to have children?"

Olivia's question disconcerted me. I'd never considered the possibility of having children. Why would I? I didn't see the point, but I realized that I had never spoken with Esther on the subject. I didn't know whether she wanted to be a mother or didn't bother herself with such concerns.

"That's none of your business."

"To be honest, I can't imagine you changing diapers."

"I can't imagine you doing it either."

"I'll have children one day. You can't go through life without them."

"Well, don't count on me," I warned her.

"No, I'm not counting on you. You're the last man I'd choose to be the father of my children."

If there was one thing I liked about Olivia, it was her honesty. She didn't pretend to be something she wasn't or to feel something she didn't.

"I have a surprise for you," I told her, changing the subject. "A Spanish cava company wants to promote themselves in the U.S., and Esther and Paul want to use you for the commercial."

"Cava? What's that?"

"It's like champagne. A sparkling wine, but made in Spain."

"It sounds good."

"The best thing is that it was Esther who thought of using you. She says you're very professional. You won't be the main part, but you'll be a bubble girl. Maybe the principal one."

"And who's going to be the star?" she asked grumpily.

"Esther and Paul want to use a famous actress."

"I won't be anyone until I get a part in Hollywood," she complained.

"It's not easy, sweetheart, but I'm working on it. I thought you'd like to be in another commercial. Anyway, we'll pay you well."

Olivia had a lot to offer. Not only was she good in bed, but I could talk to her. She had studied art at New York University and her friends included painters, writers, actors, sculptors, artists . . . None of them had made it and they all had insecurities, like she did.

Olivia was prepared to do anything necessary to become an actress. The first time she went to bed with a guy out of self-interest the bed had belonged to a producer of Broadway musicals. She left that bed with a small part in a musical whose run didn't last long.

But Olivia was determined and had accepted the reality that if she wanted to succeed, she had to pay a price, given that the heads of the film studios were overwhelmed with aspiring actresses. If she couldn't convince them with her talent, she would try to make her mark between the sheets as a first step toward winning the role that would make her a star. But her ambition was greater than her talent. Paul Hard had made this clear to me when I asked him to help me find her a decent part in a film. "She's a pretty girl, but she's lacking something. Don't ask me what. I don't think she'll get any further than a bit part," Paul had assured me.

Even so, she didn't give in, and I knew that if she was sleeping with me it wasn't so much so that I would pay her bills—anyone would do for that—but because she thought I could open doors for her.

I got back to the apartment late and I was worried that Esther might ask me why. But she didn't. She was working in her office, absorbed in the cava campaign.

"Oh, you're home. There's some salad and turkey in the refrigerator if you're hungry."

Either she didn't care where I might have been or she simply preferred to avoid the bitter aftertaste of a fight. It had always been like that between us. Not a complaint, nor a sign of curiosity as to where I had been.

It was around that time that Grandpa James died. Esther had told me about a month earlier that my grandfather had been admitted to the Mayo Clinic and that we should go and see him.

I didn't ask her who had told her; there was no need, it would have been Jaime. It was also he who called her again to tell her that my grandfather had died. She insisted that we should offer our condolences to Grandma Dorothy, Aunt Emma, and Jaime. But I refused and I asked her not to reach out to them either.

"But you can't be unmoved by your grandfather's death. He always loved you," said Esther.

"He threw me out, remember?"

"Well, you weren't exactly behaving well at that moment either . . . Please, Thomas, don't be bitter. Your grandfather always considered you his grandson."

"You said it. He considered me his grandson, but I wasn't. Esther, don't ask me to be an imposter. I'm not going to be one, even for you," I said firmly.

She bit her lower lip and looked at me sadly, as she usually did when she didn't know how to reply to me.

"At least let me talk to them. Don't tell me not to."

I conceded. I didn't want to play the villain in front of her.

What neither of us imagined was that a few months later, Grandma Dorothy and Aunt Emma would be killed in a car accident.

Aunt Emma had brought my grandmother to live with her. One weekend they were in the car on their way to Newport and had a head-on collision with another car. Both lost their lives.

Esther cried when we found out. Her tears irritated me. Why should she shed them for two women she'd seen only half a dozen times in her entire life?

She begged me to call Jaime to express our sympathies and to stand by his side at the funerals. I refused once again.

"Esther, I love you. But I beg you, do not force me to do things I don't want to do. You shouldn't care about the Spencer family, they aren't even friends of yours. You can't be devastated by what's happened."

"What about Jaime? Imagine how your brother must be feeling! You're practically all alone now. Now all you have left is each other."

"I've always been alone and it hasn't been easy. He'll have to learn."

"But—"

"Don't insist. We are not going to the funerals. You can send a card."

"I'll call Jaime. It's the very least I can do."

8

Did I mention that Ralph Morgan had made a place for himself in our lives? The candidate for Congress gave us more work than we'd expected. This didn't come as a surprise to me, since running a politician's campaign is like being married to him, but it was a revelation for Esther.

Nicholas Carter, Morgan's campaign chief, would call several times a day requesting or demanding this or that. He wanted everything then and there, without delay.

He was trying to get Morgan's campaign off to a strong start and had spent weeks organizing it down to the smallest detail.

The starting pistol would be fired in the Bronx—a controversial decision, to say the least. But Carter assured everyone that it was a case of starting where nobody else did to win over the common people.

"The black and Hispanic votes are decisive. We need to get these votes right from the beginning. What do you think Ralph has been doing all these years, going over there to offer them free legal advice?" he explained to me and Paul. Esther was standing her ground and didn't want to know anything about the political strategy they were coming up with for Morgan.

"But New York is a complex city. Even in this district . . . There are the white yuppies, people with money. And then there

are the middle classes . . . If they see him as the black and Hispanic candidate, he'll lose other voters," Paul asserted.

"What do you think, Thomas?" asked Ralph Morgan.

"What Nicholas is suggesting is risky," I replied, "but in
doing it you'll catch the attention of the media and you'll gain
some voters anxious for someone to pay attention to them. But
Paul is right too."

"Don't play it safe, Thomas! Tell me what you would do,"
Ralph insisted.

"I'd find a balance, two parallel campaigns. And I would use
Constance and Ellen. They'll get you a lot of votes from the self-
righteous middle class."

"Constance prefers that we leave her out of all this," Ralph
commented. "It's not that she doesn't want to help, but she
doesn't want to be on the front line and she really doesn't want
to subject our daughter to the public eye."

"Well, in this country you don't win elections if you don't
show off your family. And your family will do a very good job
of convincing people that you're worth voting for. Constance is
attractive, emanates sincerity, and is the epitome of an American
middle-class woman."

"Well, you mean a white American middle-class woman,"
Paul specified.

"Yes, but she's an exemplary woman, dedicated to her sick
daughter. This will touch the hearts of all women, white, black,
or any other race," I stated frankly.

"All right, in addition to the event in the Bronx, we'll organize some alternative gathering in Manhattan," Carter agreed.
"I don't know, perhaps we could arrange a meeting between
the Morgans and other families with sick children. It would be
something moving. Ralph, you could promise them that if you
win the election, you'll be the voice in Congress for the families who feel they need better support systems to care for a sick
child. That would be good."

We did it. Yes. We did it. In spite of Esther's protests and reluctance, I became deeply involved in Morgan's campaigns. Not officially, no, but in practice. Paul and I enjoyed this job more than selling cava to middle-class Americans who could afford to pay twenty dollars a bottle.

The Bronx event was a success. Nicholas Carter hired various unknown musical groups, kids eager for their big break. They entertained the attendees until the moment Ralph Morgan took the stage. Esther hadn't wanted to come with us, but Paul and I didn't want to miss the first act in the staging of this ambitious lawyer's electoral career.

Ralph was attractive and women liked him, but he wasn't handsome enough to irritate men. Of average height, with brown eyes and hair, he had an athletic physique and was like the boyfriend all mothers dreamed of for their daughters. Furthermore, he had a great talent for communication and he got along well with people. The others didn't see it, but it seemed to me that there was a certain falseness behind the open smile and the good manners. He was too close a match with the stereotype of the good middle-class boy who had studied hard to become a lawyer and was willing to sacrifice himself for the powerless, going to the Bronx and Harlem each week, as he always did, to offer free legal counsel. Too good to be true.

"There are good people in the world," Esther said when I expressed my skepticism.

"He's too perfect," I replied.

In spite of her doubts, Constance had eventually agreed to come to the Bronx to support her husband, but she had refused to bring little Ellen.

Nicholas Carter had sensibly decided that she would sit among the public.

Carter had written an excellent speech for Ralph. Exactly the kind of speech that the people in that neighborhood, which struck such fear into white people, wanted to hear. He promised to fight so that many of the undocumented immigrants could gain legal status. He defended the need, too, for high-quality schools in those neighborhoods, which had been "left in God's hands." He promised them that, if he were elected to Congress, he would look out for them, their children, and the elderly. That he wouldn't mislead them; although he couldn't promise them that he would succeed, he would at least fight for them once he reached the Capitol.

They believed him. People got to their feet, interrupting him with their applause. Some women wept.

"He's an ace, you've got to admit it," Paul whispered.

"Yes, he is. But he's lying. He can't achieve any of what he's promised."

"He hasn't promised anything. Carter has taken great care to ensure that he only says that he will try to change things, nothing more."

At the end of his speech Morgan paused while he tried to spot Constance, as if he didn't know where she was. A spotlight followed his gaze until it settled on his wife. She couldn't hide her surprise, her discomfort at being the center of attention.

"I want to thank my wife. Without her I wouldn't be here. She has always helped me. She's been helping me since the day we met in college and she continues to every day by encouraging me to believe in myself, in my dream of changing the status quo and making our beloved country even greater and fairer.

"Constance is a selfless mother who is sacrificing her own time and energy so I can commit myself to politics with the knowledge that our darling daughter doesn't lack what's most important, her mother's love. Without Constance's generosity, I wouldn't be here today. Thank you, darling, for your bottomless support, for your love, for your loyalty. Thank you."

The people got to their feet, applauding enthusiastically while the beam of the spotlight remained fixed on Constance, who seemed stunned. She stood up and looked around, overwhelmed by the show of enthusiasm. The spotlight suddenly moved away and back to the stage, where Ralph was drying his tears.

"What an actor!" Paul whispered in my ear.

I admired Ralph for his mastery of the act. I knew that Carter had prepared this part of the rally in minute detail.

When the event was finished we met them at their campaign headquarters.

Ralph was excited. He was on an adrenaline high. Carter was sure that he'd win Harlem and the Bronx.

Constance didn't join us. She had gone home. It didn't seem to me like she had enjoyed the event. I guessed that she would refuse to take part in the campaign in the future.

"Now we have to conquer white Manhattan," said Carter. "The meeting with the families of sick children is in three days. In the meantime we've gotten a few requests for interviews here. You'll do all of them, Ralph. We can't reject a single one. The people need to get to know you."

"Has Constance agreed to this?" I asked.

"To what? She knows she has to help, that Ralph needs her," responded Carter.

"Sure, but something tells me she wasn't comfortable tonight. She looked like she wanted to hightail it out of there. You should prepare her for what's coming," I insisted.

"She'll help me, there's no doubt about it, Thomas," Ralph replied. "She knows that I'm gambling my future on these elections. She doesn't have a choice." His tone of voice hinted at some kind of tension.

"Of course. But perhaps Thomas is right and we ought to try to work with her," Carter appealed.

"You have to find someone she can confide in. I don't think she likes you much, Carter," I said, tossing out this assertion with nothing whatsoever to support it.

Ralph and Carter looked at each other. I was right. Constance must blame the campaign chief for directing her husband toward a life she didn't want.

"Perhaps you could take on that role. She likes you," said Carter.

"Me? Impossible. Esther doesn't want the agency to get involved in anything beyond ensuring that the balloons stay up and the spotlights shine. Furthermore, I don't know Constance; I wouldn't know where to start," I said, hoping the others would try to convince me of the opposite.

"I'm sure you're the right person," Carter replied. "The day we were all in your office she mentioned to me that you seemed like a guy we could trust. These things happen. You click with a stranger without knowing why and the stranger ends up having more sway over you than people you've known your whole life," Carter concluded. He had already decided that I would take care of Constance, with whom it was increasingly clear he didn't get along well.

"I'll have to talk to Esther about it first," I objected, so that they didn't think that I was too eager for the role.

"I'll ask her," said Ralph.

"You? I'm not sure that's a good idea," Carter commented.

"Yes, it is; it'll be harder for her to say no to me," insisted Ralph.

I wasn't surprised that he wanted to be the one to deal with Esther. He liked her. He liked my wife in the same way I liked his. He didn't acknowledge it—probably not even to himself—but that was the truth. I wasn't so cynical, or at least I didn't fool myself. I was already savoring the possibility of having an affair with Constance.

Paul told me later why Morgan's wife hated Carter. It seems that the three of them had not only met in college but had been very close friends until Constance got pregnant and Ralph asked for Carter's advice. He advised him that it would be best if she terminated the pregnancy, that he couldn't chain himself to her for the rest of his life just because of a moment of passion in the backseat of a car.

Ralph had hesitated. In reality he would have liked to follow

Carter's advice, and he asked Constance to consider the possibility of an abortion. She refused, and he didn't dare break up with her. He was about to finish school and, thanks to his excellent academic record, he had a job waiting for him in a senator's office. He himself dreamed of getting into politics one day and he knew that any hiccups in his life would become common knowledge sooner or later. If Constance didn't end the pregnancy, the child would become his sword of Damocles, hanging over his head for the rest of his life. He married her. But though she had won the battle, Constance never forgave Carter for the advice he had given Ralph.

"And how did you find all that out?" I asked him, truly astonished.

"You have to know everything about your clients," Paul replied, downplaying the importance of this information.

"He likes Esther," I said, to see whether he had noticed.

"Yes, he likes independent women who are confident, strong, and compelling. And your wife has really improved physically. You have to acknowledge that money suits her. She looks very attractive in those high heels she's started wearing."

"Ralph isn't Esther's type," I told him, annoyed.

"You can never tell with women . . ." he remarked. "But I suppose that Esther must have married you for something other than your money, although I have to admit that I can't find a single virtue in your character to justify what she's done." He laughed with more sincerity than I would have liked.

Esther was upset with Paul and me. Ralph invited her to lunch and we both asked her to accept the invitation without giving her any clues as to what our candidate wanted.

When she got back from lunch she was furious. She walked straight into my office without knocking.

"Don't ever do that to me again, Thomas, not you or that crook Paul. You set a trap for me."

"I don't know what you mean . . . Have a seat and tell me

STORY OF A SOCIOPATH

what's up," I said, pretending not to know what she was talking about.

"I will not agree to advising Constance. That's Carter's job. I've already told Ralph Morgan that we are not going to change our position. We are not going to get involved in politics, not for him or for anyone else."

"And advising Constance is getting involved in politics? Come on, Esther, don't exaggerate! It's a matter of explaining to her how valuable her help is, how much Ralph needs her, nothing more. No need to be so mad."

"Nothing more? Do you think I'm stupid? They need Constance to play the part of self-sacrificing wife and mother, for her to parade her sick daughter around. It's disgusting!"

"That's what campaigns are like, it all adds up," I replied, shrugging my shoulders.

"Then Carter can do it—he's the campaign manager. I don't know why you have to do it."

"Well, it seems that Constance likes me, and Carter says she'll listen to me."

"Yes, that's what Ralph says. But it's not a good enough reason. You're not going to become her personal adviser. No way."

"They've asked us a favor, Esther, one very simple favor: that I have a conversation with Constance and make her see how important she is to the campaign. That's all."

"Someone else can do it," she replied furiously.

"Ralph says it's more likely that Constance will listen to someone external. Furthermore . . . well, from what Paul's told me, she doesn't get along with Carter, so she'll try to boycott anything he suggests."

"Haven't you learned your lesson? When you got personally involved with Roy and Suzi Parker, it led to undesirable consequences for us. Morgan and his wife are both grown-ups. We are not going to get mixed up in their personal issues. Not this time, Thomas. If you do it . . ."

"Then what?" I asked her in a low voice.

"I'll resign; I will no longer work on this campaign. You and Paul will do it all."

We looked at each other, sizing each other up. We both knew that if there was a clash between us it could spell the end of our relationship. If she had been another woman I would have hit her, but I held myself back as on so many other occasions. I took a deep breath, buying myself time before replying.

"All right, Esther. I won't do anything you don't like. You're placing too much significance on whether or not I have a conversation with Constance, but if it bothers you so much, I won't do it. Happy?"

"It's not about being happy, Thomas. I want you to understand . . ." Esther's tone of voice indicated that she was somewhat placated.

"I've got a lot of work. Let's forget about it."

I had no intention of respecting her wishes, of course. I liked Constance and her husband had opened the door of their home to me. I would have to have been very stupid not to try to seduce his wife.

I called Carter to tell him that I couldn't meet with Constance officially. Esther had vetoed our intervention in the political part of the campaign.

"If you arrange a way for me to see her, I'll try to make her understand how important it is for her to support Ralph. But it can't be official. Tell Ralph."

Carter told me that Ralph was fascinated by Esther.

"If you weren't both happily married and he weren't a candidate for Congress, I would tell you to be careful. He says that your wife has a great personality. Just what his wife lacks."

His tone of voice was cutting. He seemed irritated that Ralph should find Esther irresistible.

"You said it, Carter, we're both happily married. Ralph would need to be more than a guy with ambition for Esther to pay him any attention. Don't assume the whole world is as in love with him as you are."

He was silent. I listened to his breathing on the telephone line. I had been right without expecting to be, without realizing what I had said. Perhaps my subconscious had noticed what I hadn't: that Nicholas Carter was in love with Ralph Morgan.

"Let's leave it, Thomas." And he hung up.

When I told Paul, he started laughing at me.

"Come on, son, don't tell me that you hadn't realized until now. It seems to me that Carter's still in the closet, at least mostly. He must have always been in love with Ralph, and Ralph knows it and plays with his head. It's not that he gives him hope, but you know there's nothing more enduring than an impossible love."

"You could have told me," I said.

"Well, it's not like Carter walks around with a sign declaring that he's gay. In fact, he tries to hide it. And I'm not entirely sure he is, even though he isn't married and he doesn't have a girlfriend. Plus, I don't go around telling people about other people's sexual preferences."

"I'm not people, Paul. You should have told me, just as you told me why Constance doesn't like him."

"I'm not entirely certain it's true. It's just intuition. I've watched them. Carter looks at Ralph like he's besotted and Ralph lets himself be loved. He pats him on the knee, he puts an arm around his shoulders like they're two pals who've just left a baseball game. At one point I even started wondering if . . . well, it's stupid."

"Do you think they're seeing each other? That really would be something!"

"No, I don't think so, but . . . they're a very strange trio. Constance hates Carter too much for it to be solely because he gave Ralph some questionable advice many years ago. And it wasn't such a crazy thing to suggest—it's what any friend would say in a situation like that."

"So those two . . . A pair of queens!" I said, laughing.

"Don't get ahead of yourself, Thomas. Don't turn my conjectures into truths. Watch them and draw your own conclusions."

Esther thought she'd won the battle so we didn't talk about either Constance or Ralph again. She continued managing the logistics of his public appearances while I waited for the right moment to make my move on Constance. I hadn't heard from Carter since our phone conversation. Or Ralph. That's why I was surprised when, a couple of weeks later, Esther told me that the Morgans had invited us to a barbecue at their home.

"Why?" I asked.

"Well, it's spring and it seems he wants to have a party for everyone who's been working on his campaign, including us. It seemed wrong to reject the invitation. If you don't want to go, I can go with Paul."

"We'll go. If you think it's a good idea, we'll go."

"There's nothing wrong with going to their home on an occasion like this," Esther insisted.

"Of course not."

Paul came to pick us up. He had just bought himself a new car, the latest model Ford Mustang. He wanted to show it to us.

The Morgans had invited around thirty guests—young men and women who were enthusiastic collaborators on the campaign. Ralph greeted us at the door with his best smile. Constance stood at his side with a bored expression and her gaze fixed on her daughter, Ellen.

A couple of waiters were wandering around the garden carrying trays of drinks while a chef concentrated on arranging large steaks on the grill.

Everyone seemed happy. The young people were bubbling with enthusiasm and looked at Ralph with admiration. He doled out smiles and affectionate gestures to one after another.

Esther went over to Constance. She suddenly seemed very interested in talking to her. I watched them out of the corner of my eye; they were chatting in a friendly manner. Ellen joined her mother. She seemed tired.

In the meantime Paul was busy making a play for one of the girls who worked on Morgan's campaign, a brunette with long legs and short hair.

Carter came over to me. He looked at me, trying to transform his grimace of disgust into a hypocritical smile.

"It's good to see you, Thomas."

"Looks like a fun party," I commented, to fill the silence.

"I thought Ralph needed to open his home to the team. This will motivate them even more because they'll feel like they're being given special treatment, like they're more than just cogs in the electoral machine, which is what they are."

"And Constance?" I asked.

"Ah, she agreed. Unwillingly, but at least she didn't say no. She even agreed to let Ellen stay for a while. She seems very absorbed in her conversation with your wife."

Yes, the two seemed to be enjoying their conversation. I saw Constance laugh at something Esther was saying to her.

What could they be talking about? The two women couldn't have been more different.

Constance was a typical middle-class American woman, white skin, smooth blonde hair, perfect teeth. Neither very stupid nor very smart. Married to a man with a promising future.

Esther was a fighter. Everything she had achieved had been through her own efforts, her hard work and her talent. And she had paid a price for all of it. I was part of that price.

No, they had nothing in common and yet there they were, chatting as if they were friends.

Ralph went over to them and Constance took Ellen by the hand. She went into the house with her daughter.

I followed them as far as the kitchen, where a woman was arranging clean glasses on a tray.

"Well, I didn't expect to find you here. I wanted a glass of water. There's only beer and whiskey out there," I said unconvincingly.

The woman in charge of the kitchen handed me a glass of water without saying anything.

"I'm going to give Ellen a glass of milk and then she'll go take a nap. She's tired," replied Constance, as if I'd asked her what she was doing there.

"Of course, that's best. Do you like stories, Ellen?" I asked her, unsure of what else to say to the kid.

"Yes, my mom tells me one every night. But that won't be possible tonight; she needs to stay with the guests. She'll tell me two tomorrow."

"That sounds fair. Sleep well, beautiful."

They left the kitchen and I stayed where I was, lingering. I was hoping that Constance would come back. She did—sooner than expected.

"Don't you want to be in the garden?" she asked, without looking at me.

I followed her. She stopped at the doorway that led from the family room to the garden. I didn't move either.

"You don't seem to be enjoying yourself much," I stated.

"No, not really. This party is Carter's idea."

"And don't you think it's a good idea? I do. This will help to energize the young people working for the campaign. You make a very charming family."

"Do we? Well, we put on a good show."

I didn't respond. I knew that if I did, she would backtrack. Constance needed to unburden herself, but if anyone insisted on it, she would clam up.

"Will my husband become a congressman?" she asked without enthusiasm.

"He's got a lot of good qualities as a candidate and has a good chance. If he doesn't make any mistakes . . ."

"Why would he make mistakes? Carter conducts the orchestra and we all play our parts. We don't improvise."

"Well, it's just that you don't seem exactly happy . . ."

"Should I?"

"It would really help. But it's up to you. I'm not the head of the campaign, so I'll refrain from offering advice."

"Your wife said the same, that your agency isn't involved in politics, that that's Carter's area."

"I saw you talking earlier, you seemed to be getting along well."

"Yes . . . Well, we barely know each other, but she seems like a very understanding woman. I like her. You're lucky."

"Yes, I think so. How about you?"

"Me?"

"Yes. Are you lucky? Are you happy?"

"Two very personal questions for a mere acquaintance to ask." Her voice was severe, like a teacher scolding a student.

"You're right. Pardon me . . . I hope I haven't offended you," I apologized.

She kept staring at me. She was sizing me up, deciding whether she ought to reply. She sighed as if she weren't sure what she should do.

"I don't know if I'm lucky. Am I lucky to be married to a handsome guy? Am I lucky that he always does his duty? Am I lucky that all that connects us is Ellen's illness? Am I lucky that he's pleasant and well-mannered? Am I lucky that he never criticizes me for anything? Yes, you could say that I'm lucky. Ralph never does anything wrong."

"Well, then you're lucky," I admitted.

"Yes, perhaps. As for whether I'm happy . . . I'm married to the man I chose. He's a good father and a pleasant husband."

"That's not an answer."

"What do you want me to say? I don't know what happiness

is . . . Well, when I was younger I had a rough idea. To me, being in love seemed exciting, I thought that it would mean living in paradise forever. I imagined a relationship full of passion, of . . . What stupid things I'm saying! I don't know why we're talking about all this."

"Well, I'm interested in what you're saying. You know something? The first day I saw you I realized that you were different . . . I don't know, but you haven't seemed happy, and I don't just mean because of Ellen's illness. Forgive me for being so honest. I don't have the right to say such personal things to you."

"No, you don't."

Paul came over to us. He was holding the hand of the leggy brunette. He winked at me, wanting to make it clear that he had hooked up with the girl.

"A wonderful party, Mrs. Morgan. It's a pleasure to see so many young people working toward the same dream. May's been telling me how much they all admire Ralph." Paul looked enthusiastically at the girl.

"You can't do anything without a dream," Constance murmured.

"Of course not," May joined in, "and I assure you, Mrs. Morgan, that Ralph has infected us with his dream. We know that when he gets to Capitol Hill he'll bring the voice of the people," she declared very seriously.

"Well, let's leave the politics for another time. This is a party—we should be celebrating. Don't you think so?" I interrupted them, hoping that Paul would go off with his brunette and leave me alone with Constance.

Paul looked at me and gave a smile. He'd gotten the message.

"Thomas is right, sweetheart. Let's go get another beer and another couple of ribs. They're delicious."

When we were alone I saw that Constance was smiling. She seemed relieved not to have to string together a conversation with Paul and the girl.

"You got them to leave you in peace," she murmured.

"Yes, banalities irritate me and the terrible thing about these parties is that all you say and hear are banalities."

"Aren't you a banal man?"

"I hope not, Constance."

"And are you happy?"

"You're asking me my own question?"

"Are you happy with your wife?"

"You said it before, I'm lucky to be married to her. She's an exceptional woman, intelligent, hardworking, a good companion."

"I'm talking about love, Thomas."

"I know, Constance, and I'm saying what I can say. Let's leave it there."

I was being more sincere than she could imagine. But more importantly, I was casting my net so she would let herself be caught. That woman was crying out for an affair, something that would take her away from her routine, her boring life, and her emotionally distant husband.

Ralph had been watching us. He didn't seem disturbed to see us together. He waved and smiled from the other end of the garden. Carter was beside him. He said something to him. Who knows what?

The next day Paul turned up in my office. He had bags under his eyes. He still smelled of alcohol but he seemed happy.

"What a night! That girl was worth it. Don't you go thinking it was easy to get her into my bed."

"I'm not surprised—you'd have to be pretty desperate to get into your bed and she didn't seem too desperate to me."

"Don't be unpleasant, Thomas. How about you? Tell me everything. Mrs. Morgan was delighted with you. She didn't take her eyes off you after your little chat. I think her husband noticed, but he doesn't seem particularly worried."

"Don't talk trash, Paul."

"Listen, you can't fool me. You'll get her into bed if you can. And I don't think you'll find it difficult. That woman is practically begging for a man to pay her some attention."

"She has a husband."

"So what? Make sure Esther doesn't find out."

"What is there for her to find out?"

"That you've set your sights on Constance Morgan. Esther may be playing the fool when it comes to Olivia, but she isn't one."

"Olivia doesn't mean anything to me."

"I know. You just screw her."

Paul knew too much about me. He could read me like an open book. I didn't bother denying my relationship with Olivia, although I hadn't realized that it was so obvious. I was worried that it might also be to Esther.

"Do you think Esther knows about Olivia?"

"I don't think Esther's worried. She doesn't consider her a rival."

It seemed that Nicholas Carter had also realized that, if nobody prevented it, something might happen between me and Constance. And he was content with the prospect.

I wasn't surprised when he called me a few days later to invite me for a drink.

We arranged to meet on the terrace of Rockefeller Center, a place to see and be seen and where it was difficult to talk, but we did.

"We've got a crisis on our hands. Constance is refusing to be a part of the campaign. And she's said that she won't drag Ellen into it either. We've agreed to do a feature for *Vanity Fair*: the whole family, at home, like any other middle-class American family. But she won't do it."

"Well, I imagine Ralph could convince her."

"No, he's tried but he can't."

"What about you?" I asked sarcastically.

"Don't be stupid, Thomas. You know she can't stand me."

"What have you done to her?"

"I suppose I've just tried to prevent her husband from being a poor loser who earns fifty dollars an hour working for a third-rate legal practice."

"Nothing else?"

"What have they told you?" he asked suspiciously.

"They haven't told me anything. Is there anything to tell?"

"Don't lie, Thomas. We're on the same team."

"I don't know who your team is, Carter. My team is me alone, so we're not on the same team. My company takes care of the nuts and bolts of the campaign, nothing more."

"Talk to her," he said defiantly.

"To whom?"

"To Constance. She likes you. It's obvious. She'll listen to you. We need her to do this damned feature for *Vanity Fair*."

"She doesn't like me, Carter; it's just that she doesn't see me as an enemy like she does you."

"I don't care about the reason. Ralph and I both agree that she'll listen to you. Call her, invite her to lunch, whatever you want."

"Ralph wants me to invite his wife to lunch?"

"Whatever, Thomas, I've already told you."

"It's an advantage to have the go-ahead from the husband," I replied, laughing.

"What about Esther?" he asked.

"It's too noisy here. We'll catch up again soon."

When we'd parted ways I began to laugh. I really let go, chuckling loudly. The situation seemed surreal.

I let a few days pass, enough for Carter and Ralph to get nervous. Then I called Constance without saying anything to Esther or Paul.

I invited her to lunch and she refused, but she agreed to have coffee with me in the morning after she had dropped Ellen off at school.

We agreed to meet at the bar at the Waldorf. I hadn't been able to come up with a better place, but it was clearly a mistake, because anyone could have seen us there.

When I saw her come in I knew that she had dressed up for me. She was wearing a floral dress cinched in at the waist with a belt, and shoes with high enough heels to really lengthen her legs. Her clean, loose hair shone.

We sat at a table at the far end of the bar. We could talk there without anyone disturbing us.

"So, what's this important thing you need to tell me?"

"I'm not trying to trick you, Constance, I don't want to, so I'll tell you why I called you. Your husband needs you to do the feature for *Vanity Fair*. He and Carter thought that perhaps I could change your mind, make you understand how important this feature will be for the campaign."

"So you're here in your capacity as a public image expert . . ." she said, disappointed.

"Well, they gave me an excuse to call you and I'm delighted to be able to do so. But if you want to know the truth, I've been thinking about how I might be able to see you again for days."

"Would you have called me?"

"Yes, I would have; although I must confess I've been going out of my mind trying to think of a good excuse."

"Why? Why do you want to see me?"

"What about you, Constance, why do you want to see me?"

"You told me it was important . . ."

"And it is. It seems very important for me to tell you that . . . well, after our conversation I haven't stopped thinking about you. To be honest I haven't stopped since the day you came to our office with your husband. I don't know why you had such an effect on me, but you did. I don't want to think about you, but I do. And there you go, I've told you."

I held out my hand and she took it. I felt her shaking. I knew that I'd won her over.

"This isn't right."

"No, it's not right. You have a husband who loves you and I have a wife who's done nothing wrong. It's not right, but I don't think either of them make our hearts beat faster when we see them, or make us eager to go running to the bedroom, or . . . Well, at least that's how I feel. But you know what, Constance? Life doesn't give you many chances, and when a person feels that they've found someone special, when just thinking about that person gives them butterflies . . . then I think it's worth it . . . I don't know. I don't know what to say to you."

I was a good actor. I always have been. I guess it comes down to my skill at lying.

"Do you think I should do this feature?"

"I think you should do what you want. There's no doubt that it's important to Ralph's campaign, but if you don't do it, you have your reasons."

"He doesn't love me, Thomas. He's never loved me."

"I know."

"You know?"

"Yes."

"Who told you?"

"Nobody had to tell me. It's clear in the way he looks at you. I'm not saying that he doesn't appreciate you. He's a good father to Ellen, but he doesn't love you the way you need to be loved."

"It's my fault. I fought to hold on to him."

"And now?"

"Now I'm bound to him by Ellen. My daughter is sick, and we need money to treat her. There are days when she can't go to school, weeks when she has to be in the hospital. She needs me by her side."

"And I need to hold you right now."

"Thomas! Don't say that . . ."

"And you want me to."

She lowered her head. I knew she was defeated. This woman was desperate for a good afternoon of sex and affection.

"This is wrong. Please, let's leave it here."

Her look was a supplication. Yes, she wanted to sleep with me, but at the same time she hoped that I would be able to stop her. I didn't. If I weren't a bastard I could have. The scene would have been completely different:

"Constance, I'm here to ask you to do the Vanity Fair *feature."*

She would have argued against it, and might have even told me off for trying to convince her.

"I don't know why they put you up to this."

"I guess it's because they know I get along with you."

But I wouldn't have said another word. Not a hint of romance.

"I'm fed up with them trying to manipulate me," she would have said.

"I'm not trying to manipulate you, I've told you the truth. It's up to you, Constance."

"You don't mind?"

"I'm not in your shoes, it doesn't matter what I think. You have to decide what's best for you, what's best for both of you."

"What's good for Ralph isn't necessarily good for me."

"He's your husband, Constance, and he's a good man."

"If you only knew . . ."

"I don't want to know anything. But what I will say is that if you're with him you ought to support him. For your daughter, for yourself."

"I want to live, Thomas, to feel like I'm alive."

"Please, Constance, I'm not the person who should hear you say such things. They only asked me to explain how important

this Vanity Fair *feature is because I'm a public image expert and perhaps you might want to listen to me."*

"That's the only reason you're here?"

"That's the only reason."

"I thought that you and I . . ."

"You have a husband and I have a wife. We owe them, if not love, then at least loyalty. I understand your dissatisfaction; you dreamed your marriage would be different . . . Well, that happens. But I'm not going to be the one who drags you into a situation that would make you even more unhappy in the long run."

"I'm fed up, Thomas."

"Life isn't easy, but we have to face it as it comes. You've got more than you think. Ralph would never do anything to upset you and your daughter needs you both. Sometimes men don't know how to show our emotions, but that doesn't signify a lack of love."

"If you only knew . . ."

Yes, the conversation could have gone like that. I didn't have to lay siege to her until she gave in. I shouldn't have taken her hand. I shouldn't have insinuated that together we might enjoy something she had never enjoyed until that moment.

I knew that the opposite was true—that what we were about to do would sully her, that it would make her even more unhappy. But that didn't bother me. I'm not a good person, I never have been; I've always put my desires before anything else. She was just an appetizing morsel that I wanted to devour.

So I didn't say any of what I should have said and I persuaded her that we should go up to a room that I had booked there at the Waldorf, just in case.

I shouldn't have propositioned her. I could even have back-tracked: "No, I'm sorry, I don't know what I was thinking. I'm sorry, I don't want to compromise you or take advantage of the situation . . . You must forgive me. I don't know what made me suggest something like this to you. You deserve better. Forget about me, and I'll try to forget about you."

But instead I kissed her in the elevator and when we entered the room we fell onto the sofa and from there onto the floor.

Why did she give in to me that day at the hotel? I asked Olivia a few hours later when I went to see her at her apartment.

I told her what had happened. I've never had to pretend with Olivia. She knows that I don't love her and I know that she doesn't love me either, so for all these years I've been able to speak openly with her, without lies. I think that a financial contract is stronger than love and that's what has joined me to Olivia: a contract by which I have access to her whenever I want, and in return I fund her life.

I explained to her what had happened in detail—not to show off in front of her; I didn't need to—but because I was genuinely curious as to why it had been so easy to seduce Constance.

"Her marriage must just be a show. A man marries her because he's nothing but ambition and doesn't want to leave any skeletons to be discovered. What would the voters say if he hadn't done it and they found out about a young woman abandoned with a sick child?

"I don't like Ralph Morgan, everything about him seems fake. His choirboy face, his unruly mop of hair, his suits that fit him like a glove but aren't so expensive that they'll alienate the voters in the Bronx, the years he's been going to the neighborhoods to offer free legal advice . . . In truth, Constance is perfect for him. The people are moved to know that his kid is sick and that, despite getting better grades than he did in college, his wife sacrifices herself to her daughter's illness. Morgan is a fake, a good fake, yes, but there's not a drop of humanity in him."

"But you don't know him!" I protested.

"I've seen him on TV, and from what you've told me about that poor woman . . . I'm not surprised she slept with you; she needs someone to make her feel alive. She can use you for revenge; it's a private revenge, but it is revenge."

"So you don't think she did it because she likes me, then?" I asked, knowing the reply.

"Come on, Thomas! You're no Adonis and you know that well. The women who sleep with you have their reasons, but none of them has anything to do with you being an attractive guy. You're not even nice. You're the person Constance has closest at hand, so she picked you. She can't do it with Carter because he's gay; if not, she would have preferred to hurt her husband with someone closer to him. But be careful. That woman could become a problem."

"I don't see why."

"Because she's desperate, angry, bored, and she's going to stick to you like a barnacle. You'll see."

Olivia was right. Constance would become a burden that was difficult to bear.

I hadn't yet left Olivia's when my cell phone rang. I was surprised to hear Constance's voice. She wanted to know where and when we would see each other the next day. Her tone was such that her question was effectively an order.

But I found it amusing to deceive Ralph Morgan and Constance was really something in bed.

For the first few months I enjoyed our furtive liaisons, and I would be laughing inside when I met Ralph Morgan, remembering the intimate moments I had spent with his wife.

I tried to meet up with her at least a couple of times a week. In the beginning we would meet at hotels, but I convinced her that we should carry on with the affair at her house, in the bed she shared with Ralph. I would usually go to see her midmorning, knowing that Ralph would be immersed in his campaign at that time, his faithful Carter following him like a shadow, the perfect Cerberus.

I asked Olivia to go and observe Ralph Morgan during a meeting he held with young artists. I introduced her to him at the end. Morgan was enchanted with her. Not just because he recognized her from the ads but because I told him she was a good friend of mine.

Olivia stayed and waited for me while I debriefed with Carter and Ralph. She had moved away a bit, but not so far that she couldn't hear what we were saying. She was doing what I had asked her to: carefully observing Morgan and Carter.

It was lunchtime when we finished and I invited her to join me at an Italian restaurant.

"What did you think of them close up?" I wanted to know.

"Those two . . . I don't know . . . I don't think Morgan's interested in men, but he manages Carter's emotions well in the knowledge that he's in love with him. Have you noticed how he smiles at him? Carter melts when Morgan looks at him or gives him a pat on the back."

"Do you think there's anything between them?" I asked, eager to know her opinion.

"Pfff! I would say no. The fact is, Morgan is a manipulator. He uses people as it suits him. He does it with Carter and with everyone else. I noticed him flirting with that redhead who's showing her work at a gallery in SoHo, but then he got carried away praising that boring blonde who's in a Broadway musical, and he sucked up to that wacko who directs an orchestra in Harlem. He spoke to each of them as if they were important to him, as if they were unique. He establishes an emotional connection, as if nothing else exists. Morgan's very smart. He even treats you as if he really appreciates you and needs your advice."

"So you don't think he and Carter are messing around."

"Who knows? Maybe when they first met in college . . .

There may have been the occasional threesome ... But what do I know? I'm more inclined to believe the explanation I gave you. Morgan is an emotional manipulator, he knows how to get people on his side by making them think that he's on their side."

"Maybe you should become a psychologist rather than trying to be an actress," I told her sincerely.

"It would have made my father happy, but, as you know, I studied art and here I am, hoping that you'll actually do something for me for once." She gave me a meaningful look.

"Paying your bills is enough already," I replied curtly.

"You told me that you'd be able to get me a part on Broadway soon. If that vapid blonde is in a musical, I don't see why I couldn't be."

"Paul has promised me that he's working on it."

"I'll end up asking Esther. At least she's sensitive and likes helping people."

"I don't want to see you anywhere near my wife."

"You know what, Thomas? I sometimes think that Esther knows about us, but it doesn't bother her. I can understand that. You're too intense to deal with all the time."

She did. She asked Esther to help her. That's what Olivia was like. She would stop at nothing.

Esther told me about it. "Olivia called me. We should help her." Esther went ahead and managed to get a hold of something neither Paul nor myself could: a role for Olivia in an experimental play. Olivia even sang a sad and melancholy song. She wasn't a bad singer. She wasn't brilliant, but she wasn't any worse than many actresses on Broadway.

Not only did Esther get her that role, but she also hired Olivia for a new perfume ad we were working on.

The ad was a success. The director was able to get the best

out of Olivia; the camera fell in love with her green eyes and her milky white skin. She was suggestive and elegant at the same time. But not even the success of the commercial satisfied her yearning to become an actress.

I couldn't stop wondering if Olivia was right when she said that Esther knew we were sleeping together and didn't really care. I suspected it too. But if that were the case, there was no way of knowing unless I asked her directly, which I wasn't willing to do because that would have required a sincere conversation that I didn't want to have.

I was happy in my own way. I had Esther watching my back, taking care of me. She pretended to be happy, although she wasn't, no matter how rewarding she found the work and especially the fact that our agency had become a reference point in the advertising world. Esther had made a name for herself and received great acclaim, which increased the prestige of Global Communication.

As for our personal relationship, it was still governed by monotony. We were an old couple tied together by habit. But I didn't complain: habit can become very comfortable.

More than a year went by during which I couldn't bring myself to travel to London. The reports from Cooper and Evelyn were more than satisfactory. We had a small client portfolio that allowed us to pay our expenses and make a bit of a profit. Enough for Esther to be content.

Every day either Esther or I would speak on the phone to Maggie, who would update us on any administrative issues, and then either Cooper or Evelyn would inform us about work in progress.

No matter how much Esther insisted I travel to London, I didn't go. I was enjoying my life in New York. I had Esther, and I had fun with Olivia and Constance. I was too lazy to cross the Atlantic to go to a city where I didn't really have anyone.

I was also more involved with Ralph Morgan's campaign than

Esther would have liked. Officially, Nicholas Carter was campaign manager. He was the one who had the authority, and he directed Morgan, but he often sought my advice, listened to me, and little by little it became the norm for us to meet at least once a week to discuss the campaign's next steps.

Olivia used to say that Carter was grateful to me for sleeping with Constance. I was sure that Carter didn't know anything, but Olivia insisted that he did, considering that Constance had started working on the campaign without protest, and that whenever I appeared, she would run to my side, not caring what others might think.

Perhaps Olivia was right. In any case, even Ralph Morgan thanked me one day "for how well you handle Constance."

I seem to remember it was three or four weeks before the congressional elections when Roy Parker called us.

"You must come to London. I have a surprise for you," he said, laughing loudly.

There was no way to get him to say what it was about. Later Esther had to convince Maggie to tell us what Roy's surprise was.

"You asked Evelyn to find him a wife, and that's what she did," said Maggie, without further explanation. Evelyn didn't want to reveal the name of the woman Roy was going to marry either. All she said was that she hoped we liked the lucky lady.

It's true that for some time I had enjoyed Roy's company, but at that particular moment I refused to go to London. I couldn't miss the election, I didn't want to. There were only a few days left before we would find out whether Ralph Morgan had persuaded New Yorkers to vote for him. Furthermore, it would have been unprofessional for Esther and me to go away the night before the vote, even if Paul could be left in charge of the agency.

Roy protested, but in the end he admitted that we couldn't

leave our candidate by himself when he was about to cross the Rubicon.

"All right, help your man win the election like you helped me. But the day after you must come straight here. I want you to be my best man. You can't refuse."

I couldn't refuse nor could Esther not accompany me.

On the day of the election, I persuaded Esther that we should join Ralph's electoral committee to wait for the results. Carter was even more nervous than the candidate. As for Constance, she seemed indifferent about what might happen. She made me anxious with her insistence on not leaving my side. She followed me with her gaze wherever I moved, and from time to time, in an intense exercise in brashness, she would even hold my hand in front of Esther, her husband, Carter, and the rest of the team, and ask me in a mellifluous voice, "Do you really think Ralph is going to win?"

He won. Ralph was elected to Congress by a narrow margin. Carter burst into tears, and shamelessly threw his arms around Ralph. I noticed Constance's disdainful gaze as her husband gave his campaign manager a few little pats on the back, in an attempt to extricate himself from the embrace.

When Carter stopped crying we went to the room where the journalists and everyone who had worked on Ralph's campaign were waiting for him to address the voters.

I had told Constance to stand next to her husband, offering her best smile.

Ralph went in first, holding hands with his daughter, little Ellen, followed by Constance and Carter.

Esther pulled me over to a spot where we wouldn't be noticed.

"America is the land where dreams come true, and tonight dreams will begin to come true for all those who voted for me because they want change. I will do the impossible so as not to let you down. I'm grateful for the trust of all the citizens who voted for me. But I want to say that I will not only be *your* congressman—I will also pay attention to the problems and questions of those who didn't vote for me. It is my desire to become a worthy representative of the state of New York and to bring all its citizens' concerns to Washington.

"I want to thank my dear wife, Constance, for her support and late nights helping me get to where I am, and for being the best mother a man could want for his children. My daughter, Ellen, has been my inspiration, because I want to contribute to a better future for her and for everyone.

"I can assure you I will not let you down. Thank you all."

After those words Morgan kissed Constance, who received the kiss without moving a muscle, while little Ellen clapped her hands enthusiastically. Hundreds of balloons with Morgan's face on them started to float up to the ceiling as the applause thundered around the room.

Ralph whispered something into Constance's ear and she lifted her hand, waving to those present. The television cameras were trained on them.

Morgan's and Constance's parents also came out onto the stage, as Carter had arranged. Everyone was delighted to be in the supporting cast of Ralph's success.

I saw Olivia sitting in the third row. She was smiling. I had asked her to come to the event so I could talk to her about the act we were putting on.

Ralph invited us to his family's house for a late dinner. He was euphoric and needed to talk about what had happened. On Carter's initiative, Constance had arranged for a cold dinner. At first she had refused, but I convinced her to accept Carter's request. I even threatened to stop seeing her if she didn't play the role of the perfect wife.

"I like to watch you pretend, knowing that you hate your husband and that you'd rather be fucking me. It makes me want you more," I said. And it was true.

They had invited more than fifty people. We could barely fit in the living room, but because everyone was happy nobody seemed to mind not having a place to sit. The waiters came and went, passing around food and drinks from their trays.

It was nearly midnight when Esther asked me if we could go home.

"Almost everyone is drunk. We've fulfilled our obligation by coming to the party. But tomorrow morning I have a meeting at eight with the oil consortium people. I need to be awake. I don't want that campaign to pass us by."

I nodded. We'd leave, yes, but I asked for a few more minutes. I told her I needed to speak to somebody on the electoral team.

I went upstairs to the second floor. I had noticed Constance go up. She was in the bathroom; I knocked on the door and she opened it. I pushed her against the wall and I took her right there. The scene excited me. I wasn't kind to her. Afterward I went downstairs without looking at her, without saying a word.

I waited three days before I spoke with her again. I wouldn't answer her calls. Suddenly I was enjoying making her suffer. When at last I spoke to her I was cold, indifferent. I noticed the fear in her voice. Fear of losing me. I listened as she begged me to see her.

I asked her to meet me at a bar in Chinatown. She asked me to come to her house instead. She would be alone. Ralph had a meeting and Ellen was going to a classmate's birthday party. We'd have two or three hours.

I refused. The more her voice thinned into a plea, the more amused I was. I took pleasure in her suffering, just as I had enjoyed Yoko's suffering.

When we met at the bar in Chinatown she tried to hug me but I didn't let her. I rudely pushed her away and she sat down, defeated, not understanding.

"What do you want?" I asked, looking at my watch to make it clear I didn't have time for this.

"I don't understand, Thomas . . . What's the matter? You suddenly don't take my calls and . . . well, you ask me to come here."

"That's it, Constance."

"What? I don't know what you mean . . ."

"It's over. We had a nice time but that's it. Devote yourself to your husband and daughter. The congressman is going to need you to play the role of loving wife. Of course, you'll need to try harder. Stop looking so disgusted when your husband comes near you."

"But . . . what are you saying? You can't . . . you can't leave me . . . What have I done? Tell me what I've done!"

Constance had raised her voice so much that some of the bar's customers started to stare. I savored that moment. A beautiful woman pleading with an ordinary-looking man like me.

I wasn't really planning to leave her. I just wanted to make her suffer to increase her dependency on me. It greatly amused me to know that we were deceiving her husband, the flawless, newly elected congressman.

She started to cry, softly at first and then with no shyness at all. I despised her. Yes. I despised her dependency on me, knowing she was like a rag doll who would let me do whatever I pleased with her as long as she could keep me by her side. That was my power. I felt powerful with her and that was something that didn't happen with Esther or with Olivia.

Esther was my wife, but I wasn't sure how long she would remain by my side. I was indifferent about Olivia. I didn't own either of them. But Constance was wholly mine.

It took her a long time to get a hold of herself and stop crying. I looked at her, bored.

"I'm going to London with Esther," I said, knowing this would increase her desperation.

"You're leaving? Why? When will you be back?" she asked. Her anxiety was plain in her voice, in her gaze, in her clenched fists.

"Business. You know we have a branch office of Global Communication in London. There are clients we need to look after."

"Why are you going with your wife?" Her jealousy showed in her shrill tone of voice.

"Because she is my wife and my partner, but I don't need to give you explanations. You have no right to ask me anything, least of all about Esther."

"Your wife . . . I thought there was barely anything between the two of you."

"Wrong conclusion. I adore her. There is no other woman in the world like her. We will enjoy our stay in London."

"Pig!" she hissed.

"From what I can tell, you like pigs, so I will take that as a compliment."

She burst into tears again. I could feel her desperation. She was willing to do anything.

"If you leave me I'll tell everyone about us. I'll tell Ralph, and your wife; I'll call a press conference," she threatened.

I shrugged. I was sure she wasn't capable of such a stupid thing.

"Your husband will look like a cuckold, you will look like a slut, and my wife will forgive me. I'll explain to her that you seduced me, that you put your hand down my pants. We'll be able to deal with the scandal. I'll be okay, but Ralph and you won't."

It wasn't easy to forget about Constance during our stay in London. She sent me text messages continually, some supplicating, others full of threats. I didn't reply to any of them. I was determined to enjoy the trip.

Esther didn't really want to come with me, but she dutifully agreed to. Roy Parker was still our best client, and if he was getting married and had invited us to the wedding, we couldn't slight him.

Our London apartment seemed less inviting than when I had

lived there before. We had become used to having enough space for the both of us and, although neither of us said so, it was actually irritating to have to share the bathroom and not each have our own work space. We didn't feel comfortable in the bedroom even though in New York we shared a bed.

"It's so small!" Esther whispered as she unpacked suitcases.

We went to the office. Maggie was as caustic as ever. She raised an eyebrow when she saw us walk in and didn't even bother to get up to welcome us.

"Did you have a nice flight?" she asked, without enthusiasm.

We nodded, and Esther asked her to summon Evelyn and Cooper to my office.

"Cooper is having breakfast with a client and Evelyn hasn't arrived yet. She's with Roy Parker," Maggie informed us.

Esther was not willing to sit around doing nothing, so she asked Maggie to show her the accounts and all the paperwork that had to do with the company's administration.

Maggie swore under her breath at Cooper and Evelyn's absence.

I sat patiently for some time listening to Maggie repeat explanations about income and expenditure, which we already knew, but which Esther seemed determined to go over again.

Cooper finally arrived at ten. He came in whistling, oblivious to our presence. When he saw us, he seemed happy. He shook my hand, gave Esther a couple of kisses, and joined Maggie's presentation about the accounts.

As soon as I could, I diverted the conversation toward more practical issues: what they were working on, and what the new clients were like.

At eleven, Evelyn appeared. She looked as if she'd just stepped out of the shower. Her skin was radiant, her hair pulled back on her nape with a few hairpins, and she wore a red suit that hugged her figure like a glove and a pair of heels at least four inches high. Quite attractive.

She seemed happy to see us, but Evelyn wasn't one to waste any time and she joined the meeting to discuss general issues.

At one, Maggie showed signs of impatience. She was hungry. Every day at that time she had a sandwich and a cup of tea.

She refused an invitation to lunch with Cooper and Evelyn at a pub near the agency.

We made small talk, but it seemed that Cooper and Evelyn were hiding something from us. Esther also noticed it and, being Esther, asked them directly.

"I have the feeling that you have something to tell us and you don't know how." In her tone of voice there was a slight admonishment.

"Well, there is news . . . But we'll tell you later," Evelyn responded.

"I don't like surprises. Whatever you have to say, I want to hear it right now" was Esther's curt reply.

"Not now . . . No, it's not possible. Later. Roy wants to invite you both out to supper. How about seven? Cooper, you're invited as well," said Evelyn.

"Very well, we'll have dinner with Roy, but I want to know now what's going on," Esther insisted.

"It's a surprise," Cooper interrupted.

"I've told you already I don't like surprises."

"This surprise, I hope, won't disappoint you. Please, Esther, wait until the evening!" Evelyn begged her. I made a gesture to Esther asking her not to insist. What difference did it make? I didn't believe that what they had to tell us could really affect us. The agency was doing well: we didn't have huge earnings, but we did make enough for it to not be a burden. The only bad news they could give us was that Evelyn and Cooper might be thinking about leaving Global Communication to start their own business, and that wouldn't be so dramatic either. London was full of young talent eager to be discovered.

After lunch we went to the apartment to rest. I wasn't tired, but if we had to have dinner with Roy, the evening would be a long one. He wasn't the kind to go to bed straight after the meal. He would insist on having a few drinks. Perhaps Esther would be allowed to go home early, but under no circumstances would I.

At five thirty Esther whispered in my ear that it was time to get up.

"I'll get in the shower, but start getting up."

She took twenty minutes to come out of the bathroom. She was already wearing makeup and was ready to face the evening.

"What kind of restaurant is it? Do I need to dress up?"

"Le Gavroche is a place that's a little special. It's in Mayfair and people go there to see and be seen . . . I think it has a Michelin star."

"I like barbecued ribs. Why do all rich people have to be such idiots?"

"For eating at Michelin-starred restaurants?"

"Do you think all these modern executives actually like food that doesn't look like food? If they go it's because those places are fashionable, even though they would rather have a good steak. All right, what shall I wear?"

"You know, the usual in these cases: a black dress, high heels, and modern jewelry that looks sophisticated but not too formal."

"What a load of nonsense!"

She followed my advice. The heels were considerably high.

"I can't wait to meet Roy's future wife," I said on the way to the restaurant.

"Maybe we know her already," Esther suggested.

Roy was waiting for us impatiently. Cooper was wearing a tie and Evelyn a dark blue silk dress and a pair of heels that were even higher than the ones she'd worn in the morning. I started to see how beautiful she'd become.

"Will I always have to get married to get you to come to London?" Roy said as he gave Esther a hug.

"We really wanted to come and see you sooner . . . But we've had to work so hard to keep the agency running as it should in New York," I said, just for the sake of saying something when it was my turn to receive Roy's hug.

It was obvious that Roy was happy. Even rejuvenated. The suit he was wearing was from Savile Row and the shoes were Italian. Yes, he had eschewed his disheveled style in favor of clothes that were more appropriate for a member of Parliament in Her Majesty's government. Because Roy had made it. Or, more accurately, Schmidt and the lawyers had done the impossible and had enabled him to occupy a seat at Westminster. Of course, we had done our part too. I could only imagine what poor Evelyn must have had to put up with.

Roy ordered cocktails for everyone, despite Esther insisting that she preferred a glass of white wine.

"Dear, you must try the Cherry Bomb. It's got tequila, cherry marmalade, black pepper, agave, and lime. You'll like it," Roy said, not giving her much of a choice.

I had already tasted the famous cocktail a couple of times, and though it wasn't my favorite, it was stimulating.

Roy also insisted on choosing the food.

He told us endless anecdotes and gossip about government ministers. He seemed to be enjoying his position as MP and, from what he was saying, he was starting to spend more time in London than in Derbyshire.

"Evelyn doesn't like it. She says I shouldn't leave the voters unattended and I don't want to either, but I also want to enjoy life a little," he explained to us as he ordered another round of Cherry Bombs.

"You should listen to Evelyn. You're enjoying your new life thanks to your voters. Neglect them and you'll stay in the county forever," I said without holding back.

"Don't be a party pooper, Thomas. I'm making a name for myself here," he responded.

"Well, I'm sorry to burst your bubble, Roy, but here you're nobody. You represent the small Rural Party, that's all. Perhaps some minister may condescend to you so you can vote in some law, but in truth you don't matter to them. You should strengthen your party; you and I both know that it's a sham. You've been lucky, but that's it. At the next election, Labour and the Conservatives will do whatever it takes to keep you out of the game. They'll dig up your past to expose you, just as we've done before with their candidates. And you are vulnerable, Roy, very vulnerable. If somebody hired me to crush you I can assure you that it would be done easily."

There was an awkward silence at the table. Roy cleared his throat, and Evelyn lowered her gaze. I was being a killjoy. It was Esther who restored calm.

"One thing at a time, don't you think? Tomorrow we can talk about work and the future but today we are here to celebrate something. You said you were getting married and I'm hoping you will tell us to whom and, especially, that we'll get to meet her. I hope you'll be very happy."

"Thank you, Esther. Your husband is a brute but you are an angel," Roy joked.

"I think you should tell him now," Cooper interrupted.

"Yes, I think I should. Everyone, stand up, please, I'd like to propose a toast to my wedding, and to you, Thomas: you will be my best man. I hope you bring us the same luck that you've enjoyed.

"Thomas . . . Esther . . . Please meet my future wife."

I felt like an idiot. How had I not realized? Roy wrapped his right arm around Evelyn's shoulders and kissed her on the lips.

So Roy Parker was marrying Evelyn Robinson, the ambitious Radio East reporter whom I had converted into a publicist. The ugly duckling with bulging eyes who now put on the airs and graces of an executive in the City.

Esther congratulated them. First Evelyn and then Roy. She didn't seem surprised, at least not as much as I was.

"Well, I must say I suspected it. I don't know why, but . . ." said Esther.

"But we never gave you a single clue!" Evelyn responded, laughing.

"Up until today you hadn't, but when I saw you at the office this morning . . . You looked different: the way you dress, the way you move. And when we arrived at the restaurant I was absolutely sure," Esther declared.

"You are the one to blame for this, Esther. You asked Evelyn to find me a wife." Roy laughed in delight.

"Yes, and you have chosen well," said Esther. "Evelyn, you're going to be a wonderful wife and a wonderful adviser. Roy, I hope you will make Evelyn happy."

We chatted lightheartedly the rest of the evening. It wasn't the time to talk about work, much less to ask whether Roy would end his contract with us now that he had Evelyn. We needed to wait until the next day to find out.

They gave us the details of the wedding, which would be celebrated in three days. I would be the witness for Roy, and Esther for Evelyn. After the ceremony, they'd celebrate with a cocktail reception at the Dorchester with a few guests, their colleagues from the Rural Party, five or six members of Parliament, a couple of high government ministers, and a dozen friends. The celebration would be elegant but sober, Evelyn explained.

Roy insisted on taking us in his car to our apartment, hoping we would invite them up for one last drink, but Esther declined. We were both not only tired; we were also anxious to talk about the wedding. Roy was disappointed, but agreed to leave the drinks for another day.

Esther slumped onto the sofa and asked me to pour her a glass of whiskey. I poured another for myself.

"We've lost Roy," I said.

"You're wrong. Let him marry Evelyn, it's the best thing that could've happened to us," she declared.

"You're the one who's wrong. In Evelyn he'll have both a wife and a press adviser. He no longer needs us. I had a good eye when I hired her. She's intelligent and ambitious. From writing features for a local gazette, she's going on to become the wife of a member of Parliament, and she will do whatever it takes to ensure that Roy doesn't stick his foot in it."

"Precisely the reason he'll want to continue working with us. Of course you'll have to find someone to replace her in managing Roy. And it has to be someone she trusts because it'll actually be she who decides what Roy has to do."

"But don't you understand that it makes no sense for him to pay us for what his wife will do for free from now on?"

"Evelyn is going to become Mrs. Parker. She won't leave his side for a minute, but she'll still want to have a job, even if it's nominal, and be able to look after Roy's affairs at the same time. I bet you she'll ask for a change in terms, but she won't leave."

She was right. The next morning Evelyn arrived early at the office; even Maggie was surprised.

"You're getting married in a couple of days, you should be working on the wedding preparations," she scolded her.

"The only thing left to do is to collect my dress, everything else is ready. And I need to speak to Esther and Thomas."

The conversation went exactly as Esther had predicted. Evelyn told us she wanted to continue working for us, but it couldn't be on anything remotely to do with politics. Of course, she would continue to personally oversee Roy's image, although not officially, and for that purpose, she suggested that Cooper take her place.

"He's qualified, he's personable, and he gets on well with Roy. Perhaps you could hire another publicist to manage the commercial campaigns that Cooper looks after. I can give you a few names; there are lots of talented young people willing to work for almost nothing."

"And what would you do?" I wanted to know, because I couldn't quite visualize what she was going to do once she was married.

"I don't know . . . Maybe I can take care of directing institutional campaigns for NGOs and things like that."

"All right, but how many NGOs have hired us for a campaign?" I asked hesitantly.

"Until now, none," she admitted, reluctantly.

"We have a problem. We don't want to lose you or Roy, but it might be difficult for us to give you a job appropriate for your new situation. I don't know what your position would be," I said.

"She can look after the office administration," Esther suggested.

"Maggie does that already," I pointed out, shutting down the idea.

"So what could I do?" Evelyn asked, anxiety creeping into her voice.

"If you focus on PR for the agency, you'll be accused of influence peddling. Some clever journalist will reach the conclusion that if a company signs a contract with you, it'll be to get closer to Roy. No, it's not a good idea for you to have a job that's so exposed to criticism," Esther said, speaking more to herself than to us.

"Actually, she can't do anything except devote herself to being Roy's wife, which is already a job in itself," I insisted again.

"You mean I'm out. You're going to fire me." Evelyn's tense tone put me on edge.

"No, we're not going to fire you. Let me think, perhaps . . . Yes . . . That might be . . ." Esther continued speaking to herself.

"What might be?"

"We'll give the company a philanthropic angle," Esther proposed. "Each year we'll mentor young people with the best academic qualifications. They'll do internships at Global Communication and Evelyn will be their mentor, in charge of teaching them, guiding them, helping them take their first steps in the professional world. We can decide the requirements that the applicants need to meet, and we'll choose the best among them. For a couple of years they'll work here, under your management, for minimal pay. At the beginning we'll only be able to offer four or five internships; if things go well, we'll increase the number. What do you think about that?" she asked me, taking Evelyn's enthusiasm for granted.

"I don't know. You come up with some wild ideas. Do you really think we need interns?" I replied.

"If we were willing to hire a couple of young publicists, better to get four or five interns for the same price. They'll work nearly for free, and in addition, our company can check the social responsibility box. Of course, Evelyn will continue to work on the campaigns, but officially, it'll be those young interns who do it, and she'll be behind them as their teacher. Honestly, I think it's a great idea," Esther concluded.

I couldn't refuse. I would have liked to fire Evelyn but, if we did, we would lose Roy, who was still our main and safest client. I accepted. Evelyn hugged me and gave me a loud kiss on the cheek.

"You're both great! Thank you! Roy will be very happy. We were worried," Evelyn admitted.

If Maggie thought this was a good or bad idea, she didn't tell us. When we mentioned the arrangement to her, she raised an eyebrow and looked at me as she repressed a smile, which could equally mean that she considered me an idiot or that she agreed with us.

Cooper was also about to kiss me when we told him that he would now be in charge of Roy. He was eager to take the leap into political publicity because he was tired of having to come up with campaigns to sell marmalade or cologne. He thought it was more glamorous to rub shoulders with MPs. In addition, he got along well with Evelyn.

Roy called to invite me to supper, just him and me. I didn't refuse. I knew the meeting place would be Madame Agnès's house, and I was looking forward to finding out what had happened there since my last visit.

Esther didn't bat an eye when I said I was having dinner with Roy. She preferred to stay at the apartment working instead of wasting time, which is what she thought dinner with Roy would be.

"I don't like to leave you alone," I said, going through the motions.

"Don't worry, you'll have a nice time. I'd rather stay here and call Paul to see how things are going in New York."

"I'll do my best not to come home late," I said, so she understood what would happen.

"That'll be hard with Roy; after dinner he will, of course, insist on having another drink. If you get home late I won't even notice—you know I sleep like a log."

Roy picked me up at seven. He wanted to surprise me. He said we would have dinner at a restaurant that didn't look like one.

I didn't want to disappoint him, but I'd already been to the Gourmet Burger Kitchen, a quirky place that served some exceptional hamburgers.

We'd already had a couple of cocktails when I asked him about Suzi. I was curious to know how she had reacted to the news of Roy and Evelyn's wedding.

"When I told her she started to laugh like mad. She says Evelyn is a penniless journalist willing to do anything so she doesn't have to be an errand runner again for the local newspaper, and doing anything includes marrying me. She demanded an increase in her alimony, and she's turned my children against Evelyn. It could have been worse."

"And what does she do?"

"She doesn't live in Derbyshire anymore. She moved to Oxford in the hope that when the time comes our oldest son will go to university there. That's her excuse. The truth is she's having an affair with the director of a bank branch office in Oxford. My children say that this guy Harry is a good person, that he treats them well and loves their mother. Perhaps. Even so, she hates me. But all the better for her if she has someone to warm her bed at night."

"Don't you love her anymore?"

Roy was silent. He took a few seconds to reply. Whatever he said, I knew he still loved her.

"One doesn't forget a woman like Suzi . . . I was very happy with her. I never would have exchanged her for anyone else."

"And Evelyn?"

"She's a good girl. She takes care of me, she advises me well. She has become indispensable. Better to marry her, otherwise somebody might take her away."

"Good foresight."

"Come on, Thomas, you know Evelyn. Suzi is right when she says she's ambitious. She's good at her job. Things are the way they are. I'd rather have her continue working by my side, rather than leave me any old day for another job or for some guy with money who proposes. And I like her. It'll do us both good to get married. There's no deceit on either side."

Roy was practical. And just as I'd expected, he invited me to accompany him to Madame Agnès's.

"There are some new girls there, you'll like them."

"You're getting married the day after tomorrow," I reminded him, laughing.

"There is no reason why marriage should put an end to wholesome traditions."

Madame Agnès feigned joy when she saw me.

"My dear Thomas, I'm so happy to see you again. I thought you had forgotten all about us."

"Never, Madame, but business forces me to spend a lot of time in New York these days."

"Our dear Thomas is happily married, Madame. That's the main reason why he stays at arm's length," Roy added.

"Ah, marriage! It's the best thing that could happen to a man. It gives him stability and a raison d'être," Madame Agnès declared. "Single men are always getting into trouble. They don't know what they want, they think they're going to be young forever. There is nothing better for a man than marriage."

"And for a woman?" I asked, curious what answer this woman would give.

"We don't need to be married to have stability or to know who we are. We can get by alone a lot better than men can. For women, marriage is a cage, while for men, it's a liberation. They no longer have to worry about themselves; their wife will do that for them."

"And if he's the only breadwinner?" I pushed.

"Then that's what he must be, otherwise he'll feel bad about himself. No, that's not a burden shouldered for the sake of a woman, I can assure you, gentlemen. And now allow me to offer you a glass of champagne."

I followed Roy to the library, where a group of men was talking about Wimbledon. Some of them I already knew; Roy introduced me to the rest. We joined the conversation, without much enthusiasm on my part, despite the fact that tennis is the only sport that I've enjoyed playing and that has interested me all my life. I didn't stay in the library very long. Since I was there, I wanted to enjoy the rest of the night with a girl. Roy followed me; he wasn't very enthused by the conversation either.

I saw Nataly talking to an elderly man. She looked more beautiful than the last time we saw each other. Of course, that night the only thing on my mind was finding out what had happened with Yoko.

Roy chose a young woman with dark skin.

"She's Indian, and for the last few months she's been my favorite," he said, lowering his voice.

I walked up to Nataly, who was surprised to see me, although she tried to hide the grimace that appeared on her face.

I greeted her, kissing her hand, and asked the elderly gentleman to allow me to speak to "this old friend whom I haven't seen for too long." The man hesitated but in the end resigned himself to it. There were too many other pretty young ladies to talk to for it to be worth arguing over one of them, especially if she was just another girl and not his favorite.

"So, you're back. I thought we would never see you again."

"Well, here you have me, and I intend to have a nice, leisurely time with you."

"After what happened . . . I don't feel comfortable around you, Thomas. Why don't you look for another girl? Some of them are new and don't know you."

"We used to have fun together."

"I've never had fun in this house. I come here to work."

"Well, you're good at pretending."

"It comes with the money that the clients pay," she pointed out, nonchalantly.

"You're still rude."

"Just to you, Thomas."

"That means I'm different from all those other men you sleep with."

"You're the worst, Thomas."

"I don't aspire to the contrary. Let's go somewhere more private."

"I'd rather not."

"All right, but the customer is always right, and I've chosen you."

"Madame Agnès allows us to choose. None of the girls who work here do anything we don't want to do. And I don't want to be with you, Thomas."

Her gaze reflected weariness. Weariness because of me. Not even hate; just the boredom that arises with someone you don't want in your life.

"Why?"

"You're a bad person, but you knew that already. Yoko died because of you and perhaps also because of me. You bought me. And you know what? When I go up to a private room with another guy I never feel like I'm being bought. The only time I've ever sold myself was when I accepted your money in exchange for giving you information about Yoko.

"Maybe the car ran her over by accident, maybe you pushed her and nobody saw you, or maybe she decided to take her own life. In any case, I feel responsible. I'll never forgive you for corrupting me—and I don't mean in bed. You were feeding my ambition. You got me to help you make Yoko your victim."

I laughed. Suddenly I felt contempt for her. Nataly had a very guilty conscience, and it tormented her. Most of the time she was probably able to forget about Yoko and what had happened. But when she saw me it was like looking in the mirror and seeing her own sin reflected.

I, however, had no regrets. I would do the same thing again a thousand times, even knowing that the end result would be Yoko's death.

Nataly looked at me, awaiting my answer. She didn't know what to expect from me.

If I were a good man, I would have put my hand on her shoulder and offered words that would have helped to restore her inner peace:

"Don't blame yourself, dear, you had nothing to do with what happened. The information you gave me was irrelevant, it was

within anyone's reach. Do you think it would have been difficult to find out that Yoko had a boyfriend?

"Yes, she felt overwhelmed by me and I never loosened my grip. It's not something I'm proud of; I shouldn't have gotten involved in her life. But that's my responsibility, not yours. Don't blame yourself for anything, there's no reason to. Yoko chose to die to get away from me. You had nothing to do with her decision.

"I'm not going to insist that you come to a private room with me. You're right, we both remind each other of Yoko. I give you my word, I won't bother you again."

But I didn't say any of that. What I did was grab her by the wrists and pull her toward me to whisper in her ear that if she didn't come with me, I would tell Madame Agnès and the rest of the girls that she had sold out Yoko, that she had spied on her for me.

"You know what'll happen. Madame Agnès will fire you and the girls won't ever forgive you. Madame does not allow indiscretions, much less a girl spying on another in exchange for a client's money.

"If you don't come with me you'll never be able to work here again. Oh, and I'll make sure your family and friends at school find out that you're a prostitute."

Nataly went pale. Her eyes filled with tears and I relished the thought that I'd broken her. But what happened next was something I never would have imagined.

She didn't even give me time to react. Little Nataly punched me, causing me more embarrassment than pain. I felt all eyes upon us. The other customers and girls were silent, watching us, waiting to see what we would do.

Nataly was also waiting. She wasn't scared. She didn't even seem worried.

"If I were you, Thomas, I'd leave now and never come back

to this house. But if what you want is to get back at me, be my guest. I myself will help you tell Madame Agnès and the girls what a miserable pair we are. I gave you my dignity once, but you won't have it again."

Madame Agnès marched toward us. She was livid. There had never been a scene like this at her house.

"What the devil is going on here? Nataly, you'll need to explain yourself . . . And you, Mr. Spencer . . . Please, both of you, meet me in the library."

Madame turned on her heel, smiling at the gentlemen and girls who were craning their heads for an explanation.

"Nothing to worry about, ladies and gentlemen. Please, carry on talking."

Nataly darted to the library ahead of us. I sauntered after her, savoring the moment. I took for granted that I could humiliate Nataly and that Madame Agnès would fire her immediately.

Roy approached me, looking furious. "What is wrong with you? Have you gone mad? How could you think of starting a scandal with that girl?"

"Don't worry, it's all right," I said, trying to downplay the significance of what had happened.

"You've managed to get everyone to notice us and the worst thing is that tonight there are a couple of members of Parliament here who know me. Care to explain what happened?"

"Nothing of consequence, nothing that can affect your good reputation. Let me sort this out, Roy. Go and enjoy the night with that brunette you're with."

He did as I said, and left me to it. But I couldn't ignore the stares along my way. Some men looked at me in disgust and the girls seemed upset.

When I went into the library Madame Agnès closed the door. Nataly was standing, waiting expectantly, but did not seem afraid.

"Nataly just told me something that . . . my God, I should have realized!" Madame Agnès lamented.

"I don't know what this girl told you," I said with marked contempt, looking at Nataly.

"That she spied on Yoko for you in exchange for money. You turned Yoko's life into a living hell until the poor girl . . . had the tragic accident. And tonight . . . tonight your behavior has been anything but gentlemanly, Mr. Spencer. You know that as a norm in this house my guests act freely, both the gentlemen and the young ladies. Nobody is obliged to do anything."

"Madame Agnès, leave the euphemisms aside. You run a whorehouse. Nataly is a whore and she is the one I want to sleep with tonight. I won't take no for an answer from a whore, not even from you."

But I had been mistaken about what would happen. Madame Agnès gulped and then looked daggers at me with her feline eyes. She seemed at a loss for words and hesitated for a second. When she did speak, she struck me down.

"Mr. Spencer, get out of my house and don't ever come back again. You are no longer welcome. I always thought you were not really a gentleman—that you were nothing but a rich con man. Your behavior has been deplorable tonight, and many other nights as well, I'm afraid. I don't even want to find out what Nataly told you about Yoko, but now I know why she seemed nervous every time she saw you. She didn't like you. I noticed this and on one occasion even reminded her that she didn't have to be with you. She told me not to worry. And now, unfortunately, she is gone. Get out of my house."

"I see, so now the queen of the whorehouse is playing Boston Brahmin. Don't do that, Madame, you look like a cartoon. You were a hooker in your youth and now you're their procurer. I'm paying to be here, and if you don't want to cause a major scandal, don't even think of trying to kick me out. I will leave when I want to and return whenever I please." I looked at her with such scorn that she took a step back, but she soon recovered.

"Mr. Spencer, get out. If I have to call the police, I will. And if I have to ask a friend of mine to investigate Yoko's death again,

I will. I don't think your wife would like to see your face in the *Times* in relation to the death of a girl."

"And yours, Madame? Do you think you can keep your house from being found out for what it is, a den of whores?"

"I told you he wasn't a good person," Nataly spat, looking me over disdainfully.

"You be quiet. What you did to Yoko is unforgivable. I don't ever want you here again either. I'll pay you for tonight and I hope this will be the last I see of you," Madame Agnès told Nataly.

We were both silent, gazing measuredly at each other. Madame Agnès left the library without another word and returned two minutes later accompanied by Roy Parker, in which time Nataly took the opportunity to get away.

"Madame Agnès has sent me to ask you to leave. Get out of here, Thomas." Roy's tone was marked by violence.

"What if I don't want to leave?"

"I will personally kick you out. You decide. I thought you were smarter than this, that you could tell when you've outstayed your welcome. Don't create trouble for me, Thomas. This will not benefit any of us. Get out."

I weighed his gaze and saw that he was willing to punch me if necessary. In his eyes there wasn't an iota of understanding or sympathy toward me.

I didn't say goodbye. I left. I realized that Roy had no choice but to turn against me. I decided that there would be payback later.

When I got back to the apartment, Esther was reading in bed. She was surprised to see me. She said she thought I would be back late, considering that Roy was the kind who never wanted to go home. I was in a foul mood and ignored her. She glanced at me without emotion. She couldn't care less about the cause of my agitation.

I sat in the living room for a long time, knocking back a few whiskeys, but not enough to get blind drunk.

Esther got up early. She didn't ask me who was calling my cell with such insistence and why I wasn't picking up.

I looked at the screen; it was Constance. She hadn't stopped calling me since I'd left New York. I hadn't returned her calls, and the voice messages she'd been leaving me were pathetic.

She'd say she loved me more than she loved her husband and her own daughter, begging me to take her back, and then she'd insult me, threatening to tell everyone about our relationship. I put the phone on mute and decided to continue sleeping for a while longer, at least until Esther came out of the bathroom.

I didn't talk to Roy again until his wedding, which I attended without any enthusiasm. For Esther it was also a formality that we had to see through. She thanked Evelyn for choosing her as a witness, but in reality she was indifferent.

Roy and I exchanged a tense handshake and waited at the door of the venue for Evelyn to arrive with Esther. We had to wait ten minutes, and if it hadn't been for Cooper and Maggie, Roy and I would not have said a single word. We were angry at each other. Not a definitive fallout, but we didn't feel at ease. The ceremony was brief and, to my surprise, Maggie got emotional. I guess the witch had a heart after all and appreciated Evelyn, whom she had seen go from ugly duckling to lucky swan.

As Evelyn was saying I do, my phone started to vibrate. Later I saw that the call had been from Constance. In her voice message she said that I had one hour to respond or she would do something terrible. I believed her.

As soon as we arrived at the Dorchester I looked for a quiet place where I could speak to her. I was scared when I heard her. Her voice was croaky. She said she had taken a couple of pills to calm down. She started to cry. I had to promise her that we would see each other as soon as I got back to New York.

"When will that be?" she sobbed.

"I have work, Constance. I can't just drop everything. I think we'll be in London for a few more days."

"But how many days?" she insisted.

"Three or four, I don't know. Don't worry, we'll talk when I get back."

"You're not going to leave me, are you?"

"Please, Constance. I'm at the Dorchester, at a friend's wedding. I can't talk at all now, much less about personal issues."

"Tell me you're not going to leave me!" she shrieked, hysterical.

"If you scream and don't calm yourself down we won't see each other again," I threatened, knowing that it was the only thing I could do to keep her under control.

"I am calm . . . I am calm . . . But we have to talk. I'm leaving Ralph."

"Don't do anything, Constance, don't say anything; wait for me to get back. Promise me you won't do anything until we talk, or you won't see me again. I don't like being pressured or having people threaten me. You know that."

"I promise, Thomas. Do you love me?"

"How could you ask me that question?" I responded, to avoid having to confirm what she feared.

A midafternoon cocktail reception has the advantage of not lasting very long. A couple of hours later we were done. The newlyweds were planning to have dinner alone. They were flying to Delhi the next day. Evelyn wanted to spend her honeymoon in India.

Neither Esther nor I wanted to stay in London any longer, so we remained for only one more day. "You barely ever come," Cooper complained, under Maggie's watchful gaze. Although she didn't utter a single word, her facial expression was a declaration of what she was thinking.

What really bothered Cooper was having to wait for Evelyn's return to recruit interns, whose mere presence would make him feel important because, officially, he was going to be the head of the agency.

Cooper had a few ideas to grow our business and needed people, but Evelyn's work was more flexible: she was now just in charge of training the interns. Without that duty, her presence at the agency would no longer make sense. In fact, she knew it was a sham job and that if we hadn't fired her it was only to keep Roy as a client. What Roy Parker paid us monthly covered the entire running costs of the agency.

I was starting to prefer New York more and more. Though I didn't have any especially pleasant childhood memories tying me to it, it was my city. I suppose my attachment to it has been due, in the past as in the present, to the fact that New Yorkers are more communicative and less formal than the British.

As soon as we landed at the airport and went through customs I asked Esther to wait a few minutes while I went to the bathroom. I was worried that Constance would follow through with one of her threats. I wanted to call her to let her know that I was already in the city. Perhaps that would calm her down.

I called a few times, but she didn't answer. I feared the worst. That birdbrain was capable of anything.

When we arrived at home, I felt immediately at ease. I could take refuge in my office and not feel Esther's eyes upon me all the time. I guess she felt the same. It had become a necessity for each of us to have our own space.

I called Constance again. I was startled to hear the voice of Ralph Morgan.

"Who is this?" he roared, though of course my name had appeared on the screen.

"It's Thomas Spencer, Ralph. We just got back from London and we have a present for Ellen. I wanted to ask Constance whether there's a good time for us to bring it."

"Nice to hear from you, Thomas, and thank you for thinking of Ellen. Constance isn't home; she left her phone behind and that's why I answered. I'll tell her to call you and I hope we see each other soon. Carter says we should continue to work with your agency. You guys are good. How is Esther, by the way?"

"Well, she's looking forward to seeing you and Constance soon."

"We'll meet up soon, Thomas. We'll call you."

When he hung up I sighed with relief. The lie I improvised seemed to have worked, although now I'd have to find some present that said "Made in England" to give to little Ellen.

Later I told Esther that we should have gotten a present for the Morgans' daughter.

"Why should we have done that? They aren't our friends, we've only done a campaign for them."

Esther drew a clear line between work and personal relationships. She liked the Morgans, but they were in the work circle, and although she was sorry about Ellen's illness, she didn't feel emotionally close to the family.

"You see, I told the girl once that if I went to London I would bring her a present. It was silly and I only now realize that I didn't, but I wouldn't want to disappoint her. The Morgans will continue to be our clients and they'll like it if we're considerate of their daughter."

"Especially Constance. She's a strange woman, although she likes you. Okay, I'll figure out where we can get some British trinket. Are you going to sleep for a bit or are you coming to the agency?"

"I'd rather work from home. I'll go in in the afternoon. Unless there's something urgent that requires us to go now?"

"Paul wants me to look over a campaign before presenting it to the clients. You know, the one for the washing machines."

"You don't need me for that, so if you don't mind I'll stay at home."

She didn't mind. She had showered and was dressed in a pantsuit, ready to work her fingers to the bone.

As soon as she left the house I thought about going to the Morgans' house. But I didn't. I knew that would be reckless. I phoned Olivia, who, without enthusiasm, invited me for brunch at her apartment. Well, actually, my apartment, because I was the one who was paying for it. On the way to her house I stopped by a store specializing in tea. I thought I might find something typically British in there. I bought a teacup with a saucer. It had a childish design, I think with a teddy bear wearing a Union Jack.

Talking to Olivia was always liberating. I didn't need to lie to her about my relations with other women. She knew I'd been sleeping with Constance for months, and it didn't worry her in the slightest. She had actually become my best adviser and didn't mind suggesting ways I could seduce the women I wanted to sleep with.

Olivia knew that her intelligence tied me to her more than her creamy skin and green eyes. Those I could have found in others, but what I couldn't do was open up to just anyone.

"Constance has become a problem and if you want to get rid of her you will have to make her believe she is the one who is leaving you," she suggested, as she nibbled on a slice of toast with salmon.

"And how can I convince her? That woman has lost her mind. I think she'll end up telling her husband that she's been sleeping with me, and if that happens, Esther will find out."

"Which is the only thing that worries you," she remarked, throwing me a very serious look.

"I'm not going to lose Esther because of Constance or any other woman. I'd sooner see the other woman dead."

"Very dramatic, but illogical. You know something? The only woman in the world who disconcerts me is your wife. Esther must be extraordinary for a guy like you to be trembling at the possibility of losing her. She's the only chink in your armor."

"I wasn't joking when I said I'd be capable of murder if someone tried to separate me from Esther."

She believed me. She read in my face that I really was capable of anything if it meant keeping Esther.

"You should go for women who are less difficult, like me. Women who know what to expect with you, who can keep a cool head and not depend on you emotionally. Poor Constance must be very lonely and very desperate to love you. Anyway, what's important now is for you to find a way out of this mess."

"Any ideas?" I asked, in the hope that she might help me.

"Well, I don't know . . . Perhaps you could convince her how much her husband loves her and insist that her daughter needs her and that it would be harmful to them if she abandoned them. Tell her that if she does that, she'll never forgive you, and that you won't be able to build your happiness together on others' misfortune. Something like that might work."

"She's insane. She told me on the phone she was willing to abandon her daughter."

"She probably doesn't intend to do that, it's just her way of putting pressure on you."

The sound of my cell phone interrupted the conversation. It was Constance.

"Where are you? Ralph said you called. We need to see each other right away." Her anguish was evident in her voice.

"Yes, of course we'll see each other, but your husband is at home, so we'll have to wait until tomorrow when he's not in."

"He's gone now. Carter just came by to pick him up. This morning he stayed longer because he had to finish writing his speech and didn't want anyone to bother him. You can come, we'll be alone. Ellen is at school and then she'll go to a playdate at a friend's house. I don't have to pick her up until five."

"Won't Ralph be back?"

"There's no reason why he should. If you look at his website you'll see he has a packed day. Among other things, he has an interview with the mayor of New York."

"All right, we'll meet, but I'd rather it was somewhere other than your house."

"I'm not going to allow you to humiliate me like you did when you took me to Chinatown," she warned.

"We could meet at the Waldorf bar," I suggested.

"At my house, Thomas. We'll see each other at my house."

"I'm not going to your house, Constance. I don't know why but I have a feeling that your husband suspects something."

"Even better. If he catches us he'll divorce me immediately."

"Please, don't talk nonsense."

Olivia made a gesture with her hand to indicate that I shouldn't lose my patience.

"I'll see you at my place, Thomas."

Constance hung up the phone and I threw mine against the wall, but fortunately it fell on the sofa. Olivia gave me a worried look.

"You'll never get anywhere like that, Thomas. It's too obvious that you want to get rid of her. You have to do the opposite. Be a bit of an actor. Convince her that you love her but that you have to make a sacrifice. Work her bad conscience. Tell her your heart breaks every time you see Ralph with Ellen in his arms, and say how much you admire her for being such a good mother. Things like that."

"She won't listen to me," I protested.

"If you scream at her, she won't listen. If you hug her, kiss her, and say you love her, and say how hard it's going to be to give her up, then she might listen. Make her feel like a hero who must renounce love for the sake of her family."

"What you're proposing is cheap sentimentalism," I responded.

"You'll be better off with cheap sentimentalism than trying to make her listen to reason."

"She'll be waiting for me in bed."

"Then sleep with her and put in your best effort. If you reject her you'll make her even more mad. Men are so dumb!"

"And maybe you're being a smartass."

"Try out my advice. If it doesn't work you can always apply your own method."

The last thing I wanted that morning was to have sex with Constance. I was starting to feel the effects of the jet lag.

When I reached the Morgans' house, I saw Constance pacing back and forth in the garden. She approached me as I parked the car. I asked her to be discreet.

When we went inside she threw herself on me. I kissed her apathetically but didn't reject her. She held my hand and led me to the bedroom. I thought if I got in bed I might fall asleep, but I followed Olivia's advice. She had recommended that I make an effort and that's what I did. Constance seemed satisfied.

"Promise you won't leave again," she implored.

"I'll have to go again on other occasions. I can't neglect the agency in London. If I promised you I wouldn't go I'd be lying, and that's something I don't want to do."

"Do you love me?" Constance leaned her elbows on the pillow and looked me in the eye.

"If I didn't love you everything would be easier."

"Why did you tell me you wanted to leave me?"

"Don't you understand?"

"No."

"Because you're too important to me. I don't want to rip your life apart. That's why I told you we should leave it. I thought if I behaved rudely it would be easier, and you would find it easier to accept. I was wrong. I'm sorry. The last thing I want is to make you suffer."

She sighed and seemed to relax. At least the tension dissipated from her face and from her body. She hugged and kissed me. I didn't have the energy or the strength for another round and I nudged her away gently. But she tensed up again.

"Why are you pushing me away?"

"I'm not. I want to talk to you. Anyway you should have mercy on me, I haven't slept in twenty-four hours." I laughed.

"There's nothing to talk about. We'll stay together. But we need to tell our families the truth. You have to tell Esther, and I'll tell Ralph. People get divorced all the time. They'll understand."

I could have been sincere. I simply could have told her that I didn't truly care, that I didn't feel anything for her and that I wasn't planning to stay with her a minute longer.

Yes, I could have said something like, "It's over. If you want to start a scandal, go ahead. You'll only be hurting yourself. Your husband will divorce you and keep Ellen. I don't care about you, so whatever you decide to do, it won't affect me."

But I didn't say that. The time had come to test out Olivia's theories. If they failed, I had no choice but to act in my own way.

"In London I never stopped thinking about us, our bad luck. Ralph adores you. You mean the world to him and he has shown it."

"He doesn't give a shit about me," she exclaimed.

"That's not true. If that were the case he wouldn't have married you. He did, and he's been faithful to you all these years."

"Even with Carter?" she retorted, with a strident laugh.

"What do you mean?" I asked, interested in the answer.

"Those two are thick as thieves, ever since college . . . Sometimes I wonder why Ralph slept with me instead of him . . . It may even be that he slept with both of us, only I was the one who got pregnant."

"You're insinuating that your husband is . . . Don't be ridiculous! There's nothing effeminate in Ralph—these are things that men notice. And you, like all women, are quick to think the worst; you're jealous that your husband has a good friend who is also his right-hand man."

"Carter is gay. If you haven't realized that, you're blind."

"Of course Carter's gay, but that doesn't mean that all the

men in his life are. I got along very well with Carter during the campaign. He's a smart, sharp guy who knows what needs to be done. We've had lunch together at least half a dozen times and I assure you he has not tried to seduce me."

"He's in love with Ralph," she asserted.

"That's what you think because you're in love with Ralph, and it bothers you that your husband doesn't pay as much attention to you as you want him to. So you'd rather find an excuse to justify his behavior."

"I'm not in love with Ralph, and I never have been," she remarked calmly, as if it were obvious.

"But . . . you slept with him in college, you got pregnant . . . You wanted to keep the baby. What do you call that?"

"It was actually a bet. I bet my friends I could seduce Ralph. We all had a thing against Carter. He was the smartest one, the one who studied the most and who despised us the most. He looked down on us, and Carter was especially spiteful toward me. He went out of his way to ridicule me in front of the others. I don't know why. Also, Ralph was affectionate with me, and he was the most handsome guy in the class; we all wanted him. I was the one who managed it. We slept together a few times and I didn't take the necessary precautions so I ended up pregnant."

I remained silent, analyzing what she had just said. I looked at her and saw a coldhearted harpy. Yes: this serene-looking woman, the sweet and exemplary mother, was a harpy.

"You didn't have to have the baby," I insinuated, feeling uneasy.

"I'm a Christian, I could tell you that was the reason. But it was more to make Carter a martyr than to get Ralph to marry me. I knew Carter's advice to Ralph was to ditch me, to force me to get an abortion. But Ralph, in addition to being ambitious, is too fainthearted. When we were in college he said he was going into politics; therefore he needed to assume his responsibility with a girl he had knocked up and who said she was willing to be a mother. He never loved me, and I never loved him."

I was tempted to get out of bed and phone Olivia to ask her what I should do in light of the story I had just heard. It made no sense to keep insisting that Ralph loved Constance, but even so, I decided to stick to Olivia's script.

"That's what you say now. But you know what, you're not going to convince me that Ralph doesn't love you and that you don't love him. Nobody has a child to get back at an acquaintance from college, and nobody marries a girl because he wants to go into politics. If you two got married, it was because you both felt something for each other; otherwise you would have resolved it another way."

"You're wrong, Thomas," she assured me, lowering her voice.

"Look, I think as time goes by it distorts our view of things. I don't think you were ever a frivolous or stupid girl. I don't see you that way, otherwise I wouldn't be with you. I think you were a romantic girl, sensitive, in love with the handsome guy in class, and you were afraid of being rejected, probably because of you and your friends' suspicions that he might be involved with Carter, which, from my point of view, had no basis whatsoever. Nobody stays with someone she doesn't love just because she got pregnant, at least not these days."

"You're a good person if you believe that of me."

Her laughter outraged me. I took her by the arm and twisted it. I was about to hit her, but that would have diverted me from my objective, which was to convince her that she couldn't abandon her husband and her daughter because she loved them both.

"If you're that manipulative, then I'm not interested in you. I liked you because you seemed like a sweet woman, different, with principles, responsible. You don't know how many times I've berated myself for entering your life, for dragging you into a relationship that was beneath you."

"What do you mean? The first time we agreed to meet at

the Waldorf, I went with the intention of sleeping with you. I didn't want anything else. You have no idea how boring and almost nonexistent my love life with Ralph has been . . . Actually, he . . ."

"Stop, Constance! Stop talking about your husband that way. I don't recognize you in the things you say. You're not like that."

"What am I like then? I'll tell you: I'm an idiot who married a man I didn't love and who I am now tied to because my child is sick, so I can't work and am forced to depend on him. Ellen is the chain that ties me to Ralph. If she didn't exist, do you think I'd be with him? Never!" Her voice morphed into a screech.

"I hope things aren't really the way you say they are because then . . ."

"Then . . ."

"You'd stop being important to me. I can't love someone I don't respect."

Olivia would have been proud. The phrase turned out melodramatic and effective all at once. Constance glanced at me fearfully and threw her arms around my neck, hugging me so tight I could barely breathe.

"Let me go, please. We have to clear this up once and for all," I said, undoing her embrace.

"I'm going to divorce him. I'll rent an apartment where I can live with Ellen. Then . . . I hope you do the same, that you divorce Esther and that we marry or at least live together. My daughter won't bother you. She's a very good girl."

We were silent. Constance stared at me intensely, as though she might bore into my skull. Then I hit her. A single blow . . . She started to bleed and the cheek where I hit her acquired a red color, which stood out from the paleness of the rest of her face.

She remained unfazed. Not a word of protest crossed her lips. With the back of her hand she tried to wipe away the blood that was trickling down her chin.

"Go and wash your face," I commanded.

She leapt out of bed and went to the bathroom. When she came back I noticed her cheek was swelling across to her eye.

"I'm sorry. You made me very nervous. You're trying to be a woman you're not, and if you were like that I would despise you," I mumbled, as I caressed her numb face.

"We'll live together, Thomas," she declared.

"No, Constance, we won't. You chose me to get back at Ralph for not knowing how to love you the way you would like, the way you need. If Ralph told you he loves you and can't live without you, then you would drop me like a hot potato. As for Ellen . . . I don't think you're capable of punishing a child by leaving her without a father. Ralph adores the kid, and she adores him. Separating them would be cruel. Ellen is a good girl, but she wouldn't accept me; she would grow up resenting us. She's suffered enough already, fighting against illness, for you to also tear her away from her father and from her world."

"I'll divorce him!"

"Do whatever you want, but I don't want to be the one responsible for destroying the life of a child. I'm not such a bad person that I would put my personal feelings and appetites first. And neither are you. It's natural to fantasize about how happy we could be together, but we found each other late in life and our circumstances are what they are. You owe it to yourself and to your child, and, even if you don't want to admit it because you're afraid, you owe it to Ralph. You owe him your loyalty."

"You're not going to leave me," she warned, and her cold voice alarmed me.

"I never said I'd leave you. You'll leave me. Think about what we're doing. Think it through properly. I'll always be close to you and if you need me you'll have me. Don't think I'll find it easy to be around and not ask you to meet me at the Waldorf or come over when Ralph's away. But I don't want to continue abusing your kindness, your loneliness."

The bedroom door opened with a bang. Ralph's silhouette was drawn against the light. Constance clung to me. She didn't seem concerned by the presence of her husband.

I got up, pulling the sheet with me to cover myself. I didn't know what I could say to the man as he looked us over with disgust and resignation.

"So this is what you wanted me to see . . ." he said in a neutral voice.

"Yes, that's why I called you. I wanted you to know without needing to tell you. As you can see, Thomas is my lover. I didn't think you'd be surprised."

"No, I'm not. I could sense that there was something between you two, but . . . Was it necessary for you to bring him into my bed?"

Ralph spoke as if I were not present. He ignored me. He addressed only Constance. The little slut had called her husband so that he would catch us in bed. I thought that, as things stood, there was no turning back.

"I'm sorry . . ." I mustered.

"You're sorry you're sleeping with my wife? I don't think you are," he said, without looking at me.

"It was a stupid thing to do, for both of us. These things happen but . . . well, I hope we can behave like adults. It wasn't right on our part, but . . ." I didn't know what else I could say. I felt ridiculous naked, wrapped in a sheet.

I picked up my clothes, which were strewn around the floor. At least I needed to put on some underwear and pants. Ralph's demeanor was inscrutable as I did this. He continued to stare intently at his wife.

"I hope you'll give me a divorce as soon as possible," Constance said defiantly.

"A divorce? You slept with him to get a divorce? You're so stupid!"

"I want to keep Ellen. That's all."

"The girl . . . Our daughter . . . Of course not."

Ralph's voice had acquired a harsh tone that shook me up. I felt a sense of relief when I finished zipping up my pants.

"Could we behave like civilized people?" I implored, as I put my socks on.

"Shut up," Ralph ordered, without looking at me and without even raising his voice.

"Why does he have to shut up? This concerns the three of us!" Constance proclaimed, with a hysterical screech.

She had stood up. She was naked but didn't seem to care, or maybe she didn't even realize. Her face was swelling where I'd hit her. Ralph looked right through her. His eyes were clouded over with something like rage, although he was making an effort not to shout or behave violently.

"Listen, I think we shouldn't blow this out of proportion," I intervened, ignoring Ralph's orders. "What happened between me and Constance has nothing to do with how much she loves you and your daughter. Perhaps it's her way of telling you that she needs to feel loved, that you should pay more attention to her."

"How dare you tell me that I don't pay attention to my wife? How dare you?" Ralph said, this time looking me in the eye.

"I dare because Constance and I talk, and that's the case for her . . . But I'll admit to you that I've never had the slightest doubt that she loves you. I mean nothing to her. I've only served as revenge." I tried to make my words sound convincing.

"That's not true!" she wailed. "I love you. I want the divorce so I can be with you!"

"Don't try to hurt Ralph even more. I know I mean nothing to you. I . . . well, I may have allowed myself to get carried away by the circumstances, when I realized how lonely you felt . . . But I've always known that I've only been an occasional consolation," I insisted.

Constance stood in front of me. Her nakedness made me feel uncomfortable but neither she nor Ralph seemed to notice.

"Coward! You're a coward! Are you scared of Ralph? Is that it?" she shrieked, beside herself.

"Calm down! None of this makes any sense. Of course I'm not scared of Ralph . . . You're hysterical and you don't know what you're saying."

Her hand struck my cheek and I felt the burn on my face. I couldn't help myself and I hit her as Ralph watched, unperturbed. Constance swayed but managed not to lose her footing.

I strode across the room and put on my shirt without bothering to properly do up the buttons. I picked up my jacket and lurched for the door.

"No! Don't go! You can't leave me!" she yelped, desperately pouncing on me.

Ralph held her back, trying to keep her from following me as I scampered down the stairs. I felt I couldn't breathe. I heard a blow and a scream. Constance had rushed after me and I don't know if she tripped or . . . perhaps Ralph pushed her. In any case, she fell on top of me and I still don't know how I managed to catch her and prevent us both from falling to the ground.

"Murderer!" she wailed, looking at her husband while I tried not to lose my balance with her body's weight against me.

As soon as I got my footing I unhooked myself from her arms and bolted for the door. I didn't look back. I didn't want to. Nor did I want to listen to her screams, begging me not to leave her with him.

"Murderer, you pushed me, you want to get rid of me! Don't go, Thomas, don't leave me with him, he'll kill me!"

Her words echoed around the house. I rushed to the door. Outside, the rain was pelting down onto the lawn. I careened across to the car and I wasn't able to breathe calmly until I drove off. I've never wanted so badly to get home.

Could I have done anything differently? Yes. I could have faced up to Ralph:

I should have taken off my jacket and covered Constance, lead-ing her back up the stairs.

"Calm down. It's all right."

"He pushed me . . . Murderer! Murderer!"

"Please, Constance . . . Come on, you need to get dressed."

I would have helped her up the stairs. At the top, Ralph would be staring down at us both, with clenched fists. We would have shuffled by him toward their room.

"Get dressed, please, quickly. You don't have much time left, you need to go and pick up Ellen."

"Don't leave me with him!" *she would have begged.*

"I won't. Go into the bathroom and get ready, I'll stay until you're ready. I won't let him do anything to you. Calm down."

While she got dressed I would challenge Ralph. We'd look at each other, sizing each other up to see how far we were willing to go.

"I don't know if you pushed her, but don't you dare lay a fin-ger on her again, or I will destroy you. I don't care if you decide to leave her and get divorced. Do whatever you want, but if something happens to her I will report you and I'll swear I saw you push her down the stairs. Do you understand? Be careful, Congressman."

Ralph would have looked at me hatefully, but he would have had no other choice than to admit the truth. He could accuse me of sleeping with his wife, which would only be a mild incon-venience for me. But if I accused him of attempted murder, his career would be finished forever.

"Considering what just happened, it would be best for Con-stance and Ellen to move out or for you to leave. But don't ever think of going near them again."

When Constance was dressed, I would have walked her to the door, encouraging her to go and pick up her daughter. I could have promised that we would speak later, that we both needed time to reflect after what had happened. I could have encouraged her to call her parents and tell them she was going to stay with them for a while. Her parents' house was not far from hers. And I could even have given her the number of a good lawyer.

But I didn't do any of that. I didn't even say goodbye. I was relieved when the fresh air hit my face.

The city was jammed. What time was it? Around three. Thankfully my house wasn't very far from Ralph's, even though we lived in different neighborhoods in Brooklyn. I realized that Ralph had missed his appointment with the mayor. What excuse might he have given?

As I was navigating through traffic, I was startled by the sound of my phone. Esther's number appeared on the screen.

"Where are you? I just got home. I'm going to take a bath and go to bed. I'm exhausted. You were right—not resting after a transatlantic flight is for young people."

"I won't be long. I have a problem. Don't fall asleep, please . . ."

Esther was waiting for me in bed. She could barely keep her eyes open. As soon as I saw her I calmed down.

"I'm so tired, I need to sleep; although going to bed at this time will mean we'll be up at midnight."

"Well, we'll think of something to do." I chuckled.

"What did you do today?" she asked me.

I was tempted to lie but I didn't, at least not wholly.

"I bought a teacup with a bear on it and I took it to the Morgans'. I hope Ellen likes it."

"British?"

"Yes, the saucer said 'Made in England.' It'll do the trick."

I undressed and lay by her side. Esther gave me a kiss and pulled away quickly.

"You smell like . . ."

I smelled like Constance. But she didn't finish the phrase. She just gave me a suspicious glance and wished me good night.

We sank into a deep sleep, so deep that, when my phone

started ringing, it seemed to me that the sound belonged to the world of dreams. Esther had to give me a shove for me to wake up and answer.

"Someone is desperate to speak to you."

I glanced at the clock. It was eleven. Too late for any of our friends to call. I noticed it was Carter's number.

"There is nothing that you need to tell me at this hour," I said when I answered the phone, intending to hang up and continue sleeping.

"I don't, but you will have something to tell the police," he answered in a chilling voice.

I didn't quite understand what he was saying; I was still in the fog of a dream. What had he said? Esther looked at me expectantly.

"I don't understand . . ."

"Constance Morgan is dead. She took a fall as she was going down the stairs. She probably tripped. The police are investigating what she did in the last twenty-four hours, and apparently you visited her. Ralph told the police that you were at their house this morning to deliver a present for Ellen; that you spoke about everything and nothing and then you left. Do you understand me, Thomas? Just that. Oh! And Constance has a split lip and a swollen cheek, which apparently have to do with the way she hit the floor when she fell down the stairs. I think the police will be knocking on your door in a few minutes. Ralph is devastated, but I know that, together, we will overcome this situation. You know how fond Ralph is of you, and how important your agency has been for his campaign, as it will be in the future. Good friendships last forever."

I realized that Carter was delivering a message: Ralph had not confessed any of what had happened. Not even that he'd caught me in bed with his wife, or the incident on the stairs. I was being asked not to say anything either.

I didn't know what to say. Constance was dead. I found this impossible to visualize. But Carter said she was dead. Why?

Esther grew worried when she saw how overwhelmed I was and grabbed the phone.

"Who is this?" she asked.

"I'm sorry, Esther. This is Nicholas Carter. Mrs. Morgan has had an accident. I called to let you know. I'm at the Morgans' house. Ralph is very upset."

"What kind of accident did Mrs. Morgan have?" Esther asked the question without looking at me. She seemed distant, holding the phone.

"She fell down the stairs. Apparently she was going to get something for Ellen downstairs and she tripped. She broke her neck."

"Oh my God! That's awful! When did this happen?"

"A couple of hours ago, around nine."

"I see. I'm terribly sorry. What about Ellen?"

"Ralph's parents will take care of her. As you can imagine, Constance's parents are devastated."

"We're so sorry. We'll keep in touch. Please give Ralph our condolences and let us know if there's anything at all we can do . . ."

Carter cleared his throat. He didn't know how to tell Esther that the police wanted to interrogate me. In the end he just said it.

"I'm calling because the police want to speak to Thomas. It's probably just routine."

We got up. Esther told me to take a shower. I did. We needed to clear our heads. She made me coffee while I got dressed. It wasn't until we sat down with a cup of coffee in hand that she asked me why the police wanted to speak to me.

"Carter said they're going to speak to everyone who was with her in the last few hours. I already told you I was at their house."

"If you want me to help you, you will need to tell me the truth, Thomas. The whole truth."

"Help me? Hey, I don't have anything to do with what happened to Constance."

"From what Carter said the police will knock on our door any moment now."

"Well, let them come. I can't help them. I wasn't there. Remember we were sleeping in the same bed until the telephone rang."

"What time did you arrive and how long did you stay at the Morgans'?"

"I don't know . . . I got there at around twelve thirty or one, maybe later. I stayed for a good few hours, and then I came home."

"It doesn't take long to get here from the Morgans' house even when there's traffic. You were back here before four. It's obvious you weren't there when the poor woman fell down the stairs."

"But what did you think?"

"Tell me the truth, Thomas. Apart from bringing the teacup for Ellen, did you sleep with Constance? When you got into bed you smelled like . . . well, you smelled like sex. Am I wrong?"

I panicked and broke into a sweat. If I admitted I had slept with Constance, Esther might decide to leave me. I myself would have given her the excuse she needed to get rid of me.

"Do you think I didn't notice the way she looked at you?" she asked me. "Every time we met up with the Morgans it was obvious. She followed you with her eyes; she considered you hers. I admit at some point I even thought she was a bit mentally unstable. It was all too clear that there was nothing between Constance and Ralph except for that poor kid. Constance was the kind of woman who'd die for a man to look at her. And you were the ideal candidate."

I couldn't believe that Esther was speaking so matter-of-factly, as if she were referring to someone else. I continued to debate with myself whether I should tell the truth or deny everything.

"Thomas, I know you too well. I know you wouldn't want to lose me for anything in the world, but even so, you're taking risks with affairs that don't mean anything to you but that sometimes have consequences."

"I . . . No . . . Please . . . I swear there is no other woman I care about but you . . ." I stuttered as if I were a little boy.

"I know, I know . . . But we're not talking about that now. We're talking about what happened today between you and Constance."

I didn't admit it. No. I didn't admit that I'd slept with Constance and that Ralph had caught us.

"I swear that woman pursued me . . . Today I went there to beg her not to insist anymore, to tell her I didn't want anything to do with her . . . I didn't want to upset you and that's why I came up with the idea of the present for Ellen. It's not the first time I've asked her to leave me alone . . . But she refused. She deceived me, she told me she was going to the bathroom and what she did was call her husband so that he would find us together. Ralph turned up and . . . You can imagine the scene . . ."

"Yes, I can imagine that Ralph was upset to find his dear wife with another man. And then what happened?"

"Nothing . . . I told Ralph there was nothing between Constance and me, that she loved him but she felt lonely and she meant nothing to me. I told him we should behave like adults. Then I left."

"Was that it?" Esther seemed skeptical of my version of the facts.

"Well, she ran after me. I was already halfway down the stairs and I didn't see what happened, but I realized she'd tripped and when I turned around I was able to catch her; we both could have died. I got out of there. I felt like I couldn't breathe."

"So this afternoon she fell down the stairs."

"For a moment I thought that . . . Well, it's silly."

"You thought that Ralph had pushed her."

"She started to yell. She called Ralph a murderer and asked me not to leave her alone with him. I thought that my presence there was not necessary, that I would only make the situation more difficult."

We remained silent, each thinking about what I hadn't dared to say but which Esther had spelled out. The building's night porter phoned us to say that the police were coming up.

"What should I tell them?" I asked, terrified.

"You're not to blame for anything. She fell down the stairs a couple of hours ago; it's obvious you were not there."

"I hit her," I mumbled.

"What?"

Esther's severe gaze reflected a sudden distancing from me. In her eyes, I saw something similar to contempt.

"Well, not exactly. Before Ralph arrived I wanted to go and she hung on to my neck . . . I couldn't get rid of her. It's not that I hit her exactly, just that I had to twist her arm."

I didn't tell her the truth because I realized that Esther would never have forgiven me if I had hit a woman.

"You should tell the police what happened. The whole truth. That's the best thing to do. If Ralph tried to kill Constance this afternoon it's obvious he managed to do it tonight. However, you'll have to explain yourself and we'll be in trouble. You'll be in the papers, which will have negative consequences for our agency but . . . what can we do? I'm afraid we've run out of luck. It was bound to happen eventually."

In Esther's words there was not only a rebuke, there was also disappointment and hopelessness at the idea of having to start over from scratch. In Manhattan, if you're in the crime section of the newspaper, your career is over.

A few minutes later a couple of policemen turned up at my door. The police lieutenant was nice to us. The garage attendant confirmed my time of arrival at home. Esther also confirmed it. I wasn't suspected of anything—they were only trying to reconstruct what had happened and whom Constance Morgan had been with that day. Some neighbors said that a man had visited her, and one of them even memorized my license plate number.

Under Esther's scrutiny, I explained that I had brought a gift for Mr. and Mrs. Morgan's daughter and that I had stayed for a while chatting with Mrs. Morgan, with whom I had a good friendship since our PR agency had worked on her husband's campaign.

"Yes," I declared, "Mrs. Morgan was as charming as ever. We spoke about her husband's work as a congressman and the possibility of continuing to work with him. A friendly conversation, nothing more."

The policemen left. The lieutenant seemed satisfied with my answers. If he thought that Constance's fall down the stairs had not been an accident, he could rule out that I had anything to do with it. I wasn't there. Simple as that.

"You lied to him," Esther said, with both relief and concern.

"I didn't tell them the whole truth; what I didn't say was that I suspect Morgan. But I can't accuse a congressman without proof just because I think he pushed her. Besides, if I did, we would be implicated in the scandal. I don't think either Constance or Ralph deserves to have us sacrifice ourselves for them," I observed. My voice was weary.

"But if Ralph tells them the truth . . ."

"You think he's going to turn himself in for pushing his wife? He's not that stupid, and Nicholas Carter is with him; he won't allow him to fall apart. It will all depend on what the autopsy reveals."

"I don't know, Thomas . . . I don't know if you've done well in not voicing your suspicions. If Ralph Morgan pushed Constance . . . It's horrible to think something like that could have happened."

"But I don't know for sure, I can't swear it, so I'm not going to accuse him when I don't have real proof beyond my own impressions."

I tried to sound convincing, to appease her conscience. Esther seemed ready to assuage my afflictions, but not her own. I knew she couldn't stand knowing that Ralph Morgan had murdered his wife but not telling the police.

We couldn't sleep the rest of the night. I could feel her tossing and turning in bed, uncomfortable with me and with herself. Esther thought I should have told the truth even if it ruined us, but at the same time she didn't want that to happen. She would have to live with that contradiction.

I know I didn't do what I should have done. When the police lieutenant interrogated me about how long I'd been at the Morgans' and what I'd done there, I should have had the courage to tell the truth:

"Lieutenant, what I'm about to tell you may cost me my marriage. I'm sorry, Esther, I lied to you. I hope you'll forgive me. The truth is that, for a period, I was Mrs. Morgan's lover. Today Mr. Morgan caught us in bed. We had an argument. She told him she wanted a divorce and to keep custody of their daughter. He refused. I asked them both to behave civilly. I can't be sure, but it seemed to me this afternoon that Mr. Morgan pushed his wife down the stairs. Nothing bad happened because I was able to catch her—we both stumbled, but we were all right. She screamed that he was a murderer and wanted to kill her, and begged me not to leave her alone with him. Constance Morgan was afraid of her husband.

"I left and I didn't hear anything from them until tonight when Mr. Carter called me to announce what had happened. I'm sorry. I will cooperate in any way I can so that justice is done and Mrs. Morgan's death does not go unpunished."

Yes, I could have said all this to the police lieutenant. Esther would have listened. My confession would have overwhelmed her. I would have sensed her growing aversion toward me as she learned of my lies. The lieutenant might have asked me to

*accompany him to cross-examine Ralph. An opportunity to dem-
onstrate that I had courage and that I was capable of owning up
to my responsibilities.*

But I didn't, and once again I got off scot-free.

The autopsy was inconclusive. It was impossible to know
whether Constance Morgan had broken her neck due to an acci-
dental fall or if someone had pushed her. But who could have
done that? It had just been the family at home. Ellen was in her
room; her mother was reading her a story while Mr. Morgan
watched television in his room. The girl told the police that her
mother had gone to get her a glass of milk.

The official version of events was that Constance Morgan had
tripped and fallen down the stairs, breaking her neck. The newspapers went on to photograph the heartbroken congressman
and his daughter. They were described as the perfect American
family, the picture of love.

We went to the funeral. We had to. Ralph avoided my gaze
when I offered my condolences.

Nicholas Carter remained by his side at all times. Whenever
he noticed Ralph breaking down he would wrap his arm around
his shoulders in a protective gesture. I couldn't get the thought
that Ralph had pushed her out of my mind. That it had been the
second time he had pushed her. The first was when I was leaving
their house and I'd been able to keep her from falling, but the
second time, there hadn't been anyone there to catch her.

Ellen said she'd heard her mother scream and that she'd
jumped out of bed and run to the stairs. She'd found her father at
the top of the stairs, and he'd picked her up in his arms. They'd
gone down to the bottom step, and there was her mother, lying
very still.

Constance's parents were overwhelmed by the loss of their
only daughter and also by the fact that the young man she had

met in college was now a prominent congressman, and therefore the burial was attended by high-ranking politicians they'd seen on television. As for Ralph's parents, despite their grief, they couldn't hide how proud they were of their son for becoming such an important person.

I couldn't feel anything. Neither sorrow nor dread; I didn't even feel liberated by Constance's death. My only worry was what might happen with Esther. Since the night Constance died, Esther seemed distant, although she hadn't left me alone for an instant, always staying alert for anything that might implicate me. She was protective, the way she had been from the day we met, but I understood once again that something between us had broken. What I didn't know was the significance of the situation.

For three or four days I didn't dare to ask her anything, until Friday night, when we were both at home, each of us on a sofa, reading. I had suggested we go out to dinner but she said she was too tired. Tuesday had been Constance's funeral and what had happened weighed heavily on us.

The moment I lifted my gaze from my book, our eyes met. She had been watching me for a while.

I smiled at her. I couldn't think of anything else to do to clear the heavy silence.

"What are you thinking about?" I asked her.

"I'm thinking there are too many girls who die around you . . . Too many. First it was Lisa, poor stupid Lisa. Then that Japanese girl, Yoko? I think you said her name was Yoko . . . And now Constance Morgan. You attract death, Thomas. I hope I won't be the next one."

For a few seconds I froze. I knew it was only a matter of time before she decided to leave me. I shuffled over to where she was sitting, and slumped down onto the floor, hugging her legs. She started to caress my head but she did so mechanically. She wasn't there.

———

Olivia was upset about Constance's death. I couldn't understand why, as she barely knew her, but when I went to see her at her apartment a few days later, she burst into tears.

"Poor woman! What did you do to her, Thomas?" she asked, as if she had no doubt that I was to blame for Constance's death.

I was furious. I wasn't in the mood to put up with tears or accusations, and I threatened to leave her forever.

"I don't have time for silliness. Everything the papers said about Constance's death is true. It was an accident, a tragic accident."

"You're a strange guy, Thomas. One day I looked up information about you and apparently years ago your first girlfriend died under strange circumstances . . . And then that girl . . . the London prostitute you told me about . . . You said she was in a car accident. You attract death, Thomas. Women aren't safe around you."

I was startled to hear Olivia say the same thing that Esther had said. I was tempted to hit her, but I didn't.

After Constance's death, I made a decision that I have stuck to till this day. I promised myself not to initiate a stable relationship with any more women. I would only pay for the services of prostitutes. One night and no more. No matter how much I might like one in particular. I had grown attached to Olivia, more than I had anticipated.

I threw myself back into a routine. Weekdays at the agency, weekends with Esther with outings to the theater or some concert, even the usual monthly dinner with her parents and brother at the family restaurant. I found those encounters boring, but if I had tried to make any excuse not to go, my marriage would not have lasted this long. Esther had a strong sense of belonging with her family; she was connected to them in a way she would never be with me. If she had to choose, she wouldn't hesitate.

Sundays were spent at home, reading or working, each of us wrapped up in our own thoughts, barely speaking but aware of each other's presence.

No, I didn't want the life I had built for myself to go up in smoke. I'd say that living this way was the closest thing to happiness that I've ever experienced. I became calmer and more settled. I never wanted anything else.

DECLINE

9

Years went by without us noticing. Esther devoted her efforts and talent to Global Communication. I was all right. From time to time we traveled to London, where the agency functioned reasonably well. We would meet with some important new client. We would have supper with Evelyn and Roy, who had consolidated his political career. The Rural Party even won three seats in Parliament. Cooper and Maggie did fine without us. Esther found it difficult to leave the Big Apple. We earned more money than we could spend.

But, suddenly, the world we'd known—the world in which we were in our element—changed very rapidly. Our business was hit the hardest.

The crisis affected us more than we could have anticipated. Suddenly, our clients started to consider advertising something they could do without, or at the very least pay less for than they had been paying until then. Our income dwindled, although we had enough money to cope with the blow. We had invested wisely. Even so, Esther subjected us to wartime rations. She imposed drastic cuts in spending at the agency. She would not allow us to spend one dollar that wasn't strictly necessary. I proposed that we do what everyone else was doing: fire part of the staff. They could still work for us but as self-employed contractors; that way, they wouldn't be such a burden to the company. Esther wouldn't allow it.

"That's immoral, Thomas, we're not bankrupt."

"But the company isn't doing well."

"We have money."

"Yes, our money, which we have earned. Don't mix up the company with us, Esther."

But to her they were one and the same. This was part of her Catholic morality. So, reluctantly, I had to accept her austerity plan, not only for the agency but in our personal life. Esther thought it indecent to spend money on self-indulgences when many of our friends had gone bankrupt.

The agency's London branch was also doing poorly, even worse than the New York office. We couldn't keep it going with only a dozen clients who paid late and never enough. Roy had decided to take advantage of the circumstances to reduce his contribution. In all truth, he no longer needed us—he could make do with Evelyn.

I tried to convince Esther to at least close the agency's London office, but she refused to consider it, although she was willing to impose some budget restrictions that made it nearly impossible to survive.

There are years that go by quicker than others. For some, the years of the crisis became interminable. For me, they were tedious—the most tedious of my life—and that's considering I had enough reasons to feel fulfilled. We managed to ride out the crisis without huge losses, and gradually began to win back our clients from previous years, who were starting to spend money again on advertising and publicity.

Lately, when I look in the mirror, I find it hard to recognize the man I see there. My hair is turning white. My skin has become more sallow. I have love handles and my arms are flabby due to lack of exercise. But my bed is still visited by beautiful women whom I pay generously.

Through Paul, I got a hold of a phone number you can call to have young ladies sent to you for three hundred dollars an hour. Payment is cash in hand. You don't have to give your name and nobody asks for it. The girls always seem to be in good spirits. For a long time, I've been infatuated with a young girl who, like Olivia used to, dreams of making it big in New York. In fact, more than a few like her have visited my bed. The sweet angels believe that the shortest path to success is to sleep with men like me, who can pull strings for them in advertising, film, or theater. A few have actually managed to get something out of the situation. Of course these chance encounters didn't interfere with my relationship with Olivia. I felt at ease with her, and, in addition, she indulged my gluttony. She was becoming a better and better cook.

One day, Paul took us by surprise and announced that he wanted to retire.

"I'll be seventy soon. I've taught you everything I know and now it's my turn to rest. Thanks to Esther I'll have a nice retirement. I want to spend the rest of my days playing golf in Miami."

"But you don't know anyone in Miami to play golf with," I replied, fearing he might actually leave.

"But I'll meet them. There are plenty of people like me who want to enjoy their last years in a place where they're not constantly shivering from cold. I'll join some country club. You can come and visit when you have time."

Seventy. Yes, Paul was going to be seventy years old, but I didn't see him as a useless old man. Esther reminded me that over the years Paul had spent less and less time at the agency. It's not that Paul's presence was unnecessary. The agency functioned fine on its own or, rather, thanks to Esther's talent and hard work, but Paul always had a piece of advice, a valuable opinion to give. It was true, he had taught us everything he knew, and most importantly, he had given us the keys to success in the advertising world. The Big Apple is a jungle where only a few manage to triumph; the rest have to make do with crumbs.

"We're going to miss him a lot. It was reassuring to know I could always ask him how to solve a problem," Esther confessed on the day Paul was leaving.

"I'm sad too. But apparently playing golf makes him happy, and from what he said, it sounds like he found a beautiful apartment in Coral Gables."

"But he's alone. At the party he organized there won't be anyone who isn't from the office or friends from other agencies. He doesn't have a family, or parents, or siblings, or a wife, or children. He'll die alone at some hospital."

I thought about myself. I was like Paul, except I had Esther, but would she always be with me? She had a big family—parents, a brother, nieces and nephews, cousins—but what about me? I hadn't heard anything from Jaime in years. Nor had I taken any interest in my maternal grandparents before they died or in my uncle Oswaldo, whom I knew was slowly dying in a nursing home. I removed them from my life, putting them out of my mind. As if they had never belonged to my world and my relationship with them were part of another life.

Uncle Oswaldo had tried to get in touch with me a few times. But I didn't return those calls and my secretary had been briefed to tell him I was out of town. How many years had gone by since I'd last seen him? I think it was at John's funeral.

Paul had organized a party at a bar in SoHo, a kind of garage decorated with paintings by artists who hadn't yet succeeded. He had invited a few important people from the advertising scene and all the hangers-on that move around it. Especially models. He even insisted on inviting Olivia.

"You're lucky to have two good women for yourself. Others get the scraps," he said, laughing.

"I don't know if it's a good idea for you to invite Olivia. I think Esther suspects that there's always been something between us."

"She doesn't suspect, she's sure of it, but she won't tell you.

It's one of her secret weapons, which she will use against you when the time comes," he assured me with such conviction that I believed him.

So Olivia came to the party. Esther didn't react to her presence. It's not that it was strange that she was there—after all, Olivia was a model and had worked on a few of our campaigns. That was the kind of favor Paul always did for me.

Esther was glum because Paul was leaving. She was going to miss him. So was I.

Paul is a survivor. He never deceived anyone. You knew what to expect from him. I think his only weakness had been Esther.

That night at the party he confessed that he had always been secretly in love with Esther.

"If I had had anything to offer when she started giving classes at my school, I assure you I would have stolen her from you. But I always knew she was out of my league. What I've never understood is why she loved you. But that's what women are like."

"Don't speak in the past tense; she loves me."

"You know she doesn't. But let's not talk about anything that will put a damper on the party. It's my night, Thomas. Let's have a few drinks, and in my case one of these beauties who have come to see me."

Olivia arrived late. A few days earlier she had debuted in a comedy on Broadway in which Paul had gotten her a small role. I still hadn't been to see her perform.

First she greeted Paul, giving him a package that was beautifully wrapped. Paul was very touched and started to gesticulate as he unwrapped it.

It was a V-neck cotton sweater of the sort that golfers wear. Esther praised Olivia's good taste and asked a waiter to bring her a drink. Perhaps Paul was right and to Esther it represented not a secret but a liberation to know that Olivia shared a bed with me. Our love life had never been gratifying. I'd never dared to try anything too risqué. Esther wasn't the kind of woman who sought new experiences. For her, it was probably a relief that I turned to Olivia with my fantasies instead of her.

When one of the guests beckoned Esther, Paul and I stayed and chatted with Olivia for a while. She seemed more cheerful than usual.

"You're more beautiful than ever tonight, you're wearing a special smile," Paul said.

"I have an admirer," she boasted. "He's been coming to see the show every night since the premiere. He's already sent me flowers a few times."

"Be careful, Thomas, or he'll steal the girl," Paul teased.

I didn't find it funny at all. It truly irritated me that Olivia would brag in front of Paul about a guy who was head over heels for her. I didn't say anything. I downed my drink and held her arm so tightly I knew I would leave a bruise on her pale white skin.

Paul took his leave, realizing that I was annoyed and that I didn't want a spectator at that moment.

"So you have an admirer and you like that," I said in a neutral tone.

"Yes, Thomas, and because there are no secrets between us, I wanted to let you know. You still haven't come to see the show, and you haven't been by the apartment for a week, so I wasn't able to tell you sooner."

"Is there something to tell? There's a guy who likes you, so what? He's not the first nor will he be the last." I twisted her arm again.

"Stop it! Stop hurting me. You don't seem to understand, Thomas. I think Jerry is serious."

"Jerry? His name is Jerry? Wow!"

"His name is Jerry King. He's from Texas but has been living in New York for many years. He owns a few hardware shops. He does well."

"You're going to tell me his biography now? I don't give a

damn where he's from and you shouldn't either. If he comes back to the theater tell him you don't want him to bother you. It's that simple."

"No. You're not getting it. Maybe Jerry is my chance."

"Your chance? What are you talking about?" I yelled at her, ignoring the fact that people around us were staring.

"If you continue to scream and twist my arm your wife will realize that something is up. I made a mistake. I felt I had to be loyal to you and tell you as soon as possible. I should have waited until you came to the apartment."

"What are you trying to tell me, Olivia?"

"Well, that I don't have a future with you. You pay for my apartment and living expenses. You got me a few minor roles and from time to time you hire me for some ad, but nothing worthwhile. I'm coming up on forty, Thomas. I need to think about my future."

"And you think your future is a guy who sells screws?"

"He admires me. He's seen me in a few commercials and says I'm a wonderful actress. He'd be delighted to be in a serious relationship with me. Jerry is the kind who marries."

"Oh, is he? You know him well enough to know that?"

"He recently became a widower. He was married to the same woman for thirty years, and they didn't even have children."

Esther walked up to us. Her face revealed a certain anxiety about the scene I was putting on with Olivia.

"Is something the matter?" she asked gravely.

"Of course not," I replied, drily.

"We're in the middle of a friendly argument. You know that Thomas is very protective," Olivia said, trying to muster a smile.

"I see. Well, I don't think this is the time or the place to argue. It's Paul's party," Esther said without hiding her anger.

"You're right. I'm sorry." Olivia excused herself.

She left me with Esther, which made me even more furious. Esther was especially upset at me.

"Look, Thomas, I don't know why you were arguing with Olivia, nor do I care to know, but it's not very considerate of you to make a scene. You owe me some respect," she said.

"You're right. It was silly. But this girl is singularly foolish. Everything we've done to help her is no use. She has no talent as an actress but she insists that she does."

"It's all right for her to believe in herself and to not give up. That shouldn't annoy you," she said.

I held back. I gulped and smiled. The last thing I wanted was to arouse Esther's suspicion with the stupid argument I'd just had with Olivia.

"You're right. Let's forget it, it's not important. I got mad at her because I appreciate her and it bothers me when she makes bad choices in her career. Look, there are the Sullivans . . . Let's go and say hi."

The next day we went to Miami. Paul had invited us to join him for his first weekend as a retiree. We didn't talk about Olivia. Esther did not refer to her again and Paul was smart enough not to mention her.

We enjoyed the warm weather and a surprise fishing trip on Paul's new boat. The three of us had a nice time, and we promised Paul that we'd come again.

On Monday, when we returned to New York, I called Olivia to tell her I would come to see her at her apartment at lunchtime. Esther had a lunch meeting with a potential client, so I had enough time to clear things up with Olivia.

She received me coolly, not wearing any makeup and looking nervous. She had made some sandwiches. Nothing special, which irritated me deeply because I had grown used to her elaborate dishes. She tried to turn the conversation to trivial matters such as the fact that her neighbor from across the way had taken a fall and broken a leg, and that the super's son had found a job as a plumber on the other side of the city. Nothing that either of us cared about.

"Enough of the bullshit. I didn't come here to talk about your neighbor. Tell me what's going on."

"Thomas, we've been together for a number of years. You have paid for exclusivity and I have enjoyed the arrangement, although each dollar you give me is hard-earned because you're not a man who is easy to get along with, and . . . well, I've had to put up with your idiosyncrasies. So we are at peace."

"At peace? What do you mean?"

"I mean it's over. You don't owe me anything, and I don't owe you. We can be friends if you like, if you're capable of having friends, but the agreement that bound us together had an expiration date."

"You've got that wrong. I'll be the one who says when I end things with you."

"I'm under no illusion about the future. If I still haven't managed to succeed, it's not likely I'll do it now. I do boring roles onstage, I'm a TV commercial girl, but soon I won't be good enough even for that. There are plenty of girls who are younger and prettier. Until now I've been begging at the table. I need to think about the rest of my life, and if there's someone who'll give me an opportunity to be taken care of, I'm not going to waste it."

I laughed. For a good while I laughed heartily. I couldn't picture Olivia married to the hardware store guy, playing housewife. To me it was a disappointment; despite her lack of artistic talent I'd always thought she had ambition.

"I don't know why you're laughing, Thomas. I only have three or four years until men no longer give me a second glance. You'll trade me in for a younger woman and then what will I do? I don't want to be out on the street, scraping together a living or prostituting myself with just anyone to be able to eat."

"That's what you're doing now," I retorted harshly.

Olivia bit her lower lip, pondering her reply. She looked me in the eye and smiled.

"Yes, you're right, that's what I do now. But you pay well, and so I only have to put up with you. If it goes on like this, then when I'm forty or fifty years old I'll have to put up with other guys like you or even worse. Before that time comes I'm retiring from the scene. Wasn't it Marlon Brando who said his mistake was to keep acting when the audience had already gone? Well, that's it. I'd rather leave before I'm left. Jerry seems to be a good guy and I know I can get him to propose."

Silently we measured each other up. Olivia nibbled her sandwich. She didn't seem to be hungry.

"You're not going to marry him," I said sharply.

"You think Jerry won't want to marry me? You're wrong. To him it's a dream to be able to marry the girl from the washing machine ad who he's also seen in a play on Broadway. Jerry is the kind who gets married, Thomas. Also, I'm not sleeping with him until he puts a ring on my finger."

"Stop fantasizing, Olivia. There will be no wedding. I demand that you stop talking to the hardware store guy. I told you at Paul's party: when he comes to the theater you need to say that you don't want to see him."

"I'm not going to do that, Thomas. Jerry will come tonight, as he did over the weekend. I told him that if I'm not too tired I might have a drink with him."

I stood up and approached her. She closed her eyes. She knew I was going to hit her. I hit her so hard that a blood vessel burst in her eye.

"Look at yourself in the mirror. The theater adventure is over. You won't be able to go out onstage," I crowed. She didn't shed a tear. She got up and went to the bathroom. Afterward she went to the freezer to get ice, wrapped it in a cloth, and put it on her eye.

She sat down in front of me. I thought about hitting her again when I saw the look in her good eye that said she was determined to go ahead with her plan.

"This is the last time you hit me, Thomas. The last time. If you do it again I will report you to the police. But first I will tell Esther you've been sleeping with me. I'll also explain to your colleagues in the industry what kind of a man you are and what your romantic inclinations are. You'll be the talk of Manhattan."

She was threatening me. Her voice didn't break once, nor did she raise her volume. She spoke with determination.

"You see, Olivia, you won't do any of those things. I'll be the one who will tell Jerry what kind of a woman you are. Tonight I'll show up at the theater and tell him that you're a prostitute. Well paid, but a prostitute. I think he'll find it interesting to know what you're capable of in bed. This hardware store guy will run for the hills."

"You're a pig, Thomas."

"I am, Olivia. I don't pretend to be anything else."

"Why?"

"Because I bought you and you're still useful to me. I don't know for how long, but I still want to enjoy you. And I'll leave you, yes—I'll leave you when the wrinkles become more visible on your face and your body starts to sag. Then, you'll be free, you'll be your own master. But until that moment, if you try to cut loose you know I won't allow it. Normal men don't marry whores, and if this man is what you say he is, he'll flee as soon as he finds out what you do for a living."

"I'll tell Esther."

My guffaw echoed around the living room.

"You know something, Olivia? Esther doesn't ignore what kind of a man I am and she has come to terms with it. To her, it wouldn't be a shock to find out that we're sleeping together. But your Jerry will bolt. And I'll make sure that any man who comes near you knows immediately what you are. You'll end up walking the streets, charging ten dollars to every guy who mounts you."

She looked at me with her green eyes, but her gaze had no expression. I didn't know what she was thinking. I supposed she hated me, but I wasn't sure. I noticed that she gulped before she spoke again.

"We can reach an agreement. Let me see Jerry, I'll string him along . . . Let him slowly fall in love with me. It's always easier to get a man to propose on impulse, but I can try to make him wait a little. I know he's the insurance policy for my old age. How many more years will you want to be with me? Two, three . . . ? You've told me yourself that you like younger women. It's normal—with them you feel powerful. We can carry on until you replace me with one of those young ladies you pay so well. But give me back my freedom, Thomas. Do it, because other-wise we will destroy each other. You'll chase Jerry away, but I can assure you that, if I talk, you won't come out the other side unharmed. We both know we have a lot to lose. I have more, yes. You've never given me enough money to be able to save up, to ensure my future; you've been very clever. You paid for the apartment, you fed me, you bought me designer clothes, but never jewelry I could sell if I ran into trouble."

"There is no deal, Olivia. You will stay with me."

"And with Jerry. I will start a relationship with Jerry. I'll string him along, but I won't break up with him. Get over it, Thomas, or we will go to war. We will destroy each other, you know it, but I am willing."

She was. I knew she was willing to destroy herself if I forced her, but she would drag me down with her. She removed the ice and cloth. The lower part of her eye was swollen. It must have been painful.

"Don't mention weddings again to me. We'll see when I con-sider our relationship done." It was my way of not opposing her relationship with Jerry and not losing face. "Don't threaten me again, Olivia."

When I stepped out of her apartment, exhaustion hit me. The confrontation with her had given me a stomachache. It was the first time we'd had an argument. I wondered why I didn't want to give her back her freedom. I didn't love her. I wouldn't have cared if she had died that very day. So?

I wandered around for a long time in search of answers. I called Paul; he was playing golf, but listened patiently. I told him what had happened. I needed someone to explain to me why I didn't want to let her go.

"With Olivia you get the same thing as with me, you don't need to pretend to be something you're not. You're not afraid of us judging you as others do. With Esther you're in permanent tension. You're afraid she might leave you, so you spend all day trying to please her and you're not you, because if you behaved like yourself, your wife would not think twice about closing the book on you forever. With Olivia you feel comfortable in your own skin, you can brag about your exploits. I think that if you're with her it isn't because you like her more, but because with her you can talk, tell her what you really think and do. If you lose Olivia you'll be lonely, and what you fear most is loneliness."

"Don't talk garbage, Paul. I've never been lonely."

"Of course you have. It has been your own fault, but you've been lonely. And you've clung to Esther as if she were your mother, and to Olivia as if she were the best friend you could have apart from me."

"Pop psychology, Paul."

"I don't know if it's psychology, it's just the way it is. I know you, Thomas, I know what you're like. You should live and let that girl live. The hardware store guy is a good solution. For once, be generous."

"I'm not going to allow it, Paul."

"I know. But if I were you, I would. That girl is capable of making things difficult for you. I think Esther knows you're sleeping with Olivia, but if someone tells her, she'll have no choice but to act as wives do. She'll leave you. That's what my last wife did to me. I'll tell you something else. Esther is loyal to you, but if you give her an excuse to leave you, she will."

He was right. I knew Paul was right and that I should follow his advice. I shouldn't tighten the strings too much or I'd break them. I continued wandering in search of other answers that only I could give myself. I could have done things differently. When Olivia told me she wanted to marry Jerry because it was an opportunity to safeguard her future, I could have answered differently:

"I understand, dear, this moment was bound to come. Don't think it makes me happy, but that's the way things are. I don't have anything to offer you except this apartment and some money to cover your bills. You deserve better and you couldn't be more right, the years are starting to weigh on you. Soon it'll be difficult to find a man who'll take notice of you."

She would have hugged me, thanking me. She may even have cried.

"Thank you, Thomas. You'll always be my best friend. I knew you would understand. Listen, this thing with Jerry shouldn't mean we can't continue seeing each other any time you like. I will have to be prudent, but you and I don't need to break up forever; well, at least until I get married. Even then . . . perhaps on some occasion, who knows."

"Come on, Olivia, if you want to get married you'll need to behave the proper way. But thank you for telling me I can count on you. Our conversations make me feel at ease. I know I can trust you—you've always given me good advice. You are very intuitive. You know, I'd like to meet Jerry."

"Well, I don't know . . . I don't think that's a good idea. He isn't stupid, he'll realize what there is between us."

"There's no reason why he should. Tell him part of the truth, that I am the owner of the agency that hires you for the ads, that

we have a good friendship. Something like that would be okay and he would have no reason to suspect."

"And the apartment? When do I have to leave?" she'd ask, fearfully.

"You don't have to leave immediately. Wait until Jerry proposes, and when he does, tell him this place is too expensive. You'll move in with him, and you won't need this apartment anymore. I'll pay for it for a couple more months, if that suits you. Consider it my wedding gift."

Yes, I could have said all of those things. She would have thanked me the best way she knew how, in bed. We wouldn't need to break up immediately. Until then I had cheated on Esther; now it was about cheating on Jerry. It wasn't so difficult. Olivia and I were capable of pulling it off. I could even have told Esther that Olivia was getting married. She would have been surprised.

"I'm happy for her, she's a nice girl. Who is he?"

Esther would have liked it that Jerry was a hardware store entrepreneur. She respected people who got ahead through their own hard work.

But that's not what happened. I didn't say anything to Olivia, nor to Esther. I didn't even consider it. All I felt was rage and the result of that rage was now visible in Olivia's bruised eye. She'd need to cover it with makeup, but I wasn't sure that would fully conceal it.

I continued seeing Olivia. I knew she was seeing the guy from Texas, but she was able to divide her time between the two of us.

Jerry took only a couple of months to propose. Olivia responded that they still needed to give each other time, to truly get to know each other before taking the leap. She was hoping that in the meantime I'd tire of her. That I'd feel disgusted about sharing her with another. But to me it was all the same. When I met her she was already earning a living sleeping with rich guys. I went on to form a part of her rotation until I decided to buy her exclusivity.

In truth, I could have left her, but I took pleasure in mortifying her. By that time, I had long been infatuated with Doris, a young lady from Buffalo, willing to do anything to become a model. She dreamed of becoming the next Kate Moss. Her cherublike appearance was alluring. I had promised her that I would hire her for an upcoming ad, but I was charging her upfront with long and intense sessions in bed, which left me little time to attend to Olivia.

It was around that time when Esther upset our routine. It was a Saturday. Yes, I'm sure it was a Saturday. She was checking the agency accounts and I was getting bored, pretending to read. I had suggested going to dinner somewhere and to my surprise she accepted. It's not that I had much of a hankering to go anywhere, but at least the weekend wouldn't seem so long.

We went to a trendy restaurant.

After the main course, while we waited for dessert, Esther laid everything out.

"This morning I spoke to Jaime, he is devastated. Eleanor lost the battle against cancer. She died early this morning. Poor thing."

I paused, trying to process what she had just told me. She had spoken to my brother? My brother's wife had been sick and had died of cancer? Yes, that's what Esther had said, in a monotone, as if she were giving me her opinion about the duck à l'orange that she had just had.

"I'm sorry, but I don't know what you're talking about," I replied, more harshly than I'd wanted to.

"Poor Eleanor was diagnosed with pancreatic cancer six months ago. For your brother, it was devastating. He took her to the best specialists, but they all agreed on the diagnosis: there was nothing that could be done. For Jaime these months have

STORY OF A SOCIOPATH 759

been a nightmare. His children are still teenagers, you can imagine how much they'll suffer for losing their mother."

"Children? So Jaime has children . . ." I muttered.

"Two wonderful kids, Charles and Geoffrey."

I glared at her, baring the anger I felt. I refused to hide it.

"So you know my brother has two sons and that his wife was sick . . . That's interesting, because I didn't know anything. Obviously he had no reason to tell me, but how do you know?"

"Because I know. You can't tell me you're surprised. You know that he usually checks in on my birthday and always calls on Thanksgiving to see how we are."

"You never told me you were up to date on his personal life," I retorted.

"No, I never told you. What for? The day I tried to tell you that your grandfather James was in the hospital you said that it wasn't your problem and that you didn't care if he died. When your grandma moved in with your aunt Emma, you told me you couldn't care less, and when both of them died in that accident, you refused to go to the funerals and you didn't even call Jaime. You've told me on many occasions that you didn't want to hear anything about your family, and when I tried to tell you about them you didn't want to listen."

"And now you're telling me my brother has just become a widower. I must say, that is remarkable."

"I had to tell you, Thomas. Even if you don't care, it's best that you find out through me and not through an obituary in the *New York Times*."

"You could have told me," I replied, bitterly.

"Would you have let me?"

"You know what, Esther? You haven't been altogether loyal to me. You've always kept the door open for the Spencers even while knowing that I didn't want anything to do with them. I don't understand why you would care about my grandparents or Aunt Emma . . . Although in the case of my brother . . . Anyway, I thought that, being married, you and he would not have much to say to each other."

Esther wasn't affected by my criticism. She smiled at the waiter as he placed her chocolate mousse in front of her.

"In fact, we haven't spoken much over the years, I told you already; greetings for Thanksgiving, Christmas, or my birthday, and little else. Although six months ago, when Eleanor was diagnosed with pancreatic cancer, Jaime called me; he was at his wit's end."

"You met up."

"No. Well, not immediately. Actually, since then, we've been speaking occasionally. It was me who called him from time to time to ask after Eleanor. And yes, we saw each other once; I assure you it was by chance. I was at a restaurant having lunch with a client and he was also having lunch there, I think with one of the doctors who was treating Eleanor."

"That was it?"

"I don't know what you mean."

"You didn't see each other again?"

"No, Thomas, even if you have trouble believing it. We only spoke over the phone. And the only reason I told you about Eleanor is so that you'll call him. He only has you now. The rest of your family is gone. He needs someone to support him."

Esther has always disconcerted me, but I had trouble understanding what we were doing in that restaurant talking about Eleanor's death. I couldn't comprehend why she hadn't told me at home that morning and had waited until dinner.

"We haven't seen each other in many years. We have nothing to say to each other," I fumed.

"I'm going to the funeral, Thomas. I know it's what I should do."

"I don't understand . . . I don't understand you. I don't know why you decided to tell me now, or what you expect from me."

"I spent all day thinking about how to tell you; well, this moment was as good as any other. You had to know."

"So the very beautiful Eleanor Hudson is dead, leaving two sons half-orphaned . . . I feel nothing, Esther, I don't care. I never liked Eleanor and those boys don't mean anything to me. They're half nephews, only that. As for Jaime . . . I couldn't care less."

"I'm not trying to tell you that you should feel more, just that it would be a nice gesture for you to call your brother. If you don't want to, don't do it; you've always made your own decisions regarding your family."

"And I've asked you a thousand times not to call the Spencers my family. John was not my father, he was my mother's husband."

"But Jaime is your brother, you can't deny that."

"Half brother."

"I'm tired of useless arguments, Thomas. I'll support Jaime as much as I can. He doesn't have anyone."

"It seems he has you," I countered, furiously.

She looked at me. She shrugged. At that moment I started to get dizzy and a wave of cold sweat shook through my body. I was scared. A deep fear shrank my stomach and made me want to vomit. I got up and went to the bathroom. I was shaking. Suddenly I was overcome by an acute pain that went from my chest to my stomach. I couldn't breathe. I tried to calm down, make sense of what was happening to me. I fell to the ground. I can't remember much else, except that Esther's face was very close to mine, and people around us were trying to pick me up off the floor. They took me to the hospital in an ambulance. I think the medic who was taking care of me said something about a heart attack. I grasped Esther's hand. I squeezed it with all the strength I was capable of. I felt her fingers caress my face in an attempt to comfort me.

I was in the hospital for several days: first in the cardiac care unit, then I was transferred to a room. Although the doctors were optimistic, I felt that life was starting to slip away from me. Esther didn't budge from my side. She wasn't able to go to Eleanor's funeral or to offer any consolation to Jaime, and that was the only thing that gave me a sense of relief during those uncertain times.

While I was in the cardiac unit I had nightmares. I thought I could see Constance and Yoko looking at me from behind the glass that separated me from visitors. When I emerged from that semi-unconscious state I laughed at myself. I had been hallucinating. Yoko and Constance were properly dead. The ghost of Lisa didn't scare me as much. But my mind had played a bad trick on me, menacing me with the faces of those two women who had died violently because of me. I couldn't get that image out of my head.

Seven days later I walked out of the hospital on my own two feet, holding Esther's arm and bringing with me an endless list of orders from the doctor, among them a diet that was impossible to follow: no tobacco, no alcohol, lean meats, no sweets, no condiments. Plus a bunch of prescriptions for pills that I'd have to take from now on.

I would get better. That's what they told me at the hospital. My cardiologist said that my heart would be all right if I followed his recommendations: I would have nothing to worry about, apart from having to get my blood analyzed every week for something called INR, to determine the amount of anticoagulant medication I'd need to take for the rest of my life, along with the clopidogrel and the pills for my hypertension, blood sugar, and cholesterol. I protested. Being on medication for the rest of my life seemed like too much. I told the doctor that I was forgetful and wanted to know what would happen if I didn't take some of the pills he had prescribed. Dr. Douglas patiently explained that an excess of anticoagulants may provoke an internal hemorrhage and, conversely, too low a dose could cause thrombosis.

"Thomas, you cannot afford to forget to take the anticoagulants. You will live many more years if you follow my instructions to the letter," he warned.

Esther promised the doctor that she herself would make sure I took the pills without fail, and would even force me to go to the hospital each week.

When exactly did Esther meet Jaime? I think it was a few weeks after I was discharged from the hospital. She didn't try to hide it, she simply let me know one morning.

"I'm going to your brother's house this afternoon. He invited me to tea with him and his sons. He wants me to meet them."

"Why do you have to go?" I asked, again feeling the fear that had caused my heart attack.

"Because I sincerely appreciate Jaime, because I wasn't able to support him recently, especially at Eleanor's funeral, because he's lonely, because he doesn't know how to face the future . . . Because of all that, Thomas."

"And because you care about him, because you still have feelings for him," I said, with foreboding.

When Esther didn't want to lie she went quiet or responded with something other than what was asked. She was silent until she found the right words, and replied: "Listen, Thomas, right now the most important thing to me is that you get better. So do that and don't think too much about anything that isn't your own recovery.

"If you want, you can come with me to see Jaime. I'll call him and tell him; I don't think it would be an inconvenience. You may find it hard to believe, but he has been worried about you. Despite what has happened between you, you are his brother and the only thing he wants is for you to get better soon."

I could have told her that I would come with her to console my brother and my nephews. Esther would have been surprised at my decision, but she would have gritted her teeth and called Jaime to announce that we would both be visiting him:

I can imagine the scene. My brother would be nervous and awkward, but incapable of playing the villain in front of Esther.

He'd be waiting for us, his sons by his side, on the doorstep of his beautiful home.

"Thomas, it's been a long time . . . I'm happy to see that you've recovered well. Boys, this is your uncle Thomas. Charles, Geoffrey, say hello."

The two little brats would shake my hand. Jaime would invite us in.

We'd speak about the weather and other superficial things.

"I know from Esther about your successes, you have one of the best ad agencies in Manhattan. Who would have thought?"

"Well, you've done all right yourself. You've taken your father's place at his law firm."

Esther would look at me with apprehension, asking me to lead the conversation down a different path.

Charles and Geoffrey would witness the family scene with curiosity at first, then with impatience.

We wouldn't stay long. There wouldn't be anything to say, so one hour later Esther and I would be back at home. She would be very satisfied with herself for having managed to reunite Jaime and me.

"That was nice, a good start. You know what, Thomas? Now you'll have a family again."

"You're my family, Esther."

"I am, but I'm not enough. I also have you, but I like to see my brother and my nieces and nephews, I like to be reminded that life doesn't end with me. And you also seem to enjoy it when we have dinner with my parents and my brother, and that's because you wish you had something like that."

I wouldn't tell her I despised her brother and his boring wife, that I thought they were tedious and uninteresting and that all they cared about was running the restaurant.

"Yes, perhaps you're right. I promise I'll do everything I can so that things go well with Jaime from now on."

But we didn't experience a scene like that. I didn't go with her. I didn't have the strength to play the part of the brother who returns to his family like the prodigal son. I felt an even more profound hatred toward Jaime now that he was a widower. His freedom appeared to me as the greatest of threats. When Eleanor was alive I was sure that Jaime would not interfere in our lives. My brother could not conceive of disloyalty, and whether or not he loved Eleanor she was his wife, and he would never have done anything to offend her.

I was in a foul mood for the rest of the afternoon. Since the heart attack, Esther had decided that we needed someone to be at our home permanently. She hired Mrs. Morrison, a divorced, middle-aged African-American woman, who, according to Esther, knew how to do everything, and could drive, which Esther deemed an advantage.

I found her tiresome, especially because Esther had asked her not to let me out of her sight when she wasn't at home, and Mrs. Morrison had taken this directive literally. She wouldn't allow more than twenty or thirty minutes to pass without coming to ask me if I needed anything.

There were shooting pains in my chest, probably due to apprehension, because Esther took more time than I deemed necessary. She didn't get back home until seven. She seemed happy.

"Mrs. Morrison has informed me that you have been very quiet all afternoon. I called her a couple of times to ask how you were doing."

"I have pains in my chest," I said, to stoke her conscience.

She didn't think twice before calling Dr. Douglas, who ordered her to take me directly to the hospital. One hour later, the doctor examined me and concluded that there was no reason to be alarmed.

"Try to make sure he doesn't get upset about anything. I think he had an anxiety attack. Perhaps something was worrying him. Apart from that, his vital signs are excellent. However, if he feels unwell again don't hesitate to bring him to the hospital immediately," Dr. Douglas told Esther, then turned to me. "By the way, are you following the diet I prescribed? I hope you won't drink a single drop of alcohol. I already warned you that you can't drink while you're taking your medication. And your breath smells of tobacco."

"Well, I enjoy a few indulgences," I replied.

"An exception from time to time is fine, but I must insist that diet is important, Thomas. And I repeat: no tobacco or alcohol. For God's sake, Thomas, you are not a child! Esther, you should keep an eye on him."

I saw in Esther's eyes something like repentance. Blaming herself for going to see Jaime, she thought that her absence had caused an alteration in my delicate state of health. The fright meant that she didn't mention my brother again for some time.

Two months later I went back to work. Esther insisted that I not tire myself out, but Dr. Douglas had discharged me and among his recommendations was a moderate amount of exercise. Esther knew that I lacked the willpower to do things I didn't like, so she imposed on herself the obligation to come with me on an hour-long walk every morning. Then we would head to the agency, where they tried not to overwhelm me with any issues that emerged. It was me who decided I should resume a regular schedule. I didn't want to be an invalid forever. Besides, Dr. Douglas had advised that I should try to live a normal life.

When Esther felt sure that my heart was no longer in danger she told me she was going to see Jaime again.

"He has a few errands to run in the area. We've arranged to meet for coffee. It seems that he's having some trouble with his sons. He's finding it difficult to raise them without Eleanor. They were very attached to their mother. Your brother works a lot and blames himself for not spending enough time with them," she offered, as an excuse.

"And what do you care? You can't do anything—let him figure it out by himself."

"Well, nothing bad will come of having coffee and listening to him. It's not about me being willing or able to do anything, but sometimes people need someone to listen. Perhaps you could come and have coffee with us."

I didn't reply and stormed out of her office. I knew that she had decided to see Jaime and that nothing would persuade her to do otherwise.

It was not the first time. From then on, Esther never missed a chance to tell me that she was going to my brother's house, whether it was to bring a cake to his sons or because she had arranged to meet him for coffee. "He needs someone to talk to," she would say as an excuse.

In time, Jaime became a part of our marriage. At first his presence was occasional, but little by little it became constant. Even on weekends, when Esther and I were relaxing at home, her phone would ring and I'd hear her talking to one of Jaime's sons, who'd call to ask her about something.

"You get along well with those boys," I said to her, one Sunday afternoon after she'd spent a long time talking to Charles, the older son.

"They're good kids, Thomas. They miss their mother and sometimes Jaime is too strict with them. Charles wants to go fishing in Newport with some of his friends but your brother won't let him go up by himself. You know what these things are like."

"And what do you have to do with that?"

"Well, Charles called me to ask me to convince his father."

I was out of the game, a game that went on without anyone

missing me. What worried me was that Esther was becoming more and more involved in Jaime's life. I was sure she wasn't sleeping with him—she was too loyal, and Jaime was too much of a gentleman to try—but they were weaving a relationship in which I wasn't needed.

The following weekend we went to Miami to see Paul. He was in the hospital with pneumonia and the doctors didn't seem optimistic about the prognosis. But the pneumonia hadn't taken away an iota of Paul's wit and humor.

Esther went to the cafeteria, and I took advantage of those few minutes to get some things off my chest.

"Esther wants a family, Thomas, don't you see?"

"She has a family. I'm her family, and she has her parents and her brother, her sister-in-law and her nieces and nephews."

"I mean a family of her own. You never had children. Why?"

I was silent for a while, thinking. I didn't have an answer. I'd never been interested in having children, but Esther hadn't seemed to want them either. Or that's what it seemed like to me. But Paul was suggesting now that she regretted not becoming a mother.

"Your brother and his children are offering her the opportunity to be the mother she never was. And she likes that, she finds it rewarding, it makes her feel important," said Paul.

"If she wanted to become a mother then why didn't she tell me?" I contended.

"I don't have an answer to that, Thomas. Your marriage has always been peculiar. Any other woman would have left you a long time ago."

"We're a bit old to play mommy and daddy, don't you think?"

"Of course Esther is too old to give birth. But there are your brother's sons, who allow her to fulfill her yearning for motherhood. If I were you . . . Anyway . . . I don't want to worry you, Thomas, especially since you've just recovered from the heart attack, but if you were smart you'd turn the situation around.

Make amends with your brother, play the role of complacent uncle for the sake of his sons; get properly involved in those family afternoons where Esther is the stand-in mother. If you're there she won't be able to play any role other than auntie."

"I can't stand my brother! He's such a hypocrite. He has always wanted to take Esther away from me."

"Up until now he hasn't achieved it, but don't forget that women like to act as the savior. Jaime's situation is perfect—Esther will feel irreplaceable."

He was right. Paul has always been able to see what the rest of us couldn't. But I didn't follow his advice. Out of pride? Because I didn't want to cave in? I don't know, but I didn't want to be cast as the black sheep who comes back to the pen, forced to make amends with his brother and to pretend to be an uncle to some nephews he has no interest in.

On the afternoons when Esther met Jaime and his children I went to Olivia's apartment. She was the only person I could vent my fury with, although I was getting more and more irritated by her lack of interest in what was happening to me. Olivia was absorbed in her relationship with Jerry and was trying to bring ours to an end. We would exchange a few threats, aware that if either of us took one step against the other, it would mean our mutual destruction.

I couldn't give Esther any reasons to leave me, especially not now. If Olivia made our relationship public, my wife would not hesitate to do it, not because she cared or didn't already know, but because she wouldn't be able to tolerate being openly insulted.

In the same way, Olivia knew that Jerry wouldn't be able to stand knowing that I supported her and that her meager acting career didn't rake in enough to pay even half of the rent for her apartment. Nor would Jerry like to know that Olivia had earned a living as an escort for mature gentlemen who visited New York for business or pleasure. We both had plenty of ammunition to annihilate the other.

One of those afternoons, when Esther went to Jaime's house to play sympathetic auntie because my brother was once again upset with Charles for getting bad grades at school, I called Olivia to tell her that I was coming to see her. I knew it was her day off from the theater.

"I wasn't planning on seeing you today, Thomas. Jerry called me. He's going to pick me up for dinner. He wants me to meet a couple who he says are his best friends. It's important to him that they like me; they were also very good friends of his late wife."

"Tell him you can't make it, Olivia. Make something up."

"No, Thomas, I can't. I want to marry him, and I know I need the approval of the people who are important to him, and these friends are."

I insulted her for a long time. Olivia listened to me patiently. I guessed she was filing her nails or waxing her legs the whole time. That's how she was. But she didn't budge. We were both being very stubborn. If there were to be an ending it would be like that of the fable of the scorpion and the frog. We would both perish, and she knew that I did not want to perish.

I telephoned Doris, the young and charming Doris, who never said no and did her best to please me as long as I paid generously.

I spent the afternoon with Doris; I've actually been spending many afternoons in the past two or three years with her. I suspect she thinks she's getting the better of me and I find it amusing to allow her to believe that.

She listens rapturously to anything I have to say and looks at me as if I were the most attractive man on earth, but I know that what she sees in me is power. On one occasion Olivia explained to me why young and beautiful women sometimes fall in love with guys like me. "It's because of power," she said. In the case of Doris it was the power to turn her into a somebody in the concrete jungle. The power to open my wallet and give her a three-thousand-dollar Gucci handbag; the power that emanates from a man who drives a Ferrari Testarossa. That's why in her eyes my love handles fade away, and she doesn't pay attention to the mottled skin around my torso, arms, and legs, nor does she look at my hair, which has been thinning for some time.

In reality, when she embraces me she isn't embracing me, she's embracing my money, my car, who I am in Manhattan.

Doris is twenty-three years old; she has soft skin, blue eyes, and a spectacular body. I labor under no illusion, I'm not like those mature gentlemen who believe they've really made a young lady fall in love with them. I assume she goes to bed with what I have, not with my aged body.

There really is nothing more ridiculous than a man of advanced age who believes that he has won the heart of a younger woman. No—I don't want to deceive myself. That's why I prefer to admit to myself that my young lady sells herself for the sake of the reward she'll obtain. It's better than indulging in the childish illusion that a twenty-three-year-old girl might prefer my flaccid body to that of a young man in the prime of life. This is one of the lessons I learned from Olivia.

My relationship with Esther began to deteriorate. She didn't need me. My place in her life was diminishing. She found the weekends as interminable as I did. In my case because I got bored with her; in hers because she wanted to be at Jaime's home with him and his sons, playing the wife and the mother she was not.

She made no secret of the fact that she spoke with them several times each weekend. She even took her phone to the bathroom in case they called her. And they did.

One Sunday morning, I began to feel alarmed. Esther got up early and made breakfast. Sundays were Mrs. Morrison's day off, and she went to sing at a church in Harlem.

"I'll be back for lunch, I'll try not to be late," Esther announced, hurrying to the door and leaving me gobsmacked.

"Where are you going?"

"Geoffrey, your brother's youngest son, is playing an important basketball game and asked me to come. He wants me to see how good he is."

"You could have let me know sooner."

"You're right. The truth is I was hesitating but I thought you wouldn't mind me being away for a couple of hours. I'll be back for lunch. I can't say no to Geoffrey. Charles is a lot better at basketball than he is, and, well, he needs someone to encourage and support him."

"You're not their mother, Esther," I said harshly.

She bit her lip. I saw it all in her expression: she was sorry she wasn't the mother of those two boys but sometimes thought she was.

"I know, Thomas. I can't take Eleanor's place. Those boys adored their mother. I'm only trying to lend a hand."

"You can't keep devoting yourself to them as if you had a responsibility to meet; they're abusing your kindness."

"No, it's not like that . . . It actually makes me happy to be with them."

She regretted putting it like that. I know because she lowered her gaze, and if she could have, she would have erased what she had just said.

"So I should be jealous of them. I wish it made you happy to be with me."

She approached me and threw her arms around my neck while she ran her fingers through my hair.

"Please, Thomas, don't ruin it!"

Ruin it? What was I ruining? I didn't ask her and she left without giving me time to respond.

She arrived a little before lunchtime. We spent the rest of the afternoon together but in reality she was miles away, still with Jaime and his sons. She even called them a couple of times.

I started to build up a contained anger toward both Esther

and Olivia. With Olivia I could occasionally release it, but with Esther I had to pretend.

But while Esther seemed to have infinite patience for our situation, and had even stopped insisting that I accompany her to Jaime's house, Olivia was pressuring me to end our relationship. She was terrified at the possibility of losing Jerry.

Destiny weighed in on my side and allowed me to take revenge on both of them.

One morning when I was at the office dictating a few letters to my secretary, Esther interrupted us. Her intense gaze revealed that she was preoccupied.

"Thomas, something terrible has happened."

At first I was alarmed. I thought Paul had died or that one of our best clients had gone over to one of our competitors. But fortunately it wasn't either of those two things.

"Jaime phoned me. The poor thing couldn't take it anymore . . . He had to tell someone."

"Tell what?" I snapped.

"Well, it seems that the bank is about to seize his assets. It's not that things aren't going well at the office, but he invested everything he earned with Lehman Brothers and he's lost everything. He hadn't told me anything until now. Eleanor's father helped them at first, made their bank give them a loan to help cope with the situation . . . But things haven't gone the way he was hoping and . . . Well, he told me he mortgaged his home, and even the house he inherited from your aunt in Newport. It was repossessed a few days ago. He lost it. That beautiful house . . . I'm so sorry, I loved it so much! But the worst thing is that he still owes the bank a large amount of money and he doesn't have it, and Eleanor's father doesn't want to help him. He has agreed to pay his grandsons' expenses but nothing more. I think that . . . well, I think we should help him."

"Help him? You want us to give away our money to him?" I asked, raising my voice.

"No, it's not about that, but you could speak to somebody at the bank, offer some kind of guarantee so they stop pressuring Jaime and let him get back on his feet. You could also talk to his father-in-law, ask him to help, say that you can act as a guarantor for your brother. Eleanor's father knows that our company is solvent. We can do that, can't we? That's what I want."

I couldn't believe that Esther was asking me to save Jaime, that brother of mine I'd always compared myself with as a child, feeling I was ugly and clumsy. The brother praised by everyone as a good boy, a good student, and, on top of everything, good-looking. The brother sought after by all the best colleges, who went to Harvard Law and graduated with honors. The brother praised by all the newspapers as a brilliant lawyer. The brother who married the right woman, Eleanor Hudson, an East Coast aristocrat as proud as she was beautiful. And now Esther had just revealed to me that this upstanding man was a failure. I had to hold back a chuckle. Nothing could make me happier than what I had just heard. James "Jaime" Spencer was bankrupt. Not only had he lost his wife, he had also lost his fortune.

I imagined his suffering when the bank took control of the Newport house. Aunt Emma's house, where the Spencers had been happy, where I myself had spent some of my best childhood moments. The only place where I didn't feel the impatient, fretful gaze of my mother, because Aunt Emma wanted her house to be a space for freedom, even for the young ones.

No, I wasn't planning on helping him. I wouldn't lift a finger to free him from the suffering he was experiencing and restore his sense of peace.

Esther looked at me expectantly. She knew I never said no to anything she asked—I had never done that—but she also knew that asking me to save Jaime might be more than I'd be willing to concede.

I could have done it. Yes, I could have told Esther not to worry; I could have sworn to bail Jaime out:

"Don't worry, dear, of course we'll do anything in our power to help out my brother and my nephews. I'll talk to the bank—the president holds us in great esteem. He knows that we're solvent. As for Mr. Hudson, well, I don't know Eleanor's father very well, but I could go and see him. Perhaps between the two of us we can fix this. Are you happy?"

She would have hugged me gratefully, feeling guilty for not loving me as she should, willing to continue to sacrifice her life next to mine, a price she'd have to pay in order to save Jaime.

Yes, I could have told her I would do what she wanted. But I didn't. In fact I didn't agree to anything, although I didn't refuse outright. I was going to play my cards in a way that would destroy Jaime and make Esther suffer along the way, at least a little, for making me suffer on Jaime's account. Since he had installed himself in our lives, I felt Esther grow more distant with each day that went by. It was only a matter of time before she would abandon me for the opportunity to act as Jaime's savior, which according to Paul is what women are like: they give it all, expecting nothing in return. And there was nothing more romantic than trying to save a widower and his two sons from ruin.

"Will you do it, Thomas? Tell me you will." Her voice carried a note of supplication.

It took me a few seconds to respond as I searched for the right words—words that wouldn't oblige me to do anything I didn't plan to do.

"I'll interest myself in his situation."

"That's not enough," Esther said sharply.

"First, I want to know exactly what situation he's in, before we commit to something we can't follow through with. Don't ask the impossible, Esther."

"You're right . . . Yes, that's the sensible thing to do. Talk to the bank, they'll advise you on what can be done, and we'll take their advice into consideration. Thank you, Thomas. I knew I could count on you."

She hugged me. For a few moments she held me close, breathing on my neck. I felt her warmth and her agitation.

I've always forgiven Esther for not truly loving me. It was enough to have her nearby, to believe that I could share my life with her. She never deceived me about her feelings toward me or toward Jaime. In some ways she had loved me, yes, but the love she felt for me was a pale reflection of what she had always felt for Jaime. Again I remembered that Paul used to say that women sublimate the impossible, and Jaime had always been impossible, at least until he became a widower. From that moment on, Esther began to dream about the possibility of sharing a life with Jaime. It was just a dream, but a dream that fully occupied her mind, a dream that she devoted all her energy to. She was making it come true in a sense by formalizing her status as concerned and generous sister-in-law to my brother and his sons. She still didn't dare to take the big leap, but if I lowered my guard, she would.

Esther was still talking, but I wasn't listening. I was thinking about my revenge, and I was startled when I heard her mention Olivia.

"I'll call her. If that's all right with you?" she asked me.

"I'm sorry . . . I didn't quite catch what you were saying."

"Poor thing! You're thinking about Jaime, thank you, dear! Well, I was saying that I'm thinking about using Olivia for the diamond commercial."

"We've used her too many times," I replied.

"Yes, but in this case she'll be perfect, she has beautiful hands, don't you think? I thought the camera could follow some woman's hands throughout the day . . . Getting out of bed, putting on makeup, hugging her son before he goes to school, running a meeting, at a romantic dinner. The figure of the woman will be out of focus, we won't really see her features, and the important thing will be her hands, the diamond ring glinting on one of her fingers. It'll be subtle and elegant."

I realized that Esther was trying to repay me for the effort she was asking me to expend in helping Jaime. Paul was right. My wife knew what was going on between Olivia and me. The most painful part was that she didn't seem to mind and was willing to be gracious to me by hiring my lover once again.

"Do whatever you want, I don't care," I replied drily.

"Yes, we'll hire her," she insisted.

That same afternoon I called Mr. Hudson. When I told his secretary who I was, she hesitated before putting the call through.

"What do you want, Spencer?" he offered as a greeting. His tone of voice was icy.

"To speak to you. I won't take up much of your time."

"About what?"

"About my brother's financial situation."

"Talk to him. I have nothing to do with your brother's ill-judged decisions . . . Don't even think about asking me for one dollar."

"I'm not planning to do that, Mr. Hudson, believe me."

He asked me to meet him the next morning at eight at his office, warning me that he would not waste his time with me for "more than ten minutes."

Hudson had grown old since I'd last seen him. The death of Eleanor, his only daughter, had turned him into an old man, although he kept telling the same terrible jokes that he had told throughout his life.

I got straight to the point. I wanted to know my brother's real financial situation: loans, mortgages, investments, bonds, everything.

He told me. To my surprise, he gave me a detailed report on Jaime's precarious financial situation.

"Your brother wanted to blow Eleanor away, to prove that he could give her the same kind of life she'd had before they were married. The fool! He couldn't think of a better way than to mortgage all the properties he had and invest the money in options that turned out to be a disaster. He lost everything. The worst thing is that he asked my advice beforehand and I warned him not to buy junk bonds. When they went bankrupt, my daughter asked me to help her and that's what I did while she was alive. I made sure that they were able to continue enjoying the same lifestyle. I wasn't going to allow my Eleanor not to be able to afford even going to the hairdresser. So I subsidized all their domestic expenses. I also asked his banker, an old friend of mine, to give him a loan. Eleanor was convinced that her husband would get back on his feet. But your brother made another mistake: he thought that if he speculated with that money he could suddenly recover everything he had lost. He didn't consult with me and ignored the recommendations of his banker. He invested and lost. Everything. My daughter suffered at the end because of what was happening to them. Your brother paid no attention to me when I asked him to not add financial worries to her illness. But he is a weak man and told her how badly things were going. He needed my daughter's strength, even knowing that she needed what little strength she had left to fight cancer.

"A few days before she died she made me promise I would never abandon her two sons. I swore I wouldn't and I will keep my promise. They are my only grandchildren, in both of them there is a part of Eleanor. But I will not save your brother. He ruined her. She died in anguish.

"I've proposed to your brother to have my grandsons come live with me. They won't lack anything. If he doesn't accept, then I'll do what I've done over the past few months: pay their school tuition, buy them clothes, invite them on vacation . . . And don't say any nonsense like 'the boys need their father.' "

"I wasn't planning on saying that, Mr. Hudson," I admitted.

"So what do you want?"

"Only to know the details of my brother's financial situation. The extent of the debt, what banks he has issues with . . . that kind of thing."

"What for?" he asked me distrustfully.

I wasn't sure if I should lie to him. I concluded that it wasn't fully necessary to lie, so I decided to tell him almost the whole truth.

"Mr. Hudson, I have been working hard all these years. My companies have withstood the crisis. We have not had losses. I am not willing to lose my money, not even for my brother. That's why I want to know it all, because he has asked for my help."

"I know your brother is very close to your wife," he said spitefully.

"If you say so."

"My Eleanor didn't like your wife."

"There was no reason why she should have. I didn't like your daughter either. But I'm not here to talk about personal affinities."

"Are you going to lend him money? I don't think he'll be able to pay it back, he even owes money to his partners at the law firm."

"If what you say is true, I obviously won't put my money at stake. Can you assure me you won't save him, even for the sake of your grandsons?"

"I will always look after my grandsons, but I don't give a damn what happens to James Spencer. Is that clear?"

One hour later I went to the office of the investment bank that handled my brother's assets. It was the company that had managed the Spencers' affairs for almost a century. Even when I cut off my family, they continued to manage my assets.

I was greeted by a vice president. Without beating around the bush, I told him what he needed to know. I made him believe that I was willing to help my brother.

"Your brother allowed himself to get carried away in an

environment in which people thought that money was always within reach. We advised him against certain investments. As you know, our investment proposals are always very conservative, that's why they are safe. But he wouldn't listen. In confidence, I will say that in my opinion he was trying to impress his beautiful wife. He invested everything he had in junk bonds and, sadly, our forecasts were accurate. He lost everything."

"How much does he owe?"

"I don't know if I should tell you. You are his brother, but that is confidential information."

"I need to know if I can help him, that's why it's necessary for me to know the extent of the debt."

"You have trusted us ... Through all these years we've invested your money, satisfactorily, I believe, because you've even made profits when others had losses. Your capital is important but ... Anyway, however painful you find it, my obligation as your financial adviser is to recommend you don't waste your money to save anyone from something that cannot be remedied.

"Your brother had a significant portfolio of properties, as you know: the residence he inherited from his parents here in New York, in addition to the two owned by his grandparents, one in Manhattan and one in Florida, plus your aunt Emma's property in Newport. And the office, yes, the office on Madison Avenue ... He thought that if he mortgaged all these assets and invested the money he could triple the capital. As you know, there was a time when the banks were overpricing real estate properties, so he was given more money than the properties were really worth. He refused to listen to us. Within a month the bank will repossess the office, as it has done with the residences, except for the one he still owns on Seventy-Second Street, his parents' home, where you lived as a child. He won't be able to keep it for very long. In two months it will belong to the bank. Your brother is bankrupt, he can't even pay our fees."

"How much does he need?" I insisted.

"Your brother's problems amount to a sum in excess of twenty million dollars."

"Thank you for your trust. I'll see what I can do."

"You shouldn't do anything, unless you want to give away twenty million dollars."

I could have told him I didn't plan to leave my brother in the hands of his creditors. I should have ordered him to make available that quantity to cover Jaime's debt. Or asked him to restructure the debt so that Jaime could repay it little by little. Yes, I could have helped Jaime. Or at least mitigated his situation. That is what I had promised Esther.

"I will act as a guarantor for his debt. Do everything you can so that my brother can at least keep his office and home; the rest can go up for auction. But I won't allow him and his children to be put out on the street, much less let the office that belonged to my grandparents and then my father pass into the hands of anyone who is not a Spencer."

"A noble gesture, but are you sure? It's a lot of money and I don't think your brother is in a position to pay it back. He is a good lawyer but he is a terrible businessman. And all this . . . Anyway, it has damaged his reputation. You must know that many clients have abandoned him."

"I won't allow the Spencers' name to be tarnished. Prepare all the papers, I will sign as soon as they're ready."

"Your wife will need to sign too."

"She will. Don't worry about her."

But I didn't say any of these words. I was overjoyed to hear of Jaime's disrepute. My brother was about to have to depend on welfare and his father-in-law's charity.

When I stepped out into the street I felt the fresh air flood my lungs. At last I could feel superior to Jaime. The blond boy once adored by everyone, the upstanding student preferred by our teachers, the loving and loyal son who was always willing to offer a smile, the generous friend . . . Yes, he had suddenly become a failure, somebody who no longer mattered, who could no longer saunter into the tennis club in Newport looking self-satisfied, or attract the secret admiration of all the women who watched him as he hoisted the halyard on Aunt Emma's boat.

What would my mother think if she saw him like this? Would John be surprised to see his son's downfall while his stepson triumphed in the Big Apple?

I didn't see Esther the rest of the day. I called Olivia but she didn't pick up, so I tried Doris and invited her to lunch; I didn't care if somebody saw us. The girl looked at me gratefully; we had never met outside the four walls of some hotel or the apartment in Tribeca I'd just begun renting for her.

When I arrived home at around seven Esther was waiting for me impatiently.

"Well, tell me. I've been waiting for a call from you all day. You must have six or seven missed calls from me on your cell."

"I'm sorry, it hasn't been an easy day."

"What did Mr. Hudson say? Will he help Jaime?"

I spared none of Mr. Hudson's scornful comments about my brother. Esther seemed disheartened. She didn't like it when anyone doubted Jaime. I even exaggerated. I took pleasure in her indignation, her suffering.

"So he's not going to do anything."

"Not exactly. He told me he was willing to give his grandsons the life they deserve. He wants Jaime to allow them to go and live with him."

"But that would be terrible! The kids need to be with their father, they've suffered enough by losing their mother. It will break Jaime's heart if he has to be separated from his sons."

"This isn't about Jaime's heart but the future of those boys," I said, cruelly.

"No parent could bear to be asked to give up his children," she contended.

"Some parents are irresponsible, and that's what Jaime has been. If he's in this situation, it's his own fault."

"How could you say that? Your brother has been unlucky, like so many others who went bankrupt during the crisis. It's not his fault but the fault of those vultures on Wall Street, those crooks who've destroyed countless people." Esther started to get upset and looked at me, furious.

"He did the wrong things to try to impress Eleanor. He wanted to prove that he was smarter than Mr. Hudson, that he could earn a fortune. And he lost. That's what happened."

"But . . . it's not like that . . . it's not like that . . . Jaime wanted the best for his family. He did what so many others did—invest."

"And he made a mistake. In fact, Jaime had a complex about the Hudsons. I guess it wasn't easy to live with a woman whose father has one of the great fortunes of the East Coast. He wanted to prove to Eleanor what he was worth . . . and . . . he did."

"You're saying that Jaime isn't worth anything? I can't believe you think of him that way! You had your differences in the past, but you have to admit that your brother has integrity. He's a great man."

Her words were defiant. I realized how little she trusted me. And more importantly, that she wouldn't give up on Jaime. If I helped him, she would sacrifice herself, but if I didn't, she would leave me, willing to share my brother's fate. In that instant I hated her. I hated her with all my being. I hated her because I needed her, I hated her because I had been so afraid to lose her for so many years, which had forced me to conceal my deepest self so as not to scare her.

Esther looked at me fearfully, as if she had seen a monster. I wanted to laugh, to tell her I was sick of pretending, of walking the tightrope, trying not to do anything that might push her away from me.

"If you don't do something, I will. I'll sell my share of the company, I'll sell everything I have. That's what I'll do. But I won't allow those vultures from the banks to win this battle."

"They already have, Esther. As for selling . . . May I remind you that you can't sell anything without my consent? The company, the earnings, the bonds, our home, absolutely everything belongs to both of us and you can't dispose of anything without my signature. That's what you wanted, remember? I wanted to give you everything I had, but you said we'd share it all. That's what we did. You can't sell your share of the company to anyone without my authorization and I won't give it to you because I'm not willing to let Jaime drag us down with him."

Her face had contracted into a grimace of disbelief. If in that moment I hated her, she hated me even more.

"I've worked hard all these years, Thomas. I'm not asking you for a penny I haven't earned. Everything you had before we became partners is yours, I don't want it, but I demand you give me the fruit of my labor."

"No."

"You can't refuse."

"Yes, I can. I'm not going to allow Jaime to take advantage of your weakness, or allow you to give away the earnings you've worked so hard for, destroying our business to help him. I'm sorry, Esther, but I'm going to protect you from yourself. I'm going to protect us both."

"I'll divorce you," she said defiantly, knowing it was the only thing that could hurt me.

"I can't stop you. You'll hurt me, you know that, but I won't do anything to prevent that. Not this time. And even so, you wouldn't be able to use the money as you please. You signed the papers, Esther, and we both agreed that, whatever happened between us, we wouldn't divide the company or anything we own. The money is well invested."

The end result of the argument was that I smoked three packs of cigarettes and drank a bottle of whiskey.

That day she moved into the guest room. I didn't knock on

her door, nor did I utter a word of reproach. I wanted her to suffer. But still I trembled at the thought that she might leave me.

She didn't speak to me for several days. Not even when we were both at the agency. The employees seemed concerned, perhaps wondering whether what was happening between us might jeopardize their jobs.

I got used to the new situation. We became two strangers sharing a living space, a place we no longer considered a home. The only thing that didn't change was that every morning I found the pills I had to take for my heart on a saucer next to my breakfast. At night, if she was getting home late, she called Mrs. Morrison in advance so she would give me the pills I needed to take.

Days went by. We weren't capable of finding the right moment or way to forgive each other.

Olivia called me one morning, inviting me to lunch at her apartment. I imagined she wanted to talk in private, because she preferred going out to restaurants.

When I got to her apartment she was setting the table. She was nervous, I could tell, because she wouldn't stop talking.

"What kind of surprise are you going to give me?" I asked, as I lit a cigarette.

She thought I was talking about the food and she said with a smile that she'd made a lobster bisque and roast, accompanied by a salad, which she usually adorned with aromatic herbs and flowers.

The bisque was on the boil, so I poured myself a glass of wine and I asked her what she had to tell me that was so urgent.

"As you know, Esther hired me for the diamond commercial. I'm very excited about it. We start shooting tomorrow. This is good news for me—I'm grateful to you both."

"That's why you invited me?"

"I actually wanted to tell you that I'm marrying Jerry. I'm not going to postpone the wedding any longer. Jerry bought a house. He says he wants us to start a new life together, so he sold the house that he lived in with his wife. He's very considerate. He asked me to decorate the new place any way I want. We're doing a small renovation because I want to have my own space. You know, I've been living alone for so many years, and I wouldn't want to share the bathroom or the closet. I think the house will be ready in three months at most, and then we'll get married. You have to come to terms with it, Thomas. It's over. I don't care if I have to leave this apartment, I'll find a place to stay until the wedding. But it's over."

She gave me a self-satisfied glance. She was proud of her own decisiveness.

She wasn't expecting it; not even I knew I was about to do what I did. I picked up the pot and threw its contents over her hands. Olivia shrieked. The bisque covered her beautiful hands and I couldn't help chuckling when I saw the stupor on her face; it gave me satisfaction to watch her suffer.

She wouldn't stop wailing in pain, she didn't seem to know what to do. She got up and ran to the bathroom, putting her hands under the cold tap. Tears were streaming down her face. I drew near, and stood behind her.

"Never, do you hear me? Never tell me you're going to do something I don't want you to do. I warned you that if you dare take one step without my approval I'll tell Jerry what you are. Don't you dare, Olivia, don't you dare tell me that you're going to leave me again. Be careful."

On my way home I felt dizzy. I had burned her hands. The beautiful hands that were going to star in the ad Esther had hired her for. She would no longer be able to do the ad. Or go onstage.

The next morning I found out that she'd had to go to the hospital. She had been injected with painkillers. Both hands were in bandages. She couldn't do anything. The doctors explained that the burns were severe and would leave scarring.

It was Esther who told me. My wife broke the silence between us, announcing that Olivia had suffered an accident, which meant that the shoot had to be canceled and Esther had to find another model.

"That's so unfortunate," I remarked.

"Yes, so unfortunate . . ." She was silent for a moment. "She told me it was a deliberate attack—a man had wanted to hurt her. I told her to report him to the police."

"She should," I replied, unperturbed.

"I'd like to know what kind of wicked man would do such a thing. There are men who just mean trouble for women," she said, looking me steadily in the eye.

I didn't respond. I assumed she suspected it was me who had caused Olivia's burns.

After that exchange we were on speaking terms again, at least when it came to the essentials. We even had the odd dinner together when we got home from work. What didn't change was that Esther continued to sleep in the guest room.

One morning I found our aide, Mrs. Morrison, moving some of Esther's things to her new room. I felt a jabbing pain in my stomach. I couldn't deceive myself about our relationship, there was no going back now. We continued to live together, but every day I found Esther to be more of a stranger to me, as I was to her.

I visited Olivia two weeks later. One night, at dinnertime, I turned up at her apartment without notice. I turned the key and went in. She was lying on the sofa watching TV. Her hands and part of her arms were bandaged. She got up when she saw me and stood in front of me, looking at me hatefully.

"What do you want?" she demanded.

"I've come to see you" was my reply, as I sat in an armchair in front of the sofa.

She sat in front of me. She had dark circles under her green eyes, from suffering, from pain, from sleepless nights.

"We have nothing to say to each other, Thomas. The only thing that's left for you to do is kill me. Are you going to do it?" Her voice was defiant.

"I don't plan to. What about Jerry?" I wanted to know.

"He thinks I tripped and spilled the pot myself."

"Fantastic."

"Fantastic? What's fantastic about Jerry thinking I'm useless and I burned my hands myself?" Olivia nearly screamed.

"If you don't break the rules, there's no reason why anything should go wrong. It all depends on you. I told you already, it will be me who will say when I want to break up with you. Until then, smile. You cost me a lot of money and it's the least you can do."

She sat on the sofa and closed her eyes. I contemplated her for a few seconds and what I saw was not a woman who had given up but a woman who was willing to fight for her freedom.

I forced her to sleep with me. She couldn't prevent it because her hands were bandaged and she couldn't even try to defend herself. She let me. It was like I had a corpse in my arms. But I didn't care. I wanted to humiliate her.

When we were done I poured myself a whiskey and turned on the television. I didn't even offer her a glass of water.

"How do you manage if you can't use your hands?" I was curious.

"The aide comes in the morning and helps me bathe and makes me food. My neighbor comes by three or four times a day, to give me my medication. She feeds me dinner. Jerry also comes. He insists on helping me, although I've told him I'd rather he didn't come until I've recovered. But he's not the kind to sit around twiddling his thumbs. He wants to help me."

"I told you I don't want him to set foot in here," I warned.

"Don't worry. I'd never sleep with him in the bed where I've had to put up with you. They're only courtesy visits."

I said nothing and fixed my attention on the TV. What channel was it? Discovery? I can't quite remember. But something caught our attention because we were both silent as we contemplated the screen. A documentary about poisons was on. It went back even before antiquity, saying that ever since prehistoric times humankind has known about the deadly power of plants.

A botanist listed an endless number of plants that look innocuous but can cause death. A professor at New York University explained that a mixture of certain components can be lethal, and that even the medications we take every day, depending on the dosage, can cause death. An anthropologist described how in the Amazon rain forest it was easy to find roots and plants that could strike down humans and animals. A criminologist was interviewed and recounted the details of many cases of homicide in which poisons may have been used: some had been confirmed, others hadn't, because, as he explained, there are poisons that kill slowly and others that have an immediate effect. An ex–police officer said that during the Cold War, Bulgarian spies killed their opponents by poking them with an umbrella whose tip had been laced with poison.

The program lasted an hour and a half and Olivia and I didn't say a word. We stared at the screen in fascination.

Olivia said she was tired. I was also sleepy and, although another episode in the series was coming up, I decided to leave.

When I arrived home, Esther was in the living room. I was surprised to find her watching television because it was late.

"You're not in bed yet?" I asked as I poured myself a whiskey.

"I got home late. I had to finish planning the campaign for that supermarket brand. Mrs. Morrison prepared dinner trays before she left, and I sat down to watch TV for a while."

I don't know why exactly, but I was startled when I glanced at the screen and noticed that Esther was watching the second part of the same show that Olivia and I had been watching. I sat by her side and finished watching it with her. We both sat in silence, absorbed in the screen, lost in thought.

When we switched off the television I was surprised that Esther said good night, kissing me on the cheek.

"Have a good night, Thomas. See you tomorrow."

Some time has passed since Esther, Olivia, and I saw that show on TV. I haven't forgotten about it; they never talk about it. But since then I haven't trusted either of them. It was fifteen days after the documentary about poisons that I started to feel bad.

Nausea, headaches, anxiety, arrhythmia, heart pain that spread to my neck and my throat . . . I started to have little nosebleeds, and I sometimes bleed from my gums when I brush my teeth.

Dr. Douglas said that these episodes are connected to my heart disease, and that they happen because I don't follow his recommendations. He adjusted my dosage of anticoagulants again. I drink and smoke and eat whatever I want. But I don't think that whatever's happening to me is a result of my excesses. Perhaps Esther is not giving me the right dosage of anticoagulants or perhaps Olivia has decided to take revenge on me, and what better way than by poisoning me slowly through my food, via those wonderful stews that I cannot resist?

Yes, I think that one of them has decided to reduce the amount of time I have left. Or perhaps both of them? I don't know, but one day Esther told me that she had met Olivia for lunch.

"Poor thing," she said. "She's going through a lot with the burns on her hands. They'll never be the same again."

All I know is that since watching that documentary, they have changed, and I am racked with pains that not even Dr. Douglas can diagnose. He says that every illness is different and I should follow his recommendations. The damn diet. But I know that my wife, or perhaps my mistress, is slipping me something that affects my health.

And Jaime lost everything he had left. He couldn't even keep his father's house. I know that Esther sold all the jewelry I've given her over the years we've been married. A couple of Cartier gold watches, a Van Cleef one with diamonds, a necklace of diamonds and emeralds, a solitaire from Tiffany that cost me one hundred thousand dollars, some sapphire earrings . . . I've been generous to Esther. And she cashed it all in to give money to Jaime. Money that's now being used to pay the rent on a SoHo apartment. My wife told me this without caring what I might think.

"I'm just glad that you couldn't sell the firm on a whim, or else we'd be a wreck," I spat back at her when she told me about selling her jewelry.

"You could have helped him, Thomas. I didn't have any other options."

"Of course you have another option: be loyal to me."

She was silent while she absorbed my attack. I think that it had its effect, that for an instant she felt miserable for not having loved me, for having sacrificed me for Jaime.

"I never cheated on you," she said finally.

"No, you never did, and what good did it do you?"

"That's what loyalty is, not cheating on a person," she said in a thin voice.

"Loyalty means not letting down the person you love, not humiliating him, giving him as much as you receive. That's what loyalty is," I said bluntly.

"I'm sorry, Thomas. I'm truly sorry for not living up to your expectations. Perhaps you expect too much . . . I tried to make things work, to make our marriage worthwhile."

She was being sincere. She was speaking from her heart, and from her gut. Her eyes showed just how much she regretted everything.

"And it's been worthwhile. I wouldn't have exchanged our years together for anything. They've been the best years of my life. But once again Jaime has come along and stolen what was mine." I was speaking sincerely as well.

"No, please don't say that! It's not his fault. I . . . Although it's hard for you to believe, there's nothing going on between us. He refuses to . . . You know he promised your father that he would never meddle in your life and that he would give me up, as much as he loved me. You'll always be there between us."

"He did promise John that, but he must have forgotten, or else he wouldn't be ruining my life."

"You still don't want to call John your father? He's the only one you ever had. And don't try to blame Jaime. If anyone's guilty here, it's me. He . . . For God's sake, Thomas, I'm the guilty one, not Jaime! I wanted to help him, I got involved in his life, I insisted on being there for him and his children. Jaime has never asked me for anything."

"But he accepts everything you give him without a second thought, as if it were his right. He's used to having people love him and smooth his way for him, to getting everything simply by smiling. He never needed to ask."

"Thomas . . ." Esther came to me and put her hand on my shoulder.

I shook her off. I wanted her to feel guilty. I saw how upset she was, but I remained unmoved.

"You know what, Esther? My brother destroyed my life. He ruined my childhood and now he wants to take the only thing I have away from me."

"It's me . . . I'm the guilty one!"

Esther also confessed to me that, because Jaime had lost his office as well, she had rented for him not only his apartment but a couple of rooms in an office building up near Harlem. And so Jaime's clients had stopped being Manhattan brokers and had become local tradesmen. I didn't feel any sympathy for him or for her. She was trapped in a spider's web, and she didn't know how to break free.

I didn't ask her what she wanted to do. I was afraid that she would ask for a divorce. I didn't want to hear her say that she loved Jaime. I knew it already, but I couldn't bear to hear her say it.

"Your nephews will spend the summer with their grandfather. He'll take them to Europe. Paris, London, Madrid, Rome . . . And when they get back they'll go to the Hudsons' house near Newport."

"And then what?" I wanted to know.

"I don't know . . . Mr. Hudson says his grandchildren will

live with him. It depends on whether Jaime can pull himself together. He can't take care of the kids by himself."

No, my brother couldn't take care of his children, but my wife could. I realized that if the children weren't around, it wouldn't take long before Esther went to Jaime's bed. They had waited many years. Once it happened, even though Jaime would feel remorse for breaking his promise to his father, he would end up accepting Esther into his home, his life.

"I've got a deal for you," I said without thinking too much about it.

"A deal?"

"Yes. I'll help Jaime, but you have to give him up."

"What? I don't know what you're talking about."

"Yes, you do. I'll help him financially, but whatever happens, you'll stay with me. We'll rent him a decent house where he can live with his kids, we'll pay for a woman to take care of them, I'll send clients his way."

"And the price is me." Esther's voice left no doubt that she would accept.

"Yes. The price is you."

"I'm not a child anymore, and whether . . ."

"Yes, I know, whether you go now or later doesn't make any difference. But you have to make up your mind."

Her eyes clouded. It was hard for her to hold back her tears. I knew then that she had decided to leave me. I kept the pressure on her; I was prepared to win.

For a few seconds she was quiet, distant, fighting with herself. When she replied, she did so in a whisper: "All right, Thomas. You win. Help Jaime."

"I will. But I'll keep my hands on the controls. I'm not so stupid as to sacrifice ourselves for him."

I kept my word. All this time I've kept my word and I will keep it till the end. I pay Jaime's bills and make his situation easier. But

I haven't saved him from everything. The banks still have my parents' home, and my grandparents' houses, and Aunt Emma's. But at least he has money to keep his children comfortable.

When was it? I can remember the day I realized I was starting to die, that all the sickness I had felt up to this moment was turning into something more.

That day, as always, I had breakfast with Esther. Whole wheat bread and decaffeinated coffee. She made it every morning and then forced me to take the pills for my ruined heart. Then, despite her continued protests, I would smoke a cigarette. In fact, it wasn't the first one of the day, because I had already smoked two before sitting down to breakfast. I started to feel odd at midmorning. Nothing hurt, but I wasn't feeling well. I went to the bathroom and was scared to see that my urine contained threads of blood. I didn't say anything. I barely ate lunch. I couldn't get anything down.

"Are you all right? You don't look too good," Esther said when she came by the office in the middle of the afternoon to tell me that she would be home late because she had a meeting with the creatives.

"I don't know . . . the coffee didn't go down all that well this morning."

"You should watch what you eat; it'll do you good. I saw a bottle of whiskey this morning in the living room, nearly empty, and a bunch of leftover pizza. You know you can't eat that stuff. Dr. Douglas told you that it's just pouring fat into your arteries."

Anyone who overheard her would have thought that she was just being a worried wife, but I knew her well and could sense the coldness in her gaze and her annoyed tone of voice.

I said nothing. I wasn't going to give up drinking, let alone eating.

I left the agency and decided to go to Olivia's. Esther wouldn't be home for a while, so I would be able to have my fun. Also, I liked turning up at the apartment unexpectedly. I knew it upset

Olivia, even though she seemed to be resigned to sticking with me. I asked myself why. She had suddenly become as docile as she used to be cold in her dealings with me. And yes, when we talked, it was plain to see that she was trying to conceal her boredom. She didn't care about anything I might say to her. She had turned into purely a piece of meat that I could mistreat without her protesting. Nothing she said ever showed a flicker of wit. She was silent whenever I asked for her opinion on anything. She wasn't present at all.

She kept making meals for me that I could not resist. She should have trained as a chef instead of wasting so much energy on becoming an actress. She even made such amazing dressings for the simplest salads that there was no way I could pass them up, even though I thought that one of the herbs she used was bound to affect my heart problem.

"And Jerry?" I asked her that evening.

"Jerry will wait for me. We'll be together soon enough," she said.

I was scared. Yes, her certainty scared me. She looked at me haughtily even though she knew what my response would be. She didn't turn her face away when she saw me lift my hand to strike her. She didn't care. She didn't bother to say anything, she just poured me another whiskey.

I felt dizzy again that night when I left her apartment. Too much whiskey, I thought, because I had drunk four or five glasses as well as smoking a whole pack of cigarettes.

When I got home, I vomited. My heart was beating wildly and I felt ill. I went to bed. The next day I woke up a little woozy, but not so bad as to stop me from going in to the agency. I thought about calling Dr. Douglas, but I didn't. He would just ask me what I had been eating and drinking instead of really looking into my condition. My cardiologist seemed to blame everything on my bad habits. But I did go to see him the next day. I told him about the blood in my urine and he changed my dosage of Coumadin, the anticoagulant I took every day. He insisted that I come in every week for a checkup. I found ways to ignore his advice, even under Esther's watch.

Esther has kept her promise, but still sees Jaime and takes care of his children as often as she can. She decided to get rid of Mrs. Morrison, who now lives with them. We have to make do with a maid who comes in the morning and leaves at night and who, if Esther gets home late, makes sure I eat and take the pills my wife has left out for me. The worst of it is that the woman scarcely knows how to cook.

Doris, dear sweet little Doris, says that even though I eat a lot, I don't look well and should take care of myself. I spend more and more time with her. Sometimes I see a little spark of disgust in her eyes. My body has grown old, I have flab hanging around my waist, my flesh is soft as butter, and I have found the smell of my own breath disgusting for some time now. But she puts up with me without complaining. I pay her well to pretend that she likes me, and one day she even said that she loved me, but I gave her a good slap and warned her not to take me for a fool.

"I said it to please you, Thomas. Of course I don't love you. I'm with you for your money, but sometimes you have to put a bit of romance into your relationships. Other men like it, but if you don't then there's no need to worry."

I know that when she looks into my eyes she's seeing my wallet stuffed full of bills. I know that when she smiles she doesn't see me. I know that she thinks of other bodies whenever her body comes close to mine. I know that when she moans she's faking it. But that's the deal and I keep my side of it.

I really do despise men who think they've managed to seduce young and attractive women, and who think that they're admired or even loved. Poor fools!

But let's go back to that day. I've thought, more than once, that my sickness—the same illness I've had ever since—was not like anything I had felt before.

I've been back to the doctor a few times since that day, and he's given me a couple of exhaustive checkups, insisting that the pills he prescribes are not enough for me to maintain my health. He scolds me as if I were a child because I won't give up smoking, or bacon and eggs, or drinking half a bottle of whiskey a day. But what would my life be without those little pleasures?

Dr. Douglas says that I work too hard as well.

"You're stressed, like all the executives in Manhattan. I can give you a checkup whenever you want, but the conclusion will always be the same: your main enemy is yourself, Thomas. I'll tell you again: stop drinking, stop smoking, and eat vegetables, grilled meat, and fish. And no desserts. And go on vacation! You need to rest."

He adjusted the dosage of anticoagulants again, because I kept having nosebleeds and bleeding gums, as well as blood in my urine.

The doctor is optimistic, or perhaps useless. I don't dare to ask him to check my blood for poison. He'd laugh at me, say that I was paranoid. I haven't said anything for the time being and I haven't shared my suspicions with anyone, but if things go on like this . . . I know I'm dying slowly, and not from natural causes.

There are days when I feel better, others when I feel my stomach turning, but I never throw up.

Esther is solicitous. She asks me how I feel every day, as if she were waiting for me to tell her that I was going to die. And Olivia too, she asks me about my health every day. She says it's because my skin is turning yellow. Even so, I take the pills Esther gives me for my heart and eat the food that Olivia makes for me. Ever since Mrs. Morrison left there hasn't been much in the refrigerator. I go to Olivia's apartment for lunch, and she feeds me her ever more sophisticated culinary creations.

Olivia's hands are covered in scars and have lost both their beauty and their former smoothness. I can't stop myself from looking at them and she never hides them. In fact she makes a point of showing them off so I never forget that I am the cause of this damage.

She hasn't had work in months, but she doesn't seem worried. I keep paying her bills and she keeps herself busy by project managing the house Jerry is renovating. She hasn't given up on marrying him, although she hasn't mentioned it again.

Actually, I feel good only when I'm with Doris. Little Doris, whom I recently managed to get a part for in a low-budget movie: she knew how to thank me for that.

Olivia knows that Doris exists, and I think Esther does too. They both realized who she was during the Effie Awards ceremony at the Waldorf Astoria. Doris wanted to come and I got invitations for her and a friend. I didn't worry about the boy; he's gay and works occasionally as a model.

Doris was wearing one of those over-the-top Versace dresses. It was impossible not to look at her. Anyway, she came over to where I was standing with Esther. Doris put on her best smile and said to Esther that she admired her work as an executive a great deal and was thankful that Esther had taken her on for the cat food ad. Esther said she would be sure to count on Doris again in the future.

Olivia interrupted us. She and Esther greeted each other affectionately, as if they were old friends with shared secrets. They moved away from us and whispered between themselves. They left Doris to one side. I heard them laugh. The laughter was enough to make me uneasy. Then I saw everything clearly. They were poisoning me. Sometimes I think it's Esther who gives me the poison, and at other times I think it's Olivia, but maybe both of them have decided to gang up on me and get rid of me.

Doris looked at them admiringly, as did her young friend, Ronald. Esther was a star in the ad world, and Olivia had done several ads, enough for people at the ceremony to recognize her.

"She's fabulous!" Ronald said, looking at Olivia.

"She was. This is what's left of her beauty. She's quite old," I said grumpily.

"She must be at least forty," Doris said bluntly.

"I don't think so, and even if she were, she's attractive and elegant. She's got class. You should learn from her," Ronald said to Doris, trying to provoke her.

I walked away. I didn't want to get caught in a fight between two starving people who were like stray dogs, ready to roll over for the first person who threw them a bone.

Esther was adored and respected by everyone she knew, and our table was visited by all the advertising hotshots, who didn't hesitate to pay tribute to her talent.

Once again, Esther won a prize at the gala, on this occasion for the best television spot, a commercial for baby formula.

It was not new for her to win awards. When she went up to collect it I looked at her carefully. I thought that it would be hard for me to recognize the scruffy, insecure woman from Paul's academy in this strong, smiling woman.

She was not blessed with beauty, but she was intelligent and, like all intelligent women, she knew how to get the best out of herself. Doris was beautiful, but vulgar. Esther was elegant. She had not always been so, but she was now. She knew how to dress, what jewelry to wear, how to move with grace. Everything about her radiated serenity.

Olivia had sat down near us. She smiled happily as she watched Esther accept the award. It was clear that they were friends and liked each other.

I felt nauseated. I made an effort to keep myself upright; I even managed to applaud Esther's speech. I felt Olivia's eyes on me and I was surprised at her smile. I had been at her apartment the day before and she had not smiled at me then with the strength that she displayed in this moment. Was she the murderer?

I made a decision. I would go see Paul in Miami. I would tell him of my suspicions. He would know what to say, how to guide me through the labyrinth that Esther and Olivia were building together and where I was, for the first time, lost. I would take Doris with me. I didn't want to travel alone. If I felt ill I would at least have someone there to look after me.

I sent Doris a text message. She lifted her head, looked at me, and nodded.

I sent another message to Paul, telling him that I would be visiting him soon. I asked him to make me a doctor's appointment, without Esther finding out. Paul wrote back at once. He'd do it. When Esther got back to the table she looked at me expectantly. I think she had seen me engrossed in my cell phone while she was onstage.

I don't know how I made it through the rest of the night. But I did. On the way home, Esther would not stop talking about the ceremony. I didn't listen to her. I was so dizzy that my vision started to blur. I felt pressure moving from my heart up my throat. I didn't even say good night when we got home. I went to my room and threw myself down on the bed. I don't know how long I was there, but suddenly I jerked awake. I looked over at the door and there she was, very serious, looking at me.

"Are you all right, Thomas?" she asked in a cold, indifferent voice.

"I drank too much to celebrate your success. I'll be fine tomorrow."

"I don't know . . . You look odd. Do you want me to help you get into your pajamas?"

"Go to sleep. I don't need anything."

"Good night, Thomas. If it turns out you do need anything, just call me," she said, with a half-smile that scared me.

I spent the rest of the night lying in bed. I could barely feel my legs or my arms and I felt so nauseated I couldn't move. I must have fallen asleep because the maid's voice woke me.

"Sorry, I thought you had left already. I'll do your room later."

I sat up. My head was no longer spinning. A shower woke me

up completely. Although the maid insisted, I didn't want to eat anything.

"Your wife made coffee and left your pills. She asked me to make sure you take them," she said.

The one thing I didn't want to do was take any medicine that had come through Esther's hands.

I went to see Dr. Douglas. After running several tests for the umpteenth time, he concluded that I wasn't taking the right dosage of anticoagulants, and again changed my prescription.

"Sometimes a particular medicine doesn't fit well with an individual patient," he said. "And we're not getting the dosage of anticoagulants right. But we have a lot of different medicines nowadays, so let's try another one. Jantoven: I hope it works better. Of course it's essential that you stick with the diet I recommended. A man with a heart condition can't eat what he wants, much less smoke and drink."

I had scarcely recovered when I came to a decision. Given that Dr. Douglas was incapable of diagnosing what was happening to me, I would find a doctor who could give me an explanation before I headed to Miami.

It wasn't hard for me to find the name and place of work of the expert who had appeared in the Discovery Channel documentary on poisons. Professor Johnson was a famous professor at NYU, an expert in botany and pharmacology.

I got in touch with the university and had several meetings in which I made it clear that I had a yen for philanthropy and had decided to donate a certain amount of money for scholarships, but didn't know where to funnel it. I was given several options; the university officials were eager to receive several hundreds of thousands of dollars from me. But I already knew that my money was destined for Professor Johnson's department. If they thought it was strange, they said nothing. Money is money, after all. In the end they arranged for me to meet Johnson and he agreed to see me, thanks to the significant donation I was making.

I listened to his explanations patiently for half an hour, as he told me what his department did and how my money would help them. Then, when he expected me to get up and leave, I surprised him by asking a question: "Professor, I have a very significant personal reason for wanting to find out more about the poisonous capacities of certain plants."

The man could not hide his surprise and seemed to shrink back behind the table. I smiled at him to calm him down.

"I know it might seem silly to you, but I'm giving your department a donation because I saw you a few months ago in a TV show, on the Discovery Channel I think it was. Do you remember? A surprising documentary about poisons."

"Ah, yes, I remember, they asked my opinion. I don't suppose you want to poison anyone ..." he said, laughing, but slightly nervously.

"Of course not. What a thing to imagine! It was just that I was so impressed by you. That's why I wanted my money to go to your department, which I know is in need of funds."

"And my department is very grateful to you," he said warily.

"Professor, what I want to know is if, as you explained in the show, there are substances that can put people's lives at risk."

"Well, it's not impossible, but it's not easy either. But if you tell me exactly what it is you want to know ... I think that ... well ... you have a special interest in this topic."

"It's confidential, professor. I can't offer you a detailed explanation. But I'll give you an example. What about a middle-aged man with a weak heart, who suddenly starts to feel extremely ill because of the anticoagulants he's taking?"

"Anticoagulants can kill, Mr. Spencer. Doctors lose a number of patients by administering improper levels of medication. It happens every day, although no one talks about it, of course."

"And so ..."

"Medicine can cure, but it can also kill. Everything depends on the dosage, the patient, on so many other factors ... Anticoagulants are necessary, are vital in the treatment of certain illnesses. The doctor needs to know what dosage each patient needs."

"And so, if the patient should ideally take half a pill and he's prescribed a whole one . . ."

"Well, if he doesn't need the whole pill then he could have an internal hemorrhage, but if he needs a pill and a half and doesn't take it, he could suffer a coronary thrombosis."

"And if he dies . . ."

"Bad luck."

"Just that?"

"Well, I don't know what else I can tell you. Sometimes if the dosage of anticoagulants isn't correct there can be internal 'mini hemorrhages' that aren't picked up."

"And that happens?"

"Of course it happens, but it's not anyone's fault. And today we can very carefully control the dosage that a patient needs to take, so there's no need to be scared. If this is your case, then you should try to talk honestly to your doctor."

"And can you kill someone using plants?"

Professor Johnson looked at me worriedly, but he must have thought about my generous donation and, although the tenor of the conversation must have upset him, he decided to continue and answer my questions.

"Well, Mr. Spencer, there are plants that can cause a great deal of trouble depending on how you take them. Have you ever taken ginkgo biloba? I'm sure you've seen it advertised. It's a Chinese plant, also known as 'the tree of forty shields.' It has an anticoagulant effect and it's used to help with circulation; it's also used for the nervous system, for Parkinson's disease, even for hair loss, but it can have side effects. If the dosage is wrong, it can cause anxiety, vomiting, diarrhea . . . And if you mix it with other anticoagulants, like Coumadin or others, it can lead to hemorrhages. The same thing happens with ginger and garlic. As you can see, plants can have beneficial as well as unpleasant effects. And when combined with other drugs, they can affect our health. But this doesn't mean that ginger, or garlic, or ginkgo biloba themselves are harmful. Quite the contrary."

"But ginkgo biloba is freely available?" I asked in fright.

"Of course. There are lots of people who take it and feel great."

I asked him what would happen if one mixed an anticoagulant with plants that also had an anticoagulant effect.

"As I said, it depends on the dosage, but it could cause an internal hemorrhage or . . . well, imagine a worst-case scenario."

He spoke to me a little about Saint-John's-wort. Apparently people take it for depression.

"It's a woodland plant, although it's forbidden in certain countries precisely because of its secondary effects."

"Well, if plants can be that dangerous . . ."

"But you can cause a great deal of damage just with a few simple blackberries."

"Blackberries?"

"If you pick blackberries when they're green or white, and eat them, you can suffer hallucinations because your nervous system becomes overstimulated. Green and white blackberries are filled with a toxin, a saponin, which is like latex. Or oleanders: their leaves, their flowers, their seeds are all poisonous. If you eat them, after a few hours you'll start to get dizzy, throw up, have diarrhea . . . But no adult would ever think of eating them. I'm talking about plants that are not in the food chain to any extent. I'm sure you've seen a lot of philodendrons."

"Well, no, I don't know what that is."

"I'm sure you do. A houseplant that you might even have in your own home. It's ornamental. Here, I've got one by the window."

I looked at it. He was right, I had seen them in people's houses from time to time; Olivia had one in her apartment.

"No one would ever think that they should eat a philodendron leaf. If you did, you'd have serious stomach pains, liver failure, and even a seizure. All because of the calcium oxalate it contains."

I wondered if Olivia might have slipped a philodendron leaf into one of her elaborate salads.

I turned my attention back to Professor Johnson, who was now talking about nutmeg.

"The nutmeg peel contains myristicin, an insecticide that is a potent neurotoxin and causes nausea, vomiting, headaches, paranoia . . . Solanine is a toxic glycoalkaloid which you find in unripe tomatoes and eggplants; it also causes vomiting and diarrhea. And there's ricin, of course. Yes, *Ricinus communis,* which comes from a bush. It has dark leaves and its seeds are toxic because of an albumin called ricin that can, even in small quantities, cause death. Hydrangeas—so pretty—they have a compound called hydragin in them that is a cyanogenic glycoside, which can be dangerous. Or *brugmansia,* 'angels' trumpets' . . . or even common laurel . . . the flowers smell like vanilla but they're toxic; they contain oleandrin, which is a glycoside that can cause an irregular heartbeat, tachycardia, and even cardiac arrest."

Professor Johnson's explanations made my hair stand on end. Many of the symptoms I was suffering were similar to those caused by the plants he was describing. Symptoms that occasionally appeared after Olivia had prepared me a sumptuous meal. And as for the anticoagulants that Esther was giving me, I had never bothered to check if the dosage was correct. All I did was put the pills in my mouth and swallow them with a bit of water. After Professor Johnson's lesson, I felt that my intuition had been confirmed: the anticoagulants that Esther gave me every morning, and the food that Olivia cooked for me, with their spices and odd herbs, could be causing this deterioration in my health. But was either of them really capable of doing something like this? I was suspicious of them, but at the same time I said to myself that they weren't brave enough to kill me, because they both had consciences. Or maybe I didn't know them as well as

I thought I did. They might have conspired together to do this without raising suspicions. A few hydrangea seeds, a slightly higher dosage of anticoagulant . . .

Had my wife and my lover found a way to kill me without leaving any trace? At least, that's what they thought.

Professor Johnson seemed to be enthusiastic as he spoke about a series of plants I did not know: *Melia azedarach, Datura stramonium, Ficus carica, Ilex aquifolium, Conium maculatum* . . . Impossible names that I barely managed to retain in my head.

I don't know how long we spoke, but I remember there was a moment when I felt dizzy.

"Are you all right?" he asked.

"A little tired. But thank you for your explanations. It's been interesting and instructive to hear what you have to say."

"Well, you're a benefactor for my department, and if all you want is for me to help satisfy your curiosity . . . I never would have imagined that the documentary would have this much of an impact."

"Well, that documentary is exactly what brought me to you."

When I left Professor Johnson's office, I booked two tickets to Miami on the first afternoon flight. I sent a message to Doris to tell her when to meet me at the airport.

I felt better. I packed my suitcase and called a cab to take me to the agency.

I went into Esther's office, even though she was in a meeting with a couple of creatives and I knew she hated it when she was interrupted while she was working.

"Could you give me a moment?"

She frowned, but got up and left her office.

"What is it?"

"I'm going to Miami. We have a potential client there and I think it would do me good to have a bit of a rest. Plus, I want to catch up with Paul. I'll be away for a few days."

"Who's the client?" she asked without any interest.

"A man who runs a chain of hotels. He said Paul had referred him to me . . . We'll see if he's worth the trouble."

"Well, take care and give Paul my regards. I'll come with you next time—I want to see him too."

Doris was waiting impatiently for me at the airport. With no makeup and in jeans she was even more attractive than when she got all dressed up. She was excited when she saw that we were traveling business class.

Paul had booked us a hotel in Miami Beach, sure that this was what a girl like Doris would want. He was right. He invited us to the best seafood restaurant in town, right by the ocean. He was the owner's friend, so we were seated at a table set slightly aside, where I could smoke without attracting judgmental glances. The waves beat against the shore, and some surfers were defying the first shades of dusk. We chatted about inconsequential matters. What I needed to tell him would have to remain between the two of us.

"Thomas, I'm worried that you're not taking care of yourself . . . You should stop smoking; you've gone through half a pack in the two hours we've been here. And don't drink so much; you're on your fourth whiskey," my old friend said reproachfully.

The next morning I sent Doris to the beach and gave her a couple hundred dollars to go shopping if she got bored tanning in the sun. I said I had a few business meetings to get to and might not be back until the evening. She didn't care. She was young, she was in Miami Beach, and for a few hours she could pretend she was free to do whatever she wanted.

Paul was waiting for me at his apartment, where a beautiful young woman looked after him. You didn't need to be a psychic to know that there was something more than a professional relationship between them.

We sat on the terrace and the girl brought us two glasses of white wine and a plate of seafood.

"Since when do you drink wine in the morning?" I asked.

"It's better than gin or whiskey. Come on, have a drink, just a glass, it'll make you feel better. Now tell me what it is that has you so worried you needed to come and see me in person."

"They're poisoning me."

Paul started to laugh so aggressively that the girl came out to see what was going on. He waved her away, but didn't stop laughing.

"You're nuts, Thomas! Who's poisoning you?" he asked when he finally regained control.

"I don't know, Esther or Olivia, or the pair of them . . . But I know they're poisoning me."

"Right. And how do you know?"

I told him about the documentary, and how each of them had watched it by chance and how I had become a witness to what they had seen.

"If you'd only seen how interested they were when they were watching it. I saw the first half of the show with Olivia, but when I got home I found Esther caught up in it as well, watching the second part. And since then . . ."

"Okay, I'll write the rest. Esther and Olivia went to the Amazon to pick strange roots and turn them into powder, which they've started putting into your food or drinks. Is that what you're telling me, Thomas?" Paul seemed about to laugh again.

"I didn't say that they went to the Amazon . . . I guess anyone can buy any kind of poison nowadays over the Internet. I don't know if it's Esther or Olivia, or the pair of them; all I know is that it could only be the two of them who have a strong interest in getting me out of the picture."

"Are you serious, Thomas? Look, I've booked you an appointment with Dr. Taylor for a checkup, but I think he'll send you to the psychiatrist when you tell him that you think your wife and your lover are poisoning you."

"Paul, I'm serious. I . . . I have no one else to turn to." My voice trembled and my eyes grew vague and I think at this moment Paul started to take my fears seriously.

"Come on, come on. I'm sure there's an explanation for whatever it is that's happening to you. Have you seen Dr. Douglas?"

"I've spent months feeling like death and Dr. Douglas has seen me twice. The only thing he says is that I'm feeling bad because the amount of medicine I'm taking needs to be changed. Apparently we're not hitting the right level of anticoagulant for my needs. Otherwise, he says, I'm in good health—aside from suffering a heart attack and two or three 'cardiac episodes,' as he stupidly calls them. He says I'm stressed and should go on a diet. A diet that would involve dying of hunger."

"And he's right, I'm sure he's right. You're a rational man, so you can't actually believe that Esther and Olivia have decided to poison you simply because they saw a show about poisons on TV."

"I think the show gave them an idea about how to get rid of me."

"But, Thomas, do you really think Esther is capable of killing you? Or Olivia? Please! They're not psychopaths. They might have grudges against you. You haven't made Olivia's life easy."

"Esther loves Jaime, I know that. We've been sleeping in different bedrooms for months now. She sold her jewelry to help him and in the end I had to give in as well and give money to my stupid brother."

"In exchange for what?" Paul asked, knowing that I didn't give things away for free.

"In exchange for her not abandoning me. I don't care if she doesn't love me, you know that, but I don't want to lose her."

"You know what? I think that instead of a cardiologist you should go to a good psychiatrist, as I've spent years telling you. Your childhood traumas are following you around even today. You aren't upset that Esther doesn't love you, but you can't bear for her to be with your brother. You should have gotten divorced years ago."

"I don't want to get divorced."

"Everyone gets divorced, you don't need to be an exception to the rule. I've been divorced three times."

"I'm not going to let Jaime get her."

"That's exactly the kind of thing that's making you sick. And as for Olivia, why don't you leave her alone? She has the right to a life and you won't give her one. Let her marry that hardware store guy."

"I'm not going to do that. I've kept her all these years and I'll be the one to end it."

"You really ruin these girls, Thomas, but that doesn't mean that they've decided to poison you. I think you're sick from the poison you generate. You're getting obsessed and making yourself ill."

"I'm not throwing up because of an obsession; this is real. I'm not imagining feeling nauseous, or having tachycardia. I'm being poisoned, Paul. I don't know what they're using, but I know it's what they're doing."

"I'm sorry, Thomas, but you're not going to convince me that Esther has become a murderer in order to run off with Jaime, or that Olivia is one either. I'll come with you to Dr. Taylor's tomorrow. I hope he'll be able to give you a real diagnosis."

"Why don't you believe me, Paul?"

"Because I know the three of you and I know what you're capable of. No one turns into a murderer just because they saw something on TV."

"So who's poisoning me, Paul?"

"No one, that's what you won't accept—that no one is trying to kill you. But I want you to tell Dr. Taylor the truth. Tell him what you think, and he'll know what to do. And now, let me give you some more advice: Don't torture them anymore. What kind of a man are you, keeping a woman who you know doesn't love you? Or two women, in your case. You're destroying their lives and losing your own. There are a lot of girls out there."

"I know, Paul, but I'm not interested in that kind of girl."

"Olivia isn't Mother frickin' Teresa, Thomas."

"Olivia isn't just a whore. She's intelligent, she's been to college, she's been beautiful, she still is. And, most importantly, she knows how to listen to me. She knows how to listen to me without prejudice, without judging, she even gives me good advice."

"And she gets along well with your wife. Yes, you've been lucky. And now you've brought this beauty along with you to visit me."

"Doris is no Olivia, she's only good in the sack. She's fairly dumb."

"I think she's cleverer than she looks, but she's very young. Just give her time."

"The only thing she cares about is money," I said disdainfully.

"You weren't expecting her to love you. Why should she? You're not really a lovable guy. You're . . ."

He fell suddenly silent. What did Paul think about me that he didn't dare say to my face?

"What am I, Paul?"

"You're a complicated man, full of complexes, insecure, wicked. And it's not like you have a perfect body. You're a scoundrel."

We sat without speaking for a while, looking each other straight in the eye.

"And you're still my friend?"

"Because I've always been out of your jurisdiction. You've never been able to hurt me, Thomas, because you've never really paid me any attention."

His clarity surprised me. He was right, I had never thought of him as particularly valuable. He was there; he was useful to me, and nothing more.

"And so . . . Why have you helped me all these years?"

"Well, it's not that I've helped you. I've just been around to tell you the truth. Nothing else."

An hour later I found Doris at the hotel swimming pool talking to a kid her age with a muscled body and a stupid smile. She seemed to be having a good time. Her face darkened when she saw me. I went over to where they sat.

"Is this your dad?" the boy asked. "Pleased to meet you, sir."

"I'm not her father, I'm the man who's paying for her to stay in this hotel, and for the bikini she's wearing. Get out of here. You're old enough to be able to recognize a slut."

The kid looked at me aggressively, then over at Doris. She had turned red and didn't say anything, which confirmed that I had spoken the truth: she was a whore.

When we were alone together, Doris shot me a look full of anger, or perhaps hatred.

"Why did you do that to me? We were only talking."

"I pay you to smile at me, not to have fun with any handsome young thing who happens to be bobbing around. If you want a guy like that, then all you need to do is give up whatever I give you. You can leave right now. I don't need you. One phone call and I can have another model just like you."

She pouted. It looked like she was about to cry but she stopped herself. I guess she must have known that if she caused a scene, I would hit her as soon as we were in the hotel room together.

"All right, Thomas, I'm sorry for upsetting you. That guy was nothing to me. We were just talking."

The next day Paul took me to the doctor's office and then left, winking as he did so. He had already done more for me than I deserved.

Dr. Taylor looked through all the tests they had performed.

"I really don't know why you want me to give you a checkup;

you're already in the best of hands, Mr. Spencer. Dr. Douglas is an expert when it comes to heart problems. But if you insist . . ."

He left me in the care of a nurse who led me through the hospital all morning, from one room to the next. It took me seven hours to get through all the tests and checkups and meetings with doctors. I was exhausted.

Dr. Taylor told me that he needed a few days to get the results, so I spent that time getting drunk with Paul and enjoying Doris's splendid body. She was a very patient girl.

"You shouldn't worry, Mr. Spencer," Dr. Taylor said when I went to his office three days later.

"Are you going to tell me I'm fine?"

"For someone who's had a heart attack and several cardiac episodes, you could be worse. Your liver is swollen, your kidneys aren't working one hundred percent, your blood sugar level is too high . . . I can't say anything other than what Dr. Douglas has been recommending. You have to change your lifestyle. You have to stop smoking and drinking and eating fatty food; all of that is hurting you. Also, you're on the wrong dose of anticoagulants, which you should still be taking as well. But that's not uncommon. As soon as we get the dose right, you'll feel better."

"It can't be," I said in anguish.

"What do you mean?"

I confessed all my fears. I overcame my reticence and told him that I was scared that someone was poisoning me. He listened to me very seriously and seemed worried. He insisted that I tell him whom I suspected and why. But skepticism appeared on his face when I told him about the show on the Discovery Channel and the reasons my wife and my lover might want to kill me.

"Mr. Spencer, what you're telling me is very serious. Perhaps you should go to the police," he suggested, upset by my revelations.

"I want you to find traces of poison in my body. They have to be there."

Dr. Taylor paused before speaking.

"Maybe you should see Dr. Austen, who is an excellent psychiatrist. I'll call him personally, and he can see you tomorrow morning."

"I'm not crazy, Dr. Taylor."

"I'm not saying you are, but after what you've told me . . . well . . . your relationship with your wife and your lover . . . I think you should talk to Dr. Austen, and he'll help you."

"How?"

"He'll help you get things in order in your mind, Mr. Spencer, to see if this is merely a paranoid episode. I'm sorry to put it like that, but sometimes words are more alarming than they need to be."

"I'm telling you, I'm not crazy. Give me another test, find the poison they're using to kill me."

"Dizziness, general ill feeling, vomiting, high blood pressure . . . None of these are symptoms that would lead me to think that you're being poisoned. You've told me yourself that you drink too much and it's clear that your body can't process that much alcohol. You're not following the diet that your doctor prescribed. You're smoking two packs of cigarettes a day. It's madness. Keep in mind that your personal situation might be so upsetting that it causes you to feel physically ill—these things do happen. Mental illness can have a devastating physical effect."

"I know they're poisoning me!"

"Do you hear what you're saying? You're accusing your wife of wanting to kill you. It's an extremely serious accusation."

"It's either her, or my lover, or the pair of them together."

"Look here, Mr. Spencer, the only thing I can do for you is send you to Dr. Austen. Talk to him. If the doctor thinks you're telling the truth, then come back here and I'll run all the tests again, though I don't think we'll find anything. Dr. Douglas, in his report, says that you don't follow his recommendations, and that you're stressed and urgently need rest. And I agree with him."

I saw Dr. Austen the next day. I didn't like him. He had a madman's face. He ordered me to lie down on a sofa and made me answer stupid questions. And so on for a week.

Esther called me every day. She didn't seem to worry that I was delaying my return. She encouraged me to have fun and enjoy the weather in Miami, which was always better than in New York.

"Are you well, Thomas?"

"Yes, of course, why?"

"Well, you seemed to be pretty ill before you left."

"I've felt pretty good ever since I got to Miami."

"That's odd."

"Why? Should I have kept feeling ill?" I asked suspiciously.

"No, I didn't say that. Well, let's change the subject."

"All right, let's change the subject." She was worrying me.

"You know what? I think things are starting to go better for Jaime now. He has a couple of very interesting clients. The boys are spending a lot of time with their grandfather, but Jaime isn't prepared to give up on them. He says he'll get them back, get himself back on his own two feet."

"And why should I care about that?" I asked.

"I thought you'd be pleased ... If he's doing better now, it's thanks to your help."

"I haven't changed my feelings about Jaime at all. I've just given in to your blackmail, Esther. I paid the price so you wouldn't abandon me."

I hung up and cursed myself for not having been able to keep my mouth shut. Paul was right. All I was doing was giving her excuses to distance herself from me.

I called Olivia. She wasn't at home. When she answered her cell phone, she said she was out buying curtains for the new house.

"Don't get too excited about that house, it'll be a long time before you'll be able to live in it," I warned her.

"I don't think so, Thomas. You'll see how lucky I can be. And how are you, anyway?"

"Fine, my dear, enjoying Miami with a willing girl by my side."

"Enjoy it, Thomas. While you still can."

Just as Esther had, Olivia managed to worry me. It was as if both of them had expected me to continue feeling bad. The doctors could say what they wanted; they were all a bunch of useless pricks. It was clear that Esther and Olivia wanted something to happen to me.

Dr. Austen concluded that I was stressed and was suffering from persecution mania. He prescribed me certain medicines, which, although I didn't tell him so, I had no intention of taking. While he was explaining his diagnosis to me I asked him and Dr. Taylor to give me a chance.

"A chance? What do you mean? What sort of chance could we give you?" he asked with interest.

"Doctor, I can accept that as a consequence of being poisoned I might feel a certain degree of paranoia, but I don't understand why both Dr. Taylor and you so clearly reject the possibility that what I'm saying might be the truth. If I die in a few days or a few months, will you wonder if maybe I was right after all? Will you feel bad for not having paid attention to what I'm telling you now? I'm not saying that Dr. Taylor and Dr. Douglas haven't given me extensive tests, but none of you has looked for poison in my bloodstream. I know there's something inside me that's killing me. Please, please look for it."

I convinced him. Not completely, but enough for him to come with me to his friend Dr. Taylor's office and ask him to carry out a precise analysis of my blood to make sure there was no poison in it.

At first Dr. Taylor refused. Then he accepted, warning me that we would be wasting our time.

I underwent the next round of tests. It took them four days to get the results back to Dr. Taylor.

"Mr. Spencer, my conclusion is the same as Dr. Douglas's: you're not reacting well to anticoagulants, and these are vital for your cardiovascular problems. What we need to do is find the correct medication for your particular case. Dr. Douglas said in his report that he recently changed your anticoagulant. You'll have to wait to see if the one you're taking now makes you feel any better. It's also possible that you suffer from some kind of allergy. That would explain the continuous sense of illness."

"Allergy? To what?"

"That's what we need to find out now. You could be allergic to certain types of food, or even to some of the drugs in your heart medicine, or the medicine for your hypertension, or your cholesterol, or your sugar levels. Perhaps they're interacting in some way that makes you feel unwell. I think this is more likely to be the cause, rather than poison, as you are so determined to believe." This last sentence Dr. Taylor pronounced with barely contained irony.

My doctors had settled on their conclusion, and I had reached mine. My suspicions had become certainties, although I could prove nothing. Esther, who was in charge of giving me my anticoagulants, obviously wasn't giving me the dose that the doctor had prescribed, but was killing me little by little. My inertia, because I trusted her, had led me not to check that I was being given the correct amount. All I did was put the pills in my mouth and swallow them with a little water. And the doctors had made it clear to me: anticoagulants could kill.

I suspected that Esther was not acting alone, but in conjunction with Olivia. I realized that Olivia's stews, always so highly spiced, could also be the cause of my illness because of the symptoms that tended to appear after one of her substantial meals. I was sure that my "cardiac episodes" were triggered by a combination of the anticoagulants and Olivia's meals.

There was empirical proof of this: I hadn't had any health problems at all since coming to Miami. With every day that passed I felt better, stronger.

I called Esther to tell her that I was seeing a doctor in Miami.

"But why? You just had a checkup." She seemed worried.

"Well, I figured it wouldn't hurt to have a second opinion. Now that I'm here I thought I could dedicate a bit of time to myself. Dr. Douglas said that I'm stressed and need to relax. Do you need me back there?"

"Not at all. Stay as long as necessary. We can cope without you," she said quickly, with what I thought was a hint of suppressed happiness.

"I'll call you as soon as the results are in."

"Yes, do that. It's good to know that Paul's close by."

"Don't worry about me."

Doris started to get tired of Miami. She had already bought more than she ever could have dreamed of, her tan was perfect, she'd even put on a couple of pounds from so much calm and peace. But she didn't dare ask me to take her back to New York. She was sick of me, and not of the good life she was living in Miami. Paul was fatherly and attentive toward her.

"Why don't you forget about Esther and Olivia and marry Doris? She's perfect for you. She wants to have a good life and she'll put up with you in exchange. It's a good deal," Paul suggested.

"I'm not interested. She's really dumb. She bores me. She's only good at one thing."

"That's enough, my friend. One reaches the age where one shouldn't really want anything else. Women who think are exhausting. Better Doris, who's pleased with what you have, than Esther, who doesn't need to rely on you for her next meal."

"I thought you adored Esther."

"I do adore her, I've never met a better woman than her, but she's definitely one of the ones who gives you headaches."

The results of the allergy tests were conclusive: I was allergic to Pradaxa, which I took for my heart troubles, and that was causing side effects. The doctor gave me a list of foods I was allergic to as well: milk, wheat, strawberries, pineapple . . . It was a long list.

Dr. Taylor seemed satisfied when he spoke to me.

"I'm pleased that you insisted on another round of tests, Mr. Spencer. You were right to do so. In the report I've prepared for Dr. Douglas I recommend that he try one of the latest-generation anticoagulants. It's called Eliquis. The results have been good. I can't guarantee that you're going to feel better, but you should at least try it. Oh, and you should be careful about what you eat from here on out. The tests on your food allergies are conclusive. But you also have to take better care of yourself. If you don't . . . well, you're the one killing yourself. It's all in the report. With a bit of moderation, you'll start to feel better again soon. And luckily you can abandon this ridiculous idea that your wife and mistress are trying to kill you."

"So it was the heart medicine? Well, I guess that might be, but it can't just be the pills that are killing me," I said.

"You're not dying; stop saying that. You'll feel better with the new pills. Let's talk in a few months. Now relax awhile, maintain a healthy diet, stop smoking and drinking, and go home to New York. Take up your life where you left it off."

Dr. Taylor gave me an envelope with an extensive report, detailing the tests he had performed and his recommendations.

"I took the liberty of sending it to Dr. Douglas at Mount Sinai as well," he told me.

Paul chuckled when I told him that the doctors claimed my illness was due to allergies.

"It's a shame it was a pill that almost did you in. Your theory was much more interesting. It's better to die at a woman's hands," he said, laughing.

I asked him to do me a favor, but he refused.

I wanted him to call Esther and tell her that I had suffered a severe heart attack and was unlikely to survive, and to do the same with Olivia.

"I'm not going to do anything that stupid. What are you hoping to get out of it?" he asked me angrily.

"To see how they react."

"Oh, they'll be clapping their little hands. You frickin' moron."

Even without Paul's help I decided to carry out my plan. I booked tickets for a flight the next morning and, a few hours before we boarded the plane, I made Doris call Esther and Olivia. I drilled her on what she had to say. She had to pretend to be a nurse at the hospital and to say that I had suffered a heart attack and that I was clinically dead.

"You're going to give them a real shock," Doris said, without really knowing what I wanted to do.

Or at least that's what I thought, that she didn't understand. But she did a good job. Maybe she was more skilled as an actress than I'd thought. I listened in on the conversation and waited for a sob, an exclamation, anything that would show how worried Esther was. But nothing of the kind happened.

"So my husband is clinically dead. And is there any chance that he . . . that he'll pull through?"

"No, ma'am, I'm sorry. It's impossible. The doctor will be in touch with further details. Are there any instructions you'd like to give me?"

"No, I'll wait for the doctor to call and then I'll discuss my options with the insurance company."

"Please don't concern yourself with the administrative details during this difficult time. The hospital will contact the insurance company. All you need to do is tell us if we should send the body home to you in New York, or if you prefer to come to Miami."

"Well, he's dead now, so there's not a lot I can do. Although

I may come down. It wouldn't be good for me not to do that, I suppose. When Dr. Taylor calls me I'll figure it out."

Not a sob. Not a shade of pain in anything she said. My death was her liberation.

The conversation between Doris and Olivia ran along the same lines.

"Mr. Spencer told us that in case anything happened to him we should tell his wife and you. I'm sorry to have to deliver this terrible news." Doris was extremely convincing.

"Don't worry, these things happen. Thomas has had a weak heart for years, and it's not a surprise that something like this should have happened."

"Will you come to Miami?"

"Oh no, I'm not his wife, I'm just . . . well, I'm a friend of the family. I wouldn't be any use at all. Of course I'll come to his funeral. And thank you for calling me, although there was no need."

Olivia's voice was frigid. She was entirely indifferent to my death. My two wives, as Paul called them, had hardly reacted at all to my sudden death. I hated them for that and doubled down on my resolve to continue treating them badly.

"When are you going to tell them that you aren't dead?" Doris asked.

"I'm not going to tell them. They're going to find out for themselves."

After half an hour I asked Doris to call Esther again and tell her that the hospital had spoken to the insurance company and would send my corpse to New York.

"You don't need to come, Mrs. Spencer. He'll be home tomorrow. He'll be sent to the funeral home."

"Yes . . . it's probably better for me to stay and organize the funeral. An excellent idea, thank you very much."

Paul called me, furious, to tell me that Esther had tried to reach him a couple of times to confirm that I really was dead.

"And what did you say?"

"Nothing, I didn't talk to her. The girl took the calls. The first time I was out swimming, but Esther told her what she was calling about. The second time I didn't want to answer. Leave me out of your shit, Thomas. Why the hell would you even think of doing such a thing, telling Esther that you were dead?"

We took the flight to New York. Doris had a couple of suitcases filled with new clothes. I gave her money for a taxi and went directly home.

Esther wasn't there. The rooms were empty and I felt a stab of nostalgia.

I was changing my clothes when the maid came in. I hadn't heard her. The woman gave a shriek that made me jump.

"Are you crazy? Why are you screaming?"

"You're dead! Jesus . . ."

"I'm not a ghost. What are you saying?"

"You're dead . . ." she managed to say.

I laughed heartily. The woman was terrified. I asked where Esther was.

"She didn't sleep here. She called me first thing in the morning to tell me you had died . . ."

I didn't want to know anything else. I could guess where my wife had slept. I decided to try Olivia, although it wasn't hard to guess that she wouldn't be all that pleased to see me.

I went to her apartment. I put the key in the lock, trying not to make any noise; I wanted to surprise her.

I heard her talking to someone in the kitchen and went up behind her carefully. She had her cell phone in one hand and was putting the coffeepot on the burner with the other. I stopped dead in my tracks as I listened.

"Of course, darling, I think it's an excellent idea to have your brother as the best man. It would be a really lovely gesture on his part to give us the rings. I can't wait. Yes, I promise there's nothing that'll delay us any longer. We'll see each other tonight.

They'll bring the missing furniture first thing; I think you'll like how it all looks. Goodbye, my love."

"Hello," I said.

Olivia turned around and swallowed a scream. Her face reflected the terror she felt at seeing me.

"It can't be! You're dead!"

"Unluckily for you, I'm alive."

Her face screwed up into a grimace of anguish. She knew what she could expect from me.

"Yes, unluckily for me, you're alive," she said.

She looked like she was about to faint. She sat down. First she lifted her hands to her face, then let her arms fall in a gesture of resignation.

"I guess you're the one who's not looking so well."

"When's this going to end, Thomas? When?" she asked me, holding back her tears.

I didn't answer. She was a broken woman. Exhausted by the battle she had fought with me.

I could have said that I was there to free her; that I didn't care if she married Jerry and exited my life forever:

"It's over, Olivia, get out of here. I don't care. I'm tired of you. You have to be out of the apartment by tomorrow, I'm not going to pay for a single day more. I just came to tell you."

She would have regarded me with disbelief, and then with gratitude.

"Oh, Thomas, I knew you couldn't be as bad as you pretend to be!"

"I'm not giving you another day, Olivia. They'll throw you out of the apartment tomorrow," I would have warned her again.

"Of course. I'll pack my bags, I'll be out of here today. Thank you, Thomas . . . Thank you."

I would have left the apartment, and our relationship, forever.

If I had done so, then Olivia would have forgiven me—and who knows, maybe I would have saved my own life.

But that scene didn't take place. I didn't say any of the words that might have meant her freedom.

I treated her violently, so she could see just how alive I was. I left her breathless on the bed, cursing me.

I arrived at the agency at midday. There were screams as I walked past the desks. No one was prepared to see a dead man. I walked into Esther's office, and she looked at me in fright.

"Christ! It's you . . . I thought that you . . ."

"Aren't you happy to see me? Apparently some stupid nurse got me confused with another patient. You see, I couldn't be healthier."

"That's impossible!" she stammered.

"Of course it's possible, dear, here I am."

Esther stared at me, shocked, as if she were seeing her nightmares turned into flesh. There I was, tanned by the Miami sun, looking fit as a fiddle, enjoying her stunned expression.

"But . . . I don't understand!"

"A nurse mistook me for another patient."

"But why were you in the hospital?" she managed to ask.

"I told you on the phone, they were doing another checkup. I wasn't happy with Dr. Douglas. Wasn't that the right thing to do? Health is the most important thing at our age."

Esther seemed incapable of reacting. I saw that she was trembling, that it was hard for her to control herself.

"Dr. Douglas is a good doctor, Thomas, and he told you that if you take care of yourself, take your medicine and relax, you can live a good many years more," she said, breathlessly.

The secretary's voice on the intercom added to her suffering.

"Mrs. Spencer, it's Mr. Spencer on the phone, shall I put him through? He wants to know if he should come pick you up or if you're going straight to his apartment."

Esther looked at me in terror and I smiled bitterly. Of course, the Mr. Spencer on the other end of the line was my brother, Jaime.

"Tell him not to come. I'll call him when I can."

"How considerate my brother is. Maybe he was consoling you for my failed death?" I asked sarcastically.

"Jesus, Thomas, that's not funny!"

"No, it isn't. So, I'm dead and here you are, working as if nothing happened and preparing to go and spend the night with my brother. Why? Do you need to go and feed his children? Take them out to the ball game? Oh, and get in bed with Jaime, that's right. If I'm gone, then the problem's gone as well. My brother wouldn't be breaking the promise he made to his dad," I said, unable to hide how much her relationship with my brother affected me.

"We have to stop this . . . We can't keep on like this. I . . . I'm sorry, Thomas, but I can't control my feelings. I'm happy you're alive, but . . . I can't keep on like this, I'm going to go insane. I don't know how to tell you, but we have to sort this out between ourselves. Jaime and I . . ."

She stopped, unable to say what she had wanted to say to me for so long. I could have been generous with her, yielded to the evidence.

Yes, that could have been the moment I set her free:

"All right, Esther, we'll sort things out as best we can. I'll call our lawyers to draw up a divorce settlement. You understand that I'm not going to give you the agency or put everything we built together into your hands for you to waste it on Jaime, or with him. All our property is held in common, so let's see what you're left with."

Knowing her as well as I did, I'm sure she would have said, "Thank you for your generosity. We don't need to argue about money. I'll be reasonable. I will always be in your debt. You have been very generous to me."

"I'm glad you acknowledge that."

"And as for me and Jaime . . . We'll always love you and be grateful that you've allowed us to be together. You can always count on us; we'll be your family. We are *your family, Thomas.*"

But Esther could say none of this because I didn't let this conversation take place. I wasn't ready for her to be happy with Jaime. If she wanted a divorce, she would have to ask for it and we would have to fight over it in the courts. I would leave her out on the street and would ruin my brother, for good this time.

Perhaps God was punishing me, or maybe my heart really was damaged. Or else Esther went back to giving me a higher dose of the new anticoagulant, or Olivia slipped some hydrangea leaves into the salad. In any case, a few days after my return to New York, I fainted in the office and they had to take me to the hospital.

Dr. Douglas seemed more worried than before. I was in the ICU for a few days, and then they took me to a room where Esther was waiting for me.

"Are you better?" she asked, without bothering to kiss me.

"I will survive. In spite of you, I will survive," I spat.

"I don't want you to suffer, Thomas, quite the contrary. I want you to be able to be happy, but you refuse to let yourself and won't let other people be happy either."

"Right, so I'm not letting you be happy. The things I have to put up with! I thought that helping you become the best ad director in Manhattan might have made you happy, or having a huge place in Brooklyn and agencies in both New York and London might have made you happy, or my doglike devotion might have made you happy . . ."

"Please, Thomas, let's not argue! Can't we behave in a civilized way? We can discuss things calmly when you're out of the hospital. Now you need to get better, that's the most important thing. Dr. Douglas said that what you really need is rest. I think your nerves are affecting your heart."

I was discharged a few weeks later. Esther was still in the guest room and we barely saw each other. I calmly called Olivia. I didn't want her to feel like I was out of her life.

"I don't want to see you, Thomas," she said when she heard my voice.

"I don't care what you want, Olivia. I'll be at your apartment in half an hour. I don't want there to be any sign of Jerry there."

She hung up on me, but that didn't stop me from going to see her. When I entered the apartment she was waiting for me.

"I don't know what you want, Thomas, but don't you dare lay a hand on me. This is over."

She stood up and went to the kitchen. When she came back she had a plate with a piece of cake on it.

"I made it today, it's dark chocolate, your favorite. Have a piece and let's not fight."

I couldn't resist, even though I knew that the dark chocolate could be laced with one of those plants Professor Johnson had told me about.

"The chocolate's more bitter than usual," I said, to gauge her reaction.

"Really? Well, I used the same chocolate as always, I don't know . . . Maybe it's your palate, after so long in the hospital."

I stayed there awhile longer, just to annoy her, because I had no strength to do anything.

And until today I have made it a part of my routine to show up at her apartment without warning. I still eat her food, just as I allow Esther to keep giving me my pills every morning. I ask myself why I do it. Not even I understand my attitude. My wife seems eager to clarify our situation, but I refuse to talk about anything that isn't my illness or matters of business.

She reached a breaking point a few days ago.

"Thomas, this can't go on, it's over."

She played hardball, but I played harder, knowing that being with her could put my life at risk again and that death might visit me at any moment. And yes, I think that tonight might be the night.

But let's rewind a bit. I settled into my routine once again.

Paul called me on several occasions. The first time was to find out how my macabre comedy had turned out, and if my wife and my lover had forgiven me. He was upset with me because Esther had scolded him for refusing to tell her that I was alive.

"You know what, Thomas? I think you actually are going crazy. Dr. Taylor and Dr. Austen think you ought to get some treatment."

"I'm not crazy, Paul. You might find it hard to believe, but they want to poison me."

"Don't talk nonsense. It's not that you don't deserve it from both of them, given how you treat them, but they aren't murderers."

"I think you don't know women as well as you think you do," I said.

"You're sick in the head, Thomas, that's it. Dr. Taylor told me that your heart works well enough and that it will continue working, if you take care of yourself."

"Doctors don't know shit."

"Thomas, get a divorce. Accept that Esther loves Jaime, and that Olivia has the right to think about her future; it was a stroke of luck for her to meet Jerry. You win some, you lose some, but I don't think it'll be a tragedy if you give both of them up. The world is full of women, and you're still young enough to meet one who's worth the trouble. Ah, and get it straight: your wife and your lover are good people."

I know that Paul is a good friend and that he wishes me well, but he refuses to accept the evidence. He thinks too highly of Esther and feels sorry for Olivia, so he can't see their true nature.

They're a pair of desperate women whose only chance of being free is to make me disappear. If I stepped aside voluntarily, I'm sure they would let me live. But things have come to a head, and now it's either their lives or mine. My clarity scares me.

Six months have gone by since I got back from Miami, and during this time I've suffered another "serious episode," as my cardiologist says. General poor health, headaches, nausea; my hands and my feet have turned purple. I bleed from my gums, and there's blood in my urine again. Dr. Douglas says it's just because I don't follow his advice, and that the way I carry on, the medicine won't be enough to take the burden off my heart.

"You have to accept, once and for all, that you cannot have four or five whiskeys every day. And I think that's a low estimate of your consumption. As for food . . . To be frank, Thomas, you're a glutton. You don't exercise either. You have to walk, at least an hour a day. It's not much. I'm telling you, you're killing yourself."

He's wrong. It was to be expected that something would happen to me again, given that Esther is still solicitous, and is careful to give me the anticoagulants in the morning, along with the pills for high cholesterol and high blood pressure. Oh, and for my glucose levels as well. Also, knowing that I can't resist her cooking, Olivia has devoted herself to making food so appetizing that even though I know it contains poison I eat it happily. Why do I let this happen? Why can't I take my medicine without letting my wife intercept it? Why do I accept Olivia's food?

The two of them keep asking for their freedom, but I don't want to give it to them.

I wonder why I insist on this fatal struggle. Why do I do it?

Do I want to die? Am I punishing myself? Paul says I'm a son of a bitch. I know that Esther and Olivia call him to let off steam, and that at his age their tears have softened his heart.

"Let them live, Thomas," he keeps saying. "Just stop messing with their lives. If you had any dignity you wouldn't want to be with women who don't love you."

I still have Doris. I can buy the company of hundreds of girls like Doris while there are dollars left in my bank account. In that case, why? Why? Why?

I don't have an answer to that. All I know is that I don't want to let them be happy. I don't want them to have what I will never have. Why should I give them the gift of happiness? They knew who I was and what I was like when they decided to tie their fortunes to mine. Neither of them was ever disgusted by my money. They enjoyed what they got. I gave them a position in society. They owe me, yes—everything they have, they have thanks to me. They can't have been so stupid as to think that I would give them what they got for free, or that they could pay for it with a few sessions between the sheets. There are things that can't be bought, not even with that.

I went to see Professor Johnson again. I sent a check for another twenty thousand dollars to his department before I went. I knew that it was the key that would open his door to me at once.

Johnson received me with an air of resignation. I knew that he thought that I was an eccentric, or a madman, or paranoid.

"Thank you for supporting the department. Your help is inestimable," he said as we shook hands.

"I think it's you who's doing the inestimable work," I answered, just to say something.

"Well, Mr. Spencer, what can I do for you?"

"Well, I'd like to ask some questions. I hope I'm not inconveniencing you."

"If they are questions I can answer . . ." he said cautiously.

"I want to know if there's any type of chemical analysis, any test that can tell if a man is being killed, and if it is with medicine or with some of those plants you told me about."

He sighed as he gave me a sidelong glance and tried to gather his thoughts. If I hadn't been a generous donor, he would have asked me to leave his office.

"I've already explained to you that various drugs can complicate a patient's situation with their side effects. All drugs have side effects, although there are people who are more susceptible than others, and doctors always weigh the cost-benefit ratio. For example, statins have adverse effects on a lot of people. But allow me to ask you a question. What medications are you on?"

I could see that this conversation was making him uncomfortable, and the question he had dared to ask me had only made things worse.

"I've had two heart attacks, and several other 'episodes.' I take anticoagulants. And I don't respond well to them. I've had to switch to different brands on a couple of occasions."

I told him the names of the medicine I was taking—the statins to lower my cholesterol, the glucose pills, and the medication for hypertension. He listened to me carefully, without moving a muscle, concentrating on what I was saying.

"I'll be honest with you, Mr. Spencer. I think I've already hinted as much in our previous conversation. Medicines are invaluable, they represent a great step forward in human history, they fight disease and save lives, but sometimes they can provoke reactions that . . . Well, there are accidents along the way. They're giving you the correct treatment. The most common anticoagulant in the United States is the one you take, warfarin, which is the main active ingredient in Coumadin and Jantoven. In Europe, the most common anticoagulants are acenocoumarol and sintrom. In both cases, the effects are the same and have been demonstrated. They do have secondary effects and they can interact with other medicines and even with some foods. But I'm sure that your cardiologist has told you what to do to prevent that from happening. With rigorous control, there shouldn't be any problems. As far as the glucose pills go, from what you told me they prescribed repaglinide first, and then later changed it to metformin. Both of them react with alcohol and can have a harmful effect on the patient."

He looked at me, trying to see if this was a reason they had changed my prescription. I confirmed nothing. I remained silent while he continued his explanation.

"The pills you take for your blood pressure are angiotensin receptor blockers. They're commonly prescribed. You're on Januvia and Altace as well. And as for the statins, it's like I said: there are a lot of people who can't cope with them, but cardiologists are reluctant to stop prescribing them. Cost-benefit, that's what it's about."

"And the plants?" I asked him.

"The plants? I don't know what you're talking about."

"What if someone were to adulterate a person's food with plants that are harmful to a person's health and might even cause death?"

"We've already had this conversation, and what you're suggesting is absurd," he complained, and sighed again. "It's true that some plants may cause harm if ingested. But people don't eat these plants. I insist, they are not in the food chain."

"Is poison something that an analysis of a person's blood might be able to establish?"

"Well, Mr. Spencer, there is proof that can only be established afterward."

"I don't understand."

"Sometimes it's only with the autopsy that the truth comes out, but for that to be the case you'd have . . . well, you'd have to die first," he said, trying to avoid making his words sound too somber.

"So, someone could be poisoning you and you wouldn't know until you were dead. Is that what you're telling me?"

"Yes, that's possible. You could take your anticoagulant and feel terrible, have a hemorrhage even. You have a weak heart . . .

No one would think, if you died, that they were . . . that they were . . . Well, it's something that happens every day, Mr. Spencer."

"But the autopsy . . ."

"Yes, that would be the only conclusive proof."

I left Professor Johnson's office dumbstruck. So, they could be killing me, and unless they really did something wrong, there would be no way to find out until I was dead, and even then, only if someone decided that it was worthwhile to carry out an autopsy.

I followed Esther a few days ago. It wasn't anything premeditated, but I caught the tail end of a conversation. It was in the morning, during breakfast.

Her cell phone rang and she looked distractedly at the screen, but when she saw what number was calling she answered it immediately, although what surprised me was that she got up at once and went down the hallway to speak with whoever had called.

"Yes, yes . . . of course. The best thing would be for us to see each other. I can't cope anymore either . . . Yes, we have to do something definitive . . . It's useless to try to reason, you know that . . . All right, let's see each other in fifteen minutes."

That was what I managed to overhear. My wife came into the kitchen to tell me that she had an unexpected appointment with a client and that she had to leave right away.

"Of course, dear, work is work. Go to your meeting."

I followed her out. She was so wrapped up in her thoughts that she didn't realize it.

She walked toward a café near our house. There weren't usually many people early in the morning. And then I saw her. Yes, Olivia was walking rapidly toward the very same café. I hid, worried that they might see me. I was lucky. So it was Olivia who had called Esther, and the call and the meeting were not innocent, or else my wife would have told me about them.

I looked for a place where I could keep an eye on the entrance to the café without being seen. They took a long time to come out. From where I was sitting, I saw them hugging each other goodbye. They seemed to be cheering each other up. I was surprised to see that Olivia was crying. Then each went off in a different direction, and I slipped into a bookstore to avoid being seen.

I took longer than usual to get to the agency. I went straight to Esther's office.

"How was your meeting?" I asked, trying to appear nonchalant.

Esther's eyes showed worry, and as she looked at me I noticed her hesitating for a few seconds.

"All right, nothing important. I have to have lunch with a client today. And then I've got things to do. I'll be home late."

"That's not news, darling," I said as I walked out of her office.

I went to mine and closed the door as I called Olivia's cell phone. She sounded listless.

"Why don't you make me some nice barbecue chops for lunch?" I said, without even saying hello.

I heard her sigh, long and desperate, over the telephone.

"I'm very tired, Thomas, and I haven't slept well."

"Oh, and a nice bottle of red to go with the chops," I said.

"Thomas, can't it be tomorrow? Today . . ."

"At midday, Olivia, and you know I don't like waiting."

She hung up the phone in resignation. She knew that nothing she did would make me change my mind.

I told my secretary not to put any calls through to my office and not to let anyone in to see me. I needed to think. What had Esther and Olivia been talking about? They had not been behaving like acquaintances, but rather like people who had a great deal in common. Above all, I couldn't get out of my head Olivia's gesture of despair and the determination in Esther's eyes.

But that wasn't the only surprise. A few days later, Esther told me that she was planning to use Doris in a perfume ad.

"But she's completely talentless," I said sincerely.

"She comes across well on-camera and I want to help her, since she's a friend of yours," she said without apparent irony.

"How considerate!" I retorted.

I thought that my wife was making fun of me. How long had she known that I was sleeping with Doris?

"And I'm going to use Olivia as well."

"Olivia? For a perfume ad? Do you want it to be a failure? The pair of them are worthless."

She shrugged and looked me straight in the eye, holding back a smile.

"Leave it to me . . . I'm the creative. You'll see. We'll come up with something great between the three of us."

"You've never liked doing perfume ads, for all the imagination you have. Olivia's ass is getting bigger and Doris . . . Well, Doris is only ambitious. It's not a good mix of people." I was annoyed at the thought that Esther was laughing at me.

"Don't worry, Thomas. We'll figure it out," she said.

I don't know why, but I felt that some kind of judgment had been passed on me, even though nothing special happened over the next few days. Esther kept giving me my heart medicine. Olivia seemed resigned to being my cook and didn't complain when I turned up at her apartment, and Doris had been extremely demonstrative of her gratitude that my wife had hired her.

What I really hated was seeing the three of them together. Esther called Doris and Olivia into the agency to sign the contract and discuss how the perfume commercial was going to be shot.

They spent a long time locked away and then said goodbye to me frostily, mentioning that they were going to have lunch together.

For a week Esther kept my two lovers busy with the shoot. According to the other creatives at the agency, the result couldn't have been better.

Olivia appears on the screen holding a bottle of the perfume in her hands, the same perfume she used as a teenager, and puts it in her daughter's, Doris's, room. Esther's idea was that the viewers would understand that these are little daily inheritances that pass from mother to daughter.

It was straightforward, but I didn't say anything because Esther had never made a mistake. She's very good at her job.

Esther's decision to choose Olivia and Doris was intentional. It had the benefit of annoying me as well as allowing her to spend time with them.

I saw a change in the behavior of stupid little Doris. It was subtle, but noticeable, and made clear to me that there was something going on apart from the commercial.

Doris would not stop singing Esther's praises.

"I'm not surprised you married her; your wife is wonderful. So intelligent, so affectionate, so convincing," the little bitch said, and not to flatter me, but because she sincerely admired Esther.

I couldn't get a word out of her beyond these accolades. It seemed to me that she was getting progressively dumber.

I tried to pressure her by asking if she talked about anything special after work with Esther and Olivia, and she opened her eyes wide, smiled, and put her arms around my neck.

"Yes, of course . . . Esther's giving me good advice on how to get into the ad world. She says I have a future and that a good model can make a lot of money. And Olivia is so friendly! She's always cracking jokes. She told me where I could buy some cheap vintage clothes, and promised to introduce me to her hair-stylist. She says a good haircut is key."

"And you don't talk about anything else? Don't they say anything about me?"

"About you? No. Esther doesn't mention you, and Olivia . . . well, she doesn't talk about you either. Should they talk about you?" she asked in her most innocent voice.

"Well, if Esther chose you it's because I've talked about you," I said.

"Of course, of course, darling . . . If it weren't for you . . ." she said, but there was a tinge of irony in her words that shocked me.

I couldn't get anything out of Olivia. Well, she did say one thing that worried me.

"It's always great to work with Esther, she brings out the best in you," she said sincerely.

"And Doris? She's a disaster, right?"

"She's got a great future ahead of her."

"Doris? What are you saying?"

"She knows what she wants and knows how to get it."

"And what does she want? Right, to make it in Manhattan and then make the leap into Hollywood, just like you wanted to do. New York is full of girls like you, untalented and condemned to failure. You need more than a good body to succeed."

"I don't think Doris wants to be an artist, but rather to . . ."

She fell silent. I looked at her and she knew that if she didn't say anything, then I would try to force her to. She sighed.

"Doris's vocation is to be rich. To live well. She left Buffalo to make it, and she knows that her strongest weapon is her beauty, a weapon she only has for the time being, but she also knows that she has to hurry because if she doesn't make it now, then the years will pass and it'll get difficult . . ."

"So you're the example that she shouldn't follow."

"That's right, Thomas, I'm a perfect example of what Doris doesn't want. In fact, she's already shown herself to be smarter than I was. You've given her some valuable jewelry and you give her enough money every month for her to splash it around a bit, and you've rented her an apartment in Tribeca. My place in SoHo is nice, but pretty modest."

"Are you complaining, Olivia?"

"Oh no! Why would I do that? I admire the girl. She'll be rich before she's thirty," Olivia said with absolute conviction.

Her words struck me. How could Doris make herself rich if she had no talent at all? She only had one way out—for a stupid, rich man to fall in love with her. Or had Esther promised her money if she helped to . . . ? No, my wife is too intelligent to trust someone like Doris.

Esther took them out to dinner once the commercial was edited. First she organized a small meeting with the agency team, to which she invited Olivia and Doris. Then the three of them went out to eat at Cipriani.

"Doesn't it seem a bit much to take them to Cipriani?" I complained, a little upset at being left out.

"When did you start to worry about the money we spend on softening up the people we work with? Olivia and Doris have done a good job: you've seen the ad. I'm sure it'll be successful."

"This is the first time you've taken a couple of models to Cipriani," I persisted.

"Well, they're more than a couple of models. Or aren't they?" My wife looked at me defiantly.

"If you say so."

"Come on, Thomas, don't antagonize me. They were great in the shoot. Plus, going to Cipriani is a way for them to be seen by people who matter. Let's leave it at that."

And so my wife and my two lovers are having a great time together and I know there's a link between them: the extent to which they hate me. Although I try to resist thinking that Doris hates me. She might be apathetic toward me, but I haven't given her any reason to hate me aside from a couple of slaps whenever her stupidity irritates me too much.

But I'm not going to let Esther and Olivia win the match. I've decided to play it to the end, even if I lose my life in the attempt. If they manage to kill me they won't be able to enjoy my absence, at least not right away. After my last conversation with Professor Johnson, I made a few decisions.

I handed a sealed envelope to my lawyer with instructions to request an autopsy in the case of my death. My lawyer will have to give a copy of the autopsy report to the district attorney along with a letter in which I assign responsibility for anything that might have happened to me to Esther and Olivia. If I die, then it will be investigated. Maybe they won't find any proof to use against them, but at least they won't be able to celebrate their freedom for a good while. They will be under suspicion for murder. Esther won't be able to use our money to pay for lawyers and Olivia . . . Well, I don't think Jerry is going to help her. Jerry is a simple, self-made man who won't be able to deal with someone under suspicion of committing a crime.

As for Jaime, I know him well: he's a coward and he would be horrified to think that Esther could have killed me. He might regret it, but he'll leave her. I know. My brother is too principled. He wouldn't be able to look at Esther without thinking that she might have caused my death. My stupid, kindhearted brother, who looks so much like good old John. His father, my stepfather.

I'll leave all my money to Professor Johnson. Well, to his department at NYU. The university's lawyers will fight to make sure that they don't miss out on a single dollar. Esther will fight them, and will call in Dr. Douglas and Dr. Taylor. They'll say that I suffered from a persecution complex and will call on Dr. Austen to bear witness to their claim, as well as Paul Hard. But the shadow of suspicion will be difficult to lift.

This is my revenge. I might die, but they won't win the game.

They'll hate me, yes, they'll hate me, but can they really hate me any more than they already do? Paul says that Olivia has reasons to hate me, but Esther simply doesn't love me. What does he know? I can see it in my wife's eyes. I know her well. I've suppressed my own nature to have her by my side.

How much time has passed since I last thought I was dying? Barely a couple of weeks. Esther has breakfast with me every morning, and even has dinner with me every now and then, watching me carefully to see if she can detect the shadow of death on my face. I go to see Olivia every day and scrutinize her movements as she serves me whiskey or a piece of cake that she doesn't try herself.

Yes, they are poisoning me. Perhaps they put something in my food, or my coffee, or the whiskey I love so much. They know that I know.

A few days ago Dr. Douglas insisted that I see a psychiatrist, and even gave me phone numbers for a couple of them, but I became angry and asked him to test my blood for the poison they're using to kill me. It's a useless dialogue we've been having for months. He shrugs. He thinks I'm crazy, even though I had another "episode" a few weeks back that affected me more than usual and put me in the hospital for a week. While I was unconscious I felt the presence of Yoko and Constance next to me again. They told me that soon I would be with them, that the next time they would come and find me and take me away for good. Lisa was there as well. She held out her hand and laughed at me.

Esther and Olivia came to see me. They entered the room together and said they had run into each other in the elevator. There was nothing in their eyes that could be considered a sentiment akin to love, or affection, or even compassion. Nothing apart from impatience. I paid Doris well to spend time with me in the room. Esther didn't seem to mind the girl's presence; she even seemed pleased that there was someone other than her who would watch over me at the hospital. My wife explained that she couldn't stay for very long because she had so much work at the agency. She praised Doris for keeping me company.

"It's lucky for us that Doris is such a good friend. That girl's a treasure," she said, and added, with a touch of cynicism, "When I'm at work it puts me at ease knowing that she's here with you."

Dr. Douglas didn't want to believe me when I insisted in a faint voice that my collapse had not been spontaneous.

"Thomas, if you continue to say these horrible things, I will have to ask you to find another doctor. Your wife calls me every day to find out how you're progressing. She's very worried that you're having these cardiac episodes."

"The anticoagulant, Doctor . . ."

"You're on the right dosage; it's completely under control. I don't know how to make you understand that your lifestyle is what's hurting you."

The day he let me leave the hospital he treated me like a naughty little boy, slapping me on the back and giving me the same speech as always.

"Nothing's going to happen to you, Thomas. I'm sure that if you look after yourself your health will flourish. No one in his right mind with heart problems would eat a bowl of spaghetti carbonara and a T-bone steak in a single sitting, much less smoke two packs of cigarettes a day. I really think the problem is in your head as well. If you don't address your own obsessions then something really will happen to you," the stupid doctor preached.

Esther insisted that I do nothing and devote myself instead to relaxing. It was her way of making it clear that my presence at the agency was not essential and that if we continued making money, it was due to her. I didn't care. I let her work. At the end of the day I check all the accounts and there's not a single dollar that escapes my scrutiny.

She's been sleeping at home ever since I left the hospital. She gets back late, it's true. I know that when she leaves the agency she goes to my brother's house and spends a good deal of time with him and the children. When she gets home, she's absent. She asks me mechanically how I am and whether I need anything. After giving me the pills I need for the night, she retreats to the guest bedroom.

I felt bad again four days ago. It was after having lunch at Olivia's. She'd invited me, asking me to come and try her latest culinary creation, meat cooked with pineapple and other tropical fruits and with a sauce whose flavor I didn't recognize. Even so, I ate it all and the next day I came over without warning. But instead of getting annoyed she offered to make me something to eat, because, as she said, "You look terrible. I'm sure having something to eat will help." In fact, quite the opposite. Scarcely had I finished eating before I had to go home. I was sweating profusely and felt so dizzy and nauseated that I was shaking.

This morning, when my wife gave me my anticoagulants, I caught her looking at me, and there was a special gleam in her eye. She said she would be working late that night. I know she knows I don't believe her. She'll be at Jaime's, because one of his kids is sick, or he's organized a family dinner.

I've called Doris. And here I am in the apartment I've been renting for her, right in one of Manhattan's prime neighborhoods. I like the place. It costs me a fortune, but it's more comfortable than going from hotel room to hotel room. I'm not going to live much longer and it's good for me to spend my money on these little caprices. But tonight is dragging on forever. I told Doris to watch some television. In the meantime I'm going to try to put down some of my memories in writing, and I can't stop asking myself if this life would have been better, the one I didn't want to live because I preferred to be a son of a bitch. Yes, I had a choice. But I never wanted to be anything other than what I am. Would I have known? What would this life have been like, the one I didn't want to live? Would I have been happy?

Doris is chattering away at my side, but I don't listen to her. I've been trying to master the sickness, the cold sweat that covers my skin, the vomit that is trying to climb from my stomach to my throat, but I want to keep on writing. I'm terrified of my own thoughts. I think I could die tonight. Yes, I think I'll die tonight.

The stupid girl doesn't notice anything.

"You're a bit pale. Well, if you try to do this kind of thing, at your age, in your state . . ."

I told her to shut up. She's used to it. She stared at the television for a while and then started talking again as if nothing had happened, and offered to pour me a whiskey. "To get your spirits up," she said. I didn't pay her any attention, but I was alarmed by her look as she picked an ice cube to put in my drink. Then she stirred it. Suddenly I realized that this was what Olivia and Esther did as well. They fish around among the ice cubes, take a couple of them, and then stir them into the whiskey. Why do they stir it? Why hadn't I realized earlier? Could they be poisoning me with the ice? It's easy; I drink several whiskeys a day. Suddenly I remembered that in the documentary they said that you could kill people using ground glass, crystal. They might be killing me with ground glass in my ice cubes. Now I realize that Doris is looking for particular cubes in the ice bucket. Have Olivia and Esther made her their accomplice? But why would Doris want to kill me? Money. Olivia told me that Doris would be rich before she was thirty. Esther must have promised her a good chunk if she helps get rid of me. Yes, my wife and my lover might have bought the little bitch. She looks at me with a smile and hands me the glass and waits expectantly for me to take the first sip.

I laugh. Doris looks at me without understanding why I'm laughing. I drink the whiskey in a single gulp and ask her to pour me another one. Meanwhile, in my mind I go through the scene that will certainly take place. As soon as I die, my lawyers will open the sealed envelope with my precise instructions demanding an autopsy, and will make public my suspicions that my wife and my lover were conspiring to kill me. The district attorney will immediately get involved. My last testament will request that my suspicions be made public. Once the DA is in possession of the documents, my lawyers are obliged to inform the press. I can imagine the headlines: PROMINENT ADMAN DEAD IN SUSPICIOUS CIRCUMSTANCES: LEAVES LETTER ACCUSING HIS WIFE AND LOVER. Yes, it'll be a big scandal that will drag Esther and Olivia down, and they'll be under suspicion for the rest of their lives. Knowing that I'm able to destroy them is what makes the idea of death not so terrible. I'm enjoying their suffering in advance. I still have time to put Doris's name into the documents. No, she won't escape either; I won't let her enjoy my money.

They are killing me, even though no one believes me. Or am I mad? Maybe both at the same time. There will be no real answer until the day after my death.

ONE YEAR LATER

All right, Mrs. Spencer, once these last formalities are out of the way you'll be able to access the money and the accounts that have been frozen up to now. The autopsy and the police report exonerate you from . . . from your late husband's unfounded suspicions."

The lawyer, looking straight at Esther, couldn't find a single flicker of emotion on her face. Her impassivity made him nervous.

"I'm sorry for what you have had to go through, but you must understand that our obligation was to fulfill Mr. Spencer's wishes. If you would be kind enough to sign these papers . . ."

Esther took the documents that the lawyer held out to her and read them slowly, as if she had all the time in the world.

"Yes, it has been a difficult few months," the lawyer murmured, addressing himself to Paul Hard this time, who was sitting silently next to Esther.

"Yes, indeed it has, Mr. Hill," Paul agreed.

"The important thing is that it's all over," the lawyer insisted in his honeyed voice.

Paul glared at him. The man was trying to minimize the importance of what had happened.

"An exhaustive investigation of Mrs. Esther Spencer and

Ms. Olivia White as a result of an unfounded accusation of poisoning . . . as well as forcing several important doctors to make statements, with me myself brought into it as well, and the scandal in the papers . . . All because Mr. Spencer wouldn't listen to his doctors' instructions and refused to follow the proper regimen for his heart condition, thus making his illness worse." Paul's voice betrayed his indignation.

"We can't do anything apart from carrying out our client's instructions."

Esther lifted her eyes from the papers and seemed to hesitate for a few seconds before signing them. Once she had done so, she handed them over to the lawyer.

"Well, that's it. Of course, Mrs. Spencer, we will be at your disposal for whatever you might require. We would like to continue serving your interests in the same way that we have up to now."

Esther said nothing. She stood up and, taking Paul by the arm, left Thomas's lawyer's office. When they reached the street she looked at Paul and gave him a kiss.

"Thank you for coming with me, thank you for being by my side all these months, thank you for helping me face this nightmare," she said, hugging him.

"I don't know about you, but I can't forgive Thomas for what he did . . . To accuse you and Olivia of trying to kill him! And all because he didn't eat what he should, drank like a fish, and didn't follow any of his doctors' recommendations."

"The anticoagulants didn't agree with him; he had to change them several times," Esther said.

"Are you really trying to excuse his wretchedness?"

She didn't reply. They walked slowly to Rockefeller Center. Paul had lost some of his former vigor and leaned on a cane.

Olivia and Doris were waiting for them impatiently, sitting at a table.

"It's over," Esther said as a greeting.

Paul ordered a couple of gin and tonics for himself and for Esther. Olivia and Doris already had theirs.

The three women looked at one another and raised their glasses in a silent toast. They were drinking to their freedom, and in the face of Paul's confusion, they all burst out laughing.